Ray Bradbury, one of the greatest writers of fantasy and horror fiction in the world today, was born in Waukegan, Illinois, USA in 1920. As a child, he was fascinated by monsters, circuses, dinosaurs and the red planet, Mars. He started writing short stories in 1932 after an encounter with a carnival 'Mr Electrico', and was making a living out of story-writing in the 1940s: in 1944 he sold about forty stories for a total of $800.

His tales set on Mars were collected into *The Martian Chronicles*. His famous *Fahrenheit 451* was filmed by Truffaut in 1966, and many of his stories have been adapted successfully for TV and the cinema. The film based on his book *Something Wicked This Way Comes* is being released shortly.

GW00496821

By the same author

Fahrenheit 451
The October Country
Dandelion Wine
The Martian Chronicles
The Illustrated Man
Something Wicked This Way Comes
The Golden Apples of the Sun
The Day It Rained Forever
I Sing the Body Electric!
The Halloween Tree
The Machineries of Joy
The Wonderful Ice Cream Suit
R is for Rocket
S is for Space
When Elephants Last in the Dooryard Bloomed
Long After Midnight
Where Robot Mice and Robot Men Run Round in Robot Towns

The Stories of

Ray Bradbury

VOLUME 2

with an introduction by the author

GRANADA

London Toronto Sydney New York

Published in paperback by Granada Publishing Limited in 1983

ISBN 0 586 05749 8

First published in Great Britain by
Granada Publishing Limited 1981

Published by arrangement with Alfred A. Knopf, Inc.

Most of the stories in this book were previously published in the
following books:
The Illustrated Man, The Martian Chronicles, R is for Rocket,
The Machineries of Joy, S is for Space, The Golden Apples of the
Sun. A Medicine for Melancholy, Fahrenheit 451, I Sing the Body
Electric!, Dandelion Wine, Long After Midnight, Dark Carnival
and The October Country.

and in the following magazines:
American Mercury, Arkham Sampler, Charm, Collier's, Ellery
Queen's Mystery Magazine, Eros, Esquire, Famous Fantastic
Mysteries, Galaxy, Harper's, McCall's, Maclean's, Mademoiselle,
Magazine of Fantasy and Science Fiction, Marvel Science Fiction,
Penthouse, Planet Stories, Playboy, Saint Detective, Saturday Eve-
ning Post, Seventeen, Shenandoah, Star Science Fiction Stories 3,
Startling Stories, Super Science Fiction Stories, Thrilling Wonder
Stories, Today and Weird Tales.

'Punishment Without Crime' was originally published in Other
Worlds. Copyright 1950 by Other Worlds.
'The Blue Bottle' was originally published in Planet Stories. Copy-
right 1946, 1950 by Love Romances Publishing Company, Inc.

Granada Publishing Limited
Frogmore, St Albans, Herts AL2 2NF
and
36 Golden Square, London W1R 4AH
515 Madison Avenue, New York, NY 10022, USA
117 York Street, Sydney, NSW 2000, Australia
100 Skyway Avenue, Rexdale, Ontario, M9W 3A6, Canada
61 Beach Road, Auckland, New Zealand

Printed and bound in Great Britain by
Cox & Wyman Ltd, Reading
Set in Plantin

Granada ®
Granada Publishing ®

And this one, with love,
for Nancy Nicolas and Robert Gottlieb,
whose arguments about favourites
put this book together

Contents

Drunk, and in Charge of a Bicycle

an introduction by Ray Bradbury

In 1953 I wrote an article for *The Nation* defending my work as a science-fiction writer, even though that label only applied to perhaps one third of my output each year.

A few weeks later, in late May, a letter arrived from Italy. On the back of the envelope, in a spidery hand, I read these words:

> B Berenson
> I Tatti, Settignano
> Firenze, Italia

I turned to my wife and said, 'My God, this can't be from *the* Berenson, can it, the great art historian?!'

'Open it,' said my wife.

I did, and read:

> Dear Mr Bradbury:
>
> In 89 years of life, this is the first fan letter I have written. It is to tell you that I have just read your article in *The Nation* — 'Day After Tomorrow.' It is the first time I have encountered the statement by an artist in any field, that to work creatively he must put flesh into it, and enjoy it as a lark, or as a fascinating adventure.
>
> How different from the workers in the heavy industry that professional writing has become!
>
> If you ever touch Florence, come to see me.
>
> Sincerely yours. B. BERENSON.

Thus, at the age of thirty-three, I had my way of seeing, writing and living approved of by a man who became a second father to me.

I needed that approval. We all need someone higher, wiser, older to tell us we're not crazy after all, that what we're doing is all right. All right, hell, *fine*!

But it is easy to doubt yourself, because you look around at a community of notions held by other writers, other intellectuals, and they make you blush with guilt. Writing is supposed to be difficult, agonizing, a dreadful exercise, a terrible occupation.

But you see, my stories have led me through life. They shout, I follow. They run up and bite me on the leg — I respond by writing down everything that goes on during the bite. When I finish, the idea lets go, and runs off.

That is the kind of life I've had. Drunk, and in charge of a bicycle, as an Irish police report once put it. Drunk with life, that is, and not knowing where off to next. But you're on your way before dawn. And the trip? Exactly one half terror, exactly one half exhilaration.

When I was three my mother snuck me in and out of movies two or three times a week. My first film was Lon Chaney in *The Hunchback of Notre Dame*. I suffered permanent curvature of the spine *and* of my imagination that day a long time ago in 1923. From that hour on, I knew a kindred and wonderfully grotesque compatriot of the dark when I saw one. I ran off to see all the Chaney films again and again to be deliciously frightened. The Phantom of the Opera stood astride my life with his scarlet cape. And when it wasn't the Phantom it was the terrible hand that gestured from behind the bookcase in *The Cat and the Canary*, bidding me to come find more darkness hid in books.

I was in love, then, with monsters and skeletons and

circuses and carnivals and dinosaurs and, at last, the red planet, Mars.

From these primitive bricks I have built a life and a career. By my staying in love with all of these amazing things, all of the good things in my existence have come about.

In other words, I was *not* embarrassed at circuses. Some people are. Circuses are loud, vulgar, and smell in the sun. By the time many people are fourteen or fifteen, they have been divested of their loves, their ancient and intuitive tastes, one by one, until when they reach maturity there is no fun left, no zest, no gusto, no flavour. Others have criticized, and they have criticized themselves, into embarrassment. When the circus pulls in at five of a dark cold summer morn, and the calliope sounds, they do not rise and run, they turn in their sleep, and life passes by.

I did rise and run. I learned that I was right and everyone else wrong when I was nine. Buck Rogers arrived on scene that year, and it was instant love. I collected the daily strips, and was madness maddened by them. Friends criticized. Friends made fun. I tore up the Buck Rogers strips. For a month I walked through my fourth-grade classes, stunned and empty. One day I burst into tears, wondering what devastation had happened to me. The answer was: Buck Rogers. He was gone, and life simply wasn't worth living. The next thought was: Those are not my friends, the ones who got me to tear the strips apart and so tear my own life down the middle; those are my enemies.

I went back to collecting Buck Rogers. My life has been happy ever since. For that was the beginning of my writing science fiction. Since then, I have never listened to anyone who criticized my taste in space-travel, sideshows or gorillas. When such occurs, I pack up my dinosaurs and leave the room.

For, you see, it is all mulch. If I hadn't stuffed my eyes and stuffed my head with all of the above for a lifetime, when it came round to word-associating myself into story ideas, I would have brought up a ton of ciphers and a half-ton of zeros.

'The Veldt,' collected herein, is a prime example of what goes on in a headful of images, myths, toys. Back some thirty years ago I sat down to my typewriter one day and wrote these words: 'The Playroom.' Playroom where? The Past? No. The Present? Hardly. The Future? Yes! Well, then, what would a Playroom in some future year be like? I began typing, word-associating around the Room. Such a Playroom must have wall-to-wall television in each wall, and in the ceiling. Walking into such an environment, a child could shout: River Nile! Sphinx! Pyramids! and they would appear, surrounding him, in full colour, full sound, and, why not? glorious warm scents and smells and odours, pick one, for the nose!

All this came to me in a few seconds of fast typing. I knew the Room, now I must put characters in the Room. I typed out a character named George, brought him into a future-time kitchen, where his wife turned and said:

'George, I wish you'd look at the Playroom. I think it's broken – '

George and his wife go down the hall. I follow them, typing madly, not knowing what will happen next. They open the door of the Playroom and step in.

Africa. Hot sun. Vultures. Dead meats. Lions.

Two hours later the lions leaped out of the walls of the Playroom and devoured George and his wife, while their TV-dominated children sat by and sipped tea.

End of word-association. End of story. The whole thing complete and almost ready to send out, an explosion of idea, in something like 120 minutes.

The lions in that room, where did they come from?

From the lions I found in the books in the town library

when I was ten. From the lions I saw in the real circuses when I was five. From the lion that prowled in Lon Chaney's film *He Who Gets Slapped* in 1924!

1924! you say, with immense doubt. Yes, 1924. I didn't see the Chaney film again until a year ago. As soon as it flashed on the screen I knew that that was where my lions in 'The Veldt' came from. They had been hiding out, waiting, given shelter by my intuitive self, all these years.

For I am that special freak, the man with the child inside who remembers all. I remember the day and the hour I was born. I remember being circumcised on the second day after my birth. I remember suckling at my mother's breast. Years later I asked my mother about the circumcision. I had information that couldn't have been told me, there would be no reason to tell a child, especially in those still-Victorian times. Was I circumcised somewhere away from the lying-in hospital? I was. My father took me to the doctor's office. I remember the doctor. I remember the scalpel.

I wrote the story 'The Small Assassin' twenty-six years later. It tells of a baby born with all its senses operative, filled with terror at being thrust out into a cold world, and taking revenge on its parents by crawling secretly about at night and at last destroying them.

When did it all really begin? The writing, that is. Everything came together in the summer and fall and early winter of 1932. By that time I was stuffed full of Buck Rogers, the novels of Edgar Rice Burroughs, and the night-time radio serial *Chandu the Magician*. Chandu said magic and the psychic summons and the Far East and strange places which made me sit down every night and from memory write out the scripts of each show.

But the whole conglomeration of magic and myths and falling downstairs with brontosaurs only to arise with La of Opar, was shaken into a pattern by one man, Mr Electrico.

He arrived with a seedy two-bit carnival, The Dill

Brothers Combined Shows, during Labor Day weekend of 1932, when I was twelve. Every night for three nights, Mr Electrico sat in his electric chair, being fired with ten billion volts of pure blue sizzling power. Reaching out into the audience, his eyes flaming, his white hair standing on end, sparks leaping between his smiling teeth, he brushed an Excalibur sword over the heads of the children, knighting them with fire. When he came to me, he tapped me on both shoulders and then the tip of my nose. The lightning jumped into me. Mr Electrico cried: '*Live forever!*'

I decided that was the greatest idea I had ever heard. I went to see Mr Electrico the next day, with the excuse that a nickel magic trick I had purchased from him wasn't in working order. He fixed it, and toured me around the tents, shouting at each, 'Clean up your language,' before we entered to meet the dwarfs, acrobats, fat women, and Illustrated Men waiting there.

We walked down to sit by Lake Michigan where Mr Electrico spoke his small philosophies and I talked my big ones. Why he put up with me, I'll never know. But he listened, or it seemed he listened, maybe because he was far from home, maybe because he had a son somewhere in the world, or had no son at all and wanted one. Anyway he was a defrocked Presbyterian minister, he said, and lived down in Cairo, Illinois, and I could write him there, any time I wished.

Finally he gave me some special news.

'We've met before,' he said. 'You were my best friend in France in 1918, and you died in my arms in the battle of the Ardennes forest that year. And here you are, born again, in a new body, with a new name. Welcome back!'

I staggered away from that encounter with Mr Electrico wonderfully uplifted by two gifts: the gift of having lived once before (and of being told about it) . . . and the gift of trying somehow to live forever.

A few weeks later I started writing my first short stories

about the planet Mars. From that time to this, I have never stopped. God bless Mr Electrico, the catalyst, wherever he is.

I consider every aspect of all the above, my beginnings almost inevitably had to be in the attic. From the time I was twelve until I was twenty-two or -three, I wrote stories long after midnight — unconventional stories of ghosts and haunts and things in jars that I had seen in sour armpit carnivals, of friends lost to the tides in lakes, and of consorts of three in the morning, those souls who had to fly in the dark in order not to be shot in the sun.

It took me many years to write myself down out of the attic, where I had to make do with my own eventual mortality (a teenager's preoccupation), make it to the living room, then out to the lawn and sunlight where the dandelions had come up, ready for wine.

Getting out on the front lawn with my Fourth of July relatives gave me not only my Green Town, Illinois, stories, it also shoved me off towards Mars, following Edgar Rice Burroughs' and John Carter's advice, taking my childhood luggage, my uncles, aunts, my mom, dad, and brother with me. When I arrived on Mars I found them, in fact, waiting for me, or Martians who looked like them, pretending me into a grave. The Green Town stories that found their way into an accidental novel titled *Dandelion Wine* and the Red Planet stories that blundered into another accidental novel called *The Martian Chronicles* were written, alternately, during the same years that I ran to the rainbarrel outside my grandparents' house to dip out all the memories, the myths, the word-associations of other years.

Along the way, I also re-created my relatives as vampires who inhabited a town similar to the one in *Dandelion Wine*, dark first cousin to the town on Mars where the Third Expedition expired. So, I had my life three ways, as town explorer, space-traveller, and wanderer with Count

Dracula's American cousins.

I realize I haven't talked half enough, as yet, about one variety of creature you will find stalking this collection, rising here in nightmares to founder there in loneliness and despair: dinosaurs. From the time I was seventeen until I was thirty-two, I wrote some half-dozen dinosaur stories.

One night when my wife and I were walking along the beach in Venice, California, where we lived in a thirty-dollar-a-month newlyweds' apartment, we came upon the bones of the Venice Pier and the struts, tracks, and ties of the ancient roller-coaster collapsed on the sand and being eaten by the sea.

'What's that dinosaur doing lying here on the beach?' I said.

My wife, very wisely, had no answer.

The answer came the next night when, summoned from sleep by a voice calling, I rose up, listened, and heard the lonely voice of the Santa Monica bay fog horn blowing over and over and over again.

Of course! I thought. The dinosaur heard that lighthouse fog horn blowing, thought it was another dinosaur arisen from the deep past, came swimming in for a loving confrontation, discovered it was only a fog horn, and died of a broken heart there on the shore.

I leaped from the bed, wrote the story, and sent it to the *Saturday Evening Post* that week, where it appeared soon after under the title 'The Beast from 20,000 Fathoms.' That story, titled 'The Fog Horn' in this collection, became a film two years later.

The story was read by John Huston in 1953, who promptly called to ask if I would like to write the screenplay for his film *Moby Dick*. I accepted, and moved from one beast to the next.

Because of *Moby Dick*, I re-examined the life of Melville and Jules Verne, compared their mad captains in an essay written to reintroduce a new translation of *20,000 Leagues Beneath the Sea*, which, read by the 1964 New York World's Fair people, put me in charge of conceptualizing the entire upper floor of the United States Pavilion.

Because of the Pavilion, the Disney organization hired me to help plan the dreams that went into Spaceship Earth, part of Epcot, a permanent world's fair, now building to open in 1982. In that one building, I have crammed a history of mankind, coming and going back and forth in time, then plunging into our wild future in space.

Including dinosaurs.

All of my activities, all of my growing, all of my new jobs and new loves, caused and created by that original primitive love of the beasts I saw when I was five and dearly cherished when I was twenty and twenty-nine and thirty.

Look around among these stories and you will probably find only one or two that actually happened to me. I have resisted, most of my life, being given assignments to go somewhere and 'sponge up' the local colour, the natives, the look and feel of the land. I learned long ago that I am not seeing directly, that my subconscious is doing most of the 'sponging' and it will be years before any usable impressions surface.

As a young man I lived in a tenement in the Chicano section of Los Angeles. Most of my Latino stories were written years after I had moved from the tenement, with one terrifying, on-the-spot, exception. In late 1945, with World War II freshly over, a friend of mine asked me to accompany him to Mexico City in an old beat-up Ford V-8. I reminded him of the vow of poverty that circumstances had forced on me. He rebutted by calling me a coward, wondering why I didn't rev up my courage and send out three or four stories which I had hidden away. Reason for the hiding: the stories had been rejected once or twice by various magazines. Pummelled by my friend, I dusted the stories off and mailed them out, under the pseudonym William Elliott. Why the pseudonym? Because I feared that some Manhattan editors might have seen the name Bradbury on the covers of *Weird Tales* and would be prejudiced against this 'pulp' writer.

I mailed off three short stories to three different magazines, in the second week of August 1945. On August 20, I sold one story to *Charm*, on August 21, I sold a story to *Mademoiselle*, and on August 22, my twenty-fifth birthday, I sold a story to *Collier's*. The total monies amounted to $1,000 which would be like having $10,000 arrive in the mail today.

I was rich. Or so close to it I was dumbfounded. It was a turning point in my life, of course, and I hastened to write to the editors of those three magazines confessing my true name.

All three stories were listed in *The Best American Short Stories of 1946* by Martha Foley, and one of them was published in Herschel Brickell's O. Henry Memorial Award *Prize Stories* the following year.

That money took me to Mexico, to Guanajuato, and the mummies in the catacombs. The experience so wounded and terrified me, I could hardly wait to flee Mexico. I had nightmares about dying and having to remain in the halls of the dead with those propped and wired bodies. In order to purge my terror, instantly, I wrote 'The Next in Line.' One of the few times that an experience yielded results almost on the spot.

Enough of Mexico. What about Ireland?

There is every kind of Irish story here because after living in Dublin for six months I saw that most of the Irish I met had a variety of ways of making do with that dreadful beast Reality. You can run into it head-on, which is a dire business, or you can skirt around it, give it a poke, dance for it, make up a song, write you a tale, prolong the gab, fill up the flask. Each partakes of Irish cliché, but each, in the foul weather and the foundered politics, is true.

I got to know every beggar in the streets of Dublin, the ones near O'Connell's Bridge with maniac pianolas grinding more coffee than tunes and the ones who loaned out a single baby among a whole tribe of rainsoaked mendicants, so you saw the babe one hour at the top of Grafton Street and the next by the Royal Hibernian Hotel, and at midnight down by the river, but I never thought I would write of them. Then the need to howl and give an angry weep made me rear up one night and write 'McGillahee's Brat' out of terrible suspicions and the begging of a rainwalking ghost that had to be laid. I visited some of the old burnt-out estates of the great Irish landowners, and heard tales of one 'burning' that had not quite come off, and so wrote 'The Terrible Conflagration up at the Place'.

'The Anthem Sprinters', another Irish encounter, wrote itself down years later when, one rainy night, I recalled the countless times my wife and I had sprinted out of Dublin cinemas, dashing for the exit, knocking children and old folks to left and right, in order to make it to the exit before the National Anthem was played.

But how did I begin? Starting in Mr Electrico's year, I wrote a thousand words a day. For ten years I wrote at least one short story a week, somehow guessing that a day would finally come when I truly got out of the way and let it happen.

The day came in 1942 when I wrote 'The Lake'. Ten years of doing everything wrong suddenly became the right idea, the right scene, the right characters, the right day, the right creative time. I wrote the story sitting outside, with my typewriter, on the lawn. At the end of an hour the story was finished, the hair on the back of my neck was standing up, and I was in tears. I knew I had written the first really good story of my life.

All during my early twenties I had the following schedule. On Monday morning I wrote the first draft of a new story. On

Tuesday I did a second draft. On Wednesday a third. On Thursday a fourth. On Friday a fifth. And on Saturday at noon I mailed out the sixth and final draft to New York. Sunday? I thought about all the wild ideas scrambling for my attention, waiting under the attic lid, confident at last that, because of 'The Lake', I would soon let them out.

If this all sounds mechanical, it wasn't. My ideas drove me to it, you see. The more I did, the more I wanted to do. You grow ravenous. You run fevers. You know exhilarations. You can't sleep at night, because your beast-creature ideas want out and turn you in your bed. It is a grand way to live.

There was another reason to write so much: I was being paid twenty to forty dollars a story, by the pulp magazines. High on the hog was hardly my way of life. I had to sell at least one story, or better two, each month in order to survive my hot-dog, hamburger, trolley-car-fare life.

In 1944 I sold some forty stories, but my total income for the year was only $800.

It suddenly strikes me that there is much in this collection I haven't commented on yet. 'The Black Ferris' is of interest here because early one autumn twenty-three years ago it changed itself from a short story into a screenplay and then into a novel, *Something Wicked This Way Comes*.

'The Day It Rained Forever' was another word-association I handed myself one afternoon, thinking about hot suns, deserts, and harps that could change the weather.

'The Leave-Taking' is the true story of my great-grandmother who nailed shingles on rooftops well into her seventies, then took herself up to bed when I was three and said farewell to everyone and went to sleep.

'Calling Mexico' sprang into being because I visited a friend of mine one afternoon in the summer of 1946 and, as I entered the room, he handed me the telephone and said, 'Listen.' I listened and heard the sound of Mexico City coming from two thousand miles away. I went home and wrote about my telephone experience to a friend in Paris. Halfway through my letter, the letter turned into the story, which went off in the mail that day.

'Skeleton' happened because I went to my doctor when I was twenty-two, complaining that my neck, my throat, felt strange. I touched all around the tendons and muscles of my neck. The doctor did likewise and said, 'You know what you're suffering from?'

'What?'

'A bad case,' he said, 'of discovery of the larynx. We all discover, at one time or another, various tendons, various bones, in our bodies we never noticed before. That's you. Take an aspirin and go home.'

I went home, feeling my elbows, my ankles, my ribs, my throat, and my medulla oblongata.

'Skeleton', a contest between a man and his hidden bones, wrote itself that night.

'The Picasso Summer' was the result of my walking on the shoreline with friends and my wife one late afternoon. I picked up a Popsicle stick, drew pictures in the sand and said: 'Wouldn't it be awful, if you'd wanted to own a Picasso all your life, and suddenly bumped into him here, drawing mythological beasts in the sand . . . your very own Picasso "etching" right in front of you . . . '

I finished the story, about Picasso on the beach, at two in the morning.

Hemingway. 'The Parrot Who Met Papa.' One night in 1952 I drove across Los Angeles with friends to invade the printing plant where *Life* was publishing their issue with Hemingway's *Old Man and the Sea* in it. We grabbed copies, hot off the presss, sat in the nearest bar, and talked about Papa, Finca Vigía, Cuba, and, somehow, a parrot who had lived in that bar and talked to Hemingway every night. I went home, made a notation about the parrot, and put it away for sixteen years. Prowling my file folders in 1968 I came upon just the note for a title: 'The Parrot Who Met Papa.'

My God, I thought, Papa's been dead eight years. If that parrot is still around, remembers Hemingway, can speak with his voice, he's worth millions. And what if someone kidnapped the parrot, held it for ransom?

'The Haunting of the New' happened because John Godley, Lord Kilbracken, wrote me from Ireland describing his visit to a house that had burned and been replaced, stone by stone, brick by brick, in imitation of the original. Within half a day of reading Kilbracken's postcard, I had first-drafted the tale.

Enough now. There you have it. Here are one hundred stories from almost forty years of my life, containing half the damning truths I suspected at midnight, and half of the saving truths I re-found next noon. If anything is taught here, it is simply the charting of the life of someone who started out to somewhere — and went. I have not so much thought my way through life as done things and found what it was and who I was after the doing. Each tale was a way of finding selves. Each self found each day slightly different from the one found twenty-four hours earlier.

It all started that autumn day in 1932 when Mr Electrico gave me the two gifts. I don't know if I believe in previous lives, I'm not sure I can live forever. But that young boy believed in both and I have let him have his head. He has written my stories and books for me. He runs the Ouija Board and says Aye or Nay to submerged truths or half-truths. He is the skin through which, by osmosis, all the stuffs pass and put themselves on paper. I have trusted his passions, his fears, and his joys. He has, as a result, rarely failed me. When it is a long damp November in my soul, and I think too much and perceive too little, I know it is high time to get back to that boy with the tennis shoes, the high fevers, the multitudinous joys, and the terrible nightmares. I'm not sure where he leaves off and I start. But I'm proud of the tandem team. What else can I do but wish him well, and at the same time acknowledge and wish two other people well? In the same month that I married my wife Marguerite, I became affiliated with my literary representative and closest friend, Don Congdon. Maggie typed and criticized my stories, Don criticized and sold the results. With the two of them as teammates these past thirty-three years, how could I have failed? We are the Connemara Lightfoots, the Queen's Own Evaders. And we're still sprinting for that exit.

Here are the stories. Turn the page.

The Stories of

RAY BRADBURY

The Wonderful Ice Cream Suit

In the summer twilight in the city, and out front of the quiet-clicking pool hall three young Mexican-American men breathed the warm air and looked around at the world. Sometimes they talked and sometimes they said nothing at all but watched the cars glide by like black panthers on the hot asphalt or saw trolleys loom up like thunderstorms, scatter lightning, and rumble away into silence.

'Hey,' sighed Martínez at last. He was the youngest, the most sweetly sad of the three. 'It's a swell night, huh? Swell.'

As he observed the world it moved very close and then drifted away and then came close again. People, brushing by, were suddenly across the street. Buildings five miles away suddenly leaned over him. But most of the time everything — people, cars, and buildings — stayed way out on the edge of the world and could not be touched. On this quiet warm summer evening Martínez's face was cold.

'Nights like this you wish . . . lots of things.'

'Wishing,' said the second man, Villanazul, a man who shouted books out loud in his room but spoke only in whispers on the street. 'Wishing is the useless pastime of the unemployed.'

'Unemployed?' cried Vamenos, the unshaven. 'Listen to him! We got no jobs, no money!'

'So,' said Martínez, 'we got friends.'

'True.' Villanazul gazed off towards the green plaza where the palm trees swayed in the soft night wind. 'Do you know what I wish? I wish to go into that plaza and speak among the businessmen who gather there nights to talk big talk. But dressed as I am, poor as I am, who would listen? So,

Martínez, we have each other. The friendship of the poor is real friendship. We − '

But now a handsome young Mexican with a fine thin moustache strolled by. And on each of his careless arms hung a laughing woman.

'*Madre mía!*' Martínez slapped his own brow. 'How does that one rate *two* friends?'

'It's his nice new white summer suit.' Vamenos chewed a black thumbnail. 'He looks sharp.'

Martínez leaned out to watch the three people moving away, and then looked at the tenement across the street, in one fourth-floor window of which, far above, a beautiful girl leaned out, her dark hair faintly stirred by the wind. She had been there forever, which was to say for six weeks. He had nodded, he had raised a hand, he had smiled, he had blinked rapidly, he had even bowed to her, on the street, in the hall when visiting friends, in the park, downtown. Even now, he put his hand up from his waist and moved his fingers. But all the lovely girl did was let the summer wind stir her dark hair. He did not exist. He was nothing.

'*Madre mía!*' He looked away and down the street where the man walked his two friends around a corner. 'Oh, if just I had one suit, one! I wouldn't need money if I *looked* okay.'

'I hesitate to suggest,' said Villanazul, 'that you see Gómez. But he's been talking some crazy talk for a month now about clothes. I keep on saying I'll be in on it to make him go away. That Gómez.'

'Friend,' said a quiet voice.

'Gómez!' Everyone turned to stare.

Smiling strangely, Gómez pulled forth an endless thin yellow ribbon which fluttered and swirled on the summer air.

'Gómez,' said Martínez, 'what are you doing with that tape measure?'

Gómez beamed. 'Measuring people's skeletons.'

'Skeletons!'

'Hold on.' Gómez squinted at Martínez. '*Caramba!* Where you *been* all my life! Let's try *you!*'

Martínez saw his arm seized and taped, his leg measured, his chest encircled.

'Hold still!' cried Gómez. 'Arm — perfect. Leg — chest — *perfecto*! Now quick, the height! There! Yes! Five foot five! You're in! Shake!' Pumping Martínez's hand, he stopped suddenly. 'Wait. You got . . . ten bucks?'

'I have!' Vamenos waved some grimy bills. 'Gómez, measure me!'

'All I got left in the world is nine dollars and ninety-two cents.' Martínez searched his pockets. 'That's enough for a new suit? Why?'

'Why? Because you got the right skeleton, that's why!'

'*Señor* Gómez. I don't hardly know you — '

'Know me? You're going to live with me! Come on!'

Gómez vanished into the poolroom. Martínez, escorted by the polite Villanazul, pushed by an eager Vamenos, found himself inside.

'Domínguez!' said Gómez.

Domínguez, at a wall telephone, winked at them. A woman's voice squeaked on the receiver.

'Manulo!' said Gómez.

Manulo, a wine bottle tilted bubbling to his mouth, turned.

Gómez pointed at Martínez.

'At last we found our fifth volunteer!'

Domínguez said, 'I got a date, don't bother me — ' and stopped. The receiver slipped from his fingers. His little black telephone book full of fine names and numbers went quickly back into his pocket. 'Gómez, you —'

'Yes, yes! Your money, now! *Ándale!*'

The woman's voice sizzled on the dangling phone.

Domínguez glanced at it uneasily.

Manulo considered the empty wine bottle in his hand and

the liquor-store sign across the street.

Then very reluctantly both men laid ten dollars each on the green velvet pool table.

Villanazul, amazed, did likewise, as did Gómez, nudging Martínez. Martínez counted out his wrinkled bills and change. Gómez flourished the money like a royal flush.

'Fifty bucks! The suit costs sixty! All we need is ten bucks!'

'Wait,' said Martínez. 'Gómez, are we talking about *one* suit? *Uno?*'

'*Uno!*' Gómez raised a finger. 'One wonderful white ice cream summer suit! White, white as the August moon!'

'But who will own this one suit?'

'Me!' said Manulo.

'Me!' said Domínguez.

'Me!' said Villanazul.

'Me!' cried Gómez. '*And* you, Martínez, let's show him. Line up!'

Villanazul, Manulo, Domínguez, and Gómez rushed to plant their backs against the poolroom wall.

'Martínez, you too, the other end, line up! Now, Vamenos, lay that billiard cue across our heads!'

'Sure, Gómez, sure!'

Martínez, in line, felt the cue tap his head and leaned out to see what was happening. 'Ah!' he gasped.

The cue lay flat on all their heads, with no rise or fall, as Vamenos slid it along, grinning.

'We're all the same height!' said Martínez.

'The same!' Everyone laughed.

Gómez ran down the line, rustling the yellow tape measure here and there on the men so they laughed even more wildly.

'Sure!' he said. 'It took a month, four weeks, mind you, to find four guys the same size and shape as me, a month of running around measuring. Sometimes I found guys with five-foot skeletons, sure, but all the meat on their bones was too much or not enough. Sometimes their bones were too long in the legs or too short in the arms. Boy, all the bones! I tell you! But now, five of us, same shoulders, chests, waists, arms, and as for weight? Men!'

Manulo, Domínguez, Villanazul, Gómez, and at last Martínez stepped on to the scales which flipped ink-stamped cards at them as Vamenos, still smiling wildly, fed pennies. Heart pounding, Martínez read the cards.

'One hundred thirty-five pounds . . . one thirty-six . . . one thirty-three . . . one thirty-four . . . one thirty-seven . . . a miracle!'

'No,' said Villanazul simply, 'Gómez.'

They all smiled upon that genius who now circled them with his arms.

'Are we not fine?' he wondered. 'All the same size, all the same dream — the suit. So each of us will look beautiful one night each week, eh?'

'I haven't looked beautiful in years,' said Martínez. 'The girls run away.'

'They will run no more, they will freeze,' said Gómez, 'when they see you in the cool white summer ice cream suit.'

'Gómez,' said Villanazul, 'just let me ask one thing.'

'Of course, *compadre*.'

'When we get this nice new white ice cream summer suit, some night you're not going to put it on and walk down to the Greyhound bus in it and go live in El Paso for a year in it, are you?'

'Villanazul, Villanazul, how can you say that?'

'My eyes sees and my tongue moves,' said Villanazul. 'How about the *Everybody Wins!* Punchboard Lotteries you ran and you kept running when nobody won? How about the United Chili Con Carne and Frijole Company you were going to organize and all that ever happened was the rent ran out on a two-by-four office?'

'The errors of a child now grown,' said Gómez. 'Enough!

In this hot weather someone may buy the special suit that is made just for us that stands waiting in the window of Shumway's Sunshine Suits! We have fifty dollars. Now we need just one more skeleton!'

Martínez saw the men peer around the pool hall. He looked where they looked. He felt his eyes hurry past Vamenos, then come reluctantly back to examine his dirty shirt, his huge nicotined fingers.

'Me!' Vamenos burst out at last. 'My skeleton, measure it, it's great! Sure, my hands are big, and my arms, from digging ditches! But —'

Just then Martínez heard passing on the sidewalk outside that same terrible man with his two girls, all laughing together.

He saw anguish move like the shadow of a summer cloud on the faces of the other men in this poolroom.

Slowly Vamenos stepped on to the scales and dropped his penny. Eyes closed, he breathed a prayer.

'*Madre mía*, please . . . '

The machinery whirred: the card fell out. Vamenos opened his eyes.

'Look! One thirty-five pounds! Another miracle!'

The men stared at his right hand and the card, at his left hand and a soiled ten-dollar bill.

Gómez swayed. Sweating, he licked his lips. Then his hand shot out, seized the money.

Yelling, everyone ran from the poolroom.

'The clothing store! The suit! *Vamos!*'

The woman's voice was still squeaking on the abandoned telephone. Martínez, left behind, reached out and hung the voice up. In the silence he shook his head. '*Santos*, what a dream! Six men,' he said, 'one suit. What will come of this? Madness? Debauchery? Murder? But I go with God. Gómez, wait for me!'

Martínez was young. He ran fast.

Mr Shumway, of Shumway's Sunshine Suits, paused while adjusting a tie rack, aware of some subtle atmospheric change outside his establishment.

'Leo,' he whispered to his assistant, 'Look . . . '

Outside, one man, Gómez, strolled by, looking in. Two men, Manulo and Domínguez, hurried by, staring in. Three men, Villanazul, Martínez and Vamenos, jostling shoulders, did the same.

'Leo,' Mr Shumway swallowed. 'Call the police!'

Suddenly six men filled the doorway.

Martínez, crushed among them, his stomach slightly upset, his face feeling feverish, smiled so wildly at Leo that Leo let go the telephone.

'Hey,' breathed Martínez, eyes wide. 'There's a great suit over there!'

'No.' Manulo touched a lapel. '*This* one!'

'There is only one suit in all the world!' said Gómez coldly. 'Mr Shumway, the ice cream white, size thirty-four, was in your window just an hour ago! It's gone! You didn't –'

'Sell it?' Mr Shumway exhaled. 'No, no. In the dressing room. It's still on the dummy.'

Martínez did not know if he moved and moved the crowd or if the crowd moved and moved him. Suddenly they were all in motion. Mr Shumway, running, tried to keep ahead of them.

'This way, gents. Now which of you . . . ?'

'All for one, one for all!' Martínez heard himself say, and laughed. 'We'll all try it on!'

'All?' Mr Shumway clutched at the booth curtain as if his shop were a steamship that had suddenly tilted in a great swell. He stared.

That's it, thought Martínez, look at our smiles. Now, look at the skeletons behind our smiles! Measure here, there, up, down, yes, do you *see*?

Mr Shumway saw. He nodded. He shrugged.

'All!' He jerked the curtain. 'There! Buy it, and I'll throw in the dummy free!'

Martínez peered quietly into the booth, his motion drawing the others to peer to.

The suit was there.

And it was white.

Martínez could not breathe. He did not want to. He did not need to. He was afraid his breath would melt the suit. It was enough, just looking.

But at last he took a great trembling breath and exhaled, whispering. '*Ay. Ay, caramba!*'

'It puts out my eyes,' murmured Gómez.

'Mr Shumway,' Martínez heard Leo hissing. 'Ain't it dangerous precedent to sell it? I mean, what if everybody bought *one* suit for *six* people?'

'Leo,' said Mr Shumway, 'you ever hear one single fifty-nine-dollar suit make so many people happy at the same time before?'

'Angels' wings,' murmured Martínez. 'The wings of white angels.'

Martínez felt Mr Shumway peering over his shoulders into the booth. The pale glow filled his eyes.

'You know something, Leo?' he said in awe. 'That's a *suit!*'

Gómez, shouting, whistling, ran up to the third-floor landing and turned to wave to the others, who staggered, laughed, stopped, and had to sit down on the steps below.

'Tonight!' cried Gómez. 'Tonight you move in with me, eh? Save rent as well as clothes, eh? Sure! Martínez, you got the suit?'

'Have I?' Martínez lifted the white gift-wrapped box high. 'From us to us! *Ay-hah!*'

'Vamenos, you got the dummy?'

'Here!'

Vamenos, chewing an old cigar, scattering sparks, slipped.

The dummy, falling, toppled, turned over twice, and banged down the stairs.

'Vamenos! Dumb! Clumsy!'

They seized the dummy from him. Stricken, Vamenos looked about as if he'd lost something.

Manulo snapped his fingers. 'Hey, Vamenos, we got to celebrate! Go borrow some wine!'

Vamenos plunged downstairs in a whirl of sparks.

The others moved into the room with the suit. Leaving Martínez in the hall to study Gómez's face.

'Gómez, you look sick.'

'I am,' said Gómez. 'For what have I done?' He nodded to the shadows in the room working about the dummy. 'I pick Domínguez, a devil with the women. All right. I pick Manulo, who drinks, yes, but who sings as sweet as a girl, eh? Okay. Villanazul reads books. You, you wash behind your ears. But then what do I do? Can I wait? No! I got to buy that suit! So the last guy I pick is a clumsy slob who has the right to wear *my* suit −' He stopped, confused. 'Who gets to wear *our* suit one night a week, fall down in it, or not come in out of the rain in it! Why, why, why did I *do* it!'

'Gómez,' whispered Villanazul from the room. 'The suit is ready. Come see if it looks as good using *your* light bulb.'

Gómez and Martínez entered.

And there on the dummy in the centre of the room was the phosphorescent, the miraculously white-fired ghost with the incredible lapels, the precise stitching, the neat buttonholes. Standing with the white illumination of the suit upon his cheeks, Martínez suddenly felt he was in church. White! White! It was white as the whitest vanilla ice cream, as the bottled milk in tenement halls at dawn. White as a winter cloud all alone in the moonlit sky late at night. Seeing it here in the warm summer-night room made their breath almost show on the air. Shutting his eyes, he could see it printed on his lids. He knew what colour his dreams would be this night.

'White . . . ' murmured Villanazul. 'White as the snow on that mountain near our town in Mexico, which is called the Sleeping Woman.'

'Say that again,' said Gómez.

Villanazul, proud yet humble, was glad to repeat his tribute.

' . . . white as the snow on the mountain called –'

'I'm back!'

Shocked, the men whirled to see Vamenos in the door, wine bottles in each hand.

'A party! Here! Now tell us, who wears the suit first tonight? Me?'

'It's too late!' said Gómez.

'Late! It's only nine-fifteen!'

'Late?' said everyone, bristling. 'Late?'

Gómez edged away from these men who glared from him to the suit to the open window.

Outside and below it was, after all, thought Martínez, a fine Saturday night in a summer month and through the calm warm darkness the women drifted like flowers on a quiet stream. The men made a mournful sound.

'Gómez, a suggestion.' Villanazul licked his pencil and drew a chart on a pad. 'You wear the suit from nine-thirty to ten, Manulo till ten-thirty, Domínguez till eleven, myself till eleven-thirty, Martínez till midnight, and – '

'Why me *last*?' demanded Vamenos, scowling.

Martínez thought quickly and smiled. 'After midnight is the *best* time, friend.'

'Hey,' said Vamenos, 'that's right. I never thought of that. Okay.'

Gómez smiled. 'All right. A half hour each. But from now on, remember, we each wear the suit just one night a week. Sundays we draw the straws for who wears the suit the extra night.'

'Me!' laughed Vamenos. 'I'm lucky!'

Gómez held on to Martínez, tight.

'Gómez,' urged Martínez, 'you first. Dress.'

Gómez could not tear his eyes from that disreputable
Vamenos. At last, impulsively, he yanked his shirt off over
his head. 'Ay-yeah!' he howled. 'Ay-*yeee*!'

Whisper rustle . . . the clean shirt.

'Ah . . . !'

How clean the new clothes feel, thought Martínez, holding
the coat ready. How clean they sound, how clean they smell!

Whisper . . . the pants . . . the tie, rustle . . . the suspenders. Whisper . . . now Martínez let loose the coat,
which fell in place on flexing the shoulders.

'*Ole!*'

Gómez turned like a matador in his wondrous suit-of-
lights.

'*Ole*, Gómez, *ole!*'

Gómez bowed and went out the door.

Martínez fixed his eyes to his watch. At ten sharp he heard
someone wandering about in the hall as if they had forgotten
where to go. Martínez pulled the door open and looked out.

Gómez was there, heading for nowhere.

He looks sick, thought Martínez. No, stunned, shook up,
surprised, many things.

'Gómez! This is the place!'

Gómez turned around and found his way through the
door.

'Oh, friends, friends,' he said. 'Friends, what an experience! This suit! This suit!'

'Tell us, Gómez!' said Martínez.

'I can't, how can I say it!' He gazed at the heavens, arms
spread, palms up.

'*Tell* us, Gómez!'

'I have no words, no words. You must see, yourself. Yes,
you must see — ' And here he lapsed into silence shaking his

head until at last he remembered they all stood watching him. 'Who's next? Manulo?'

Manulo stripped to his shorts, leapt forward.

'Ready!'

All laughed, shouted, whistled.

Manulo, ready, went out the door. He was gone twenty-nine minutes and thirty seconds. He came back holding to doorknobs, touching the wall, feeling his own elbows, putting the flat of his hand to his face.

'Oh, let me tell you,' he said. '*Compadres.* I went to the bar, eh, to have a drink? But no. I did not go in the bar, do you hear? I did not drink. For as I walked I began to laugh and sing. Why, why? I listened to myself and asked this. Because. The suit made me feel better than wine ever did. The suit made me drunk, drunk! So I went to the Guadalajara Refritería instead and played the guitar and sang four songs, very high! The suit, ah, the suit!'

Domínguez, next to be dressed, moved out through the world, came back from the world.

The black telephone book! thought Martínez. He had it in his hands when he left! Now, he returns, hands empty! What? What?

'On the street,' said Domínguez, seeing it all again, eyes wide, 'on the street I walked, a woman cried, "Domínguez, is that *you!*" Another said, "Domínguez? No, Quetzalcoatl, the Great White God come from the East," do you hear? And suddenly I didn't want to go with six women or eight, no. One, I thought. One! And to this one, who knows *what* I would say? "Be mine!" Or "Marry me!" *Caramba!* This suit is dangerous! But I did not care! I live, I live! Gómez, did it happen this way with you?'

Gómez, still dazed by the events of the evening, shook his head. 'No, no talk. It's too much. Later. Villanazul . . . ?'

Villanazul moved shyly forward.

Villanazul went shyly out.

Villanazul came shyly home.

'Picture it,' he said, not looking at them, looking at the floor, talking to the floor. 'The green plaza, a group of elderly businessmen gathered under the stars and they are talking, nodding, talking. Now one them whispers. All turn to stare. They move aside, they make a channel through which a white-hot light burns its way as through ice. At the centre of the great light is this person. I take a deep breath. My stomach is jelly. My voice is very small, but it grows louder. And what do I say? I say, "Friends. Do you know Carlyle's *Sartor Resartus*? In that book we find *his* Philosophy of Suits . . . " '

And at last it was time for Martínez to let the suit float him out to haunt the darkness.

Four times he walked around the block. Four times he paused beneath the tenement porches, looking up at the window where the light was lit; a shadow moved, the beautiful girl was there, not there, away and gone, and on the fifth time there she was on the porch above, driven out by the summer heat, taking the cooler air. She glanced down. She made a gesture.

At first he thought she was waving to him. He felt like a white explosion that had riveted her attention. But she was not waving. Her hand gestured and the next moment a pair of dark-framed glasses sat upon her nose. She gazed at him.

Ah, ah, he thought, so that's it. So! Even the blind may see this suit! He smiled up at her. He did not have to wave. And at last she smiled back. She did not have to wave either. Then, because he did not know what else to do and he could not get rid of this smile that had fastened itself to his cheeks, he hurried, almost ran, around the corner, feeling her stare after him. When he looked back she had taken off her glasses and gazed now with the look of the nearsighted at what, at most, must be a moving blob of light in the great darkness here. Then for good measure he went around the block again, through a city so suddenly beautiful he wanted to yell, then laugh, then yell again.

Returning, he drifted, oblivious, eyes half closed, and seeing him in the door, the others saw not Martínez but themselves come home. In that moment, they sensed that something had happened to them all.

'You're late!' cried Vamenos, but stopped. The spell could not be broken.

'Somebody tell me,' said Martínez. 'Who am I?'

He moved in a slow circle through the room.

Yes, he thought, yes, it's the suit, yes, it had to do with the suit and them altogether in that store on this fine Saturday night and then here, laughing and feeling more drunk without drinking as Manulo said himself, as the night ran and each slipped on the pants and held, toppling, to the others and, balanced, let the feeling get bigger and warmer and finer as each man departed and the next took his place in the suit until now here stood Martínez all splendid and white as one who gives orders and the world grows quiet and moves aside.

'Martínez, we borrowed three mirrors while you were gone. Look!'

The mirrors, set up as in the store, angled to reflect three Martínezes and the echoes and memories of those who had occupied this suit with him and known the bright world inside this thread and cloth. Now, in the shimmering mirror, Martínez saw the enormity of this thing they were living together and his eyes grew wet. The others blinked. Martínez touched the mirrors. They shifted. He saw a thousand, a million white-armoured Martínezes march off into eternity, reflected, re-reflected, forever, indomitable, and unending.

He held the white coat out on the air. In a trance, the others did not at first recognize the dirty hand that reached to take the coat. Then:

'Vamenos!'

'Pig!'

'You didn't wash!' cried Gómez. 'Or even shave, while you waited! *Compadres*, the bath!'

'The bath!' said everyone.

'No!' Vamenos flailed. 'The night air! I'm dead!'

They hustled him yelling out and down the hall.

Now here stood Vamenos, unbelievable in white suit, beard shaved, hair combed, nails scrubbed.

His friends scowled darkly at him.

For was it not true, thought Martínez, that when Vamenos passed by, avalanches itched on mountaintops? If he walked under windows, people spat, dumped garbage, or worse. Tonight now, this night, he would stroll beneath ten thousand wide-opened windows, near balconies, past alleys. Suddenly the world absolutely sizzled with flies. And here was Vamenos, a fresh-frosted cake.

'You sure look keen in that suit, Vamenos,' said Manulo sadly.

'Thanks,' Vamenos twitched, trying to make his skeleton comfortable where all their skeletons had so recently been. In a small voice Vamenos said, 'Can I go now?'

'Villanazul!' said Gómez. 'Copy down these rules.'

Villanazul licked his pencil.

'First,' said Gómez, 'don't fall down in that suit, Vamenos!'

'I won't.'

'Don't lean against buildings in that suit.'

'No buildings.'

'Don't walk under trees with birds in them in that suit. Don't smoke. Don't drink – '

'Please,' said Vamenos, 'can I *sit down* in this suit?'

'When in doubt, take the pants off, fold them over a chair.'

'Wish me luck,' said Vamenos.

'Go with God, Vamenos.'

He went out. He shut the door.

There was a ripping sound.

'Vamenos!' cried Martínez.

He whipped the door open.

Vamenos stood with two halves of a handkerchief torn in

his hands, laughing.

'Rrrip! Look at your faces! Rrrip!' He tore the cloth again. 'Oh, oh, your faces, your faces! Ha!'

Roaring, Vamenos slammed the door, leaving them stunned and alone.

Gómez put both hands on top of his head and turned away. 'Stone me. Kill me. I have sold our souls to a demon!'

Villanazul dug in his pockets, took out a silver coin, and studied it for a long while.

'This is my last fifty cents. Who else will help me buy back Vamenos' share of the suit?'

'It's no use,' Manulo showed them ten cents. 'We got only enough to buy the lapels and the buttonholes.'

Gómez, at the open window, suddenly leaned out and yelled. 'Vamenos! No!'

Below on the street, Vamenos, shocked, blew out a match and threw away an old cigar butt he had found somewhere. He made a strange gesture to all the men in the window above, then waved airily and sauntered on.

Somehow, the five men could not move away from the window. They were crushed together there.

'I bet he eats a hamburger in that suit,' mused Villanazul. 'I'm thinking of the mustard.'

'Don't!' cried Gómez. 'No, no!'

Manulo was suddenly at the door.

'I need a drink, bad.'

'Manulo, there's wine here, that bottle on the floor —'

Manulo went out and shut the door.

A moment later Villanazul stretched with great exaggeration and strolled about the room.

'I think I'll walk down to the plaza, friends.'

He was not gone a minute when Domínguez, waving his black book at the others, winked and turned the doorknob.

'Domínguez,' said Gómez.

'Yes?'

'If you see Vamenos, by accident,' said Gómez, 'warn him away from Mickey Murrillo's Red Rooster Café. They got fights not only *on* TV but *out front* of the TV too.'

'He wouldn't go into Murillo's,' said Domínguez. 'That suit means too much to Vamenos. He wouldn't do anything to hurt it.'

'He'd shoot his mother first,' said Martínez.

'Sure he would.'

Martínez and Gómez, alone, listened to Domínguez's footsteps hurry away down the stairs. They circled the undressed window dummy.

For a long while, biting his lips, Gómez stood at the window, looking out. He touched his shirt pocket twice, pulled his hand away, and then at last pulled something from the pocket. Without looking at it, he handed it to Martínez.

'Martínez, take this.'

'What is it?'

Martínez looked at the piece of folded pink paper with print on it, with names and numbers. His eyes widened.

'A ticket on the bus to El Paso three weeks from now!'

Gómez nodded. He couldn't look at Martínez. He stared out into the summer night.

'Turn it in. Get the money,' he said. 'Buy us a nice white panama hat and a pale blue tie to go with the white ice cream suit, Martínez. Do that.'

'Gómez — '

'Shut up. Boy, is it hot in here! I need air.'

'Gómez. I am touched. Gómez — '

But the door stood open. Gómez was gone.

Mickey Murrillo's Red Rooster Café and Cocktail Lounge was squashed between two big brick buildings and, being narrow, had to be deep. Outside, serpents of red and sulphur-green neon fizzed and snapped. Inside, dim shapes loomed and swam away to lose themselves in a swarming night sea.

Martínez, on tiptoe, peeked through a flaked place on the red-painted front window.

He felt a presence on his left, heard breathing on his right. He glanced in both directions.

'Manulo! Villanazul!'

'I decided I wasn't thirsty,' said Manulo. 'So I took a walk.'

'I was just on my way to the plaza,' said Villanazul, 'and decided to go the long way around.'

As if by agreement, the three men shut up now and turned together to peer on tiptoe through various flaked spots on the window.

A moment later, all three felt a new very warm presence behind them and heard still faster breathing.

'Is our white suit in there?' asked Gómez's voice.

'Gómez!' said everybody, surprised. 'Hi!'

'Yes!' cried Domínguez, having just arrived to find his own peephole. 'There's the suit! And, praise God, Vamenos is still *in* it!'

'I can't see!' Gómez squinted, shielding his eyes. 'What's he *doing*?'

Martínez peered. Yes! There, way back in the shadows, was a big chunk of snow and the idiot smile of Vamenos winking above it, wreathed in smoke.

'He's smoking!' said Martínez.

'He's drinking!' said Domínguez.

'He's eating a taco!' reported Villanazul.

'A *juicy* taco,' added Manulo.

'No,' said Gómez. 'No, no, no . . . '

'Ruby Escuadrillo's with him!'

'Let me see that!' Gómez pushed Martínez aside.

Yes, there was Ruby! Two hundred pounds of glittering sequins and tight black satin on the hoof, her scarlet fingernails clutching Vamenos' shoulder. Her cowlike face, floured with powder, greasy with lipstick, hung over him!

'That hippo!' said Domínguez. 'She's crushing the shoulder pads. Look, she's going to sit on his lap!'

'No, no, not with all that powder and lipstick!' said Gómez. 'Manulo, inside! Grab that drink! Villanazul, the cigar, the taco! Domínguez, date Ruby Escuadrillo, get her away. *Ándale*, men!'

The three vanished, leaving Gómez and Martínez to stare, gasping, through the peephole.

'Manulo, he's got the drink, he's *drinking* it!'

'*Ay*! There's Villanazul, he's got the cigar, he's eating the taco!'

'Hey, Domínguez, he's got Ruby! What a *brave* one!'

A shadow bulked through Murrillo's front door, travelling fast.

'Gómez!' Martínez clutched Gómez's arm. 'That was Ruby Escuadrillo's boyfriend, Toro Ruíz. If he finds her with Vamenos, the ice cream suit will be covered with blood, *covered* with blood — '

'Don't make me nervous,' said Gómez. 'Quickly!'

Both ran. Inside they reached Vamenos just as Toro Ruíz grabbed about two feet of the lapels of that wonderful ice cream suit.

'Let go of Vamenos!' cried Martínez.

'Let go that *suit*!' corrected Gómez.

Toro Ruíz, tap-dancing Vamenos, leered at these intruders.

Villanazul stepped up shyly.

Villanazul smiled. 'Don't hit him. Hit me.'

Toro Ruíz hit Villanazul smack on the nose.

Villanazul holding his nose, tears stinging his eyes, wandered off.

Gómez grabbed one of Toro Ruíz's arms, Martínez the other.

'Drop him, let him go, *cabrón, coyote, vaca!*'

Toro Ruíz twisted the ice cream suit material until all six men screamed in mortal agony. Grunting, sweating, Toro Ruíz dislodged as many as climbed on. He was winding up to hit Vamenos when Villanazul wandered back, eyes streaming.

'Don't hit him. Hit me!'

As Toro Ruíz hit Villanazul on the nose, a chair crashed on Toro's head.

'Ay!' said Gómez.

Toro Ruíz swayed, blinking, debating whether to fall. He began to drag Vamenos with him.

'Let go!' cried Gómez. 'Let go!'

One by one, with great care, Toro Ruíz's bananalike fingers let loose of the suit. A moment later he was ruins at their feet.

'*Compadres*, this way!'

They ran Vamenos outside and set him down where he freed himself of their hands with injured dignity.

'Okay, okay. My time ain't up. I still got two minutes and, let's see — ten seconds.'

'What!' said everybody.

'Vamenos,' said Gómez, 'you let a Guadalajara cow climb on you, you pick fights, you smoke, you drink, you eat tacos, and *now* you have the nerve to say your time ain't up?'

'I got two minutes and one second left!'

'Hey, Vamenos, you sure look sharp!' Distantly a woman's voice called from across the street.

Vamenos smiled and buttoned the coat.

'It's Ramona Álvarez! Ramona, wait!' Vamenos stepped off the kerb.

'Vamenos,' pleaded Gómez. 'What can you do in one minute and' — he checked his watch — 'forty seconds!'

'Watch! Hey, Ramona!'

Vamenos loped.

'Vamenos, look out!'

Vamenos, surprised, whirled, saw a car, heard the shriek of brakes.

'No,' said all five men on the sidewalk.

Martínez heard the impact and flinched. His head moved up. It looks like white laundry, he thought, flying through the air. His head came down.

Now he heard himself and each of the men make a different sound. Some swallowed too much air. Some let it out. Some choked. Some groaned. Some cried aloud for justice. Some covered their faces. Martínez felt his own fist pounding his heart in agony. He could not move his feet.

'I don't want to live,' said Gómez quietly. 'Kill me, someone.'

Then, shuffling, Martínez looked down and told his feet to walk, stagger, follow one after the other. He collided with other men. Now they were trying to run. They ran at last and somehow crossed a street like a deep river through which they could only wade, to look down at Vamenos.

'Vamenos!' said Martínez. 'You're alive!'

Strewn on his back, mouth open, eyes squeezed tight, tight, Vamenos motioned his head back and forth, back and forth, moaning.

'Tell me, tell me, oh, tell me, tell me.'

'Tell you what, Vamenos?'

Vamenos clenched his fists, ground his teeth.

'The suit, what have I done to the suit, the suit, the suit!'

The men crouched lower.

'Vamenos, it's . . . why, it's *okay*!'

'You lie!' said Vamenos. 'It's torn, it must be, it must be, it's torn, all around, *underneath*?'

'No,' Martínez knelt and touched here and there. 'Vamenos, all around, underneath even, it's okay!'

Vamenos opened his eyes to let the tears run free at last. 'A miracle,' he sobbed. 'Praise the saints!' He quieted at last. 'The car?'

'Hit and run.' Gómez suddenly remembered and glared at the empty street. 'It's good he didn't stop. We'd have – '

Everyone listened.

Distantly a siren wailed.

'Someone's phoned for an ambulance.'

'Quick!' said Vamenos, eyes rolling. 'Set me up! Take off our coat!'

'Vamenos – '

'Shut up, idiots!' cried Vamenos. 'The coat, that's it! Now, the pants, the pants, quick, quick *peones*! Those doctors! You seen movies? They rip the pants with razors to get them off! They don't *care*! They're maniacs! Ah, God, quick, quick!'

The siren screamed.

The men panicking, all handled Vamenos at once.

'Right leg, *easy*, hurry, cows! Good! Left leg, now, left, you hear, there, easy, *easy*! Ow, God! Quick! Martínez, your pants, take them off!'

'What?' Martínez froze.

The siren shrieked.

'Fool!' wailed Vamenos. 'All is lost! Your pants! Give me!'

Martínez jerked at his belt buckle.

'Close in, make a circle!'

Dark pants, light pants flourished on the air.

'Quick, here come the maniacs with the razors! Right leg on, left leg, *there*!'

'The zipper, cows, zip my zipper!' babbled Vamenos.

The siren died.

'*Madre mía*, yes, just in time! They arrive.' Vamenos lay back down and shut his eyes. '*Gracias*.'

Martínez turned, nonchalantly buckling on the white pants as the interns brushed past.

'Broken leg,' said one intern as they moved Vamenos on to a stretcher.

'*Compadres*,' said Vamenos, 'don't be mad with me.'

Gómez snorted. 'Who's mad?'

In the ambulance, head tilted back, looking out at them upside down Vamenos faltered.

'*Compadres*, when . . . when I come from the hospital . . . am I still in the bunch? You won't kick me out? Look, I'll give up smoking, keep away from Murrillo's, swear off women – '

'Vamenos,' said Martínez gently, 'don't promise nothing.'

Vamenos, upside down, eyes brimming wet, saw Martínez there, all white now against the stars.

'Oh, Martínez, you sure look great in that suit. *Compadres*, don't he look *beautiful*?'

Villanazul climbed in beside Vamenos. The door slammed. The four remaining men watched the ambulance drive away.

Then surrounded by his friends, inside the white suit, Martínez was carefully escorted back to the kerb.

In the tenement, Martínez got out the cleaning fluid and the others stood around, telling him how to clean the suit and, later, how not to have the iron too hot and how to work the lapels and the crease and all. When the suit was cleaned and pressed so it looked like a fresh gardenia just opened, they fitted it to the dummy.

'Two o'clock,' murmured Villanazul. 'I hope Vamenos sleeps well. When I left him at the hospital, he looked good.'

Manulo cleared his throat. 'Nobody else is going out with that suit tonight, huh?'

The others glared at him.

Manulo flushed. 'I mean . . . it's late. We're tired. Maybe no one will use the suit for forty-eight hours, huh? Give it a rest. Sure. Well. Where do we sleep?'

The night being still hot and the room unbearable, they

carried the suit on its dummy out and down the hall. They brought with them also some pillows and blankets. They climbed the stairs towards the roof of the tenement. There, thought Martínez, is the cooler wind, and sleep.

On the way, they passed a dozen doors that stood open, people still perspiring and awake, playing cards, drinking pop, fanning themselves with movie magazines.

I wonder, thought Martínez. I wonder if — Yes!

On the fourth floor, a certain door stood open.

The beautiful girl looked up as the men passed. She wore glasses and when she saw Martínez she snatched them off and hid them under her book.

The others went on, not knowing they had lost Martínez, who seemed stuck fast in the open door.

For a long moment he could say nothing. Then he said:

'José Martínez.'

And she said:

'Celia Obregón.'

And then both said nothing.

He heard the men moving up on the tenement roof. He moved to follow.

She said quickly, 'I saw you tonight!'

He came back.

'The suit,' he said.

'The suit,' she said, and paused. 'But not the suit.'

'Eh?' he said.

She lifted the book to show the glasses lying in her lap. She touched the glasses.

'I do not see well. You would think I would wear my glasses, but no. I walk around for years now, hiding them, seeing nothing. But tonight, even without the glasses, I see. A great whiteness passes below in the dark. So white! And I put on my glasses quickly!'

'The suit, as I said,' said Martínez.

'The suit for a little moment, yes, but there is another

whiteness above the suit.'

'Another?'

'Your teeth! Oh, such white teeth, and so many!'

Martínez put his hand over his mouth.

'So happy, Mr Martínez,' she said. 'I have not often seen such a happy face and such a smile.'

'Ah,' he said, not able to look at her, his face flushing now.

'So, you see,' she said quietly, 'the suit caught my eye, yes, the whiteness filled the night below. But the teeth were much whiter. Now, I have forgotten the suit.'

Martínez flushed again. She, too, was overcome with what she had said. She put her glasses on her nose, and then took them off, nervously, and hid them again. She looked at her hands and at the door above his head.

'May I – ' he said, at last.

'May you – '

'May I call for you,' he asked, 'when next the suit is mine to wear?'

'Why must you wait for the suit?' she said.

'I thought – '

'You do not need the suit,' she said.

'But – '

'If it were just the suit,' she said, 'anyone would be fine in it. But no, I watched. I saw many men in that suit, all different, this night. So again I say, you do not need to wait for the suit.'

'*Madre mía, madre mía!*' he cried happily. And then, quieter, 'I will need the suit for a little while. A month, six months, a year. I am uncertain. I am fearful of many things. I am young.'

'That is as it should be,' she said.

'Good night, Miss – '

'Celia Obregón.'

'Celia Obregón,' he said, and was gone from the door.

The others were waiting on the roof of the tenement.

Coming up through the trap door, Martínez saw they had placed the dummy and the suit in the centre of the roof and put their blankets and pillows in a circle around it. Now they were lying down. Now a cooler night wind was blowing here, up in the sky.

Martínez stood alone by the white suit, smoothing the lapels, talking half to himself.

'Ay, *caramba*, what a night! Seems ten years since seven o'clock, when it all started and I had no friends. Two in the morning, I got all *kinds* of friends . . . ' He paused and thought, Celia Obregón. Celia Obregón. ' . . . All kinds of friends,' he went on. 'I got a room, I got clothes. You tell *me*. You know what?' He looked around at the men lying on the rooftop, surrounding the dummy and himself. 'It's funny. When I wear this suit, I know I will win at pool, like Gómez. A woman will look at me like Domínguez. I will be able to sing like Manulo, sweetly. I will talk fine politics like Villanazul. I'm strong as Vamenos. So? So, tonight, I am more than Martínez. I am Gómez, Manulo, Domínguez, Villanazul, Vamenos. I am everyone. Ay . . . ay . . . ' He stood a moment longer by this suit which could save all the ways they sat or stood or walked. This suit which could move fast and nervous like Gómez or slow and thoughtfully like Villanazul or drift like Domínguez, who never touched ground, who always found a wind to take him somewhere. This suit which belonged to them but which also owned them all. This suit that was — what? A parade.

'Martínez,' said Gómez. 'You going to sleep?'

'Sure, I'm just thinking.'

'What?'

'If we ever get rich,' said Martínez softly, 'it'll be kind of sad. Then we'll all have suits. And there won't be no more nights like tonight. It'll break up the old gang. It'll never be the same after that.'

The men lay thinking of what had just been said.

Gómez nodded gently.

'Yeah . . . it'll never be the same . . . after that.'

Martínez lay down on his blanket. In darkness, with the others, he faced the middle of the roof and the dummy, which was the centre of their lives.

And their eyes were bright, shining, and good to see in the dark as the neon lights from nearby buildings flicked on, flicked off, flicked on, flicked off, revealing and then vanishing, revealing and then vanishing, their wonderful white vanilla ice cream summer suit.

Dark They Were
and Golden-Eyed

The rocket metal cooled in the meadow winds. Its lid gave a
bulging *pop*. From its clock interior stepped a man, a woman,
and three children. The other passengers whispered away
across the Martian meadow, leaving the man alone among his
family.

The man felt his hair flutter and the tissues of his body
draw tight as if he were standing at the centre of a vacuum.
His wife, before him, seemed almost to whirl away in smoke.
The children, small seeds, might at any instant be sown to all
the Martian climes.

The children looked up at him, as people look to the sun to
tell what time of their life it is. His face was cold.

'What's wrong?' asked his wife.

'Let's get back on the rocket.'

'Go back to Earth?'

'Yes! Listen!'

The wind blew as if to flake away their identities. At any
moment the Martian air might draw his soul from him, as
marrow comes from a white bone. He felt submerged in a
chemical that could dissolve his intellect and burn away his
past.

They looked at Martian hills that time had worn with a
crushing pressure of years. They saw the old cities, lost in
their meadows, lying like children's delicate bones among
the blowing lakes of grass.

'Chin up, Harry,' said his wife. 'It's too late. We've come
over sixty million miles.'

The children with their yellow hair hollered at the deep
dome of Martian sky. There was no answer but the racing

hiss of wind through the stiff grass.

He picked up the luggage in his cold hands. 'Here we go,' he said — a man standing on the edge of a sea, ready to wade in and be drowned.

They walked into town.

Their name was Bittering. Harry and his wife Cora; Dan, Laura and David. They built a small white cottage and ate good breakfasts there, but the fear was never gone. It lay with Mr Bittering and Mrs Bittering, a third unbidden partner at every midnight talk, at every dawn awakening.

'I feel like a salt crystal,' he said, 'in a mountain stream, being washed away. We don't belong here. We're Earth people. This is Mars. It was meant for Martians. For heaven's sake, Cora, let's buy tickets for home!'

But she only shook her head. 'One day the atom bomb will fix Earth. Then we'll be safe here.'

'Safe and insane!'

Tick-tock, seven o'clock sang the voice-clock; *time to get up*. And they did.

Something made him check everything each morning — warm hearth, potted blood-geraniums — precisely as if he expected something to be amiss. The morning paper was toast-warm from the 6 A.M. Earth rocket. He broke its seal and tilted it at his breakfast place. He forced himself to be convivial.

'Colonial days all over again,' he declared. 'Why, in ten years there'll be a million Earth Men on Mars. Big cities, everything! They said we'd fail. Said the Martians would resent our invasion. But did we find any Martians? Not a living soul! Oh, we found their empty cities, but no one in them. Right?'

A river of wind submerged the house. When the windows ceased rattling Mr Bittering swallowed and looked at the children.

'I don't know,' said David. 'Maybe there're Martians around we don't see. Sometimes nights I think I hear 'em. I hear the wind. The sand hits my window. I get scared. And I see those towns way up in the mountains where the Martians lived a long time ago. And I think I see things moving around those towns, Papa. And I wonder if those Martians *mind* us living here. I wonder if they won't do something to us for coming here.'

'Nonsense!' Mr Bittering looked out the windows. 'We're clean, decent people.' He looked at his children. 'All dead cities have some kind of ghosts in them. Memories. I mean.' He stared at the hills. 'You see a staircase and you wonder what Martians looked like climbing it. You see Martian paintings and you wonder what the painter was like. You make a little ghost in your mind, a memory. It's quite natural. Imagination.' He stopped. 'You haven't been prowling up in those ruins, have you?'

'No, Papa.' David looked at his shoes.

'See that you stay away from them. Pass the jam.'

'Just the same,' said little David. 'I bet something happens.'

Something happened that afternoon.

Laura stumbled through the settlement crying. She dashed blindly on to the porch.

'Mother, Father — the war, Earth!' she sobbed. 'A radio flash just came. Atom bombs hit New York! All the space rockets blown up. No more rockets to Mars, ever!'

'Oh, Harry!' The mother held on to her husband and daughter.

'Are you sure, Laura?' asked the father quietly.

Laura wept. 'We're stranded on Mars, forever and ever!'

For a long time there was only the sound of the wind in the late afternoon.

Alone, thought Bittering. Only a thousand of us here. No

way back. No way. No way. Sweat poured from his face and his hands and his body; he was drenched in the hotness of his fear. He wanted to strike Laura, cry, 'No, you're lying! The rockets will come back!' Instead, he stroked Laura's head against him and said, 'The rockets will get through some-day.'

'Father, what will we do?'

'Go about our business, of course. Raise crops and children. Wait. Keep things going until the war ends and the rockets come again.'

The two boys stepped out on to the porch.

'Children,' he said, sitting there, looking beyond them, 'I've something to tell you.'

'We know,' they said.

In the following days, Bittering wandered often through the garden to stand alone in his fear. As long as the rockets had spun a silver web across space, he had been able to accept Mars. For he had always told himself: Tomorrow, if I want, I can buy a ticket and go back to Earth.

But now: The web gone, the rockets lying in jigsaw heaps of molten girder and unsnaked wire. Earth people left to the strangeness of Mars, the cinnamon dusts and wine airs, to be baked like gingerbread shapes in Martian summers, put into harvested storage by Martian winters. What would happen to him, the others? This was the moment Mars had waited for. Now it would eat them.

He got down on his knees in the flower bed, a spade in his nervous hands. Work, he thought, work and forget.

He glanced up from the garden to the Martian mountains. He thought of the proud old Martian names that had once been on those peaks. Earth Men, dropping from the sky, had gazed upon hills, rivers. Martian seas left nameless in spite of names. Once Martians had built cities, named cities; climbed mountains, named mountains; sailed seas, named seas.

Mountains melted, seas drained, cities tumbled. In spite of this, the Earth Men had felt a silent guilt at putting new names to these ancient hills and valleys.

Nevertheless, man lives by symbol and label. The names were given.

Mr Bittering felt very alone in his garden under the Martian sun, anachronism bent here, planting Earth flowers in a wild soil.

Think. Keep thinking. Different things. Keep your mind free of Earth, the atom war, the lost rockets.

He perspired. He glanced about. No one watching. He removed his tie. Pretty bold, he thought. First your coat off, now your tie. He hung it neatly on a peach tree he had imported as a sapling from Massachusetts.

He returned to his philosophy of names and mountains. The Earth Men had changed names. Now there were Hormel Valleys, Roosevelt Seas, Ford Hills, Vanderbilt Pleataux, Rockefeller Rivers, on Mars. It wasn't right. The American settlers had shown wisdom, using old Indian prairie names: Wisconsin, Minnesota, Idaho, Ohio, Utah, Milwaukee, Waukegan, Osseo. The old names, the old meanings.

Staring at the mountains wildly, he thought: Are you up there? All the dead ones, you Martians? Well, here we are, alone, cut off! Come down, move us out! We're helpless.

The wind blew a shower of peach blossoms.

He put out his sun-browned hand, gave a small cry. He touched the blossoms, picked them up. He turned them, he touched them again and again. Then he shouted to his wife.

'Cora!'

She appeared at a window. He ran to her.

'Cora, these blossoms!'

She handled them.

'Do you see? They're different. They've changed! They're not peach blossoms any more!'

'Look all right to me,' she said.

'They're not. They're *wrong*! I can't tell how. An extra petal, a leaf, something, the colour, the smell!'

The children ran out in time to see their father hurrying about the garden, pulling up radishes, onions, and carrots from their beds.

'Cora, come look!'

They handled the onions, the radishes, the carrots among them.

'Do they look like carrots?'

'Yes . . . no.' She hesitated. 'I don't know.'

'They're changed.'

'Perhaps.'

'You know they have! Onions but not onions, carrots but not carrots. Taste: the same but different. Smell: not like it used to be.' He felt his heart pounding, and he was afraid. He dug his fingers into the earth. 'Cora, what's happening? What is it? We've got to get away from this.' He ran across the garden. Each tree felt his touch. 'The roses. The roses. They're turning green!'

And they stood looking at the green roses.

And two days later Dan came running. 'Come see the cow. I was milking her and I saw it. Come on!'

They stood in the shed and looked at their one cow.

It was growing a third horn.

And the lawn in front of their house very quietly and slowly was colouring itself like spring violets. Seed from Earth but growing up a soft purple.

'We must get away,' said Bittering. 'We'll eat this stuff then we'll change — who knows to what? I can't let it happen. There's only one thing to do. Burn this food!'

'It's not poisoned.'

'But it is. Subtly, very subtly. A little bit. A very little bit. We mustn't touch it.'

He looked with dismay at their house. 'Even the house. The wind's done something to it. The air's burned it. The fog at night. The boards, all warped out of shape. It's not an Earth Man's house any more.'

'Oh, your imagination!'

He put on his coat and tie. 'I'm going into town. We've got to do something now. I'll be back.'

'Wait, Harry!' his wife cried.

But he was gone.

In town, on the shadowy step of the grocery store, the men sat with their hands on their knees, conversing with great leisure and ease.

Mr Bittering wanted to fire a pistol in the air.

What are you doing, you fools! he thought. Sitting here! You've heard the news — we're stranded on this planet. Well, move! Aren't you frightened? Aren't you afraid? What are you going to do?

'Hello, Harry,' said everyone.

'Look,' he said to them. 'You did hear the news, the other day, didn't you?'

They nodded and laughed. 'Sure. Sure, Harry.'

'What are you going to do about it?'

'Do, Harry, do? What *can* we do?'

'Build a rocket, that's what!'

'A rocket, Harry? To go back to all that trouble? Oh, Harry!'

'But you *must* want to go back. Have you noticed the peach blossoms, the onions, the grass?'

'Why, yes, Harry, seems we did,' said one of the men.

'Doesn't it scare you?'

'Can't recall that it did much, Harry.'

'Idiots!'

'Now, Harry.'

Bittering wanted to cry. 'You've got to work with me. If we stay here, we'll all change. The air. Don't you smell it? Something in the air. A Martian virus, maybe: some seed, or a pollen. Listen to me!'

They stared at him.

'Sam,' he said to one of them.

'Yes, Harry?'

'Will you help me build a rocket?'

'Harry, I got a whole load of metal and some blueprints. You want to work in my metal shop on a rocket, you're welcome. I'll sell you that metal for five hundred dollars. You should be able to construct a right pretty rocket, if you work alone, in about thirty years.'

Everyone laughed.

'Don't laugh.'

Sam looked at him with quiet good humour.

'Sam,' Bittering said. 'Your eyes — '

'What about them, Harry?'

'Didn't they used to be grey?'

'Well now, I don't remember.'

'They were, weren't they?'

'Why do you ask, Harry?'

'Because now they're kind of yellow-coloured.'

'Is that so, Harry?' Sam said, casually.

'And you're taller and thinner — '

'You might be right, Harry.'

'Sam, you shouldn't have yellow eyes.'

'Harry, what colour eyes have *you* got?' Sam said.

'My eyes? They're blue of course.'

'Here you are, Harry.' Sam handed him a pocket mirror. 'Take a look at yourself.'

Mr Bittering hesitated, and then raised the mirror to his face.

There were little, very dim flecks of new gold captured in the blue of his eyes.

'Now look what you've done,' said Sam a moment later. 'You've broken my mirror.'

Harry Bittering moved into the metal shop and began to

build the rocket. Men stood in the open door and talked and joked without raising their voices. Once in a while they gave him a hand on lifting something. But mostly they just idled and watched him with their yellowing eyes.

'It's suppertime, Harry,' they said.

His wife appeared with his supper in a wicker basket.

'I won't touch it,' he said. 'I'll eat only food from our Deepfreeze. Food that came from Earth. Nothing from our garden.'

His wife stood watching him. 'You can't build a rocket.'

'I worked in a shop once, when I was twenty. I know metal. Once I get it started, the others will help,' he said, not looking at her, laying out the blueprints.

'Harry, Harry,' she said, helplessly.

'We've got to get away, Cora. We've *got* to!'

The nights were full of wind that blew down the empty moonlit sea meadows past the little white chess cities lying for their twelve-thousandth year in the shallows. In the Earth Men's settlement, the Bittering house shook with a feeling of change.

Lying abed, Mr Bittering felt his bones shifted, shaped, melted like gold. His wife, lying beside him, was dark from many sunny afternoons. Dark she was, and golden-eyed, burnt almost black by the sun, sleeping, and the children metallic in their beds, and the wind roaring forlorn and changing through the old peach trees, the violet grass, shaking out green rose petals.

The fear would not be stopped. It had his throat and heart. It dripped in a wetness of the arm and the temple and the trembling palm.

A green star rose in the east.

A strange word emerged from Mr Bittering's lips.

'*Iorrt. Iorrt.*' He repeated it.

It was a Martian word. He knew no Martian.

In the middle of the night he arose and dialled a call through to Simpson, the archaeologist.

'Simpson, what does the word *Iorrt* mean?'

'Why, that's the old Martian word for our planet Earth. Why?'

'No special reason.'

The telephone slipped from his hand.

'Hello, hello, hello, hello,' it kept saying while he sat gazing out at the green star. 'Bittering? Harry, are you there?'

The days were full of metal sound. He laid the frame of the rocket with the reluctant help of three indifferent men. He grew very tired in an hour or so and had to sit down.

'The altitude,' laughed a man.

'Are you *eating*, Harry?' asked another.

'I'm eating,' he said, angrily.

'From your Deepfreeze?'

'Yes!'

'You're getting thinner, Harry.'

'I'm not!'

'And taller.'

'Liar!'

His wife took him aside a few days later. 'Harry, I've used up all the food in the Deepfreeze. There's nothing left. I'll have to make sandwiches using food grown on Mars.'

He sat down heavily.

'You must eat,' she said. 'You're weak.'

'Yes,' he said.

He took a sandwich, opened it, looked at it, and began to nibble at it.

'And take the rest of the day off,' she said. 'It's hot. The children want to swim in the canals and hike. Please come along.'

'I can't waste time. This is a crisis!'

'Just for an hour,' she urged. 'A swim'll do you good.'

He rose, sweating. 'All right, all right. Leave me alone. I'll come.'

'Good for you, Harry.'

The sun was hot, the day quiet. There was only an immense staring burn upon the land. They moved along the canal, the father, the mother, the racing children in their swim suits. They stopped and ate meat sandwiches. He saw their skin baking brown. And he saw the yellow eyes of his wife and his children, their eyes that were never yellow before. A few tremblings shook him, but were carried off in waves of pleasant heat as he lay in the sun. He was too tired to be afraid.

'Cora, how long have your eyes been yellow?'

She was bewildered. 'Always, I guess.'

'They didn't change from brown in the last three months?'

She bit her lips. 'No. Why do you ask?'

'Never mind.'

They sat there.

'The children's eyes,' he said. 'They're yellow, too.'

'Sometimes growing children's eyes change colour.'

'Maybe *we're* children, too. At least to Mars. That's a thought.' He laughed. 'Think I'll swim.'

They leaped into the canal water, and he let himself sink down and down to the bottom like a golden statue and lie there in green silence. All was water-quiet and deep, all was peace. He felt the steady, slow current drift him easily.

If I lie here long enough, he thought, the water will work and eat away my flesh until the bones show like coral. Just my skeleton left. And then the water can build on that skeleton — green things, deep water things, red things, yellow things. Change. Change. Slow, deep, silent change. And isn't that what it is up *there*?

He saw the sky submerged above him, the sun made Martian by atmosphere and time and space.

Up there, a big river, he thought, a Martian river, all of us lying deep in it, in our pebble houses, in our sunken boulder houses, like crayfish hidden, and the water rushing away our old bodies and lengthening the bones and —

He let himself drift up through the soft light.

Dan sat on the edge of the canal, regarding his father seriously.

'*Utha*,' he said.

'What?' asked his father.

The boy smiled. 'You know. *Utha*'s the Martian word for "father".'

'Where did you learn it?'

'I don't know. Around. *Utha!*'

'What do you want?'

The boy hesitated. 'I — I want to change my name.'

'Change it?'

'Yes.'

His mother swam over. 'What's wrong with Dan for a name?'

Dan fidgeted. 'The other day you called, Dan, Dan, Dan. I didn't even hear. I said to myself, That's not my name. I've a new name I want to use.'

Mr Bittering held to the side of the canal, his body cold and his heart pounding slowly. 'What's is this new name?'

'Linnl. Isn't that a good name? Can I use it? Can't I, please?'

Mr Bittering put his hand on his head. He thought of the silly rocket, himself working alone, himself alone even among his family, so alone.

He heard his wife say. 'Why not?'

He heard himself say, 'Yes, you can use it.'

'Yaaa!' screamed the boy. 'I'm Linnl, Linnl!'

Racing down the meadowlands, he danced and shouted.

Mr Bittering looked at his wife. 'Why did we do that?'

'I don't know,' she said. 'It just seemed like a good idea.'

They walked into the hills. They strolled on old mosaic

paths, beside still-pumping fountains. The paths were covered with a thin film of cool water all summer long. You kept your bare feet cool all the day, splashing as in a creek, wading.

They came to a small deserted Martian villa with a good view of the valley. It was on top of a hill. Blue marble halls, large murals, a swimming pool. It was refreshing in this hot summertime. The Martians hadn't believed in large cities.

'How nice,' said Mrs Bittering, 'if we could move up here to this villa for the summer.'

'Come on,' he said. 'We're going back to town. There's work to be done on the rocket.'

But as he worked that night, the thought of the cool blue marble villa entered his mind. As the hours passed, the rocket seemed less important.

In the flow of days and weeks, the rocket receded and dwindled. The old fever was gone. It frightened him to think he had let it slip this way. But somehow the heat, the air, the working conditions –

He heard the men murmuring on the porch of his metal shop.

'Everyone's going. You heard?'

'All going. That's right.'

Bittering came out. 'Going where?' He saw a couple of trucks, loaded with children and furniture, drive down the dusty street.

'Up to the villas,' said the man.

'Yeah, Harry. I'm going. So is Sam. Aren't you, Sam?'

'That's right, Harry. What about you?'

'I've got work to do here.'

'Work! You can finish that rocket in the autumn, when it's cooler.'

He took a breath. 'I got the frame all set up.'

'In the autumn is better.' Their voices were lazy in the heat.

'Got to work,' he said.

'Autumn,' they reasoned. And they sounded so sensible, so right.

Autumn would be best, he thought. Plenty of time, then.

No! cried part of himself, deep down, put away, locked tight, suffocating. No! No!

'In the autumn,' he said.

'Come on, Harry,' they all said.

'Yes,' he said, feeling his flesh melt in the hot liquid air. 'Yes, in the autumn. I'll begin work again then.'

'I got a villa near the Tirra Canal,' said someone.

'You mean the Roosevelt Canal, don't you?'

'Tirra. The old Martian name.'

'But on the map — '

'Forget the map. It's Tirra now. Now I found a place in the Pillan mountains — '

'You mean the Rockefeller range,' said Bittering.

'I mean the Pillan mountains,' said Sam.

'Yes,' said Bittering, buried in the hot, swarming air. 'The Pillan mountains.'

Everyone worked at loading the truck in the hot, still afternoon of the next day.

Laura, Dan and David carried packages. Or, as they preferred to be known. Ttil, Linnl, and Werr carried packages.

The furniture was abandoned in the little white cottage.

'It looked just fine in Boston,' said the mother. 'And here in the cottage. But up at the villa? No. We'll get it when we come back in the autumn.'

Bittering himself was quiet.

'I've some ideas on furniture for the villa,' he said after a time. 'Big, lazy furniture.'

'What about your encyclopaedia? You're taking it along, surely?'

Mr Bittering glanced away. 'I'll come and get it next week.'

They turned to their daughter. 'What about your New York dresses?'

The bewildered girl stared. 'Why, I don't want them any more.'

They shut off the gas, the water, they locked the doors and walked away. Father peered into the truck.

'Gosh, we're not taking much,' he said. 'Considering all we brought to Mars, this is only a handful!'

He started the truck.

Looking at the small white cottage for a long moment, he was filled with a desire to rush to it, touch it, say good-bye to it, for he felt as if he were going away on a long journey, leaving something to which he could never quite return, never understand again.

Just then Sam and his family drove by in another truck.

'Hi, Bittering! Here we go!'

The truck swung down the ancient highway out of town. There were sixty others travelling the same direction. The town filled with a silent, heavy dust from their passage. The canal waters lay blue in the sun, and a quiet wind moved in the strange trees.

'Good-bye, town,' said Mr Bittering.

'Good-bye, good-bye,' said the family, waving to it.

They did not look back again.

Summer burned the canals dry. Summer moved like flame upon the meadows. In the empty Earth settlement, the painted houses flaked and peeled. Rubber tyres upon which children had swung in back yards hung suspended like stopped clock pendulums in the blazing air.

At the metal shop, the rocket frame began to rust.

In the quiet autumn Mr Bittering stood, very dark now, very golden-eyed, upon the slope above his villa, looking at the valley.

'It's time to go back,' said Cora.

'Yes, but we're not going,' he said quietly. 'There's nothing there any more.'

'Your books,' she said. 'Your fine clothes.'

'Your *llles* and your fine *ior uele rre*,' she said.

'The town's empty. No one's going back,' he said. 'There's no reason to, none at all.'

The daughter wove tapestries and the sons played songs on ancient flutes and pipes, their laughter echoing in the marble villa.

Mr Bittering gazed at the Earth settlement far away in the low valley. 'Such odd, such ridiculous houses the Earth people built.'

'They didn't know any better,' his wife mused. 'Such ugly people. I'm glad they've gone.'

They both looked at each other, startled by all they had just finished saying. They laughed.

'Where did they go?' he wondered. He glanced at his wife. She was golden and slender as his daughter. She looked at him, and he seemed almost as young as their eldest son.

'I don't know,' she said.

'We'll go back to town maybe next year, or the year after, or the year after that,' he said calmly. 'Now — I'm warm. How about taking a swim?'

They turned their backs to the valley. Arm in arm they walked silently down a path of clear-running spring water.

Five years later a rocket fell out of the sky. It lay steaming in the valley. Men leaped out of it, shouting.

'We won the war on the Earth! We're here to rescue you! Hey!'

But the American-built town of cottages, peach trees, and theatres was silent. They found a flimsy rocket frame rusting in an empty shop.

The rocket men searched the hills. The captain established headquarters in an abandoned bar. His lieutenant came back to report.

'The town's empty, but we found native life in the hills, sir. Dark people. Yellow eyes. Martians. Very friendly. We talked a bit, not much. They learn English fast. I'm sure our relations will be most friendly with them, sir.'

'Dark, eh?' mused the captain. 'How many?'

'Six, eight hundred, I'd say, living in those marble ruins in the hills, sir. Tall, healthy. Beautiful women.'

'Did they tell you what became of the men and women who built this Earth settlement, Lieutenant?'

'They hadn't the foggiest notion of what happened to this town or its people.'

'Strange. You think those Martians killed them?'

'They look surprisingly peaceful. Chances are a plague did this town in, sir.'

'Perhaps. I suppose this is one of those mysteries we'll never solve. One of those mysteries you read about.'

The captain looked at the room, the dusty windows, the blue mountains rising beyond, the canals moving in the light, and he heard the soft wind in the air. He shivered. Then, recovering, he tapped a large fresh map he had thumbtacked to the top of an empty table.

'Lots to be done, Lieutenant.' His voice droned on and quietly on as the sun sunk behind the blue hills. 'New settlements. Mining sites, minerals to be looked for. Bacteriological specimens taken. The work, all the work. And the old records were lost. We'll have a job of remapping to do, renaming the mountains and rivers and such. Calls for a little imagination.

'What do you think of naming those mountains the Lincoln Mountains, this canal the Washington Canal, those hills — we can name those hills for you, Lieutenant. Diplomacy. And you, for a favour, might name a town for

me. Polishing the apple. And why not make this the Einstein
Valley, and further over . . . are you *listening*, Lieutenant?'

The lieutenant snapped his gaze from the blue colour and
the quiet mist of the hills far beyond the town.

'What? Oh, *yes*, sir!'

The Strawberry Window

In his dream he was shutting the front door with its strawberry windows and lemon windows and windows like white clouds and windows like clear water in a country stream. Two dozen panes squared round the one big pane, coloured of fruit wines and gelatines and cool water ices. He remembered his father holding him up as a child. 'Look!' And through the green glass the world was emerald, moss, and summer mint. 'Look!' The lilac pane made livid grapes of all the passersby. And at last the strawberry glass perpetually bathed the town in roseate warmth, carpeted the world in pink sunrise, and made the cut lawn seem imported from some Persian rug bazaar. The strawberry window, best of all, cured people of their paleness, warmed the cold rain, and set the blowing shifting February snows afire.

'Yes, yes! There — !'

He awoke.

He heard his boys talking before he was fully out of his dream and he lay in the dark now, listening to the sad sound their talk made, like the wind blowing the white sea-bottoms into the blue hills, and then he remembered.

We're on Mars, he thought.

'What?' His wife called out in her sleep.

He hadn't realized he had spoken: he lay as still as he possibly could. But now, with a strange kind of numb reality, he saw his wife rise to haunt the room, her pale face staring through the small, high windows of their quonset hut at the clear but unfamiliar stars.

'Carrie,' he whispered.

She did not hear.

'Carrie,' he whispered. 'There's something I want to tell you. For a month now I've been wanting to say . . . tomorrow . . . tomorrow morning, there's going to be . . . '

But his wife sat all to herself in the blue starlight and would not look at him.

If only the sun stayed up, he thought, if only there was no night. For during the day he nailed the settlement town together, the boys were in school, and Carrie had cleaning, gardening, cooking to do. But when the sun was gone and their hands were empty of flowers or hammers and nails and arithmetics, their memories, like night birds, came home in the dark.

His wife moved, a slight turn of her head.

'Bob,' she said at last. 'I want to go home.'

'Carrie!'

'This isn't home,' she said.

He saw that her eyes were wet and brimming. 'Carrie, hold on awhile.'

'I've got no fingernails from holding on now!'

As if she still moved in her sleep, she opened her bureau drawers and took out layers of handkerchiefs, shirts, under-clothing, and put it all on top of the bureau, not seeing it, letting her fingers touch and bring it out and put it down. The routine was long familiar now. She would talk and put things out and stand quietly awhile, and then later put all the things away and come, dry-faced, back to bed and dreams. He was afraid that some night she would empty every drawer and reach for the few ancient suitcases against the wall.

'Bob . . . ' Her voice was not bitter, but soft, featureless, and as uncoloured as the moonlight that showed what she was doing. 'So many nights for six months I've talked this way; I'm ashamed. You work hard building houses in town. A man who works so hard shouldn't have to listen to a wife gone sad on him. But there's nothing to do but talk it out. It's the little things I miss most of all. I don't know — silly things.

Our front-porch swing. The wicker rocking chair, summer nights. Looking at the people walk or ride by those evenings, back in Ohio. Our black upright piano, out of tune. My Swedish cut glass. Our parlour furniture – oh, it was like a herd of elephants, I know, and all of it old. And the Chinese hanging crystals that hit when the wind blew. And talking to neighbours there on the front porch, July nights. All those crazy, silly things . . . they're not important. But it seems those are things that come to mind around three in the morning. I'm sorry.'

'Don't be,' he said. 'Mars is a far place. It smells funny, looks funny, and feels funny. I think to myself nights too. We came from a nice town.'

'It was green,' she said. 'In the spring and summer. And yellow and red in the fall. And ours was a nice house; my, it was old, eighty-ninety years or so. Used to hear the house talking at night, whispering away. All the dry wood, the banisters, the front porch, the sills. Wherever you touched, it talked to you. Every room a different way. And when you had the whole house talking, it was a family around you in the dark, putting you to sleep. No other house, the kind they build nowadays, can be the same. A lot of people have got to go through and live in a house to make it mellow down all over. This place here, now, this hut, it doesn't know I'm in it, doesn't care if I live or die. It makes a noise like tin, and tin's cold. It's got no pores for the years to sink in. It's got no cellar for you to put things away for next year and the year after that. It's got no attic where you keep things from last year and all the other years before you were born. If we only had a little bit up here that was familiar. Bob, then we could make room for all that's strange. But when everything, *every single thing* is strange, then it takes forever to make things familiar.'

He nodded in the dark. 'There's nothing you say that I haven't thought.'

She was looking at the moonlight where it lay upon the suitcases against the wall. He saw her move her hand down towards them.

'Carrie!'

'What?'

He swung his legs out of bed. 'Carrie, I've done a crazy damn-fool thing. All these months I heard you dreaming away, scared, and the boys at night and the wind, and Mars out there, the sea-bottoms and all, and . . . ' He stopped and swallowed. 'You got to understand what I did and why I did it. All the money we had in the bank a month ago, all the money we saved for ten years, I spent.'

'Bob!'

'I threw it away, Carrie, I swear, I threw it away on nothing. It was going to be a surprise. But now, tonight, there you are, and there are those damned suitcases on the floor and . . . '

'Bob,' she said, turning around. 'You mean we've gone through all *this*, on Mars, putting away extra money every week, only to have you burn it up in a few hours?'

'I don't know,' he said. 'I'm a crazy fool. Look, it's not long till morning. We'll get up early. I'll take you down to see what I've done. I don't want to tell you. I want you to see. And if it's no go, then, well, there's always those suitcases and the rocket to Earth four times a week.'

She did not move. 'Bob, Bob,' she murmured.

'Don't say any more,' he said.

'Bob, Bob . . . ' She shook her head slowly, unbelievingly. He turned away and lay back down on his own side of the bed, and she sat on the other side, and for a moment did not lie down, but only sat looking at the bureau where her handkerchiefs and jewellery and clothing lay ready in neat stacks where she had left them. Outside a wind the colour of moonlight stirred up the sleeping dust and powdered the air.

At last she lay back, but said nothing more and was a cold weight in the bed, staring down the long tunnel of night towards the faintest sign of morning.

They got up in the very first light and moved in the small quonset hut without a sound. It was a pantomime prolonged almost to the time when someone might scream at the silence, as the mother and father and the boys washed and dressed and ate a quiet breakfast of toast and fruit juice and coffee, with no one looking directly at anyone and everyone watching someone in the reflective surfaces of toaster, glassware, or cutlery, where all their faces were melted out of shape and made terribly alien in the early hour. Then, at last, they opened the quonset door and let in the air that blew across the cold blue-white Martian seas, where only the sand tides dissolved and shifted and made ghost patterns, and they stepped out under a raw and staring cold sky and began their walk towards a town, which seemed no more than a motion-picture set far on ahead of them on a vast, empty stage.

'What part of town are we going to?' asked Carrie.

'The rocket depot,' he said. 'But before we get there, I've a lot to say.'

The boys slowed down and moved behind their parents, listening. The father gazed ahead, and not once in all the time he was talking did he look at his wife or sons to see how they were taking all that he said.

'I believe in Mars,' he began quietly. 'I guess I believe some day it'll belong to us. We'll nail it down. We'll settle in. We won't turn tail and run. It came to me one day a year ago, right after we first arrived. Why did we come? I asked myself. Because I said, because. It's the same thing with the salmon every year. The salmon don't know why they go where they go, but they go, anyway. Up rivers they don't remember, up streams, jumping waterfalls, but finally making it to where they propagate and die, and the whole thing starts again. Call it racial memory, instinct, call it nothing, but there it is. And here we are.'

They walked in the silent morning with the great sky watching them and the strange blue and steam-white sands sifting about their feet on the new highway

'So here we are. And from Mars where? Jupiter, Neptune, Pluto, and on out? Right. *And on out*. Why? Some day the sun will blow up like a leaky furnace. Boom — there goes Earth. But maybe Mars won't be hurt; or if Mars is hurt maybe Pluto won't be, or if Pluto's hurt, then where'll *we* be, our sons' sons, that is?'

He gazed steadily up into that flawless shell of plum-coloured sky.

'Why, we'll be on some world with a number maybe; planet 6 of star system 97, planet 2 of system 99! So damn far off from here you need a nightmare to take it in! We'll be gone, do you see, gone off away and safe! And I thought to myself, ah, ah. So that's the reason we came to Mars, so *that*'s the reason men shoot off their rockets.'

'Bob — '

'Let me finish; not to make money, no. Not to see the sights, no. Those are the lies men tell, the fancy reasons they give themselves. Get rich, get famous, they say. Have fun, jump around, they say. But all the while, inside, something else is ticking along the way it ticks in salmon or whales, the way it ticks, by God, in the smallest microbe you want to name. And that little clock that ticks in everything living, you know what it says? It says get away, spread out, move along, keep swimming. Run to so many worlds and build so many towns that *nothing* can ever kill man. You *see*, Carrie? It's not just us come to Mars, it's the race, the whole darn human race, depending on how *we* make out in our lifetime. This thing is so big I want to laugh, I'm so scared stiff of it.'

He felt the boys walking steadily behind him and he felt Carrie beside him and he wanted to see her face and how she was taking all this, but he didn't look there, either.

'All this is no different than me and Dad walking the fields when I was a boy, casting seed by hand when our seeder broke down and we'd no money to fix it. It had to be done, somehow, for the later crops. My God, Carrie, my God, you *remember* those Sunday-supplement articles, "The Earth Will Freeze in a Million Years?" I bawled once, as a boy, reading articles like that. My mother asked why. I'm bawling for all those poor people up ahead, I said. Don't worry about them, Mother said. But, Carrie, that's my whole point; we *are* worrying about them. Or we wouldn't be here. It matters if Man with a capital M keeps going. There's nothing better than Man with a capital M in my books. I'm prejudiced, of course, because I'm one of the breed. But if there's any way to get hold of that immortality men are always talking about, this is the way — spread out — seed the universe. Then you got a harvest against crop failures anywhere down the line. No matter if Earth has famines or the rust comes in. You got the new wheat lifting on Venus or where-in-hell-ever man gets to in the next thousand years. I'm crazy with the idea. Carrie, crazy. When I finally hit on it I got so excited I wanted to grab people, you, the boys, and tell them. But hell, I knew that wasn't necessary. I knew a day or night would come when you'd hear that ticking in yourselves too, and then you'd see, and no one'd have to say anything again about all this. It's big talk, Carrie, I know, and big thoughts for a man just short of five feet five, but by all that's holy, it's true.'

They moved through the deserted streets of the town and listened to the echoes of their walking feet.

'And this morning?' said Carrie.

'I'm coming to this morning,' he said. 'Part of *me* wants to go home too. But the other part says if we go, everything's lost. So I thought, what bothers us most? Some of the things we once had. Some of the boys' things, your things, mine.

And I thought, if it takes an old thing to get a new thing started, by God, I'll use the old thing. I remember from history books that a thousand years ago they put charcoals in a hollowed-out cow horn, blew on them during the day, so they carried their fire on marches from place to place, to start a fire every night with the sparks left over from morning. Always a new fire, but always something of the old in it. So I weighed and balanced it off. Is the Old worth all our money? I asked. No! It's only the things we *did* with the Old that have any worth. Well, then, is the New worth *all* our money? I asked. Do you feel like investing in the day after the middle of next week? Yes! I said. If I can fight this thing that makes us want to go back to Earth, I'd dip my money in kerosene and strike a match!'

Carrie and the two boys did not move. They stood on the street, looking at him as if he were a storm that had passed over and around, almost blowing them from the ground, a storm that was now dying away.

'The freight rocket came in this morning,' he said, quietly. 'Our delivery's on it. Let's go and pick it up.'

They walked slowly up the three steps into the rocket depot and across the echoing floor towards the freight room that was just sliding back its doors, opening for the day.

'Tell us again about the salmon,' said one of the boys.

In the middle of the warm morning they drove out of town in a rented truck filled with great crates and boxes and parcels and packages, long ones, tall ones, short ones, flat ones, all numbered and neatly addressed to one Robert Prentiss, New Toledo, Mars.

They stopped the truck by the quonset hut and the boys jumped down and helped their mother out. For a moment Bob sat behind the wheel, and then slowly got out himself to walk around and look into the back of the truck at the crates.

And by noon all but one of the boxes were opened and their contents placed on the sea-bottom where the family stood among them.

'Carrie . . .'

And he led her up the old porch steps that now stood uncrated on the edge of town.

'Listen to 'em, Carrie.'

The steps squeaked and whispered underfoot.

'What do they say, tell me what they say?'

She stood on the ancient wooden steps, holding to herself, and could not tell him.

He waved his hand. 'Front porch here, living room there, dining room, kitchen, three bedrooms. Part we'll build new, part we'll bring. Of course all we got here now is the front porch, some parlour furniture, and the old bed.'

'All that money, Bob!'

He turned smiling. 'You're not mad, now, look at me! You're not mad. We'll bring it all up, next year, five years! The cut-glass vases, that Armenian carpet your mother gave us in 1961! Just *let* the sun explode!'

They looked at the other crates, numbered and lettered: Front-porch swing, front-porch wicker rocker, hanging Chinese crystals . . .

'I'll blow them myself to make them ring.'

They set the front door, with its little panes of coloured glass, on top of the stairs, and Carrie looked through the strawberry window.

'What do you see?'

But he knew what she saw, for he gazed through the coloured glass, too. And there was Mars, with its cold sky warmed and its dead seas fired with colour, with its hills like mounds of strawberry ice, and its sands like burning charcoals sifted by wind. The strawberry window, the strawberry window, breathed soft rose colours on the land and filled the mind and the eye with the light of a never-ending dawn. Bent there, looking through, he heard himself say:

'The town'll be out this way in a year. This'll be a shady street, you'll have your porch, and you'll have friends. You won't *need* all this so much, then. But starting right here, with this little bit that's familiar, watch it spread, watch Mars change so you'll know it as if you've known it all your life.'

He ran down the steps to the last and as yet unopened canvas-covered crate. With his pocket knife he cut a hole in the canvas. 'Guess!' he said.

'My kitchen stove? My furnace?'

'Not in a million years.' He smiled very gently. 'Sing me a song,' he said.

'Bob, you're clean off your head.'

'Sing me a song worth all the money we had in the bank and now don't have, but who gives a blast in hell,' he said.

'I don't know anything but "Genevieve, Sweet Genevieve"!'

'Sing that,' he said.

But she could not open her mouth and start the song. He saw her lips move and try, but there was no sound.

He ripped the canvas wider and shoved his hand into the crate and touched around for a quiet moment, and started to sing the words himself until he moved his hand a last time and then a single clear piano chord sprang out on the morning air.

'There,' he said. 'Let's take it right on to the end. Everyone! Here's the harmony.

A Scent of Sarsaparilla

Mr William Finch stood quietly in the dark and blowing attic all morning and afternoon for three days. For three days in late November, he stood alone, feeling the soft, white flakes of Time falling out of the infinite cold steel sky, silently, softly, feathering the roof and powdering the eaves. He stood, eyes shut. The attic, wallowed in seas of wind in the long sunless days, creaked every bone and shook down ancient dusts from its beams and warped timbers and lathings. It was a mass of sights and torments that ached all about him where he stood sniffing its elegant dry perfumes and feeling of its ancient heritages. Ah. Ah.

Listening, downstairs, his wife Cora could not hear him walk or shift or twitch. She imagined she could only hear him breathe, slowly out and in, like a dusty bellows, alone up there in the attic, high in the windy house.

'Ridiculous,' she muttered.

When he hurried down for lunch the third afternoon, he smiled at the bleak walls, the chipped plates, the scratched silverware, and even at his wife!

'What's all the excitement?' she demanded.

'Good spirits is all. Wonderful spirits!' he laughed. He seemed almost hysterical with joy. He was seething in a great warm ferment which, obviously, he had trouble concealing. His wife frowned.

'What's that *smell*?'

'Smell, smell, smell?'

'Sarsaparilla.' She sniffed suspiciously. 'That's what it is!'

'Oh, it couldn't be!' His hysterical happiness stopped as quickly as if she'd switched him off. He seemed stunned, ill at ease, and suddenly very careful.

'Where did you go this morning?' she asked.

'You *know* I was cleaning the attic.'

'Mooning over a lot of trash. I didn't hear a sound. Thought maybe you weren't in the attic at all. What's that?' She pointed.

'Well, now how did *those* get there?' he asked the world.

He peered down at the pair of black spring-metal bicycle clips that bound his thin pants cuffs to his bony ankles.

'Found them in the attic,' he answered himself. 'Remember when we got out on the gravel road in the early morning on our tandem bike, Cora, forty years ago, everything fresh and new?'

'If you don't finish that attic today, I'll come up and toss everything out myself.'

'Oh, no,' he cried. 'I have everything the way I want it!'

She looked at him coldly.

'Cora,' he said, eating his lunch, relaxing, beginning to enthuse again, 'you know what attics are? They're Time Machines, in which old, dim-witted men like me can travel back forty years to a time when it was summer all year round and children raided ice wagons. Remember how it tasted? You held the ice in your handkerchief. It was like sucking the flavour of linen and snow at the same time.'

Cora fidgeted.

It's not impossible, he thought, half closing his eyes, trying to see it and build it. Consider an attic. It's very atmosphere is Time. It deals in other years, the cocoons and chrysalises of another age. All the bureau drawers are little coffins where a thousand yesterdays lie in state. Oh, the attic's a dark, friendly place, full of Time, and if you stand in the very centre of it, straight and tall, squinting your eyes, and thinking and thinking, and smelling the Past, and putting out your hands to feel of Long Ago, why, it . . .

He stopped, realizing he had spoken some of this aloud.

Cora was eating rapidly.

'Well, wouldn't it be interesting,' he asked the parting in her hair, 'if Time Travel *could* occur? And what more logical, proper place for it to happen than in an attic like *ours*, eh?'

'It's not always summer back in the old days,' she said. 'It's just your crazy memory. You remember all the good things and forget the bad. It wasn't always summer.'

'Figuratively speaking, Cora, it was.'

'Wasn't.'

'What I mean is this,' he said, whispering excitedly, bending forwards to see the image he was tracing on the blank dining room wall. 'If you rode your unicycle carefully between the years, balancing, hands out, careful, careful, if you rode from year to year, spent a week in 1909, a day in 1900, a month or a fortnight somewhere else, 1905, 1898, you could stay with summer the rest of your life.'

'Unicycle?'

'You know, one of those tall chromium one-wheeled bikes, single-seater, the performers ride in vaudeville shows, juggling. Balance, true balance, it takes, not to fall off, to keep the bright objects flying in the air, up and up, a light, a flash, a sparkle, a bomb of brilliant colours, red, yellow, blue, green, white, gold: all the Junes and Julys and Augusts that ever were, in the air, about you, at once, hardly touching your hands, flying, suspended, and you, smiling, among them. Balance, Cora, *balance*.'

'Blah,' she said, 'blah, blah.' And added. 'Blah!'

He climbed the long cold stairs to the attic, shivering.

There were nights in winter when he woke with porcelain in his bones, with cool chimes blowing in his ears, with frost piercing his nerves in a raw illumination like white-cold fireworks exploding and showering down in flaming snows upon a silent land deep in his subconscious. He was cold, cold, cold, and it would take a score of endless summers, with their green torches and bronze suns, to thaw him free of his wintry sheath. He was a great tasteless chunk of brittle ice, a snowman put to bed each night, full of confetti dreams, tumbles of crystal and flurry. And there lay winter outside forever, a great leaden wine press smashing down its colourless lid of sky, squashing them all like so many grapes, mashing colour and sense and being from everyone, save the children who fled on skis and toboggans down mirrored hills which reflected the crushing iron shield that hung lower above town each day and every eternal night.

Mr Finch lifted the attic trap door. But here, *here*. A dust of summer sprang up about him. The attic dust simmered with heat left over from other seasons. Quietly, he shut the trap door down.

He began to smile.

The attic was quiet as a thundercloud before a storm. On occasion, Cora Finch heard her husband murmuring, murmuring, high up there.

At five in the afternoon, singing 'My Isle of Golden Dreams', Mr Finch flipped a crisp new straw hat in the kitchen door. 'Boo!'

'Did you sleep all afternoon?' snapped his wife. 'I called up at you four times and no answer.'

'Sleep?' He considered this and laughed, then put his hand quickly over his mouth. 'Well, I guess I did.'

Suddenly she saw him. 'My God!' she cried, 'where'd you get that coat?'

He wore a red candy-striped coat, a high white, choking collar and ice cream pants. You could smell the straw hat like a handful of fresh hay fanned in the air.

'Found 'em in an old trunk.'

She sniffed. 'Don't smell of moth balls. Looks brandnew.'

'Oh, no!' he said hastily. He looked stiff and uncomfortable as she eyed his costume.

'This isn't summer-stock company,' she said.

'Can't a fellow have a little fun?'

'That's all you've ever had.' She slammed the oven door. 'While I've stayed home and knitted, Lord knows, you've been down at the store helping ladies' elbows in and out doors.'

He refused to be bothered. 'Cora.' He looked deep into the crackling straw hat. 'Wouldn't it be nice to take a Sunday walk the way we used to do, with your silk parasol and your long dress whishing along, and sit on those wire-legged chairs at the soda parlour and smell the drugstore the way they used to smell? Why don't drugstores smell that way any more? And order two sarsaparillas for us, Cora, and then ride out in our 1910 Ford to Hannahan's Pier for a box supper and listen to the brass band. How about it?'

'Supper's ready. Take that dreadful uniform off.'

'If you could make a wish and take a ride on those oak-lined country roads like they had before cars started rushing, would you *do* it?' he insisted, watching her.

'Those old roads were dirty. We came home looking like Africans. Anyway' — she picked up a sugar jar and shook it — 'this morning I had forty dollars here. Now it's gone! Don't tell me you ordered those clothes from a costume house. They're brand new: they didn't come from any trunk!'

'I'm — ' he said.

She raved for half an hour, but he could not bring himself to say anything. The November wind shook the house and as she talked, the snows of winter began to fall again in the cold sky.

'Answer me!' she cried. 'Are you crazy, spending our money that way, on clothes you can't wear?'

'The attic,' he started to say.

She walked off and sat in the living room.

The snow was falling fast now and it was a cold dark November evening. She heard him climb up the stepladder, slowly, into the attic, into that dusty place of other years, into that black place of costumes and props and Time, into a world separate from this world below.

He closed the trap door down. The flashlight, snapped on, was company enough. Yes, here was all of Time compressed in a Japanese-paper flower. At the touch of memory, everything would unfold into the clear water of the mind, in beautiful blooms, in spring breezes, larger than life. Each of the bureau drawers slid forth, might contain aunts and cousins and grandmamas, ermined in dust. Yes, Time was here. You could feel it breathing, an atmospheric instead of a mechanical clock.

Now the house below was as remote as another day in the Past. He half shut his eyes and looked and looked on every side of the waiting attic.

Here, in prismed chandelier, were rainbows and mornings and noons as bright as new rivers flowing endlessly back through Time. His flashlight caught and flickered them alive, the rainbows leapt up to curve the shadows back with colours, with colours like plums and strawberries and Concord grapes, with colours like cut lemons and the sky where the clouds drew off after storming and the blue was there. And the dust of the attic was incense burning and all of Time burning, and all you need do was peer into the flames. It was indeed a great machine of Time, this attic, he knew, he felt, he was sure, and if you touched prisms here, doorknobs there, plucked tassels, chimed crystals, swirled dust, punched trunk hasps and gusted the vox humana of the old hearth bellows until it puffed the soot of a thousand ancient fires into your eyes, if, indeed, you played this instrument, this warm machine of parts, if you fondled all of its bits and pieces, its levers and changers and movers, then, then, *then*!

He thrust out his hands to orchestrate, to conduct, to flourish. There was music in his head, in his mouth shut tight, and he played the great machine, the thunderously silent organ, bass, tenor, soprano, low, high, and at last, at last, a chord that shuddered him so that he had to shut his eyes.

'About nine o'clock that night she heard him calling, 'Cora!' She went upstairs. His head peered down at her from above, smiling at her. He waved his hat. 'Good-bye, Cora.'

'What do you mean?' she cried.

'I've thought it over for three days and I'm saying good-bye.'

'Come down out of there, you fool!'

'I drew five hundred dollars from the bank yesterday. I've been thinking about this. And then when *it* happened, well . . . Cora . . . ' He shoved his eager hand down. 'For the last time, will you come along with me?'

'In the attic? Hand down that stepladder, William Finch. I'll climb up there and run you out of that filthy place!'

'I'm going to Hannahan's Pier for a bowl of clam chowder,' he said. 'And I'm requesting the brass band to play "Moonlight Bay". Oh, come on, Cora . . . ' He motioned his extended hand.

She simply stared at his gentle, questioning face.

'Good-bye,' he said.

He waved gently, gently. Then his face was gone, the straw hat was gone.

'William!' she screamed.

The attic was dark and silent.

Shrieking, she ran and got a chair and used it to groan her way up into the musty darkness. She flourished the flashlight. 'William! William!'

The dark spaces were empty. A winter wind shook the house.

Then she saw the far west attic window, ajar.

She fumbled over to it. She hesitated, held her breath. Then, slowly, she opened it. The ladder was placed outside the window, leading down on to a porch roof.

She pulled back from the window.

Outside the opened frame the apple trees shone bright green, it was twilight of a summer day in July. Faintly, she heard explosions, firecrackers going off. She heard laughter and distant voices. Rockets burst in the warm air, softly, red, white, and blue, fading.

She slammed the window and stood reeling. 'William!'

Wintry November light glowed up through the trap in the attic floor behind her. Bent to it, she saw the snow whispering against the cold clear panes down in that November world where she would spend the next thirty years.

She did not go near the window again. She sat alone in the black attic, smelling the one smell that did not seem to fade. It lingered like a sigh of satisfaction, on the air. She took a deep, long breath.

The old familiar, the unforgettable scent of drugstore sarsaparilla.

The Picasso Summer

George and Alice Smith detrained at Biarritz one summer noon and in an hour had run through their hotel on to the beach into the ocean and back out to bake upon the sand.

To see George Smith sprawled burning there, you'd think him only a tourist flown fresh as iced lettuce to Europe and soon to be transshipped home. But here was a man who loved art more than life itself.

'There . . . ' George Smith sighed. Another ounce of perspiration trickled down his chest. Boil out the Ohio tap water, he thought, then drink down the best Bordeaux. Silt your blood with rich French sediment so you'll see with native eyes!

Why? Why eat, breathe, drink everything French? So that, given time, he might really begin to understand the genius of one man.

His mouth moved forming a name.

'George?' His wife loomed over him. 'I know what you've been thinking. I can read your lips.'

He lay perfectly still waiting.

'And?'

'Picasso,' she said.

He winced. Someday she would learn to pronounce that name.

'Please,' she said. 'Relax. I know you heard the rumour this morning, but you should see your eyes — your tic is back. All right, Picasso's here, down the coast a few miles away, visiting friends in some small fishing town. But you must forget it or our vacation's ruined.'

'I wish I'd never heard the rumour,' he said honestly.

'If only,' she said, 'you liked other painters.'

Others? Yes, there were others. He could breakfast most congenially on Caravaggio still lifes of autumn pears and midnight plums. For lunch: those fire-squirting, thick-wormed Van Gogh sunflowers, those blooms a blind man might read with one rush of scorched fingers down fiery canvas. But the great feast? The paintings he saved his palate for? There, filling the horizon like Neptune risen, crowned with limeweed, alabaster, coral, paintbrushes clenched like tridents in horn-nailed fists, and with fist-tail vast enough to fluke summer showers out over all Gibraltar – who else but the creator of *Girl Before a Mirror* and *Guernica*?

'Alice,' he said patiently, 'how can I explain? Coming down on the train, I thought, Good Lord, it's *all* Picasso country!'

But was it really? he wondered. The sky, the land, the people, the flushed pink bricks here, scrolled electric-blue ironwork balconies there, a mandolin ripe as a fruit in some man's thousand fingerprinting hands, billboard tatters blowing like confetti in night winds – how much was Picasso, how much George Smith staring round the world with wild Picasso eyes? He despaired of answering. That old man had distilled turpentines and linseed oil so thoroughly through George Smith that they shaped his being, all Blue Period at twilight, all Rose Period at dawn.

'I keep thinking,' he said aloud, 'if we saved our money . . . '

'We'll never have five thousand dollars.'

'I know,' he said quietly. 'But it's nice thinking we might bring it off someday. Wouldn't it be great to just step up to him, say "Pablo, here's five thousand! Give us the sea, the sand, that sky, or any old thing you want, we'll be happy . . . '

After a moment his wife touched his arm.

'I think you'd better go in the water now,' she said.

'Yes,' he said. 'I'd better do just that.'

White fire showered up when he cut the water.

During the afternoon George Smith came out, and went into the ocean with the vast spilling motions of now warm, now cool people who at last, with the sun's decline, their bodies all lobster colours and colours of broiled squab and guinea hen, trudged for their wedding-cake hotels.

The beach lay deserted for endless mile on mile save for two people. One was George Smith, towel over shoulder, out for a last devotional.

For along the shore another shorter, square-cut man walked alone in the tranquil weather. He was deeper-tanned, his close-shaven head dyed almost mahogany by the sun, and his eyes were clear and bright as water in his face.

So the shore-line stage was set, and in a few minutes the two men would meet. And once again Fate fixed the scales for shocks and surprises, arrivals and departures. And all the while these two solitary strollers did not for a moment think on coincidence, that unswum stream which lingers at man's elbow with every crowd in every town. Nor did they ponder the fact that if man dares dip into that stream he grabs a wonder in each hand. Like most, they shrugged at such folly and stayed well up the bank lest Fate should shove them in.

The stranger stood alone. Glancing about, he saw his aloneness, saw the waters of the lovely bay, saw the sun sliding down the late colours of the day, and then, half turning, spied a small wooden object on the sand. It was no more than the slender stick from a lime ice cream delicacy long since melted away. Smiling, he picked the stick up. With another glance around to re-ensure his solitude, the man stooped again and, holding the stick gently, with light sweeps of his hand began to do the one thing in all the world he knew best how to do.

He began to draw incredible figures along the sand.

He sketched one figure and then moved over and, still

looking down, completely focused on his work now, drew a second and a third figure, and after that a fourth and a fifth and a sixth.

George Smith, printing the shoreline with his feet, gazed here, gazed there, and then saw the man ahead. George Smith, drawing nearer, saw that the man, deeply tanned, was bending down. Nearer yet, and it was obvious what the man was up to. George Smith chuckled. Of course, of course . . . Alone on the beach this man — how old? sixty-five? seventy? — was scribbling and doodling away. How the sand flew! How the wild portraits flung themselves out there on the shore! How . . .

George Smith took one more step and stopped, very still.

The stranger was drawing and drawing and did not seem to sense that anyone stood immediately behind him and the world of his drawings in the sand. By now he was so deeply enchanted with his solitudinous creation that depth bombs set off in the bay might not have stopped his flying hand nor turned him round.

George Smith looked down at the sand. And after a long while, looking, he began to tremble.

For there on the flat shore were pictures of Grecian lions and Mediterranean goats and maidens with flesh of sand like powdered gold and satyrs piping on hand-carved horns and children dancing, strewing flowers along and along the beach with lambs gambolling after, and muscians skipping to their harps and lyres and unicorns racing youths towards distant meadows, woodlands, ruined temples, and volcanoes. Along the shore in a never-broken line, the hand, the wooden stylus of this man, bent down in fever and raining perspiration, scribbled, ribboned, looped around over and up, across, in, out, stitched, whispered, stayed, then hurried on as if this travelling bacchanal must flourish to its end before the sun was put out by the sea. Twenty, thirty yards or more the nymphs and dryads and summer founts sprang up in unravelled hieroglyphs. And the sand in the dying light was the colour of molten copper on which was now slashed a message that any man in any time might read and savour down the years. Everything whirled and poised in its own wind and gravity. Now wine was being crushed from under the grape-blooded feet of dancing vintners' daughters, now steaming seas gave birth to coin-sheathed monsters while flowered kites strewed scent on blowing clouds . . . now . . . now . . . now . . .

The artist stopped.

George Smith drew back and stood away.

The artist glanced up, surprised to find someone so near. Then he simply stood there, looking from George Smith to his own creations flung like idle footprints down the way. He smiled at last and shrugged as if to say, Look what I've done; see what a child? You will forgive me, won't you? One day or another we are all fools . . . You too, perhaps? So allow an old fool this, eh? Good! Good!

But George Smith could only look at the little man with the sun-dark skin and the clear sharp eyes and say the man's name once, in a whisper, to himself.

They stood thus for perhaps another five seconds, George Smith staring at the sand-frieze, and the artist watching George Smith with amused curiosity. George Smith opened his mouth, closed it, put out his hand, took it back. He stepped towards the pictures, stepped away. Then he moved along the line of figures, like a man viewing a precious series of marbles cast up from some ancient ruin on the shore. His eyes did not blink, his hand wanted to touch but did not dare to touch. He wanted to run but did not run.

He looked suddenly at the hotel. Run, yes! Run! What? Grab a shovel, dig, excavate, save a chunk of this all-too-crumbling sand? Find a repairman, race him back here with plaster of Paris to cast a mould of some small fragile part of these? No, no. Silly, silly. Or . . . ? His eyes flicked to his hotel window. The camera! Run, get it, get back, and hurry along the shore, clicking, changing film, clicking until . . .

George Smith whirled to face the sun. It burned faintly on his face; his eyes were two small fires from it. The sun was half underwater, and as he watched it sank the rest of the way in a matter of seconds.

The artist had drawn nearer and now was gazing into George Smith's face with great friendliness, as if he were guessing every thought. Now he was nodding his head in a little bow. Now the ice cream stick had fallen casually from his fingers. Now he was saying good night, good night. Now he was gone, walking back down the beach towards the south.

George Smith stood looking after him. After a full minute he did the only thing he could possibly do. He started at the beginning of the fantastic frieze of satyrs and fauns and wine-dipped maidens and prancing unicorns and piping youths and he walked slowly along the shore. He walked a long way, looking down at the free-running bacchanal. And when he came to the end of the animals and men he turned around and started back in the other direction, just staring down as if he had lost something and did not quite know where to find it. He kept on doing this until there was no more light in the sky or on the sand to see by.

He sat down at the supper table.

'You're late,' said his wife. 'I just had to come down alone. I'm ravenous.'

'That's all right,' he said.

'Anything interesting happen on your walk?' she asked.

'No,' he said.

'You look funny; George, you didn't swim out too far, did you, and almost drown? I can tell by your face. You *did* swim out too far, didn't you?'

'Yes,' he said.

'Well,' she said, watching him closely. 'Don't ever do that again. Now — what'll you have?'

He picked up the menu and started to read it and stopped suddenly.

'What's wrong?' asked his wife.

He turned his head and shut his eyes for a moment.

'Listen.'

She listened.

'I don't hear anything,' she said.

'Don't you?'

'No. What is it?'

'Just the tide,' he said after a while, sitting there, his eyes still shut. 'Just the tide coming in.'

The Day It
Rained Forever

The hotel stood like a hollowed dry bone under the very centre of the desert sky where the sun burned the roof all day. All night, the memory of the sun stirred in every room like the ghost of an old forest fire. Long after dusk, since light meant heat, the hotel lights stayed off. The inhabitants of the hotel preferred to feel their way blind through the halls in their never-ending search for cool air.

This one particular evening Mr Terle, the proprietor, and his only boarders, Mr Smith and Mr Fremley, who looked and smelled like two ancient rags of cured tobacco, stayed late on the long veranda. In their creaking glockenspiel rockers they gasped back and forth in the dark, trying to rock up a wind.

'Mr Terle . . . ? Wouldn't it be *really* nice . . . someday . . . if you could buy . . . air conditioning . . . ?'

Mr Terle coasted a while, eyes shut.

'Got no money for such things, Mr Smith.'

The two old boarders flushed; they hadn't paid a bill now in twenty-one years.

Much later Mr Fremley sighed a grievous sigh. 'Why, why don't we all just quit, pick up, get outa here, move to a decent city? Stop this swelterin' and fryin' and sweatin'.'

'Who'd buy a dead hotel in a ghost town?' said Mr Terle quietly. 'No. No, we'll just sit here and wait, wait for that great day, January 29.'

Slowly, all three men stopped rocking.

January 29.

The one day in all the year when it really let go and rained.

'Won't wait long.' Mr Smith tilted his gold railroad watch

like the warm summer moon in his palm. 'Two hours and nine minutes from now it'll *be* January 29. But I don't see nary a cloud in ten thousand miles.'

'It's rained every January 29 since I was born!' Mr Terle stopped, surprised at his own loud voice. 'If it's a day late this year, I won't pull God's shirttail.'

Mr Fremley swallowed hard and looked from east to west across the desert towards the hills. 'I wonder . . . will there ever be a gold rush hereabouts again?'

'No gold,' said Mr Smith. 'And what's more, I'll make you a bet — no rain. No rain tomorrow or the day after the day after tomorrow. No rain all the rest of this year.'

The three old men sat staring at the big sun-yellowed moon that burned a hole in the high stillness.

After a long while, painfully, they began to rock again.

The first hot morning breezes curled the calendar pages like a dried snake skin against the flaking hotel front.

The three men, thumbing their suspenders up over their hat-rack shoulders, came barefoot downstairs to blink out at that idiot sky.

'January 29 . . . '

'Not a drop of mercy there.'

'Day's young.'

'*I'm* not,' Mr Fremley turned and went away.

It took him five minutes to find his way up through the delirious hallways to his hot, freshly baked bed.

At noon, Mr Terle peered in.

'Mr Fremley . . . ?'

'Damn desert cactus, that's us!' gasped Mr Fremley, lying there, his face looking as if at any moment it might fall away in a blazing dust on the raw plank floor. 'But even the best damn cactus got to have just a sip of water before it goes back to another year of the same damn furnace. I tell you I won't move again. I'll lie here and die if I don't hear more than birds pattin' around up on that roof!'

'Keep your prayers simple and your umbrella handy,' said Mr Terle and tiptoed away.

At dusk, on the hollow roof a faint pattering sounded.

Mr Fremley's voice sang out mournfully from his bed.

'Mr Terle, that ain't rain! That's you with the garden hose sprinklin' well water on the roof! Thanks for tryin'; but cut it out now.'

The pattering sound stopped. There was a sigh from the yard below.

Coming around the side of the hotel a moment later, Mr Terle saw the calendar fly out and down in the dust.

'Damn January 29!' cried a voice. 'Twelve more months! Have to wait twelve more months, now!'

Mr Smith was standing there in the doorway. He stepped inside and brought out two dilapidated suitcases and thumped them on the porch.

'Mr Smith!' cried Mr Terle. 'You can't leave after thirty years!'

'They say it rains twenty days a month in Ireland,' said Mr Smith. 'I'll get a job there and run around with my hat off and my mouth open.'

'You can't go!' Mr Terle tried frantically to think of something; he snapped his fingers. 'You owe me nine thousand dollars' rent!'

Mr Smith recoiled; his eyes got a look of tender and unexpected hurt in them.

'I'm sorry,' Mr Terle looked away. 'I didn't mean that. Look now — you just head for Seattle. Pours two inches a week there. Pay me when you can, or never. But do me a favour; wait till midnight. It's cooler then, anyhow. Get you a good night's walk towards the city.'

'Nothin'll happen between now and midnight.'

'You got to have faith. When everything else is gone, you got to believe a thing'll happen. Just stand here with me, you don't have to sit, just stand here and think of rain. That's the last thing I'll ever ask of you.'

On the desert sudden little whirlwinds of dust twisted up, sifted down. Mr Smith's eyes scanned the sunset horizon.

'What do I think? Rain, oh you rain, come along here? Stuff like that?'

'Anything. Anything at all!'

Mr Smith stood for a long time between his two mangy suitcases and did not move. Five, six minutes ticked by. There was no sound, save the two men's breathing in the dusk.

Then at last, very firmly, Mr Smith stooped to grasp the luggage handles.

Just then, Mr Terle blinked. He leaned forwards cupping his hand to his ear.

Mr Smith froze, his hands still on the luggage.

From away among the hills, a murmur, a soft and tremulous rumble.

'Storm coming!' hissed Mr Terle.

The sound grew louder; a kind of whitish cloud rose up from the hills.

Mr Smith stood on tiptoe.

Upstairs Mr Fremley sat up like Lazarus.

Mr Terle's eyes grew wider and yet wider to take hold of what was coming. He held to the porch rail like the captain of a calm-foundered vessel feeling the first stir of some tropic breeze that smelled of lime and ice-cool white meat of coconut. The smallest wind stroked over his aching nostrils as over the flues of a white-hot chimney.

'There!' cried Mr Terle. 'There!'

And over the last hill, shaking out feathers of fiery dust, came the cloud, the thunder, the racketing storm.

Over the hill the first car to pass in twenty days flung itself down the valley with a shriek, a thud, and a wail.

Mr Terle did not dare to look at Mr Smith.

Mr Smith looked up, thinking of Mr Fremley in his room.

Mr Fremley, at the window, looked down and saw the car expire and die in front of the hotel.

For the sound that the car made was curiously final. It had come a very long way on blazing sulphur roads, across salt flats abandoned ten millions years ago by the shingling off of waters. Now, with wire-ravellings like cannibal hair sprung up from seams, with a great eyelid of canvas top thrown back and melted to spearmint gum over the rear seat, the auto, a Kissel car, vintage 1924, gave a final shuddering as if to expel its ghost upon the air.

The old woman in the front seat of the car waited patiently, looking in at the three men and the hotel as if to say, Forgive me, my friend is ill: I've known him a long while, and now I must see him through his final hour. So she just sat in the car waiting for the faint convulsions to cease and for the great relaxation of all the bones which signifies that the final process is over. She must have sat a full half minute longer listening to her car, and there was something so peaceful about her that Mr Terle and Mr Smith leaned slowly towards her. At last she looked at them with a grave smile and raised her hand.

Mr Fremley was surprised to see his hand go out the window, above, and wave back to her.

On the porch Mr Smith murmured, 'Strange. It's not a storm. And I'm not disappointed. How come?'

But Mr Terle was down the path and to the car.

'We thought you were . . . that is . . . ' He trailed off. 'Terle's my name, Joe Terle.'

She took his hand and looked at him with absolutely clear and unclouded light blue eyes like water that has melted from snow a thousand miles off and come a long way, purified by wind and sun.

'Miss Blanche Hillgood,' she said, quietly. 'Graduate of the Grinnell College, unmarried teacher of music, thirty years high-school glee club and student of orchestra conductor, Green City, Iowa, twenty years private teacher of piano, harp, and voice, one month retired and living on a pension and now, taking my roots with me, on my way to California.'

'Miss Hillgood, you don't look to be going anywhere from here.'

'I had a feeling about that.' She watched the two men circle the car cautiously. She sat like a child on the lap of a rheumatic grandfather, undecided. 'Is there nothing we can do?'

'Make a fence of the wheels, dinner gong of the brake-drums, the rest'll make a fine rock garden.'

Mr Fremley shouted from the sky. 'Dead? I say, is the car dead? I can *feel* it from here! Well — it's way past time for supper!'

Mr Terle put out his hand. 'Miss Hillgood, that there is Joe Terle's Desert Hotel, open twenty-six hours a day. Gila monsters and road runners please register before going upstairs. Get you a night's sleep, free, we'll knock our Ford off its blocks and drive you to the city come morning.'

She let herself be helped from the car. The machine groaned as if in protest at her going. She shut the door carefully with a soft click.

'One friend gone, but the other still with me. Mr Terle, could you please bring her in out of the weather?'

'Her, ma'am?'

'Forgive me, I never think of things but what they're people. The car was a man, I suppose, because it took me places. But a harp, now, don't you agree, is female?'

She nodded to the rear seat of the car. There, tilted against the sky like an ancient scrolled leather ship prow cleaving the wind, stood a case which towered above any driver who might sit up in front and sail the desert calms or the city traffics.

'Mr Smith,' said Mr Terle, 'lend a hand.'

They untied the huge case and hoisted it gingerly out between them.

'What you got there?' cried Mr Fremley from above.

Mr Smith stumbled. Miss Hillgood gasped. The case shifted in the two men's arms.

From within the case came a faint musical humming.

Mr Fremley, above, heard. It was all the answer he needed. Mouth open, he watched the lady and the two men and their boxed friend sway and vanish in the cavernous porch below.

'Watch out!' said Mr Smith. 'Some damn fool left his luggage here – ' He stopped. 'Some damn fool? *Me!*'

The two men looked at each other. They were not perspiring any more. A wind had come up from somewhere, a gentle wind that fanned their shirt collars and flapped the strewn calendar gently in the dust.

'*My* luggage . . . ' said Mr Smith.

Then they all went inside.

'More wine, Miss Hillgood? Ain't had wine on the table in years.'

'Just a touch, if you please.'

They sat by the light of a single candle which made the room an oven and struck fire from the good silverware and the uncracked plates as they talked and drank warm wine and ate.

'Miss Hillgood, get on with your life.'

'All my life,' she said, 'I've been so busy running from Beethoven to Bach to Brahms, I never noticed I was twenty-nine. Next time I looked up I was forty. Yesterday, seventy-one. Oh, there were men; but they'd given up singing at ten and given up flying when they were twelve. I always figured we were born to fly, one way or other, so I couldn't stand most men shuffling along with all the iron of the earth in their blood. I never met a man who weighed less than nine hundred pounds. In their black business suits, you could hear them roll by like funeral wagons.

'So you flew away?'

'Just in my mind, Mr Terle. It's taken sixty years to make the final break. All that time I grabbed on to piccolos and flutes and violins because they make streams in the air, you know, like streams and rivers on the ground. I rode every tributary and tried every fresh-water wind from Handel on down to a whole slew of Strausses. It's been the far way around that's brought me here.'

'How'd you finally make up your mind to leave?' asked Mr Smith.

'I looked around last week and said, "Why, look, you've been flying *alone*!" No one in all Green City really cares *if* you fly or how high you go. It's always, "Fine, Blanche," or "Thanks for the recital at the PTA tea, Miss H." But no one really listening. And when I talked a long time ago about Chicago or New York, folks swatted me and laughed. "Why be a little frog in a big pond when you can be the biggest frog in all Green City!" So I stayed on, while the folks who gave me advice moved away or died or both. The rest had wax in their ears. Just last week I shook myself and said, "Hold on! Since when do *frogs* have wings?" '

'So now you're headin' west?' said Mr Terle.

'Maybe to play in pictures or in that orchestra under the stars. But somewhere I just must play at last for someone who'll hear and really listen . . . '

They sat in the warm dark. She was finished, she had said it all now, foolish or not — and she moved back quietly in her chair.

Upstairs someone coughed.

Miss Hillgood heard, and rose.

It took Mr Fremley a moment to ungum his eyelids and make

out the shape of the woman bending down to place the tray by his rumpled bed.

'What you all talkin' about down there just now?'

'I'll come back later and tell you word for word,' said Miss Hillgood. 'Eat now. The salad's fine.' She moved to leave the room.

He said, quickly, 'You goin' to stay?'

She stopped half out the door and tried to trace the expression on his sweating face in the dark. He, in turn, could not see her mouth or eyes. She stood a moment longer, silently, then went on down the stairs.

'She must not've heard me,' said Mr Fremley.

But he knew she had heard.

Miss Hillgood crossed the downstairs lobby to fumble with the locks on the upright leather case.

'I must pay you for my supper.'

'On the house,' said Mr Terle.

'I must pay,' she said, and opened the case.

There was a sudden flash of gold.

The two men quickened in their chairs. They squinted at the little old woman standing beside the tremendous heart-shaped object which towered above her with its shining columbined pedestal atop which a calm Grecian face with antelope eyes looked serenely at them even as Miss Hillgood looked now.

The two men shot each other the quickest and most startled of glances, as if each had guessed what might happen next. They hurried across the lobby, breathing hard, to sit on the very edge of the hot velvet lounge, wiping their faces with damp handkerchiefs.

Miss Hillgood drew a chair under her, rested the golden harp gently back on her shoulder, and put her hands to the strings.

Mr Terle took a breath of fiery air and waited.

A desert wind came suddenly along the porch outside,

tilting the chairs so they rocked this way and that like boats
on a pond at night.

Mr Fremley's voice protested from above. 'What's goin'
on down there?'

And then Miss Hillgood moved her hands.

Starting at the arch near her shoulder, she played her
fingers out along the simple tapestry of wires towards the
blind and beautiful stare of the Greek goddess on her
column, and then back. Then for a moment she paused and
let the sounds drift up through the baked lobby air and into
all the empty rooms.

If Mr Fremley shouted above, no one heard. For Mr Terle
and Mr Smith were so busy jumping up to stand riven in
shadows, they heard nothing save the storming of their own
hearts and the shocked rush of all the air in their lungs. Eyes
wide, mouths dropped, in a kind of pure insanity, they stared
at the two women there, the blind Muse proud on her golden
pillar, and the seated one, gentle eyes closed, her small hands
stretched forth on the air.

Like a girl, they both thought wildly, like a little girl
putting her hands out of a window to feel what? Why, of
course, of course!

To feel the rain.

The echo of the first shower vanished down remote cause-
ways and roof drains, away.

Mr Fremley, above, rose from his bed as if pulled round by
his ears.

Miss Hillgood played.

She played and it wasn't a tune they knew at all, but it was a
tune they had heard a thousand times in their long lives,
words or not, melody or not. She played and each time her
fingers moved, the rain fell pattering through the dark hotel.
The rain fell cool at the open windows and the rain rinsed
down the baked floorboards of the porch. The rain fell on the
roof top and fell on hissing sand, it fell on rusted car and

empty stable and dead cactus in the yard. It washed the windows and laid the dust and filled the rain barrels and curtained the doors with beaded threads that might part and whisper as you walked through. But more than anything the soft touch and coolness of it fell on Mr Smith and Mr Terle. Its gentle weight and pressure moved them down and down until it had seated them again. By its continuous budding and prickling on their faces it made them shut up their eyes and mouths and raise their hands to shield it away. Seated there, they felt their heads tilt slowly back to let the rain fall where it would.

The flash flood lasted a minute, then faded away as the fingers trailed down the loom, let drop a few last bursts and squalls and then stopped.

The last chord hung in the air like a picture taken when lightning strikes and freezes a billion drops of water on their downward flight. Then the lightning went out. The last drops fell through darkness in silence.

Miss Hillgood took her hands from the strings, her eyes still shut.

Mr Terle and Mr Smith opened their eyes to see those two miraculous women way over there across the lobby somehow come through the storm untouched and dry.

They trembled. They leaned forwards as if they wished to speak. They looked helpless, not knowing what to do.

And then a single sound from high above in the hotel corridors drew their attention and told them what to do.

The sound came floating down feebly, fluttering like a tired bird beating its ancient wings.

The two men looked up and listened.

It was the sound of Mr Fremley.

Mr Fremley, in his room, applauding.

It took five seconds for Mr Terle to figure out what it was. Then he nudged Mr Smith and began, himself, to beat his palms together. The two men struck their hands in mighty explosions. The echoes ricocheted about in the hotel caverns above and below, striking walls, mirrors, windows, trying to fight free of rooms.

Miss Hillgood opened her eyes now, as if this new storm had come on her in the open, unprepared.

The men gave their own recital. They smashed their hands together so fervently it seemed they had fistfuls of fire-crackers to set off, one on another. Mr Fremley shouted. Nobody heard. Hands winged out, banged shut again and again until fingers puffed up and the old men's breath came short and they put their hands at last on their knees, a heart pounding inside each one.

Then, very slowly, Mr Smith got up and still looking at the harp, went outside and carried in the suitcases. He stood at the foot of the lobby stairs looking for a long while at Miss Hillgood. He glanced down at her single piece of luggage resting there by the first tread. He looked from her suitcase to her and raised his eyebrows questioningly.

Miss Hillgood looked at her harp, at her suitcase, at Mr Terle, and at last back to Mr Smith.

She nodded once.

Mr Smith bent down and with his own luggage under one arm and her suitcase in the other, he started the long slow climb up the stairs in the gentle dark. As he moved, Miss Hillgood put the harp back on her shoulder and either played in time to his moving or he moved in time to her playing, neither of them knew which.

Half up the flight, Mr Smith met Mr Fremley who, in a faded robe, was testing his slow way down.

Both stood there, looking deep into the lobby at the one man on the far side in the shadows, and the two women further over, no more than a motion and a gleam. Both thought the same thoughts.

The sound of the harp playing, the sound of the cool water falling every night and every night of their lives, after this.

No spraying the roof with the garden hose now any more. Only sit on the porch or lie in your night bed and hear the falling . . . the falling . . . the falling . . .

Mr Smith moved on up the stairs; Mr Fremley moved down.

The harp, the harp. Listen, listen!

The fifty years of drought were over.

The time of the long rains had come.

A Medicine for Melancholy

(*The Sovereign Remedy Revealed!*)

'Send for some leeches; bleed her,' said Doctor Gimp.

'She has no blood left!' cried Mrs Wilkes. 'Oh, Doctor, what ails our Camillia?'

'She's not right.'

'Yes, yes?'

'She's poorly.' The good doctor scowled.

'Go on, go on!'

'She's a fluttering candle flame, no doubt.'

'Ah, Doctor Gimp,' protested Mr Wilkes. 'You but tell us as you go out what we told you when you came in!'

'No, more! Give her these pills at dawn, high noon, and sunset. A sovereign remedy!'

'Damn, she's *stuffed* with sovereign remedies now!'

'Tut, tut! That's a shilling as I pass downstairs, sir.'

'Go down and send the Devil up!' Mr Wilkes shoved a coin in the good doctor's hand.

Whereupon the physician, wheezing, taking snuff, sneezing, stamped down into the swarming streets of London on a sloppy morn in the spring of 1762.

Mr and Mrs Wilkes turned to the bed where their sweet Camillia lay pale, thin, yes, but far from unlovely, with large wet lilac eyes, her hair a creek of gold upon her pillow.

'Oh,' she almost wept. 'What's to become of me? Since the start of spring, three weeks, I've been a ghost in my mirror: I frighten me. To think I'll die without seeing my twentieth birthday.'

'Child,' said the mother. 'Where do you hurt?'

'My arms. My legs. My bosom. My head. How many doctors — six? — have turned me like a beef on a spit. No more. Please, let me pass away untouched.'

'What a ghastly, what a mysterious illness,' said the mother. 'Oh, do something, Mr Wilkes!'

'What?' asked Mr Wilkes angrily. 'She won't have the physician, the apothercary, or the priest! — and Amen to that! — they've wrung me dry! Shall I run in the street then and bring the Dustman up?'

'Yes,' said a voice.

'What!' All three turned to stare.

They had quite forgotten her younger brother, Jamie, who stood picking his teeth at a far window, gazing serenely down into the drizzle and the loud rumbling of the town.

'Four hundred years ago,' he said serenely, 'it was tried, it worked. Don't bring the Dustman up, no, no. But let us hoist Camillia, cot and all, manoeuvre her downstairs, and set her up outside our door.'

'Why? What for?'

'In a single hour' — Jamie's eyes jumped, counting — 'a thousand folk rush by our gate. In one day, twenty thousand people run, hobble, or ride by. Each might eye my swooning sister, each count her teeth, pull her ear lobes, and all, all, mind you, would have a sovereign remedy to offer! One of them would just have to be right!'

'Ah,' said Mr Wilkes, stunned.

'Father!' said Jamie breathlessly. 'Have you ever known one single man who didn't think he personally wrote *Materia Medica*? This green ointment for sour throat, that ox-salve for miasma or bloat? Right now, ten thousand self-appointed apothecaries sneak off down there, their wisdom lost to us!'

'Jamie boy, you're incredible!'

'Cease!' said Mrs Wilkes. 'No daughter of mine will be put on display in this or any street — '

'Fie, woman!' said Mr Wilkes. 'Camillia melts like snow and you hesitate to move her from this hot room? Come, Jamie, lift the bed!'

'Camillia?' Mrs Wilkes turned to her daughter.

'I may as well die in the open,' said Camillia, 'where a cool breeze might stir my locks as I . . . '

'Bosh!' said the father. 'You'll not die. Jamie, heave! Ha! There! Out of the way, wife! Up, boy, *higher*!'

'Oh,' cried Camillia faintly. 'I fly, I *fly* . . . !'

Quite suddenly a blue sky opened over London. The population, surprised by the weather, hurried out into the streets, panicking for something to see, to do, to buy. Blind men sang, dogs jigged, clowns shuffled and tumbled, children chalked games and threw balls as if it were carnival time.

Down into all this, tottering, their veins bursting from their brows, Jamie and Mr Wilkes carried Camillia like a lady Pope sailing high in her sedan-chair cot, eyes clenched shut, praying.

'Careful!' screamed Mrs Wilkes. 'Ah, she's dead! No. There. Put her down. Easy . . . '

And at last the bed was tilted against the house front so that the River of Humanity surging by could see Camillia, a large pale Bartolemy Doll put out like a prize in the sun.

'Fetch a quill, ink, paper, lad,' said the father. 'I'll make notes as to symptoms spoken of and remedies offered this day. Tonight we'll average them out. Now — '

But already a man in the passing crowd had fixed Camillia with a sharp eye.

'She's sick!' he said.

'Ah,' said Mr Wilkes, gleefully. 'It begins. The quill, boy. There. Go on, sir!'

'She's not well.' The man scowled. 'She does poorly.'

'Does poorly —' Mr Wilkes wrote, then froze. 'Sir?' He looked up suspiciously. 'Are you a physician?'

'I am, sir.'

'I *thought* I knew the words! Jamie, take my cane, drive him off! Go, sir, be gone!'

The man hastened off, cursing, mightily exasperated.

'She's not well, she does poorly . . . pah!' mimicked Mr Wilkes, but stopped. For now a woman, tall and gaunt as a spectre fresh risen from the tomb, was pointing a finger at Camillia Wilkes.

'Vapours,' she intoned.

'Vapours,' wrote Mr Wilkes, pleased.

'Lung-flux,' chanted the woman.

'Lung-flux!' Mr Wilkes wrote, beaming. 'Now, that's more *like* it!'

'A medicine for melancholy is needed,' said the woman palely. 'Be there mummy ground to medicine in your house? The best mummies are: Egyptian, Arabian, Hirasphatos, Libyan, all of great use in magnetic disorders. Ask for me, the Gypsy, at the Flodden Road. I sell stone parsley, male frankincense —'

'Flodden Road, stone parsley — slower, woman.'

'Opobalsam, pontic valerian —'

'Wait, woman! Opobalsam, yes! Jamie, stop her!'

But the woman, naming the medicine, glided on.

A girl no more than seventeen, walked up now and stared at Camillia Wilkes.

'She —'

'One moment!' Mr Wilkes scribbled feverishly. '— Magnetic disorders — pontic valerian — drat! Well, young girl, now. What do you see in my daughter's face? You fix her with your gaze, you hardly breathe. So?'

'She —' The strange girl searched deep into Camillia's eyes, flushed, and stammered. 'She suffers from . . . from . . . '

'Spit it out!'

'She . . . she . . . oh!'

And the girl, with a last look of deepest sympathy, darted off through the crowd.

'Silly girl!'

'No, Papa,' murmured Camillia, eyes wide. 'Not silly. She *saw*. She *knew*. Oh, Jamie, run fetch her, make her tell!'

'No, she offered nothing! Whereas, the Gypsy, see her list!'

'I know it, Papa.' Camillia, paler, shut her eyes.

Someone cleared his throat.

A butcher, his apron a scarlet battleground, stood bristling his fierce moustaches there.

'I have seen cows with this look,' he said. 'I have saved them with brandy and three new eggs. In winter I have saved myself with the same elixir —'

'My daughter is no cow, sir!' Mr Wilkes threw down his quill. 'Nor is she a butcher, nor is it January! Step back, sir, others wait!'

And indeed, now a vast crowd clamoured, drawn by the others, aching to advise their favourite swig, recommend some country site where it rained less and shone more sun than in all England or your South of France. Old men and women, especial doctors as all the aged are, clashed by each other in bristles of canes, in phalanxes of crutches and hobble sticks.

'Back!' cried Mrs Wilkes, alarmed. 'They'll crush my daughter like a spring berry!'

'Stand off!' Jamie seized canes and crutches and threw them over the mob, which turned on itself to go seek their missing members.

'Father, I fail, I fail,' gasped Camillia.

'Father!' cried Jamie. 'There's but one way to stop this riot! Charge them! Make them pay to give us their mind on this ailment!'

'Jamie, you are my son! Quick, boy, paint a sign! Listen, people! Tuppence! Queue up please, a line! Tuppence to speak your piece! Get your money out, yes! That's it. You, sir. You, madame. And you, sir. Now, my quill! Begin!'

The mob boiled in like a dark sea.

Camillia opened one eye and swooned again.

Sundown, the streets almost empty, only a few strollers now. Camillia moth-fluttered her eyelids at a familiar clinking jingle.

'Three hundred and ninety-nine, four hundred pennies!' Mr Wilkes counted the last money into a bag held by his grinning son. 'There!'

'It will buy me a fine black funeral coach,' said the pale girl.

'Hush! Did you imagine, family, so many people, two hundred, would pay to give us their opinion?'

'Yes,' said Mrs Wilkes. 'Wives, husbands, children, are deaf to each other. So people gladly pay to have someone listen. Poor things, each today thought he and he alone knew quinsy, dropsy, glanders, could tell the slaver from the hives. So tonight we are rich and two hundred people are happy, having unloaded their full medical kit at our door.'

'Gods, instead of quelling the riot, we had to drive them off snapping like pups.'

'Read us the list, Father,' said Jamie, 'of two hundred remedies. Which one is true?'

'I care not,' whispered Camillia, sighing. 'It grows dark. My stomach is queasy from listening to the names! May I be taken upstairs?'

'Yes, dear. Jamie, lift!'

'Please,' said a voice.

Half-bent, the men looked up.

There stood a Dustman of no particular size or shape, his face masked with soot from which shone water-blue eyes and a white slot of an ivory smile. Dust sifted from his sleeves and his pants as he moved, as he talked quietly, nodding.

'I couldn't get through the mob earlier,' he said, holding his dirty cap in his hands. 'Now, going home, here I am. Must I pay?'

'No, Dustman, you need not,' said Camillia gently.

'Hold on –' protested Mr Wilkes.

But Camillia gave him a soft look and he grew silent.

'Thank you, ma'am.' The Dustman's smile flashed like warm sunlight in the growing dusk. 'I have but one advice.'

He gazed at Camillia. She gazed at him.

'Be this Saint Bosco's Eve, sir, ma'am?'

'Who knows? Not *me*, sir!' said Mr Wilkes.

'I think it *is* Saint Bosco's Eve, sir. Also, it is the night of the full moon. So,' said the Dustman humbly, unable to take his eyes from the lovely haunted girl, 'you must leave your daughter out in the light of that rising moon.'

'Out under the moon!' said Mrs Wilkes.

'Doesn't that make the lunatic?' asked Jamie.

'Beg pardon, sir.' The Dustman bowed. 'But the full moon soothes all sick animals, be they human or plain field beast. There is a serenity of colour, a quietude of touch, a sweet sculturing of mind and body in full moonlight.'

'It may rain –' said the mother uneasily.

'I swear,' said the Dustman quickly. 'My sister suffered this same swooning paleness. We set her like a potted lily out one spring night with the moon. She lives today in Sussex, the soul of reconstituted health!'

'Reconstituted! Moonlight! And will cost us not a penny of the four hundred we collected this day, Mother, Jamie, Camillia.'

'No!' said Mrs Wilkes. 'I won't have it!'

'Mother,' said Camillia.

She looked earnestly at the Dustman.

From his grimed face the Dustman gazed back, his smile like a little scimitar in the dark.

'Mother,' said Camillia. 'I feel it. The moon will cure me,

it will, it will . . . '

The mother sighed. 'This is not my day, nor night. Let me kiss you for the last time, then. There.'

And the mother went upstairs.

Now the Dustman backed off, bowing courteously to all.

'All night now, remember, beneath the moon, not the slightest disturbance until dawn. Sleep well, young lady. Dream, and dream the best. Good night.'

Soot was lost in soot: the man was gone.

Mr Wilkes and Jamie kissed Camillia's brow.

'Father, Jamie,' she said. 'Don't worry.'

And she was left alone to stare off where at a great distance she thought she saw a smile hung by itself in the dark blink off and on, then go round a corner, vanishing.

She waited for the rising of the moon.

Night in London, the voices growing drowsier in the inns, the slamming of doors, drunken farewells, clocks chiming. Camillia saw a cat like a woman stroll by in her furs, saw a woman like a cat stroll by, both wise, both Egyptian, both smelling of spice. Every quarter hour or so a voice drifted down from above:

'You all right, child?'

'Yes, Father.'

'Camillia?'

'Mother, Jamie, I'm fine.'

And at last. 'Good night.'

'Good night.'

The last lights out. London asleep.

The moon rose.

And the higher the moon, the larger grew Camillia's eyes as she watched the alleys, the courts, the streets, until at last, at midnight, the moon moved over her to show her like a marble atop an ancient tomb.

A motion in darkness.

Camillia pricked her ears.

A faint melody sprang out on the air.

A man stood in the shadows of the court.

Camillia gasped.

The man stepped forth into moonlight, carrying a lute which he strummed softly. He was a man well-dressed, whose face was handsome and, now anyway, solemn.

'A troubadour,' said Camillia aloud.

The man, his finger on his lips, moved slowly forwards and soon stood by her cot.

'What are you doing out so late?' asked the girl, unafraid but not knowing why.

'A friend sent me to make you well.' He touched the lute strings. They hummed sweetly. He was indeed handsome there in the silver light.

'That cannot be,' she said, 'for it was told me, the *moon* is my cure.'

'And so it will be, maiden.'

'What songs do you sing?'

'Songs of spring nights, aches and ailments without name. Shall I name your fever, maiden?'

'If you know it, yes.'

'First, the symptoms: raging temperatures, sudden cold, heart fast then slow, storms of temper, then sweet calms, drunkenness from having sipped only well water, dizziness from being touched only *thus* —'

He touched her wrist, saw her melt towards delicious oblivion, drew back.

'Depressions, elations,' he went on. 'Dreams — '

'Stop!' she cried, enthralled. 'You know me to the letter. Now, name my ailment!'

'I will.' He pressed his lips to the palm of her hand so she quaked suddenly. 'The name of the ailment is Camillia Wilkes.'

'How strange.' She shivered, her eyes glinting lilac fires.

'Am I then my own affliction? How sick I make myself? Even now, feel my heart!'

'I feel it, so.'

'My limbs, they burn with summer heat!'

'Yes. They scorch my fingers.'

'But now, the night wind, see how I shudder, cold! I die, I swear it, I die!'

'I will not let you,' he said quietly.

'Are you a doctor, then?'

'No, just your plain, your ordinary physician, like another who guessed your trouble this day. The girl who would have named it but ran off in the crowd.'

'Yes, I saw in her eyes she knew what had seized me. But, now, my teeth chatter. And no extra blanket!'

'Give room, please. There. Let me see: two arms, two legs, head and body. I'm all here!'

'What, sir!'

'To warm you from the night, of course.'

'How like a hearth! Oh, sir, sir, do I *know* you? Your name?'

Swiftly above her, his head shadowed hers. From it his merry clear-water eyes glowed as did his white ivory slot of a smile.

'Why, Bosco, of course,' he said.

'Is there not a saint by that name?'

'Given an hour, you will call me so, yes.'

His head bent closer. Thus sooted in shadow, she cried with joyous recognition to welcome her Dustman back.

'The world spins! I pass away! The cure, sweet Doctor, or all is lost!'

'The cure,' he said. 'And the cure is *this* . . . '

Somewhere, cats sang. A shoe, shot from a window, tipped them off a fence. Then all was silence and the moon . . .

'Shh . . . '

Dawn. Tiptoeing downstairs. Mr and Mrs Wilkes peered into their courtyard.

'Frozen stone dead from the terrible night, I *know* it!'

'No, wife, look! Alive! Roses in her cheeks! No, more! Peaches, persimmons! She glows all rosy-milky! Sweet Camillia, alive and well, made whole again!'

They bent by the slumbering girl.

'She smiles, she dreams: what's that she says?'

'The sovereign,' sighed the girl, 'remedy.'

'What, what?'

The girl smiled again, a white smile, in her sleep.

'A medicine,' she murmured, 'for melancholy.'

She opened her eyes.

'Oh, Mother, Father!'

'Daughter! Child! Come upstairs!'

'No.' She took their hands, tenderly. 'Mother? Father?'

'Yes?'

'No one will see. The sun but rises. Please. Dance with me.'

They did not want to dance.

But, celebrating they knew not what, they did.

The Shoreline
at Sunset

Tom, knee-deep in the waves, a piece of driftwood in his hand, listened.

The house, up towards the Coast Highway in the late afternoon, was silent. The sounds of closets being rummaged, suitcase locks snapping, vases being smashed, and of a final door crashing shut, all had faded away.

Chico, standing on the pale sand, flourished his wire strainer to shake out a harvest of lost coins. After a moment, without glancing at Tom, he said, 'Let her go.'

So it was every year. For a week or a month, their house would have music swelling from the windows, there would be new geraniums potted on the porch rail, new paint on the doors and steps. The clothes on the wire line changed from harlequin pants to sheath dresses to handmade Mexican frocks like white waves breaking behind the house. Inside, the paintings on the walls shifted from imitation Matisse to pseudo-Italian Renaissance. Sometimes, looking up, he would see a woman drying her hair like a bright yellow flag on the wind. Sometimes the flag was black or red. Sometimes the woman was tall, sometimes short, against the sky. But there was never more than one woman at a time. And, at last, a day like today came . . .

Tom placed his driftwood on the growing pile near where Chico sifted the billion footprints left by people long vanished from their holidays.

'Chico. What are we doing here?'

'Living the life of Riley, boy!'

'I don't feel like Riley, Chico.'

'Work at it, boy!'

Tom saw the house a month from now, the flowerpots blowing dust, the walls hung with empty squares, only sand carpeting the floors. The rooms would echo like shells in the wind. And all night every night bedded in separate rooms he and Chico would hear a tide falling away and away down a long shore, leaving no trace.

Tom nodded, imperceptibly. Once a year he himself brought a nice girl here, knowing she was right at last and that in no time they would be married. But his women always stole silently away before dawn, feeling they had been mistaken for someone else, not being able to play the part. Chico's friends left like vacuum cleaners, with a terrific drag, roar, rush, leaving no lint unturned, no clam unprised of its pearl, taking their purses with them like toy dogs which Chico had petted as he opened their jaws to count their teeth.

'That's four women so far this year.'

'Okay, referee.' Chico grinned. 'Show me the way to the showers.'

'Chico —' Tom bit his lower lip, then went on. 'I been thinking. Why don't we split up?'

Chico just looked at him.

'I mean,' said Tom, quickly, 'maybe we'd have better luck, alone.'

'Well, I'll be goddamned,' said Chico slowly, gripping the strainer in his big fists before him. 'Look here, boy, don't you know the facts? You and me, we'll be here come the year 2000. A couple of crazy dumb old gooney-birds drying their bones in the sun. Nothing's ever going to happen to us now, Tom, it's too late. Get that through your head and shut up.'

Tom swallowed and looked steadily at the other man. 'I'm thinking of leaving — next week.'

'Shut up, shut up, and get to work!'

Chico gave the sand an angry showering rake that tilled him forty-three cents in dimes, pennies, and nickels. He stared blindly at the coins shimmering down the wires like a pinball game all afire.

Tom did not move, holding his breath.

They both seemed to be waiting for something.

The something happened.

'Hey . . . hey . . . hey . . . '

From a long way off down the coast a voice called.

The two men turned slowly.

'Hey . . . hey . . . oh, hey . . . !'

A boy was running, yelling, waving, along the shore two hundred yards away. There was something in his voice that made Tom feel suddenly cold. He held on to his own arms, waiting.

'Hey!'

The boy pulled up, gasping, pointing back along the shore.

'A woman, a funny woman, by the North Rock!'

'A woman!' The words exploded from Chico's mouth and he began to laugh. 'Oh, no, no!'

'What you mean, a "funny" woman?' asked Tom.

'I don't know,' cried the boy, his eyes wide. 'You got to come see! Awful funny!'

'You mean "drowned"?'

'Maybe! She came out of the water, she's lying on the shore, you got to see, yourself . . . funny . . . ' The boy's voice died. He gazed off north again. 'She's got a fish's tail.'

Chico laughed. 'Not before supper, please.'

'Please!' cried the boy, dancing now. 'No lie! Oh, hurry!'

He ran off, sensed he was not followed, and looked back in dismay.

Tom felt his lips move. 'Boy wouldn't run this far for a joke, would he, Chico?'

'People have run further for less.'

Tom started walking. 'All right, son.'

'Thanks, mister, oh thanks!'

The boy ran. Twenty yards up the coast. Tom looked

back. Behind him, Chico squinted, shrugged, dusted his hands wearily, and followed.

They moved north along the twilight beach, their skin weathered in tiny folds about their burnt pale eyes, looking younger for their hair cut close to the skull so you could not see the grey. There was a fair wind and the ocean rose and fell with prolonged concussions.

'What,' said Tom, 'what if we get to North Rock and it's true? The ocean *has* washed some *thing* up?'

But before Chico could answer, Tom was gone, his mind racing down coasts littered with horseshoe crabs, sand dollars, starfish, kelp, and stone. From all the times he'd talked on what lives in the sea, the names, returned with the breathing fall of waves. Argonauts, they whispered, codlings, pollacks, houndfish, tautog, tench, sea elephant, they whispered, gillings, flounders, and beluga, the white whale, and grampus, the sea dog . . . always you thought how these must look from their deep-sounding names. Perhaps you would never in your life see them rise from the salt meadows beyond the safe limits of the shore, but they were there, and their names, with a thousand others, made pictures. And you looked and wished you were a frigate-bird that might fly nine thousand miles around to return some year with the full size of the ocean in your head.

'Oh, quick!' The boy had run back to peer in Tom's face. 'It might be gone '

'Keep your shirt on, boy,' said Chico.

They came around the North Rock. A second boy stood there, looking down.

Perhaps from the corner of his eye, Tom saw something on the sand that made him hesitate to look straight at it, but fix instead on the face of the boy standing there. The boy was pale and he seemed not to breathe. On occasion he remembered to take a breath, his eyes focused, but the more they saw there on the sand the more they took time off from focusing and turned blank and looked stunned. When the ocean came in over his tennis shoes, he did not move or notice.

Tom glanced away from the boy to the sand.

And Tom's face, in the next moment, became the face of the boy. His hands assumed the same curl at his sides and his mouth moved to open and stay half open and his eyes, which were light in colour, seemed to bleach still more with so much looking.

The setting sun was ten minutes above the sea.

'A big wave came in and went out,' said the first boy, 'and here she was.'

They looked at the woman lying there.

Her hair was very long and it lay on the beach like the threads of an immense harp. The water stroked along the threads and floated them up and let them down, each time in a different fan and silhouette. The hair must have been five or six feet long and now it was strewn on the hard wet sand and it was the colour of limes.

Her face . . .

The men bent half down in wonder.

Her face was white sand sculpture, with a few water drops shimmering on it like summer rain upon a cream-coloured rose. Her face was that moon which when seen by day is pale and unbelievable in the blue sky. It was milk-marble veined with faint violet in the temples. The eyelids, closed down upon the eyes, were powdered with a faint water colour, as if the eyes beneath gazed through the fragile tissue of the lids and saw them standing there above her, looking down and looking down. The mouth was a pale flushed sea-rose, full and closed upon itself. And her neck was slender and white and her breasts were small and white, now covered, un-covered, covered, uncovered in the flow of water, the ebb of water, the flow, the ebb, the flow. And the breasts were flushed at their tips, and her body was startlingly white, almost an illumination, a white-green lightning against the sand. And as the water shifted her, her skin glinted like the surface of a pearl.

The lower half of her body changed itself from white to very pale blue, from very pale blue to pale green, from pale green to emerald green, to moss and lime green, to scintillas and sequins all dark green, all flowing away in a fount, a curve, a rush of light and dark, to end in a lacy fan, a spread of foam and jewel on the sand. The two halves of this creature were so joined as to reveal no point of fusion where pearl woman, woman of whiteness made of cream-water and clear sky, merged with that half which belonged to the amphibious slide and rush of current that came up on the shore and shelved down the shore, tugging its half towards its proper home. The woman was the sea, the sea was woman. There was no flaw or seam, no wrinkle or stitch; the illusion, if illusion it was, held perfectly together and the blood from one moved into and through and mingled with what must have been the ice waters of the other.

'I wanted to run get help.' The first boy seemed not to want to raise his voice. 'But Skip said she was dead and there's no help for that. Is she?'

'She was never alive,' said Chico. 'Sure,' he went on, feeling their eyes on him suddenly. 'It's something left over from a movie studio. Liquid rubber skinned over a steel frame. A prop, a dummy.'

'Oh, no, it's real!'

'We'll find a label somewhere,' said Chico. 'Here.'

'Don't!' cried the first boy.

'Hell.' Chico touched the body to turn it, and stopped. He knelt there, his face changing.

'What's the matter?' asked Tom.

Chico took his hand away and looked at it. 'I was wrong.' His voice faded.

Tom took the woman's wrist. 'There's a pulse.'

'You're feeling your own heartbeat.'

'I just don't know . . . maybe . . . maybe . . .'

The woman was there and her upper body was all moon pearl and tidal cream and her lower body all slithering ancient green-black coins that slid upon themselves in the shift of wind and water.

'There's a trick somewhere!' cried Chico, suddenly.

'No. No!' Just as suddenly Tom burst out in laughter. 'No trick! My God, my God, I feel great! I haven't felt so great since I was a kid!'

They walked slowly around her. A wave touched her white hand so the fingers faintly, softly waved. The gesture was that of someone asking for another and another wave to come in and lift the fingers and then the wrist and then the arm and then the head and finally the body and take all of them together back down out to sea.

'Tome.' Chico's mouth opened and closed. 'Why don't you go get our truck?'

Tom didn't move.

'You hear me?' said Chico.

'Yes, but —'

'But what?' We could sell this somewhere, I don't know — the university, that aquarium at Seal Beach or . . . well, hell, why couldn't we just set up a place? Look.' He shook Tom's arm. 'Drive to the pier. Buy us three hundred pounds of chipped ice. When you take anything out of the water you *need* ice, don't you?'

'I never thought.'

'Think about it! Get moving!'

'I don't know, Chico.'

'What do you mean? She's real, isn't she?' He turned to the boys. '*You* say she's real, don't you? Well, then, what are we waiting for?'

'Chico,' said Tom. 'You better go get the ice yourself.'

'Someone's got to stay and make sure she don't go back out with the tide!'

'Chico,' said Tom. 'I don't know how to explain. I don't want to get that ice for you.'

'I'll go myself, then. Look, boys, build the sand up here to keep the waves back. I'll give you five bucks apiece. Hop to it!'

The sides of the boys' faces were bronze-pink from the sun which was touching the horizon now. Their eyes were a bronze colour looking at Chico.

'My God!' said Chico. 'This is better than finding ambergris!' He ran to the top of the nearest dune, called, 'Get to work!' and was gone.

Now Tom and the two boys were left with the lonely woman by the North Rock and the sun was one-fourth of the way below the western horizon. The sand and the woman were pink-gold.

'Just a little line,' whispered the second boy. He drew his fingernail along under his own chin, gently. He nodded to the woman. Tom bent again to see the faint line under either side of her firm white chin, the small, almost invisible line where the gills were or had been and were now almost sealed shut, invisible.

He looked at the face and the great strands of hair spread out in a lyre on the shore.

'She's beautiful,' he said.

The boys nodded without knowing it.

Behind them, a gull leaped up quickly from the dunes. The boys gasped and turned to stare.

Tom felt himself trembling. He saw the boys were trembling too. A car horn hooted. Their eyes blinked, suddenly afraid. They looked up towards the highway.

A wave poured about the body, framing it in a clear white pool of water.

Tom nodded the boys to one side.

The wave moved the body an inch in and two inches out towards the sea.

The next wave came and moved the body two inches in and six inches out towards the sea.

'But —' said the first boy.

Tom shook his head.

The third wave lifted the body two feet down towards the sea. The wave after that drifted the body another foot down the shingles and the next three moved it six feet down.

The first boy cried out and ran after it.

Tom reached him and held his arm. The boy looked helpless and afraid and sad.

For a moment there were no more waves. Tom looked at the woman, thinking. She's true, she's real, she's mine . . . but . . . she's dead. Or will be if she stays here.

'We can't let her go,' said the first boy. 'We can't, we just can't!'

The other boy stepped between the woman and the sea. 'What would we do with her,' he wanted to know, looking at Tom, 'if we kept her?'

The first boy tried to think. 'We could — we could —' He stopped and shook his head. 'Oh, my gosh.'

The second boy stepped out the way and left a path from the woman to the sea.

The next wave was a big one. It came in and went out and the sand was empty. The whiteness was gone and the black diamonds and the great threads of the harp.

They stood by the edge of the sea, looking out, the man and the two boys, until they heard the truck driving up on the dunes behind them.

The last of the sun was gone.

They heard footsteps running on the dunes and someone yelling.

They drove back down the darkening beach in the light truck with the big treaded tyres in silence. The two boys sat in the rear on the bags of chipped ice. After a long while, Chico began to swear steadily, half to himself, spitting out the window.

'Three hundred pounds of ice. Three hundred *pounds* of ice! What do I do with it now? And I'm soaked to the skin, soaked! You didn't even move when I jumped in and swam out to look around! Idiot, idiot! You haven't changed! Like every other time, like always, you do nothing, nothing, just stand there, stand there, do nothing, nothing, just stare!'

'And what did you do, I ask, what?' said Tom, in a tired voice, looking ahead. 'The same as you always did, just the same, no different, no different at all. You should've seen yourself.'

They dropped the boys off at their beach house. The younger spoke in a voice you could hardly hear against the wind. 'Gosh, nobody'll ever believe . . .'

The two men drove down the coast and parked.

Chico sat for two or three minutes waiting for his fists to relax on his lap, and then he snorted.

'Hell. I guess things turn out for the best.' He took a deep breath. 'It just came to me. Funny. Twenty, thirty years from now, middle of the night, our phone'll ring. It'll be one of those boys, grown-up, calling long-distance from a bar somewhere. Middle of the night, them calling to ask one question. "It's *true*, isn't it?" they'll say. "It *did* happen, didn't it? Back in 1958, it really happened to *us*?" And we'll sit there on the edge of the bed, middle of the night, saying, "Sure, boy, sure, it really happened to us in 1958." And they'll say, "Thanks," and we'll say, "Don't mention it, any old time." And we'll all say good night. And maybe they won't call again for a couple of years.'

The two men sat on their front-porch steps in the dark.

'Tom?'

'What?'

Chico waited a moment.

'Tom, next week — you're not going away.'

It was not a question but a quiet statement.

Tom thought about it, his cigarette dead in his fingers. And he knew that now he could never go away. For tomorrow and the day after the day after that he would walk down and go swimming there in all the green and white fires and the dark caverns in the hollows under the strange waves. Tomorrow and tomorrow and tomorrow.

'No, Chico I'm staying here.'

Now the silver looking glasses advanced in a crumpling line all along the coast from a thousand miles north to a thousand miles south. The mirrors did not reflect so much as one building or one tree or one highway or one car or even one man himself. The mirrors reflected only the quiet moon and then shattered into a billion bits of glass that spread out in a glaze on the shore. Then the sea was dark awhile, preparing another line of mirrors to rear up and surprise the two men who sat there for a long time never once blinking their eyes, waiting.

Fever Dream

They put him between fresh, clean, laundered sheets and there was always a newly squeezed glass of thick orange juice on the table under the dim pink lamp. All Charles had to do was call and Mom or Dad would stick their heads into his room to see how sick he was. The acoustics of the room were fine; you could hear the toilet gargling its porcelain throat of mornings, you could hear rain tap the roof or sly mice run in the secret walls or the canary singing in its cage downstairs. If you were very alert, sickness wasn't too bad.

He was thirteen, Charles was. It was mid-September, with the land beginning to burn with autumn. He lay in bed for three days before the terror overcame him.

His hand began to change. His right hand. He looked at it and it was hot and sweating there on the counterpane alone. It fluttered, it moved a bit. Then it lay there, changing colour.

That afternoon the doctor came and tapped his chest like a little drum. 'How are you?' asked the doctor, smiling. 'I know, don't tell me: "My *cold* is fine, Doctor, but *I* feel awful!" Ha!' He laughed at his own oft-repeated joke.

Charles lay there and for him that terrible and ancient jest was becoming a reality. The joke fixed itself in his mind. His mind touched and drew away from it in a pale terror. The doctor did not know how cruel he was with his jokes! 'Doctor,' whispered Charles, lying flat and colourless. 'My *hand*, it doesn't *belong* to me any more. This morning it *changed* into something else. I want you to change it back, Doctor. Doctor!'

The doctor showed his teeth and patted the boy's hand. 'It looks fine to me, son. You just had a little fever dream.'

'But it changed, Doctor, oh, Doctor,' cried Charles, pitifully, holding up his pale and wild hand. 'It *did*!'

The doctor winked. 'I'll give you a pink pill for that.' He popped a tablet on to Charles's tongue. 'Swallow!'

'Will it make my hand change back and become *me*, again?'

'Yes, yes.'

The house was silent when the doctor drove off down the road in his car under the quiet, blue September sky. A clock ticked far below in the kitchen world. Charles lay, looking at his hand.

It did not change back. It was still something else.

The wind blew outside. Leaves fell against the cool window.

At four o'clock his other hand changed. It seemed almost to become a fever. It pulsed and shifted, cell by cell. It beat like a warm heart. The fingernails turned blue and then red. It took about an hour for it to change and when it was finished, it looked just like any ordinary hand. But it was not ordinary. It no longer was him any more. He lay in a fascinated horror and then fell into an exhausted sleep.

Mother brought the soup up at six. He wouldn't touch it. 'I haven't any hands,' he said, eyes shut.

'Your hands are perfectly good,' said Mother.

'No,' he wailed. 'My hands are gone. I feel like I have stumps. Oh, Mama, Mama, hold me, hold me, I'm scared!'

She had to feed him herself.

'Mama,' he said, 'get the doctor, please, again. I'm so sick.'

'The doctor'll be here tonight at eight,' she said, and went out.

At seven, with night dark and close around the house, Charles was sitting up in bed when he felt the thing happening to first one leg and then the other. 'Mama! Come quick!' he screamed.

But when Mama came the thing was no longer happening.

When she went downstairs, he simply lay without fighting as his legs beat and beat, grew warm, red-hot, and the room filled with the warmth of his feverish change. The glow crept up from his toes to his ankles and then to his knees.

'May I come in?' The doctor smiled in the doorway.

'Doctor!' cried Charles. 'Hurry, take off my blankets!'

The doctor lifted the blankets tolerantly. 'There you are. Whole and healthy. Sweating, though. A little fever. I told you not to move around, bad boy.' He pinched the moist pink cheek. 'Did the pills help? Did your hand change back?'

'No, no, now it's my other hand and my legs?'

'Well, well, I'll have to give you three more pills, one for each limb, eh, my little peach?' laughed the doctor.

'Will they help me? Please, please. What've I *got*?'

'A mild case of scarlet fever, complicated by a slight cold.'

'Is it a germ that lives and has more little germs in me?'

'Yes.'

'Are you *sure* it's scarlet fever? You haven't taken any tests!'

'I guess I know a certain fever when I see one,' said the doctor, checking the boy's pulse with cool authority.

Charles lay there, not speaking until the doctor was crisply packing his black kit. Then in the silent room, the boy's voice made a small, weak pattern, his eyes alight with remembrance. 'I read a book once. About petrified trees, wood turning to stone. About how trees fell and rotted and minerals got in and built up and they look just like trees, but they're not, they're stone.' He stopped. In the quiet warm room his breathing sounded.

'Well?' asked the doctor.

'I've been thinking,' said Charles after a time. 'Do germs ever get big? I mean, in biology class they told us about one-celled animals, amoebas and things, and how millions of years ago they got together until there was a bunch and they made the first body. And more and more cells got together and got bigger and then finally maybe there was a fish and finally here *we* are, and all we are is a bunch of cells that decided to get together, to help each other out. Isn't that right?' Charles wet his feverish lips.

'What's all this about?' The doctor bent over him.

'I've got to tell you this. Doctor, oh, I've got to!' he cried. 'What would happen, oh just pretend, please pretend, that just like in the old days, a lot of microbes got together and wanted to make a bunch, and reproduced and made *more* —'

His white hands were on his chest now, crawling towards his throat.

'And they decided to *take over* a person!' cried Charles.

'Take over a person?'

'Yes, *become* a person. *Me*, my hands, my feet! What if a disease somehow knew how to kill a person and yet live after him?'

He screamed.

The hands were on his neck.

The doctor moved forward, shouting.

At nine o'clock the doctor was escorted out to his car by the mother and father, who handed him his bag. They conversed in the cool night wind for a few minutes. 'Just be sure his hands are kept strapped to his legs,' said the doctor. 'I don't want him hurting himself.'

'Will he be all right, Doctor?' The mother held to his arm a moment.

He patted her shoulder. 'Haven't I been your family physician for thirty years? It's the fever. He imagines things.'

'But those bruises on his throat, he almost choked himself.'

'Just you keep him strapped: he'll be all right in the morning.'

The car moved off down the dark September road.

*   *   *

At three in the morning, Charles was still awake in his small black room. The bed was damp under his head and his back. He was very warm. Now he no longer had any arms or legs, and his body was beginning to change. He did not move on the bed, but looked at the vast blank ceiling space with insane concentration. For a while he had screamed and thrashed, but now he was weak and hoarse from it, and his mother had got up a number of times to soothe his brow with a wet towel. Now he was silent, his hands strapped to his legs.

He felt the walls of his body change, the organs shift, the lungs catch fire like burning bellows of pink alcohol. The room was lighted up as with the flickerings of a hearth.

Now he had no body. It was all gone. It was under him, but it was filled with a vast pulse of some burning, lethargic drug. It was as if a guillotine had neatly lopped off his head, and his head lay shining on a midnight pillow while the body, below, still alive, belonged to somebody else. The disease had eaten his body and from the eating had reproduced itself in feverish duplicate. There were little hand hairs and the fingernails and the scars and the toenails and the tiny mole on his right hip, all done again in perfect fashion.

I am dead, he thought. I've been killed, and yet I live. My body is dead, it is all disease and nobody will know. I will walk around and it will not be me, it will be something else. It will be something all bad, all evil, so big and so evil it's hard to understand or think about. Something that will buy shoes and drink water and get married some day maybe and do more evil in the world than has ever been done.

Now the warmth was stealing up his neck, into his cheeks, like a hot wine. His lips burned, his eyelids, like leaves, caught fire. His nostrils breathed out blue flame, faintly, faintly.

This will be all, he thought. It'll take my head and my brain and fix each eye and every tooth and all the marks in my brain, and every hair and every wrinkle in my ears, and there'll be nothing left of me.

He felt his brain fill with a boiling mercury. He felt his left eye clench in upon itself and, like a snail, withdraw, shift. He was blind in his left eye. It no longer belonged to him. It was enemy territory. His tongue was gone, cut out. His left cheek was numbed, lost. His left ear stopped hearing. It belonged to someone else now. This thing that was being born, this mineral thing replacing the wooden log, this disease replacing healthy animal cell.

He tried to scream and he was able to scream loud and high and sharply in the room, just as his brain flooded down, his right eye and right ear were cut out, he was blind and deaf, all fire, all terror, all panic, all death.

His scream stopped before his mother ran through the door to his side.

It was a good, clear morning, with a brisk wind that helped carry the doctor up the path before the house. In the window above, the boy stood, fully dressed. He did not wave when the doctor waved and called, 'What's this? Up? My God!'

The doctor almost ran upstairs. He came gasping into the bedroom.

'What are you doing out of bed?' he demanded of the boy. He tapped his thin chest, took his pulse and temperature. 'Absolutely amazing! Normal. Normal, by God!'

'I shall never be sick again in my life,' declared the boy, quietly, standing there, looking out the wide window. 'Never.'

'I hope not. Why, you're looking fine, Charles.'

'Doctor?'

'Yes, Charles?'

'Can I go to school *now*?' asked Charles.

'Tomorrow will time enough. You sound positively eager.'

'I am. I like school. All the kids. I want to play with them and wrestle with them, and spit on them and play with the girls' pigtails and shake the teacher's hand, and rub my hands on all the cloaks in the cloakroom, and I want to grow up and travel and shake hands with people all over the world, and be married and have lots of children, and go to libraries and handle books and – *all* of that I want to!' said the boy, looking off into the September morning. 'What's the name you called me?'

'What?' The doctor puzzled. 'I called you nothing but Charles.'

'It's better than no name at all, I guess.' The boy shrugged.

'I'm glad you want to go back to school,' said the doctor.

'I really anticipate it,' smiled the boy. 'Thank you for your help, Doctor. Shake hands.'

'Glad to.'

They shook hands gravely, and the clear wind blew through the open window. They shook hands for almost a minute, the boy smiling up at the old man and thanking him.

Then, laughing, the boy raced the doctor downstairs and out to his car. His mother and father followed for the happy farewell.

'Fit as a fiddle!' said the doctor. 'Incredible!'

'And strong,' said the father. 'He got out of his straps himself during the night. Didn't you, Charles?'

'Did I?' said the boy.

'You did! How?'

'Oh,' the boy said, 'that was a long time ago.'

'A long time ago!'

They all laughed, and while they were laughing, the quiet boy moved his bare foot on the sidewalk and merely touched, brushed against a number of red ants that were scurrying about on the sidewalk. Secretly, his eyes shining, while his parents chatted with the old man, he saw the ants hesitate, quiver, and lie still on the cement. He sensed they were cold now.

'Good-bye!'

The doctor drove away, waving.

The boy walked ahead of his parents. As he walked he looked away towards the town and began to hum 'School Days' under his breath.

'It's good to have him well again,' said the father.

'Listen to him. He's so looking forward to school!'

The boy turned quietly. He gave each of his parents a crushing hug. He kissed them both several times.

Then without a word he bounded up the steps into the house.

In the parlour, before the others entered, he quickly opened the bird cage, thrust his hand in, and petted the yellow canary, *once*.

Then he shut the cage door, stood back, and waited.

The Town Where
No One Got Off

Crossing the continental United States by night, by day, on the train, you flash past town after wilderness town where nobody ever gets off. Or rather, no person who doesn't *belong*, no person who hasn't roots in these country graveyards ever bothers to visit their lonely stations or attend their lonely views.

I spoke of this to a fellow passenger, another salesman like myself, on the Chicago – Los Angeles train as we crossed Iowa.

'True,' he said. 'People get off in Chicago; everyone gets off there. People get off in New York, get off in Boston, get off in L.A. People who don't live there go there to see and come back to tell. But what tourist ever just got off at Fox Hill, Nebraska, to *look* at it? You? Me? No! I don't know anyone, got no business there, it's no health resort, so why bother?'

'Wouldn't it be a fascinating change,' I said, 'some year to plan a really different vacation? Pick some village lost on the plains where you don't know a soul and go there for the hell of it?'

'You'd be bored stiff.'

'I'm not bored thinking of it!' I peered out the window. 'What's the next town coming up on this line?'

'Rampart Junction.'

I smiled. 'Sounds good. I might get off there.'

'You're a liar and a fool. What you want? Adventure? Romance? Go ahead, jump off the train. Ten seconds later you'll call yourself an idiot, grab a taxi, and race us to the next town.'

'Maybe!'

I watched telephone poles flick by, flick by, flick by. Far

ahead I could see the first faint outlines of a town.

'But I don't think so,' I heard myself say.

The salesman across from me looked faintly surprised.

For slowly, very slowly, I was rising to stand. I reached for my hat. I saw my hand fumble for my one suitcase. I was surprised myself.

'Hold on!' said the salesman. 'What're you doing?'

The train rounded a curve suddenly. I swayed. Far ahead I saw one church spire, a deep forest, a field of summer wheat.

'It looks like I'm getting off the train,' I said.

'Sit down,' he said.

'No,' I said. 'There's something about that town up ahead. I've got to go and see. I've got the time. I don't have to be in L.A. really, until next Monday. If I don't get off the train now, I'll always wonder what I missed, what I let slip by when I had the chance to see it.'

'We were just talking. There's nothing there.'

'You're wrong,' I said. 'There is.'

I put my hat on my head and lifted the suitcase in my hand.

'By God,' said the salesman, 'I think you're really going to do it.'

My heart beat quickly. My face was flushed.

The rain whistled. The train rushed down the track. The town was near!

'Wish me luck,' I said.

'Luck!' he cried.

I ran for the porter, yelling.

There was an ancient flake-painted chair tilted back against the station-platform wall. In this chair, completely relaxed so he sank into his clothes, was a man of some seventy years whose timbers looked as if he'd been nailed there since the station was built. The sun had burned his face dark and tracked his cheek with lizard folds and stitches that held his eyes in a perpetual squint. His hair smoked ash-white in the summer wind. His blue shirt, open at the neck to show white clock springs, was bleached like the staring late afternoon sky. His shoes were blistered as if he had held them, uncaring, in the mouth of a stove, motionless, forever. His shadow under him was stencilled a permanent black.

As I stepped down, the old man's eyes flicked every door on the train and stopped, surprised, at me.

I thought he might wave.

But there was only a sudden colouring of his secret eyes; a chemical change that was recognition. Yet he had not twitched so much as his mouth, an eyelid, a finger. An invisible bulk had shifted inside him.

The moving train gave me an excuse to follow it with my eyes. There was no one else on the platform. No autos waited by the cobwebbed, nailed-shut office. I alone had departed the iron thunder to set foot on the choppy waves of platform lumber.

The train whistled over the hill.

Fool! I thought. My fellow passenger had been right. I would panic at the boredom I already sensed in this place. All right, I thought, fool, yes, but run, no!

I walked my suitcase down the platform, not looking at the old man. As I passed, I felt his thin bulk shift again, this time so I could hear it. His feet were coming down to touch and tap the mushy boards.

I kept walking.

'Afternoon,' a voice said faintly.

I knew he did not look at me but only at that great cloudless spread of shimmering sky.

'Afternoon,' I said.

I started up the dirt road towards the town. One hundred yards away, I glanced back.

The old man, still seated there, stared at the sun, as if posing a question.

I hurried on.

I moved through the dreaming late afternoon town, utterly

anonymous and alone, a trout going upstream, not touching the banks of a clear-running river of life that drifted all about me.

My suspicions were confirmed: it was a town where nothing happened, where occurred only the following events:

At four o'clock sharp, the Honneger Hardware door slammed as a dog came out to dust himself in the road. Four-thirty, a straw sucked emptily at the edge of a soda glass, making a sound like a great cataract in the drugstore silence. Five o'clock, boys and pebbles plunged in the town river. Five-fifteen, ants paraded in the slanting light under some elm trees.

And yet — I turned in a slow circle — somewhere in this town there must be something worth seeing, I knew it was there. I knew I had to keep walking and looking. I knew I would find it.

I walked. I looked.

All through the afternoon there was only one constant and unchanging factor: the old man in the bleached blue pants and shirt was never far away. When I sat in the drugstore he was out front spitting tobacco that rilled itself into tumble-bugs in the dust. When I stood by the river he was crouched downstream making a great thing of washing his hands.

Along about seven-thirty in the evening, I was walking for the seventh or eighth time through the quiet streets when I heard footsteps beside me.

I looked over, and the old man was pacing me, looking straight ahead, a piece of dried grass in his stained teeth.

'It's been a long time,' he said gently.

We walked along in the twilight.

'A long time,' he said, 'waitin' on that station platform.'

'You?' I said.

'Me.' He nodded in the tree shadows.

'Were you waiting for someone at the station?'

'Yes,' he said. 'You.'

'Me?' The surprise must have shown in my voice. 'But why . . . ? You never saw me before in your life.'

'Did I say I did? I just said I was waitin'.'

We were on the edge of town now. He had turned and I had turned with him along the darkening riverbank towards the trestle where the night trains ran over going east, going west, but stopping rare few times.

'You want to know anything about me?' I asked suddenly. 'You the sheriff?'

'No, not the sheriff. And no, I don't want to know nothin' about you.' He put his hands in his pockets. The sun was set now. The air was suddenly cool. 'I'm just surprised you're here at last, is all.'

'Surprised?'

'Surprised,' he said, 'and . . . pleased.'

I stopped abruptly and looked straight at him.

'How long have you been sitting on that station platform?'

'Twenty years, give or take a few.'

I knew he was telling the truth; his voice was as easy and quiet as the river.

'Waiting for me?' I said.

'Or someone like you,' he said.

We walked on in the growing dark.

'How you like our town?'

'Nice, quiet,' I said.

'Nice, quiet.' He nodded. 'Like the people?'

'People look nice and quiet.'

'They are,' he said. 'Nice, quiet.'

I was ready to turn back but the old man kept talking and in order to listen and be polite I had to walk with him in the vaster darkness, the tides of field and meadow beyond town.

'Yes,' said the old man, 'the day I retired, twenty years ago, I sat down on that station platform and there I been sittin', doin' nothin', waitin' for somethin' to happen. I didn't know what, I didn't know, I couldn't say. But when it finally happened, I'd know it. I'd look at it and say. Yes, sir, that's what I was waitin' for. Train wreck? No. Old woman friend come back to town after fifty years? No. No. It's hard to say. Someone. Somethin'. And it seems to have somethin' to do with you. I wish I could say —,

'Why don't you try?' I said.

The stars were coming out. We walked on.

'Well,' he said slowly, 'you know much about your own insides?'

'You mean my stomach or you mean psychologically?'

'That's the word. I mean your head, your brain, you know much about *that*?'

The grass whispered under my feet. 'A little.'

'You hate many people in your time?'

'Some.'

'We all do. It's normal enough to hate, ain't it, and not only hate but, while we don't talk about it, don't we sometimes want to hit people who hurt us, even *kill* them?'

'Hardly a week passes we don't get that feeling,' I said, 'and put it away.'

'We put away all our lives,' he said. 'The town says thus and so, Mom and Dad say this and that, the law says such and such. So you put away one killin' and another and two more after that. By the time you're my age, you got lots of that kind of stuff between your ears. And unless you went to war, nothin' ever happened to get rid of it.'

'Some men trapshoot or hunt ducks,' I said. 'Some men box or wrestle.'

'And some don't. I'm talkin' about them that don't. Me. All my life I've been saltin' down those bodies, puttin' em' away on ice in my head. Sometimes you get mad at a town and the people in it for makin' you put things aside like that. You like the old cave men who just gave a hell of a yell and whanged someone on the head with a club.'

'Which all leads up to . . . ?'

'Which all leads up to: Everybody'd like to do one killin' in his life, to sort of work off that big load of stuff, all those killin's in his mind he never did have the guts to do. And once in a while a man has a chance. Someone runs in front of his car and he forgets the brakes and keeps goin'. Nobody can prove nothin' with that sort of thing. The man don't even tell himself he did it. He just didn't get his foot on the brake in time. But you know and I know what really happened, don't we?'

'Yes,' I said.

The town was far away now. We moved over a small stream on a wooden bridge, just near the railway embankment.

'Now,' said the old man, looking at the water, 'the only kind of killin' worth doin' is the one where nobody can guess who did it or why they did it or who they did it to, right? Well, I got this idea maybe twenty years ago. I don't think about it every day or every week. Sometimes months go by, but the idea's this: Only one train stops here each day, sometimes not even that. Now, if you wanted to kill someone you'd have to wait, wouldn't you, for years and years, until a complete and actual stranger came to your town, a stranger who got off the train for no reason, a man nobody knows and who don't know nobody in the town. Then, and only then, I thought, sittin' there on the station chair, you could just go up and when nobody's around, kill him and throw him in the river. He'd be found miles downstream. Maybe he'd never be found. Nobody would ever think to come to Rampart Junction to find him. He wasn't goin' there. He was on his way someplace else. There, that's my whole idea. And I'd know that man the minute he got off the train. Know him, just as clear . . .'

I had stopped walking. It was dark. The moon would not be up for an hour.

'Would you?' I said.

'Yes,' he said. I saw the motion of his head looking at the stars. 'Well, I've talked enough.' He sidled close and touched my elbow. His hand was feverish, as if he had held it to a stove before touching me. His other hand, his right hand, was hidden, tight and bunched, in his pocket. 'I've talked enough.'

Something screamed.

I jerked my head.

Above, a fast-flying express razored along the unseen tracks, flourished light on hill, forest, farm, town dwellings, field, ditch, meadow, ploughed earth and water, then, raving high, cut off away, shrieking, gone. The rails trembled for a little while after that. Then, silence.

The old man and I stood looking at each other in the dark. His left hand was still holding my elbow. His other hand was still hidden.

'May I say something?' I said at last.

The old man nodded.

'About myself,' I said. I had to stop. I could hardly breathe. I forced myself to go on. 'It's funny. I've often thought the same way as you. Sure, just today, going cross-country, I thought, How perfect, how perfect, how really perfect it could be. Business has been bad for me, lately. Wife sick. Good friend died last week. War in the world. Full of boils, myself. It would do me a world of good —'

'What?' the old man said, his hand on my arm.

'To get off this train in a small town,' I said, 'where nobody knows me, with this gun under my arm, and find someone and kill them and bury them and go back down to the station and get on and go home and nobody the wiser and nobody ever to know who did it, ever. Perfect, I thought, a perfect crime. And I got off the train.'

We stood there in the dark for another minute, staring at each other. Perhaps we were listening to each other's heart beating very fast, very fast indeed.

The world turned under me. I clenched my fists. I wanted to fall. I wanted to scream like the train.

For suddenly I saw that all the things I had just said were not lies put forth to save my life.

All the things I had just said to this man were true.

And now I knew why I had stepped from the train and walked up through this town. I knew what I had been looking for.

I heard the old man breathing hard and fast. His hand was tight on my arm as if he might fall. His teeth were clenched. He leaned towards me as I leaned towards him. There was a terrible silent moment of immense strain as before an explosion.

He forced himself to speak at last. It was the voice of a man crushed by a monstrous burden.

'How do I know you got a gun under your arm?'

'You don't know.' My voice was blurred. 'You can't be sure.'

He waited. I thought he was going to faint.

'That's how it is?' he said.

'That's how it is,' I said.

He shut his eyes tight. He shut his mouth tight.

After another five seconds, very slowly, heavily, he managed to take his hand away from my own immensely heavy arm. He looked down at his right hand then, and took it, empty, out of his pocket.

Slowly, with great weight, we turned away from each other and started walking blind, completely blind, in the dark.

The midnight passenger-to-be-picked-up flare sputtered on the tracks. Only when the train was pulling out of the station did I lean from the open Pullman door and look back.

The old man was seated there with his chair tilted against the station wall, with his faded blue pants and shirt and his sun-baked face and his sun-bleached eyes. He did not glance at me as the train slid past. He was gazing east along the empty rails where tomorrow or the next day or the day after the day after that, a train, some train, any train, might fly by here, might slow, might stop. His face was fixed, his eyes were blindly frozen, towards the east. He looked a hundred years old.

The train wailed.

Suddenly old myself, I leaned out, squinting.

Now the darkness that had brought us together stood between. The old man, the station, the town, the forest, were lost in the night.

For an hour I stood in the roaring blast staring back at all that darkness.

All Summer in a Day

'Ready?'

'Ready.'

'Now?'

'Soon.'

'Do the scientists really know? Will it happen today, will it?'

'Look, look: see for yourself!'

The children pressed to each other like so many roses, so many weeds, intermixed, peering out for a look at the hidden sun.

It rained.

It had been raining for seven years: thousands upon thousands of days compounded and filled from one end to the other with rain, with the drum and gush of water, with the sweet crystal fall of showers and the concussion of storms so heavy they were tidal waves come over the islands. A thousand forests had been crushed under the rain and grown up a thousand times to be crushed again. And this was the way life was forever on the planet Venus, and this was the schoolroom of the children of the rocket men and women who had come to a raining world to set up civilization and live out their lives.

'It's stopping, it's stopping!'

'Yes, yes!'

Margot stood apart from them, from these children who could never remember a time when there wasn't rain and rain and rain. They were all nine years old, and if there had been a day, seven years ago, when the sun came out for an hour and showed its face to the stunned world, they could not recall. Sometimes, at night, she heard them stir, in remembrance, and she knew they were dreaming and remembering gold or a yellow crayon or a coin large enough to buy the world with. She knew they thought they remembered a warmness, like a blushing in the face, in the body, in the arms and legs and trembling hands. But then they always awoke to the tatting drum, the endless shaking down of clear bead necklaces upon the roof, the walk, the gardens, the forests, and their dreams were gone.

All day yesterday they had read in class about the sun. About how like a lemon it was, and how hot. And they had written small stories or essays or poems about it:

> *I think the sun is a flower,*
> *That blooms for just one hour.*

That was Margot's poem, read in a quiet voice in the still classroom while the rain was falling outside.

'Aw, you didn't write that!' protested one of the boys.

'I did,' said Margot. 'I *did*.'

'William!' said the teacher.

But that was yesterday. Now the rain was slackening, and the children were crushed in the great thick windows.

'Where's the teacher?'

'She'll be back.'

'She'd better hurry, we'll miss it!'

They turned on themselves, like a feverish wheel, all tumbling spokes.

Margot stood alone. She was a very frail girl who looked as if she had been lost in the rain for years and the rain had washed out the blue from her eyes and the red from her mouth and the yellow from her hair. She was an old photograph dusted from an album, whitened away, and if she spoke at all her voice would be a ghost. Now she stood, separate, staring at the rain and the loud wet world beyond the huge glass.

'What're *you* looking at?' said William.

Margot said nothing.

'Speak when you're spoken to.' He gave her a shove. But she did not move; rather she let herself be moved only by him and nothing else.

They edged away from her, they would not look at her. She felt them go away. And this was because she would play no games with them in the echoing tunnels of the underground city. If they tagged her and ran, she stood blinking after them and did not follow. When the class sang songs about happiness and life and games her lips barely moved. Only when they sang about the sun and the summer did her lips move as she watched the drenched windows.

And then, of course, the biggest crime of all was that she had come here only five years ago from Earth and she remembered the sun and the way the sun was and the sky was when she was four in Ohio. And they, they had been on Venus all their lives, and they had been only two years old when last the sun came out and had long since forgotten the colour and heat of it and the way it really was. But Margot remembered.

'It's like a penny,' she said once, eyes closed.

'No, it's not!' the children cried.

'It's like a fire,' she said, 'in the stove.'

'You're lying, you don't remember!' cried the children.

But she remembered and stood quietly apart from all of them and watched the patterning windows. And once, a month ago, she had refused to shower in the school shower rooms, had clutched her hands to her ears and over her head, screaming the water mustn't touch her head. So after that, dimly, dimly, she sensed it, she was different and they knew her difference and kept away.

There was talk that her father and mother were taking her back to Earth next year; it seemed vital to her that they do so, though it would mean the loss of thousands of dollars to her family. And so, the children hated her for all these reasons of big and little consequence. They hated her pale snow face, her waiting silence, her thinness, and her possible future.

'Get away!' The boy gave her another push. 'What're you waiting for?'

Then, for the first time, she turned and looked at him. And what she was waiting for was in her eyes.

'Well, don't wait around here!' cried the boy savagely. 'You won't see nothing!'

Her lips moved.

'Nothing!' he cried. 'It was all a joke, wasn't it?' He turned to the other children. 'Nothing's happening today. *Is* it?'

They all blinked at him and then, understanding, laughed and shook their heads. 'Nothing, nothing!'

'Oh, but,' Margot whispered, her eyes helpless. 'But this is the day, the scientists predict, they say, they *know*, the sun . . . '

'All a joke!' said the boy, and seized her roughly. 'Hey, everyone, let's put her in a closet before teacher comes!'

'No,' said Margot, falling back.

They surged about her, caught her up and bore her, protesting, and then pleading, and then crying, back into a tunnel, a room, a closet, where they slammed and locked the door. They stood looking at the door and saw it tremble from her beating and throwing herself against it. They heard her muffled cries. Then, smiling, they turned and went out and back down the tunnel, just as the teacher arrived.

'Ready, children?' She glanced at her watch.

'Yes!' said everyone.

'Are we all here?'

'Yes!'

The rain slackened still more.

They crowded to the huge door.

The rain stopped.

It was as if, in the midst of a film concerning an avalanche, a tornado, a hurricane, a volcanic eruption, something had, first, gone wrong with the sound apparatus, thus muffling and finally cutting off all noise, all of the blasts and repercussions and thunders, and then, second, ripped the film from the projector and inserted in its place a peaceful tropical slide which did not move or tremor. The world ground to a standstill. The silence was so immense and unbelievable that you felt your ears had been stuffed or you had lost your hearing altogether. The children put their hands to their ears. They stood apart. The door slid back and the smell of the silent, waiting world came in to them.

The sun came out.

It was the colour of flaming bronze and it was very large. And the sky around it was a blazing blue tile colour. And the jungle burned with sunlight as the children, released from their spell, rushed out, yelling, into the springtime.

'Now, don't go too far,' called the teacher after them. 'You've only two hours, you know. You wouldn't want to get caught out!'

But they were running and turning their faces up to the sky and feeling the sun on their cheeks like a warm iron: they were taking off their jackets and letting the sun burn their arms.

'Oh, it's better than the sun lamps, isn't it?'

'Much, much better!'

They stopped running and stood in the great jungle that covered Venus, that grew and never stopped growing, tumultuously, even as you watched it. It was a nest of octopi, clustering up great arms of fleshlike weed, wavering, flowering in this brief spring. It was the colour of rubber and ash, this jungle, from the many years without sun. It was the colour of stones and white cheeses and ink, and it was the colour of the moon.

The children lay out, laughing, on the jungle mattress, and heard it sigh and squeak under them, resilient and alive. They ran among the trees, they slipped and fell, they pushed each other, they played hide-and-seek and tag, but most of all they squinted at the sun until tears ran down their faces, they put their hands up to that yellowness and that amazing blueness and they breathed of the fresh, fresh air and listened and listened to the silence which suspended them in a blessed sea of no sound and no motion. They looked at everything and savoured everything. Then, wildly, like animals escaped from their caves, they ran and ran in shouting circles. They ran for an hour and did not stop running.

And then –

In the midst of their running one of the girls wailed.

Everyone stopped.

The girl, standing in the open, held out her hand.

'Oh, look, look,' she said, trembling.

They came slowly to look at her opened palm.

In the centre of it, cupped and huge, was a single raindrop.

She began to cry, looking at it.

They glanced quietly at the sky.

'Oh. Oh.'

A few cold drops fell on their noses and their cheeks and their mouths. The sun faded behind a stir of mist. A wind blew cool around them. They turned and started to walk back towards the underground house, their hands at their sides, their smiles vanishing away.

A boom of thunder startled them and like leaves before a new hurricane, they tumbled upon each other and ran. Lightning struck ten miles away, five miles away, a mile, a half mile. The sky darkened into midnight in a flash.

They stood in the doorway of the underground for a moment until it was raining hard. Then they closed the door and heard the gigantic sound of the rain falling in tons and avalanches, everywhere and for ever.

'Will it be seven more years?'

'Yes. Seven.'

Then one of them gave a little cry.

'Margot!'

'What?'

'She's still in the closet where we locked her.'

'Margot.'

They stood as if someone had driven them, like so many stakes, into the floor. They looked at each other and then looked away. They glanced out at the world that was raining now and raining and raining steadily. They could not meet each other's glances. Their faces were solemn and pale. They looked at their hands and feet, their faces down.

'Margot.'

One of the girls said. 'Well . . . ?'

No one moved.

'Go on,' whispered the girl.

They walked slowly down the hall in the sound of cold rain. They turned through the doorway to the room in the sound of the storm and thunder, lightning on their faces, blue and terrible. They walked over to the closet door slowly and stood by it.

Behind the closed door was only silence.

They unlocked the door, even more slowly, and let Margot out.

Frost and Fire

I

During the night, Sim was born. He lay wailing upon the
cold cave stones. His blood beat through him a thousand
pulses each minute. He grew, steadily.

Into his mouth his mother with feverish hands put the
food. The nightmare of living was begun. Almost instantly at
birth his eyes grew alert, and then, without half understanding why, filled with bright, insistent terror. He gagged
upon the food, choked and wailed. He looked about, blindly.

There was a thick fog. It cleared. The outlines of the cave
appeared. And a man loomed up, insane and wild and
terrible. A man with a dying face. Old, withered by winds,
baked like adobe in the heat. The man was crouched in a far
corner of the cave, his eyes whitening to one side of his face,
listening to the far wind trumpeting up above on the frozen
night planet.

Sim's mother, trembling now and again, staring at the
man, fed Sim pebblefruits, valley-grasses and ice-nipples
broken from the cavern entrance, and eating, eliminating,
eating again, he grew larger, larger.

The man in the corner of the cave was his father! The
man's eyes were all that was alive in his face. He held a crude
stone dagger in his withered hands and his jaw hung loose
and senseless.

Then, with a widening focus, Sim saw the old people
sitting in the tunnel beyond this living quarter. And as he
watched, they began to die.

Their agonies filled the cave. They melted like waxen
images, their faces collapsed inward on their sharp bones,
their teeth protruded. One minute their faces were mature,

fairly smooth, alive, electric. The next minute a desiccation and burning away of their flesh occurred.

Sim thrashed in his mother's grasp. She held him. 'No, no,' she soothed him, quietly, earnestly, looking to see if this, too, would cause her husband to rise again.

With a soft swift padding of naked feet, Sim's father ran across the cave. Sim's mother screamed. Sim felt himself torn loose from her grasp. He fell upon the stones, rolling, shrieking with his new, moist lungs!

The webbed face of his father jerked over him, the knife was poised. It was like one of those prenatal nightmares he'd had again and again while still in his mother's flesh. In the next few blazing, impossible instants questions flicked through his brain. The knife was high, suspended, ready to destroy him. But the whole question of life in this cave, the dying people, the withering and the insanity, surged through Sim's new, small head. How was it that he understood? A newborn child? Can a newborn child think, see, understand, interpret? No. It was wrong! It was impossible. Yet it was happening! To him. He had been alive an hour now. And in ths next instant perhaps dead!

His mother flung herself upon the back of his father, and beat down the weapon. Sim caught the terrific backwash of emotion from both their conflicting minds. 'Let me kill him!' shouted the father, breathing harshly, sobbingly. 'What has he to live for?'

'No, no!' insisted the mother, and her body, frail and old as it was, stretched across the huge body of the father, tearing at his weapon. 'He must live! There may be a future for him! He may live longer than us, and be young!'

The father fell back against a stone crib. Lying there, staring, eyes glittering. Sim saw another figure inside that stone crib. A girl-child, quietly feeding itself, moving its delicate hands to procure food. His sister.

The mother wrenched the dagger from her husband's

grasp, stood up, weeping and pushing back her cloud of stiffening-grey hair. Her mouth trembled and jerked. 'I'll kill you!' she said, glaring down at her husband. 'Leave my children alone.'

The old man spat tiredly, bitterly, and looked vacantly into the stone crib, at the little girl. 'One eighth of *her* life's over, already,' he gasped. 'And she doesn't know it. What's the use?'

As Sim watched, his own mother seemed to shift and take a tortured, smokelike form. The thin bony face broke out into a maze of wrinkles. She was shaken with pain and had to sit by him, shuddering and cuddling the knife to her shrivelled breasts. She, like the old people in the tunnel, was ageing, dying.

Sim cried steadily. Everywhere he looked was horror. A mind came to meet his own. Instinctively he glanced towards the stone crib. Dark, his sister, returned his glance. Their minds brushed like straying fingers. He relaxed somewhat. He began to learn.

The father sighed, shut his lids down over his green eyes. 'Feed the child,' he said, exhaustedly. 'Hurry. It is almost dawn and it is our last day of living, woman. Feed him. Make him grow.'

Sim quieted, and images, out of the terror, floated to him.

This was a planet next to the sun. The nights burned with cold, the days were like torches of fire. It was a violent, impossible world. The people lived in the cliffs to escape the incredible ice and the day of flame. Only at dawn and sunset was the air breath-sweet, flower-strong, and then the cave peoples brought their children out into a stony, barren valley. At dawn the ice thawed into creeks and rivers, at sunset the day fire died and cooled. In the intervals of even, livable temperature the people lived, ran, played, loved, free of the caverns; all life on the planet jumped, burst into life. Plants grew instantly, birds were flung like pellets across the sky. Smaller, legged animal life rushed frantically through the rocks; everything tried to get its living down in the brief hour of respite.

It was an unbearable planet. Sim understood this, a matter of hours after birth. Racial memory bloomed in him. He would live his entire life in the caves, with two hours a day outside. Here, in stone channels of air he would talk, talk incessantly with his people, sleep never, think, think and lie upon his back, dreaming; but never sleeping.

And he would live exactly eight days.

The *violence* of this thought! Eight days. Eight *short* days. It was wrong, impossible, but a fact. Even while in his mother's flesh some racial knowledge or some strange far wild voice had told him he was being formed rapidly, shaped and propelled out swiftly.

Birth was quick as a knife. Childhood was over in a flash. Adolescence was a sheet of lightning. Manhood was a dream, maturity a myth, old age an inescapably quick reality, death a swift certainty.

Eight days from now he'd stand half-blind, withering, dying, as his father now stood, staring uselessly at his own wife and child.

This day was an eighth part of his total life! He must enjoy every second of it. He must search his parents' thoughts for knowledge.

Because in a few hours they'd be dead.

This was so impossibly unfair. Was this all of life? In his prenatal state hadn't he dreamed of *long* lives, valleys not of blasted stone but green foliage and temperate clime? Yes! And if he'd dreamed then there must be truth in the visions. How could he seek and find the long life? Where? And how could he accomplish a life mission that huge and depressing in eight short, vanishing days?

How had his people got into such a condition?

As if at a button pressed, he saw an image. Metal seeds, blown across space from a distant green world, fighting with long flames, crashing on this bleak planet. From their shattered hulls tumbled men and women.

When? Long ago. Ten thousand days. The crash victims hid in the cliffs from the sun. Fire, ice and floods washed away the wreckage of the huge metal seeds. The victims were shaped and beaten like iron upon a forge. Solar radiations drenched them. Their pulses quickened, two hundred, five hundred, a thousand beats a minute. Their skins thickened, their blood changed. Old age came rushing. Children were born in the caves. Swifter, swifter, swifter the process. Like all this world's wild life, the men and women from the crash lived and died in a week, leaving children to do likewise.

So this is life, thought Sim. It was not spoken in his mind, for he knew no words, he knew only images, old memory, an awareness, a telepathy that could penetrate flesh, rock, metal. Somewhere along the line, they *had* developed telepathy, plus racial memory, the only good gifts, the only hope in all this terror. So, thought Sim, I'm the five-thousandth in a long line of futile sons? What can I do to save myself from dying eight days from now? Is there escape?

His eyes widened, another image came to focus.

Beyond this valley of cliffs, on a low mountain, lay a perfect, unscarred metal seed. A metal ship, not rusted or touched by the avalanches. The ship was deserted, whole, intact. It was the only ship of all these that had crashed that was still a unit, still usable. But it was so far away. There was no one in it to help. This ship, on the far mountain, was the destiny towards which he would grow. There was his only hope of escape.

His mind flexed.

In this cliff, deep down in a confinement of solitude, worked a handful of Scientists. To these men, when he was old enough and wise enough, he must go. They, too, dreamed of escape, of long life, of green valleys and temperate weathers. They, too, stared longingly at that distant ship upon its high mountain, its metal so perfect it did not rust or age.

The cliff groaned.

Sim's father lifted his eroded, lifeless face.

'Dawn's coming,' he said.

II

Morning relaxed the mighty granite cliff muscles. It was the time of the avalanche.

The tunnels echoed to running bare feet. Adults, children pushed with eager, hungry eyes towards the outside dawn. From far out, Sim heard a rumble of rock, a scream, a silence. Avalanches fell into valley. Stones that had been biding their time, not quite ready to fall, for a million years let go their bulks, and where they had begun their journey as single boulders they smashed upon the valley floor in a thousand shrapnel and friction-heated nuggets.

Every morning at least one person was caught in the downpour.

The cliff people dared the avalanches. It added one more excitement to their lives, already too short, too headlong, too dangerous.

Sim felt himself seized up by his father. He was carried brusquely down the tunnel for a thousand yards, to where the daylight appeared. There was a shining insane light in his father's eyes. Sim could not move. He sensed what was going to happen. Behind his father, his mother hurried, bringing with her little sister, Dark. 'Wait! Be careful!' she cried to her husband.

Sim felt his father crouch, listening.

High in the cliff was a tremor, a shivering.

'Now!' bellowed his father, and leaped out.

An avalanche fell down at them!

Sim had accelerated impressions of plunging walls, dust,

confusion. His mother screamed! There was a jolting, a plunging.

With one last step, Sim's father hurried him forwards into the day. The avalanche thundered behind him. The mouth of the cave, where Mother and Dark stood back out of the way, was choked with rubble and two boulders that weighed a hundred pounds each.

The storm thunder of the avalanche passed away to a trickle of sand. Sim's father burst out into laughter. 'Made it! By the Gods! Made it alive!' And he looked scornfully at the cliff and spat, 'Pagh!'

Mother and sister Dark struggled through the rubble. She cursed her husband. 'Fool! You might have killed Sim!'

'I may yet,' retorted the father.

Sim was not listening. He was fascinated with the remains of an avalanche afront of the next tunnel. Blood trickled out from under a rise of boulders, soaking into the ground. There was nothing more to be seen. Someone else had lost the game.

Dark ran ahead on lithe, supple feet, naked and certain.

The valley air was like a wine filtered between mountains. The heaven was a restive blue: not the pale scorched atmosphere of full day, nor the bloated, bruised black-purple of night, ariot with sickly shining stars.

This was a tide pool. A place where waves of varying and violent temperatures struck, receded. Now the tide pool was quiet, cool, and its life moved abroad.

Laughter! Far away, Sim heard it. Why laughter! How could any of his people find time for laughing? Perhaps later he would discover why.

The valley suddenly blushed with impulsive colour. Plant life, thawing in the precipitant dawn, shoved out from most unexpected sources. It flowered as you watched. Pale green tendrils appeared on scoured rocks. Seconds later, ripe globes of fruit twitched upon the blade-tips. Father gave Sim to his mother and harvested the momentary, volatile crop, thrust scarlet, blue, yellow fruits into a fur sack which hung at his waist. Mother tugged at the moist new grasses, laid them on Sim's tongue.

His senses were being honed to a fine edge. He stored knowledge thirstily. He understood love, marriage, customs, anger, pity, rage, selfishness, shadings and subtleties, realities and reflections. One thing suggested another. The sight of green plant life whirled his mind like a gyroscope, seeking balance in a world where lack of time for explanations made a mind seek and interpret on its own. The soft burden of food gave him knowledge of his system, of energy, of movement. Like a bird newly cracking its way from a shell, he was almost a unit, complete, all-knowing. Heredity and telepathy that fed upon every mind and every wind had done all this for him. He grew excited with his ability.

They walked, Mother, Father and the two children, smelling the smells, watching the birds bounce from wall to wall of the valley like scurrying pebbles and suddenly the father said a strange thing:

'Remember?'

Remember what? Sim lay cradled. Was it any effort for them to remember, when they'd lived only seven days!

The husband and wife looked at each other.

'Was it only three days ago?' said the woman, her body shaking, her eyes closing to think. 'I can't believe it. It is so unfair.' She sobbed, then drew her hand across her face and bit her parched lips. The wind played at her grey hair. 'Now it is my turn to cry. An hour ago it was you!'

'An hour is half a life.'

'Come.' She took her husband's arm. 'Let us look at everything, because it will be our last looking.'

'The sun'll be up in a few minutes,' said the old man. 'We must turn back now.'

'Just one more moment,' pleaded the woman.

'The sun will catch us.'

'Let it catch me then!'

'You don't mean that.'

'I mean nothing, nothing at all,' cried the woman.

The sun was coming fast. The green in the valley burnt away. Searing wind blasted from over the cliffs. Far away where the sun bolts hammered battlements of cliff, the huge stone faces shook their contents: those avalanches not already powdered down were now released and fell like mantles.

'Dark!' shouted the father. The girl sprang over the warm floor of the valley, answering, her hair a black flag behind her. Hands full of green fruits, she joined them.

The sun rimmed the horizon with flame, the air convulsed dangerously with it, and whistled.

The cave people bolted, picking up their fallen children, bearing vast loads of fruit and grass with them back to their deep hideouts. In moments the valley was bare. Except for one small child someone had forgotten. He was running far out on the flatness, but he was not strong enough, and engulfing heat was drifting down from the cliffs even as he was half across the valley.

Flowers were burnt into effigies, grasses sucked back into rocks like singed snakes. Flower seeds whirled and fell in the sudden furnace blast of wind, sown far into gullies and crannies, ready to blossom at sunset tonight, and then go to seed and die again.

Sim's father watched that child running, alone, out on the floor of the valley. He and his wife and Dark and Sim were safe in the mouth of their tunnel.

'He'll never make it,' said Father. 'Do not watch him, woman. It's not a good thing to watch.'

They turned away. All except Sim, whose eyes had caught a glint of metal far away. His heart hammered in him, and his eyes blurred. Far away, atop a low mountain, one of those metal seeds from space reflected a dazzling ripple of light! It was like one of his intra-embryo dreams fulfilled! A metal space seed, intact, undamaged, lying on a mountain! There was his future! There was his hope for survival! There was where he would go in a few days, when he was — strange thought — a grown man!

The sun plunged into the valley like molten lava.

The little running child screamed, the sun burned, and the screaming stopped.

Sim's mother walked painfully, with sudden age, down the tunnel, paused, reached up, broke off two last icicles that had formed during the night. She handed one to her husband, kept the other. 'We will drink one last toast. To you, to the children.'

'To *you*.' He nodded to her. 'To the children.' They lifted the icicles. The warmth melted the ice down into their thirsty mouths.

III

All day the sun seemed to blaze and erupt into the valley. Sim could not see it, but the vivid pictorials in his parents' minds were sufficient evidence of the nature of the day fire. The light ran like mercury, sizzling and roasting the caves, poking inward, but never penetrating deeply enough. It lighted the caves. It made the hollows of the cliff comfortably warm.

Sim fought to keep his parents young. But no matter how hard he fought with mind and image, they became like mummies before him. His father seemed to dissolve from one stage of oldness to another. This is what will happen to me soon, thought Sim in terror.

Sim grew upon himself. He felt the digestive-eliminatory movements of his body. He was fed every minute, he was continually swallowing, feeding. He began to fit words to images and processes. Such a word was 'love'. It was not an abstraction, but a process, a stir of breath, a smell of morning air, a flutter of heart, the curve of arm holding him, the look in the suspended face of his mother. He saw the processes, then searched behind her suspended face and there was the word, in her brain, ready to use. His throat prepared to speak. Life was pushing him, rushing him along towards oblivion.

He sensed the expansion of his fingernails, the adjustments of his cells, the profusion of his hair, the multiplication of his bones and sinew, the grooving of the soft pale wax of his brain. His brain at birth as clear as a circle of ice, innocent, unmarked, was, an instant later, as if hit with a thrown rock, cracked and marked and patterned in a million crevices of thought and discovery.

His sister, Dark, ran in and out with other little hothouse children, forever eating. His mother trembled over him, not eating, she had no appetite, her eyes were webbed shut.

'Sunset,' said his father, at last.

The day was over. The light faded, a wind sounded.

His mother arose. 'I want to see the outside world once more . . . just once more . . . ' She stared blindly, shivering.

His father's eyes were shut, he lay against the wall.

'I cannot rise,' he whispered faintly. 'I cannot.'

'Dark!' The mother croaked, the girl came running. 'Here,' and Sim was handed to the girl. 'Hold Sim, Dark, feed him, care for him.' She gave Sim one last fondling touch.

Dark said not a word, holding Sim, her great green eyes shining wetly.

'Go now,' said the mother. 'Take him out into the sunset time. Enjoy yourselves. Pick foods, eat. Play.'

Dark walked away without looking back. Sim twisted in her eager grasp, looking over his shoulder with unbelieving, tragic eyes. He cried out and somehow summoned from his lips the first word of existence:

'Why . . . ?'

He saw his mother stiffen. 'The child spoke!'

'Aye,' said his father. 'Did you hear what he said?'

'I heard,' said the mother quietly.

The last thing Sim saw of his living parents was his mother weakly, swayingly, slowly moving across the floor to lie beside her silent husband. That was the last time he ever saw them move.

IV

The night came and passed and then started the second day.

The bodies of all those who had died during the night were carried in a funeral procession to the top of a small hill. The procession was long, the bodies numerous.

Dark walked in the procession, holding the newly walking Sim by one hand. Only an hour before dawn Sim had learned to walk.

At the top of the hill, Sim saw once again the far-off metal seed. Nobody ever looked at it, or spoke of it. Why? Was there some reason? Was it a mirage? Why did they not run towards it? Worship it? Try to get to it and fly away into space?

The funeral words were spoken. The bodies were placed upon the ground where the sun, in a few minutes, would cremate them.

The procession then turned and ran down the hill, eager to have their few minutes of free time running and playing and laughing in the sweet air.

Dark and Sim, chattering like birds, feeding among the rocks, exchanged what they knew of life. He was in his second day, she in her third. They were driven, as always, by the mercurial speed of their lives.

Another piece of his life opened wide.

Fifty young men ran down the cliffs, holding sharp stones and rock daggers in their thick hands. Shouting, they ran off towards distant black, low lines of small rock cliffs.

'War!'

The thought stood in Sim's brain. It shocked and beat at

him. These men were running to fight, to kill, over there in those small black cliffs where other people lived.

But why? Wasn't life short enough without fighting, killing?

From a great distance he heard the sound of conflict, and it made his stomach cold. 'Why, Dark, why?'

Dark didn't know. Perhaps they would understand tomorrow. Now, there was the business of eating to sustain and support their lives. Watching Dark was like seeing a lizard forever flicking its pink tongue, forever hungry.

Pale children ran on all sides of them One beetlelike boy scuttled up the rocks, knocking Sim aside, to take from him a particularly luscious red berry he had found growing under an outcrop.

The child ate hastily of the fruit before Sim could gain his feet. Then Sim hurled himself unsteadily, the two of them fell in a ridiculous jumble, rolling, until Dark pried them, squalling, apart.

Sim bled. A part of him stood off, like a god, and said, 'This should not be. Children should not be this way. It is wrong!'

Dark slapped the little intruding boy away. 'Get on!' she cried. 'What's your name, bad one?'

'Chion!' laughed the boy. 'Chion, Chion, Chion!'

Sim glared at him with all the ferocity in his small, unskilled features. He choked. This was his enemy. It was as if he'd waited for an enemy of person as well as scene. He had already understood the avalanches, the heat, the cold, the shortness of life, but these were things of places, of scene — mute, extravagant manifestations of unthinking nature, not motivated save by gravity and radiation. Here, now, in this stridulant Chion he recognized a thinking enemy!

Chion darted off, turned at a distance, tauntingly:

'Tomorrow I will be big enough to kill you!'

And he vanished around a rock.

More children ran, giggling, by Sim. Which of them would be friends, enemies? How could friends and enemies come about in this impossible, quick lifetime? There was no time to make either, was there?

Dark, knowing his thoughts, drew him away. As they searched for food, she whispered fiercely in his ear. 'Enemies are made over things like stolen foods: gifts of long grasses make friends. Enemies come, too, from opinions and thoughts. In five seconds you've made an enemy for life. Life's so short enemies must be made quickly.' And she laughed with an irony strange for one so young, who was growing older before her rightful time. 'You must fight to protect yourself. Others, superstitious ones, will try killing you. There is a belief, a ridiculous belief, that if one kills another, the murderer partakes of the life energy of the slain, and therefore will live an extra day. You see? As long as that is believed, you're in danger.'

But Sim was not listening. Bursting from a flock of delicate girls who tomorrow would be tall, quieter, and who the day after that would become shapely and the next day take husbands, one small girl whose hair was a violet-blue flame caught Sim's sight.

She ran past, brushed Sim, their bodies touched. Her eyes, white as silver coins, shone at him. He knew then that he'd found a friend, a love, a wife, one who would a week from now lie with him atop the funeral pyre as sunlight undressed their flesh from bone.

Only the glance, but it held them in mid-motion, one instant.

'Your name?' he shouted after her.

'Lyte!' she called laughingly back.

'I'm Sim,' he answered, confused and bewildered.

'Sim!' she repeated it, flashing on. 'I'll remember!'

Dark nudged his ribs. 'Here, *eat*,' she said to the distracted boy. 'Eat or you'll never get big enough to catch her.'

From nowhere, Chion appeared, running by. 'Lyte!' he mocked, dancing malevolently along and away. 'Lyte! I'll remember Lyte, too!'

Dark stood tall and reed-slender, shaking her dark ebony clouds of hair, sadly. 'I see your life before you, little Sim. You'll need weapons soon to fight for this Lyte one. Now, hurry – the sun's coming!'

They ran back to the caves.

V

One fourth of his life was over! Babyhood was gone. He was now a young boy! Wild rains lashed the valley at nightfall. He watched new river channels cut in the valley, out past the mountain of the metal seed. He stored the knowledge for later use. Each night there was a new river, a bed newly cut.

'What's beyond the valley?' wondered Sim.

'No one's ever been beyond it,' explained Dark. 'All who tried to reach the plain were frozen to death or burnt. The only land we know's within half an hour's run. Half an hour out and half an hour back.'

'No one has ever reached the metal seed, then?'

Dark scoffed. 'The Scientists, they try. Silly fools. They don't know enough to stop. It's no use. It's too far.'

The Scientists. The word stirred him. He had almost forgotten the vision he had in the moments before and after birth. His voice was eager. 'Where are the Scientists?'

Dark looked away from him. 'I wouldn't tell you if I knew. They'd kill you, experimenting! I don't want you joining them! Live your life, don't cut it in half trying to reach that silly metal thing on the mountain.'

'I'll find out where they are from someone else, then!'

'No one'll tell you! They hate the Scientists. You'll have to find them on your own. And then what? Will you save us? Yes, save us, little boy!' Her face was sullen; already half her life was gone.

'We can't just sit and talk and eat,' he protested. 'And

nothing else.' He leapt up.

'Go find them!' she retorted acidly. 'They'll help you forget. Yes, yes.' She spat it out. 'Forget your life's over in just a few more days!'

Sim ran through the tunnels, seeking. Sometimes he half imagined where the Scientists were. But then a flood of angry thought from those around him, when he asked the direction to the Scientists' cave, washed over him in confusion and resentment. After all, it was the Scientists' fault that they had been placed upon this terrible world! Sim flinched under the bombardment of oaths and curses.

Quietly he took his seat in a central chamber with the children to listen to the grown men talk. This was the time of education, the Time of Talking. No matter how he chafed at delay, or how great his impatience, even though life slipped fast from him and death approached like a black meteor, he knew his mind needed knowledge. Tonight, then, was the night of school. But he sat uneasily. Only *five* more days of life.

Chion sat across from Sim, his thin-mouthed face arrogant.

Lyte appeared between the two. The last few hours had made her firmer-footed, gentler, taller. Her hair shone brighter. She smiled as she sat beside Sim, ignoring Chion. And Chion became rigid at this and ceased eating.

The dialogue crackled, filled the room. Swift as heartbeats, one thousand, two thousand words a minute. Sim learned, his head filled. He did not shut his eyes, but lapsed into a kind of dreaming that was almost intra-embryonic in lassitude and drowsy vividness. In the faint background the words were spoken, and they wove a tapestry of knowledge in his head.

He dreamed of green meadows free of stones, all grass, round and rolling and rushing easily towards a dawn with no taint of freezing, merciless cold or smell of boiled rock or scorched monument. He walked across the green meadow. Overhead the metal seeds flew by in a heaven that was a steady, even temperature. Things were slow, slow, slow.

Birds lingered upon gigantic trees that took a hundred, two hundred, five thousand days to grow. Everything remained in its place, the birds did not flicker nervously at a hint of sun, nor did the trees suck back frightenedly when a ray of sunlight poured over them.

In this dream people strolled, they rarely ran, the heart rhythm of them was evenly languid, not jerking and insane. The grass remained and did not burn away in torches. The dream people talked always of tomorrow and living and not tomorrow and dying. It all seemed so familiar that when Sim felt someone take his hand he thought it simply another part of the dream.

Lyte's hand lay inside his own. 'Dreaming?' she asked.

'Yes.'

'Things are balanced. Our minds, to even things, to balance the unfairness of our living, go back in on ourselves, to find what there is that is good to see.'

He beat his hand against the stone floor again and again. 'It does not make things fair! I hate it! It reminds me that there is something better, something I have missed! Why can't we be ignorant! Why can't we live and die without knowing that this is an abnormal living?' And his breath rushed harshly from his half-open, constricted mouth.

'There is purpose in everything,' said Lyte. 'This gives us purpose, makes us work, plan, to try to find a way.'

His eyes were hot emeralds in his face. 'I walked up a hill of grass, very slowly,' he said.

'The same hill of grass I walked an hour ago?' asked Lyte.

'Perhaps. Close enough to it. The dream is better than the reality.' He flexed his eyes, narrowed them. 'I watched people and they did not eat.'

'Or talk?'

'Or talk, either. And we always are eating, always talking. Sometimes those people in the dream sprawled with their eyes shut, not moving a muscle.'

As Lyte stared down into his face a terrible thing happened. He imagined her face blackening, wrinkling, twisting into knots of agedness. The hair blew out like snow about her ears, the eyes were like discoloured coins caught in a web of lashes. Her teeth sank away from her lips, the delicate fingers hung like charred twigs from her atrophied wrists. Her beauty was consumed and wasted even as he watched, and when he seized her, he cried out, for he imagined his own hand corroded, and, in terror, he choked back a cry.

'Sim, what's wrong?'

The saliva in his mouth dried at the taste of the words.

'Five more days . . .'

'The Scientists.'

Sim started. Who'd spoken? In the dim light a tall man talked. 'The Scientists crashed us on this world, and now have wasted thousands of lives and time. It's no use. Tolerate them but give them none of your time. You only live once, remember.'

Where were these hated Scientists? Now, after the Learning, the Time of Talking, he was ready to find them. Now, at least, he knew enough to begin his fight for freedom, for the ship!

'Sim, where're you going?'

But Sim was gone. The echo of his running feet died away down a shaft of polished stone.

It seemed that half the night was wasted. He blundered into a dozen dead ends. Many times he was attacked by the insane young men who wanted his life energy. Their superstitious ravings echoed after him. The gashes of their hungry fingernails covered his body.

He found what he looked for.

A half dozen men gathered in a small basalt cave deep down in the cliff lode. On a table before them lay objects which, though unfamiliar, struck harmonious chords in Sim.

The Scientists worked in sets, old men doing important work, young men learning, asking questions; and at their feet were three small children. They were a process. Every eight days there was an entirely new set of Scientists working on any one problem. The amount of work done was terribly inadequate. They grew old, fell dead just when they were beginning their creative period. The creative time of any one individual was perhaps a matter of twelve hours out of his entire span. Three quarters of one's life was spent learning, a brief interval of creative power, then senility, insanity, death.

The men turned as Sim entered.

'Don't tell me we have a recruit?' said the eldest of them.

'I don't believe it,' said another, younger one. 'Chase him away. He's probably one of those warmongers.'

'No, no,' objected the elder one, moving with little shuffles of his bare feet towards Sim. 'Come in, come in, boy.' He had friendly eyes, slow eyes, unlike those of the swift inhabitants of the upper caves. Grey and quiet. 'What do you want?'

Sim hesitated, lowered his head, unable to meet the quiet, gentle gaze. 'I want to live,' he whispered.

The old man laughed quietly. He touched Sim's shoulder. 'Are you a new breed? Are you sick?' he queried of Sim, half seriously. 'Why aren't you playing? Why aren't you readying yourself for the time of love and marriage and children? Don't you know that tomorrow night you'll be almost grown? Don't you realize that if you are not careful you'll miss all of life?' He stopped.

Sim moved his eyes back and forth with each query. He

blinked at the instruments on the table top. 'Shouldn't I be here?' he asked.

'Certainly,' roared the old man, sternly. 'But it's a miracle you are. We've had no volunteers from the rank and file for a thousand days! We've had to breed our own scientists, a closed unit! Count us! Six men! And three children! Are we not overwhelming?' The old man spat upon the stone floor. 'We ask for volunteers and the people shout back at us, "Get someone else!" or "We have no time!" And you know why they say that?'

'No.' Sim flinched.

'Because they're selfish. They'd like to live longer, yes, but they know that anything they do cannot possible ensure their *own* lives any extra time. It might guarantee longer life to some future offspring of theirs. But they won't give up their love, their brief youth, give up one interval of sunset or sunrise!'

Sim leaned against the table, earnestly. 'I understand.'

'You do?' The old man stared at him blindly. He sighed and slapped the child's arm gently. 'Yes, of course, you do. It's too much to expect anyone to understand, any more. You're rare.'

The others moved in around Sim and the old man.

'I am Dienc. Tomorrow night Cort here will be in my place. I'll be dead by then. And the night after that someone else will be in Cort's place, and then you, if you work and believe — but first, I give you a chance. Return to your playmates if you want. There is someone you love? Return to her. Life is short. Why should you care for the unborn to come? You have a right to youth. Go now, if you want. Because if you stay you'll have no time for anything but working, and growing old and dying at your work. But it is good work. Well?'

Sim looked at the tunnel. From a distance the wind roared and blew, the smells of cooking and the patter of naked feet sounded, and the laughter of young people was an increasingly good thing to hear. He shook his head, impatiently, and his eyes were wet.

'I will stay,' he said.

VI

The third night and third day passed. It was the fourth night. Sim was drawn into their living. He learned about that metal seed upon the top of the far mountain. He heard of the original seeds — things called 'ships' that crashed and how the survivors hid and dug in the cliffs, grew old swiftly and in their scrabbling to barely survive, forgot all science. Knowledge of mechanical things had no chance of survival in such a volcanic civilization. There was only NOW for each human.

Yesterday didn't matter, tomorrow stared them vividly in their very faces. But somehow the radiations that had forced their ageing had also induced a kind of telepathic communication whereby philosophies and impressions were absorbed by the newborn. Racial memory, growing instinctively, preserved memories of another time.

'Why don't we go to that ship on the mountain?' asked Sim.

'It is too far. We would need protection from the sun,' explained Dienc.

'Have you tried to make protection?'

'Salves and ointments, suits of stone and bird-wing and, recently, crude metals. None of which worked. In ten thousand more lifetimes perhaps we'll have made a metal in which will flow cool water to protect us on the march to the ship. But we work so slowly, so blindly. This morning, mature, I took up my instruments. Tomorrow, dying, I lay them down. What can one man do in one day? If we had ten thousand men, the problem would be solved . . . '

'I will go to the ship,' said Sim.

'Then you will die,' said the old man. A silence had fallen on the room at Sim's words. Then the men stared at Sim.

'You are a very selfish boy.'

'Selfish!' cried Sim, resentfully.

The old man patted the air. 'Selfish in a way I like. You want to live longer, you'll do anything for that. You will try for the ship. But I tell you it is useless. Yet, if you want to, I cannot stop you. At least you will not be like those among us who go to war for an extra few days of life.'

'War?' asked Sim. 'How can there be war here?'

And a shudder ran through him. He did not understand.

'Tomorrow will be time enough for that,' said Dienc. 'Listen to me, now.'

The night passed.

VII

It was morning. Lyte came shouting and sobbing down a corridor, and ran full into his arms. She had changed again. She was older, again, more beautiful. She was shaking and she held to him. 'Sim, they're coming after you!'

Bare feet marched down the corridor, surged inwards at the opening. Chion stood grinning there, taller, too, a sharp rock in either of his hands. 'Oh, there you are, Sim!'

'Go away!' cried Lyte, savagely whirling on him.

'Not until we take Sim with us,' Chion assured her. Then, smiling at Sim. '*If*, that is, he is with us in the fight.'

Dienc shuffled forwards, his eyes weakly fluttering, his birdlike hands fumbling in the air. 'Leave!' he shrilled angrily. 'This boy is a Scientist now. He works with us.'

Chion ceased smiling. 'There is better work to be done. We go now to fight the people in the farthest cliffs.' His eyes glittered anxiously. 'Of course, you will come with us, Sim?'

'No, no!' Lyte clutched at his arm.

Sim patted her shoulder, then turned to Chion. 'Why are you attacking these people?'

'There are three extra days for those who go with us to fight.'

'Three extra days! Of living?'

Chion nodded firmly. 'If we win, we live eleven days instead of eight. The cliffs they live in, something about the mineral in them that protects you from radiation! Think of it, Sim, three long, good days of life. Will you join us?'

Dienc interrupted. 'Get along without him. Sim is my pupil!'

Chion snorted. 'Go die, old man. By sunset tonight you'll be charred bone. Who are you to order us? We are young, we want to live longer.'

Eleven days. The words were unbelievable to Sim. Eleven days. Now he understood why there was war. Who wouldn't fight to have his life lengthened by almost half its total. So many more days of living! Yes. Why not, indeed!

'Three extra days,' called Dienc, stridently, '*if* you live to enjoy them. If you're not killed. *If. If!* You have never won yet. You have always lost!'

'But this time,' Chion declared sharply, 'we'll win!'

Sim was bewildered. 'But we are all of the same ancestors. Why don't we all share the best cliffs?'

Chion laughed and adjusted a sharp stone in his hand. 'Those who live in the best cliffs think they are better than us. That is always man's attitude when he has power. The cliffs, there, besides, are small, there's room for only three hundred people in them.'

Three extra days.

'I'll go with you,' Sim said to Chion.

'Fine!' Chion was very glad, much too glad at the decision.

Dienc gasped.

Sim turned to Dienc and Lyte. 'If I fight, and win, I will be half a mile closer to the ship. And I'll have three extra days in which to strive to reach the ship. That seems the only thing for me to do.'

Dienc nodded, sadly. 'It *is* the only thing. I believe you. Go along now.'

'Good-bye,' said Sim.

The old man looked surprised, then he laughed as at a little joke on himself. 'That's right — I won't see you again, will I? Good-bye, then.' And they shook hands.

They went out. Chion, Sim, and Lyte, together, followed by the others, all children growing swiftly into fighting men. And the light in Chion's eyes was not a good thing to see.

Lyte went with him. She chose his rocks for him and carried them. She would not go back, no matter how he pleaded. The sun was just beyond the horizon and they marched across the valley.

'Please, Lyte, go back!'

'And wait for Chion to return?' she said. 'He plans that when you die I will be his mate.' She shook out her un-believable blue-white curls of hair defiantly. 'But I'll be with you. If you fall, I fall.'

Sim's face hardened. He was tall. The world had shrunk during the night. Children packs screamed by hilarious in their food searching and he looked at them with alien wonder: could it be only four days ago he'd been like these? Strange. There was a sense of many days in his mind, as if he'd really lived a thousand days. There was a dimension of incident and thought so thick, so multicoloured, so richly diverse in his head that it was not to be believed so much could happen in so short a time.

The fighting men ran in clusters of two or three. Sim looked ahead at the rising line of small ebon cliffs. This, then, he said to himself, is my fourth day. And still I am no closer to the ship, or to anything, not even — he heard the light tread of Lyte beside him — not even to her who bears my weapons and picks me ripe berries.

One half of his life was gone. Or a third of it — If he won this battle. *If.*

He ran easily, lifting, letting fall his legs. This is the day of my physical awareness, as I run I feed, as I feed I grow and as

I grow I turn my eyes to Lyte with a kind of dizzying vertigo. And she looks upon me with the same gentleness of thought. This is the day of our youth. Are we wasting it? Are we losing it on a dream, a folly?

Distantly he heard laughter. As a child he'd questioned it. Now he understood laughter. This particular laughter was made of climbing high rocks and plucking the greenest blades and drinking the headiest vintage from the morning ices and eating of the rock-fruits and tasting of young lips in new appetite.

They neared the cliffs of the enemy.

He saw the slender erectness of Lyte. The new surprise of her neck where if you touched you could time her pulse: the fingers which cupped in your own were animate and supple and never still; the . . .

Lyte snapped her head to one side. 'Look ahead!' she cried. 'See what is to come — look only ahead.'

He felt that they were racing by part of their lives, leaving their youth on the pathside, without so much as a glance.

'I am blind with looking at stones,' he said, running.

'Find new stones, then!'

'I see stones — ' His voice grew gentle as the palm of her hand. The landscape floated under him. Everything was like a fine wind, blowing dreamily. 'I see stones that make a ravine that lies in a cool shadow where the stone-berries are thick as tears. You touch a boulder and the berries fall in silent red avalanches, and the grass is very tender . . . '

'I do not see it!' She increased her pace, turning her head away.

He saw the floss upon her neck, like the small moss that grows silvery and light on the cool side of pebbles, that stirs if you breathe the lightest breath upon it. He looked upon himself, his hands clenched as he heaved himself forwards towards death. Already his hands were veined and youth-swollen.

Lyte handed him food to eat.

'I am not hungry,' he said.

'Eat, keep your mouth full,' she commanded sharply, 'so you will be strong for battle.'

'Gods!' he roared, anguished. 'Who cares for battles!'

Ahead of them, rocks hailed down, thudding. A man fell with his skull split wide. The war was begun.

Lyte passed the weapons to him. They ran without another word until they entered the killing ground.

The boulders began to roll in a synthetic avalanche from the battlements of the enemy!

Only one thought was in his mind now. To kill, to lessen the life of someone else so he could live, to gain a foothold here and live long enough to make a stab at the ship. He ducked, he weaved, he clutched stones and hurled them up. His left hand held a flat stone shield with which he diverted the swiftly plummeting rocks. There was a spatting sound everywhere. Lyte ran with him, encouraging him. Two men dropped before him, slain, their breasts cleaved to the bone, their blood springing out in unbelievable founts.

It was a useless conflict. Sim realized instantly how insane the venture was. They could never storm the cliff. A solid wall of rocks rained down. A dozen men dropped with shards of ebony in their brains, a half dozen more showed drooping, broken arms. One screamed and the upthrust white joint of his knee was exposed as the flesh was pulled away by two successive blows of well-aimed granite. Men stumbled over one another.

The muscles in his cheeks pulled tight and he began to wonder why he had ever come. But his raised eyes, as he danced from side to side, weaving and bobbing, sought always the cliffs. He wanted to live there so intensely, to have his chance. He would have to stick it out. But the heart was gone from him.

Lyte screamed piercingly. Sim, his heart panicking, twisted and saw that her hand was loose at the wrist, with an ugly wound bleeding profusely on the back of the knuckles. She clamped it under her armpit to soothe the pain. The anger rose in him and exploded. In his fury he raced forwards, throwing his missiles with deadly accuracy. He saw a man topple and flail down, falling from one level to another of the caves, a victim of his shot. He must have been screaming, for his lungs were bursting open and closed and his throat was raw, and the ground spun madly under his racing feet.

The stone that clipped his head sent him reeling and plunging back. He ate sand. The universe dissolved into purple whorls. He could not get up. He lay and knew that this was his last day, his last time. The battle raged around him, dimly he felt Lyte over him. Her hands cooled his head, she tried to drag him out of range, but he lay gasping and telling her to leave him.

'Stop!' shouted a voice. The whole war seemed to give pause. 'Retreat!' commanded the voice swiftly. And as Sim watched, lying upon his side, his comrades turned and fled back towards home.

'The sun is coming, our time is up!' He saw their muscled backs, their moving, tensing, flickering legs go up and down. The dead were left upon the field. The wounded cried for help. But there was no time for the wounded. There was only time for swift men to run the gauntlet home and, their lungs aching and raw with heated air, burst into their tunnels before the sun burnt and killed them.

The sun!

Sim saw another figure racing towards him. It was Chion! Lyte was helping Sim to his feet, whispering helpfully to him. 'Can you walk?' she asked. And he groaned and said, 'I think so.' 'Walk then,' she said. 'Walk slowly, and then faster and faster. We'll make it. Walk slowly, start carefully. We'll make it. I know we will.'

Sim got to his feet, stood swaying. Chion raced up, a strange expression cutting lines in his cheeks, his eyes shining with battle. Pushing Lyte abruptly aside he seized upon a rock and dealt Sim a jolting blow upon his ankle that laid wide the flesh. All of this was done quite silently.

Now he stood back, still not speaking, grinning like an animal from the night mountains, his chest panting in and out, looking from the thing he had done, to Lyte, and back. He got his breath. 'He'll never make it.' He nodded at Sim. 'We'll have to leave him here. Come along, Lyte.'

Lyte, like a cat-animal, sprang upon Chion, searching for his eyes, shrieking through her exposed, hard-pressed teeth. Her fingers stroked great bloody furrows down Chion's arms and again, instantly, down his neck. Chion, with an oath, sprang away from her. She hurled a rock at him. Grunting, he let it miss him, then ran off a few yards. 'Fool!' he cried, turning to scorn her. 'Come along with me. Sim will be dead in a few minutes. Come along!'

Lyte turned her back on him. 'I will go if you carry me.'

Chion's face changed. His eyes lost their gleaming. 'There is no time. We would both die if I carried you.'

Lyte looked through and beyond him. 'Carry me, then, for that's how I wish it to be.'

Without another word, glancing fearfully at the sun, Chion fled. His footsteps sped away and vanished from hearing. 'May he fall and break his neck,' whispered Lyte, savagely glaring at his form as it skirted a ravine. She returned to Sim. 'Can you walk?'

Agonies of pain shot up his leg from the wounded ankle. He nodded ironically. 'We could make it to the cave in two hours, walking. I have an idea, Lyte. Carry me.' And he smiled with the grim joke.

She took his arm. 'Nevertheless we'll walk. Come.'

'No,' he said. 'We're staying here.'

'But why?'

'We came to seek a home here. If we walk we will die. I would rather die here. How much time have we?'

Together they measured the sun. 'A few minutes,' she said, her voice flat and dull. She held close to him.

The black rocks of the cliff were paling into deep purples and browns as the sun began to flood the world.

What a fool he was! He should have stayed and worked with Dienc, and thought and dreamed.

With the sinews of his neck standing out defiantly he bellowed upwards at the cliff holes.

'Send me down one man to do battle!'

Silence. His voice echoed from the cliff. The air was warm.

'It's no use,' said Lyte. 'They'll pay no attention.'

He shouted again. 'Hear me!' He stood with his weight on his good foot, his injured left leg throbbing and pulsating with pain. He shook a fist. 'Send down a warrior who is no coward! I will not turn and run home! I have come to fight a fair fight! Send a man who will fight for the right to his cave! Him I will surely kill!'

More silence. A wave of heat passed over the land, receded.

'Oh, surely,' mocked Sim, hands on naked hips, head back, mouth wide, 'surely there's one among you not afraid to fight a cripple!' Silence. 'No?' Silence.

'Then I have miscalculated you. I'm wrong. I'll stand here, then, until the sun shucks the flesh off my bone in black scraps, and call you the filthy names you deserve.'

He got an answer.

'I do not like being called names,' replied a man's voice.

Sim leaned forward, forgetting his crippled foot.

A huge man appeared in a cave mouth on the third level.

'Come down,' urged Sim. 'Come down, fat one, and kill me.'

The man scowled seriously at his opponent a moment, then lumbered slowly down the path, his hands empty of any weapons. Immediately every cave above clustered with heads. An audience for this drama.

The man approached Sim. 'We will fight by the rules, if you know them.'

'I'll learn them as we go,' replied Sim.

This pleased the man and he looked at Sim warily, but not unkindly. 'This much I will tell you,' offered the man generously. 'If you die, I will give your mate shelter and she will live as she pleases, because she is the wife of a good man.'

Sim nodded swiftly. 'I am ready,' he said.

'The rules are simple. We do not touch each other, save with stones. The stones and the sun will do either of us in. Now is the time —'

VIII

A tip of the sun showed on the horizon. 'My name is Nhoj,' said Sim's enemy, casually taking up a handful of pebbles and stones, weighing them. Sim did likewise. He was hungry. He had not eaten for many minutes. Hunger was the curse of this planet's peoples — a perpetual demanding of empty stomachs for more, more food. His blood flushed weakly, shot tinglingly through veins in jolting throbs of heat and pressure, his rib cage shoved out, went in, shoved out again, impatiently.

'Now!' roared the three hundred watchers from the cliffs. 'Now!' they clamoured, the men and women and children balanced, in turmoil on the ledges. 'Now! Begin!'

As if at a cue, the sun arose. It smote them a blow as with a flat, sizzling stone. The two men staggered under the molten impact, sweat broke from their naked thighs and loins, under their arms and on their faces was a glaze like fine glass.

Nhoj shifted his huge weight and looked at the sun as if in no hurry to fight. Then, silently, with no warning, he snapped out a pebble with a startling trigger-flick of thumb and forefinger. It caught Sim flat on the cheek, staggered him back, so that a rocket of unbearable pain climbed up his crippled foot and burst into nervous explosion at the pit of his stomach. He tasted blood from his bleeding cheek.

Nhoj moved serenely. Three more flicks of his magical hands and three tiny, seemingly harmless bits of stone flew like whistling birds. Each of them found a target, slammed it. The nerve centres of Sim's body! One hit his stomach so that ten hours' eating almost slid up his throat. A second got his forehead, a third his neck. He collapsed to the boiling sand. His knee made a wrenching sound on the hard earth. His face was colourless and his eyes, squeezed tight, were pushing tears out from the hot, quivering lids. But even as he had fallen he had let loose, with wild force, his handful of stones!

The stones purred in the air. One of them, and only one, struck Nhoj. Upon the left eyeball. Nhoj moaned and laid his hands in the next instant to his shattered eye.

Sim choked out a bitter, sighing laugh. This much triumph he had. The eye of his opponent. It would give him . . . Time. Oh, Gods, he thought, his stomach retching sickly, fighting for breath, this is a world of Time. Give me a little more, just a trifle!

Nhoj, one-eyed, weaving with pain, pelted the writhing body of Sim, but his aim was off now, the stones flew to one side or if they struck at all they were weak and spent and lifeless.

Sim forced himself half erect. From the corners of his eyes he saw Lyte, waiting, staring at him, her lips breathing words of encouragement and hope. He was bathed in sweat, as if a rain spray had showered him down.

The sun was now fully over the horizon. You could smell it. Stones glinted like mirrors, the sand began to roil and bubble. Illusions sprang up everywhere in the valley. Instead of one warrior Nhoj he was confronted by a dozen, each in an upright position, preparing to launch another missile. A dozen irregular warriors who shimmered in the golden menace of day, like bronze gongs smitten, quivered in one vision!

Sim was breathing desperately. His nostrils flared and sucked and his mouth drank thirstily of flame instead of oxygen. His lungs took fire like silk torches and his body was consumed. The sweat spilled from his pores to be instantly evaporated. He felt himself shrivelling, shrivelling in on himself, he imagined himself looking like his father, old, sunken, slight, withered! Where was the sand? Could he move? Yes. The world wriggled under him, but now he was on his feet.

There would be no more fighting.

A murmur from the cliff told this. The sunburnt faces of the high audience gaped and jeered and shouted encouragement to their warrior. 'Stand straight, Nhoj, save your strength now! Stand tall and perspire!' they urged him. And Nhoj stood, swaying lightly, swaying slowly, a pendulum in an incandescent fiery breath from the skyline. 'Don't move, Nhoj, save your heart, save your power!'

'The test, the test!' said the people on the heights. 'The test of the sun.'

And this was the worst part of the fight. Sim squinted painfully at the distorted illusion of cliff. He thought he saw his parents; father with his defeated face, his green eyes burning, mother with her hair blowing like a cloud of grey smoke in the fire wind. He must get up to them, live for and with them!

Behind him, Sim heard Lyte whimper softly. There was a whisper of flesh against the sand. She had fallen. He did not dare turn. The strength of turning would bring him thundering down in pain and darkness.

His knees bent. If I fall, he thought, I'll lie here and become ashes. Where was Nhoj? Nhoj was there, a few yards from him, standing bent, slick with perspiration, looking as if he were being hit over the spine with great hammers of destruction.

Fall, Nhoj! Fall! thought Sim. Fall, fall! Fall so I can take your place!

But Nhoj did not fall. One by one the pebbles in his half-loose left hand plummeted to the broiling sands and Nhoj's lips peeled back, the saliva burned away from his lips and his eyes glazed. But he did not fall. The will to live was strong in him. He hung as if by a wire.

Sim fell to one knee!

'Ahh!' wailed the knowing voices from the cliff. They were watching death. Sim jerked his head up, smiling mechanically, foolishly, as if caught in the act of doing something silly. 'No, no,' he insisted drowsily, and got back up again. There was so much pain he was all one ringing numbness. A whirring, buzzing, frying sound filled the land. High up, an avalanche came down like a curtain on a drama, making no noise. Everything was quiet except for a steady humming. He saw fifty images of Nhoj now, dressed in armours of sweat, eyes puffed with torture, cheeks sunken, lips peeled back like the rind of a drying fruit. But the wire still held him.

'Now,' muttered Sim, sluggishly, with a thick, baked tongue between his blazing teeth. 'Now I'll fall and lie and dream.' He said it with slow, thoughtful pleasure. He planned it. He knew how it must be done. He would do it accurately. He lifted his head to see if the audience was watching.

They were gone!

The sun had driven them back in. All save one or two brave ones. Sim laughed drunkenly and watched the sweat gather on his dead hands, hesitate, drop off, plunge down towards sand and turn to steam halfway there.

Nhoj fell.

The wire was cut. Nhoj fell upon his stomach, a gout of blood kicked from his mouth. His eyes rolled back into a white, senseless insanity.

All across the valley the winds sang and moaned and Sim saw a blue lake with a blue river feeding it and low white houses near the river with people going and coming in the houses and among the tall green trees. Trees taller than seven men, beside the river mirage.

He fell forward.

He was shocked when he felt the hands eagerly stop him in mid-plunge, lift him, hurry him off, high in the hungry air, like a torch held and waved, ablaze.

How strange death is, he thought, and blackness took him.

He awakened to the flow of cool water on his cheeks.

He opened his eyes fearfully. Lyte held his head upon her lap, her fingers were moving food to his mouth. He was tremendously hungry and tired, but fear squeezed both of these things away. He struggled upward, seeing the strange cave contours overhead.

'What time is it?' he demanded.

'The same day as the contest. Be quiet,' she said.

'The same day!'

She nodded amusedly. 'You've lost nothing of your life. This is Nhoj's cave. We are inside the black cliff. We will live three extra days. Satisfied? Lie down.'

'Nhoj is dead?' He fell back, panting, his heart slamming his ribs. He relaxed slowly. 'I won. I won,' he breathed.

'Nhoj is dead. So were we, almost. They carried us in from outside only in time.'

He ate ravenously. 'We have no time to waste. We must get strong. My leg —' He looked at it, tested it. There was a swath of long yellow grasses around it and the ache had died away. Even as he watched, the terrific pulsings of his body went to work and cured away the impurities under the bandages. It *has* to be strong by sunset, he thought. It *has* to be.

He got up and limped around the cave like a captured animal. He felt Lyte's eyes upon him. He could not meet her gaze. Finally, helplessly, he turned.

She interrupted him. 'You want to go on to the ship?' she asked, softly. 'Tonight? When the sun goes down?'

He took a breath, exhaled it. 'Yes.'

'You couldn't possibly wait until morning?'

'No.'

'Then I'll go with you.'

'No!'

'If I lag, behind, let me. There's nothing here for me.'

They stared at each other a long while. He shrugged wearily.

'All right,' he said, at last. 'I couldn't stop you, I know that. We'll go together.'

IX

They waited in the mouth of their new cave. The sun set. The stones cooled so that one could walk on them. It was almost time for the leaping out and the running towards the distant, glittering metal seed that lay on the far mountain.

Soon would come the rains. And Sim thought back over all the times he had watched the rains thicken into creeks, into rivers that cut new beds each night. One night there would be a river running north, the next a river running northeast, the third night a river running due west. The valley was continually cut and scarred by the torrents. Earthquakes and avalanches filled the old beds. New ones were the order of the day. It was this idea of the river and the directions of the river that he had turned over in his head for many hours. It might possibly — Well, he would wait and see.

He noticed how living in this new cliff had slowed his pulse, slowed everything. A mineral result, protection against the solar radiations. Life was still, swift, but not as swift as before.

'Now, Sim!' cried Lyte.

They ran. Between the hot death and the cold one. Together, away from the cliffs, out towards the distant, beckoning ship.

Never had they run this way in their lives. The sound of their feet running was a hard, insistent clatter over vast oblongs of rock, down into ravines, up the sides, and on again. They raked the air in and out of their lungs. Behind them the cliffs faded into things they could never turn back to now.

They did not eat as they ran. They had eaten to the bursting point in the cave, to save time. Now it was only running, a lifting of legs, a balancing of bent elbows, a convulsion of muscles, a slaking in of air that had been fiery and was now cooling.

'Are they watching us?'

Lyte's breathless voice snatched at his ears above the pound of his heart.

Who? But he knew the answer. The cliff peoples, of course. How long had it been since a race like this one? A thousand days? Ten thousand? How long since someone had taken the chance and sprinted with an entire civilization's eyes upon their backs, into gullies, across cooling plain. Were there lovers pausing in their laughter back there, gazing at the two tiny dots that were a man and woman running towards destiny? Were children eating of new fruits and stopping in their play to see the two people racing against time? Was Dienc still living, narrowing hairy eyebrows down over fading eyes, shouting them on in a feeble, rasping voice, shaking a twisted hand? Were there jeers? Were they being called fools, idiots? And in the midst of the name-calling, were people praying them on, hoping they would reach the ship?

Sim took a quick glance at the sky, which was beginning to bruise with the coming night. Out of nowhere clouds materialized and a light shower trailed across a gully two hundred yards ahead of them. Lightning beat upon distant mountains and there was a strong scent of ozone on the disturbed air.

'The halfway mark,' panted Sim, and he saw Lyte's face half turn, longingly looking back at the life she was leaving. 'Now's the time, if we want to turn back, we still have time. Another minute –'

Thunder snarled in the mountains. An avalanche started out small and ended up huge and monstrous in a deep fissure. Light rain dotted Lyte's smooth white skin. In a minute her hair was glistening and soggy with rain.

'Too late, now,' she shouted over the patting rhythm of her own naked feet. 'We've got to go ahead!'

And it was too late. Sim knew, judging the distances, that there was no turning back now.

His leg began to pain him. He favoured it, slowing. A wind came up swiftly. A cold wind that bit into the skin. But it came from the cliffs behind them, helped rather than hindered them. An omen? he wondered. No.

For as the minutes went by it grew upon him how poorly he had estimated the distance. Their time was dwindling out, but they were still an impossible distance from the ship. He said nothing, but the impotent anger at the slow muscles in his legs welled up into bitterly hot tears in his eyes.

He knew that Lyte was thinking the same as himself. But she flew along like a white bird, seeming hardly to touch ground. He heard her breath go out and in her throat, like a clean, sharp knife in its sheath.

Half the sky was dark. The first stars were peering through lengths of black cloud. Lightning jiggled a path along a rim just ahead of them. A full thunderstorm of violent rain and exploding electricity fell upon him.

They slipped and skidded on moss-smooth pebbles. Lyte fell, scrambled up again with a burning oath. Her body was scarred and dirty. The rain washed over her.

The rain came down and cried on Sim. It filled his eyes and ran in rivers down his spine and he wanted to cry with it.

Lyte fell and did not rise, sucking her breath, her breasts quivering.

He picked her up and held her. 'Run, Lyte, please, run!'

'Leave me, Sim. Go ahead!' The rain filled her mouth. There was water everywhere. 'It's no use. Go on without me.'

He stood there, cold and powerless, his thoughts sagging, the flame of hope blinking out. All the world was blackness, cold falling sheaths of water, and despair.

'We'll walk, then,' he said. 'And keep walking, and resting.'

They walked for fifty yards, easily, slowly, like children out for a stroll. The gully ahead of them filled with water that went sliding away with a swift wet sound, towards the horizon.

Sim cried out. Tugging at Lyte he raced forward. 'A new channel,' he said, pointing. 'Each day the rain cuts a new channel. Here, Lyte!' He leaned over the floodwaters.

He dived in, taking her with him.

The flood swept them like bits of wood. They fought to stay upright, the water got into their mouths, their noses. The land swept by on both sides of them. Clutching Lyte's fingers with insane strength, Sim felt himself hurled end over end, saw flicks of lightning on high, and a new fierce hope was born in him. They could no longer run — well, then they would let the water do the running for them.

With a speed that dashed them against rocks, split open their shoulders, abraded their legs, the new, brief river carried them. 'This way!' Sim shouted over a salvo of thunder and steered frantically towards the opposite side of the gully. The mountain where the ship lay was just ahead. They must not pass it by. They fought in the transporting liquid and were slammed against the far side. Sim leaped up, caught an overhanging rock, locked Lyte in his legs, and drew himself hand over hand upwards.

As quickly as it had come, the storm was gone. The lightning faded. The rain ceased. The clouds melted and fell away over the sky. The wind whispered into silence.

'The ship!' Lyte lay upon the ground. 'The ship, Sim. This is the mountain of the ship!'

Now the cold came. The killing cold.

They forced themselves drunkenly up the mountain. The cold slid along their limbs, got into their arteries like a chemical and slowed them.

Ahead of them, with a fresh-washed sheen, lay the ship. It was a dream. Sim could not believe that they were actually so near it. Two hundred yards. One hundred and seventy yards.

The ground became covered with ice. They slipped and fell again and again. Behind them the river was frozen into a blue-white snake of cold solidity. A few last drops of rain from somewhere came down as hard pellets.

Sim fell against the bulk of the ship. He was actually touching it. Touching it! He heard Lyte whimpering in her constricted throat. This was the metal, the ship. How many others had touched it in the long days? He and Lyte had made it!

Then, as cold as the air, his veins were chilled.

Where was the entrance?

You run, you swim, you almost drown, you curse, you sweat, you work, you reach a mountain, you go up it, you hammer on metal, you shout with relief, and then — you can't find the entrance.

He fought to control himself. Slowly, he told himself, but not too slowly, go around the ship. The metal slid under his searching hands, so cold that his hands, sweating, almost froze to it. Now, far around to the side, Lyte moved with him. The cold held them like a fist. It began to squeeze.

The entrance.

Metal. Cold, immutable metal. A thin line of opening at the sealing point. Throwing all caution aside, he beat at it. He felt his stomach seething with cold. His fingers were numb, his eyes were half frozen in their sockets. He began to beat and search and scream against the metal door. 'Open up! Open up!' He staggered. He had struck something . . . A *click*!

The air lock sighed. With a whispering of metal on rubber beddings, the door swung softly sidewise and vanished back.

He saw Lyte run forward, clutch at her throat, and drop inside a small shiny chamber. He shuffled after her, blankly.

The air-lock door sealed shut behind him.

He could not breathe. His heart began to slow, to stop.

They were trapped inside the ship now, and something was happening. He sank down to his knees and choked for air.

The ship he had come to for salvation was now slowing his pulse, darkening his brain, poisoning him. With a starved, faint kind of expiring terror, he realized he was dying.

Blackness.

He had a dim sense of time passing, of thinking, struggling, to make his heart go quick, quick . . . To make his eyes focus. But the fluid in his body lagged quietly through his settling veins and he heard his pulses thud, pause, thud, pause and thud again with lulling intermissions.

He could not move, not a hand or leg or finger. It was an effort to lift the tonnage of his eyelashes. He could not shift his face even, to see Lyte lying beside him.

From a distance came her irregular breathing. It was like the sound a wounded bird makes with his dry, unravelled pinions. She was so close he could almost feel the heat of her; yet she seemed a long way removed.

I'm getting cold! he thought. Is this death? This slowing of blood, of my heart, this cooling of my body, this drowsy thinking of thoughts?

Staring at the ship's ceiling he traced its intricate system of tubes and machines. The knowledge, the purpose of the ship, its actions, seeped into him. He began to understand in a kind of revealing lassitude just what these things were his eyes rested upon. Slow. Slow.

There was an instrument with a gleaming white dial.

Its purpose?

He drudged away at the problem, like a man under water.

People had used the dial. Touched it. People had repaired it. Installed it. People had dreamed of it before the building, before the installing, before the repairing and touching and using. The dial contained memory of use and manufacture, its very shape was a dream-memory telling Sim why and for what it had been built. Given time, looking at anything, he could draw from it the knowledge he desired. Some dim part of him reached out, dissected the contents of things, analysed them.

This dial measured time!

Millions of hours of time!

But how could that be? Sim's eyes dilated, hot and glittering. Where were humans who needed such an instrument?

Blood thrummed and beat behind his eyes. He closed them.

Panic came to him. The day was passing. I am lying here, he thought, and my life slips away. I cannot move. My youth is passing. How long before I can move?

Through a kind of porthole he saw the night pass, the day come, the day pass, and again another night. Stars danced frostily.

I will lie here for four or five days, wrinkling and withering, he thought. This ship will not let me move. How much better if I had stayed in my home cliff, lived, enjoyed this short life. What good has it done to come here? I'm missing all the twilights and dawns. I'll never touch Lyte, though she's here at my side.

Delirium. His mind floated up. His thoughts whirled through the metal ship. He smelled the razor-sharp smell of joined metal. He heard the hull contract with night, relax with day.

Dawn.

Already — another dawn!

Today I would have been fully grown. His jaw clenched. I must get up. I must move. I must enjoy this time.

But he didn't move. He felt his blood pump sleepily from chamber to red chamber in his heart, on down and around through his dead body, to be purified by his folding and unfolding lungs.

The ship grew warm. From somewhere a machine clicked. Automatically the temperature cooled. A controlled gust of air flushed the room.

Night again. And then another day.

He lay and saw four days of his life pass.

He did not try to fight. It was no use. His life was over.

He didn't want to turn his head now. He didn't want to see Lyte with her face like his tortured mother's — eyelids like grey ash flakes, eyes like beaten, sanded metal, cheeks like eroded stones. He didn't want to see a throat like parched thongs of yellow grass, hands the pattern of smoke risen from a fire, breasts like desiccated rinds and hair stubbly and unshorn as moist grey weeds!

And himself? How did *he* look? Was his jaw sunken, the flesh of his eyes pitted, his brow lined and age-scarred?

His strength began to return. He felt his heart beating so slow that it was amazing. One hundred beats a minute. Impossible. He felt so cool, so thoughtful, so easy.

His head fell over to one side. He stared at Lyte. He shouted in surprise.

She was young and fair.

She was looking at him, too weak to say anything. Her eyes were like tiny silver medals, her throat curved like the arm of a child. Her hair was blue fire eating at her scalp, fed by the slender life of her body.

Four days had passed and still she was young . . . no, younger than when they had entered the ship. She was still adolescent.

He could not believe it.

Her first words were, 'How long will this last?'

He replied carefully, 'I don't know.'

'We are still young.'

'The ship. Its metal is around us. It cuts away the sun and the things that came from the sun to age us.'

Her eyes shifted thoughtfully. 'Then, if we stay here — '

'We'll remain young.'

'Six more days? Fourteen more? Twenty?'

'More than that, maybe.'

She lay there, silently. After a long time, she said, 'Sim?'

'Yes.'

'Let's stay here. Let's not go back. If we go back now, you know what'll happen to us . . . ?'

'I'm not certain.'

'We'll start getting old again, won't we?'

He looked away. He stared at the ceiling and the clock with the moving finger. 'Yes. We'll grow old.'

'What if we grow old — instantly. When we step from the ship won't the shock be too much?'

'Maybe.'

Another silence. He began to move his limbs, testing them. He was very hungry. 'The others are waiting,' he said.

Her next words made him gasp. 'The others are dead,' she said. 'Or will be in a few hours. All those we knew back there are old.'

He tried to picture them old. Dark, his sister, bent and

senile with time. He shook his head, wiping the picture away. 'They may die,' he said. 'But there are others who've been born.'

'People we don't even know.'

'But, nevertheless, *our* people,' he replied. 'People who'll live only eight days, or eleven days unless we help them.'

'But we're *young*, Sim! We can *stay* young!'

He didn't want to listen. It was too tempting a thing to listen to. To stay here. To live. 'We've already had more time than the others,' he said. 'I need workers. Men to heal this ship. We'll get on our feet now, you and I, and find food, eat, and see if the ship is movable. I'm afraid to try to move it myself. It's so big. I'll need help.'

'But that means running back all that distance!'

'I know.' He lifted himself weakly. 'But I'll do it.'

'How will you get them back here?'

'We'll use the river.'

'*If* it's there. It *may* be somewhere else.'

'We'll wait until there *is* one, then. I've got to go back, Lyte. The son of Dienc is waiting for me, my sister, your brother, are old people, ready to die, and waiting for some word from us —'

After a long while he heard her move, dragging herself tiredly to him. She put her head upon his chest, her eyes closed, stroking his arm. 'I'm sorry. Forgive me. You have to go back. I'm a selfish fool.'

He touched her cheek, clumsily. 'You're human. I understand you. There's nothing to forgive.'

They found food. They walked through the ship. It was empty. Only in the control room did they find the remains of a man who must have been the chief pilot. The others had evidently bailed out into space in emergency lifeboats. This pilot, sitting at his controls, alone, had landed the ship on a mountain within sight of other fallen and smashed crafts. Its location on high ground had saved it from the floods. The pilot himself had died, probably of heart failure, soon after landing. The ship had remained here, almost within reach of the other survivors, perfect as an egg, but silent, for – how many thousand days? If the pilot had lived, what a different thing life might have been for the ancestors of Sim and Lyte. Sim, thinking of this, felt the distant, ominous vibration of war. How had the war between worlds come out? Who had won? Or had both planets lost and never bothered trying to pick up survivors? Who had been right? Who was the enemy? Were Sim's people of the guilty or innocent side? They might never know.

He checked the ship hurriedly. He knew nothing of its workings, yet as he walked its corridors, patted its machines, he learned from it. It needed only a crew. One man couldn't possibly set the whole thing running again. He laid his hand upon one round, snoutlike machine. He jerked his hand away, as if burnt.

'Lyte!'

'What is it?'

He touched the machine again, caressed it, his hand trembled violently, his eyes welled with tears, his mouth opened and closed, he looked at the machine, loving it, then looked at Lyte.

'With this machine –' he stammered, softly, incredulously. 'With – With this machine I can –'

'What, Sim?'

He inserted his hand into a cuplike contraption with a lever inside. Out of the porthole in front of him he could see the distant line of cliffs. 'We were afraid there might never be another river running by this mountain, weren't we?' he asked, exultantly.

'Yes, Sim, but –'

'There *will* be a river. And I *will* come back, tonight! And I'll bring men with me. Five hundred men! Because with this machine I can blast a river bottom all the way to the cliffs, down which the waters will rush, giving myself and the men a swift, sure way of travelling back!' He rubbed the machine's barrellike body. 'When I touched it, the life and method of it burnt into me! Watch!' He depressed the lever.

A beam of incandescent fire lanced out from the ship, screaming.

Steadily, accurately, Sim began to cut away a riverbed for the storm waters to flow in. The night was turned to day by its hungry eating.

The return to the cliffs was to be carried out by Sim alone. Lyte was to remain in the ship, in case of any mishap. The trip back seemed, at first glance, to be impossible. There would be no river rushing to cut his time, to sweep him along towards his destination. He would have to run the entire distance in the dawn, and the sun would get him, catch him before he'd reached safety.

'The only way to do it is to start *before* sunrise.'

'But you'd be frozen, Sim.'

'Here.' He made adjustments on the machine that had just finished cutting the riverbed in the rock floor of the valley. He lifted the smooth snout of the gun, pressed the lever, left it down. A gout of fire shot towards the cliffs. He fingered the range control, focused the flame end three miles from its source. Done. He turned to Lyte. 'But I don't understand,' she said.

He opened the air-lock door. 'It's bitter cold out, and half an hour yet till dawn. If I run parallel to the flame from the machine, close enough to it, there'll not be much heat, but enough to sustain life, anyway.'

'It doesn't sound safe,' Lyte protested.

'*Nothing* does, on this world.' He moved forward. 'I'll have a half-hour start. That should be enough to reach the cliffs.'

'But if the machine should fail while you're still running near its beam?'

'Let's not think of that,' he said.

A moment later he was outside. He staggered as if kicked in the stomach. His heart almost exploded in him. The environment of his world forced him into swift living again. He felt his pulse rise, kicking through his veins.

The night was cold as death. The heat ray from the ship sliced across the valley, humming, solid and warm. He moved next to it, very close. One misstep in his running and —

'I'll be back,' he called to Lyte.

He and the ray of light went together.

In the early morning the peoples of the caves saw the long finger of orange incandescence and the weird whitish apparition floating, running along beside it. There was a muttering and moaning and many sighs of awe.

And when Sim finally reached the cliffs of his childhood he saw alien peoples swarming there. There were no familiar faces. Then he realized how foolish it was to expect familiar faces. One of the older men glared down at him. 'Who're you?' he shouted. 'Are you from the enemy cliff? What's your name?'

'I am Sim, the son of Sim!'

'Sim!'

An old woman shrieked from the cliff above him. She came hobbling down the stone pathway. 'Sim, Sim, it *is* you!'

He looked at her, frankly bewildered. 'But I don't know you,' he murmured.

'Sim, don't you recognize me? Oh, Sim, it's me! Dark!'

'Dark!'

He felt sick at his stomach. She fell into his arms. This old, trembling woman with the half-blind eyes, his sister.

Another face appeared above. That of an old man. A cruel, bitter face. It looked down at Sim and snarled. 'Drive him away!' cried the old man. 'He comes from the cliff of the enemy. He's lived there! He's still young! Those who go there can never come back among us. Disloyal beast!' And a rock hurtled down.

Sim leaped aside, pulling the old woman with him.

A roar came from the people. They ran towards Sim, shaking their fists. 'Kill him, kill him!' raved the old man, and Sim did not know who he was.

'Stop!' Sim held out his hands. 'I come from the ship!'

'The ship?' The people slowed. Dark clung to him, looking up into his young face, puzzling over his smoothness.

'Kill him, kill him, kill him!' croaked the old man, and picked up another rock.

'I offer you ten days, twenty days, thirty more days of life!'

The people stopped. Their mouths hung open. Their eyes were incredulous.

'Thirty days?' It was repeated again and again. 'How?'

'Come back to the ship with me. Inside it, one can live forever!'

The old man lifted high a rock, then, choking, fell forward in an apoplectic fit, and tumbled down the rocks to lie at Sim's feet.

Sim bent to peer at the ancient one, at the raw, dead eyes, the loose, sneering lips, the crumpled, quiet body.

'Chion!'

'Yes,' said Dark behind him, in a croaking, strange voice. 'Your enemy. Chion.'

That night two hundred men started for the ship. The water ran in the new channel. One hundred of them were drowned or lost behind in the cold. The others, with Sim, got through to the ship.

Lyte awaited them, and threw wide the metal door.

The weeks passed. Generations lived and died in the cliffs, while the Scientists and workers laboured over the ship, learning its functions and its parts.

On the last day, two dozen men moved to their stations

within the ship. Now there was a destiny of travel ahead.

Sim touched the control plates under his fingers.

Lyte, rubbing her eyes, came and sat on the floor next to him, resting her head against his knee, drowsily. 'I had a dream,' she said, looking off at something far away. 'I dreamed I lived in caves in a cliff on a cold-hot planet where people grew old and died in eight days.'

'What an impossible dream,' said Sim. 'People couldn't possibly live in such a nightmare. Forget it. You're awake now.'

He touched the plates gently. The ship rose and moved into space.

Sim was right.

The nightmare was over at last.

The Anthem Sprinters

'There's no doubt of it, Doone's the best.'

'Devil take Doone!'

'His reflex is uncanny, his lope on the incline extraordinary, he's off and gone before you reach for your hat.'

'Hoolihan's better, any day!'

'Day, hell. Why not *now*?'

I was at the far end of the bar at the top of Grafton Street listening to the tenors singing, the concertinas dying hard, and the arguments prowling the smoke, looking for opposition. The pub was the Four Provinces and it was getting on late at night, for Dublin. So there was the sure threat of everything shutting at once, meaning spigots, accordions, piano lids, soloists, trios, quartets, pubs, sweet shops and cinemas. In a great heave like the Day of Judgement, half Dublin's population would be thrown out into raw lamplight, there to find themselves wanting in gum-machine mirrors. Stunned, their moral and physical sustenance plucked from them, the souls would wander like battered moths for a moment, then wheel about for home.

But now here I was listening to a discussion the heat of which, if not the light, reached me at fifty paces.

'Doone!'

'Hoolihan!'

Then the smallest man at the far end of the bar, turning, saw the curiosity enshrined in my all too open face and shouted, 'You're American, of course! And wondering what we're up to? Do you trust my looks? Would you bet as I told you on a sporting event of great local consequence? If "Yes" is your answer, come here!'

So I strolled my Guinness the length of the Four Provinces to join the shouting men, as one violinist gave up destroying a tune and the pianist hurried over, bringing his chorus with him.

'Name's Timulty!' The little man took my hand.

'Douglas,' I said. 'I write for the cinema.'

'Fillums!' cried everyone.

'Films,' I admitted modestly.

'What luck! Beyond belief!' Timulty seized me tighter. 'You'll be the best judge ever, as well as bet! Are you much for sports? Do you know, for instance, the cross-country, the four-forty, and such man-on-foot excursions?'

'I've witnessed two Olympic Games.'

'Not just fillums, but the world competition!' Timulty gasped. 'You're the rare one. Well, now what do you know of the special all-Irish decathlon event which has to do with picture theatres?'

'What event is that?'

'What indeed! Hoolihan!'

An even littler fellow, pocketing his harmonica, leaped forward, smiling, 'Hoolihan, that's me. The best Anthem Sprinter in all Ireland!'

'*What* sprinter?' I asked.

'A-n-t,' spelled Hoolihan, much too carefully, '-h-e-m. Anthem. Sprinter. The fastest.'

'Since you been in Dublin,' Timulty cut in, 'have you attended the cinema?'

'Last night,' I said. 'I saw a Clark Gable film. Night before, an old Charles Laughton —'

'Enough! You're a fanatic, as are all the Irish. If it weren't for cinemas and pubs to keep the poor and workless off the street or in their cups, we'd have pulled the cork and let the isle sink long ago. Well.' He clapped his hands. 'When the picture ends each night, have you observed a peculiarity of the breed?'

'End of the picture?' I mused. 'Hold on! You can't mean the national anthem, can you?'

'*Can* we, boys?' cried Tumulty.

'We can!' cried all.

'Any night, every night, for tens of dreadful years, at the end of each damn fillum, as if you'd never heard the baleful tune before,' grieved Timulty, 'the orchestra strikes up for Ireland. And what happens *then*?'

'Why,' said I, falling in with it, 'if you're any man at all, you try to get out of the theatre in those few precious moments between the end of the film and the start of the anthem.'

'You've nailed it!'

'Buy the Yank a drink!'

'After all,' I said casually, 'I'm in Dublin four months now. The anthem has begun to pale. No disrespect meant,' I added faintly.

'And none taken!' said Timulty. 'Or given by any of us patriotic IRA veterans, survivors of the Troubles and lovers of country. Still, breathing the same air ten thousand times makes the senses reel. So, as you've noted, in that God-sent three- or four-second interval any audience in its right mind beats it the hell out. And the best of the crowd is —'

'Doone,' I said. 'Or Hoolihan. Your Anthem Sprinters!'

They smiled at me. I smiled at them.

We were all so proud of my intuition that I bought them a round of Guinness.

Licking the suds from our lips, we regarded each other with benevolence.

'Now,' said Timulty, his voice husky with emotion, his eyes squinted off at the scene, 'at this very moment, not one hundred yards down the slight hill, in the comfortable dark of the Grafton Theatre, seated on the aisle of the fourth row centre is —'

'Doone,' said I.

'The man's eerie,' said Hoolihan, lifting his cap to me.

'Well' — Timulty swallowed his disbelief — 'Doone's there all right. He's not seen the fillum before, it's a Deanna Durbin brought back by the asking, and the time is now . . . '

Everyone glanced at the wall clock.

'Ten o'clock!' said the crowd.

'And in just fifteen minutes the cinema will be letting the customers out for good and all.'

'And?' I asked.

'And,' said Timulty. 'And! If we should send Hoolihan here in for a test of speed and agility, Doone would be ready to meet the challenge.'

'He didn't go to the show just for an Anthem Sprint, did he?'

'Good grief, no. He went for the Deanna Durbin songs and all. Doone plays the piano here, for sustenance. But if he should casually note the entrance of Hoolihan here, who would make himself conspicuous by his late arrival just across from Doone, well, Doone would know what was up. They would salute each other and both sit listening to the dear music until FINIS hove in sight.'

'Sure,' Hoolihan danced lightly on his toes, flexing his elbows. 'Let me at him, let me *at* him!'

Timulty peered close at me. 'Mr Douglas, I observe your disbelief. The details of the sport have bewildered you. How is it, you ask, that full-grown men have time for such as this? Well, time is the one thing the Irish have plenty of lying about. With no jobs at hand, what's minor in your country must be made to look major in ours. We have never seen the elephant, but we've learned a bug under a microscope is the greatest beast on earth. So while it hasn't passed the border, the Anthem Sprint's a high-blooded sport once you're in it. Let me nail down the rules!'

'First,' said Hoolihan reasonably, 'knowing what he

knows now, find out if the man wants to bet.'

Everyone looked at me to see if their reasoning had been wasted.

'Yes,' I said.

All agreed I was better than a human being.

'Introductions are in order,' said Timulty. 'Here's Fogarty, exit-watcher supreme. Nolan and Clannery, aisle-superintendent judges. Clancy, timekeeper. And general spectators O'Neill, Bannion and the Kelly boys, count 'em! Come on!'

I felt as if a vast street-cleaning machine, one of those brambled monsters all moustache and scouring brush, had seized me. The amiable mob floated me down the hill towards the multiplicity of little blinking lights where the cinema lured us on. Hustling, Timulty shouted the essentials:

'Much depends on the character of the theatre, of course!'

'Of course!' I yelled back.

'There be the liberal free-thinking theatres with grand aisles, grand exits and even grander, more spacious latrines. Some with so much porcelain, the echoes alone put you in shock. Then there's the parsimonious mousetrap cinemas with aisles that squeeze the breath from you, seats that knock your knees, and doors best sidled out of on your way to the men's lounge in the sweet shop across the alley. Each theatre is carefully assessed, before, during and after a sprint, the facts set down. A man is judged then, and his time reckoned good or inglorious, by whether he had to fight his way through men and women *en masse*, or mostly men, mostly women, or, the worst, children at the flypaper matinees. The temptation with children, of course, is to lay into them as you'd harvest hay, tossing them in windrows to left and right, so we've stopped that. Now mostly it's nights here at the Grafton!'

The mob stopped. The twinkling theatre lights sparkled in

our eyes and flushed our cheeks.

'The ideal cinema,' said Fogarty.

'Why?' I asked.

'Its aisles,' said Clannery, 'are neither too wide nor too narrow, its exits well placed, the door hinges oiled, the crowds a proper mixture of sporting bloods and folks who mind enough to leap aside should a Sprinter, squandering his energy, come dashing up the aisle.'

I had a sudden thought. 'Do you — handicap your runners?'

'We do! Sometimes by shifting exits when the old are known too well. Or we put a summer coat on one, a winter coat on another. Or seat one chap in the sixth row, while the other takes the third. And if a man turns terrible feverish swift, we add the greatest known burden of all — '

'Drink?' I said.

'What else? Now, Doone, being fleet, is a two-handicap man. Nolan!' Timulty held forth a flask. 'Run this in. Make Doone take two swigs, big ones.'

Nolan ran.

Timulty pointed. 'While Hoolihan here, having already gone through all Four Provinces of the pub this night, is amply weighted. Even all!'

'Go now, Hoolihan,' said Fogarty. 'Let our money be a light burden on you. We'll see you bursting out that exit five minutes from now, victorious and first!'

'Let's synchronize watches!' said Clancy.

'Synchronize my back-behind,' said Timulty. 'Which of us has more than dirty wrists to stare at? It's you alone, Clancy, has the time. Hoolihan, inside!'

Hoolihan shook hands with us all, as if leaving for a trip around the world. Then, waving, he vanished into the cinema darkness.

At which moment, Nolan burst back out, holding high the half-empty flask. 'Doone's handicapped!'

'Fine! Clannery, go check the contestants, be sure they sit opposite each other in the fourth row, as agreed, caps on, coats half buttoned, scarves properly furled. Report back to me.'

Clannery ran into the dark.

'The usher, the ticket taker?' I said.

'Are inside, watching the fillum,' said Timulty. 'So much standing is hard on the feet. They won't interfere.'

'It's ten-thirteen,' announced Clancy. 'In two more minutes —'

'Post time,' I said.

'You're a dear lad,' admitted Timulty.

Clannery came hot-footing out.

'All set! In the right seats and everything!'

' 'Tis almost over! You can tell — towards the end of any fillum the music has a way of getting out of hand.'

'It's loud, all right,' agreed Clannery. 'Full orchestra and chorus behind the singing maid now. I must come tomorrow for the entirety. Lovely.'

'Is it?' said Clancy, and the others.

'What's the tune?'

'Ah, off with the tune!' said Timulty. 'One minute to go and you ask the tune! Lay the bets. Who's for Doone? Who Hoolihan?' There was a multitudinous jabbering and passing back and forth of money, mostly shillings.

I held out four shillings.

'Doone,' I said.

'Without having seen him?'

'A dark horse,' I whispered.

'Well said!' Timulty spun about. 'Clannery, Nolan, inside, as aisle judges! Watch sharp there's no jumping the FINIS.'

In went Clannery and Nolan, happy as boys.

'Make an aisle, now. Mr Douglas, you over here with me!'

The men rushed to form an aisle on each side of the two

closed main entrance — exit doors.

'Fogarty, lay your ear to the door!'

This Fogarty did. His eyes widened.

'The damn music is extra loud!'

One of the Kelly boys nudged his brother. 'It will be over soon. Whoever is to die is dying this moment. Whoever is to live is bending over him.'

'Louder still!' announced Fogarty, head up against the door panel, hands twitching as if he were adjusting a radio. 'There! That's the grand *ta-ta* for sure that comes just as FINIS or THE END jumps on the screen.'

'They're off!' I murmured.

'Stand!' said Timulty.

We all stared at the door.

'There's the Anthem!'

' 'Tenshun!'

We all stood erect. Someone saluted.

But still we stared at the door.

'I hear feet running,' said Fogarty.

'Whoever it is had a good start before the anthem —'

The door burst wide.

Hoolihan plunged to view, smiling such a smile as only breathless victors know.

'Hoolihan!' cried the winners.

'Doone!' cried the losers. 'Where's Doone?'

For, while Hoolihan was first, a competitor was lacking.

The crowd was dispersing into the street now.

'The idiot didn't come out the wrong door?'

We waited. The crowd was soon gone.

Timulty ventured first into the empty lobby.

'Doone?'

No one there.

'Could it be he's in *there*?'

Someone flung the men's room door wide. 'Doone?'

No echo, no answer.

'Good grief,' cried Timulty, 'it can't be he's broken a leg and lies on the slope somewhere with the mortal agonies?'

'That's it!'

The island of men, heaving one way, changed gravities and heaved the other, towards the inner door, through it, and down the aisle, myself following.

'Doone!'

Clannery and Nolan were there to meet us and pointed silently down. I jumped into the air twice to see over the mob's head. It was dim in the vast theatre. I saw nothing.

'Doone!'

Then at last we were bunched together near the fourth row on the aisle. I heard their boggled exclamations as they saw what I saw:

Doone, still seated in the fourth row on the aisle, his hands folded, his eyes shut.

Dead?

None of that.

A tear, large, luminous and beautiful, fell on his cheek. Another tear, larger and more lustrous, emerged from his other eye. His chin was wet. It was certain he had been crying for some minutes.

The men peered into his face, circling, leaning.

'Doone, are ya sick?'

'Is it fearful news?'

'Ah, God,' cried Doone. He shook himself to find the strength, somehow, to speak.

'Ah, God,' he said at last, 'she has the voice of an angel.'

'Angel?'

'That one up there.' He nodded.

They turned to stare at the empty silver screen.

'Is it Deanna Durbin?'

Doone sobbed. 'The dear dead voice of my grandmother come back —'

'Your grandma's behind!' exclaimed Timulty. 'She had no such voice as that!'

'And who's to know, save me?' Doone blew his nose, dabbed at his eyes.

'You mean to say it was just the Durbin lass kept you from the sprint?'

'Just!' said Doone. 'Just! Why, it would be sacrilege to bound from a cinema after a recital like that. You might also then jump full tilt across the altar during a wedding, or waltz about at a funeral.'

'You could've at least warned us it was no contest.' Timulty glared.

'How could I? It just crept over me in a divine sickness. That last bit she sàng, "The Lovely Isle of Innisfree", was it not, Clannery?'

'What else did she sing?' asked Fogarty.

'What else did she sing?' cried Timulty. 'He's just lost half of our day's wages and you ask what else she sang! Get off!'

'Sure, it's money runs the world,' Doone agreed, seated there, closing up his eyes. 'But it is music that holds down the friction.'

'What's going on there?' cried someone above.

A man leaned down from the balcony, puffing a cigarette. 'What's all the rouse?'

'It's the projectionist,' whispered Timulty. Aloud: 'Hello, Phil, darling! It's only the Team! We've a bit of a problem here, Phil, in ethics, not to say aesthetics. Now, we wonder if, well, could it be possible to run the anthem over.'

'Run it over?'

There was a rumble from the winners, a mixing and shoving of elbows.

'A lovely idea,' said Doone.

'It is,' said Timulty, all guile. 'An act of God incapacitated Doone.'

'A tenth-run flicker from the year 1937 caught him by the short hairs is all,' said Fogarty.

'So the fair thing is' — here Timulty, unperturbed, looked to heaven — 'Phil, dear boy, also is the last reel of the Deanna Durbin fillum still there?'

'It ain't in the ladies' room,' said Phil, smoking steadily.

'What a wit the boy has. Now, Phil, do you think you could just thread it back through the machine there, and give us the FINIS again?'

'Is that what you all want?' asked Phil.

There was a hard moment of indecision. But the thought of another contest was too good to be passed, even though already-won money was at stake. Slowly everyone nodded.

'I'll bet myself, then,' Phil called down. 'A shilling on Hoolihan!'

The winners laughed and hooted; they looked to win again. Hoolihan waved graciously. The losers turned on their man.

'Do you hear the insult, Doone? Stay awake, man!'

'When the girl sings, damn it, go deaf!'

'Places, everyone!' Timulty jostled about.

'There's no audience,' said Hoolihan. 'And without them there's no obstacles, no real contest.'

'Why' — Fogarty blinked around — 'let's all of us be the audience.'

'Fine!' Beaming, everyone threw himself into a seat.

'Better yet,' announced Timulty, up front, 'why not make it teams? Doone and Hoolihan, sure, but for every Doone man or Hoolihan man that makes it out before the anthem freezes him on his hobnails, an extra point, right?'

'Done!' cried everyone.

'Pardon,' I said. 'There's no one outside to judge.'

Everyone turned to look at me.

'Ah,' said Timulty. 'Well, Nolan, outside!'

Nolan trudged up the aisle, cursing.

Phil stuck his head from the projection booth above.

'Are ya clods down there ready?'

'If the girl is and the anthem is!'

And the lights went out.

I found myself seated next in from Doone, who whispered fervently, 'Poke me, lad, keep me alert to practicalities instead of ornamentation, eh?'

'Shut up!' said someone. 'There's the mystery.'

And there indeed it was, the mystery of song and art and life, if you will, the young girl singing on the time-haunted screen.

'We lean on you, Doone,' I whispered.

'Eh?' he replied. He smiled ahead. 'Ah, look, ain't she lovely? Do you hear?'

'The bet, Doone,' I said. 'Get ready.'

'All right,' he groused. 'Let me stir my bones. Jesus save me.'

'What?'

'I never thought to test. My right leg. Feel. Naw, you can't. It's dead, it is!'

'Asleep, you mean?' I said, appalled.

'Dead or asleep, hell, I'm sunk! Lad, lad, you must run for me! Here's my cap and scarf!'

'Your cap — ?'

'When victory is yours, show them, and we'll explain you ran to replace this fool leg of mine!'

He clapped the cap on, tied the scarf.

'But look here —' I protested.

'You'll do brave! Just remember, it's FINIS and no sooner! The song's almost up. Are you tensed?'

'God, *am* I!' I said.

'It's blind passions that win, boy. Plunge straight. If you step on someone, do not look back. There!' Doone held his legs to one side to give clearance. 'The song's done. He's kissing her —'

'The FINIS!' I cried.

I leaped into the aisle.

I ran up the slope. I'm first! I thought. I'm ahead! It can't be! There's the door!

I hit the door as the anthem began.

I slammed into the lobby — safe!

I won! I thought, incredulous, with Doone's cap and scarf like victory laurels upon and about me. Won! Won for the Team!

Who's second, third, fourth?

I turned to the door as it swung shut.

Only then did I hear the shouts and yells inside.

Good Lord! I thought, six men have tried the wrong exit at once, someone tripped, fell, someone else piled on. Otherwise, why am I the first and only? There's a fierce silent combat in there this second, the two teams locked in mortal wrestling attitudes, asprawl, akimbo, above and below the seats, that *must* be it!

I've won! I wanted to yell, to break it up.

I threw the door wide.

I stared into the abyss where nothing stirred.

Nolan came to peer over my shoulder.

'That's the Irish for you,' he said, nodding. 'Even more than the race, it's the Muse they like.'

For what were the voices yelling in the dark?

'Run it again! Over! That last song! Phil!'

'No one move. I'm in heaven. Doone, how right you were!'

Nolan passed me, going in to sit.

I stood for a long moment looking down along at all the rows where the teams of Anthem Sprinters sat, none having stirred, wiping their eyes.

'Phil, darling?' called Timulty, somewhere up front.

'It's done!' said Phil.

'And this time,' added Timulty, '*without* the anthem.'

Applause for this.

The dim lights flashed off. The screen glowed like a great warm hearth.

I looked back out at the bright sane world of Grafton Street, the Four Provinces pub, the hotels, shops and night-wandering folk. I hesitated.

Then, to the tune of 'The Lovely Isle of Innisfree', I took off the cap and scarf, hid these laurels under a seat, and slowly, luxuriously, with all the time in the world, sat myself down . . .

And So Died Riabouchinska

The cellar was cold cement and the dead man was cold stone and the air was filled with an invisible fall of rain, while the people gathered to look at the body as if it had been washed in on an empty shore at morning. The gravity of the earth was drawn to a focus here in this single basement room — a gravity so immense that it pulled their faces down, bent their mouths at the corners and drained their cheeks. Their hands hung weighted and their feet were planted so they could not move without seeming to walk underwater.

A voice was calling, but nobody listened.

The voice called again and only after a long time did the people turn and look, momentarily, into the air. They were at the seashore in November and this was a gull crying over their heads in the grey colour of dawn. It was a sad crying, like the birds going south for the steel winter to come. It was an ocean sounding the shore so far away that it was only a whisper of sand and wind in a seashell.

The people in the basement room shifted their gaze to a table and a golden box resting there, no more than twenty-four inches long, inscribed with the name RIABOUCHINSKA. Under the lid of this small coffin the voice at last settled with finality, and the people stared at the box, and the dead man lay on the floor, not hearing the soft cry.

'Let me out, let me out, oh, please, please, someone let me out.'

And finally Mr Fabian, the ventriloquist, bent and whispered to the golden box, 'No, Ria, this is serious business. Later. Be quiet, now, that's a good girl.' He shut his eyes and tried to laugh.

From under the polished lid her calm voice said, 'Please don't laugh. You should be much kinder now after what's happened.'

Detective Lieutenant Krovitch touched Fabian's arm. 'If you don't mind, we'll save your dummy act for later. Right now there's all *this* to clean up.' He glanced at the woman, who had now taken a folding chair. 'Mrs Fabian.' He nodded to the young man sitting next to her. 'Mr Douglas, you're Mr Fabian's press agent and manager?'

The young man said he was. Krovitch looked at the face of the man on the floor. 'Fabian, Mrs Fabian, Mr Douglas – all of you say you don't know this man who was murdered here last night, never heard the name Ockham before. Yet Ockham earlier told the stage manager he knew Fabian and had to see him about something vitally important.'

The voice in the box began again quietly.

Krovitch shouted. '*Damn* it, Fabian!'

Under the lid, the voice laughed. It was like a muffled bell ringing.

'Pay no attention to her, Lieutenant,' said Fabian.

'Her? Or *you*, damn it! What is this? Get together, you two!'

'We'll never be together,' said the quiet voice, 'never again after tonight.'

Krovitch put out his hand. 'Give me the key, Fabian.'

In the silence there was the rattle of the key in the small lock, the squeal of the miniature hinges as the lid was opened and laid back against the table top.

'Thank you,' said Riabouchinska.

Krovitch stood motionless, just looking down and seeing Riabouchinska in her box and not quite believing what he saw.

The face was white and it was cut from marble or from the whitest wood he had ever seen. It might have been cut from snow. And the neck that held the head which was as dainty as a porcelain cup with the sun shining through the thinness of it, the neck was also white. And the hands could have been ivory and they were thin small things with tiny fingernails and whorls on the pads of the fingers, little delicate spirals and lines.

She was all white stone, with light pouring through the stone and light coming out of the dark eyes with blue tones beneath like fresh mulberries. He was reminded of milk glass and of cream poured into a crystal tumbler. The brows were arched black and thin and the cheeks were hollowed and there was a faint pink vein in each temple and a faint blue vein barely visible above the slender bridge of the nose, between the shining dark eyes.

Her lips were half parted and it looked as if they might be slightly damp, and the nostrils were arched and modelled perfectly, as were the ears. The hair was black and it was parted in the middle and drawn behind the cars and it was real — he could see every single strand of hair. Her gown was as black as her hair and draped in such a fashion as to show her shoulders, which were carved wood as white as a stone that has lain a long time in the sun. She was very beautiful. Krovitch felt his throat move and then he stopped and did not say anything.

Fabian took Riabouchinska from her box. 'My lovely lady,' he said. 'Carved from the rarest imported woods. She's appeared in Paris, Rome, Istanbul. Everyone in the world loves her and thinks she's really human, some sort of incredibly delicate midget creature. They won't accept that she was once part of many forests growing far away from cities and idiotic people.'

Fabian's wife, Alyce, watched her husband, not taking her eyes from his mouth. Her eyes did not blink once in all the time he was telling of the doll he held in his arms. He in turn seemed aware of no one but the doll; the cellar and its people were lost in a mist that settled everywhere.

But finally the small figure stirred and quivered. 'Please, don't talk about me! You know Alyce doesn't like it.'

'Alyce never has liked it.'

'Shh, don't!' cried Riabouchinska. 'Not here, not now.' And then, swiftly, she turned to Krovitch and her tiny lips moved. 'How did it all happen? Mr Ockham, I mean, Mr Ockham.'

Fabian said, 'You'd better go to sleep now, Ria.'

'But I don't want to,' she replied. 'I've as much right to listen and talk, I'm as much a part of this murder as Alyce or – or Mr Douglas even!'

The press agent threw down his cigarette. 'Don't drag me into this, you –' And he looked at the doll as if it had suddenly become six feet tall and were breathing there before him.

'It's just that I want the truth to be told,' Riabouchinska turned her head to see all of the room. 'And if I'm locked in my coffin there'll be no truth, for John's a consummate liar and I must watch after him, isn't that right, John?'

'Yes,' he said, his eyes shut, 'I suppose it is.'

'John loves me best of all the women in the world and I love him and try to understand his wrong way of thinking.'

Krovitch hit the table with his fist. 'God damn, oh, God *damn* it, Fabian! If you think you can – '

'I'm helpless,' said Fabian.

'But she's –'

'I know, I know what you want to say,' said Fabian quietly, looking at the detective. 'She's in my throat, is that it? No, no. She's not in my throat. She's somewhere else. I don't know. Here, or here.' He touched his chest, his head.

'She's quick to hide. Sometimes there's nothing I can do. Sometimes she is only herself, nothing of me at all. Sometimes she tells me what to do and I must do it. She stands guard, she reprimands me, is honest where I am dishonest, good when I am wicked as all the sins that ever were. She lives a life apart. She's raised a wall in my head and lives there, ignoring me if I try to make her say improper things, co-operating if I suggest the right words and pantomime.' Fabian sighed. 'So if you intend going on I'm afraid Ria must be present. Locking her up will do no good, no good at all.'

Lieutenant Krovitch sat silently for the better part of a minute, then made his decision. 'All right. Let her stay. It just may be, by God, that before the night's over I'll be tired enough to ask even a ventriloquist's dummy questions.'

Krovitch unwrapped a fresh cigar, lit it and puffed smoke. 'So you don't recognize the dead man, Mr Douglas?'

'He looks vaguely familiar. Could be an actor.'

Krovitch swore. 'Let's all stop lying, what do you say? Look at Ockham's shoes, his clothing. It's obvious he needed money and came here tonight to beg, borrow or steal some. Let me ask you this, Douglas. Are you in love with Mrs Fabian?'

'Now, wait just a moment!' cried Alyce Fabian.

Krovitch motioned her down. 'You sit there, side by side, the two of you. I'm not exactly blind. When a press agent sits where the husband should be sitting, consoling the wife, well! The way you look at the marionette's coffin, Mrs Fabian, holding your breath when she appears. You make fists when she talks. Hell, you're obvious.'

'If you think for one moment I'm jealous of a stick of wood!'

'Aren't you?'

'No, no, I'm not!'

Fabian moved. 'You needn't tell him anything, Alyce.'

'Let her!'

They all jerked their heads and stared at the small figurine, whose mouth was now slowly shutting. Even Fabian looked at the marionette as if it had struck him a blow.

After a long while Alyce Fabian began to speak.

'I married John seven years ago because he said he loved me and because I loved him and I loved Riabouchinska. At first, anyway. But then I began to see that he really lived all of his life and paid most of his attentions to her and I was a shadow waiting in the wings every night.

'He spent fifty thousand dollars a year on her wardrobe – a hundred thousand dollars for a doll's house with gold and silver and platinum furniture. He tucked her in a small satin bed each night and talked to her. I thought it was all an elaborate joke at first and I was wonderfully amused. But when it finally came to me that I was indeed merely an assistant in his act I began to feel a vague sort of hatred and distrust – not for the marionette, because after all it wasn't her doing, but I felt a terrible growing dislike and hatred for John, because it *was* his fault. He, after all, was the control, and all of his cleverness and natural sadism came out through his relationship with the wooden doll.

'And when I finally became very jealous, how silly of me! It was the greatest tribute I could have paid him and the way he had gone about perfecting the art of throwing his voice. It was all so idiotic, it was all so strange. And yet I knew that something had hold of John, just as people who drink have a hungry animal somewhere in them, starving to death.

'So I moved back and forth from anger to pity, from jealousy to understanding. There were long periods when I didn't hate him at all, and I never hated the thing that Ria was in him, for she was the best half, the good part, the honest and the lovely part of him. She was everything that he never let himself try to be.'

Alyce Fabian stopped talking and the basement room was silent.

'Tell about Mr Douglas,' said a voice, whispering.

Mrs Fabian did not look up at the marionette. With an effort she finished it out. 'When the years passed and there was so little love and understanding from John, I guess it was natural I turned to — Mr Douglas.'

Krovitch nodded. 'Everything begins to fall into place. Mr Ockham was a very poor man, down on his luck, and he came to this theatre tonight because he knew something about you and Mr Douglas. Perhaps he threatened to speak to Mr Fabian if you didn't buy him off. That would give you the best of reasons to get rid of him.'

'That's even sillier than all the rest,' said Alyce Fabian tiredly. 'I didn't kill him.'

'Mr Douglas might have and not told you.'

'Why kill a man?' said Douglas. 'John knew all about us.'

'I did indeed,' said John Fabian, and laughed.

He stopped laughing and his hand twitched, hidden in the snowflake interior of the tiny doll, and her mouth opened and shut, opened and shut. He was trying to make her carry the laughter on after he had stopped, but there was no sound, save the little empty whisper of her lips moving and gasping, while Fabian stared down at the little face and perspiration came out, shining, upon his cheeks.

The next afternoon Lieutenant Krovitch moved through the theatre darkness backstage, found the iron stairs and climbed with great thought, taking as much time as he deemed necessary on each step, up to the second-level dressing rooms. He rapped on one of the thin-panelled doors.

'Come in,' said Fabian's voice from what seemed a great distance.

Krovitch entered and closed the door and stood looking at the man who was slumped before his dressing mirror. 'I have something I'd like to show you,' Krovitch said. His face showing no emotion whatever, he opened a manilla folder and pulled out a glossy photograph, which he placed on the dressing table.

John Fabian raised his eyebrows, glanced quickly up at Krovitch and then settled slowly back in his chair. He put his

fingers to the bridge of his nose and massaged his face carefully, as if he had a headache. Krovitch turned the picture
over and began to read from the typewritten data on the back.
'Name, Miss Ilyana Riamonova. One hundred pounds. Blue
eyes. Black hair. Oval face. Born 1914, New York City.
Disappeared 1934. Believed a victim of amnesia. Of Russo-
Slav parentage. Etcetera. Etcetera.'

Fabian's lip twitched.

Krovitch laid the photograph down, shaking his head
thoughtfully. 'It was pretty silly of me to go through police
files for a picture of a marionette. You should have heard the
laughter at headquarters. *God*. Still, here she is —
Riabouchinska. *Not* papier-mâché, *not* wood, *not* a puppet,
but a woman who once lived and moved around and —
disappeared.' He looked steadily at Fabian. 'Suppose you
take it from there?'

Fabian half smiled. 'There's nothing to it at all. I saw this
woman's picture a long time ago, liked her looks and copied
my marionette after her.'

'Nothing to it at all.' Krovitch took a deep breath and
exhaled, wiping his face with a huge handkerchief. 'Fabian,
this very morning I shuffled through a stack of *Billboard*
magazines that high. In the year 1934 I found an interesting
article concerning an act which played on a second-rate cir-
cuit, known as Fabian and Sweet William. Sweet William
was a little boy dummy. There was a girl assistant — Ilyana
Riamonova. No picture of her in the article, but I at least had
a name, the name of a real person, to go on. It was simple to
check police files then and dig up this picture. The resem-
blance, needless to say, between the live woman on one hand
and the puppet on the other is nothing short of incredible.
Suppose you go back and tell your story over again, Fabian.'

'She was my assistant, that's all. I simply used her as a
model.'

'You're making me sweat,' said the detective. 'Do you

think I'm a fool? Do you think I don't know love when I see it? I've watched you handle the marionette, I've seen you talk to it, I've seen how you make it react to you. You're in love with the puppet naturally, because you loved the original woman very, very much. I've lived too long not to sense that. Hell, Fabian, stop fencing around.'

Fabian lifted his pale slender hands, turned them over, examined them and let them fall.

'All right. In 1934 I was billed as Fabian and Sweet William. Sweet William was a small bulb-nosed boy dummy I carved a long time ago. I was in Los Angeles when this girl appeared at the stage door one night. She'd followed my work for years. She was desperate for a job and she hoped to be my assistant . . . '

He remembered her in the half light of the alley behind the theatre and how startled he was at her freshness and eagerness to work with and for him and the way the cool rain touched softly down through the narrow alleyway and caught in small spangles through her hair, melting in dark warmness, and the rain beaded upon her white porcelain hand holding her coat together at her neck.

He saw her lips' motion in the dark and her voice, separated off on another sound track, it seemed, speaking to him in the autumn wind, and he remembered that without his saying yes or no or perhaps she was suddenly on the stage with him, in the great pouring bright light, and in two months he, who had always prided himself on his cynicism and disbelief, had stepped off the rim of the world after her, plunging down a bottomless place of no limit and no light anywhere.

Arguments followed, and more than arguments – things said and done that lacked all sense and sanity and fairness. She had edged away from him at last, causing his rages and remarkable hysterias. Once he burned her entire wardrobe in a fit of jealousy. She had taken this quietly. But then one night he handed her a week's notice, accused her of monstrous disloyalty, shouted at her, seized her, slapped her again and again across the face, bullied her about and thrust her out the door, slamming it!

She disappeared that night.

When he found the next day that she was really gone and there was nowhere to find her, it was like standing in the centre of a titanic explosion. All the world was smashed flat and all the echoes of the explosion came back to reverberate at midnight, at four in the morning, at dawn, and he was up early, stunned with the sound of coffee simmering and the sound of matches being struck and cigarettes lit and himself trying to shave and looking at mirrors that were sickening in their distortion.

He clipped out all the advertisements that he took in the papers and pasted them in neat rows in a scrapbook — all the ads describing her and telling about her and asking for her back. He even put a private detective on the case. People talked. The police dropped by to question him. There was more talk.

But she was gone like a piece of white incredibly fragile tissue paper, blown over the sky and down. A record of her was sent to the largest cities, and that was the end of it for the police. But not for Fabian. She might be dead or just running away, but wherever she was he knew that somehow and in some way he would have her back.

One night he came home, bringing his own darkness with him, and collapsed upon a chair, and before he knew it he found himself speaking to Sweet William in the totally black room.

'William, it's all over and done. I can't keep it up!'

And William cried, 'Coward! Coward!' from the air above his head, out of the emptiness. 'You can get her back if you want!'

Sweet William squeaked and clappered at him in the night.

'Yes, you can! *Think!*' he insisted. 'Think of a way. You can do it. Put me aside, lock me up. Start all over.'

'Start all over?'

'Yes,' whispered Sweet William, and darkness moved within darkness. 'Yes. Buy wood. Buy fine new wood. Buy hard-grained wood. Buy beautiful fresh new wood. And carve. Carve slowly and carve carefully. Whittle away. Cut delicately. Make the little nostrils so. And cut her thin black eyebrows round and high, so, and make her cheeks in small hollows. Carve, carve . . . '

'No! It's foolish. I could never do it!'

'Yes, you could. Yes you could, could, could, could . . . '

The voice faded, a ripple of water in an underground stream. The stream rose up and swallowed him. His head fell forward. Sweet William sighed. And then the two of them lay like stones buried under a waterfall.

The next morning, John Fabian bought the hardest, finest-grained piece of wood that he could find and brought it home and laid it on the table, but could not touch it. He sat for hours staring at it. It was impossible to think that out of this cold chunk of material he expected his hands and his memory to re-create something warm and pliable and familiar. There was no way even faintly to approximate that quality of rain and summer and the first powderings of snow upon a clear pane of glass in the middle of a December night. No way, no way at all to catch the snowflakes without having it melt swiftly in your clumsy fingers.

And yet Sweet William spoke out, sighing and whispering, after midnight, 'You can do it. Oh, yes, yes, you can do it!'

And so he began. It took him an entire month to carve her hands into things as natural and beautiful as shells lying in the sun. Another month and the skeleton, like a fossil imprint he was searching out, stamped and hidden in the wood, was revealed, all febrile and so infinitely delicate as to suggest the veins in the white flesh of an apple.

And all the while Sweet William lay mantled in dust in his box that was fast becoming a very real coffin. Sweet William croaking and wheezing some feeble sarcasm, some sour criticism, some hint, some help, but dying all the time, fading, soon to be untouched, soon to be like a sheath moulted in summer and left behind to blow in the wind.

As the weeks passed and Fabian moulded and scraped and polished the new wood, Sweet William lay longer and longer in stricken silence, and one day as Fabian held the puppet in his hand Sweet William seemed to look at him a moment with puzzled eyes and then there was a death rattle in his throat.

And Sweet William was gone.

Now as he worked, a fluttering, a faint motion of speech began far back in his throat, echoing and re-echoing, speaking silently like a breeze among dry leaves. And then for the first time he held the doll in a certain way in his hands and memory moved down his arms and into his fingers and from his fingers into the hollowed wood and the tiny hands flickered and the body became suddenly soft and pliable and her eyes opened and looked up at him.

And the small mouth opened the merest fraction of an inch and she was ready to speak and he knew all of the things that she must say to him, he knew the first and the second and the third things he would have her say. There was a whisper, a whisper, a whisper.

The tiny head turned this way gently, that way gently. The mouth half opened again and began to speak. And as it spoke he bent his head and he could feel the warm breath — of *course* it was there! — coming from her mouth, and when he listened very carefully, holding her to his head, his eyes shut, wasn't *it* there, too, softly, *gently* — the beating of her heart?

Krovitch sat in a chair for a full minute after Fabian stopped talking. Finally he said, 'I *see*. And your wife?'

'Alyce? She was my second assistant, of course. She

worked very hard and God help her, she loved me. It's hard now to know why I ever married her. It was unfair of me.'

'What about the dead man – Ockham?'

'I never saw him before you showed me his body in the theatre basement yesterday.'

'Fabian,' said the detective.

'It's the truth!'

'Fabian.'

'The truth, the truth, damn it, I swear it's the truth!'

'The truth.' There was a whisper like the sea coming in on the grey shore at early morning. The water was ebbing in a fine lace on the sand. The sky was cold and empty. There were no people on the shore. The sun was gone. And the whisper said again, 'The truth.'

Fabian sat up straight and took hold of his knees with his thin hands. His face was rigid. Krovitch found himself making the same motion he had made the day before – looking at the grey ceiling as if it were a November sky and a lonely bird going over and away, grey within the cold greyness.

'The truth.' Fading. 'The truth.'

Krovitch lifted himself and moved as carefully as he could to the far side of the dressing room where the golden box lay open and inside the box the thing that whispered and talked and could laugh sometimes and could sometimes sing. He carried the golden box over and set it down in front of Fabian and waited for him to put his living hand within the gloved delicate hollowness, waited for the fine small mouth to quiver and the eyes to focus. He did not have to wait long.

'The first letter came a month ago.'

'No.'

'The first letter came a month ago.'

'No, *no*!'

'The letter said, "Riabouchinska, born 1914, died 1934. Born again in 1935." Mr Ockham was a juggler. He'd been on the same bill with John and Sweet William years before.

He remembered that once there had been a woman, before there was a puppet.'

'No, that's not true!'

'Yes,' said the voice.

Snow was falling in silences and even deeper silences through the dressing room. Fabian's mouth trembled. He stared at the blank walls as if seeking some new door by which to escape. He half rose from his chair. 'Please . . . '

'Ockham threatened to tell about us to everyone in the world.'

Krovitch saw the doll quiver, saw the fluttering of the lips, saw Fabian's eyes widen, and fix and his throat convulse and tighten as if to stop the whispering.

'I − I was in the room when Mr Ockham came. I lay in my box and I listened and heard, and I *know*.' The voice blurred, then recovered and went on. 'Mr Ockham threatened to tear me up, burn me into ashes if John didn't pay him a thousand dollars. Then suddenly there was a falling sound. A cry. Mr Ockham's head must have struck the floor. I heard John cry out and I heard him swearing. I heard him sobbing. I heard a gasping and a choking sound.'

'You heard nothing! You're deaf, you're blind! You're wood!' cried Fabian.

'But I *hear*!' she said, and stopped as if someone had put a hand to her mouth.

Fabian had leaped to his feet now and stood with the doll in his hand. The mouth clapped twice, three times, then finally made words. 'The choking sound stopped. I heard John drag Mr Ockham down the stairs under the theatre to the old dressing rooms that haven't been used in years. Down, down, down, I heard them going away and away − down . . . '

Krovitch stepped back as if he were watching a motion picture that had suddenly grown monstrously tall. The figures terrified and frightened him, they were immense,

they towered! They threatened to inundate him with size.
Someone had turned up the sound so that it screamed.

He saw Fabian's teeth, a grimace, a whisper, a clenching.
He saw the man's eyes squeeze shut.

Now the soft voice was so high and faint it trembled
towards nothingness.

'I'm not made to live this way. This way. There's nothing
for us now. Everyone will know, everyone will. Even when
you killed him and I lay asleep last night, I dreamed, I knew,
I realized. We both knew, we both realized that these would
be our last days, our last hours. Because while I've lived with
your weakness and I've lived with your lies, I can't live with
something that kills and hurts in killing. There's no way to go
on from here. How *can* I live alongside such knowledge? . . . '

Fabian held her into the sunlight which shone dimly
through the small dressing-room window. She looked at him
and there was nothing in her eyes. His hand shook and in
shaking made the marionette tremble, too. Her mouth closed
and opened, closed and opened, closed and opened, again
and again and again. Silence.

Fabian moved his fingers unbelievingly to his own mouth.
A film slid across his eyes. He looked like a man lost in the
street, trying to remember the number of a certain house,
trying to find a certain window with a certain light. He
swayed about, staring at the walls, at Krovitch, at the doll, at
his free hand, turning the fingers over, touching his throat,
opening his mouth. He listened.

Miles away in a cave, a single wave came in from the sea
and whispered down in foam. A gull moved soundlessly, not
beating its wings – a shadow.

'She's gone. She's gone. I can't find her. She's run off. I
can't find her. I can't find her. I try, I try, but she's run off
far. Will you help me find her?'

Riabouchinska slipped bonelessly from his limp hand,

folded over and glided noiselessly down to lie upon the cold floor, her eyes closed, her mouth shut.

Fabian did not look at her as Krovitch led him out of the door.

Boys! Raise Giant Mushrooms in Your Cellar!

Hugh Fortnum woke to Saturday's commotions and lay, eyes shut, savouring each in its turn.

Below, bacon in a skillet; Cynthia waking him with fine cookings instead of cries.

Across the hall, Tom *actually* taking a shower.

Far off in the bumblebee dragonfly light, whose voice was already damning the weather, the time, and the tides? Mrs Goodbody? Yes. That Christian giantess, six-foot tall with her shoes off, the gardener extraordinary, the octogenarian dietician and town philosopher.

He rose, unhooked the screen and leaned out to hear her cry, 'There! Take *that*! *This'll* fix you! Hah!'

'Happy Saturday, Mrs Goodbody!'

The old woman froze in clouds of bug spray pumped from an immense gun.

'Nonsense!' she shouted. 'With these fiends and pests to watch for?'

'What kind *this* time?' called Fortnum.

'I don't want to shout it to the jaybirds, but' — she glanced suspiciously around — 'what would you say if I told you I was the first line of defence concerning flying saucers?'

'Fine,' replied Fortnum. 'There'll be rockets between the worlds any year now.'

'There already *are*!' She pumped, aiming the spray under the hedge. 'There! Take that!'

He pulled his head back in from the fresh day, somehow not as high-spirited as his first response had indicated. Poor soul, Mrs Goodbody. Always the essence of reason. And now what? Old age?

The doorbell rang.

He grabbed his robe and was half down the stairs when he heard a voice say, 'Special delivery, Fortnum?' and saw Cynthia turn from the front door, a small packet in her hand.

'Special delivery airmail for your son.'

Tom was downstairs like a centipede.

'Wow! That must be from the Great Bayou Novelty Green-house!'

'I wish I were as excited about ordinary mail,' observed Fortnum.

'Ordinary?!' Tom ripped the cord and paper wildly. 'Don't you read the back pages of *Popular Mechanics*? Well, here *they* are!'

Everyone peered into the small open box.

'Here,' said Fortnum, '*what* are?'

'The Sylvan Glade Jumbo-Giant Guaranteed Growth Raise-Them-in-Your Cellar-for-Big-Profit-Mushrooms!'

'Oh, of course,' said Fortnum. 'How silly of me.'

Cynthia squinted. 'Those little teeny bits?'

' "Fabulous growth in twenty-four hours." ' Tom quoted from memory. ' "Plant them in your cellar . . . " '

Fortnum and wife exchanged glances.

'Well,' she admitted, 'it's better than frogs and green snakes.'

'Sure is!' Tom ran.

'Oh, Tom,' said Fortnum lightly.

Tom paused at the cellar door.

'Tom,' said his father. 'Next time, fourth-class mail would do fine.'

'Heck,' said Tom. 'They must've made a mistake, thought I was some rich company. Airmail special, who can afford that?'

The cellar door slammed.

Fortnum bemused, scanned the wrapper a moment then dropped it into the wastebasket. On his way to the kitchen, he opened the cellar door.

Tom was already on his knees, digging with a hand rake in the dirt.

He felt his wife beside him, breathing softly, looking down into the cool dimness.

'Those *are* mushrooms, I hope. Not . . . toadstools?'

Fortnum laughed. 'Happy harvest, farmer!'

Tom glanced up and waved.

Fortnum shut the door, took his wife's arm and walked her out to the kitchen, feeling fine.

Towards noon, Fortnum was driving towards the nearest market when he saw Roger Willis, a fellow Rotarian and a teacher of biology at the town high school, waving urgently from the sidewalk.

Fortnum pulled his car up and opened the door.

'Hi, Roger, give you a lift?'

Willis responded all too eagerly, jumping in and slamming the door.

'Just the man I want to see. I've put off calling for days. Could you play psychiatrist for five minutes, God help you?'

Fortnum examined his friend for a moment as he drove quietly on.

'God help you, yes. Shoot.'

Willis sat back and studied his fingernails. 'Let's just drive a moment. There. Okay. Here's what I want to say: Something's wrong with the world.'

Fortnum laughed easily. 'Hasn't there always been?'

'No, no, I mean . . . something strange — something unseen — is happening.'

'Mrs Goodbody,' said Fortnum, half to himself, and stopped.

'Mrs Goodbody?'

'This morning, gave me a talk on flying saucers.'

'No.' Willis bit the knuckle of his forefinger nervously.

'Nothing like saucers. At least, I don't think. Tell me, what exactly is intuition?'

'The conscious recognition of something that's been subconscious for a long time. But don't quote this amateur psychologist!' He laughed again.

'Good, good!' Willis turned, his face lighting. He readjusted himself in the seat. 'That's it! Over a long period, things gather, right? All of a sudden, you have to spit, but you don't remember saliva collecting. Your hands are dirty, but you don't know how they got that way. Dust falls on you every day and you don't feel it. But when you get enough dust collected up, there it is, you see and name it. That's intuition, as far as I'm concerned. Well, what kind of dust has been falling on *me*? A few meteors in the sky at night? funny weather just before dawn? I don't know. Certain colours, smells, the way the house creaks at three in the morning? Hair prickling on my arms? All I know is the damn dust has collected. Quite suddenly I know.'

'Yes,' said Fortnum, disquieted. 'But what *is* it you know?'

Willis looked at his hands in his lap. 'I'm afraid. I'm not afraid. Then I'm afraid again, in the middle of the day. Doctor's checked me. I'm A-one. No family problems. Joe's a fine boy, a good son. Dorothy? She's remarkable. With her I'm not afraid of growing old or dying.'

'Lucky man.'

'But beyond my luck now. Scared stiff, really, for myself, my family; even right now, for you.'

'Me?' said Fortnum.

They had stopped now by an empty lot near the market. There was a moment of great stillness, in which Fortnum turned to survey his friend. Willis's voice had suddenly made him cold.

'I'm afraid for everybody,' said Willis. 'Your friends, mine, and their friends, on out of sight. Pretty silly, eh?'

Willis opened the door, got out and peered in at Fortnum.

Fortnum felt he had to speak. 'Well, what do we do about it?'

Willis looked up at the sun burning in the sky. 'Be aware,' he said slowly. 'Watch everything for a few days.'

'Everything?'

'We don't use half what God gave us, ten per cent of the time. We ought to hear more, feel more, smell more, taste more. Maybe there's something wrong with the way the wind blows these weeds there in the lot. Maybe it's the sun up on those telephone wires or the cicadas singing in the elm trees. If only we could stop, look, listen, a few days, a few nights, and compare notes. Tell me to shut up then, and I will.'

'Good enough,' said Fortnum, playing it lighter than he felt. 'I'll look around. But how do I know the thing I'm looking for when I see it?'

Willis peered in at him, sincerely. 'You'll know. You've got to know. Or we're done for, all of us,' he said quietly.

Fortnum shut the door and didn't know what to say. He felt a flush of embarrassment creeping up his face. Willis sensed this.

'Hugh, do you think I'm . . . off my rocker?'

'Nonsense!' said Fortnum, too quickly. 'You're just nervous, is all. You should take a week off.'

Willis nodded. 'See you Monday night?'

'Any time. Drop around.'

'I hope I will, Hugh. I really hope I will.'

Then Willis was gone, hurrying across the dry weed-grown lot towards the side entrance of the market.

Watching him go, Fortnum suddenly did not want to move. He discovered that very slowly he was taking deep breaths, weighing the silence. He licked his lips, tasting the salt. He looked at his arm on the doorsill, the sunlight burning the golden hairs. In the empty lot the wind moved all alone to itself. He leaned out to look at the sun, which stared back with one massive stunning blow of intense power that made him jerk his head in. Then he laughed out loud. Then he drove away.

The lemonade glass was cool and deliciously sweaty. The ice made music inside the glass, and the lemonade was just sour enough, just sweet enough on his tongue. He sipped, he savoured, he tilted back in the wicker rocking chair on the twilight front porch, his eyes closed. The crickets were chirping out on the lawn. Cynthia, knitting across from him on the porch, eyed him curiously; he could feel her attention.

'What are you up to?' she said at last.

'Cynthia,' he said, 'is your intuition in running order? Is this earthquake weather? Is the land going to sink? Will war be declared? Or is it only that our delphinium will die of the blight?'

'Hold on. Let me feel my bones.'

He opened his eyes and watched Cynthia in turn closing hers and sitting absolutely statue-still, her hands on her knees. Finally she shook her head and smiled.

'No. No war declared. No land sinking. Not even a blight. Why?'

'I've met a lot of doom talkers today. Well, two anyway, and – '

The screen door burst wide. Fortnum's body jerked as if he had been struck.

'What – !'

Tom, a gardener's wooden flat in his arms, stepped out on the porch.

'Sorry,' he said. 'What's wrong, Dad?'

'Nothing,' Fortnum stood up, glad to be moving. 'Is that the crop?'

Tom moved forward eagerly. 'Part of it. Boy, they're

doing great. In just seven hours, with lots of water, look how big the darn things are!' He set the flat on the table between his parents.

The crop was indeed plentiful. Hundreds of greyish-brown mushrooms were sprouting up in the damp soil.

'I'll be damned,' said Fortnum, impressed.

Cynthia put out her hand to touch the flat, then took it away uneasily.

'I hate to be a spoilsport, but . . . there's no way for these to be anything else but mushrooms, is there?'

Tom looked as if he had been insulted. 'What do you think I'm going to feed you? Poisoned fungoids?'

'That's just it,' said Cynthia quickly. 'How do you tell them apart?'

'Eat 'em,' said Tom. 'If you live, they're mushrooms. If you drop dead — *well*!'

He gave a great guffaw, which amused Fortnum but only made his mother wince. She sat back in her chair.

'I — I don't like them,' she said.

'Boy, oh, boy.' Tom seized the flat angrily. 'When are we going to have the next wet-blanket sale in *this* house?'

He shuffled morosely away.

'Tom —' said Fortnum.

'Never mind,' said Tom. 'Everyone figures they'll be ruined by the boy entrepreneur. To heck with it!'

Fortnum got inside just as Tom heaved the mushrooms, flat and all, down the cellar stairs. He slammed the cellar door and ran out the back door.

Fortnum turned back to his wife, who, stricken, glanced away.

'I'm sorry,' she said. 'I don't know why, I just *had* to say that to Tom. I —'

The phone rang. Fortnum brought it outside on its extension cord.

'Hugh?' It was Dorothy Willis's voice. She sounded suddenly very old and very frightened. 'Hugh, Roger isn't there, is he?'

'Dorothy? No.'

'He's gone!' said Dorothy. 'All his clothes were taken from the closet.' She began to cry.

'Dorothy, hold on, I'll be there in a minute.'

'You must help oh, you must. Something's happened to him, I know it,' she wailed. 'Unless you do something, we'll never see him alive again.'

Very slowly he put the receiver back on its hook, her voice weeping inside it. The night crickets quite suddenly were very loud. He felt the hairs, one by one, go up on the back of his neck.

Hair can't do that, he thought. Silly, silly. It can't do that, not in *real* life, it can't!

But, one by slow prickling one, his hair did.

The wire hangers were indeed empty. With a clatter, Fortnum shoved them aside and down along the rod, then turned and looked out of the closet at Dorothy Willis and her son Joe.

'I was just walking by,' said Joe, 'and saw the closet empty, all Dad's clothes gone!'

'Everything was fine,' said Dorothy. 'We've had a wonderful life. I don't understand. I don't, I don't!' She began to cry again, putting her hands to her face.

Fortnum stepped out of the closet.

'You didn't hear him leave the house?'

'We were playing catch out front, said Joe. 'Dad said he had to go in for a minute. I went around back. Then he was gone!'

'He must have packed quickly and walked wherever he was going, so we wouldn't hear a cab pull up in front of the house.'

They were moving out through the hall now.

'I'll check the train depot and the airport.' Fortnum hesitated. 'Dorothy, is there anything in Roger's background —'

'It wasn't insanity took him.' She hesitated. 'I feel, somehow, he was kidnapped.'

Fortnum shook his head. 'It doesn't seem reasonable he would arrange to pack, walk out of the house and go meet his abductors.'

Dorothy opened the door as if to let the night or the night wind move down the hall as she turned to stare back through the rooms, her voice wandering.

'No. Somehow they came into the house. Right in front of us, they stole him away.'

And then: 'A terrible thing has happened.'

Fortnum stepped out into the night of crickets and rustling trees. The doom talkers, he thought, talking their dooms. Mrs Goodbody, Roger, and now Roger's wife. Something terrible *has* happened. But what, in God's name? And how?

He looked from Dorothy to her son. Joe, blinking the wetness from his eyes, took a long time to turn, walk along the hall and stop, fingering the knob of the cellar door.

Fortnum felt his eyelids twitch, his irises flex, as if he were snapping a picture of something he wanted to remember.

Joe pulled the cellar door wide, stepped down out of sight, gone. The door tapped shut.

Fortnum opened his mouth to speak, but Dorothy's hand was taking his now, he had to look at her.

'Please,' she said. 'Find him for me.'

He kissed her cheek. 'If it's humanly possible.'

If it's humanly possible. Good Lord, why had he picked *those* words?

He walked off into the summer night.

A gasp exhalation, an asthmatic insuck, a vapouring sneeze. Somebody dying in the dark? No.

Just Mrs Goodbody, unseen beyond the hedge, working

late, her hand pump aimed, her bony elbow thrusting. The sick-sweet smell of bug spray enveloped Fortnum as he reached his house.

'Mrs Goodbody? Still at it?'

From the black hedge her voice leaped. 'Damn it, yes! Aphids, water bugs, woodworms, and now the *Marasmius oreades*. Lord, it grows fast!'

'What does?'

'The *Marasmius oreades*, of course! It's me against them, and I intend to win! There! There! There!'

He left the hedge, the gasping pump, the wheezing voice, and found his wife waiting for him on the porch almost as if she were going to take up where Dorothy had left off at her door a few minutes ago.

Fortnum was about to speak when a shadow moved inside. There was a creaking noise. A knob rattled.

Tom vanished into the basement.

Fortnum felt as if someone had set off an explosion in his face. He reeled. Everything had the numbed familiarity of those waking dreams where all motions are remembered before they occur, all dialogue known before it falls from the lips.

He found himself staring at the shut basement door. Cynthia took him inside, amused.

'What? Tom? Oh, I relented. The darn mushrooms, meant so much to him. Besides, when he threw them into the cellar they did nicely, just lying in the dirt —'

'Did they?' Fortnum heard himself say.

Cynthia took his arm. 'What about Roger?'

'He's gone, yes.'

'Men, men, men,' she said.

'No, you're wrong,' he said. 'I've seen Roger nearly every day the last ten years. When you know a man that well, you can tell how things are at home, whether things are in the oven or the Mixmaster. Death hadn't breathed down his neck yet; he wasn't running scared after his immortal youth, picking peaches in someone else's orchards. No, no, I swear. I'd bet my last dollar on it, Roger —'

The doorbell rang behind him. The delivery boy had come up quietly on to the porch and was standing there with a telegram in his hand.

'Fortnum?'

Cynthia snapped on the hall light as he ripped the envelope open and smoothed it out for reading.

TRAVELLING NEW ORLEANS. THIS TELEGRAM POSSIBLE OFF-GUARD MOMENT. YOU MUST REFUSE, REPEAT REFUSE, ALL SPECIAL-DELIVERY PACKAGES. ROGER.

Cynthia glanced up from the paper.

'I don't understand. What does he mean?'

But Fortnum was already at the telephone, dialling swiftly, once. 'Operator? The police, and hurry!'

At ten-fifteen that night the phone rang for the sixth time during the evening, Fortnum got it and immediately gasped. 'Roger! Where are you?'

'Where am I, hell,' said Roger lightly, almost amused. 'You know very well where I am, you're responsible for this. I should be angry!'

Cynthia, at his nod, had hurried to take the extension phone in the kitchen. When he heard the soft click, he went on.

'Roger, I swear I don't know. I got that telegram from you —'

'What telegram?' said Roger jovially. 'I sent no telegram. Now, of a sudden, the police come pouring on to the south-bound train, pull me off in some jerk-water, and I'm calling you to get them off my neck. Hugh, if this is some joke.'

'But, Roger, you just vanished!'

'On a business trip, if you can call that vanishing. I told Dorothy about this, and Joe.'

'This is all very confusing, Roger. You're in no danger? Nobody's blackmailing you, forcing you into this speech?'

'I'm fine, healthy, free and unafraid.'

'But Roger, your premonitions?'

'Poppycock! Now, look, I'm being very good about this, aren't I?'

'Sure, Roger – '

'Then play the good father and give me permission to go. Call Dorothy and tell her I'll be back in five days. How *could* she have forgotten?'

'She did, Roger. See you in five days, then?'

'Five days, I swear.'

The voice indeed was winning and warm, the old Roger again. Fortnum shook his head.

'Roger,' he said, 'this is the craziest day I've ever spent. You're not running off from Dorothy? Good Lord, you can tell *me*.'

'I love her with all my heart. Now here's Lieutenant Parker of the Ridgetown police. Good-bye, Hugh.'

'Good –'

But the lieutenant was on the line, talking, talking angrily. What had Fortnum meant putting them to this trouble? What was going on? Who did he think he was? Did or didn't he want this so-called friend held or released?

'Released,' Fortnum managed to say somewhere along the way, and hung up the phone and imagined he heard a voice call 'All aboard' and the massive thunder of the train leaving the station two hundred miles south in the somehow increasingly dark night.

Cynthia walked very slowly to the parlour.

'I feel so foolish,' she said.

'How do you think I feel?'

'Who could have sent that telegram, and why?'

He poured himself some Scotch and stood in the middle of the room looking at it.

'I'm glad Roger is all right,' his wife said at last.

'He isn't,' said Fortnum.

'But you just said —'

'I said nothing. After all, we couldn't very well drag him off that train and truss him up and send him home, could we, if he insisted he was okay? No. He sent that telegram, but changed his mind after sending it. Why, why, why?' Fortnum paced the room, sipping the drink. 'Why warn us against special-delivery packages? The only package we've got this *year* which fits that description is the one Tom got this morning . . . ' His voice trailed off.

Before he could move, Cynthia was at the wastepaper basket taking out the crumpled wrapping paper with the special-delivery stamps on it.

The postmark read: NEW ORLEANS, L.A.

Cynthia looked up from it. 'New Orleans. Isn't that where Roger is heading right now?'

A doorknob rattled, a door opened and closed in Fortnum's mind. Another doorknob rattled, another door swung wide and then shut. There was a smell of damp earth.

He found his hand dialling the phone. After a long while Dorothy Willis answered at the other end. He could imagine her sitting alone in a house with too many lights on. He talked quietly with her for a while, then cleared his throat and said, 'Dorothy, look, I know it sounds silly. Did any special-delivery packages arrive at your house the last few days?'

Her voice was faint. 'No.' Then: 'No, wait. Three days ago. But I thought you *knew*! All the boys on the block are going in for it.'

Fortnum measured his words carefully.

'Going in for what?'

'But why ask?' she said. 'There's nothing wrong with

raising mushrooms, is there?'

Fortnum closed his eyes.

'Hugh? Are you still there?' asked Dorothy. 'I said there's nothing wrong with –'

'Raising mushrooms?' said Fortnum at last. 'No. Nothing wrong. Nothing wrong.'

And slowly he put down the phone.

The curtains blew like veils of moonlight. The clock ticked. The after-midnight world flowed into and filled the bedroom. He heard Mrs Goodbody's clear voice on this morning's air, a million years gone now. He heard Roger putting a cloud over the sun at noon. He heard the police damning him by phone from downstate. Then Roger's voice again, with the locomotive thunder hurrying him away and away, fading. And, finally, Mrs Goodbody's voice behind the hedge:

'Lord, it grows fast!'

'What does?'

'The *Marasmius oreades*!'

He snapped his eyes open. He sat up.

Downstairs, a moment later, he flicked through the unabridged dictionary.

His forefinger underlined the words:

'*Marasmius oreades*: A mushroom commonly found on lawns in summer and early autumn . . . '

He let the book fall shut.

Outside, in the deep summer night, he lit a cigarette and smoked quietly.

A meteor fell across space, burning itself out quickly. The trees rustled softly.

The front door tapped shut.

Cynthia moved towards him in her robe.

'Can't sleep?'

'Too warm, I guess.'

'It's not warm.'

'No,' he said, feeling his arms. 'In fact, it's cold.' He sucked on the cigarette twice, then, not looking at her, said, 'Cynthia, what if . . . ' He snorted and had to stop. 'Well, what if Roger was right this morning. Mrs Goodbody, what if she's right, too? Something terrible *is* happening. Like, well,' – he nodded at the sky and the million stars – 'Earth being invaded by things from other worlds, maybe.'

'Hugh –'

'No, let me run wild.'

'It's quite obvious we're not being invaded, or we'd notice.'

'Let's say we've only half noticed, become uneasy about something. What? How could we be invaded? By what means would creatures invade?'

Cynthia looked at the sky and was about to try something when he interrupted.

'No, not meteors or flying saucers, things we can see. What about bacteria? That comes from outer space, too, doesn't it?'

'I read once, yes.'

'Spores, seeds, pollens, viruses probably bombard our atmosphere by the billions every second and have done so for millions of years. Right now we're sitting out under an invisible rain. It falls all over the country, the cities, the towns, and right now, our lawn.'

'*Our* lawn?'

'*And* Mrs Goodbody's. But people like her are always pulling weeds, spraying poison, kicking toadstools off their grass. It would be hard for any strange life form to survive in cities. Weather's a problem, too. Best climate might be south: Alabama, Georgia, Louisiana. Back in the damp bayous they could grow to a fine size.'

But Cynthia was beginning to laugh now.

'Oh, really, you don't believe, do you, that this Great

Bayou or Whatever Greenhouse Novelty Company that sent Tom his package is owned and operated by six-foot-tall mushrooms from another planet?'

'If you put it that way, it sounds funny.'

'Funny! It's hilarious!' She threw her head back, deliciously.

'Good grief!' he cried, suddenly irritated. '*Something's* going on! Mrs Goodbody is rooting out and killing *Marasmius oreades*. What is *Marasmius oreades*? A certain kind of mushroom. Simultaneously, and I suppose *you'll* call it coincidence, by special delivery, what arrives the same day? Mushrooms for Tom! What *else* happens? Roger fears he may soon cease to be! Within hours, he vanishes, then tele-graphs us, warning us not to accept what? The special-delivery mushrooms for Tom! Has Roger's son got a similar package in the last few days? He has! Where do the packages come from? New Orleans! And where is Roger going when he vanishes? New Orleans! Do you see, Cynthia, do you see? I wouldn't be upset if all these separate things didn't lock together! Roger, Tom, Joe, mushrooms, Mrs Goodbody, packages, destinations, everything in one pattern!'

She was watching his face now, quieter, but still amused. 'Don't get angry.'

'I'm not!' Fortnum almost shouted. And then he simply could not go on. He was afraid that if he did he would find himself shouting with laughter too, and somehow he did not want that. He stared at the surrounding houses up and down the block and thought of the dark cellars and the neighbour boys who read *Popular Mechanics* and sent their money in by the millions to raise the mushrooms hidden away. Just as he, when a boy, had mailed off for chemicals, seeds, turtles, numberless salves and sickish ointments. In how many million American homes tonight were billions of mushrooms rousing up under the ministrations of the innocent?

'Hugh?' His wife was touching his arm now. 'Mushrooms,

even big ones, can't think, can't move, don't have arms and legs. How could they run a mail-order service and "take over" the world? Come on, now, let's look at your terrible friends and monsters!'

She pulled him towards the door. Inside, she headed for the cellar, but he stopped, shaking his head, a foolish smile shaping itself somehow to his mouth. 'No, no, I know what we'll find. You win. The whole thing's silly. Roger will be back next week and we'll all get drunk together. Go on up to bed now and I'll drink a glass of warm milk and be with you in a minute.'

'That's better!' she kissed him on both cheeks, squeezed him and went away up the stairs.

In the kitchen, he took out a glass, opened the refrigerator, and was pouring the milk when he stopped suddenly.

Near the front of the top shelf was a small yellow dish. It was not the dish that held his attention, however. It was what lay in the dish.

The fresh-cut mushrooms.

He must have stood there for half a minute, his breath frosting the air, before he reached out, took hold of the dish, sniffed it, felt the mushrooms, then at last, carrying the dish, went out into the hall. He looked up the stairs, hearing Cynthia moving about in the bedroom, and was about to call up to her, 'Cynthia, did you put *these* in the refrigerator?' Then he stopped. He knew her answer. She had not.

He put the dish of mushrooms on the newel-upright at the bottom of the stairs and stood looking at them. He imagined himself in bed later, looking at the walls, the open windows, watching the moonlight sift patterns on the ceiling. He heard himself saying, Cynthia? And her answering, Yes? And him saying, There *is* a way for mushrooms to grow arms and legs. What? she would say, silly, silly man, what? And he would gather courage against her hilarious reaction and go on. What

if a man wandered through the swamp, picked the mushrooms and *ate* them . . . ?

No response from Cynthia.

Once inside the man, would the mushrooms spread
through his blood, take over every cell and change the man
from a man to a — Martian? Given this theory, would the
mushrooms *need* its own arms and legs? No, not when it
could borrow people, live inside and become them. Roger ate
mushrooms given him by his son. Roger became 'something
else'. He kidnapped himself. And in one last flash of sanity,
of being himself, he telegraphed us, warning us not to accept
the special-delivery mushrooms. The 'Roger' that tele-
phoned later was no longer Roger but a captive of what he
had eaten! Doesn't that figure, Cynthia, doesn't it, doesn't
it?

No, said the imagined Cynthia, no, it doesn't figure, no,
no, no . . .

There was the faintest whisper, rustle, stir from the cellar.
Taking his eyes from the bowl, Fortnum walked to the cellar
door and put his ear to it.

'Tom?'

No answer.

'Tom, are you down there?'

No answer.

'Tom?'

After a long while, Tom's voice came up from below.

'Yes, Dad?'

'It's after midnight,' said Fortnum, fighting to keep his
voice from going high. 'What are you doing down there?'

No answer.

'I said —'

'Tending to my crop,' said the boy at last, his voice cold
and faint.

'Well, get the hell *out* of there! You hear me?'

Silence.

'Tom? Listen! Did you put some mushrooms in the refrigerator tonight? If so, why?'

Ten seconds must have ticked by before the boy replied from below, 'For you and Mom to eat, of course.'

Fortnum heard his heart moving swiftly and had to take three deep breaths before he could go on.

'Tom? You didn't . . . that is, you haven't by any chance *eaten* some of the mushrooms yourself, *have* you?'

'Funny you ask that,' said Tom. 'Yes. Tonight. On a sandwich. After supper. Why?'

Fortnum held the doorknob. Now it was his turn not to answer. He felt his knees beginning to melt and he fought the whole silly senseless fool thing. No reason, he tried to say, but his lips wouldn't move.

'Dad?' called Tom, softly from the cellar. 'Come on down.' Another pause. 'I want you to see the harvest.'

Fortnum felt the knob slip in his sweaty hand. The knob rattled. He gasped.

'Dad?' called Tom softly.

Fortnum opened the door.

The cellar was completely black below.

He stretched his hand in towards the light switch.

As if sensing this from somewhere, Tom said, 'Don't. Light's bad for the mushrooms.'

He took his hand off the switch.

He swallowed. He looked back at the stair leading up to his wife. I suppose, he thought, I should go say good-bye to Cynthia. But why should I think that! Why, in God's name, should I think that at all? No reason, *is* there?

None.

'Tom?' he said, affecting a jaunty air. 'Ready or not, here I come!'

And stepping down in darkness, he shut the door.

The Vacation

It was a day as fresh as grass growing up and clouds going over and butterflies coming down can make it. It was a day compounded from silences of bee and flower and ocean and land, which were not silences at all, but motions, stirs, flutters, risings, fallings, each in its own time and matchless rhythm. The land did not move, but moved. The sea was not still, yet was still. Paradox flowed into paradox, stillness mixed with stillness, sound with sound. The flowers vibrated and the bees fell in separate and small showers of golden rain on the clover. The seas of hill and the seas of ocean were divided, each from the other's motion, by a railroad track, empty, compounded of rust and iron marrow, a track on which, quite obviously, no train had run in many years. Thirty miles north it swirled on away to further mists of distance, thirty miles south it tunnelled islands of cloud-shadow that changed their continental positions on the sides of far mountains as you watched.

Now, suddenly, the railroad track began to tremble.

A blackbird, standing on the rail, felt a rhythm grow faintly, miles away, like a heart beginning to beat.

The blackbird leaped up over the sea.

The rail continued to vibrate softly until, at long last, around a curve and along the shore came a small workman's handcar, its two-cylinder engine popping and spluttering in the great silence.

On top of this small four-wheeled car, on a double-sided bench facing in two directions and with a little surrey roof above for shade, sat a man, his wife and their small seven-year-old son. As the handcar travelled through lonely stretch after lonely stretch, the wind whipped their eyes and blew their hair, but they did not look back but only ahead. Sometimes they looked eagerly as a curve unwound itself, sometimes with great sadness, but always watchful, ready for the next scene.

As they hit a level straightaway, the machine engine gasped and stopped abruptly. In the now crushing silence, it seemed that the quiet of earth, sky and sea itself, by its friction, brought the car to a wheeling halt.

'Out of gas.'

The man sighing, reached for the extra can in the small storage bin and began to pour it into the tank.

His wife and son sat quietly looking at the sea, listening to the muted thunder, the whisper, the drawing back of huge tapestries of sand, gravel, green weed, and foam.

'Isn't the sea nice?' said the woman.

'I like it,' said the boy.

'Shall we picnic here, while we're at it?'

The man focused some binoculars on the green peninsula ahead.

'Might as well. The rails have rusted badly. There's a break ahead. We may have to wait while I set a few back in place.'

'As many as there are,' said the boy, 'we'll have picnics!'

The woman tried to smile at this, then turned her grave attention to the man. 'How far have we come today?'

'Not ninety miles.' The man still peered through the glasses, squinting. 'I don't like to go farther than that any one day, anyway. If you rush, there's no time to see. We'll reach Monterey day after tomorrow, Palo Alto the next day, if you want.'

The woman removed her great shadowing straw hat, which had been tied over her golden hair with a bright yellow ribbon, and stood perspiring faintly, away from the machine. They had ridden so steadily on the shuddering handcar that the motion was sewn in their bodies. Now, with the stopping, they felt odd, on the verge of unravelling.

'Let's eat!'

The boy ran the wicker lunch basket down to the shore.

The boy and the woman were already seated by a spread tablecloth when the man came down to them, dressed in his business suit and vest and tie and hat as if he expected to meet someone along the way. As he dealt out the sandwiches and exhumed the pickles from their cool green Mason jars, he began to loosen his tie and unbutton his vest, always looking around as if he should be careful and ready to button up again.

'Are we all alone, Papa?' said the boy, eating.

'Yes.'

'No one else, anywhere?'

'No one else.'

'Were there people before?'

'Why do you keep asking that? It wasn't that long ago. Just a few months. You remember.'

'Almost. If I try hard, then I don't remember at all.' The boy let a handful of sand fall through his fingers. 'Were there as many people as there is sand here on the beach? What *happened* to them?'

'I don't know,' the man said, and it was true.

They had wakened one morning and the world was empty. The neighbours' clothes-line was still strung with blowing white wash, cars gleamed in front of other seven-a.m. cottages, but there were no farewells, the city did not hum with its mighty arterial traffics, phones did not alarm themselves, children did not wail in sunflower wildernesses.

Only the night before, he and his wife had been sitting on the front porch when the evening paper was delivered, and, not even daring to open the headlines out, he had said, 'I wonder when He will get tired of us and just rub us all out?'

'It has gone pretty far,' she said. 'On and on. We're such

fools, aren't we?'

'Wouldn't it be nice' — he lit his pipe and puffed it — 'if we woke tomorrow and everyone in the world was gone and everything was starting over?' He sat smoking, the paper folded in his hand, his head resting back on the chair.

'If you could press a button right now and make it happen, would you?'

'I think I would,' he said. 'Nothing violent. Just have everyone vanish off the face of the earth. Just leave the land and the sea and the growing things, like flowers and grass and fruit trees. And the animals, of course, let them stay. Everything except man, who hunts when he isn't hungry, eats when full, and is mean when no one's bothered him.'

'Naturally, we would be left.' She smiled quietly.

'I'd like that,' he mused. 'All of time ahead. The longest summer vacation in history. And us out for the longest picnic-basket lunch in memory. Just you, me and Jim. No commuting. No keeping up with the Joneses. Not even a car. I'd like to find another way of travelling, an older way. Then, a hamper full of sandwiches, three bottles of pop, pick up supplies where you need them from empty grocery stores in empty towns, and summertime forever up ahead . . . '

They sat a long while on the porch in silence, the newspaper folded between them.

At last she opened her mouth.

'Would we be *lonely*?' she said.

So that's how it was the morning of the new world. They had awakened to the soft sounds of an earth that was now no more than a meadow, and the cities of the earth sinking back into seas of sabregrass, marigold, marguerite and morning-glory. They had taken it with remarkable calm at first, perhaps because they had not liked the city for so many years, and had had so many friends who were not truly friends, and had lived a boxed and separate life of their own within a mechanical hive.

The husband arose and looked out the window and observed very calmly, as if it were a weather condition, 'Everyone's gone,' knowing this just by the sounds the city had ceased to make.

They took their time over breakfast, for the boy was still asleep, and then the husband sat back and said, 'Now I must plan what to do.'

'Do? Why . . . why, you'll go to work, of course.'

'You still don't believe it, do you?' He laughed. 'That I won't be rushing off each day at eight-ten, that Jim won't go to school ever again. School's out for all of us! No more pencils, no more books, no more boss's sassy looks! We're let out, darling, and we'll never come back to the silly damn dull routines. Come on!'

And he had walked her through the still and empty city streets.

'They didn't die,' he said. 'They just . . . went away.'

'What about the other cities?'

He went to an outdoor phone booth and dialled Chicago, then New York, then San Francisco.

Silence. Silence. Silence.

'That's it,' he said, replacing the receiver.

'I feel guilty,' she said. 'Them gone and us here. And . . . I feel happy. Why? I *should* be unhappy.'

'Should you? It's no tragedy. They weren't tortured or blasted or burned. They went easily and they didn't know. And now we owe nothing to no one. Our only responsibility is being happy? Thirty more years of happiness, wouldn't that be good?'

'But . . . then we must have more children!'

'To repopulate the world?' He shook his head slowly, calmly. 'No. Let Jim be the last. After he's grown and gone let the horses and cows and ground squirrels and garden spiders have the world. They'll get on. And someday some other species that can combine a natural happiness with a natural curiosity will build cities that won't even look like cities to us, and survive. Right now, let's go pack a basket, wake Jim, and get going on that long thirty-year summer vacation. I'll beat you to the house!'

He took a sledge hammer from the small handcar, and while he worked alone for half an hour fixing the rusted rails into place, the woman and the boy ran along the shore. They came back with dripping shells, a dozen or more, and some beautiful pink pebbles, and sat and the boy took school from the mother, doing homework on a pad with a pencil for a time, and then at high noon the man came down, his coat off, his tie thrown aside, and they drank orange pop, watching the bubbles surge up, glutting, inside the bottles. It was quiet. They listened to the sun tune the old iron rails. The smell of hot tar on the ties moved about them in the salt wind, as the husband tapped his atlas map lightly and gently.

'We'll go to Sacramento next month, May, then work up towards Seattle. Should make that by July first, July's a good month in Washington, then back down as the weather cools, to Yellowstone, a few miles a day, hunt here, fish there . . . '

The boy, bored, moved away to throw sticks into the sea and wade out like a dog to retrieve them.

The man went on: 'Winter in Tucson, then, part of the winter, moving towards Florida, up the coast in the spring, and maybe New York by June. Two years from now, Chicago in the summer. Winter, three years from now, what about Mexico City? Anywhere the rails lead us, anywhere at all, and if we come to an old offshoot rail line we don't know anything about, what the hell, we'll just take it, go down it, to see where it goes. And some year, by God, we'll boat down the Mississippi, always wanted to do that. Enough to last us a lifetime. And that's just how long I want to take to do it all . . . '

His voice faded. He started to fumble the map shut, but, before he could move, a bright thing fell through the air and hit the paper. It rolled off into the sand and made a wet lump.

His wife glanced at the wet place in the sand and then swiftly searched his face. His solemn eyes were too bright. And down one cheek was a track of wetness.

She gasped. She took his hand and held it, tight.

He clenched her hand very hard, his eyes shut now, and slowly he said, with difficulty. 'Wouldn't it be nice if we went to sleep tonight and in the night, somehow, it all came back. All the foolishness, all the noise, all the hate, all the terrible things, all the nightmares, all the wicked people and stupid children, all the mess, all the smallness, all the confusion, all the hope, all the need, all the love. Wouldn't it be nice.'

She waited and nodded her head once.

Then both of them started.

For standing between them, they knew not for how long, was their son, an empty pop bottle in one hand.

The boy's face was pale. With his free hand he reached out to touch his father's cheek, where the single tear had made its track.

'You,' he said. 'Oh, Dad, you. You haven't anyone to play with, *either*.'

The wife started to speak.

The husband moved to take the boy's hand.

The boy jerked back. 'Silly! Oh, silly! Silly fools! Oh, you dumb, dumb!' And, whirling, he rushed down to the ocean and stood there crying loudly.

The wife rose to follow him, but the husband stopped her.

'No. Let him.'

And then they both grew cold and quiet. For the boy, below on the shore, crying steadily, now was writing on a piece of paper and stuffing it in the pop bottle and ramming the cap back on and taking the bottle and giving it a great glittering heave up in the air and out into the tidal sea.

What, thought the wife, what did he write on the note? What's in the bottle?

The bottle moved out in the waves.

The boy stopped crying.

After a long while he walked up the shore, to stand looking at his parents. His face was neither bright nor dark, alive nor dead, ready nor resigned; it seemed a curious mixture that simply made do with time, weather and these people. They looked at him and beyond to the bay, where the bottle containing the scribbled note was almost out of sight now, shining in the waves.

Did he write what *we* wanted? thought the woman. Did he write what he heard us just wish, just say?

Or did he write something for only himself, she wondered, that tomorrow he might wake and find himself alone in an empty world, no one around, no man, no woman, no father, no mother, no fool grownups with fool wishes, so he could trudge up to the railroad tracks and take the handcar motoring, a solitary boy, across the continental wilderness, on eternal voyages and picnics?

Is that what he wrote in the note?

Which?

She searched his colourless eyes, could not read the answer; dared not ask.

Gull shadows sailed over and kited their faces with sudden passing coolness.

'Time to go,' someone said.

They loaded the wicker basket on to the rail car. The woman tied her large bonnet securely in place with its yellow ribbon, they set the boy's pail of shells on the floorboards, then the husband put on his tie, his vest, his coat, his hat, and they all sat on the benches of the car looking out at the sea where the bottled note was far out, blinking, on the horizon.

'Is asking enough?' said the boy. 'Does wishing work?'

'Sometimes . . . *too* well.'

'It depends on what you ask for.'

The boy nodded, his eyes far away.

They looked back at where they had come from, and then ahead to where they were going.

'Good-bye, place,' said the boy, and waved.

The car rolled down the rusty rails. The sound of it dwindled, faded. The man, the woman, the boy dwindled with it in distance, among the hills.

After they were gone, the rail trembled faintly for two minutes, and ceased. A flake of rust fell. A flower nodded.

The sea was very loud.

The Illustrated Woman

When the new patient wanders into the office and stretches out to stutter forth a compendious ticker tape of free association, it is up to the psychiatrist immediately beyond, behind and above to decide at just which points of the anatomy the client is in touch with the couch.

In other words, where does the patient make contact with reality?

Some people seem to float half an inch above any surface whatsoever. They have not seen earth in so long, they have become somewhat airsick.

Still others so firmly weight themselves down, clutch, thrust, heave their bodies towards reality, that long after they are gone you find their tiger shapes and claw marks in the upholstery.

In the case of Emma Fleet, Dr George C. George was a long time deciding which was furniture and which was woman and where what touched which.

For, to begin with, Emma Fleet resembled a couch.

'Mrs Emma Fleet, Doctor,' announced his receptionist.

Dr George C. George gasped.

For it was a traumatic experience, seeing this woman shunt herself through the door without benefit of railroad switchman or the ground crews who rush about under Macy's Easter balloons, heaving on lines, guiding the massive images to some eternal hangar off beyond.

In came Emma Fleet, as quick as her name, the floor shifting like a huge set of scales under her weight.

Dr George must have gasped again, guessing her at four

hundred on the hoof, for Emma Fleet smiled as if reading his mind.

'Four hundred two and a half pounds, to be exact,' she said.

He found himself staring at his furniture.

'Oh, it'll hold all right,' said Mrs Fleet intuitively.

She sat down.

The couch yelped like a cur.

Dr George cleared his throat. 'Before you make yourself comfortable,' he said, 'I feel I should say immediately and honestly that we in the psychiatrical field have had little success in inhibiting appetites. The whole problem of weight and food has so far eluded our ability for coping. A strange admission, perhaps, but unless we put our frailties forth, we might be in danger of fooling ourselves and thus taking money under false pretences. So, if you are here seeking help for your figure, I must list myself among the nonplussed.'

'Thank you for your honesty, Doctor,' said Emma Fleet. 'However, I don't wish to lose. I'd prefer your helping me *gain* another one hundred or two hundred pounds.'

'Oh, no!' Dr George exclaimed.

'Oh, yes. But my heart will not allow what my deep dear soul would most gladly endure. My physical heart might fail at what my loving heart and mind would ask of it.'

She sighed. The couch sighed.

'Well, let me brief you. I'm married to Willy Fleet. We work for the Dillbeck-Horsemann Travelling Shows. I'm known as Lady Bountiful. And Willy . . .'

She swooned up out of the couch and glided or rather escorted her shadow across the floor. She opened the door.

Beyond, in the waiting room, a cane in one hand, a straw hat in the other, seated rigidly, staring at the wall, was a tiny man with tiny feet and tiny hands and tiny bright-blue eyes in a tiny head. He was, at the most, one would guess, three feet high, and probably weighed sixty pounds in the rain. But there was a proud, gloomy, almost violent look of genius blazing in that small but craggy face.

'That's Willy Fleet,' said Emma lovingly, and shut the door.

The couch, sat on, cried again.

Emma beamed at the psychiatrist, who was still staring, in shock, at the door.

'No children, of course,' he heard himself say.

'No children.' Her smile lingered. 'But that's not my problem, either. Willy, in a way, is my child. And I, in a way, besides being his wife, am his mother. It all has to do with size, I imagine, and we're happy with the way we've balanced things off.'

'Well, if your problem isn't children, or your size or his, or controlling weight, then what . . . ?'

Emma Fleet laughed lightly, tolerantly. It was a nice laugh, like a girl's somehow caught in that great body and throat.

'Patience, Doctor. Mustn't we go back down the road to where Willy and I first met?'

The doctor shrugged, laughed quietly himself and relaxed, nodding. 'You must.'

'During high school,' said Emma Fleet, 'I weighed one-eighty and tipped the scales at two-fifty when I was twenty-one. Needless to say, I went on few summer excursions. Most of the time I was left in drydock. I had many girl friends, however, who liked to be seen with me. They weighed one-fifty, most of them, and I made them feel svelte. But that's a long time ago. I don't worry over it any more. Willy changed all that.'

'Willy sounds like a remarkable man,' Dr George found himself saying, against all the rules.

'Oh, he is, he is! He *smoulders* – with ability, with talent as

yet undiscovered, untapped!' she said, quickening warmly.
'God bless him, he leaped into my life like summer lightning!
Eight years ago I went with my girl friends to the visiting
Labor Day carnival. By the end of the evening, the girls had
all been seized away from me by the running boys who,
rushing by, grabbed and took them off into the night. There I
was alone with three Kewpie Dolls, a fake alligator handbag
and nothing to do but make the Guess Your Weight man
nervous by looking at him every time I went by and pretending like at any moment I might pay my money and dare him
to guess.

'But the Guess Your Weight man *wasn't* nervous! After I
had passed three times I saw him staring at me. With awe,
yes, with admiration! And who was this Guess Your Weight
man? Willy Fleet, of course. The fourth time I passed he
called to me and said I could get a prize free if only I'd let him
guess my weight. He was all feverish and excited. He danced
around. I'd never been made over so much in my life. I
blushed. I felt good. So I sat in the scales chair. I heard the
pointer whizz up around and I heard Willy whistle with
honest delight.

' "Two hundred and eighty-nine pounds!" he cried. "Oh
boy, you're lovely!"

' "I'm *what*?" I said.

' "You're the loveliest woman in the whole world," said
Willy, looking me right in the eye.

'I blushed again. I laughed. We both laughed. Then I must
have cried, for the next thing, sitting there, I felt him touch
my elbow with concern. He was gazing into my face, faintly
alarmed.

' "I haven't said the wrong thing?" he asked.

' "No," I sobbed, and then grew quiet. "The right thing,
only the right thing. It's the first time anyone ever . . . . "

' "What?" he said.

' "Ever put up with my fat," I said.

' "You're not fat," he said. "You're large, you're big, you're wonderful. Michelangelo would have loved you. Titian would have loved you. Da Vinci would have loved you. They knew what they were doing in those days. Size. Size is everything. I should know. Look at me. I travelled with Singer's Midgets for six seasons, known as Jack Thimble. And oh my God, dear lady, you're right out of the most glorious part of the Renaissance, Bernini, who built those colonnades around the front of Saint Peter's and inside at the altar, would have lost his everlasting soul just to know someone like you."

' "Don't!" I cried. "I wasn't meant to feel this happy. It'll hurt so much when you stop."

' "I won't stop, then," he said. "Miss . . . ?"

' "Emma Gertz."

' "Emma," he said, "are you married?"

' "Are you kidding?" I said.

' "Emma, do you like to travel?"

' "I've never travelled."

' "Emma," he said, "this old carnival's going to be in your town one more week. Come down every night, every day, why not? Talk to me, know me. At the end of the week, who can tell, maybe you'll travel with me."

' "What are you suggesting?" I said, not really angry or irritated or anything, but fascinated and intrigued that anyone would offer anything to Moby Dick's daughter.

' "I mean marriage!" Willy Fleet looked at me, breathing hard, and I had the feeling that he was dressed in a mountaineer's rig, alpine hat, climbing boots, spikes, and a rope slung over his baby shoulder. And if I should ask him, "Why are you saying this?" he might well answer, "Because you're *there*."

'But I didn't ask, so he didn't answer. We stood there in the night, at the centre of the carnival, until at last I started off down the midway, swaying. "I'm drunk!" I cried. "Oh, so very drunk, and I've had nothing to drink."

' "Now that I've found you," called Willy Fleet after me, "you'll never escape me, remember!" '

'Stunned and reeling, blinded by his large man's words sung out in his soprano voice, I somehow blundered from the carnival grounds and trekked home.

'The next week we were married.'

Emma Fleet paused and looked at her hands.

'Would it bother you if I told you about the honeymoon?' she asked shyly.

'No,' said the doctor, then lowered his voice, for he was responding all too quickly to the details. 'Please *do* go on.'

'The honeymoon,' Emma sounded her *vox humana*. The response from all the chambers of her body vibrated the couch, the room, the doctor, the dear bones within the doctor.

'The honeymoon . . . was not usual.'

The doctor's eyebrows lifted the faintest touch. He looked from the woman to the door beyond which, in miniature, sat the image of Edward Hillary, he of Everest.

'You have never seen such a rush as Willy spirited me off to his home, a lovely doll's house, really, with one large normal-sized room that was to be mine, or, rather, ours. There, very politely, always the kind, the thoughtful, the quiet gentleman, he asked for my blouse, which I gave him, my skirt, which I gave him. Right down the list, I handed him the garments that he named, until at last . . . Can one blush from head to foot? One can. One did. I stood like a veritable hearthfire stoked by a blush of all-encompassing and ever-moving colour that surged and resurged up and down my body in tints of pink and rose and then pink again.

' "My God!" cried Willy, "you're the loveliest grand camellia that ever did unfurl!" Whereupon new tides of blush moved in hidden avalanches within, showing only to colour the tent of my body, the outermost and, to Willy anyway, most precious skin.

'What did Willy do then? Guess.'

'I daren't,' said the doctor, flustered himself.

'He walked around and around me.'

'*Circled* you?'

'Around and around, like a sculptor gazing at a huge block of snow-white granite. He said so himself. Granite or marble from which he might shape images of beauty as yet unguessed. Around and around he walked, sighing and shaking his head happily at his fortune, his little hands clasped, his little eyes bright. Where to begin, he seemed to be thinking, where, where to begin!?

'He spoke at last. "Emma," he asked, "why, why do you think I've worked for years as the Guess Your Weight man at the carnival? Why? Because I have been searching my lifetime through for such as you. Night after night, summer after summer, I've watched those scales jump and twitter! And now at last I've the means, the way, the will, the canvas, whereby to express my genius!"

'He stopped walking and looked at me, his eyes brimming over.

' "Emma," he said softly, "may I have permission to do anything absolutely whatsoever at all with you?"

' "Oh, Willy, Willy," I cried. "Anything!" '

Emma Fleet paused.

The doctor found himself out at the edge of his chair. 'Yes, yes. And *then*?'

'And then,' said Emma Fleet, 'he brought out all his boxes and bottles of inks and stencils and his bright silver tattoo needles.'

'Tattoo needles?'

The doctor fell back in his chair. 'He . . . tattooed you?'

'He tattooed me.'

'He was a tattoo artist?'

'He was, he is, an artist. It only happens that the form his art takes happens to be the tattoo.'

'And you,' said the doctor slowly, 'were the canvas for which he had been searching much of his adult life?'

'I was the canvas for which he had searched *all* of his life.'

She let it sink, and it *did* sink, and keep on sinking, into the doctor. Then when she saw it had struck bottom and stirred up vast quantities of mud, she went serenely on.

'So our grand life began! I loved Willy and Willy loved me and we both loved this thing that was larger than ourselves that we were doing together. Nothing less than creating the greatest picture the world has ever seen. "Nothing less than perfection!" cried Willy. "Nothing less than perfection!" cried myself in response.

'Oh, it was a happy time. Ten thousand cosy busy hours we spent together. You can't imagine how proud it made me to be the vast shore along which the genius of Willy Fleet ebbed and flowed in a tide of colours.

'One year alone we spent on my right arm and my left, half a year on my right leg, eight months on my left, in preparation for the grand explosion of bright detail which erupted out along my collarbone and shoulderblades, which fountained upwards from my hips to meet in a glorious July celebration of pinwheels, Titian nudes, Giorgione landscapes and El Greco cross-indexes of lightning on my façade, prickling with vast electric fires up and down my spine.

'Dear me, there never has been, there never will be, a love like ours again, a love where two people so sincerely dedicated themselves to one task, of giving beauty to the world in equal portions. We flew to each other day after day, and I ate more, grew larger, with the years. Willy approved, Willy applauded. Just that much more room, more space for his configurations to flower in. We could not bear to be apart, for we both felt, were certain, that once the Masterpiece was finished we could leave circus, carnival, or vaudeville forever. It was grandiose, but we knew that once finished, I could be toured through the Art Institute in Chicago, the Kress Collection in Washington, the Tate Gallery in London, the Louvre, the Uffizi, the Vatican Museum! For the rest of our lives we would travel with the sun!

'So it went, year on year. We didn't need the world or the people of the world, we had each other. We worked at our ordinary jobs by day, and then, till after midnight, there was Willy at my ankle, there was Willy at my elbow, there was Willy exploring up the incredible slope of my back towards the snowy-talcumed crest. Willy wouldn't let me see, most of the time. He didn't like me looking over his shoulder, he didn't like me looking over *my* shoulder, for that matter. Months passed before, curious beyond madness, I would be allowed to see his progress slow inch by inch as the brilliant inks inundated me and I drowned in the rainbow of his inspirations. Eight years, eight glorious wondrous years. And then at last it was done, it was finished. And Willy threw himself down and slept for forty-eight hours straight. And I slept near him, the mammoth bedded with the black lamb. That was just four weeks ago. Four short weeks back, our happiness came to an end.'

'Ah, yes,' said the doctor. 'You and your husband are suffering from the creative equivalent of the "baby blues", the depression a mother feels after her child is born. Your work is finished. A listless and somewhat sad period invariably follows. But, now, consider, you will reap the rewards of your long labour, surely? You *will* tour the world?'

'No,' cried Emma Fleet, and a tear sprang to her eye. 'At any moment, Willy will run off and never return. He has begun to wander about the city. Yesterday I caught him brushing off the carnival scales. Today I found him working, for the first time in eight years, back at his Guess Your Weight booth!'

'Dear me,' said the psychiatrist. 'He's . . . ?'

'Weighing new women, yes! Shopping for new canvas! He hasn't said, but I know, I know! This time he'll find a heavier woman yet, five hundred, six hundred pounds! I guessed this would happen, a month ago, when we finished the Masterpiece. So I ate still more, and stretched my skin more, so that little places appeared here and there, little open patches that Willy had to repair, fill in with fresh detail. But now I'm done, exhausted, I've stuffed to distraction, the last fill-in work is done. There's not a millionth of an inch of space left between my ankles and my Adam's apple where we can squeeze in one last demon, dervish or baroque angel. I am, to Willy, work over and done. Now he wants to move on. He will marry, I fear, four more times in his life, each time to a larger woman, a greater extension for a greater mural, and the grand finale of his talent. Then, too, in the last week, he has become critical.'

'Of the Masterpiece with a capital *M*?' asked the doctor.

'Like all artists, he is a superb perfectionist. Now he finds little flaws, a face here done slightly in the wrong tint or texture, a hand there twisted slightly askew by my hurried diet to gain more weight and thus give him new space and renew his attention. To him, above all, I was a beginning. Now he must move on from his apprenticeship to his true masterworks. Oh, Doctor, I am about to be abandoned. What is there for a woman who weighs four hundred pounds and is laved with illustrations? If he leaves, what shall I do, where go, who would want me now? Will I be lost again in the world as I was before my wild happiness?'

'A psychiatrist,' said the psychiatrist, 'is not supposed to give advice. But . . . '

'But, but, but?' she cried, eagerly.

'A psychiatrist is supposed to let the patient discover and cure himself. Yet, in this case . . . '

'This case, yes, go on!'

'It seems so simple. To keep your husband's love . . . '

'To keep his love, yes?'

The doctor smiled. 'You must destroy the Masterpiece.'

'What?'

'Erase it, get rid of it. Those tattoos *will* come off, won't they? I read somewhere once that —'

'Oh, Doctor!' Emma Fleet leaped up. 'That's *it*! It can be done! And, best of all, Willy can do it! It will take three months alone to wash me clean, rid me of the very Masterpiece that irks him now. Then, virgin white again, we can start another eight years, after that another eight and another. Oh, Doctor, I know he'll do it! Perhaps he was only waiting for me to suggest — and I too stupid to guess! Oh, Doctor, Doctor!

And she crushed him in her arms.

When the doctor broke happily free, she stood off, turning in a circle.

'How strange,' she said. 'In half an hour you solve the next three thousand days and beyond of my life. You're very wise. I'll pay you anything!'

'My usual modest fee is sufficient,' said the doctor.

'I can hardly wait to tell Willy! But first,' she said, 'since you've been so wise, you deserve to see the Masterpiece before it is destroyed.'

'That's hardly necessary, Mrs —'

'You must discover for yourself the rare mind, eye and artistic hand of Willy Fleet, before it is gone forever and we start anew!' she cried, unbuttoning her voluminous coat.

'It isn't really —'

'There!' she said, and flung her coat wide.

The doctor was somehow not surprised to see that she was stark naked beneath her coat.

He gasped. His eyes grew large. His mouth fell open. He sat down slowly, though in reality he somehow wished to stand, as he had in the fifth grade as a boy, during the salute

to the flag, following which three dozen voices broke into an
awed and tremulous song:

> *O beautiful for spacious skies*
> *For amber waves of grain,*
> *For purple mountain majesties*
> *Above the fruited plain . . .*

But, still seated, overwhelmed, he gazed at the continental
vastness of the woman.

Upon which, nothing whatsoever was stitched, painted,
water-coloured or in any way tattooed.

Naked, unadorned, untouched, unlined, unillustrated.

He gasped again.

Now she had whipped her coat back about her with a
winsome acrobat's smile, as if she had just performed a
towering feat. Now she was sailing towards the door.

'Wait −' said the doctor.

But she was out the door, in the reception room, babbling,
whispering, 'Willy, Willy!' and bending to her husband,
hissing in his tiny ear until *his* eyes flexed wide, and his
mouth firm and passionate dropped open and he cried aloud
and clapped his hands with elation.

'Doctor, Doctor, thank you, thank you!'

He darted forward and seized the doctor's hand and shook
it, hard. The doctor was surprised at the fire and rock
hardness of that grip. It was the hand of a dedicated artist, as
were the eyes burning up at him darkly from the wildly
illuminated face.

'Everything's going to be fine!' cried Willy.

The doctor hesitated, glancing from Willy to the great
shadowing balloon that tugged at him wanting to fly off
away.

'We won't have to come back again, ever?'

Good Lord, the doctor thought, does *he* think that *he* has illustrated her from stem to stern, and does she humour him about it? Is *he* mad?

Or does *she* imagine that he has tattooed her from neck to toe-bone, and does he humour her? Is *she* mad?

Or, most strange of all, do they *both* believe that he has swarmed as across the Sistine Chapel ceiling, covering her with rare and significant beauties? Do they both believe, know, humour each other in their specially dimensioned world?

'Will we have to come back again?' asked Willy Fleet a second time.

'No.' The doctor breathed a prayer. 'I think not.'

Why? Because, by some idiot grace, he had done the right thing, hadn't he? By prescribing for a half-seen cause he had made a full cure, yes? Regardless if she believed or he believed or both believed in the Masterpiece, by suggesting the pictures be erased, destroyed, the doctor had made her a clean, lively and inviting canvas again, if *she* needed to be. And if he, on the other hand, wished a new woman to scribble, scrawl and pretend to tattoo on, well, that worked, too. For new and untouched she would be.

'Thank you, Doctor, oh thank you, thank you!'

'Don't thank me,' said the doctor. 'I've done nothing.' He almost said, It was all a fluke, a joke, a surprise! I fell downstairs and landed on my feet!

'Good-bye, good-bye!'

And the elevator slid down, the big woman and the little man sinking from sight into the now suddenly not-too-solid earth, where the atoms opened to let them pass.

'Good-bye, thanks, thanks . . . thanks . . .'

Their voices faded, calling his name and praising his intellect long after they had passed the fourth floor.

The doctor looked around and moved unsteadily back into his office. He shut the door and leaned against it.

'Doctor,' he murmured, 'heal thyself.'

He stepped forward. He did not feel real. He must lie down, if but for a moment.

Where?

On the couch, of course, on the couch.

Some Live Like Lazarus

You won't believe it when I tell you I waited more than sixty years for a murder, hoped as only a woman can hope that it might happen, and didn't move a finger to stop it when it finally drew near. Anna Marie, I thought, you can't stand guard forever. Murder, when ten thousand days have passed, is more than a surprise, it is a miracle.

'Hold on! Don't let me fall!'

Mrs Harrison's voice.

Did I ever, in half a century, hear it whisper? Was it always screaming, shrieking, demanding, threatening?

Yes, always.

'Come along, Mother. There you are, Mother.'

Her son Roger's voice.

Did I ever in all the years hear it rise above a murmur, protest, or, even faintly birdlike, argue?

No. Always the loving monotone.

This morning, no different than any other of their first mornings, they arrived in their great black hearse for their annual Green Bay summer. There he was, thrusting his hand in to hoist the window dummy after him, an ancient sachet of bones and talcum dust that was named, surely for some terrible practical joke, Mother.

'Easy does it, Mother.'

'You're bruising my arm!'

'Sorry, Mother.'

I watched from a window of the lake pavilion as he trundled her off down the path in her wheelchair, she pushing her cane like a musket ahead to blast any Fates or Furies they might meet out of the way.

'Careful, don't run me into the flowers, thank God we'd sense not to go to Paris after all. You'd've had me in that nasty traffic. You're not disappointed?'

'No, Mother.'

'We'll see Paris next year.'

Next year . . . next year . . . no year at all, I heard someone murmur. Myself, gripping the window sill. For almost seventy years I had heard her promise this to the boy, boy-man, man, man-grasshopper and the now livid male praying mantis that he was, pushing his eternally cold and fur-wrapped woman past the hotel verandas where, in another age, paper fans had fluttered like Oriental butterflies in the hands of basking ladies.

'There, Mother, inside the cottage . . . ' his faint voice fading still more, forever young when he was old, forever old when he was very young.

How old is she now? I wondered. Ninety-eight, yes, ninety-nine wicked years old. She seemed like a horror film repeated each year because the hotel entertainment fund could not afford to buy a new one to run in the moth-flaked evenings.

So, through all the repetitions of arrivals and departures, my mind ran back to when the foundations of the Green Bay Hotel were freshly poured and the parasols were new leaf green and lemon gold, that summer of 1890 when I first saw Roger, who was five, but whose eyes already were old and wise and tired.

He stood on the pavilion grass looking at the sun and the bright pennants as I came up to him.

'Hello,' I said.

He simply looked at me.

I hesitated, tagged him and ran.

He did not move.

I came back and tagged him again.

He looked at the place where I had touched him, on the

shoulder, and was about to run after me when her voice came from a distance.

'Roger, don't dirty your clothes!'

And he walked slowly away towards his cottage, not looking back.

That was the day I started to hate him.

Parasols have come and gone in a thousand summer colours, whole flights of butterfly fans have blown away on August winds, the pavilion has burned and been built again in the selfsame size and shape, the lake has dried like a plum in its basin, and my hatred, like these things, came and went, grew very large, stopped still for love, returned, then diminished with the years.

I remember when he was seven, them driving by in their horse carriage, his hair long, brushing his poutish, shrugging shoulders. They were holding hands and she was saying, 'If you're very good this summer, next year we'll go to London. Or the year after that, at the latest.'

And my watching their faces, comparing their eyes, their ears, their mouths, so when he came in for soda pop one noon that summer I walked straight up to him and cried, 'She's not your mother!'

'What!' He looked around in panic, as if she might be near.

'She's not your aunt or your grandma, either!' I cried. 'She's a witch that stole you when you were a baby. You don't know who your mama is or your pa. You don't look anything like her. She's holding you for a million ransom which comes due when you're twenty-one from some duke or king!'

'Don't say that!' he shouted, jumping up.

'Why not?' I said angrily. 'Why do you come around here? You can't play this, can't play that, can't do nothing, what good are you? She says, she does. I know *her*! She hangs upside down from the ceiling in her black clothes in her bedroom at midnight!'

'Don't say that!' His face was frightened and pale.

'Why not say it?'

'Because,' he bleated, 'it's true.'

And he was out that door and running.

I didn't see him again until the next summer. And then only once, briefly, when I took some clean linen down to their cottage.

The summer when we were both twelve was the summer that for some time I didn't hate him.

He called my name outside the pavilion screen door and when I looked out he said, very quietly, 'Anna Marie, when I am twenty and you are twenty, I'm going to marry you.'

'Who's going to let you?' I asked.

'I'm going to let you,' he said. 'You just remember, Anna Marie. You wait for me. Promise?'

I could only nod. 'But what about –'

'She'll be dead by then,' he said, very gravely. 'She's old. She's *old*.'

And then he turned and went away.

The next summer they did not come to the resort at all. I heard she was sick. I prayed every night that she would die.

But two years later they were back, and the year after the year after that until Roger was nineteen and I was nineteen, and then at last we had reached and touched twenty, and for one of the few times in all the years, they came into the pavilion together, she in her wheelchair now, deeper in her furs than ever before, her face a gathering of white dust and folded parchment.

She eyed me as I set her ice cream sundae down before her, and eyed Roger as he said, 'Mother, I want you to meet –'

'I do not meet girls who wait on public tables,' she said. 'I acknowledge they exist, work, and are paid. But I immediately forget their names.'

She touched and nibbled her ice cream, touched and nibbled her ice cream, while Roger sat not touching his at all.

They left a day earlier than usual that year. I saw Roger as he paid the bill, in the hotel lobby. He shook my hand to say good-bye and I could not help but say, 'You've forgotten.'

He took a half step back, then turned around, patting his coat pockets.

'Luggage, bills paid, wallet, no, I seem to have everything,' he said.

'A long time ago,' I said, 'you made a promise.'

He was silent.

'Roger,' I said, 'I'm twenty now. And so are you.'

He seized my hand again, swiftly, as if he were falling over the side of a ship and it was me going away, leaving him to drown forever beyond help.

'Once more year, Anna! Two, three, at the most!'

'Oh, no,' I said forlornly.

'Four years at the outside! The doctors say −'

'The doctors don't know what I know, Roger. She'll live forever. She'll bury you and me and drink wine at our funerals.'

'She's a sick woman, Anna! My God, she *can't* survive!'

'She will, because we give her strength. She knows we want her dead. That really gives her the power to go on.'

'I can't talk this way, I can't!' Seizing his luggage, he started down the hall.

'I won't wait, Roger,' I said.

He turned at the door and looked at me so helplessly, so palely, like a moth pinned to the wall, that I could not say it again.

The door slammed shut.

The summer was over.

The next year Roger came directly to the soda fountain, where he said, 'Is it true? Who is he?'

'Paul,' I said. 'You know Paul. He'll manage the hotel someday. We'll marry this fall.'

'That doesn't give me much time,' said Roger.

'It's too late,' I said. 'I've already promised.'

'Promised, hell! You don't love him!'

'I think I do.'

'Think, hell! Thinking's one thing, knowing's another. You *know* you love me!'

'Do I, Roger?'

'Stop relishing the damn business so much! You know you do! Oh, Anna, you'll be miserable!'

'I'm miserable now,' I said.

'Oh, Anna, Anna, wait!'

'I have waited, most of my life. But I know what will happen.'

'Anna!' He blurted it out as if it had come to him suddenly. 'What if — what if she died *this* summer?'

'She won't.'

'But if she did, if she took a turn for the worse, I mean, in the next two months —' He searched my face. He shortened it. 'The next month, Anna, two weeks, listen, if she died in two short weeks, would you wait that long, would you marry me then?'

I began to cry. 'Oh, Roger, we've never even kissed. This is ridiculous.'

'Answer me, if she died one week, seven days from now . . . ' He grabbed my arms.

'But how can you be sure?'

'I'll *make* myself sure! I swear she'll be dead a week from now, or I'll never bother you again with this!'

And he flung the screen doors wide, hurrying off into the day that was suddenly too bright.

'Roger, don't —' I cried.

But my mind thought, Roger *do*, do something, anything, to start it all or end it all.

That night in bed I thought, What ways are there for murder that no one could know? Is Roger, a hundred yards away this moment, thinking the same? Will he search the woods tomorrow for toadstools resembling mushrooms, or drive the car too fast and fling her door wide on a curve? I saw the wax-dummy witch fly through the air in a lovely soaring arc, to break like ridiculous peanut brittle on an oak, an elm, a maple. I sat up in bed. I laughed until I wept. I wept until I laughed again. No, no, I thought, he'll find a better way. A night burglar will shock her heart into her throat. Once in her throat, he will not let it go down again, she'll choke on her own panic.

And then the oldest, the darkest, most childish thought of all. There's only one way to finish a woman whose mouth is the colour of blood. Being what she is, no relative, not an aunt or great-grandmother, surprise her with a stake driven through her heart!

I heard her scream. It was so loud, all the night birds jumped from the trees to cover the stars.

I lay back down. Dear Christian Anna Marie, I thought, what's this? Do you want to kill? Yes, for why not kill a killer, a woman who strangled her child in his crib and has not loosened the throttling cord since? He is so pale, poor man, because he has not breathed free air, all of his life.

And then, unbidden, the lines of an old poem stood up in my head. Where I had read them or who had put them down, or if I had written them myself, within my head over the years, I could not say. But the lines were there and I read them in the dark:

> *Some live like Lazarus*
> *In a tomb of life*
> *And come forth curious late to twilight hospitals*
> *And mortuary rooms.*

The lines vanished. For a while I could recall no more, and then, unable to fend it off, for it came of itself, a last fragment appeared in the dark:

Better cold skies seen bitter to the North
Than stillborn stay, all blind and gone to ghost.
If Rio is lost, well, love the Arctic Coast!
O ancient Lazarus
Come ye forth.

There the poem stopped and let me be. At last I slept, restless, hoping for the dawn, and good and final news.

The next day I saw him pushing her along the pier and thought, Yes, that's it! She'll vanish and be found a week from now, on the shore, like a sea monster floating, all face and no body.

That day passed. Well, surely, I thought, tomorrow . . .

The second day of the week, the third, the fourth and then the fifth and sixth passed, and on the seventh day one of the maids came running up the path, shrieking.

'Oh, it's terrible, terrible!'

'Mrs Harrison?' I cried. I felt a terrible and quite uncontrollable smile on my face.

'No, no, her *son*! He's hung himself!'

'Hung himself?' I said ridiculously, and found myself, stunned, explaining, to her. 'Oh, no, it wasn't *him* was going to die, it was —' I babbled. I stopped, for the maid was clutching, pulling my arm.

'We cut him down, oh, God, he's still alive, quick!'

Still alive? He still breathed, yes, and walked around through the other years, yes, but alive? No.

It was she who gained strength and lived through his attempt to escape her. She never forgave his trying to run off.

'What do you mean by that, what do you mean?' I remember her screaming at him as he lay feeling his throat, in the cottage, his eyes shut, wilted, and I hurried in the door. 'What do you mean doing that, what, what?'

And looking at him there I knew he had tried to run away from both of us, we were both impossible to him. I did not forgive him that either, for a while. But I did feel my old hatred of him become something else, a kind of dull pain, as I turned and went back for a doctor.

'What do you mean, you silly boy?' she cried.

I married Paul that autumn.

After that, the years poured through the glass swiftly. Once each year, Roger led himself into the pavilion to sit eating mint ice with his limp empty-gloved hands, but he never called me by my name again, nor did he mention the old promise.

Here and there in the hundreds of months that passed I thought, For his own sake now, for no one else, sometime, somehow he must simply up and destroy the dragon with the hideous bellows face and the rust-scaled hands. For Roger and only for Roger, Roger must do it.

Surely *this* year, I thought, when he was fifty, fifty-one, fifty-two. Between seasons I caught myself examining occasional Chicago papers, hoping to find a picture of her lying slit like a monstrous yellow chicken. But no, but no, but no . . .

I'd almost forgotten them when they returned this morning. He's very old now, more like a doddering husband than a son. Baked grey clay he is, with milky blue eyes, a toothless mouth, and manicured fingernails which seem stronger because the flesh has baked away.

At noon today, after a moment of standing out, a lone grey wingless hawk staring at a sky in which he had never soared or flown, he came inside and spoke to me, his voice rising.

'Why didn't you tell me?'

'Tell you what?' I said, scooping out his ice cream before he asked for it.

'One of the maids just mentioned, your husband died five years ago! You should have told me!'

'Well, now you know,' I said.

He sat down slowly. 'Lord,' he said, tasting the ice cream and savouring it, eyes shut, 'this is bitter.' Then, a long time later, he said, 'Anna, I never asked. Were there ever any children?'

'No,' I said. 'And I don't know why. I guess I'll never know why.'

I left him sitting there and went to wash the dishes.

At nine tonight I heard someone laughing by the lake. I hadn't heard Roger laugh since he was a child, so I didn't think it was him until the doors burst wide and he entered, flinging his arms about, unable to control his almost weeping hilarity.

'Roger!' I asked. 'What's wrong?'

'Nothing! Oh, nothing!' he cried. 'Everything's lovely! A root beer, Anna! Take one yourself! Drink with me!'

We drank together, he laughed, winked, then got immensely calm. Still smiling, though, he looked suddenly, beautifully young.

'Anna,' he whispered intensely, leaning forward, 'guess what? I'm flying to China tomorrow! Then India! Then London, Madrid, Paris, Berlin, Rome, Mexico City!'

'*You* are, Roger?'

'I am,' he said. 'I, I, I, not we, we, we, but I, Roger Bidwell Harrison, I, I, *I*!'

I stared at him and he gazed quietly back at me, and I must have gasped. For then I knew what he had finally done tonight, this hour, within the last few minutes.

Oh, no, my lips must have murmured.

Oh, but yes, yes, his eyes upon me replied, incredible miracle of miracles, after all these waiting years. Tonight at last. Tonight.

I let him talk. After Rome it was Vienna and Stockholm, he'd saved thousands of schedules, flight charts and hotel bulletins for forty years; he knew the moons and tides, the goings and comings of everything on the sea and in the sky.

'But best of all,' he said at last, 'Anna, Anna, will you come along with me? I've lots of money put away, don't let me run on! Anna, tell me, *will* you?'

I came around the counter slowly and saw myself in the mirror, a woman in her seventieth year going to a party half a century late.

I sat down beside him and shook my head.

'Oh, but, Anna, why not, there's no reason why!'

'There is a reason,' I said. 'You.'

'Me, but I don't count!'

'That's just it, Roger, you do.'

'Anna, we could have a wonderful time —'

'I daresay. But, Roger, you've *been* married for seventy years. Now, for the first time, you're not married. You don't want to turn around and get married again right off, do you?'

'*Don't* I?' he asked, blinking.

'You don't, you really don't. You deserve a little while, at least, off by yourself, to see the world, to know who Roger Harrison is. A little while away from women. Then, when you've gone around the world and come back, is time to think of other things.'

'If you *say* so —'

'No. It mustn't be anything I say or know or tell you to do. Right now it must be you telling yourself what to know and see and do. Go have a grand time. If you can, be happy.'

'Will you be here waiting for me when I come back?'

'I haven't it in me any more to wait, but I'll be here.'

He moved towards the door, then stopped and looked at me as if surprised by some new question that had come into his mind.

'Anna,' he said, 'if all this had happened forty, fifty years ago, would you have gone away with me then? Would you really have married me?'

I did not answer.

'Anna?' he asked.

After a long while I said, 'There are some questions that should never be asked.'

Because, I went on, thinking, there can be no answers. Looking down the years towards the lake, I could not remember, so I could not say, whether we could have ever been happy. Perhaps even as a child, sensing the impossible in Roger, I had clenched the impossible, and therefore the rare, to my heart, simply because it was impossible and rare. He was a sprig of farewell summer pressed in an old book, to be taken out, turned over, admired, once a year, but more than that? Who could say? Surely not I, so long, so late in the day. Life is questions, not answers.

Roger had come very close to read my face, my mind, while I thought all this. What he saw there made him look away, close his eyes, then take my hand and press it to his cheek.

'I'll be back, I swear I will!'

Outside the door he stood bewildered for a moment in the moonlight, looking at the world and all its directions, east, west, north, south, like a child out of school for his first summer not knowing which way to go first, just breathing, just listening, just seeing.

'Don't hurry!' I said fervently. 'Oh, God, whatever you do, please enjoy yourself, don't hurry!'

I saw him run off towards the limousine near the cottage where I am supposed to rap in the morning and where I will get no answer. But I know that I will not go to the cottage and that I'll keep the maids from going there because the old lady has given orders not to be bothered. That will give Roger the chance, the start he needs. In a week or two or three, I might call the police. Then if they met Roger coming back on the boat from all those wild places, it won't matter.

Police? Perhaps not even them. Perhaps she died of a heart attack and poor Roger only thinks he killed her and now proudly sails off into the world, his pride not allowing him to know that only her own self-made death released him.

But then again, if at last all the murder he put away for seventy years forced him tonight to lay hands on and kill the hideous turkey, I could not find it in my heart to weep for her but only for the great time it has taken to act out the sentence.

The road is silent. An hour has passed since the limousine roared away down the road.

Now I have just put out the lights and stand alone in the pavilion looking out at the shining lake where in another century, under another sun, a small boy with an old face was first touched to play tag with me and now, very late, has tagged me back, has kissed my hand and run away, and this time myself, stunned, not following.

Many things I do not know, tonight.

But one thing I'm sure of.

I do not hate Roger Harrison any more.

The Best of All
Possible Worlds

The two men sat swaying side by side, unspeaking for the long while it took for the train to move through cold December twilight, pausing at one country station after another. As the twelfth depot was left behind, the older of the two men muttered, 'Idiot, Idiot!' under his breath.

'What?' The younger man glanced up from his *Times*.

The old man nodded bleakly. 'Did you see that damn fool rush off just now, stumbling after that woman who smelled of Chanel?'

'Oh, her?' The young man looked as if he could not decide whether to laugh or be depressed. 'I followed her off the train once myself.'

The old man snorted and closed his eyes. 'I too, five years ago.'

The young man stared at his companion as if he had found a friend in a most unlikely spot.

'Did — did the same thing happen once you reached the end of the platform?'

'Perhaps. Go on.'

'Well, I was twenty feet behind her and closing up fast when her husband drove into the station with a carload of kids! Bang! The car door slammed, I saw her Cheshire-cat smile as she drove away. I waited half an hour, chilled to the bone, for another train. It taught me something, by God!'

'It taught you nothing whatsoever,' replied the older man dryly. 'Idiot bulls, that's all of us, you, me, them, silly boys jerking like laboratory frogs if someone scratches our itch.'

'My grandpa once said. "Big in the hunkus, small in the brain, that is man's fate." '

'A wise man. But now, what do you make of *her*?'

'That woman? Oh, she likes to keep in trim. It must pep her liver to know that with a little mild eye-rolling she can make the lemmings swarm any night on this train. She has the best of all possible worlds, don't you think? Husband, children, plus the knowledge she's neat packaging and can prove it five trips a week, hurting no one, least of all herself. And, everything considered, she's not much to look at. It's just she *smells* so good.'

'Tripe,' said the old man. 'It won't wash. Purely and simply, she's a woman. All women are women, all men are dirty goats. Until you accept that, you will be rationalizing your glands all your life. As it is, you will know no rest until you are seventy or thereabouts. Meanwhile, self-knowledge may give you whatever solace can be had in a sticky situation. Given all these essential and inescapable truths, few men ever strike a balance. Ask a man if he is happy and he will immediately think you are asking if he is *satisfied*. Satiety is most men's Edenic dream. I have known only one man who came heir to the very best of all possible worlds, as you used the phrase.'

'Good Lord,' said the young man, his eyes shining, 'I wouldn't mind hearing about him.'

'I hope there's time. This chap is the happiest ram, the most carefree bull, in history. Wives and girl friends galore, as the sales pitch says. Yet he has no qualms, guilts, no feverish nights of lament and self-chastisement.'

'Impossible,' the young man put in. 'You can't eat your cake and digest it, too!'

'He did, he does, he will! Not a tremor, not a trace of moral seasickness after an all-night journey over a choppy sea of innersprings! Successful businessman. Apartment in New York on the best street, the proper height above traffic, plus a long-weekend Bucks County place on a more than correct little country stream where he herds his nannies, the happy farmer. But I met him first at his New York apartment last year, when he had just married. At dinner, his wife was truly gorgeous, snow-cream arms, fruity lips, an amplitude of harvest land below the line, a plenitude above. Honey in the horn, the full apple barrel through winter, she seemed thus to me *and* her husband, who nipped her bicep in passing. Leaving, at midnight, I found myself raising a hand to slap her on the flat of her flank like a thoroughbred. Falling down in the elevator, life floated out from under me. I nickered.'

'Your powers of description,' said the young commuter, breathing heavily, 'are incredible.'

'I write advertising copy,' said the older. 'But to continue. I met let us call him Smith again not two weeks later. Through sheer coincidence I was invited to crash a party by a friend. When I arrived in Bucks County, whose place should it turn out to be but Smith's! And near him, in the centre of the living room, stood this dark Italian beauty, all tawny panther, all midnight and moonstones, dressed in earth colours, browns, siennas, tans, ambers, all the tones of a riotously fruitful autumn. In the babble I lost her name. Later I saw Smith crush her like a great sunwarmed vine of lush October grapes in his arms. Idiot fool, I thought. Lucky dog, I thought. Wife in town, mistress in country. He is tramping out the vintage, et cetera, and all that. Glorious. But I shall not stay for the wine festival, I thought, and slipped away, unnoticed.'

'I can't stand too much of this talk,' said the young commuter, trying to raise the window.

'Don't interrupt,' said the older man. 'Where was I?'

'Trampled. Vintage.'

'Oh, yes! Well, as the party broke up, I finally caught the lovely Italian's name. *Mrs* Smith!'

'He'd married again, eh?'

'Hardly. Not enough time. Stunned, I thought quickly: He must have two sets of friends. One set knows his city wife.

The other set knows this mistress whom he *calls* wife. Smith's too smart for bigamy. No other answer. Mystery.'

'Go on, go on,' said the young commuter feverishly.

'Smith, in high spirits, drove me to the train station that night. On the way he said. "What do you think of my wives?"

' "Wives, plural?" he said.

' "Plural, hell," he said. "I've had twenty in the last three years, each better than the last! Twenty, count them, twenty! Here!" As we stopped at the station he pulled out a thick photo wallet. He glanced at my face as he handed it over. "No, no," he laughed, "I'm not Bluebeard with a score of old theatre trunks in the attic crammed full of former mates. Look!"

'I flipped the pictures. They flew by like an animated film. Blondes, brunettes, redheads, the plain, the exotic, the fabulously impertinent or the sublimely docile gazed out at me, smiling, frowning. The flutter-flicker hypnotized, then haunted me. There was something terribly familiar about each photo.

' "Smith," I said, "you must be very rich to afford all these wives."

' "Not rich, no. Look again!"

'I flipped the montage in my hands. I gasped. I knew.

' "The Mrs Smith I met tonight, the Italian beauty, is the one and only Mrs Smith," I said. "But, at the same time, the woman I met in New York two weeks ago is also the one and only Mrs Smith. It can only follow that both women are one and the same!"

' "Correct!" cried Smith, proud of my sleuthing.

' "Impossible!" I blurted out.

' "No," said Smith, elated. "My wife is amazing. One of the finest off-Broadway actresses when I met her. Selfishly I asked her to quit the stage on pain of severance of our mutual insanity, our rampaging up one side of a chaise-lounge and down the other. A giantess made dwarf by love, she slammed the door on the theatre, to run down the alley with me. The first six months of our marriage, the earth did not move, it shook. But, inevitably, fiend that I am, I began to watch various other women ticking by like wondrous pendulums. My wife caught me noting the time. Meanwhile, she had begun to cast her eyes on passing theatrical billboards. I found her nesting with the *New York Times* next-morning reviews, desperately tearful. Crisis! How to combine two violent careers, that of passion-dishevelled actress and that of anxiously rambling ram?"

' "One night," said Smith, "I eyed a peach Melba that drifted by. Simultaneously, an old playbill blew in the wind and clung to my wife's ankle. It was as if these two events, occurring within the moment, had shot a window shade with a rattling snap clear to the top of its roll. Light *poured* in! My wife seized my arm. Was she or was she not an actress? She was! Well, then, well! She sent me packing for twenty-four hours, wouldn't let me in the apartment, as she hurried about some vast and exciting preparations. When I returned home the next afternoon at the blue hour, as the French say in their always twilight language, my wife had vanished! A dark Latin put out her hand to me. 'I am a friend of your wife's,' she said and threw herself upon me, to nibble my ears, crack my ribs, until I held her off and, suddenly suspicious, cried, 'This is no woman I'm with — this is my *wife!*' And we both fell laughing to the floor. This *was* my wife, with a different cosmetic, different couturier, different posture and intonation. 'My actress!' I said. 'Your actress!' she laughed. 'Tell me what I should be and I'll be it. Carmen? All right, I'm Carmen. Brunhilde? Why not? I'll study, create and, when you grow bored, re-create. I'm enrolled at the Dance Academy. I'll learn to sit, stand, walk, ten thousand ways. I'm chin deep in speech lessons, I'm signed at the Berlitz! I am also a member of the Yamayuki Judo Club —' 'Good Lord,' I cried, 'what for?' 'This!' she replied, and tossed me head over heels into bed!"

' "Well," said Smith, "from that day on I've lived Riley and nine other Irishmen's lives! Unnumbered fancies have passed me in delightful shadow plays of women all colours, shapes, sizes, fevers! My wife, finding her proper stage, our parlour, and audience, me, has fulfilled her need to be the greatest actress in the land. Too small an audience? No! For I, with my ever-wandering tastes, am there to meet her, whichever part she plays. My jungle talent coincides with her wide-ranging genius. So, caged at last, yet free, loving her I love everyone. It's the best of all possible worlds, friend, the best of all possible worlds." '

There was a moment of silence.

The train rumbled down the track in the new December darkness.

The two commuters, the young and the old, were thoughtful now, considering the story just finished.

At last the young man swallowed and nodded in awe. 'Your friend Smith solved his problem, all right.'

'He did.'

The young man debated a moment, then smiled quietly. 'I have a friend, too. His situation was similar, but – different. Shall I call him Quillan?'

'Yes,' said the old man, 'but hurry. I get off soon.'

'Quillan,' said the young man quickly, 'was in a bar one night with a fabulous redhead. The crowd parted before her like the sea before Moses. Miraculous, I thought, revivifying, beyond the senses! A week later, in Greenwich, I saw Quillan ambling along with a dumpy little woman, his own age, of course, only thirty-two, but she'd gone to seed young. Tatty, the English would say; pudgy, snouty-nosed, not enough make-up, wrinkled stockings, spider's-nest hair, and immensely quiet; she was content to walk along, it seemed, just holding Quillan's hand. Ha, I thought, here's his poor little parsnip wife who loves the earth he treads, while other nights he's out winding up that incredible robot redhead! How sad, what a shame. And I went on my way.

'A month later I met Quillan again. He was about to dart into a dark entranceway in MacDougal Street, when he saw me. "Oh, God!" he cried, sweating. "Don't tell on me! My wife must never know!"

'I was about to swear myself to secrecy when a woman called to Quillan from a window above.

'I glanced up. My jaw dropped.

'There in the window stood the dumpy, seedy little woman!!

'So suddenly it was clear. The beautiful redhead was his *wife*! She danced, she sang, she talked loud and long, a brilliant intellectual, the goddess Siva, thousand-limbed, the finest throw pillow ever sewn by mortal hand. Yet she was strangely − tiring.

'So my friend Quillan had taken this obscure Village room where, two nights a week, he could sit quietly in the mouse-brown silence or walk on the dim streets with this good homely dumpy comfortably mute woman who was not his wife at all, as I had quickly supposed, but his mistress!

'I looked from Quillan to his plump companion in the window above and wrung his hand with new warmth and understanding. "Mum's the word!" I said. The last I saw of them, they were seated in a delicatessen, Quillan and his mistress their eyes gently touching each other, saying nothing, eating pastrami sandwiches. He too had, if you think about it, the best of all possible worlds.'

The train roared, shouted its whistle and slowed. Both men, rising, stopped and looked at each other in surprise. Both spoke at once:

'You get off at *this* stop?'

Both nodded, smiling.

Silently they made their way back and, as the train stopped in the chill December night, alighted and shook hands.

'Well, give my best to Mr Smith.'

'And mine to Mr Quillan!'

Two horns honked from opposite ends of the station. Both men looked at one car. A beautiful woman was in it. Both looked at the other car. A beautiful woman was in it.

They separated, looking back at each other like two schoolboys, each stealing a glance at the car towards which the other was moving.

'I wonder,' thought the old man, 'if that woman down there is . . . '

'I wonder,' thought the young man, 'if that lady in his car could be . . . '

But both were running now. Two car doors slammed like pistol shots ending a matinee.

The cars drove off. The station platform stood empty. It being December and cold, snow soon fell like a curtain.

The One Who Waits

I live in a well. I live like smoke in a well. Like vapour in a stone throat. I don't move. I don't do anything but wait. Overhead I see the cold stars of night and morning, and I see the sun. And sometimes I sing old songs of this world when it was young. How can I tell you what I am when I don't know? I cannot. I am simply waiting. I am mist and moonlight and memory. I am sad and I am old. Sometimes I fall like rain into the well. Spiders' webs are startled into forming where my rain falls fast, on the water surface. I wait in cool silence and there will be a day when I no longer wait.

Now it is morning. I hear a great thunder. I smell fire from a distance. I hear a metal crashing. I wait. I listen.

Voices. Far away.

'All right!'

One voice. An alien voice. An alien tongue I cannot know. No word is familiar. I listen.

'Send the men out!'

A crunching in crystal sands.

'Mars! So this is it!'

'Where's the flag?'

'Here, sir.'

'Good, good.'

The sun is high in the blue sky and its golden rays fill the well and I hang like a flower pollen, invisible and misting in the warm light.

Voices.

'In the name of the Government of Earth, I proclaim this to be the Martian Territory, to be equally divided among the member nations.'

What are they saying? I turn in the sun, like a wheel, invisible and lazy, golden and tireless.

'What's over here?'

'A well!'

'No!'

'Come on. Yes!'

The approach of warmth. Three objects bend over the well mouth, and my coolness rises to the objects.

'Great!'

'Think it's good water?'

'We'll see.'

'Someone get a lab test bottle and a dropline.'

'I will!'

A sound of running. The return.

'Here we are.'

I wait.

'Let it down. Easy.'

Glass shines, above, coming down on a slow line.

The water ripples softly as the glass touches and fills. I rise in the warm air towards the well mouth.

'Here we are. You want to test this water, Regent?'

'Let's have it.'

'What a beautiful well. Look at that construction. How old you think it is?'

'God knows. When we landed in that other town yesterday. Smith said there hasn't been life on Mars in ten thousand years.'

'Imagine.'

'How is it, Regent? The water.'

'Pure as silver. Have a glass.'

The sound of water in the hot sunlight. Now I hover like a dust, a cinnamon, upon the soft wind.

'What's the matter, Jones?'

'I don't know. Got a terrible headache. All of sudden.'

'Did you drink the water yet?'

'No, I haven't. It's not that. I was just bending over the well and all of a sudden my head split. I feel better now.'

Now I know who I am.

My name is Stephen Leonard Jones and I am twenty-five years old and I have just come in a rocket from a planet called Earth and I am standing with my good friends Regent and Shaw by an old well on the planet Mars.

I look down at my golden fingers, tan and strong. I look at my long legs and at my silver uniform and at my friends.

'What's wrong, Jones?' they say.

'Nothing,' I say, looking at them. 'Nothing at all.'

The food is good. It has been ten thousand years since food. It touches the tongue in a fine way and the wine with the food is warming. I listen to the sound of voices. I make words that I do not understand but somehow understand. I test the air.

'What's the matter, Jones?'

I tilt this head of mine and rest my hands holding the silver utensils of eating. I feel everything.

'What do you mean?' this voice, this new thing of mine, says.

'You keep breathing funny. Coughing,' says the other man.

I pronounce exactly. 'Maybe a little cold coming on.'

'Check with the doc later.'

I nod my head and it is good to nod. It is good to do several things after ten thousand years. It is good to breathe the air and it is good to feel the sun in the flesh deep and going deeper and it is good to feel the structure of ivory, the fine skeleton hidden in the warming flesh, and it is good to hear sounds much clearer and more immediate than they were in the stone deepness of a well. I sit enchanted.

'Come out of it, Jones. Snap to it. We got to move!'

'Yes,' I say, hypnotized with the way the word forms like water on the tongue and falls with slow beauty out into the air.

I walk and it is good walking. I stand high and it is a long way to the ground when I look down from my eyes and my head. It is like living on a fine cliff and being happy there.

Regent stands by the stone well, looking down. The others have gone murmuring to the silver ship from which they came.

I feel the fingers of my hand and the smile of my mouth.

'It is deep,' I say.

'Yes.'

'It is called a Soul Well.'

Regent raises his head and looks at me. 'How do you know that?'

'Doesn't it look like one?'

'I never heard of a Soul Well.'

'A place where waiting things, things that once had flesh, wait and wait,' I say, touching his arm.

The sand is fire and the ship is silver fire in the hotness of the day and the heat is good to feel. The sound of my feet in the hard sand. I listen. The sound of the wind and the sun burning the valleys. I smell the smell of the rocket boiling in the noon. I stand below the port.

'Where's Regent?' someone says.

'I saw him by the well,' I reply.

One of them runs towards the well. I am beginning to tremble. A fine shivering tremble, hidden deep, but becoming very strong. And for the first time I hear it, as if it too were hidden in a well. A voice calling deep within me, tiny and afraid. And the voice cries, *Let me go, let me go*, and there is a feeling as if something is trying to get free, a pounding of labyrinthine doors, a rushing down dark corridors and up passages, echoing and screaming.

'Regent's in the well!'

The men are running, all five of them. I run with them but now I am sick and the trembling is violent.

'He must have fallen. Jones, you were here with him. Did you see? Jones? Well, speak up, man.'

'What's wrong, Jones?'

I fall to my knees, the trembling is so bad.

'He's sick. Here, help me with him.'

'The sun.'

'No, not the sun,' I murmur.

They stretch me out and the seizures come and go like earthquakes and the deep hidden voice in me cries. *This is Jones, this is* me, *that's not him, that's not him, don't believe him, let me out, let me out*! And I look up at the bent figures and my eyelids flicker. They touch my wrists.

'His heart is acting up.'

I close my eyes. The screaming stops. The shivering ceases.

I rise, as in a cool well, released.

'He's dead,' says someone.

'Jones is dead.'

'From what?'

'Shock, it looks like.'

'What kind of shock?' I say, and my name is Sessions and my lips move crisply, and I am the captain of these men. I stand among them and I am looking down at a body which lies cooling on the sands. I clap both hands to my head.

'Captain!'

'It's nothing,' I say, crying out. 'Just a headache. I'll be all right. There. There,' I whisper. 'It's all right now.'

'We'd better get out of the sun, sir.'

'Yes,' I say, looking down at Jones. 'We should never have come. Mars doesn't want us.'

We carry the body back to the rocket with us, and a new voice is calling deep in me to be let out.

Help, help. Far down in the moist earthen-works of the body. *Help, help!* in red fathoms, echoing and pleading.

The trembling starts much sooner this time. The control is less steady.

'Captain, you'd better get in out of the sun, you don't look too well, sir.'

'Yes,' I say. 'Help,' I say.

'What, sir?'

'I didn't say anything.'

'You said "Help," sir.'

'Did I, Matthews, did I?'

The body is laid out in the shadow of the rocket and the voice screams in the deep underwater catacombs of bone and crimson tide. My hands jerk. My mouth splits and is parched. My nostrils fasten wide. My eyes roll. *Help, help, oh help, don't, don't, let me out, don't, don't.*

'Don't,' I say.

'What, sir?'

'Never mind,' I say. 'I've got to get free,' I say. I clap my hand to my mouth.

'How's that, sir?' cries Matthews.

'Get inside, all of you, go back to Earth!' I shout.

A gun is in my hand. I lift it.

'Don't sir!'

An explosion. Shadows run. The screaming is cut off. There is a whistling sound of falling through space.

After ten thousand years, how good to die. How good to feel the sudden coolness, the relaxation. How good to be like a hand within a glove that stretches out and grows wonderfully cold in the hot sand. Oh, the quiet and the loveliness of gathering, darkening death. But one cannot linger on.

A crack, a snap.

'Good God, he's killed himself!' I cry, and open my eyes and there is the captain lying against the rocket, his skull split by a bullet, his eyes wide, his tongue protruding between his white teeth. Blood runs from his head. I bend to him and touch him. 'The fool,' I say. 'Why did he do that?'

The men are horrified. They stand over the two dead men and turn their heads to see the Martian sands and the distant well where Regent lies lolling in deep waters. A croaking comes out of their dry lips, a whimpering, a childish protest against this awful dream.

The men turn to me.

After a long while, one of them says, 'That makes you captain, Matthews.'

'I know,' I say slowly.

'Only six of us left.'

'Good God, it happened so quick!'

'I don't want to stay here, let's get out!'

The men clamour. I go to them and touch them now, with a confidence which almost sings in me. 'Listen,' I say, and touch their elbows or their arms or their hands.

We all fall silent.

We are one.

No, no, no, no, no, no! Inner voices crying, deep down and gone into prisons beneath exteriors.

We are looking at each other. We are Samuel Matthews and Raymond Moses and William Spaulding and Charles Evans and Forrest Cole and John Summers, and we say nothing but look upon each other and our white faces and shaking hands.

We turn, as one, and look at the well.

'Now,' we say.

No, no, six voices scream, hidden and layered down and stored forever.

Our feet walk in the sand and it is as if a great hand with twelve fingers were moving across the hot sea bottom.

We bend to the well, looking down. From the cool depths six faces peer back up at us.

One by one we bend until our balance is gone, and one by

one drop into the mouth and down through cool darkness into the cold waters.

The sun sets. The stars wheel upon the night sky. Far out, there is a wink of light. Another rocket coming, leaving red marks on space.

I live in a well. I live like smoke in a well. Like vapour in a stone throat. Overhead I see the cold stars of night and morning, and I see the sun. And sometimes I sing old songs of this world when it was young. How can I tell you what I am when even I don't know? I cannot.

I am simply waiting.

Tyrannosaurus Rex

He opened a door on darkness. A voice cried, 'Shut it!' It was like a blow in the face. He jumped through. The door banged. He cursed himself quietly. The voice, with dreadful patience, intoned, 'Jesus. You Terwilliger?'

'Yes,' said Terwilliger. A faint ghost of screen haunted the dark theatre wall to his right. To his left, a cigarette wove fiery arcs in the air as someone's lips talked swiftly around it.

'You're five minutes late!'

Don't make it sound like five years, thought Terwilliger.

'Shove your film in the projection room door. Let's *move*.'

Terwilliger squinted.

He made out five vast loge seats that exhaled, breathed heavily as amplitudes of executive life shifted, leaning towards the middle loge where, almost in darkness, a little boy sat smoking.

No, thought Terwilliger, not a boy. That's him. Joe Clarence. Clarence the Great.

For now the tiny mouth snapped like a puppet's, blowing smoke. 'Well?'

Terwilliger stumbled back to hand the film to the projectionist, who made a lewd gesture towards the loges, winked at Terwilliger and slammed the booth door.

'Jesus,' sighed the tiny voice. A buzzer buzzed. 'Roll it, projection!'

Terwilliger probed the nearest loge, struck flesh, pulled back and stood biting his lips.

Music leaped from the screen. His film appeared in a storm of drums:

TYRANNOSAURUS REX: THE THUNDER LIZARD.

Photographed in stop-motion animation with mini-
atures created by John Terwilliger. A study in life-
forms on Earth one billion years before Christ.

Faint ironic applause came softly patting from the baby
hands in the middle loge.

Terwilliger shut his eyes. New music jerked him alert. The
last titles faded into a world of primeval sun, mist,
poisonous rain and lush wilderness. Morning fogs were
strewn along eternal seacoasts where immense flying dreams
and dreams of nightmare scythed the wind. Huge triangles of
bone and rancid skin, of diamond eye and crusted tooth,
pterodactyls, the kites of destruction, plunged, struck prey,
and skimmed away, meat and screams in their scissor
mouths.

Terwilliger gazed, fascinated.

In the jungle foliage now, shiverings, creepings, insect
jitterings, antennae twitchings, slim locked in oily fatted
slime, armour skinned to armour, in sun glade and shadow
moved the reptilian inhabitors of Terwilliger's mad remembrance of vengeance given flesh and panic taking wing.

Brontosaur, stegosaur, triceratops. How easily the clumsy
tonnages of name fell from one's lips.

The great brutes swung like ugly machineries of war and
dissolution through moss ravines, crushing a thousand
flowers at one footfall, snouting the mist, ripping the sky in
half with one shriek.

My beauties, thought Terwilliger, my little lovelies. All
liquid latex, rubber sponge, ball-socketed steel articulature;
all night-dreamed, clay-modelled, warped and welded,
riveted and slapped to life by hand. No bigger than my fist,
half of them; the rest no larger than this head they sprang
from.

'Good Lord,' said a soft admiring voice in the dark.

Step by step, frame by frame of film, stop motion by stop motion, he, Terwilliger, had run his beasts through their postures, moved each a fraction of an inch, photographed them, moved them another hair, photographed them, for hours and days and months. Now these rare images, this eight hundred scant feet of film, rushed through the projector.

And lo! he thought. I'll never get used to it. Look! They come *alive*!

Rubber, steel, clay, reptilian latex sheath, glass eye, porcelain fang, all ambles, trundles, strides in terrible prides through continents as yet unmanned, by seas as yet unsalted, a billion years lost away. They *do* breathe. They *do* smite air with thunders. Oh, uncanny!

I feel, thought Terwilliger, quite simply, that there stands *my* Garden, and these my animal creations which I love on this Sixth Day, and tomorrow, the Seventh, I must rest.

'Lord,' said the soft voice again.

Terwilliger almost answered, 'Yes?'

'This is beautiful footage, Mr Clarence,' the voice went on.

'Maybe,' said the man with a boy's voice.

'Incredible animation.'

'I've seen better,' said Clarence the Great.

Terwilliger stiffened. He turned from the screen where his friends lumbered into oblivion, from butcheries wrought on architectural scales. For the first time he examined his possible employers.

'Beautiful stuff.'

This praise came from the old man who sat by himself far across the theatre, his head lifted forward in amaze towards that ancient life.

'It's jerky. Look there!' The strange boy in the middle loge half rose, pointing with the cigarette in his mouth. 'Hey, was *that* a bad shot? You *see*?'

'Yes,' said the old man, tired suddenly, fading back in his chair. 'I see.'

Terwilliger crammed his hotness down upon a suffocation of swiftly moving blood.

'Jerky,' said Joe Clarence.

White light, quick numerals, darkness; the music cut, the monsters vanished.

'Glad that's over,' Joe Clarence exhaled. 'Almost lunchtime. Throw on the next reel. Walter! That's all, Terwilliger.' Silence. 'Terwilliger?' Silence. 'Is that dumb bunny still here?'

'Here,' Terwilliger ground his fists on his hips.

'Oh,' said Joe Clarence. 'It's not bad. But don't get ideas about money. A dozen guys came here yesterday to show stuff as good or better than yours, tests for our new film, *Prehistoric Monster*. Leave your bid in an envelope with my secretary. Same door out as you came in. Walter, what the hell you waiting for? Roll the next one!'

In darkness, Terwilliger barked his shins on a chair, groped for and found the door handle, gripped it tight, tight.

Behind him the screen exploded; an avalanche fell in great flourings of stone, whole cities of granite, immense edifices of marble piled, broke and flooded down. In this thunder, he heard voices from the week ahead:

'We'll pay you one thousand dollars, Terwilliger.'

'But I need a thousand for my equipment alone!'

'Look, we're giving you a break. Take it or leave it!'

With the thunder dying, he knew he would take, and he knew he would hate it.

Only when the avalanche had drained off to silence behind him and his own blood had raced to the inevitable decision and stalled in his heart, did Terwilliger pull the immensely weighted door wide to step forth into the terrible raw light of day.

Fuse flexible spine to sinuous neck, pivot neck to death's-head skull, hinge jaw from hollow cheek, glue plastic sponge over lubricated skeleton, slip snake-pebbled skin over sponge, meld seams with fire, then rear upright triumphant in a world where insanity wakes but to look on madness — Tyrannosaurus Rex!

The Creator's hands glided down out of arc-light sun. They placed the granuled monster in false green summer wilds, they waded it in broths of teeming bacterial life. Planted in serene terror, the lizard machine basked. From the blind heavens the Creator's voice hummed, vibrating the Garden with the old and monotonous tune about the foot-bone connected to the . . . anklebone, anklebone connected to the . . . legbone, legbone connected to the . . . kneebone, kneebone connected to the . . .

A door burst wide.

Joe Clarence ran in very much like an entire Cub Scout pack. He looked wildly around as if no one were there.

'My God!' he cried. 'Aren't you set up yet? This costs me money!'

'No,' said Terwilliger dryly. 'No matter how much time I take, I get paid the same.'

Joe Clarence approached in a series of quick starts and stops. 'Well, shake a leg. And make it real horrible.'

Terwilliger was on his knees beside the miniature jungle set. His eyes were on a straight level with his producer's as he said, 'How many feet of blood and gore would you like?'

'Two thousand feet of each!' Clarence laughed in a kind of gasping stutter. 'Let's look.' He grabbed the lizard.

'Careful!'

'Careful?' Clarence turned the ugly beast in careless and non-loving hands. 'It's my monster, ain't it? The contract — '

'The contract says you use this model for exploitation

advertising, but the animal reverts to me after the film's in release.'

'Holy cow,' Clarence waved the monster. 'That's wrong. We just signed the contracts four days ago –'

'It feels like four years.' Terwilliger rubbed his eyes. 'I've been up two nights without sleep finishing this beast so we can start shooting.'

Clarence brushed this aside. 'To hell with the contract. What a slimy trick. It's my monster. You and your agent give me heart attacks. Heart attacks about money, heart attacks about equipment, heart attacks about –'

'The camera you gave me is ancient.'

'So if it breaks, fix it; you got hands? The challenge of the shoestring operation is using the old brain instead of cash. Getting back to the point, this monster, it should've been specified in the deal, is my baby.'

'I never let anyone own the things I make,' said Terwilliger honestly. 'I put too much time and affection in them.'

'Hell, okay, so we give you fifty bucks extra for the beast, and throw in all this camera equipment free when the film's done, right? Then you start your own company. Compete with me, get even with me, right, using my own machines!' Clarence laughed.

'If they don't fall apart first,' observed Terwilliger.

'Another thing,' Clarence put the creature on the floor and walked around it. 'I don't like the way this monster shapes up.'

'You don't like *what*?' Terwilliger almost yelled.

'His expression. Needs more fire, more . . . goombah. More mazash!'

'Mazash?'

'The old bimbo! Bug the eyes more. Flex the nostrils. Shine the teeth. Fork the tongue sharper. You can *do* it! Uh, the monster ain't mine, huh?'

'Mine.' Terwilliger arose.

His belt buckle was now on a line with Joe Clarence's eyes. The producer stared at the bright buckle almost hypnotically for a moment.

'God damn the goddamn lawyers!'

He broke for the door.

'Work!'

The monster hit the door a split second after it slammed shut.

Terwilliger kept his hand poised in the air from his over-hand throw. Then his shoulders sagged. He went to pick up his beauty. He twisted off its head, skinned the latex fles off the skull, placed the skull on a pedestal and, painstakingly, with clay, began to reshape the prehistoric face.

'A little goombah,' he muttered. 'A touch of mazash.'

They ran the first film test on the animated monster a week later.

When it was over, Clarence sat in darkness and nodded imperceptibly.

'Better. But . . . more horrific, bloodcurdling. Let's scare the hell out of Aunt Jane. Back to the drawing board!'

'I'm a week behind schedule now,' Terwilliger protested. 'You keep coming in, change this, change that, you say, so I change it, one day the tail's all wrong, next day it's the claws — '

'You'll find a way to make me happy,' said Clarence. 'Get in there and fight the old aesthetic fight!'

At the end of the month they ran the second test.

'A near miss! Close!' said Clarence. 'The face is just almost right. Try again, Terwilliger!'

Terwilliger went back. He animated the dinosaur's mouth so that it said obscene things which only a lip reader might catch, while the rest of the audience would think the beast was only shrieking. Then he got the clay and worked until 3 a.m. on the awful face.

'That's it!' cried Clarence in the projection room the next week. 'Perfect! Now *that*'s what I call a monster!'

He leaned towards the old man, his lawyer, Mr Glass, and Maury Poole, his production assistant.

'You *like* my creature?' He beamed.

Terwilliger, slumped in the back row, his skeleton as long as the monsters he built, could feel the old lawyer shrug.

'You seen one monster, you seen 'em all.'

'Sure, sure, but this one's special!' shouted Clarence happily. 'Even *I* got to admit Terwilliger's a genius!'

They all turned back to watch the beast on the screen, in a titanic waltz, throw its razor tail wide in a vicious harvesting that cut grass and clipped flowers. The beast paused now to gaze pensively off into mists, gnawing a red bone.

'That monster,' said Mr Glass at last, squinting. 'He sure looks familiar.'

'Familiar?' Terwilliger stirred alert.

'It's got such a look,' drawled Mr Glass in the dark, 'I couldn't forget, from someplace.'

'Natural Museum exhibits?'

'No, no.'

'Maybe,' laughed Clarence, 'you read a book once, Glass?'

'Funny . . . ' Glass, unperturbed, cocked his head, closed one eye. 'Like detectives, I don't forget a face. But, that Tyrannosaurus Rex — where before did I meet *him*?'

'Who cares?' Clarence sprinted. 'He's great. And all because I booted Terwilliger's behind to make him do it right. Come on, Maury!'

When the door shut, Mr Glass turned to gaze steadily at Terwilliger. Not taking his eyes away, he called softly to the projectionist, 'Walt? Walter? Could you favour us with that beast again?'

'Sure thing.'

Terwilliger shifted uncomfortably, aware of some bleak force gathering in blackness, in the sharp light that shot forth once more to ricochet terror off the screen.

'Yeah. Sure,' mused Mr Glass. 'I almost remember. I almost know him. But . . . *who*?'

The brute, as if answering, turned and for a disdainful moment stared across one hundred thousand million years at two small men hidden in a small dark room. The tyrant machine named itself in thunder.

Mr Glass quickened forward, as if to cup his ear.

Darkness swallowed all.

With the film half finished, in the tenth week, Clarence summoned thirty of the office staff, technicians and a few friends to see a rough cut of the picture.

The film had been running fifteen minutes when a gasp ran through the small audience.

Clarence glanced swiftly about.

Mr Glass, next to him, stiffened.

Terwilliger, scenting danger, lingered near the exit, not knowing why; his nervousness was compulsive and intuitive. Hand on the door, he watched.

Another gasp ran through the crowd.

Someone laughed quietly. A woman secretary giggled. Then there was instantaneous silence.

For Joe Clarence had jumped to his feet.

His tiny figure sliced across the light on the screen. For a moment, two images gesticulated in the dark: Tyrannosaurus, ripping the leg from a pteranodon, and Clarence, yelling, jumping forward as if to grapple with these fantastic wrestlers.

'Stop! Freeze it right there!'

The film stopped. The image held.

'What's wrong?' asked Mr Glass.

'Wrong?' Clarence crept up on the image. He thrust his baby hand to the screen, stabbed the tyrant jaw, the lizard eye, the fangs, the brow, then turned blindly to the projector light so that reptilian flesh was printed on his furious cheeks. 'What goes? What *is* this?'

'Only a monster, Chief.'

'Monster, hell!' Clarence pounded the screen with his tiny fists. 'That's *me*!'

Half the people leaned forward, half the people fell back, two people jumped up, one of them Mr Glass, who fumbled for his other spectacles, flexed his eyes and moaned, 'So *that's* where I saw him before!'

'That's where you what?'

Mr Glass shook his head, eyes shut. 'That face, I *knew* it was familiar.'

A wind blew in the room.

Everyone turned. The door stood open.

Terwilliger was gone.

They found Terwilliger in his animation studio cleaning out his desk, dumping everything into a large cardboard box, the Tyrannosaurus machine-toy-model under his arm. He looked up as the mob swirled in, Clarence at the head.

'What did I do to deserve this!' he cried.

'I'm sorry, Mr Clarence.'

'You're sorry?! Didn't I pay you well?'

'No, as a matter of fact.'

'I took you to lunches —'

'Once. I picked up the tab.'

'I gave you dinner at home, you swam in my pool, and now *this*! You're fired!'

'You can't fire me, Mr Clarence. I've worked the last week free and overtime, you forgot my cheque —'

'You're fired anyway, oh, you're *really* fired! You're blackballed in Hollywood. Mr Glass!' He whirled to find the old man. 'Sue him!'

'There's nothing,' said Terwilliger, not looking up any

more, just looking down, packing, keeping in motion, 'nothing you can sue me for. Money? You never paid enough to save on. A house? Could never afford that. A wife? I've worked for people like you all my life. So wives are out. I'm an unencumbered man. There's nothing you can do to me. If you attach my dinosaurs, I'll just go hole up in a small town somewhere, get me a can of latex rubber, some clay from the river, some old steel pipe, and make new costumes. I'll buy stock film raw and cheap. I've got an old beat-up stop-motion camera. Take that away, and I'll build one with my own hands. I can do anything. And that's why you'll never hurt me again.'

'You're fired!' cried Clarence. 'Look at me. Don't look away. You're fired! You're fired!'

'Mr Clarence,' said Mr Glass, quietly, edging forward. 'Let me talk to him just a moment.'

'So talk to him!' said Clarence. 'What's the use? He just stands there with that monster under his arm and the goddamn thing looks like me, so get out of the way!'

Clarence stormed out the door. The others followed.

Mr Glass shut the door, walked over to the window and looked out at the absolutely clear twilight sky.

'I wish it would rain,' he said. 'That's one thing about California I can't forgive. It never really let's go and cries. Right now, what wouldn't I give for a little something from that sky? A bolt of lightning, even.'

He stood silent, and Terwilliger slowed in his packing. Mr Glass sagged down into a chair and doodled on a pad with a pencil, talking sadly, half aloud, to himself.

'Six reels of film shot, pretty good reels, half the film done, three hundred thousand dollars down the drain, hail and farewell. Out the window all the jobs. Who feeds the starving mouths of boys and girls? Who will face the stockholders? Who chucks the Bank of America under the chin? Anyone for Russian roulette?'

He turned to watch Terwilliger snap the locks on a brief-case.

'What hath God wrought?'

Terwilliger, looking down at his hands, turning them over to examine their texture, said, 'I didn't know I was doing it, I swear. It came out in my fingers. It was all subconscious. My fingers do everything for me. They did *this*.'

'Better the fingers had come in my office and taken me direct by the throat,' said Glass. 'I was never one for slow motion. The Keystone Kops, at triple speed, was my idea of living, or dying. To think a rubber monster has stepped on us all. We are now so much tomato mush, ripe for canning!'

'Don't make me feel any guiltier than I feel,' said Terwilliger.

'What do you want, I should take you dancing?'

'It's just,' cried Terwilliger, 'he kept at me. Do this. Do that. Do it the other way. Turn it inside out, upside down, he said. I swallowed my bile. I was angry all the time. Without knowing, I must've changed the face. But right up till five minutes ago, when Mr Clarence yelled, I didn't see it. I'll take all the blame.'

'No,' sighed Mr Glass, 'we should *all* have seen. Maybe we did and couldn't admit. Maybe we did and laughed all night in our sleep, when we couldn't hear. So where are we now? Mr Clarence, he's got investments he can't throw out. You got your career from this day forward, for better or worse, you can't throw out. Mr Clarence right now is aching to be convinced it was all some horrible dream. Part of his ache, ninety-nine per cent, is in his wallet. If you could put one per cent of your time in the next hour convincing him of what I'm going to tell you next, tomorrow morning there will be no orphan children staring out of the want ads in *Variety* and *The Hollywood Reporter*. If you would go tell him —'

'Tell me *what*?'

Joe Clarence, returned, stood in the door, his cheeks still inflamed.

'What he just told me,' Mr Glass turned calmly. 'A touching story.'

'I'm listening!' said Clarence.

'Mr Clarence.' The old lawyer weighed his words carefully. 'This film you just saw is Mr Terwilliger's solemn and silent tribute to you.'

'It's *what*?' shouted Clarence.

Both men, Clarence and Terwilliger, dropped their jaws.

The old lawyer gazed only at the wall and in a shy voice said, 'Shall I go on?'

The animator closed his jaw. 'If you want to.'

'This film' — the lawyer arose and pointed in a single motion towards the projection room — 'was done from a feeling of honour and friendship for you, Joe Clarence. Behind your desk, an unsung hero of the motion picture industry, unknown, unseen, you sweat out your lonely little life while who gets the glory? The stars. How often does a man in Atawanda Springs, Idaho, tell his wife, "Say, I was thinking the other night about Joe Clarence — a great producer, that man"? How often? Should I tell? Never! So Terwilliger brooded. How could he present the real Clarence to the world? The dinosaur is there; boom! it hits him! This is it! he thought, the very thing to strike terror to the world, here's a lonely, proud, wonderful, awful symbol of independence, power, strength, shrewd animal cunning, the true democrat, the individual brought to its peak, all thunder and big lightning. Dinosaur: Joe Clarence. Joe Clarence: Dinosaur. Man embodied in Tyrant Lizard!'

Mr Glass sat down, panting quietly.

Terwilliger said nothing.

Clarence moved at last, walked across the room, circled Glass slowly, then came to stand in front of Terwilliger, his face pale. His eyes were uneasy, shifting up along

Terwilliger's tall skeleton frame.

'You said *that*?' he asked faintly.

Terwilliger swallowed.

'To me, he said it. He's shy,' said Mr Glass. 'You ever hear him say much, ever talk back? swear? anything? He likes people, he can't say. But, immortalize them? That he can do!'

'Immortalize?' said Clarence.

'What else?' said the old man. 'Like a statue, only moving. Years from now people will say, "Remember that film, *The Monster from the Pleistocene*?" And people will say, "Sure! why?" "Because," the others say, "it was the one monster, the one brute, in all Hollywood history had real guts, real personality. And why is this? Because one genius had enough imagination to base the creature on a real-life, hard-hitting, fast-thinking businessman of A-one calibre." You're one with history, Mr Clarence. Film libraries will carry you in good supply. Cinema societies will ask for you. How lucky can you get? Nothing like this will ever happen to Immanuel Glass, a lawyer. Every day for the next two hundred, five hundred years, you'll be starring somewhere in the world!'

'*Every* day?' asked Clarence softly. 'For the next —'

'Eight hundred, even; why not?'

'I never thought of that.'

'Think of it!'

Clarence walked over to the window and looked out at the Hollywood Hills, and nodded at last.

'My God, Terwilliger,' he said. 'You really like me *that* much?'

'It's hard to put in words,' said Terwilliger, with difficulty.

'So do we finish the mighty spectacle?' asked Glass. 'Starring the tyrant terror striding the earth and making all quake before him, none other than Mr Joseph J. Clarence?'

'Yeah. Sure.' Clarence wandered off, stunned, to the door,

where he said, 'You know? I always *wanted* to be an actor!'

Then he went quietly out into the hall and shut the door.

Terwilliger and Glass collided at the desk, both clawing at a drawer.

'Age before beauty,' said the lawyer, and quickly pulled forth a bottle of whisky.

At midnight on the night of the first preview of *Monster from the Stone Age*, Mr Glass came back to the studio, where everyone was gathering for a celebration, and found Terwilliger seated alone in his office, his dinosaur on his lap.

'You weren't *there*?' asked Mr Glass.

'I couldn't face it. Was there a riot?'

'A riot? The preview cards are all superdandy extra plus! A lovelier monster nobody saw before! So now, we're talking sequels! Joe Clarence as the Tyrant Lizard in *Return of the Stone-Age Monster*, Joe Clarence and/or Tyrannosaurus Rex in, maybe, *Beast from the Old Country* – '

The phone rang. Terwilliger got it.

'Terwilliger, this is Clarence! Be there in five minutes! We've done it! Your animal! Great! Is he mine now? I mean, to hell with the contract, as a favour, can I have him for the mantel?'

'Mr Clarence, the monster's yours.'

'Better than an Oscar! So long!'

Terwilliger stared at the dead phone.

'God bless us all, said Tiny Tim. He's laughing, almost hysterical with relief.'

'So maybe I know why,' said Mr Glass. 'A little girl after the preview, asked him for an autograph.'

'An *autograph*?'

'Right there in the street. Made him sign. First autograph he ever gave in his life. He laughed all the while he wrote his name. Somebody knew him. There he was, in front of the theatre, big as life, Rex Himself, so sign the name. So he did.'

'Wait a minute,' said Terwilliger slowly, pouring drinks. 'That little girl . . . ?'

'My youngest daughter,' said Glass. 'So who knows? And who will tell?'

They drank.

'Not me,' said Terwilliger.

Then, carrying the rubber dinosaur between them, and bringing the whisky, they went to stand by the studio gate, waiting for the limousines to arrive all lights, horns and annunciations.

The Screaming Woman

My name is Margaret Leary and I'm ten years old and in the fifth grade at Central School. I haven't any brothers or sisters, but I've got a nice father and mother except they don't pay much attention to me. And anyway, we never thought we'd have anything to do with a murdered woman. Or almost, anyway.

When you're just living on a street like we live on, you don't think awful things are going to happen, like shooting or stabbing or burying people under the ground, practically in your back yard. And when it does happen you don't believe it. You just go on buttering your toast or baking a cake.

I got to tell you how it happened. It was a noon in the middle of July. It was hot and Mama said to me, 'Margaret, you go to the store and buy some ice cream. It's Saturday. Dad's home for lunch, so we'll have a treat.'

I ran out across the empty lot behind our house. It was a big lot, where kids had played baseball, and broken glass and stuff. And on my way back from the store with the ice cream I was just walking along, minding my own business, when all of a sudden it happened.

I heard the Screaming Woman.

I stopped and listened.

It was coming up out of the ground.

A woman was buried under the rocks and dirt and glass, and she was screaming, all wild and horrible, for someone to dig her out.

I just stood there, afraid. She kept screaming, muffled.

Then I started to run. I fell down, got up, and ran some more. I got in the screen door of my house and there was

Mama, calm as you please, not knowing what I knew, that there was a real live woman buried out in the back of our house, just a hundred yards away, screaming bloody murder.

'Mama,' I said.

'Don't stand there with the ice cream,' said Mama.

'But, Mama,' I said.

'Put it in the icebox,' she said.

'Listen, Mama, there's a Screaming Woman in the empty lot.'

'And wash your hands,' said Mama.

'She was screaming and screaming . . .'

'Let's see, now, salt and pepper,' said Mama, far away.

'Listen to me,' I said loud. 'We got to dig her out. She's buried under tons and tons of dirt and if we don't dig her out, she'll choke up and die.'

'I'm certain she can wait until after lunch,' said Mama.

'Mama, don't you believe me?'

'Of course, dear. Now wash your hands and take this plate of meat in to your father.'

'I don't even know who she is or how she got there,' I said. 'But we got to help her before it's too late.'

'Good gosh,' said Mama. 'Look at this ice-cream. What did you do, just stand in the sun and let it melt?'

'Well, the empty lot . . .'

'Go on, now, scoot.'

I went into the dining room.

'Hi, Dad, there's a Screaming Woman in the empty lot.'

'I never knew a woman who didn't,' said Dad.

'I'm serious,' I said.

'You look very grave,' said Father.

'We've got to get picks and shovels and excavate, like for an Egyptian mummy,' I said.

'I don't feel like an archaeologist, Margaret,' said Father. 'Now, some nice cool October day, I'll take you up on that.'

'But we can't wait that long,' I almost screamed. My heart

was bursting in me. I was excited and scared and afraid and here was Dad, putting meat on his plate, cutting and chewing and paying no attention.

'Dad?' I said.

'Mmmmm?' he said, chewing.

'Dad, you just gotta come out after lunch and help me,' I said. 'Dad, Dad, I'll give you all the money in my piggy bank!'

'Well,' said Dad. 'So it's a business proposition, is it? It must be important for you to offer your perfectly good money. How much money will you pay, by the hour?'

'I got five whole dollars it took me a year to save, and it's all yours.'

Dad touched my arm. 'I'm touched, I'm really touched. You want me to play with you and you're willing to pay for my time. Honest, Margaret, you make your old Dad feel like a piker. I don't give you enough time. Tell you what, after lunch, I'll come out and listen to your Screaming Woman, free of charge.'

'Will you, oh, will you, really?'

'Yes, ma'am, that's what I'll do,' said Dad. 'But you must promise me one thing?'

'What?'

'If I come out, you must eat all of your lunch first.'

'I promise,' I said.

'Okay.'

Mother came in and sat down and we started to eat.

'Not so fast,' said Mama.

I slowed down. Then I started eating fast again.

'You heard your mother,' said Dad.

'The Screaming Woman,' I said. 'We got to hurry.'

'I,' said Father, 'intend sitting here quietly and judiciously giving my attention first to my steak, then to my potatoes, and my salad, of course, and then to my ice cream, and after that to a long drink of iced coffee, if you don't mind. I may be a good hour at it. And another thing, young lady, if you mention her name, this Screaming Whatsis, once more at this table during lunch, I won't go out with you to hear her recital.'

'Yes, sir.'

'Is that understood?'

'Yes, sir,' I said.

Lunch was a million years long. Everybody moved in slow motion, like those films you see at the movies. Mama got up slow and down slow and forks and knives and spoons moved slow. Even the flies in the room were slow. And Dad's cheek muscles moved slow. It was so slow. I wanted to scream, 'Hurry! Oh, please, rush, get up, run around, come on out, run!'

But no, I had to sit, and all the while we sat there slowly, slowly eating our lunch, out there in the empty lot (I could hear her screaming in my mind. *Scream!*) was the Screaming Woman, all alone, while the world ate its lunch and the sun was hot and the lot was empty as the sky.

'There we are,' said Dad, finished at last.

'Now will you come out to see the Screaming Woman?' I said.

'First a little more iced coffee,' said Dad.

'Speaking of Screaming Women,' said Mother, 'Charlie Nesbitt and his wife Helen had another fight last night.'

'That's nothing new,' said Father. 'They're always fighting.'

'If you ask me, Charlie's no good,' said Mother. 'Or her either.'

'Oh, I don't know,' said Dad. 'I think she's pretty nice.'

'You're prejudiced. After all, you almost married her.'

'You going to bring that up again?' he said. 'After all, I was only engaged to her six weeks.'

'You showed some sense when you broke it off.'

'Oh, you know Helen. Always stagestruck. Wanted to

travel in a trunk. I just couldn't see it. That broke it up. She was sweet, though. Sweet and kind.'

'What did it get her? A terrible brute of a husband like Charlie.'

'Dad,' I said.

'I'll give you that, Charlie has got a terrible temper,' said Dad. 'Remember when Helen had the lead in our high school graduation play? Pretty as a picture. She wrote some songs for it herself. That was the summer she wrote that song for me.'

'Ha,' said Mother.

'Don't laugh. It was a good song.'

'You never told me about that song.'

'It was between Helen and me. Let's see, how *did* it *go*?'

'Dad,' I said.

'You'd better take your daughter out in the back lot,' said Mother, 'before she collapses. You can sing me that wonderful song later.'

'Okay, come on, you,' said Dad, and I ran him out of the house.

The empty lot was still empty and hot and the glass sparkled green and white and brown all around where the bottles lay.

'Now, where's this Screaming Woman?' laughed Dad.

'We forgot the shovels,' I cried.

'We'll get them later, after we hear the soloist,' said Dad.

I took him over to the spot. 'Listen,' I said.

We listened.

'I don't hear anything,' said Dad, at last.

'Shh,' I said. 'Wait.'

We listened some more. 'Hey, there, Screaming Woman!' I cried.

We heard the sun in the sky. We heard the wind in the trees, real quiet. We heard a bus, far away, running along. We heard a car pass.

That was all.

'Margaret,' said Father. 'I suggest you go lie down and put a damp cloth on your forehead.'

'But she was here,' I shouted. 'I heard her, screaming, and screaming and screaming. See, here's where the ground's been dug up.' I called frantically at the earth. 'Hey, there, you down there!'

'Margaret,' said Father. 'This is the place where Mr Kelly dug yesterday, a big hole, to bury his trash and garbage in.'

'But during the night,' I said, 'someone else used Mr Kelly's burying place to bury a woman. And covered it all over again.'

'Well, I'm going back in and take a cool shower,' said Dad.

'You won't help me dig?'

'Better not stay out here too long,' said Dad. 'It's hot.'

Dad walked off. I heard the back door slam.

I stamped on the ground. 'Darn,' I said.

The screaming started again.

She screamed and screamed. Maybe she had been tired and was resting and now she began it all over, just for me.

I stood in the empty lot in the hot sun and I felt like crying. I ran back to the house and banged the door.

'Dad, she's screaming again!'

'Sure, sure,' said Dad. 'Come on.' And he led me to my upstairs bedroom. 'Here,' he said. He made me lie down and put a cold rag on my head. 'Just take it easy.'

I began to cry. 'Oh, Dad, we can't let her die. She's all buried, like that person in that story by Edgar Allan Poe, and think how awful it is to be screaming and no one paying any attention.'

'I forbid you to leave the house,' said Dad, worried. 'You just lie there the rest of the afternoon.' He went out and locked the door. I heard him and Mother talking in the front room. After a while I stopped crying. I got up and tiptoed to the window. My room was upstairs. It seemed high.

I took a sheet off the bed and tied it to the bedpost and let it out the window. Then I climbed out the window and shinnied down until I touched the ground. Then I ran to the garage, quiet, and I got a couple of shovels and I ran to the empty lot. It was hotter than ever. And I started to dig, and all the while I dug, the Screaming Woman screamed . . .

It was hard work. Shoving in the shovel and lifting the rocks and glass. And I knew I'd be doing it all afternoon and maybe I wouldn't finish in time. What could I do? Run tell other people? But they'd be like Mom and Dad, pay no attention. I just kept digging, all by myself.

About ten minutes later, Dippy Smith came along the path through the empty lot. He's my age and goes to my school.

'Hi, Margaret,' he said.

'Hi, Dippy,' I gasped.

'What you doing?' he asked.

'Digging.'

'For what?'

'I got a Screaming Lady in the ground and I'm digging for her,' I said.

'I don't hear no screaming,' said Dippy.

'You sit down and wait awhile and you'll hear her scream yet. Or better still, help me dig.'

'I don't dig unless I hear a scream,' he said.

We waited.

'Listen!' I cried. 'Did you *hear* it?'

'Hey,' said Dippy, with slow appreciation, his eyes gleaming. 'That's okay. Do it again.'

'Do what again?'

'The scream.'

'We got to wait,' I said, puzzled.

'Do it again,' he insisted, shaking my arm. 'Go on.' He dug in his pocket for a brown aggie. 'Here.' He shoved it at me. 'I'll give you this marble if you do it again.'

A scream came out of the ground.

'Hot dog!' said Dippy. 'Teach *me* to do it!' He danced around as if I was a miracle.

'I don't . . . ' I started to say.

'Did you get the *Throw-Your-Voice* book for a dime from the Magic Company in Dallas, Texas?' cried Dippy. 'You got one of those tin ventriloquist contraptions in your mouth?'

'Y-yes,' I lied, for I wanted him to help. 'If you'll help me dig, I'll tell you about it later.'

'Swell,' he said. 'Give me a shovel.'

We both dug together, and from time to time the woman screamed.

'Boy,' said Dippy. 'You'd think she was right under foot. You're wonderful, Maggie.' Then he said, 'What's her name?'

'Who?'

'The Screaming Woman. You must have a name for her.'

'Oh, sure.' I thought a moment. 'Her name's Wilma Schweiger and she's a rich old woman, ninety-six years old, and she was buried by a man named Spike, who counterfeited ten-dollar bills.'

'Yes, *sir*,' said Dippy.

'And there's hidden treasure buried with her, and I, I'm a grave robber come to dig her out and get it,' I gasped, digging excitedly.

Dippy made his eyes Oriental and mysterious. 'Can I be a grave robber, too?' He had a better idea. 'Let's pretend it's the Princess Ommanatra, an Egyptian queen, covered with diamonds!'

We kept digging and I thought, Oh, we will rescue her, we *will*. If only we keep on!

'Hey, I just got an idea,' said Dippy. And he ran off and got a piece of cardboard. He scribbled on it with crayon.

'Keep digging!' I said. 'We can't stop!'

'I'm making a sign. See? SLUMBERLAND CEMETERY! We can bury some birds and beetles here, in matchboxes and stuff. I'll go find some butterflies.'

'No, Dippy!'

'It's more fun that way. I'll get me a dead cat, too, maybe . . . '

'Dippy, use your shovel! Please!'

'Aw,' said Dippy. 'I'm tired. I think I'll go home and take a nap.'

'You can't do that.'

'Who says so?'

'Dippy, there's something I want to tell you.'

'What?'

He gave the shovel a kick.

I whispered in his ear. 'There's really a woman buried here.'

'Why sure there is,' he said. 'You said it, Maggie.'

'You don't believe me, either.'

'Tell me how you throw your voice and I'll keep on digging.'

'But I can't tell you, because I'm not doing it,' I said. 'Look, Dippy, I'll stand way over here and you listen there.'

The Screaming Woman screamed again.

'Hey!' said Dippy. 'There really *is* a woman here!'

'That's what I tried to say.'

'Let's dig!' said Dippy.

We dug for twenty minutes.

'I wonder who she is?'

'I don't know.'

'I wonder if it's Mrs Nelson or Mrs Turner or Mrs Bradley. I wonder is she's pretty. Wonder what colour her hair is? Wonder if she's thirty or ninety or sixty?'

'Dig!' I said.

The mound grew high.

'Wonder if she'll reward us for digging her up.'

'Sure.'

'A quarter, do you think?'

'More than that. I bet it's a dollar.'

Dippy remembered as he dug, 'I read a book once of magic. There was a Hindu with no clothes on who crept down in a grave and slept there sixty days, not eating anything, no malts, no chewing gum or candy, no air, for sixty days.' His face fell. 'Say, wouldn't it be awful if it was only a radio buried here and us working so hard?'

'A radio's nice, it'd be all ours.'

Just then a shadow fell across us.

'Hey, you kids, what you think you're doing?'

We turned. It was Mr Kelly, the man who owned the empty lot. 'Oh, hello, Mr Kelly,' we said.

'Tell you what I want you to do,' said Mr Kelly. 'I want you to take those shovels and take that soil and shovel it right back in that hole you been digging. That's what I want you to do.'

My heart started beating fast again. I wanted to scream myself.

'But Mr Kelly, there's a Screaming Woman and . . . '

'I'm not interested. I don't hear a thing.'

'Listen!' I cried.

The scream.

Mr Kelly listened and shook his head. 'Don't hear nothing. Go on now, fill it up and get home with you before I give you my foot!'

We filled the hole all back in again. And all the while we filled it, Mr Kelly stood there, arms folded, and the woman screamed, but Mr Kelly pretended not to hear it.

When we were finished, Mr Kelly stomped off, saying, 'Go on home now. And if I catch you here again . . . '

I turned to Dippy. 'He's the one,' I whispered.

'Huh?' said Dippy.

'He *murdered* Mrs Kelly. He buried her here, after he strangled her, in a box, but she came to. Why, he stood right here and she screamed and he wouldn't pay any attention.'

'Hey,' said Dippy. 'That's right. He stood right here and lied to us.'

'There's only one thing to do,' I said. 'Call the police and have them come arrest Mr Kelly.'

We ran for the corner store telephone.

The police knocked on Mr Kelly's door five minutes later. Dippy and I were hiding in the bushes, listening.

'Mr Kelly?' said the police officer.

'Yes, sir, what can I do for you?'

'Is Mrs Kelly at home?'

'Yes, sir.'

'May we see her, sir?'

'Of course. Hey, Anna!'

Mrs Kelly came to the door and looked out. 'Yes, sir?'

'I beg your pardon,' apologized the officer. 'We had a report that you were buried out in an empty lot, Mrs Kelly. It sounded like a child made the call, but we had to be certain. Sorry to have troubled you.'

'It's those blasted kids,' cried Mr Kelly, angrily. 'If I ever catch them, I'll rip them limb from limb!'

'Cheezit!' said Dippy, and we both ran.

'What'll we do now?' I said.

'I got to go home,' said Dippy. 'Boy, we're really in trouble. We'll get a licking for this.'

'But what about the Screaming Woman?'

'To heck with her,' said Dippy. 'We don't dare go near that empty lot again. Old man Kelly'll be waiting around with his razor strap and lambast heck out'n us. And I just happened to remember, Maggie. Ain't old man Kelly sort of deaf, hard-of-hearing?'

'Oh, my gosh,' I said. 'No *wonder* he didn't hear the screams.'

'So long,' said Dippy. 'We sure got in trouble over your darn old ventriloquist voice. I'll be seeing you.'

I was left all alone in the world, no one to help me, no one to believe me at all. I just wanted to crawl down in that box with the Screaming Woman and die. The police were after me now, for lying to them, only I didn't know it was a lie, and my father was probably looking for me, too, or would be once he found my bed empty. There was only one last thing to do, and I did it.

I went from house to house, all down the street, near the empty lot. And I rang every bell and when the door opened I said: 'I beg your pardon, Mrs Griswold, but is anyone missing from your house?' or 'Hello, Mrs Pikes, you're looking fine today. Glad to see you *home*.' And once I saw that the lady of the house was home I just chatted awhile to be polite, and went on down the street.

The hours were rolling along. It was getting late. I kept thinking, oh, there's only so much air in that box with that woman under the earth, and if I don't hurry, she'll suffocate, and I got to rush! So I rang bells and knocked on doors, and it got later, and I was just about to give up and go home, when I knocked on the *last* door, which was the door of Mr Charlie Nesbitt, who lives next to us. I kept knocking and knocking.

Instead of Mrs Nesbitt, or Helen as my father calls her, coming to the door, why it was Mr Nesbitt, Charlie, *himself*.

'Oh,' he said. 'It's you, Margaret.'

'Yes,' I said. 'Good afternoon.'

'What can I do for you, kid?' he said.

'Well, I thought I'd like to see your wife, Mrs Nesbitt,' I said.

'Oh,' he said.

'May I?'

'Well, she's gone out to the store,' he said.

'I'll wait,' I said, and slipped in past him.

'Hey,' he said.

I sat down in a chair. 'My, it's a hot day,' I said, trying to be calm, thinking about the empty lot and air going out of the box, and the screams getting weaker and weaker.

'Say, listen, kid,' said Charlie, coming over to me, 'I don't think you better wait.'

'Oh, sure,' I said. 'Why not?'

'Well, my wife won't be back,' he said.

'Oh?'

'Not today, that is. She's gone to the store, like I said, but, but, she's going on from there to visit her mother. Yeah. She's going to visit her mother, in Schenectady. She'll be back, two or three days, maybe a week.'

'That's a shame,' I said.

'Why?'

'I wanted to tell her something.'

'What?'

'I just wanted to tell her there's a woman buried over in the empty lot, screaming under tons and tons of dirt.'

Mr Nesbitt dropped his cigarette.

'You dropped your cigarette, Mr Nesbitt,' I pointed out, with my shoe.

'Oh, did I? Sure. So I did,' he mumbled. 'Well, I'll tell Helen when she comes home, your story. She'll be glad to hear it.'

'Thanks. It's a real woman.'

'How do you know it is?'

'I heard her.'

'How, how you know it isn't, well, a *mandrake* root?'

'What's that?'

'You know. A mandrake. It's a kind of a plant, kid. They scream. I know, I read it once. How you know it ain't a mandrake?'

'I never thought of that.'

'You better start thinking,' he said, lighting another cigarette. He tried to be casual. 'Say, kid, you, eh, you *say* anything about this to anyone?'

'Sure. I told lots of people.'

Mr Nesbitt burned his hand on his match.

'Anybody doing anything about it?' he asked.

'No,' I said. 'They won't believe me.'

He smiled. 'Of course. Naturally. You're nothing but a kid. Why should they listen to you?'

'I'm going back now and dig her out with a spade,' I said.

'Wait.'

'I got to go,' I said.

'Stick around,' he insisted.

'Thanks, but no,' I said, frantically.

He took my arm. 'Know how to play cards, kid? Black jack?'

'Yes, sir.'

He took out a deck of cards from a desk. 'We'll have a game.'

'I got to go dig.'

'Plenty of time for that,' he said, quiet. 'Anyway, maybe my wife'll be home. Sure. That's it. You wait for her. Wait awhile.'

'You think she will be?'

'Sure, kid. Say, about that voice; is it very strong?'

'It gets weaker all the time.'

Mr Nesbitt sighed and smiled. 'You and your kid games. Here now, let's play that game of black jack, it's more fun than Screaming Women.'

'I got to go. It's late.'

'Stick around, you got nothing to do.'

I knew what he was trying to do. He was trying to keep me in his house until the screaming died down and was gone. He was trying to keep me from helping her. 'My wife'll be home in ten minutes,' he said. 'Sure. Ten minutes. You wait. You sit right there.'

We played cards. The clock ticked. The sun went down the sky. It was getting late. The screaming got fainter and fainter in my mind. 'I got to go,' I said.

'Another game,' said Mr Nesbitt. 'Wait another hour, kid.

My wife'll come yet. Wait.'

In another hour he looked at his watch. 'Well, kid, I guess you can go now.' And I knew what his plan was. He'd sneak down in the middle of the night and dig up his wife, still alive, and take her somewhere else and bury her, good. 'So long, kid. So long.' He let me go, because he thought that by now the air must all be gone from the box.

The door shut in my face.

I went back near the empty lot and hid in some bushes. What could I do? Tell my folks? But they hadn't believed me. Call the police on Mr Charlie Nesbitt? But he said his wife was away visiting. Nobody would believe me!

I watched Mr Kelly's house. He wasn't in sight. I ran over to the place where the screaming had been and just stood there.

The screaming had stopped. It was so quiet I thought I would never hear a scream again. It was all over. I was too late, I thought.

I bent down and put my ear to the ground.

And then I heard it, way down, way deep, and so faint I could hardly hear it.

The woman wasn't screaming any more. She was singing.

Something about, 'I loved you fair, I loved you well.'

It was sort of a sad song. Very faint. And sort of broken. All of those hours down under the ground in that box must have sort of made her crazy. All she needed was some air and food and she'd be all right. But she just kept singing, not wanting to scream any more, not caring, just singing.

I listened to the song.

And then I turned and walked straight across the lot and up the steps to my house and I opened the front door.

'Father,' I said.

'So there you are!' he cried.

'Father,' I said.

'You're going to get a licking,' he said.

'She's not screaming any more.'

'Don't talk about her!'

'She's singing now,' I cried.

'You're not telling the truth!'

'Dad,' I said. 'She's out there and she'll be dead soon if you don't listen to me. She's out there, singing, and this is what she's singing.' I hummed the tune. I sang a few of the words. 'I loved you fair, I loved you well . . . '

Dad's face grew pale. He came and took my arm.

'What did you say?' he said.

I sang it again: 'I loved you fair, I loved you well.'

'Where did you *hear* that song?' he shouted.

'Out in the empty lot, just now.'

'But that's *Helen's* song, the one she wrote, years ago, for *me*!' cried Father. 'You *can't* know it. *Nobody* knew it, except Helen and me. I never sang it to anyone, not you or anyone.'

'Sure,' I said.

'Oh, my God!' cried Father, and ran out the door to get a shovel. The last I saw of him he was in the empty lot, digging, and lots of other people with him, digging.

I felt so happy I wanted to cry.

I dialled a number on the phone and when Dippy answered I said, 'Hi, Dippy. Everything's fine. Everything's worked out keen. The Screaming Woman isn't screaming any more.'

'Swell,' said Dippy.

'I'll meet you in the empty lot with a shovel in two minutes,' I said.

'Last one there's a monkey! So long!' cried Dippy.

'So long, Dippy!' I said, and ran.

The Terrible Conflagration
up at the Place

The men had been hiding down by the gatekeeper's lodge for half an hour or so, passing a bottle of the best between, and then, the gatekeeper having been carried off to bed, they dodged up the path at six in the evening and looked at the great house with the warm lights lit in each window.

'That's the place,' said Riordan.

'Hell, what do you mean, "That's the place"?' cried Casey, then softly added, 'We seen it all our lives.'

'Sure,' said Kelly, 'but with the Troubles over and around us, sudden-like a place looks *different*. It's quite a toy, lying there in the snow.'

And that's what it seemed to the fourteen of them, a grand playhouse laid out in the softly falling feathers of a spring night.

'Did you bring the matches?' asked Kelly.

'Did I bring the — what do you think I *am*!'

'Well, *did* you, is all I ask.'

Casey searched himself. When his pockets hung from his suit he swore and said, 'I did not.'

'Ah, what the hell,' said Nolan. 'They'll have matches inside. We'll borrow a few. Come on.'

Going up the road, Timulty tripped and fell.

'For God's sake, Timulty,' said Nolan, 'where's your sense of romance? In the midst of a big Easter Rebellion we want to do everything just so. Years from now we want to go into a pub and tell about the Terrible Conflagration up at the Place, do we not? If it's all mucked up with the sight of you landing on your ass in the snow, that makes no fit picture of the Rebellion we are now in, does it?'

Timulty, rising, focused the picture and nodded. 'I'll mind me manners.'

'Hist! Here we are!' cried Riordan.

'Jesus, stop saying things like "That's the place" and "Here we are," ' said Casey. 'We see the damned house. Now what do we do next?'

'Destroy it?' suggested Murphy tentatively.

'Gah, you're so dumb you're hideous,' said Casey. 'Of course we destroy it, but first . . . blueprints and plans.'

'It seemed simple enough back at Hickey's Pub,' said Murphy. 'We would just come tear the damn place down. Seeing as how my wife outweighs me, I need to tear *something* down.'

'It seems to me,' said Timulty, drinking from the bottle, 'we go rap on the door and ask permission.'

'Permission!' said Murphy. 'I'd hate to have you running hell, the lost souls would never get fried! We —'

But the front door swung wide suddenly, cutting him off.

A man peered out into the night.

'I say,' said a gentle and reasonable voice, 'would you mind keeping your voices down. The lady of the house is sleeping before we drive to Dublin for the evening, and —'

The men, revealed in the hearth-light glow of the door, blinked and stood back, lifting their caps.

'Is that you, Lord Kilgotten?'

'It is,' said the man at the door.

'We will keep our voices down,' said Timulty, smiling, all amiability.

'Beg pardon, your Lordship,' said Casey.

'Kind of you,' said his Lordship. And the door closed gently.

All the men gasped.

' "Beg pardon, your Lordship." "We'll keep our voices down, your Lordship." ' Casey slapped his head. 'What

were we saying? Why didn't someone catch the door while he
was still there?'

'We was dumbfounded, that's why; he took us by surprise,
just like them damned high and mighties. I mean, we weren't
doing anything out here, were we?'

'Our voices *were* a bit high,' admitted Timulty.

'Voices, hell,' said Casey. 'The damn Lord's come and
gone from our fell clutches!'

'*Shh*, not so loud,' said Timulty.

Casey lowered his voice. 'So let us sneak up on the door,
and –'

'That strikes me as unnecessary,' said Nolan. 'He *knows*
we're here now.'

'Sneak up on the door,' repeated Casey, grinding his teeth,
'and batter it down –'

The door opened again.

The Lord, a shadow, peered out at them and the soft,
patient, frail old voice inquired, 'I say, what *are* you doing
out there?'

'Well, it's this way, your Lordship –' began Casey, and
stopped, paling.

'We come,' blurted Murphy, 'we come . . . to *burn* the
Place!'

His Lordship stood for a moment looking out at the men,
watching the snow, his hand on the doorknob. He shut his
eyes for a moment, thought, conquered a tic in both eyelids
after a silent struggle, and then said, 'Hmm, well in that case,
you had best come in.'

The men said that was fine, great, good enough, and
started off when Casey cried, 'Wait!' Then to the old man in
the doorway, 'We'll come in, when we are good and ready.'

'Very well,' said the old man. 'I shall leave the door ajar
and when you have decided the time, enter. I shall be in the
library.'

Leaving the door a half inch open, the old man started away when Timulty cried out, 'When we are *ready*? Jesus, God, when will we ever be readier? Out of the way, Casey!'

And they all ran up the porch.

Hearing this, his Lordship turned to look at them with his bland and not-unfriendly face, the face of an old hound who has seen many foxes killed and just as many escape, who has run well, and now in late years, paced himself down to a soft, shuffling walk.

'Scrape your feet, please, gentlemen.'

'Scraped they are.' And everyone carefully got the snow and mud off his shoes.

'This way,' said his Lordship, going off, his clear, pale eyes set in lines and bags and creases from too many years of drinking brandy, his cheeks bright as cherry wine. 'I will get you all a drink, and we shall see what we can do about your . . . how did you put it . . . burning the Place?'

'You're Sweet Reason itself,' admitted Timulty, following as Lord Kilgotten led them into the library, where he poured whiskey all around.

'Gentlemen.' He let his bones sink into a wing-backed chair. 'Drink.'

'We decline,' said Casey.

'Decline?' gasped everyone, the drinks almost in their hands.

'This is a sober thing we are doing and we must be sober for it,' said Casey, flinching from their gaze.

'Who do we listen to?' asked Riordan. 'His Lordship or Casey?'

For answer all the men downed their drinks and fell to coughing and gasping. Courage showed immediately in a red colour through their faces, which they turned so that Casey could see the difference. Casey drank his, to catch up.

Meanwhile, the old man sipped his whiskey, and something about his calm and easy way of drinking put them far out in

Dublin Bay and sank them again. Until Casey said, 'Your Honour, you've heard of the Troubles? I mean not just the Kaiser's war going on across the sea, but our own very great Troubles and the Rebellion that has reached even this far, to our town, our pub, and now, your Place?'

'An alarming amount of evidence convinces me this is an unhappy time,' said his Lordship. 'I suppose what must be must be. I know you all. You have worked for me. I think I have paid you rather well on occasion.'

'There's no doubt of that, your Lordship.' Casey took a step forward. 'It's just, "The old order changeth," and we have heard of the great houses out near Tara and the great manors beyond Killashandra going up in flames to celebrate freedom and —'

'Whose freedom?' asked the old man, mildly. 'Mine? From the burden of caring for this house, which my wife and I rattle around in like dice in a cup or — well, get on. *When* would you like to burn the Place?'

'If it isn't too much trouble, sir,' said Timulty, 'now.'

The old man seemed to sink deeper into his chair.

'Oh, dear,' he said.

'Of course,' said Nolan quickly, 'if it's inconvenient, we could come back later —'

'Later! What kind of talk is *that*?' asked Casey.

'I'm terribly sorry,' said the old man. 'Please allow me to explain. Lady Kilgotten is asleep now, we are going into Dublin for the opening of a play by Synge —'

'That's a damn fine writer,' said Riordan.

'Saw one of his plays a year ago,' said Nolan, 'and —'

'Stand off!' said Casey.

The men stood back. His Lordship went on with his frail moth voice. 'We have a dinner planned back here at midnight for ten people. I don't suppose — you could give us until tomorrow night to get ready?'

'No,' said Casey.

'Hold on,' said everyone else.

'Burning,' said Timulty, 'is one thing, but tickets is another. I mean, the theatre is *there*, and a dire waste not to see the play, and all that food set up, it might as well be eaten. And all the guests coming. It would be hard to notify them ahead.'

'Exactly what *I* was thinking,' said his Lordship.

'Yes, I know!' shouted Casey, shutting his eyes, running his hands over his cheeks and jaw and mouth and clenching his fists and turning around in frustration. 'But you *don't* put off burnings, you *don't* reschedule them like tea parties, you *do* them!'

'You do if you remember to bring the matches,' said Riordan under his breath.

Casey whirled and looked as if he might hit Riordan, but the impact of the truth slowed him down.

'On top of which,' said Nolan, 'the missus above is a fine lady and needs a last night of entertainment and rest.'

'Very kind of you.' His Lordship refilled the man's glass.

'Let's take a vote,' said Nolan.

'Hell,' Casey scowled around. 'I see the vote counted already. Tomorrow night will do, dammit.'

'Bless you,' said old Lord Kilgotten. 'There will be cold cuts laid out in the kitchen, you might check in there first, you shall probably be hungry, for it will be heavy work. Shall we say eight o'clock tomorrow night? By then I shall have Lady Kilgotten safely to a hotel in Dublin. I should not want her knowing until later that her home no longer exists.'

'God, you're a Christian,' muttered Riordan.

'Well, let us not brood on it,' said the old man. 'I consider it past already, and I never think of the past. Gentlemen.'

He arose. And, like a blind old sheepherder-saint, he wandered out into the hall with the flock straying and ambling and softly colliding after.

Half down the hall, almost to the door, Lord Kilgotten saw

something from the corner of his blear eye and stopped. He turned back and stood brooding before a large portrait of an Italian nobleman.

The more he looked the more his eyes began to tic and his mouth to work over a nameless thing.

Finally Nolan said, 'Your Lordship, what is it?'

'I was just thinking,' said the Lord, at last, 'you love Ireland, do you not?'

My God, yes! said everyone. Need he ask?

'Even as do I,' said the old man gently. 'And do you love all that is in it, in the land, in her heritage?'

That, too, said all, went without saying!

'I worry then,' said the Lord, 'about things like this. This portrait is by Van Dyck. It is very old and very fine and very important and very expensive. It is, gentlemen, a National Art Treasure.'

'Is *that* what it is!' said everyone, more or less, and crowded around for a sight.

'Ah, God, it's fine work,' said Timulty.

'The flesh itself,' said Nolan.

'Notice,' said Riordan, 'the way his little eyes seem to follow you?'

Uncanny, everyone said.

And were about to move on, when his Lordship said, 'Do you realize this Treasure, which does not truly belong to me, nor you, but to all the people as precious heritage, this picture will be lost forever tomorrow night?'

Everyone gasped. They had *not* realized.

'God save us,' said Timulty, 'we can't have that!'

'We'll move it out of the house, first,' said Riordan.

'Hold on!' cried Casey.

'Thank you,' said his Lordship, 'but where would you put it? Out in the weather it would soon be torn to shreds by wind, dampened by rain, flaked by hail; no, no, perhaps it is best it burns quickly —'

'None of that!' said Timulty. 'I'll take it home, myself.'

'And when the great strife is over,' said his Lordship, 'you will then deliver into the hands of the new government this precious gift of Art and Beauty from the past?'

'Er . . . every single one of those things, I'll do,' said Timulty.

But Casey was eyeing the immense canvas, and said, 'How much does the monster weigh?'

'I would imagine,' said the old man, faintly, 'seventy to one hundred pounds, within that range.'

'Then how in hell do we get it to Timulty's house?' asked Casey.

'Me and Brannahan will carry the damn treasure,' said Timulty, 'and if need be, Nolan, *you* lend a hand.'

'Posterity will thank you,' said his Lordship.

They moved on along the hall, and again his Lordship stopped, before yet two more paintings.

'These are two nudes —'

They *are* that! said everyone.

'By Renoir,' finished the old man.

'That's the French gent who made them?' asked Rooney. 'If you'll excuse the expression?'

It looks French all right, said everyone.

And a lot of ribs received a lot of knocking elbows.

'These are worth several thousand pounds,' said the old man.

'You'll get no argument from me,' said Nolan, putting out his finger, which was slapped down by Casey.

'I —' said Blinky Watts, whose fish eyes swam about continuously in tears behind his thick glasses. 'I would like to volunteer a home for the two French ladies. I thought I might tuck those two Art Treasures one under each arm and hoist them to the wee cot.'

'Accepted,' said the Lord with gratitude.

Along the hall they came to another, vaster landscape with

all sorts of monster beast-men cavorting about treading fruit and squeezing summer-melon women. Everyone craned forward to read the brass plate under it: *Twilight of the Gods.*

'Twilight, hell,' said Rooney, 'it looks more like the start of a great afternoon!'

'I believe,' said the gentle old man, 'there is irony intended both in title and subject. Note the glowering sky, the hideous figures hidden in the clouds. The gods are unaware, in the midst of their bacchanal, that Doom is about to descend.'

'I do not see,' said Blinky Watts, 'the Church or any of her girly priests up in them clouds.'

'It was a different kind of Doom in them days,' said Nolan. 'Everyone knows *that.*'

'Me and Tuohy,' said Flannery, 'will carry the demon gods to my place. Right, Tuohy?'

'Right!'

And so it went now, along the hall, the squad pausing here or there as on a grand tour of a museum, and each in turn volunteering to scurry home through the snowfall night with a Degas or a Rembrandt sketch or a large oil by one of the Dutch masters, until they came to a rather grisly oil of a man, hung in a dim alcove.

'Portrait of myself,' muttered the old man, 'done by her Ladyship. Leave it there, please.'

'You mean,' gasped Nolan, 'you want it to go up in the Conflagration?'

'Now, this next picture –' said the old man, moving on.

And finally the tour was at an end.

'Of course,' said his Lordship, 'if you really want to be saving, there are a dozen exquisite Ming vases in the house – '

'As good as collected,' said Nolan.

'A Persian carpet on the landing –'

'We will roll it and deliver it to the Dublin Museum.'

'And that exquisite chandelier in the main dining room.'

'It shall be hidden away until the Troubles are over,' sighed Casey, tired already.

'Well, then,' said the old man, shaking each hand as he passed. 'Perhaps you might start now, don't you imagine? I mean, you do indeed have a largish job preserving the National Treasures. Think I shall nap five minutes now before dressing.'

And the old man wandered off upstairs.

Leaving the men stunned and isolated in a mob in the hall below, watching him go away out of sight.

'Casey,' said Blinky Watts, 'has it crossed your small mind, if you'd remembered to bring the matches there would be no such long night of work as this ahead?'

'Jesus, where's your taste for the ass-thetics?' cried Riordan.

'Shut up!' said Casey. 'Okay, Flannery, you on one end of the *Twilight of the Gods*, you, Tuohy, on the far end where the maid is being given what's good for her. Ha! *Lift*!'

And the gods, soaring crazily, took to the air.

By seven o'clock most of the paintings were out of the house and racked against each other in the snow, waiting to be taken off in various directions towards various huts. At seven-fifteen, Lord and Lady Kilgotten came out and drove away, and Casey quickly formed the mob in front of the stacked paintings so the nice old lady wouldn't see what they were up to. The boys cheered as the car went down the drive. Lady Kilgotten waved frailly back.

From seven-thirty until ten the rest of the paintings walked out in ones and twos.

When all the pictures were gone save one, Kelly stood in the dim alcove worrying over Lady Kilgotten's Sunday painting of the old Lord. He shuddered, decided on a supreme humanitarianism, and carried the portrait safely out into the night.

At midnight, Lord and Lady Kilgotten, returning with guests, found only great shuffling tracks in the snow where Flannery and Tuohy had set off one way with the dear bacchanal; where Casey, grumbling, had led a parade of Van Dycks, Rembrandts, Bouchers, and Piranesis another; and where last of all, Blinky Watts, kicking his heels, had trotted happily into the woods with his nude Renoirs.

The dinner party was over by two. Lady Kilgotten went to bed satisfied that all the paintings had been sent out, en masse, to be cleaned.

At three in the morning, Lord Kilgotten still sat sleepless in his library alone among empty walls, before a fireless hearth, a muffler about his thin neck, a glass of brandy in his faintly trembling hand.

About three-fifteen there was a stealthy creaking of parquetry, a shift of shadows, and, after a time, cap in hand, there stood Casey at the library door.

'Hist!' he called softly.

The Lord, who had dozed somewhat, blinked his eyes wide. 'Oh dear me,' he said, 'is it time for us to go?'

'That's tomorrow night,' said Casey. 'And, anyways, it's not you that's going, it's Them is coming back.'

'Them? Your friends?'

'No, *yours*.' And Casey beckoned.

The old man let himself be led through the hall to look out the front door into a deep well of night.

There, like Napoleon's numbed dog-army of foot-weary, undecided, and demoralized men, stood the shadowy but familiar mob, their hands full of pictures — pictures leaned against their legs, pictures on their backs, pictures stood upright and held by trembling, panic-whitened hands in the drifted snow. A terrible silence lay over and among the men. They seemed stranded, as if one enemy had gone off to fight far better wars while yet another enemy, as yet unnamed, nipped silent and trackless at their behinds. They kept glancing over their shoulders at the hills and the town as if at any moment Chaos herself might unleash her dogs from there. They alone, in the infiltering night, heard the far-off baying of dismays and despairs that cast a spell.

'Is that *you*, Riordan?' called Casey, nervously.

'Ah, who the hell *would* it be!' cried a voice out beyond.

'What do they *want*?' asked the old party.

'It's not so much what *we* want as what *you* might now want from *us*,' called a voice.

'You see,' said another, advancing until all could see it was Hannahan in the light, 'considered in all its aspects, your Honour, we've decided, you're such a fine gent, we —'

'We will *not* burn your house!' cried Blinky Watts.

'Shut up and let the man talk!' said several voices.

Hannahan nodded. 'That's it. We will *not* burn your house.'

'But see here,' said the Lord, 'I'm quite prepared. Everything can easily be moved out.'

'You're taking the whole thing too lightly, begging your pardon, your Honour,' said Kelly. 'Easy for you is not easy for us.'

'I see,' said the old man, not seeing at all.

'It seems,' said Tuohy, 'we have all of us, in just the last few hours developed problems. Some to do with the home and some to do with transport and cartage, if you get my drift. Who'll explain first? Kelly? No? Casey? Riordan?'

Nobody spoke.

At last, with a sigh, Flannery edged forward. 'It's this way — ' he said.

'Yes?' said the old man, gently.

'Well,' said Flannery, 'me and Tuohy here got half through the woods, like damn fools, and was across two thirds of the bog with the large picture of the *Twilight of the Gods* when we began to sink.'

'Your strength failed?' inquired the Lord kindly.

'Sink, your Honour, just plain sink, into the *ground*,' Tuohy put in.

'Dear me,' said the Lord.

'You can say that again, your Lordship,' said Tuohy. 'Why together, me and Flannery and the demon gods must have weighed close on to six hundred pounds, and that bog out there is infirm if it's anything, and the more we walk the deeper we sink, and a cry strangled in me throat, for I'm thinking of those scenes in the old story where the Hound of the Baskervilles or some such fiend chases the heroine out in the moor and down she goes, in a watery pit, wishing she had kept at that diet, but it's too late, and bubbles rise to pop on the surface. All of this a-throttling in me mind, your Honour.'

'And so?' the Lord put it, seeing he was expected to ask.

'And so,' said Flannery, 'we just walked off and left the damn gods there in their twilight.'

'In the middle of the *bog*?' asked the elderly man, just a trifle upset.

'Ah, we covered them up. I mean we put our mufflers over the scene. The gods will not die twice, your Honour. Say, did you hear *that*, boys? The gods – '

'Ah, shut up,' cried Kelly. 'Ya dimwits. Why didn't you bring the damn portrait in off the bog?'

'We thought we would come to get two more boys to help – '

'Two more!' cried Nolan. 'That's four men, plus a parcel of gods, you'd all sink *twice* as fast, and the bubbles rising, ya nitwit!'

'Ah!' said Tuohy. 'I never thought of that.'

'It has been thought of now,' said the old man. 'And perhaps several of you will form a rescue team – '

'It's done, your Honour,' said Casey. 'Bob, you and Tim dash off and save the pagan deities.'

'You won't tell Father Leary?'

'Father Leary my behind. Get!' And Tim and Bob panted off.

His Lordship turned now to Nolan and Kelly.

'I see that you, too, have brought your rather large picture back.'

'At least we made it within a hundred yards of the door, sir,' said Kelly. 'I suppose you're wondering *why* we have returned it, your Honour?'

'With the gathering in of coincidence upon coincidence,' said the old man, going back in to get his overcoat and putting on his tweed cap so he could stand out in the cold and finish what looked to be a long converse, 'yes, I was given to speculate.'

'It's me back,' said Kelly. 'It gave out not five hundred yards down the main road. The back has been springing out and in for five years now, and me suffering the agonies of Christ. I sneeze and fall to my knees, your Honour.'

'I have suffered the selfsame delinquency,' said the old man. 'It is as if someone had driven a spike into one's spine.' The old man touched his back, carefully, remembering, which brought a gasp from all, nodding.

'The agonies of Christ, as I said,' said Kelly.

'Most understandable then that you could not finish your journey with that heavy frame,' said the old man, 'and most commendable that you were able to struggle back this far with the dreadful weight.'

Kelly stood taller immediately, as he heard his plight described. He beamed. 'It was nothing. And I'd do it again, save for the string of bones above me ass. Begging pardon, your Honour.'

But already his Lordship had passed his kind if tremulous grey-blue, unfocused gaze towards Blinky Watts who had, under either arm, like a dartful prancer, the two Renoir peach ladies.

'Ah, God, there was no trouble with sinking into bogs or

knocking my spine out of shape,' said Watts, treading the earth to demonstrate his passage home. 'I made it back to the house in ten minutes flat, dashed into the wee cot, and began hanging the pictures on the wall, when my wife came up behind me. Have ya ever had your wife come up behind ya, your Honour, and just stand there mum's the word?'

'I seem to recall a similar circumstance,' said the old man, trying to remember if he did, then nodding as indeed several memories flashed over his fitful baby mind.

'Well, your Lordship, there is no silence like a woman's silence, do you agree? And no standing there like a woman's standing there like a monument out of Stonehenge. The mean temperature dropped in the room so quick I suffered from the polar concussions, as we call it in our house. I did not dare turn to confront the Beast, or the daughter of the Beast, as I call her in deference to her mom. But finally I heard her suck in a great breath and let it out very cool and calm like a Prussian general. "That woman is naked as a jay bird," and "That other woman is raw as the inside of a clam at low tide."

' "But," said I, "these are studies of natural physique by a famous French artist."

' "Jesus-come-after-me-French," she cried; "the-skirts-half-up-to-your-bum-French. The dress-half-down-to-your-navel-French. And the-gulping-and-smothering-they-do-with-their-mouths-in-their-dirty-novels-French, and now you come home and nail 'French' on the walls, why don't you while you're at it, pull the crucifix down and nail one fat naked lady *there*?"

'Well, your Honour, I just shut up my eyes and wished my ears would fall off. "Is *this* what you want our boys to look at last thing at night as they go to sleep?" she says. Next thing I know, I'm on the path and here I am and here's the raw-oyster nudes, your Honour, beg your pardon, thanks, and much obliged.'

'They *do* seem to be unclothed,' said the old man, looking at the two pictures, one in either hand, as if he wished to find all that this man's wife said was in them. 'I had always thought of summer, looking at them.'

'From your seventieth birthday on, your Lordship, perhaps. But *before* that?'

'Uh, yes, yes,' said the old man, watching a speck of half-remembered lechery drift across one eye.

When his eye stopped drifting it found Bannock and Toolery on the edge of the far rim of the uneasy crowd. Behind each, dwarfing them, stood a giant painting.

Bannock had got his picture home only to find he could not get the damn thing through the door, nor any window.

Toolery had actually got his picture *in* the door when his wife said what a laughingstock they'd be, the only family in the village with a Rubens worth half a million pounds and not even a cow to milk!

So that was the sum, total, and substance of this long night. Each man had a similar chill, dread, and awful tale to tell, and all were told at last, and as they finished a cold snow began to fall among these brave members of the local, hard-fighting IRA.

The old man said nothing, for there was nothing really to say that wouldn't be obvious as their pale breaths ghosting the wind. Then, very quietly, the old man opened wide the front door and had the decency not even to nod or point.

Slowly and silently they began to file by, as past a familiar teacher in an old school, and then faster they moved. So in flowed the river returned, the Ark emptied out before, not after, the Flood, and the tide of animals and angels, nudes that flamed and smoked in the hands, and noble gods that pranced on wings and hoofs, went by, and the old man's eyes shifted gently, and his mouth silently named each, the Renoirs, the Van Dycks, the Lautrec, and so on until Kelly, in passing, felt a touch at his arm.

Surprised Kelly looked over.

And saw the old man was staring at the small painting beneath his arm.

'My wife's portrait of me?'

'None other,' said Kelly.

The old man stared at Kelly and at the painting beneath his arm and then out towards the snowing night.

Kelly smiled softly.

Walking soft as a burglar, he vanished out into the wilderness, carrying the picture. A moment later, you heard him laughing as he ran back, hands empty.

The old man shook his hand, once, tremblingly, and shut the door.

Then he turned away as if the event was already lost to his wandering child mind and toddled down the hall with his scarf like a gentle weariness over his thin shoulders, and the mob followed him in where they found drinks in their great paws and saw that Lord Kilgotten was blinking at the picture over the fireplace as if trying to remember, was the *Sack of Rome* there in the years past? or was it the *Fall of Troy*? Then he felt their gaze and looked full on the encircled army and said:

'Well now, what shall we *drink* to?'

The men shuffled their feet.

Then Flannery cried, 'Why, to his Lordship, of course!'

'His Lordship!' cried all, eagerly, and drank, and coughed and choked and sneezed, while the old man felt a peculiar glistering about his eyes, and did not drink at all till the commotion stilled, and then said, 'To Our Ireland,' and drank, and all said Ah God and Amen to that, and the old man looked at the picture over the hearth and then at last shyly observed, 'I do hate to mention it — that picture —'

'Sir?'

'It seems to me,' said the old man, apologetically, 'to be a trifle off-centred, on the tilt. I wonder if you might—'

'*Mightn't* we, boys!' cried Casey.

And fourteen men rushed to put it right.

Night Call, Collect

What made the old poem run in his mind he could not guess,
but run it did:

> *Suppose and then suppose and then suppose*
> *That wires on the far-slung telephone black poles*
> *Sopped up the billion-flooded words they heard*
> *Each night all night and saved the sense*
> *And meaning of it all.*

He stopped. What next? Ah, yes . . .

> *Then, jigsaw in the night,*
> *Put all together and*
> *In philosophic phase*
> *Tried words like moron child.*

Again he paused. How did the thing end? Wait —

> *Thus mindless beast*
> *All treasuring of vowels and consonants*
> *Saves up a miracle of bad advice*
> *And lets it filter whisper, heartbeat out*
> *One lisping murmur at a time.*
> *So one night soon someone sits up*
> *Hears sharp bell ring, lifts phone*
> *And hears a Voice like Holy Ghost*
> *Gone far is nebulae*
> *That Beast upon the wire,*
> *Which with sibilance and savourings*

Down continental madnesses of time
Says Hell and O
And then Hell-o.

He took a breath and finished:

To such Creation
Such dumb brute lost Electric Beast,
What is your wise reply?

He sat silently.

He sat, a man eighty years old. He sat in an empty room in an empty house on an empty street in an empty town on the empty planet Mars.

He sat as he had sat now for fifty years, waiting.

On the table in front of him lay a telephone that had not rung for a long, long time.

It trembled now with some secret preparation. Perhaps that trembling had summoned forth the poem . . .

His nostrils twitched. His eyes flared wide.

The phone shivered ever so softly.

He leaned forward, staring at it.

The phone . . . *rang*.

He leapt up and back, the chair fell to the floor. He cried out:

'No!'

The phone rang again.

'No!'

He wanted to reach out, he did reach out and knock the thing off the table. It fell out of the cradle at the exact moment of its third ring.

'No . . . oh, no, no,' he said softly, hands covering his chest, head wagging, the telephone at his feet. 'It can't be . . . can't be . . . '

For after all, he was alone in a room in an empty house in

an empty town on the planet Mars where no one was alive, only he lived, he was King of the Barren Hill . . .

And yet . . .

' . . . Barton . . . '

Someone called his name.

No. Something buzzed and made a noise of crickets and cicadas in far desertlands.

Barton? he thought. Why . . . why that's *me*!

He hadn't heard anyone say his name in so long he had quite forgot. He was not one for ambling about calling himself by name. He had never –

'Barton,' said the phone. 'Barton. Barton. Barton.'

'Shut up!!' he cried.

And kicked the receiver and bent sweating, panting, to put the phone back on its cradle.

No sooner did he do this than the damned thing rang again.

This time he made a fist around it, squeezed it, as if to throttle the sound, but at last, seeing his knuckles burn colour away to whiteness, let go and picked up the receiver.

'Barton,' said a far voice, a billion miles away.

He waited until his heart had beat another three times and then said:

'Barton here,' he said.

'Well, well,' said the voice, only a million miles away now. 'Do you know who this is?'

'Christ,' said the old man. 'The first call I've had in half a lifetime, and we play games.'

'Sorry. How stupid of me. Of course you wouldn't recognize your own voice on the telephone. No one ever does. We are accustomed all of us, to hearing our voice conducted through the bones of our head. Barton, this is Barton.'

'What?'

'Who did you think it was?' said the voice. 'A rocket captain? Did you think someone had come to rescue you?'

'No.'

'What's the date?'

'July 20, 2097.'

'Good Lord. Fifty years! Have you been sitting there *that* long waiting for a rocket to come from Earth?'

The old man nodded.

'Now, old man, do you know who I am?'

'Yes.' He trembled. 'I remember. We are one. I am Emil Barton and you are Emil Barton.'

'With one difference. You're eighty, I'm only twenty. All of life before me!'

The old man began to laugh and then to cry. He sat holding the phone like a lost and silly child in his fingers. The conversation was impossible, and should not be continued, yet he went on with it. When he got hold of himself he held the phone close and said, 'You there! Listen, oh God, if I could warn you! How can I? You're only a voice. If I could show you how lonely the years are. End it, kill yourself! Don't wait! If you knew what it is to change from the thing you are to the thing that is me, today, here, now, at *this* end.'

'Impossible!' The voice of the young Barton laughed, far away. 'I've no way to tell if you ever get this call. This is all mechanical. You're talking to a transcription, no more. This is 2037. Sixty years in your past. Today, the atom was started on Earth. All colonials were called home from Mars, by rocket, I got left behind!'

'I remember,' whispered the old man.

'Alone on Mars,' laughed the young voice. 'A month, a year, who cares? There are foods and books. In my spare time I've made transcription libraries of ten thousand words, responses, my voice, connected to phone relays. In later months I'll call, have someone to talk with.'

'Yes.'

'Sixty years from now my own tapes will ring me up. I don't really think I'll be here on Mars that long, it's just a beautifully ironic idea of mine, something to pass the time. Is that really you, Barton? Is that really *me*?'

Tears fell from the old man's eyes. 'Yes.'

'I've made a thousand Bartons, tapes, sensitive to all questions, in one thousand Martian towns. An army of Bartons over Mars, while I wait for the rockets to return.'

'Fool!' The old man shook his head, wearily. 'You waited sixty years. You grew old waiting, always alone. And now you've become me and you're still alone in the empty cities.'

'Don't expect my sympathy. You're like a stranger, off in another country. I can't be sad. I'm alive when I make these tapes. And you're alive when you hear them. Both of us, to the other, incomprehensible. Neither can warn the other, even though both respond, one to the other, one automatically, the other warmly and humanly. I'm human now. You're human later. It's insane. I can't cry, because not knowing the future I can only be optimistic. These hidden tapes can only react to a certain number of stimuli from you. Can you ask a dead man to weep?'

'Stop it!' cried the old man. He felt the familiar seizures of pain. Nausea moved through him, and blackness. 'Oh God, but you were heartless. Go away!'

'Were, old man? I *am*. As long as the tapes glide on, as long as spindles and hidden electronic eyes read and select and convert words to send to you, I'll be young and cruel. I'll go on being young and cruel long after you're dead. Good-bye.'

'Wait!' cried the old man.

Click.

Barton sat holding the silent phone a long time. His heart gave him intense pain.

What insanity it had been. In his youth how silly, how inspired, those first secluded years, fixing the telephonic brains, the tapes, the circuits, scheduling calls on time relays:

The phone bell.

'Morning, Barton. This is Barton. Seven o'clock. Rise and shine!'

Again!

'Barton? Barton calling. You're to go to Mars Town at noon. Install a telephonic brain. Thought I'd remind you.'

'Thanks.'

The bell!

'Barton? Barton. Have lunch with me? The Rocket Inn?'

'Right.'

'See you. So long!'

Brrrrinnnnng!

'That you, B? Thought I'd cheer you. Firm chin, and all that. The rescue rocket might come tomorrow, to save us.'

'Yes, tomorrow, tomorrow, tomorrow, tomorrow.'

Click.

But the years had burned into smoke. Barton had muted the insidious phones and their clever, clever repartee. They were to call him only after he was eighty, if he still lived. And now today, the phone ringing, the past breathing in his ear, whispering, remembering.

The phone!

He let it ring.

I don't have to answer it, he thought.

The bell!

There's no one there at all, he thought.

The ringing!

It's like talking to yourself, he thought. But different. Oh God, how different.

He felt his hands lift the phone.

'Hello, old Barton, this is young Barton. I'm twenty-one today! In the last year I've put voice-brains in two hundred more towns. I've populated Mars with Bartons!'

'Yes.' The old man remembered those nights six decades ago, rushing over blue hills and into iron valleys, with a truckful of machinery, whistling, happy. Another telephone, another relay. Something to do. Something clever and wonderful and sad. Hidden voices. Hidden, hidden. In those young days when death was not death, time was not time, old age a faint echo from the long cavern of years ahead. That young idiot, that sadistic fool, never thinking someday he might reap this harvest.

'Last night,' said Barton, aged twenty-one, 'I sat alone in a movie theatre in an empty town. I played an old Laurel and Hardy. God, how I laughed.'

'Yes.'

'I got an idea. I recorded my voice one thousand times on one tape. Broadcast from the town, it sounds like a thousand people. A comforting noise, the noise of a crowd. I fixed it so doors slam in town, children sing, music boxes play, all by clockworks. If I don't look out the window, if I just listen, it's all right. But if I look, it spoils the illusion. I guess I'm getting lonely.'

The old man said, 'That was your first sign.'

'What?'

'The first time you admitted you were lonely.'

'I've experimented with smells. As I walk the empty streets, the smell of bacon, eggs, ham, fillets, come from the houses. All done with hidden machines.'

'Madness.'

'Self-protection!'

'I'm tired.' Abruptly, the old man hung up. It was too much. The past drowning him . . .

Swaying, he moved down the tower stairs to the streets of the town.

The town was dark. No longer did red neons burn, music play, or cooking smells linger. Long ago he had abandoned the fantasy of the mechanical lie. Listen! Are those footsteps? Smell! Isn't that strawberry pie! He had stopped it all.

He moved to the canal where the stars shone in the quivering waters.

Under water, in row after fishlike row, rusting, were the robot population of Mars he had constructed over the years, and, in a wild realization of his own insane inadequacy, had commanded to march, one two three four! into the canal deeps, plunging, bubbling like sunken bottles. He had killed them and shown no remorse.

Faintly a phone rang in a lightless cottage.

He walked on. The phone ceased.

Another cottage ahead rang its bell as if it knew of his passing. He began to run. The ringing stayed behind. Only to be taken up by a ringing from now this house — now that, now here, there! He darted on. Another phone!

'All right!' he shrieked, exhausted. 'I'm coming!'

'Hello, Barton!'

'What do you want!'

'I'm lonely. I only live when I speak. So I must speak. You can't shut me up forever.'

'Leave me alone!' said the old man, in horror. 'Oh, my heart!'

'This is Barton, age twenty-four. Another couple of years gone. Waiting. A little lonelier. I've read *War and Peace*, drunk sherry, run restaurants with myself as waiter, cook, entertainer. Tonight, I star in a film at the Tivoli — Emil Barton in *Love's Labour Lost*, playing all the parts, some with wigs!'

'Stop calling me — or I'll kill you!'

'You can't kill me. You'll have to find me, first!'

'I'll find you!'

'You've forgotten where you hid me. I'm everywhere, in boxes, houses, cables, towers, underground! Go ahead, try! What'll you call it? Telecide? Suicide? Jealous, are you? Jealous of me here, only twenty-four, bright-eyed, strong, young. All right, old man, it's war! Between us. Between me! A whole regiment of us, all ages form against you, the real one. Go ahead, declare war!'

'I'll kill you!'

Click. Silence.

He threw the phone out the window.

In the midnight cold, the automobile moved in deep valleys. Under Barton's feet on the floorboard were revolvers, rifles, dynamite. The roar of the car was in his thin, tired bones.

I'll find them, he thought, and destroy all of them. Oh, God, how can he do this to me?

He stopped the car. A strange town lay under the late moons. There was no wind.

He held the rifle in his cold hands. He peered at the poles, the towers, the boxes. Where was this town's voice hidden? That tower? Or that one there! So many years ago. He turned his head now this way, now that, wildly.

He raised the rifle.

The tower fell with the first bullet.

All of them, he thought. All of the towers in this town will have to be cut apart. I've forgotten. Too long.

The car moved along the silent street.

A phone rang.

He looked at the deserted drugstore.

A phone.

Pistol in hand, he shot the lock off the door, and entered.

Click.

'Hello, Barton? Just a warning. Don't try to rip down all the towers, blow things up. Cut your own throat that way. Think it over . . . '

Click.

He stepped out of the phone booth slowly and moved into the street and listened to the telephone towers humming high in the air, still alive, still untouched. He looked at them and then he understood.

He could not destroy the towers. Suppose a rocket came

from Earth, impossible idea, but suppose it came tonight, tomorrow, next week? And landed on the other side of the planet, and used the phones to try to call Barton, only to find the circuits dead?

Barton dropped his gun.

'A rocket won't come,' he argued, softly with himself. 'I'm old. It's too late.'

But suppose it came, and you never knew, he thought. No, you've got to keep the lines open.

Again, a phone ringing.

He turned dully. He shuffled back into the drugstore and fumbled with the receiver.

'Hello?' A strange voice.

'Please,' said the old man, 'don't bother me.'

'Who's this, who's there? Who is it? Where are you?' cried the voice, surprised.

'Wait a minute.' The old man staggered. 'This is Emil Barton, who's that?'

'This is Captain Rockwell, Apollo Rocket 48. Just arrived from Earth.'

'No, no, no.'

'Are you there, Mr Barton?'

'No, no, it can't be.'

'Where are you?'

'You're lying!' The old man had to lean against the booth. His eyes were cold blind. 'It's you, Barton, making fun of me, lying again!'

'This is Captain Rockwell. Just landed. In New Chicago. Where are you?'

'In Green Villa,' he gasped. 'That's six hundred miles from you.'

'Look, Barton, can you come here?'

'What?'

'We've repairs on our rocket. Exhausted from the flight. Can you come help?'

'Yes, yes.'

'We're at the field outside town. Can you come by to-morrow?'

'Yes, but — '

'Well?'

The old man petted the phone. 'How's Earth? How's New York? Is the war over? Who's President now? What happened?'

'Plenty of time for gossip when you arrive.'

'Is everything fine?'

'Fine.'

'Thank God.' The old man listened to the far voice. 'Are you sure you're Captain Rockwell?'

'Dammit, man!'

'I'm sorry!'

He hung up and ran.

They were here, after many years, unbelievable, his own people who would take him back to Earth's seas and skies and mountains.

He started the car. He would drive all night. It would be worth a risk, to see people, to shake hands, to hear them again.

The car thundered in the hills.

That voice. Captain Rockwell. It couldn't be himself, forty years ago. He had never made a recording like that. Or had he? In one of his depressive fits, in a spell of drunken cynicism, hadn't he once made a false tape of a false landing on Mars with a synthetic captain, an imaginary crew? He jerked his head, savagely. No. He was a suspicious fool. Now was no time to doubt. He must run with the moons of Mars, all night. What a party they would have!

The sun rose. He was immensely tired, full of thorns and

brambles, his heart plunging, his fingers fumbling the wheel, but the thing that pleased him most was the thought of one last phone call: Hello, *young* Barton, this is *old* Barton. I'm leaving for Earth today! Rescued! He smiled weakly.

He drove into the shadowy limits of New Chicago at sundown. Stepping from his car he stood staring at the rocket tarmac, rubbing his reddened eyes.

The rocket field was empty. No one ran to meet him. No one shook his hand, shouted, or laughed.

Hs felt his heart roar. He knew blackness and a sensation of falling through the open sky. He stumbled towards an office.

Inside, six phones sat in a neat row.

He waited, gasping.

Finally: the bell.

He lifted the heavy receiver.

A voice said, 'I was wondering if you'd get there alive.'

The old man did not speak but stood with the phone in his hands.

The voice continued: 'Captain Rockwell reporting for duty. Your orders, sir?'

'You,' groaned the old man.

'How's your heart, old man?'

'No!'

'Had to eliminate you some way, so I could live, if you call a transcription living.'

'I'm going out now,' replied the old man. 'I don't care. I'll blow up everything until you're all dead!'

'You haven't the strength. Why do you think I had you travel so far, so fast? This is your last trip!'

The old man felt his heart falter. He would never make the other towns. The war was lost. He slid into a chair and made low, mournful noises with his mouth. He glared at the five other phones. As if at a signal, they burst into chorus! A nest of ugly birds screaming!

Automatic receivers popped up.

The office whirled. 'Barton, Barton, Barton!'

He throttled a phone in his hands. He choked it and still it laughed at him. He beat it. He kicked it. He furled the hot wire like serpentine in his fingers, ripped it. It fell about his stumbling feet.

He destroyed three other phones. There was a sudden silence.

And as if his body now discovered a thing which it had long kept secret, it seemed to sink upon his tired bones. The flesh of his eyelids fell away like petals. His mouth withered. The lobes of his ears were melting wax. He pushed his chest with his hands and fell face down. He lay still. His breathing stopped. His heart stopped.

After a long spell, the remaining two phones rang.

A relay snapped somewhere. The two phone voices were connected, one to the other.

'Hello, Barton?'

'Yes, Barton?'

'Aged twenty-four.'

'I'm twenty-six. We're both young. What's happened?'

'I don't know. Listen.'

The silent room. The old man did not stir on the floor. The wind blew in the broken window. The air was cool.

'Congratulate me, Barton, this is my twenty-*sixth* birthday!'

'Congratulations!'

The voices sang together, about birthdays, and the singing blew out the window, faintly, faintly, into the dead city.

The Tombling Day

It was the Tombling day, and all the people had walked up the summer road, including Grandma Loblilly, and they stood now in the green day and the high sky country of Missouri, and there was a smell of the seasons changing and the grass breaking out in flowers.

'Here we are,' said Grandma Loblilly, over her cane, and she gave them all a flashing look of her yellow-brown eyes and spat into the dust.

The graveyard lay on the side of a quiet hill. It was a place of sunken mounds and wooden markers; bees hummed all about in quietudes of sound and butterflies withered and blossomed on the clear blue air. The tall sunburnt men and ginghamed women stood a long silent time looking in at their deep and buried relatives.

'Well, let's get to work!' said Grandma, and she hobbled across the moist grass, sticking it rapidly, here and there, with her cane.

The others brought the spades and special crates, with daisies and lilacs tied brightly to them. The government was cutting a road through here in August and since this graveyard had gone unused in fifty years the relatives had agreed to untuck all the old bones and pat them snug somewhere else.

Grandma Loblilly got right down on her knees and trembled a spade in her hand. The others were busy at their own places.

'Grandma,' said Joseph Pikes, making a big shadow on her working. 'Grandma, you shouldn't be workin' on this place. This's William Simmons's grave, Grandma.'

At the sound of his voice, everyone stopped working, and

listened, and there was just the sound of butterflies on the cool afternoon air.

Grandma looked up at Pikes. 'You think I don't *know* it's his place? I ain't seen William Simmons in sixty years, but I intend to visit him today.' She patted out trowel after trowel of rich soil and she grew quiet and introspective and said things to the day and those who might listen. 'Sixty years ago, and him a fine man, only twenty-three. And me, I was twenty and all golden about the head and all milk in my arms and neck and persimmon in my cheeks. Sixty years and a planned marriage and then a sickness and him dying away. And me alone, and I remember how the earth mound over him sank in the rains — '

Everybody stared at Grandma.

'But still, Grandma — ' said Joseph Pikes.

'Gimme a hand!' she cried.

Nine men helped lift the iron box out of the earth, Grandma poking at them with her cane. 'Careful!' she shouted. 'Easy!' she cried. 'Now.' They set it on the ground. 'Now,' she said, 'if you be so kindly, you gentlemen might fetch Mr Simmons on up to my house for a spell.'

'We're takin' him on to the new cemetery,' said Joseph Pikes.

Grandma fixed him with her needle eye. 'You just trot that box right up to my house. Much obliged.'

The men watched her dwindle down the road. They looked at the box, looked at each other, and then spat on their hands.

Five minutes later the men squeezed the iron coffin through the front door of Grandma's little white house and set the box down by the potbelly stove.

She gave them a drink all around. 'Now, let's lift the lid,' she said. 'It ain't every day you see old friends.'

The men did not move.

'Well, if you won't, I will.' She thrust at the lid with her cane, again and again, breaking away the earth crust. Spiders went touching over the floor. There was a rich smell, like ploughed spring earth. Now the men fingered the lid. Grandma stood back. 'Up!' she said. She gestured her cane, like an ancient goddess. And up in the air went the lid. The men set it on the floor and turned.

There was a sound like wind sighing in October, from all their mouths.

There lay William Simmons as the dust filtered bright and golden through the air. There he slept, a little smile on his lips, hands folded, all dressed up and no place in all the world to go.

Grandma Loblilly gave a low moaning cry.

'He's all there!'

There he was, indeed. Intact as a beetle in his shell, his skin all fine and white, his small eyelids over his pretty eyes like flower petals put there, his lips still with colour to them, his hair combed neat, his tie tied, his fingernails pared clean. All in all, he was as complete as the day they shovelled the earth upon his silent case.

Grandma stood tightening her eyes, her hands up to catch the breath that moved from her mouth. She couldn't see. 'Where's my specs?' she cried. People searched. 'Can't you find 'em?' she shouted. She squinted at the body. 'Never mind,' she said, getting close. The room settled. She sighed and quavered and cooed over the open box.

'He's kept,' said one of the women. 'He ain't crumbled.'

'Things like that,' said Joseph Pikes, 'don't happen.'

'It *happened*,' said the woman.

'Sixty years underground. Stands to reason no man lasts that long.'

The sunlight was late by each window, the last butterflies were settling among flowers to look like nothing more than other flowers.

Grandma Loblilly put out her wrinkly hand, trembling.

'The earth kept him. The way the air is. That was good dry soil for keeping.'

'He's young,' wailed one of the women, quietly. 'So young.'

'Yes,' said Grandma Loblilly, looking at him. 'Him, lying there, twenty-three years old. And me, standing here, pushing eighty!' She shut her eyes.

'Now, Grandma.' Joseph Pikes touched her shoulder.

'Yes, him lyin' there, all twenty-three and fine and purty, and *me* – ' She squeezed her eyes tight. 'Me bending over him, never young agin, myself, only old and spindly, never to have a chance at being young agin. Oh, Lord! Death keeps people young. Look how kind death's been to him.' She ran her hands over her body and face slowly, turning to the others. 'Death's nicer than life. Why didn't I die then too? Then we'd both be young now, together. Me in my box, in my white wedding gown all lace, and my eyes closed down, all shy with death. And my hands making a prayer on my bosom.'

'Grandma, don't carry on.'

'I got a right to carry on! Why didn't I die, too? Then, when he came back, like he came today, to see me. I wouldn't be like *this*!'

Her hands went wildly to feel her lined face, to twist the loose skin, to fumble the empty mouth, to yank the grey hair and look at it with appalled eyes.

'What a fine coming-back he's had!' She showed her skinny arms. 'Think that a man of twenty-three years will want the likes of a seventy-nine-year-old woman with sunprot in her veins? I been cheated! Death kept him young forever. Look at me; did *Life* do so much?'

'They're compensations,' said Joseph Pikes. 'He ain't young, Grandma. He's long over eighty years.'

'You're a fool, Joseph Pikes. He's fine as a stone, not touched by a thousand rains. And he's come back to see me and he'll be picking one of the younger girls now. What would he want with an old woman?'

'He's in no way to fetch nuthin' offa nobody,' said Joseph Pikes.

Grandma pushed him back. 'Get out now, all of you! Ain't your box, ain't your lid, and it ain't your almost-husband! You leave the box here, leastwise tonight, and tomorrow you dig a new burying place.'

'Awright, Grandma; he was your beau. I'll come early tomorra. Don't you cry, now.'

'I'll do what my eyes most need to do.'

She stood stiff in the middle of the room until the last of them were out the door. After a while she got a candle and lit it and she noticed someone standing on the hill outside. It was Joseph Pikes. He'd be there the rest of the night, she reckoned, and she did not shout for him to go away. She did not look out the window again, but she knew he was there, and so was much better rested in the following hours.

She went to the coffin and looked down at William Simmons.

She gazed fully upon him. Seeing his hands was like seeing actions. She saw how they had been with reins of a horse in them, moving up and down. She remembered how the lips of him had clucked as the carriage had glided along with an even pacing of the horse through the meadowlands, the moonlight shadows all around. She knew how it was when those hands held to you.

She touched his suit. 'That's not the same suit he was buried in!' she cried suddenly. And yet she knew it was the same. Sixty years had changed not the suit but the linings of her mind.

Seized with a quick fear, she hunted a long time until she found her spectacles and put them on.

'Why, *that*'s not William Simmons!' she shouted.

But she knew this also was untrue. It was William

Simmons. 'His chin didn't go back that far!' she cried softly, logically. 'Or *did* it?' And his hair. 'It was a wonderful sorrel colour, I remember! This hair here's just plain brown. And his nose, I don't recall it being that tippy!'

She stood over this strange man and, gradually, as she watched, she knew that this indeed was William Simmons. She knew a thing she should have known all along: that dead people are like wax memory — you take them in your mind, you shape and squeeze them, push a bump here, stretch one out there, pull the body tall, shape and reshape, handle, sculpt and finish a man-memory until he's all out of kilter.

There was a certain sense of loss and bewilderment in her. She wished she had never opened the box. Or, leastwise, had the sense to leave her glasses off. She had not seen him clearly at first; just enough so she filled in the rough spots with her mind. Now, with her glasses on . . .

She glanced again and again at his face. It became slowly familiar. That memory of him that she had torn apart and put together for sixty years faded to be replaced by the man she had *really* known. And he was *fine* to look upon. The sense of having lost something vanished. He was the same man, no more, no less. This was always the way when you didn't see people for years and they came back to say howdy-do. For a spell you felt so very uneasy with them. But then, at last you relaxed.

'Yes, that's you,' she laughed. 'I see you peeking out from behind all the strangeness. I see you all glinty and sly here and there and about.'

She began to cry again. If only she could lie to herself, if only she could say, 'Look at him, he don't look the same, he's not the same man I took a fetching on!' then she could feel better. But all the little inside-people sitting around in her head would rock back in their tiny rockers and cackle and say, 'You ain't foolin' us none, Grandma.'

Yes, how easy to deny it was him. And feel better. But she

didn't deny it. She felt the great depressing sadness because here he was, young as creek water, and here she was, old as the sea.

'William Simmons!' she cried. 'Don't look at me! I know you still love me, so I'll primp myself up!'

She stirred the stove-fire, quickly put irons on to heat, used irons on her hair till it was all grey curls. Baking powder whitened her cheeks! She bit a cherry to colour her lips, pinched her cheeks to bring a flush. From a trunk she yanked old materials until she found a faded blue velvet dress which she put on.

She stared wildly in the mirror at herself.

'No, no.' She groaned and shut her eyes. 'There's nothing I can do to make me younger'n you, William Simmons! Even if I died now it wouldn't cure me of this old thing come on me, this disease – '

She had a violent wish to run forever in the woods, fall in a leaf pile and moulder down into smoking ruin with them. She ran across the room, intending never to come back. But as she yanked the door wide a cold wind exploded over her from outside and she heard a sound that made her hesitate.

The wind rushed about the room, yanked at the coffin and pushed inside it.

William Simmons seemed to stir in his box.

Grandma slammed the door.

She moved slowly back to squint at him.

He was ten years older.

There were wrinkles and lines on his hands and face.

'William Simmons!'

During the next hour, William Simmons's face tolled away the years. His cheeks went in on themselves, like clenching a fist, like withering an apple in a bin. His flesh was made of carved pure white snow, and the cabin heat melted it. It got a charred look. The air made the eyes and mouth pucker. Then, as if struck a hammer blow, the face shattered into a million wrinkles. The body squirmed in an agony of time. It was forty, then fifty, then sixty years old! It was seventy, eighty, one hundred years! Burning, burning away! There were small whispers and leaf-crackles from its face and its age-burning hands, one hundred ten, one hundred twenty years, lined upon etched, graved, line!

Grandma Loblilly stood there all the cold night, aching her bird bones, watching, cold, over the changing man. She was a witness to all improbabilities. She felt something finally let loose of her heart. She did not feel sad any more. The weight lifted away from her.

She went peacefully to sleep, standing against a chair.

Sunlight came yellow through the woodland, birds and ants and creek waters were moving, each as quiet as the other, going somewhere.

It was morning.

Grandma woke and looked down upon William Simmons.

'Ah,' said Grandma, looking and seeing.

Her very breath stirred and stirred his bones until they flaked, like a chrysalis, like a kind of candy, all whittling away, burning with an invisible fire. The bones flaked and flew, light as pieces of dust on the sunlight. Each time she shouted the bones split asunder, there was a dry flaking rustle from the box.

If there was a wind and she opened the door, he'd be blown away on it like so many crackly leaves!

She bent for a long time, looking at the box. Then she gave a knowing cry, a sound of discovery, and moved back, putting her hands first to her face and then to her spindly breasts and then travelling all up and down her arms and legs and fumbling at her empty mouth.

Her shout brought Joseph Pikes running.

He pulled up at the door only in time to see Grandma Loblilly dancing and jumping around on her yellow, high-peg shoes in a wild gyration.

She clapped her hands, laughed, flung her skirts, ran in a circle, and did a little waltz with herself, tears on her face. And to the sunlight and the flashing image of herself in the wall mirror she cried:

'I'm young! I'm eighty, but I'm younger'n *him*!'

She skipped, she hopped, and she curtsied.

'There are compensations, Joseph Pikes; you was right!' she chortled. 'I'm younger'n *all* the dead ones in the whole world!'

And she waltzed so violently the whirl of her dress pulled at the box and whispers of chrysalis leapt on the air to hang golden and powdery amid her shouts.

'Whee-*deee*!' she cried. 'Whee-*heee*!'

The Haunting
of the New

I hadn't been in Dublin for years. I'd been round the world —
everywhere but Ireland — but now within the hour of my
arrival the Royal Hibernian Hotel phone rang and on the
phone: Nora herself, God bless!

'Charles? Charlie? Chuck? Are you rich at last? And do
rich writers buy fabulous estates?'

'Nora!' I laughed. 'Don't you ever say hello?'

'Life's too short for hellos, and now there's no time for
decent good-byes. *Could* you buy Grynwood?'

'Nora, Nora, your family house, two hundred rich years
old? What would happen to wild Irish social life, the parties,
drinks, gossip? You can't throw it all away!'

'Can and shall. Oh, I've trunks of money waiting out in the
rain this moment. But, Charlie, Charles, I'm *alone* in the
house. The servants have fled to help the Aga. Now on this
final night, Chuck, I need a writer-man to see the Ghost.
Does your skin prickle? Come. I've mysteries and a home to
give away. Charlie, oh, Chuck, oh, Charles.'

Click. Silence.

Ten minutes later I roared round the snake-road through
the green hills towards the blue lake and the lush grass
meadows of the hidden and fabulous house called Grynwood.

I laughed again. Dear Nora! For all her gab, a party was
probably on the tracks this moment, lurched towards
wondrous destruction. Bertie might fly from London, Nick
from Paris, Alicia would surely motor up from Galway. Some
film director, cabled within the hour, would parachute or
helicopter down, a rather seedy manna in dark glasses.
Marion would show with his Pekingese dog troupe, which

always got drunker, and sicker, than he.

I gunned my hilarity as I gunned the motor.

You'll be beautifully mellow by eight o'clock, I thought, stunned to sleep by concussions of bodies before midnight, drowse till noon, then even more nicely potted by Sunday high tea. And somewhere in between, the rare game of musical beds with Irish and French countesses, ladies, and plain field-beast art majors crated in from the Sorbonne, some with chewable moustaches, some not, and Monday ten millions years off. Tuesday, I would motor oh so carefully back to Dublin, nursing my body like a great impacted wisdom tooth, gone much too wise with women, pain-flashing with memory.

Trembling, I remembered the first time I had drummed out to Nora's, when I was twenty-one.

A mad old Duchess with flour-talcumed cheeks, and the teeth of a barracuda had wrestled me and a sports car down this road fifteen years ago, braying into the fast weather:

'You shall love Nora's menagerie zoo and horticultural garden! Her friends are beasts and keepers, tigers and pussies, rhododendrons and flytraps. Her streams run cold fish, hot trout. Hers is a great greenhouse where brutes grow outsize, force-fed by unnatural airs; enter Nora's on Friday with clean linen, sog out with the wet-wash-soiled bedclothes Monday, feeling as if you had meantime inspired, painted, and lived through all Bosch's Temptations, Hells, Judgements, and Dooms! Live at Nora's and you reside in a great warm giant's cheek, deliciously gummed and morselled hourly. You will pass, like victuals, through her mansion. When it has crushed forth your last sweet-sour sauce and dismarrowed your youth-candied bones, you will be discarded in a cold iron-country train station lonely with rain.'

'I'm coated with enzymes?' I cried above the engine roar. 'No house can break down my elements, or take nourishment from my Original Sin.'

'Fool!' laughed the Duchess. 'We shall see most of your skeleton by sunrise Sunday!'

I came out of memory as I came out of the woods at a fine popping glide and slowed because the very friction of beauty stayed the heart, the mind, the blood, and therefore the foot upon the throttle.

There under a blue-lake sky by a blue-sky lake lay Nora's own dear place, the grand house called Grynwood. It nestled in the roundest hills by the tallest trees in the deepest forest in all Eire. It had towers built a thousand years ago by unremembered peoples and unsung architects for reasons never to be guessed. Its gardens had first flowered five hundred years back and there were outbuildings scattered from a creative explosion two hundred years gone amongst old tomb yards and crypts. Here was a convent hall become a horse barn of the landed gentry, there were new wings built on ninety years ago. Out around the lake was a hunting-lodge ruin where wild horses might plunge through minted shadow to sink away in greenwater grasses by yet further cold ponds and single graves of daughters whose sins were so rank they were driven forth even in death to wilderness, sunk traceless in the gloom.

As if in bright welcome, the sun flashed vast tintinnabulations from scores of house windows. Blinded, I clenched the car to a halt. Eyes shut, I licked my lips.

I remembered my first night at Grynwood.

Nora herself opening the front door. Standing stark naked, she announced:

'You're too late. It's all over!'

'Nonsense. Hold this, boy, and this.'

Whereupon the Duchess, in three nimble moves, peeled herself raw as a blanched oyster in the wintry doorway.

I stood aghast, gripping her clothes.

'Come in, boy, you'll catch your death.' And the bare Duchess walked serenely away among the well-dressed people.

'Beaten at my own game,' cried Nora. 'Now, to compete, I must put my clothes back on. And I was *so* hoping to shock you.'

'Never fear,' I said. 'You have.'

'Come help me dress.'

In the alcove, we waded among her clothes, which lay in misshapen pools of musky scent upon a parqueted floor.

'Hold the panties while I slip into them. You're Charles, aren't you?'

'How do you do.' I flushed, then burst into an uncontrollable fit of laughter. 'Forgive me,' I said at last, snapping her bra at the back, 'it's just here it is early evening, and I'm putting you *into* your clothes. I – '

A door slammed somewhere. I glanced around for the Duchess.

'Gone,' I murmured. 'The house has devoured her, already.'

True. I didn't see the Duchess again until the rainy Monday morn she had predicted. By then she had forgotten my name, my face, and the soul behind my face.

'My God,' I said. 'What's that, and *that?*'

Still dressing Nora, we had arrived at the library door. Inside, like a bright mirror-maze, the weekend guests turned.

'That,' Nora pointed, 'is the Manhattan Civic Ballet flown over on ice by jet stream. To the left, the Hamburg Dancers, flown the opposite way. Divine casting. Enemy ballet mobs unable, because of language, to express their scorn and vitriol. They must pantomime their cat-fight. Stand aside, Charlie. What was Valkyrie must become Rhine Maiden. And those boys *are* Rhine Maidens. Guard your flank!'

Nora was right.

The battled was joined.

The tiger lilies leapt at each other, jabbering in tongues. Then, frustrated, they fell away, flushed. With a bombardment of slammed doors, the enemies plunged off to scores of rooms. What was horror became horrible friendship and what was friendship became steamroom oven-bastings of unabashed and, thank God, hidden affection.

After that it was one grand crystal-chandelier avalanche of writer-artist-choreographer-poets down the swift-sloped weekend.

Somewhere I was caught and swept in the heaped pummel of flesh headed straight for a collision with the maiden-aunt reality of Monday noon.

Now, many lost parties, many lost years later, here I stood.

And there stood Grynwood manse, very still.

No music played. No cars arrived.

Hello, I thought. A new statue seated by the shore. Hello, again. Not a statue . . .

But Nora herself seated alone, legs drawn under her dress, face pale, staring at Grynwood as if I had not arrived, was nowhere in sight.

'Nora . . . ?' But her gaze was so steadily fixed to the house wings, its mossy roofs and windows full of empty sky, I turned to stare at it myself.

Something *was* wrong. Had the house sunk two feet into the earth? Or had the earth sunk all about, leaving it stranded forlorn in the high chill air?

Had earthquakes shaken the windows atilt so they mirrored intruders with distorted gleams and glares?

The front door of Grynwood stood wide open. From this door, the house breathed out upon me.

Subtle. Like waking by night to feel the push of warm air from your wife's nostrils, but suddenly terrified, for the scent of her breath has changed, she smells of someone else! You want to seize her awake, cry her name. Who *is* she, how, what? But heart thudding, you lie sleepless by some stranger in bed.

I walked. I sensed my image caught in a thousand windows moving across the grass to stand over a silent Nora.

A thousand of me sat quietly down.

Nora, I thought. Oh dear God, here we are again.

That first visit to Grynwood . . .

And then here and there through the years we had met like people brushing in a crowd, like lovers across the aisle and strangers on a train, and with the whistle crying the quick next stop, touched hands or allowed our bodies to be bruised together by the crowd cramming out as the doors flung wide, then, impelled, no more touch, no word, nothing for years.

Or, it was as if at high noon midsummer every year or so we ran off up the vital strand a way, never dreaming we might come back and collide in mutual need. And then somehow another summer ended, a sun went down, and there came Nora dragging her empty sandpail and here came I with scabs on my knees, and the beach empty and a strange season gone, and just us left to say hello Nora, hello Charles as the wind rose and the sea darkened as if a great herd of octopi suddenly swam by with their inks.

I often wondered if a day might come when we circled the long way round and stayed. Somewhere back perhaps twelve years ago there had been one moment, balanced like a feather upon fingertip, when our breaths from either side had held our love warmly and perfectly in poise.

But that was because I had bumped into Nora in Venice, with her roots packed, far from home, away from Grynwood, where she might truly belong to someone else, perhaps even to me.

But somehow our mouths had been too busy with each other to ask permanence. Next day, healing our lips, puffed from mutual assaults, we had not the strength to say forever-as-of-now, more tomorrows this way, an apartment, a house anywhere, not Grynwood, not Grynwood ever again, stay! Perhaps the light of noon was cruel, perhaps it showed too

many pores in people. Or perhaps, more accurately, the
nasty children were bored again. Or terrified of a prison of
two! Whatever the reason, the feather, once briefly lofted on
champagne breath, toppled. Neither knew which ceased
breathing upon it first. Nora pretended an urgent telegram
and fled off to Grynwood.

Contact was broken. The spoiled children never wrote. I
did not know what sand-castles she had smashed. She did not
know what Indian Madras had bled colour from passion's
sweat on my back. I married. I divorced. I travelled.

And now here we were again come from opposite directions late on a strange day by a familiar lake, calling to each
other without calling, running to each other without moving,
as if we had not been years apart.

'Nora.' I took her hand. It was cold. 'What's happened?'

'Happened?' She laughed, grew silent, staring away.
Suddenly she laughed again, that difficult laughter that
might instantly flush with tears. 'Oh, my dear Charlie, think
wild, think all, jump hoops and come round to maniac
dreams. Happened, Charlie, happened?!'

She grew frightfully still.

'Where are the servants, the guests —?'

'The party,' she said, 'was last night.'

'Impossible! You've never had just a Friday-night bash.
Sundays have always seen your lawn littered with demon
wretches strewn and bandaged with bedclothes. Why —?'

'Why did I invite you out today, you want to ask, Charles?'
Nora still looked only at the house. 'To give you Grynwood.
A gift, Charlie, if you can force it to let you stay, if it will put
up with you — '

'I don't want the house!' I burst in.

'Oh, it's not if you want *it*, but if it wants *you*. It threw us
all out, Charlie.'

'Last night . . . ?'

'Last night the last great party at Grynwood didn't come

off. Mag flew from Paris. The Aga sent a fabulous girl from Nice. Roger, Percy, Evelyn, Vivian, Jon were here. That bullfighter who almost killed the playwright over the ballerina was here. The Irish dramatist who falls off stages drunk was here. Ninety-seven guests teemed in that door between five and seven last night. By midnight they were gone.'

I walked across the lawn.

Yes, still fresh in the grass: the tyre marks of three dozen cars.

'It wouldn't let us have the party, Charles.' Nora called, faintly.

I turned blankly. 'It? The house?'

'Oh, the music was splendid but went hollow upstairs. We heard our laughter ghost back from the topmost halls. The party clogged. The *petits fours* were clods in our throat. The wine ran over our chins. No one got to bed for even three minutes. Doesn't it sound a lie? But, Limp Meringue Awards were given to all and they went away and I slept bereft on the lawn all night. Guess why? Go look, Charlie.'

We walked up to the open front door of Grynwood.

'What shall I look for?'

'Everything. All the rooms. The house itself. The mystery. Guess. And when you've guessed a thousand times I'll tell you why I can never live here again, must leave, why Grynwood is yours if you wish. Go in alone.'

And in I went, slowly, one step at a time.

I moved quietly on the lovely lion-yellow hardwood parquetry of the great hall. I gazed at the Aubusson wall tapestry. I examined the ancient white marble Greek medallions displayed on green velvet in a crystal case.

'Nothing,' I called back to Nora out there in the late cooling day.

'No. Everything,' she called. 'Go on.'

The library was a deep warm sea of leather smell where five thousand books gleamed their colours of hand-rubbed cherry, lime, and lemon bindings. Their gold eyes, bright titles, glittered. Above the fireplace which could have kennelled two firedogs and ten great hounds hung the exquisite Gainsborough *Maidens and Flowers* that had warmed the family for generations. It was a portal overlooking summer weather. One wanted to lean through and sniff wild seas of flowers, touch harvest of peach maiden girls, hear the machinery of bees bright-stitching up the glamorous airs.

'Well?' called a far voice.

'Nora!' I cried. 'Come here. There's nothing to fear! It's still daylight!'

'No,' said the far voice sadly. 'The sun is going down. What do you see, Charlie?'

'Out in the hall again, the spiral stairs. The parlour. Not a dust speck on the air. I'm opening the cellar door. A million barrels and bottles. Now the kitchen. Nora, this is lunatic!'

'Yes, isn't it?' wailed the far voice. 'Go back to the library. Stand in the middle of the room. See the Gainsborough *Maidens and Flowers* you always loved?'

'It's here.'

'It's not. See the silver Florentine humidor?'

'I see it.'

'You don't. See the great maroon leather chair where you drank sherry with Father?'

'Yes.'

'No,' sighed the voice.

'Yes, no? Do, don't? Nora, enough!'

'More than enough, Charlie. Can't you guess? Don't you *feel* what happened to Grynwood?'

I ached, turning. I sniffed the strange air.

'Charlie,' said Nora, far out by the open front door ' . . . four years ago,' she said faintly. 'Four years ago . . . Grynwood burned completely to the ground.'

I ran.

I found Nora pale at the door.

'It *what*?' I shouted.

'Burned to the ground,' she said. 'Utterly. Four years ago.'

I took three long steps outside and looked up at the walls and windows.

'Nora, it's standing, it's all here!'

'No, it isn't, Charlie. That's not Grynwood.'

I touched the grey stone, the red bricks, the green ivy. I ran my hand over the carved Spanish front door. I exhaled in awe. 'It can't be.'

'It is,' said Nora. 'All new. Everything from the cellar stones up. New, Charles. New, Charlie. New.'

'This *door*?'

'Sent up from Madrid, last year.'

'This pavement?'

'Quarried near Dublin two years ago. The windows from Waterford this spring.'

I stepped through the front door.

'The parqueting?'

'Finished in France and shipped over autumn last.'

'But, but, that *tapestry*!?'

'Woven near Paris, hung in April.'

'But it's all the *same*, Nora!'

'Yes, isn't it? I travelled to Greece to duplicate the marble relics. The crystal case I had made, too, in Rheims.'

'The library!'

'Every book, all bound the same way, stamped in similar gold, put back on similar shelves. The library alone cost one hundred thousand pounds to reproduce.'

'The same, the same, Nora,' I cried, in wonder, 'oh God, the same,' and we were in the library and I pointed at the silver Florentine humidor. 'That, of course, was saved out of the fire?'

'No, no. I'm an artist. I remembered. I sketched, I took the drawings to Florence. They finished the fraudulent fake in July.'

'The Gainsborough *Maidens and Flowers*!?'

'Look close! That's Fritzi's work. Fritzi, that horrible drip-dry beatnik painter in Montmartre? Who threw paint on canvas and flew them as kites over Paris so the wind and rain patterned beauty for him, which he sold for exorbitant prices? Well, Fritzi, it turns out, is a secret Gainsborough fanatic. He'd kill me if he knew I told. He painted this *Maidens* from memory, isn't it *fine*?'

'Fine, fine, oh God, Nora, are you telling the truth?'

'I wish I weren't. Do you think I've been mentally ill, Charles? Naturally you might think. Do you believe in good and evil, Charlie? I didn't used. But now, quite suddenly, I have turned old and rain-dowdy. I have hit forty, forty has hit me, like a locomotive. Do you know what I think? . . . the house destroyed *itself*.'

'It *what*?'

She went to peer into the halls where shadows gathered now, coming in from the late day.

'When I first came into my money, at eighteen, when people said Guilt I said Bosh. They cried Conscience. I cried Crapulous Nonsense! But in those days the rain barrel was empty. A lot of strange rain has fallen since and gathered in me, and to my cold surprise I find me to the brim with old sin and know there *is* conscience and guilt.

'There are a thousand young men in me, Charles.

'They thrust and buried themselves there. When they withdrew, Charles, I thought they withdrew. But no, no, now I'm sure there is not a single one whose barb, whose lovely poisoned thorn, is not caught in my flesh, one place or another. God, God, how I loved their barbs, their thorns. God, how I loved to be pinned and bruised. I thought the medicines of time and travel might heal the grip marks. But now I know I am all fingerprints. There lives no inch of my flesh, Chuck, that is not FBI file systems of palm print and Egyptian whorl of finger stigmata. I have been stabbed by a thousand lovely boys and thought I did not bleed but God I do bleed now. I have bled all over this house. And my friends who denied guilt and conscience, in a great subway heave of flesh have trammelled through here and jounced and mouthed each other and sweat upon floors and buckshot the walls with their agonies and descents, each from the other's crosses. The house has been stormed by assassins, Charlie, each seeking to kill the other's loneliness with their short swords, no one finding surcease, only a momentary groaning out of relaxation.

'I don't think there has ever been a happy person in this house, Charles, I see that now.

'Oh, it all *looked* happy. When you hear so much laughter and see so much drink and find human sandwiches in every bed, pink and white morsels to munch upon, you think: What joy! how happy-fine!

'But it is a lie, Charlie, you and I know that, and the house drank the lie in my generation and Father's before me and Grandfather beyond. It was always a happy house, which means a dreadful estate. The assassins have wounded each other here for long over two hundred years. The walls dripped. The doorknobs were gummy. Summer turned old in the Gainsborough frame. So the assassins came and went, Charlie, left sins and memories of sins which the house kept.

'And when you have caught up just so much darkness, Charles, you must vomit, mustn't you?

'My life is my emetic. I choke on my own past.

'So did this house.

'And finally, guilt-ridden, terribly sad, one night I heard the friction of old sins rubbing together in attic beds. And with this spontaneous combustion the house smouldered ablaze. I heard the fire first as it sat in the library, devouring books. Then I heard it in the cellar drinking wine. By that time I was out the window and down the ivy and on the lawn with the servants. We picnicked on the lake shore at four in

the morning with champagne and biscuits from the gatekeeper's lodge. The fire brigade arrived from town at five to
see the roofs collapse and vast fire founts of spark fly over the
clouds and the sinking moon. We gave them champagne also
and watched Grynwood die finally, at last, so at dawn there
was nothing.

'It had to destroy itself, didn't it, Charlie, it was so evil
from all my people and from me?'

We stood in the cold hall. At last I stirred myself and said,
'I guess so, Nora.'

We walked into the library where Nora drew forth blueprints and a score of notebooks.

'It was then, Charlie, I got my inspiration. Build
Grynwood again. A grey jigsaw puzzle put back together!
Phoenix reborn from the sootbin. So no one would know of
its death through sickness. Not you, Charlie, or any friends
off in the world; let all remain ignorant. My guilt over its
destruction was immense. How fortunate to be rich. You can
buy a fire brigade with champagne and the village news-
papers with four cases of gin. The news never got a mile out
that Grynwood was strewn sackcloth and ashes. Time later to
tell the world. Now! to work! And off I raced to my Dublin
solicitor's where my father had filed architectural plans and
interior details. I sat for months with a secretary, word-
associating to summon up Grecian lamps, Roman tiles. I shut
my eyes to recall every hairy inch of carpeting, every fringe,
every rococo ceiling oddment, all, all brasswork decor,
firedog, switchplates, log-bucket, and doorknob. And when
the list of thirty thousand items was compounded, I flew in
carpenters from Edinburgh, tile setters from Siena, stone-
cutters from Perugia, and they hammered, nailed, thrived,
carved, and set for four years, Charlie, and I loitered at the
factory outside Paris to watch spiders weave my tapestry and
floor the rugs. I rode to hounds at Waterford while watching
them blow my glass.

'Oh, Charles, I don't think it has ever happened, has it in history, that anyone ever put a destroyed thing back the way it was? Forget the past, let the bones cease! Well, not for me, I thought, no: Grynwood shall rise and be as ever it was. But, while looking like the old Grynwood, it would have the advantage of being really new. A fresh start, I thought, and while building it I led such a *quiet* life, Charles. The work was adventure enough.

'As I did the house over, I thought I did myself over. While I favoured it with rebirth, I favoured myself with joy. At long last, I thought, a happy person comes and goes at Grynwood.

'And it was finished and done, the last stone cut, the last tile placed, two weeks ago.

'And I sent invitations across the world, Charlie, and last night they all arrived, a pride of lion-men from New York, smelling of Saint John's breadfruit, the staff of life. A team of lightfoot Athens boys. A Negro *corps de ballet* from Johannesburg. Three Sicilian bandits, or were they actors? Seventeen lady violinists who might be ravished as they laid down their violins and picked up their skirts. Four champion polo players. One tennis pro to restring my guts. A darling French poet. Oh God, Charles, it was to be a swell grand fine re-opening of the Phoenix Estates. Nora Gryndon, proprietress. How did I know, or guess, the house would not want us here?'

'Can a house want or not want?'

'Yes, when it is very new and everyone else, no matter what age, is very old. It was freshly born. We were stale and dying. It was good. We were evil. It wished to stay innocent. So it turned us out.'

'How?'

'Why, just by being itself. It made the air so quiet, Charlie, you wouldn't believe. We all felt someone had died.

'After a while, with no one saying but everyone feeling it,

people just got in their cars and drove away. The orchestra shut up its music and sped off in ten limousines. There went the entire party, around the lake drive, as if heading for a midnight outdoor picnic, but no, just going to the airport or the boats, or Galway, everyone cold, no one speaking, and the house empty, and the servants themselves pumping away on their bikes, and me alone in the house, the last party over, the party that never happened, that never could begin. As I said, I slept on the lawn all night, alone with my old thoughts and I knew this was the end of all the years, for I was ashes, and ashes cannot build. It was the new grand lovely fine bird lying in the dark, by itself. It hated my breath in the dooryard. I was over. It had begun. There.'

Nora was finished with her story.

We sat silently for a long while in the very late afternoon as dusk gathered to fill the rooms, and put out the eyes of the windows. A wind rippled the lake.

I said, 'It can't all be true. Surely you *can* stay here.'

'A final test, so you'll not argue me again. We shall try to spend the night here.'

'Try?'

'We won't make it through till dawn. Let's fry a few eggs, drink some wine, go to bed early. But lie on top of your covers with your clothes on. You shall want your clothes, swiftly, I imagine.'

We ate almost in silence. We drank wine. We listened to the new hours striking from the new brass clocks everywhere in the new house.

At ten, Nora sent me up to my room.

'Don't be afraid,' she called to me on the landing. 'The house means us no harm. It simply fears *we* may hurt *it*. I shall read in the library. When you are ready to leave, no matter what hour, come for me.'

'I shall sleep snug as a bug,' I said.

'*Shall* you?' said Nora.

And I went up to my new bed and lay in the dark smoking, feeling neither afraid nor smug, calmly waiting for any sort of happening at all.

I did not sleep at midnight.

I was awake at one.

At three, my eyes were still wide.

The house did not creak, sigh, or murmur. It waited, as I waited, timing its breath to mine.

At three-thirty in the morning the door to my room slowly opened.

There was simply a motion of dark upon dark. I felt the wind draught over my hands and face.

I sat up slowly in the dark.

Five minutes passed. My heart slowed its beating.

And then far away below, I heard the front door open.

Again, not a creak or whisper. Just the click and shadowing change of wind motioning the corridors.

I got up and went out into the hall.

From the top of the stairwell I saw what I expected: the front door open. Moonlight flooded the new parqueting and shone upon the new grandfather clock which ticked with a fresh oiled bright sound.

I went down and out the front door.

'*There* you are,' said Nora, standing down by my car in the drive.

I went to her.

'You didn't hear a thing,' she said, 'and yet you heard something, right?'

'Right.'

'Are you ready to leave now, Charles?'

I looked up at the house. 'Almost.'

'You know now, don't you, it is all over? You feel it, surely, that it is the dawn come up on a new morning? And, feel my heart, my soul beating pale and mossy within my heart, my blood so black, Charlie, you have felt it often beating under your own body, you know how old I am. You know how full of dungeons and racks and late afternoons and blue hours of French twilight I am. Well . . . '

Nora looked at the house.

'Last night, as I lay in bed at two in the morning, I heard the front door drift open. I knew that the whole house had simply leant itself ajar to let the latch free and glide the door wide. I went to the top of the stairs. And, looking down, I saw the creek of moonlight laid out fresh in the hall. And the house so much as said, Here is the way you go, tread the cream, walk the milky new path out of this and away, go, old one, go with your darkness. You are with child. The sour-gum ghost is in your stomach. It will never be born. And because you cannot drop it, one day it will be your death. What are you waiting for?

'Well, Charles, I was afraid to go down and shut that door. And I knew it was true, I would never sleep again. So, I went down and out.

'I have a dark old sinful place in Geneva. I'll go there to live. But you are younger and fresher, Charlie, so I want this place to be yours.'

'Not so young.'

'Younger than I.'

'Not so fresh. It wants me to go, too, Nora. The door to *my* room just now. It opened, too.'

'Oh, Charlie,' breathed Nora, and touched my cheek. 'Oh, Charles,' and then, softly, 'I'm sorry.'

'Don't be. We'll go together.'

Nora opened the car door.

'Let me drive. I must drive now, very fast, all the way to Dublin. Do you mind?'

'No. But what about your luggage?'

'What's in there, the house can have. Where are you going?'

I stopped walking. 'I must shut the front door.'

'No,' said Nora. 'Leave it open.'

'But . . . people will come in.'

Nora laughed quietly. 'Yes. But only good people. So that's all right, isn't it?'

I finally nodded. 'Yes. That's all right.'

I came back to stand by my car, reluctant to leave. Clouds were gathering. It was beginning to snow. Great gentle white leaflets fell down out on the moonlit sky as harmlessly soft as the gossip of angels.

We got in and slammed the car doors. Nora gunned the motor.

'Ready?' she said.

'Ready.'

'Charlie?' said Nora. 'When we get to Dublin, will you sleep with me, I mean *sleep*, the next few days? I shall need someone the next days. Will you?'

'Of course.'

'I wish,' she said. And tears filled her eyes. 'Oh God, how I wish I could burn myself down and start over. Burn myself down so I could go up to the house now and go in and live forever like a dairy maid full of berries and cream. Oh but hell. What's the use of talk like that?'

'Drive, Nora,' I said gently.

And she drummed the motor and we ran out of the valley, along the lake, with gravel buckshotting out behind, and up the hills and through the deep snow forest, and by the time we reached the last rise, Nora's tears were shaken away, she did not look back, and we drove at seventy through the dense falling and thicker night towards a darker horizon and a cold stone city, and all the way, never once letting go, in silence I held one of her hands.

Tomorrow's Child

He did not want to be father of a small Blue Pyramid. Peter
Horn hadn't planned it that way at all. Neither he nor his wife
imagined that such a thing could happen to them. They had
talked quietly for days about the birth of their coming child,
they had eaten normal foods, slept a great deal, taken in a few
shows, and, when it was time for her to fly in the helicopter to
the hospital, her husband held her and kissed her.

'Honey, you'll be home in six hours,' he said. 'These new
birth-mechanisims do everything but father the child for
you.'

She remembered an old-time-song — 'No, no, they can't
take that away from me!' — and sang it, and they laughed as
the helicopter lifted them over the green way from country to
city.

The doctor, a quiet gentleman named Wolcott, was very
confident. Polly Ann, the wife, was made ready for the task
ahead and the father was put, as usual, out in the waiting
room where he could suck on cigarettes or take highballs
from a convenient mixer. He was feeling pretty good. This
was the first baby, but there was not a thing to worry about.
Polly Ann was in good hands.

Dr Wolcott came into the waiting room an hour later. He
looked like a man who has seen death. Peter Horn, on his
third highball, did not move. His hand tightened on the glass
and he whispered:

'She's dead.'

'No,' said Wolcott, quietly. 'No, no, she's fine. It's the
baby.'

'The baby's dead, then.'

'The baby's alive, too, but − drink the rest of that drink and come along after me. Something's happened.'

Yes, indeed, something had happened. The 'something' that had happened had brought the entire hospital out into the corridors. People were going and coming from one room to another. As Peter Horn was led through a hallway where attendants in white uniforms were standing around peering into each other's faces and whispering, he became quite ill.

'Hey, looky looky! The child of Peter Horn! Incredible!'

They entered a small clean room. There was a crowd in the room, looking down at a low table. There was something on the table.

A small Blue Pyramid.

'Why've you brought me here?' said Horn, turning to the doctor.

The small Blue Pyramid moved. It began to cry.

Peter Horn pushed forward and looked down wildly. He was very white and he was breathing rapidly. 'You don't mean that's it?'

The doctor named Wolcott nodded.

The Blue Pyramid had six blue snakelike appendages and three eyes that blinked from the tips of projecting structures.

Horn didn't move.

'It weighs seven pounds, eight ounces,' someone said.

Horn thought to himself. They're kidding me. This is some joke. Charlie Ruscoll is behind all this. He'll pop in a door any moment and cry 'April Fool!' and everybody'll laugh. That's not my child. Oh, horrible! They're kidding me.

Horn stood there, and the sweat rolled down his face.

'Get me away from here.' Horn turned and his hands were opening and closing without purpose, his eyes were flickering.

Wolcott held his elbow, talking calmly. 'This is your child. Understand that, Mr Horn.'

'No. No, it's not.' His mind wouldn't touch the thing. 'It's a nightmare. Destroy *it*!'

'You can't kill a human being.'

'Human?' Horn blinked tears. 'That's not human! That's a crime against God!'

The doctor went on, quickly. 'We've examined this — child — and we've decided that it is not a mutant, a result of gene destruction or rearrangement. It's not a freak. Nor is it sick. Please listen to everything I say to you.'

Horn stared at the wall, his eyes wide and sick. He swayed. The doctor talked distantly, with assurance.

'This child was somehow affected by the birth pressure. There was a dimensional disstructure caused by the simultaneous short-circuitings and malfunctionings of the new birth and hypnosis machines. Well, anyway,' the doctor ended lamely, 'your baby was born into — another dimension.'

Horn did not even nod. He stood there, waiting.

Dr Wolcott made it emphatic. 'Your child is alive, well, and happy. It is lying there, on the table. But because it was born into another dimension it has a shape alien to us. Our eyes, adjusted to a three-dimensional concept, cannot recognize it as a baby. But it *is*. Underneath that camouflage, the strange pyramidal shape and appendages, it is *your* child.'

Horn closed his mouth and shut his eyes. 'Can I have a drink?'

'Certainly.' A drink was thrust into Horn's hands.

'Now, let me just sit down, sit down somewhere a moment.' Horn sank wearily into a chair. It was coming clear. Everything shifted slowly into place. It was his child, no matter what. He shuddered. No matter how horrible it looked, it was his first child.

At last he looked up and tried to see the doctor. 'What'll we tell Polly?' His voice was hardly a whisper.

'We'll work that out this morning, as soon as you feel up to it.'

'What happens after that? Is there any way to – change it back?'

'We'll try. That is, if you give us permission to try. After all, it's your child. You can do anything with him you want to do.'

'Him?' Horn laughed ironically, shutting his eyes. 'How do you know it's a him?' He sank down into darkness. His ears roared.

Wolcott was visibly upset. 'Why, we – that is – well, we don't know, for sure.'

Horn drank more of his drink. 'What if you *can't* change him back?'

'I realize what a shock it is to you, Mr Horn. If you can't bear to look upon the child, we'll be glad to raise him here, at the Institute, for you.'

Horn thought it over. 'Thanks. But he still belongs to me and Polly. I'll give him a home. Raise him like I'd raise any kid. Give him a normal home life. Try to learn to love him. Treat him right.' His lips were numb, he couldn't think.

'You realize what a job you're taking on, Mr Horn. This child can't be allowed to have normal playmates; why, they'd pester it to death in no time. You know how children are. If you decide to raise the child at home, his life will be strictly regimented, he must *never* be seen by anyone. Is that clear?'

'Yes. Yes, it's clear, Doc. Doc, is he all right mentally?'

'Yes. We've tested his reactions. He's a fine healthy child as far as nervous response and such things go.'

'I just wanted to be sure. Now, the only person is Polly.'

Wolcott frowned. 'I confess that one has me stumped. You know it is pretty hard on a woman to hear that her child has been born dead. But *this*, telling a woman she's given birth to something not recognizable as human. It's not as clean as death. There's too much chance for shock. And yet I must tell her the truth. A doctor gets nowhere by lying to his patient.'

Horn put his glass down. 'I don't want to lose Polly, too. I'd be prepared now, if you destroyed the child, to take it. But I don't want Polly killed by the shock of this whole thing.'

'I think we may be able to change the child back. That's the point which makes me hesitate. If I thought the case was hopeless I'd make out a certificate of euthanasia immediately. But it's at least worth a chance.'

Horn was very tired. He was shivering quietly, deeply. 'All right, Doctor. It needs food, milk, and love until you can fix it up. It's had a raw deal so far, no reason for it to go on getting a raw deal. When will we tell Polly?'

'Tomorrow afternoon, when she wakes up.'

Horn got up and walked to the table which was warmed by a soft illumination from overhead. The Blue Pyramid sat upon the table as Horn held out his hand.

'Hello, Baby,' said Horn.

The Blue Pyramid looked up at Horn with three bright blue eyes. It shifted a tiny blue tendril, touching Horn's fingers with it.

Horn shivered.

'Hello, Baby.'

The doctor produced a special feeding bottle.

'This is woman's milk. Here we go.'

Baby looked upwards through clearing mists. Baby saw the shapes moving over him and knew them to be friendly. Baby was newborn, but already alert, strangely alert. Baby was aware.

There were moving objects above and around Baby. Six cubes of grey-white colour, bending down. Six cubes with hexagonal appendages and three eyes to each cube. Then there were two other cubes coming from a distance over a crystalline plateau. One of the cubes was white. It had three eyes too. There was something about this White Cube that Baby liked. There was an attraction. Some relation. There was an odour to the White Cube that reminded Baby of itself.

Shrill sounds came from the six bending-down Grey-White Cubes. Sounds of curiosity and wonder. It was like a kind of piccolo music, all playing at once.

Now the two newly arrived cubes, the White Cube and the Grey Cube, were whistling. After a while the White Cube extended one of its hexagonal appendages to touch Baby. Baby responded by putting out one of its tendrils from its pyramidal body. Baby liked the White Cube. Baby liked. Baby was hungry. Baby liked. Maybe the White Cube would give it food . . .

The Grey Cube produced a pink globe for Baby. Baby was now to be fed. Good. Good. Baby accepted food eagerly.

Food was good. All the Grey-White Cubes drifted away, leaving only the nice White Cube standing over Baby looking down and whistling over and over. Over and over.

They told Polly the next day. Not everything. Just enough. Just a hint. They told her the baby was not well, in a certain way. They talked slowly, and in ever-tightening circles, in upon Polly. Then Dr Wolcott gave a long lecture on the birth-mechanisms, how they helped a woman in her labour, and how, this time, they had short-circuited. There was another man of scientific means present and he gave her a dry little talk on dimensions, holding up his fingers, so! one, two, three, and four. Still another man talked of energy and matter. Another spoke of underprivileged children.

Polly finally sat up in bed and said, 'What's all the talk for? What's wrong with my baby that you should all be talking so long?'

Wolcott told her.

'Of course, you can wait a week and see it,' he said. 'Or you can sign over guardianship of the child to the Institute.'

'There's only one thing I want to know,' said Polly.

Dr Wolcott raised his brows.

'*Did I* make the child that way?' asked Polly.

'You most certainly did *not*!'

'The child isn't a monster, genetically?' asked Polly.

'The child was thrust into another continuum. Otherwise, it is perfectly normal.'

Polly's tight, lined mouth relaxed. She said, simply, 'Then, bring me my baby. I want to see him. Please. Now.'

They brought the 'child'.

The Horns left the hospital the next day. Polly walked out on her own two good legs, with Peter Horn following her, looking at her in quiet amazement.

They did not have the baby with them. That would come later. Horn helped his wife into their helicopter and sat beside her. He lifted the ship, whirring, into the warm air.

'You're a wonder,' he said.

'Am I?' she said, lighting a cigarette.

'You are. You didn't cry. You didn't do anything.'

'He's not so bad, you know,' she said. 'Once you get to know him. I can even — hold him in my arms. He's warm and he cries and he even needs his triangular diapers.' Here she laughed. He noticed a nervous tremor in the laugh, however. 'No, I didn't cry, Pete, because that's my baby. Or he will be. He isn't dead, I thank God for that. He's — I don't know how to explain — still unborn. I like to think he hasn't been born yet. We're waiting for him to show up. I have confidence in Dr Wolcott. Haven't you?'

'You're right. You're right.' He reached over and held her hand. 'You know something? You're a peach.'

'I can hold on,' she said, sitting there looking ahead as the green country swung under them. 'As long as I know something good will happen, I won't let it hurt or shock me. I'll wait six months, and then maybe I'll kill myself.'

'Polly!'

She looked at him as if he'd just come in. 'Pete, I'm sorry. But this sort of thing doesn't happen. Once it's over and the baby is finally "born'll", I'll forget it so quick it'll never have occurred. But if the doctor can't help us, then a mind can't take it, a mind can only tell the body to climb out on a roof and jump.'

'Things'll be all right,' he said, holding to the guide-wheel. 'They have to be.'

She said nothing, but let the cigarette smoke blow out of her mouth in the pounding concussion of the helicopter fan.

Three weeks passed. Every day they flew in to the Institute to visit 'Py'. For that was the quiet calm name that Polly Horn gave to the Blue Pyramid that lay on the warm sleeping-table and blinked up at them. Dr Wolcott was careful to point out that the habits of the 'child' were as normal as any others; so many hours asleep, so many awake, so much attentiveness, so much boredom, so much food, so much elimination. Polly Horn listened, and her face softened and her eyes warmed.

At the end of the third week, Dr Wolcott said, 'Feel up to taking him home now? You live in the country, don't you? All right, you have an enclosed patio, he can be out there in the sunlight, on occasion. He needs a mother's love. That's trite, but nevertheless true. He should be suckled. We have an arrangement where he's been fed by the new feed-mech; cooing voice, warmth, hands, and all.' Dr Wolcott's voice was dry. 'But still I feel you are familiar enough with him now to know he's a pretty healthy child. Are you game, Mrs Horn?'

'Yes, I'm game.'

'Good. Bring him in every third day for a checkup. Here's his formula. We're working on several solutions now, Mrs Horn. We should have some results for you by the end of the year. I don't want to say anything definite, but I have reason to believe we'll pull that boy out of the fourth dimension, like a rabbit out of a hat.'

The doctor was mildly surprised and pleased when Polly Horn kissed him, then and there.

Peter Horn took the copter home over the smooth rolling greens of Griffith. From time to time he looked at the pyramid lying in Polly's arms. She was making cooing noises at it, it was replying in approximately the same way.

'I wonder,' said Polly.

'What?'

'How do *we* look to *it*?' asked his wife.

'I asked Wolcott about that. He said we probably look funny to him, also. He's in one dimension, we're in another.'

'You mean we don't look like men and women to him?'

'If we could see ourselves, no. But remember, the baby knows nothing of men or women. To the baby whatever shape we're in, we are natural. It's accustomed to seeing us shaped like cubes or squares or pyramids, as it sees us from its separate dimension. The baby's had no other experience, no other norm with which to compare what it sees. We *are* it's norm. On the other hand, the baby seems weird to us because we compare it to our accustomed shapes and sizes.'

'Yes, I see. I see.'

Baby was conscious of movement. One White Cube held him in warm appendages. Another White Cube sat further over, within an oblong of purple. The oblong moved in the air over a vast bright plain of pyramids, hexagons, oblongs, pillars, bubbles, and multicoloured cubes.

One White Cube made a whistling noise. The other White Cube replied with a whistling. The White Cube that held him shifted about. Baby watched the two White Cubes, and watched the fleeing world outside the travelling bubble.

Baby felt — sleepy. Baby closed his eyes, settled his

pyramidal youngness upon the lap of the White Cube, and made faint little noises . . .

'He's asleep,' said Polly Horn.

Summer came, Peter Horn himself was busy with his export-import business. But he made certain he was home every night. Polly was all right during the day, but, at night, when she had to be alone with the child, she got to smoking too much, and one night he found her passed out on the davenport, an empty sherry bottle on the table beside her. From then on, he took care of the child himself nights. When it cried it made a weird whistling noise, like some jungle animal lost and wailing. It wasn't the sound of a child.

Peter Horn had the nursery soundproofed.

'So your wife won't hear your baby crying?' asked the workman.

'Yes,' said Peter Horn. 'So she won't hear.'

They had few visitors. They were afraid that someone might stumble on Py, dear sweet pyramid little Py.

'What's that noise?' asked a visitor one evening, over his cocktail. 'Sounds like some sort of bird. You didn't tell me you had an aviary, Peter.'

'Oh, yes,' said Horn, closing the nursery door. 'Have another drink. Let's drink, everyone.'

It was like having a dog or a cat in the house. At least that's how Polly looked upon it. Peter Horn watched her and observed exactly how she talked and petted the small Py. It was Py this and Py that, but somehow with some reserve, and sometimes she would look around the room and touch herself, and her hands would clench, and she would look lost and afraid, as if she were waiting for someone to arrive.

In September, Polly reported to her husband: 'He can say Father. Yes he can. Come on, Py. Say Father!'

She held the blue warm pyramid up.

'Wheelly,' whistled the little warm Blue Pyramid.

'Again,' repeated Polly.

'Wheelly!' whistled the pyramid.

'For God's sake, stop!' said Peter Horn. He took the child from her and put it in the nursery where it whistled over and over that name, that name, that name. Horn came out and poured himself a stiff drink. Polly was laughing quietly.

'Isn't that terrific?' she said. 'Even his *voice* is in the fourth dimension. Won't it be nice when he learns to talk later? We'll give him Hamlet's soliloquy to memorize and he'll say it but it'll come out like something from James Joyce! Aren't we lucky? Give me a drink.'

'You've had enough,' he said.

'Thanks, I'll help myself,' she said and did.

October, and then November. Py was learning to talk now. He whistled and squealed and made a bell-like tone when he was hungry. Dr Wolcott visited. 'When his colour is a constant bright blue,' said the doctor, 'that means he's healthy. When the colour fades, dull — the child is feeling poorly. Remember that.'

'Oh, yes, I will, I will,' said Polly. 'Robin's-egg blue for health, dull cobalt for illness.'

'Young lady,' said Wolcott. 'You'd better take a couple of these pills and come see me tomorrow for a little chat. I don't like the way you're talking. Stick out your tongue. Ah-hmm. You been drinking? Look at the stains on your fingers. Cut the cigarettes in half. See you tomorrow.'

'You don't give me much to go on,' said Polly. 'It's been almost a year now.'

'My dear Mrs Horn, I don't want to excite you continually. When we have our mechs ready, we'll let you know. We're working every day. There'll be an experiment soon. Take those pills now and shut that nice mouth.' He chucked Py under the 'chin'. 'Good healthy baby, by God! Twenty pounds if he's an *ounce*!'

Baby was conscious of the goings and comings of the two

nice White Cubes who were with him during all of his waking hours. There was another cube, a grey one, who visited on certain days. But mostly it was the two White Cubes who cared for and loved him. He looked at the one warm, rounder, softer White Cube and made the low warbling soft sound of contentment. The White Cube fed him. He was content. He grew. All was familiar and good.

The New Year, the year 1989, arrived.

Rocket ships flashed on the sky, and helicopters whirred and flourished the warm California winds.

Peter Horn carted home large plates of specially poured blue and grey polarized glass, secretly. Through these, he peered at his 'child'. Nothing. The pyramid remained a pyramid, no matter if he viewed it through X-ray or yellow cellophane. The barrier was unbreakable. Horn returned quietly to his drinking.

The big thing happened early in February. Horn, arriving home in his helicopter, was appalled to see a crowd of neighbours gathered on the lawn of his home. Some of them were sitting, others were standing, still others were moving away, with frightened expressions on their faces.

Polly was walking the 'child' in the yard.

Polly was quite drunk. She held the small Blue Pyramid by the hand and walked him up and down. She did not see the helicopter land, nor did she pay much attention as Horn came running up.

One of the neighbours turned. 'Oh, Mr Horn, it's the cutest thing. Where'd you *find* it?'

One of the others cried, 'Hey, you're quite the traveller, Horn. Pick it up in South America?'

Polly held the pyramid up. 'Say Father!' she cried, trying to focus on her husband.

'Wheel!' cried the pyramid.

'Polly!' Peter Horn said.

'He's friendly as a dog or a cat,' said Polly, moving the

child with her. 'Oh, no, he's not dangerous. He's friendly as a baby. My husband brought him from Afghanistan.'

The neighbours began to move off.

'Come back!' Polly waved at them. 'Don't you want to see my baby? Isn't he simply beautiful!'

He slapped her face.

'My baby,' she said, brokenly.

He slapped her again and again until she quit saying it and collapsed. He picked her up and took her into the house. Then he came out and took Py in and then he sat down and phoned the Institute.

'Dr Wolcott, this is Horn. You'd better have your stuff ready. It's tonight or not at all.'

There was a hesitation. Finally Wolcott sighed. 'All right. Bring your wife and the child. We'll try to have things in shape.'

They hung up.

Horn sat there studying the pyramid.

'The neighbours thought he was grand,' said his wife, lying on the couch, her eyes shut, her lips trembling . . .

The Institute hall smelled clean, neat, sterile. Dr Wolcott walked along it, followed by Peter Horn and his wife Polly, who was holding Py in her arms. They turned in at a doorway and stood in a large room. In the centre of the room were two tables with large black hoods suspended over them.

Behind the tables were a number of machines with dials and levers on them. There was the faintest perceptible hum in the room. Peter Horn looked at Polly for a moment.

Wolcott gave her a glass of liquid. 'Drink this.' She drank it. 'Now. Sit down.' They sat. The doctor put his hands together and looked at them for a moment.

'I want to tell you what I've been doing in the last few months,' he said. 'I've tried to bring the baby out of whatever hell dimension, fourth, fifth, or sixth, that it is in. Each time you left the baby for a checkup we worked on the problem.

Now, we have a solution, but it has nothing to do with bringing the baby out of the dimension in which *it* exists.'

Polly sank back. Horn simply watched the doctor carefully for anything he might say. Wolcott leaned forward.

'I can't bring Py out, but I can put you people *in*. That's it.' He spread his hands.

Horn looked at the machine in the corner. 'You mean you can send *us* into Py's dimension.'

'If you want to go badly enough.'

Polly said nothing. She held Py quietly and looked at him.

Dr Wolcott explained. 'We know what series of malfunctions, mechanical and electrical, forced Py into his present state. We can reproduce those accidents and stresses. But bringing him *back* is something else. It might take a million trials and failures before we got the combination. The combination that jammed him into another space was an accident, but luckily we saw, observed, and recorded it. There are no records for bringing one back. We have to work in the dark. Therefore, it will be easier to put *you* in the fourth dimension than to bring Py into ours.'

Polly asked, simply and earnestly, 'Will I see my baby as he really is, if I go into his dimension?'

Wolcott nodded.

Polly said, 'Then I want to go.'

'Hold on,' said Peter Horn. 'We've only been in this office five minutes and already you're promising away the rest of your life.'

'I'll be with my real baby. I won't care.'

'Dr Wolcott, what will it be like, in that dimension on the other side?'

'There will be no change that *you* will notice. You will both seem the same size and shape to one another. The pyramid will become a baby, however. You will have added an extra sense, you will be able to interpret what you see differently.'

'But won't we turn into oblongs or pyramids ourselves?

And won't you, Doctor, look like some geometrical form instead of a human?'

'Does a blind man who sees for the first time give up his ability to hear or taste?'

'No.'

'All right, then. Stop thinking in terms of subtraction. Think in terms of addition. You're gaining something. You lose nothing. You know what a human looks like, which is an advantage Py doesn't have, looking out from his dimension. When you arrive "over there" you can see Dr Wolcott as *both* things, a geometrical abstract or a human, as you choose. It will probably make quite a philosopher out of you. There's one other thing, however.'

'And that?'

'To everyone else in the world you, your wife and the child will look like abstract forms. The baby a triangle. Your wife an oblong perhaps. Yourself a hexagonal solid. The world will be shocked, not you.'

'We'll be freaks.'

'You'll be freaks. But you won't know it. You'll have to lead a secluded life.'

'Until you find a way to bring all three of us out together.'

'That's right. It may be ten years, twenty. I won't recommend it to you, you may both go quite mad as a result of feeling apart, different. If there's a grain of paranoia in you, it'll come out. It's up to you, naturally.'

Peter Horn looked at his wife, she looked back gravely.

'We'll go,' said Peter Horn.

'Into Py's dimension?' said Wolcott.

'Into Py's dimension.'

They stood up from their chairs. 'We'll lose no other sense, you're certain, Doctor? Will you be able to understand us when we talk to you? Py's talk is incomprehensible.'

'Py talks that way because that's what he thinks we sound like when our talk comes through the dimensions to him. He imitates the sound. When you are over there and talk to me, you'll be talking perfect English, because you know *how*. Dimensions have to do with senses and time and knowledge.'

'And what about Py? When we come into his stratum of existence. Will he see us as humans, immediately, and won't that be a shock to him? Won't it be dangerous?'

'He's awfully young. Things haven't got too set for him. There'll be a slight shock, but your odours will be the same, and your voices will have the same timbre and pitch and you'll be just as warm and loving, which is most important of all. You'll get on with him well.'

Horn scratched his head slowly. 'This seems such a long way around to where we want to go.' He sighed. 'I wish we could have another kid and forget all about this one.'

'This baby is the one that counts. I daresay Polly here wouldn't want any other, would you, Polly?'

'This baby, *this* baby,' said Polly.

Wolcott gave Peter Horn a meaningful look. Horn interpreted it correctly. This baby or no more Polly ever again. This baby or Polly would be in a quiet room somewhere staring into space for the rest of her life.

They moved towards the machine together. 'I guess I can stand it, if she can,' said Horn, taking her hand. 'I've worked hard for many years now, it might be fun retiring and being an abstract for a change.'

'I envy you the journey, to be honest with you,' said Wolcott, making adjustments on the large dark machine. 'I don't mind telling you that as a result of your being "over there" you may very well write a volume of philosophy that will set Dewey, Bergson, Hegel, or any of the others on their ears. I might "come over" to visit you one day.'

'You'll be welcome. What do we need for the trip?'

'Nothing. Just lie on these tables and be still.'

A humming filled the room. A sound of power and energy and warmth.

They lay on the tables, holding hands, Polly and Peter Horn. A double black hoof came down over them. They were both in darkness. From somewhere far off in the hospital, a voice-clock sang, '*Tick-tock, seven o'clock. Tick-tock, seven o'clock* . . . ' fading away in a little soft gong.

The low humming grew louder. The machine glittered with hidden, shifting, compressed power.

'Is there any danger?' cried Peter.

'None!'

The power screamed. The very atoms of the room divided against each other, into alien and enemy camps. The two sides fought for supremacy. Horn gaped his mouth to shout. His insides became pyramidal, oblong with terrific electric seizures. He felt a pulling, suckling, demanding power claw at his body. The power yearned and nuzzled and pressed through the room. The dimensions of the black hood over his torso were stretched, pulled into wild planes of incomprehension. Sweat, pouring down his face, was not sweat, but a pure dimensional essence! His limbs were wrenched, flung, jabbed, suddenly caught. He began to melt like running wax.

A clicking sliding noise.

Horn thought swiftly, but calmly. How will it be in the future with Polly and me and Py at home and people coming over for a cocktail party? How will it be?

Suddenly he knew how it would be and the thought of it filled him with a great awe and a sense of credulous faith and time. They would live in the same white house on the same quiet, green hill, with a high fence around it to keep out the merely curious. And Dr Wolcott would come to visit, park his beetle in the yard below, come up the steps and at the door would be a tall slim White Rectangle to meet him with a dry martini in its snakelike hand.

And in an easy chair across the room would sit a Salt White Oblong with a copy of Nietzsche open, reading, smoking a pipe. And on the floor would be Py, running about. And there would be talk and more friends would come in and the White Oblong and the White Rectangle would laugh and joke and offer little finger sandwiches and more drinks and it would be a good evening of talk and laughter.

That's how it would be.

Click.

The humming noise stopped.

The hood lifted from Horn.

It was all over.

They were in another dimension.

He heard Polly cry out. There was much light. Then he slipped from the table, stood blinking. Polly was running. She stopped and picked up something from the floor.

It was Peter Horn's son. A living pink-faced, blue-eyed boy, lying in her arms, gasping and blinking and crying.

The pyramidal shape was gone. Polly was crying with happiness.

Peter Horn walked across the room, trembling, trying to smile to himself, to hold on to Polly and the child, both at the same time, and weep with them.

'Well!' said Wolcott, standing back. He did not move for a long while. He only watched the White Oblong and the slim White Rectangle holding the Blue Pyramid on the opposite side of the room. An assistant came in the door.

'Shhh,' said Wolcott, hand to his lips. 'They'll want to be alone a while. Come along.' He took the assistant by the arm and tiptoed across the room. The White Rectangle and the White Oblong didn't even look up when the door closed.

I Sing the Body Electric!

Grandma!

I remember her birth.

Wait, you say, *no* man remembers his own grandma's birth.

But, yes, *we* remember the day that she was born.

For we, her grandchildren, slapped her to life. Timothy, Agatha, and I, Tom, raised up our hands and brought them down in a huge crack! We shook together the bits and pieces, parts and samples, textures and tastes, humours and distillations that would move her compass needle north to cool us, south to warm and comfort us, east and west to travel round the endless world, glide her eyes to know us, mouth to sing us asleep by night, hands to touch us awake at dawn.

Grandma. O dear and wondrous electric dream . . .

When storm lightnings rove the sky making circuitries amidst the clouds, her name flashes on my inner lid. Sometimes still I hear her ticking, humming above our beds in the gentle dark. She passes like a clock-ghost in the long halls of memory, like a hive of intellectual bees swarming after the Spirit of Summers Lost. Sometimes still I feel the smile I learned from her, printed on my cheek at three in the deep morn . . .

All right, all right! you cry. What was it like the day your damned and wondrous-dreadful-loving Grandma was born?

It was the week the world ended . . .

Our mother was dead.

One late afternoon a black car left Father and the three of us stranded on our own front drive staring at the grass, thinking:

That's not our grass. There are the croquet mallets, balls, hoops, yes, just as they fell and lay three days ago when Dad stumbled out on the lawn, weeping with the news. There are the roller skates that belonged to a boy, me, who will never be that young again. And yes, there the tyre-swing on the old oak, but Agatha afraid to swing. It would surely break. It would fall.

And the house? Oh, God . . .

We peered through the front door, afraid of the echoes we might find confused in the halls; the sort of clamour that happens when all the furniture is taken out and there is nothing to soften the river of talk that flows in any house at all hours. And now the soft, the warm, the main piece of lovely furniture was gone forever.

The door drifted wide.

Silence came out. Somewhere a cellar door stood wide and a raw wind blew damp earth from under the house.

But, I thought, we don't *have* a cellar!

'Well,' said Father.

We did not move.

Aunt Clara drove up the path in her big canary-coloured limousine.

We jumped through the door. We ran to our rooms.

We heard them shout and then speak and then shout and then speak: Let the children live with me! Aunt Clara said. They'd rather kill themselves! Father said.

A door slammed. Aunt Clara was gone.

We almost danced. Then we remembered what had happened and went downstairs.

Father sat alone talking to himself or to a remnant ghost of Mother left from the days before her illness, and jarred loose now by the slamming of the door. He mumured to his hands, his empty palms:

'The children need someone. I love them but, let's face it, I must work to feed us all. You love them, Ann, but you're gone. And Clara? Impossible. She loves but smothers. And as for maids, nurses —?'

Here Father sighed and we sighed with him, remembering.

The luck he had had with maids or live-in teachers or sitters was beyond intolerable. Hardly a one who wasn't a crosscut saw grabbing against the grain. Handaxes and hurricanes best described them. Or, conversely, they were all fallen trifle, damp soufflé. We children were unseen furniture to be sat upon or dusted or sent for reupholstering come spring and fall, with a yearly cleaning at the beach.

'What we need,' said Father, 'is a . . . '

We all leaned to his whisper.

' . . . grandmother.'

'But,' said Timothy, with the logic of nine years, 'all our grandmothers are dead.'

'Yes in one way, no in another.'

What a fine mysterious thing for Dad to say.

'Here,' he said at last.

He handed us a multifold, multicoloured pamphlet. We had seen it in his hands, off and on, for many weeks, and very often during the last few days. Now, with one blink of our eyes, as we passed the paper from hand to hand, we knew why Aunt Clara, insulted, outraged, had stormed from the house.

Timothy was the first to read aloud from what he saw on the first page:

' "I Sing the Body Electric!" '

He glanced up at Father, squinting. 'What the heck does that mean?'

'Read on.'

Agatha and I glanced guiltily about the room, afraid Mother might suddenly come in to find us with this blasphemy, but then nodded to Timothy, who read:

' "Fanto —" '

'Fantoccini,' Father prompted.

' "Fantoccini Limited. *We Shadow Forth* . . . the answer to all your most grievous problems. One Model Only, upon which a thousand times a thousand variations can be added, subtracted, subdivided, indivisible, with Liberty and Justice for all." '

'Where does it say *that*?' we all cried.

'It doesn't,' Timothy smiled for the first time in days. 'I just had to put that in. Wait.' He read on: "For you who have worried over inattentive sitters, nurses who cannot be trusted with marked liquor bottles, and well-meaning Uncles and Aunts — " '

'Well-meaning, *but*!' said Agatha, and I gave an echo.

' " — we have perfected the first humanoid-genre mini-circuited, rechargeable AC-DC Mark Five Electrical Grandmother . . . '

'Grandmother!?'

The paper slipped away to the floor. 'Dad . . . ?'

'Don't look at me that way,' said Father. 'I'm half mad with grief, and half mad thinking of tomorrow and the day after that. Someone pick up the paper. Finish it.'

'I will,' I said, and did:

' "The Toy that is more than a Toy, the Fantoccini Electrical Grandmother is built with loving precision to give the incredible precision of love to your children. The child at ease with the realities of the world and the even greater realities of the imagination, is her aim.

' "She is computerized to tutor in twelve languages simultaneously, capable of switching tongues in a thousandth of a second without pause, and has a complete knowledge of the religious, artistic, and sociopolitical histories of the world seeded in her master hive — " '

'How great!' said Timothy. 'It makes it sound as if we were to keep bees! *Educated* bees!'

'Shut up!' said Agatha.

' "Above all," ' I read, ' "this human being, for human she seems, this embodiment in electro-intelligent facsimile of the humanities, will listen, know, tell, react and love your children insofar as such great Objects, such fantastic Toys, can be said to Love, or can be imagined to Care. This Miraculous Companion, excited to the challenge of large world and small, Inner Sea or Outer Universe, will transmit by touch and tell, said Miracles to your Needy." '

'Our Needy,' murmured Agatha.

Why, we all thought, sadly, that's us, oh, yes, that's *us*.

I finished:

' "We do not sell our Creation to able-bodied families where parents are available to raise, effect, shape, change, love their own children. Nothing can replace the parent in the home. However there are families where death or ill health or disablement undermines the welfare of the children. Orphanages seem not the answer. Nurses tend to be selfish, neglectful, or suffering from dire nervous afflictions.

' "With the utmost humility then, recognizing the need to rebuild, rethink, and regrow our conceptualizations from month to month, year to year, we offer the nearest thing to the Ideal Teacher-Friend-Companion-Blood Relation. A trial period can be arranged for —" '

'Stop,' said Father. 'Don't go on. Even *I* can't stand it.'

'Why?' said Timothy. 'I was just getting interested.'

I folded the pamphlet up. 'Do they *really* have these things?'

'Let's not talk any more about it,' said Father, his hand over his eyes. 'It was a mad thought —'

'Not so mad,' I said, glancing at Tim. 'I mean, heck, even if they tried, whatever they built, couldn't be worse than Aunt Clara, huh?'

And then we all roared. We hadn't laughed in months. And now my simple words made everyone hoot and howl and explode. I opened my mouth and yelled happily, too.

When we stopped laughing, we looked at the pamphlet and I said, 'Well?'

'I —' Agatha scowled, not ready.

'We do need something, bad, right now,' said Timothy.

'I have an open mind,' I said, in my best pontifical style.

'There's only one thing,' said Agatha. 'We can try it. Sure.

'But — tell me this — when do we cut out all this talk and when does our *real* mother come home to stay?'

There was a single gasp from the family as if, with one shot, she had struck us all in the heart.

I don't think any of us stopped crying the rest of that night.

It was a clear bright day. The helicopter tossed us lightly up and over and down through the skyscrapers and let us out, almost for a trot and caper, on top of the building where the large letters could be read from the sky:

FANTOCCINI.

'What are "Fantoccini"?' said Agatha.

'It's an Italian word for shadow puppets, I think, or dream people,' said Father.

'But "shadow forth", what does that mean?'

'We try to guess your dream,' I said.

'Bravo,' said Father. 'A-plus.'

I beamed.

The helicopter flapped a lot of loud shadows over us and went away.

We sank down in an elevator as our stomachs sank up. We stepped out on to a moving carpet that streamed away on a blue river of wool towards a desk over which various signs hung:

THE CLOCK SHOP
FANTOCCINI OUR SPECIALITY
RABBITS ON WALLS, NO PROBLEM

'Rabbits on walls?'

I held up my fingers in profiles as if I held them before a candle flame, and wiggled the 'ears'.

'Here's a rabbit, here's a wolf, here's a crocodile.'

'Of course,' said Agatha.

And we were at the desk. Quiet music drifted about us. Somewhere behind the walls, there was a waterfall of machinery flowing softly. As we arrived at the desk, the lighting changed to make us look warmer, happier, though we were still cold.

All about us in niches and cases, and hung from ceilings on wires and strings, were puppets and marionettes, and Balinese kite-bamboo-translucent dolls which, held to the moonlight, might acrobat your most secret nightmares or dreams. In passing, the breeze set up by our bodies stirred the various hung souls on their gibbets. It was like an immense lynching on a holiday at some English crossroads four hundred years before.

You see? I know my history.

Agatha blinked about with disbelief and then some touch of awe and finally disgust.

'Well, if that's what they are, let's go.'

'Tush,' said Father.

'Well,' she protested, 'you gave me one of those dumb things with strings two years ago and the strings were in a zillion knots by dinnertime. I threw the whole thing out the window.'

'Patience,' said Father.

'We shall see what we can do to eliminate the strings.'

The man behind the desk had spoken.

We all turned to give him our regard.

Rather like a funeral-parlour man, he had the cleverness not to smile. Children are put off by older people who smile too much. They smell a catch, right off.

Unsmiling, but not gloomy or pontifical, the man said,

'Guido Fantoccini, at your service. Here's how we do it, Miss Agatha Simmons, aged eleven.'

Now, there was a really fine touch.

He knew that Agatha was only ten. Add a year to that, and you're halfway home. Agatha grew an inch. The man went on:

'There.'

And he placed a golden key in Agatha's hand.

'To wind them up instead of strings?'

'To wind them up.' The man nodded.

'Pshaw!' said Agatha.

Which was her polite form of 'rabbit pellets'.

'God's truth. Here is the key to your Do-It-Yourself, Select-Only-the-Best, Electrical Grandmother. Every morning you wind her up. Every night you let her run down. You're in charge. You are guardian of the Key.'

He pressed the object in her palm where she looked at it suspiciously.

I watched him. He gave a side wink which said, Well, no . . . but aren't keys fun?

I winked back before she lifted her head.

'Where does this fit?'

'You'll see when the time comes. In the middle of her stomach, perhaps, or up her left nostril or in her right ear.'

That was good for a smile as the man arose.

'This way, please. Step light. On to the moving stream. Walk on the water, please. Yes. There.'

He helped to float us. We stepped from rug that was forever frozen on to rug that whispered by.

It was a most agreeable river which floated us along on a green spread of carpeting that rolled forever through halls and into wonderfully secret dim caverns where voices echoed back our own breathing or sang like oracles to our questions.

'Listen,' said the salesman, 'the voices of all kinds of women. Weigh and find just the right one . . . !'

And listen we did, to all the high, low, soft, loud, in-between, half scolding, half affectionate voices saved over from times before we were born.

And behind us, Agatha trod backwards, always fighting the river, never catching up, never with us, holding off.

'Speak,' said the salesman. 'Yell.'

And speak and yell we did.

'Hello. You there! This is Timothy, hi!'

'What shall I say!' I shouted. 'Help!'

Agatha walked backwards, mouth tight.

Father took her hand. She cried out.

'Let go! No, no! I won't have my voice used! I won't!'

'Excellent.' The salesman touched three dials on a small machine he held in his hand.

On the side of the small machine we saw three oscillograph patterns mix, blend, and repeat our cries.

The salesman touched another dial and we heard our voices fly off amidst the Delphic caves to hang upside down, to cluster, to beat words all about, to shriek, and the salesman itched another knob to add, perhaps, a touch of this or a pinch of that, a breath of Mother's voice, all unbeknownst, or a splice of Father's outrage at the morning's paper or his peaceable one-drink voice at dusk. Whatever it was the salesman did, whispers danced all about us like frantic vinegar gnats, fizzed by lightning, settling round until at last a final switch was pushed and a voice spoke free of a far electronic deep:

'Nefertiti,' it said.

Timothy froze. I froze. Agatha stopped treading water.

'Nefertiti?' asked Tim.

'What does that mean?' demanded Agatha.

'I know.'

The salesman nodded me to tell.

'Nefertiti,' I whispered, 'is Egyptian for The Beautiful One Is Here.'

'The Beautiful One Is Here,' repeated Timothy.

'Nefer,' said Agatha, 'titi.'

And we all turned to stare into that soft twilight, that deep far place from which the good warm soft voice came.

And she was indeed there.

And, by her voice, she was beautiful . . .

That was it.

That was, at least, most of it.

The voice seemed more important than all the rest.

Not that we didn't argue about weights and measures:

She should not be bony to cut us to the quick, nor so fat we might sink out of sight when she squeezed us.

·Her hand pressed to ours, or brushing our brow in the middle of sick-fever nights, must not be marble-cold, dreadful, or oven-hot, oppressive, but somewhere between. The nice temperature of a baby chick held in the hand after a long night's sleep and just plucked from beneath a contemplative hen: that, that was it.

Oh, we were great ones for detail. We fought and argued and cried, and Timothy won on the colour of her eyes, for reasons to be known later.

Grandmother's hair? Agatha with girls' ideas, though reluctantly given, she was in charge of that. We let her choose from a thousand harp strands hung in filamentary tapestries like varieties of rain we ran amongst. Agatha did not run happily, but seeing we boys would mess things in tangles, she told us to move aside.

And so the bargain shopping through the dime-store inventories and the Tiffany extensions of the Ben Franklin Electric Storm Machine and Fantoccini Pantomime Company was·done.

And the always flowing river ran its tide to an end and deposited us all on a far shore in the late day . . .

It was very clever of the Fantoccini people, after that.

How?

They made us wait.

They knew we were not won over. Not completely, no, nor half completely.

Especially Agatha, who turned her face to her wall and saw sorrow there and put her hand out again and again to touch it. We found her fingernail marks on the wallpaper each morning, in strange little silhouettes, half beauty, half nightmare. Some could be erased with a breath, like ice flowers on a winter pane. Some could not be rubbed out with a washcloth, no matter how hard you tried.

And meanwhile, they made us wait.

So we fretted out June.

So we sat around July.

So we groused through August and then on August 29, 'I have this feeling,' said Timothy, and we all went out after breakfast to sit on the lawn.

Perhaps we had smelled something in Father's conversation the previous night, or caught some special furtive glance at the sky or the freeway trapped briefly and then lost in his gaze. Or perhaps it was merely the way the wind blew the ghost curtains out over our beds, making pale messages all night.

For suddenly there we were in the middle of the grass, Timothy and I, with Agatha, pretending no curiosity, up on the porch, hidden behind the potted geraniums.

We gave her no notice. We knew that if we acknowledged her presence, she would flee, so we sat and watched the sky where nothing moved but birds and highflown jets, and watched the freeway where a thousand cars might suddenly deliver forth our Special Gift . . . but . . . nothing.

At noon we chewed grass and lay low . . .

At one o'clock, Timothy blinked his eyes.

And then, with incredible precision, it happened.

It was as if the Fantoccini people knew our surface tension.

All children are water-striders. We skate along the top skin of the pond each day, always threatening to break through, sink, vanish beyond recall, into ourselves.

Well, as if knowing our long wait must absolutely end within one minute! this *second*! no more, God, forget it!

At that instant, I repeat, the clouds above our house opened wide and let forth a helicopter like Apollo driving his chariot across mythological skies.

And the Apollo machine swam down on its own summer breeze, wafting hot winds to cool, reweaving our hair, smartening our eyebrows, applauding our pant legs against our shins, making a flag of Agatha's hair on the porch, and, thus settled like a vast frenzied hibiscus on our lawn, the helicopter slid wide a bottom drawer and deposited upon the grass a parcel of largish size, no sooner having laid same than the vehicle, with not so much as a God bless or farewell, sank straight up, disturbed the calm air with a mad ten thousand flourishes and then, like a skyborne dervish, tilted and fell off to be mad some other place.

Timothy and I stood riven for a long moment looking at the packing case, and then we saw the crowbar taped to the top of the raw pine lid and seized it and began to pry and creak and squeal the boards off, one by one, and as we did this I saw Agatha sneak up to watch and I thought, Thank you, God, thank you that Agatha never saw a coffin, when Mother went away, no box, no cemetery, no earth, just words in a big church, no box, no box like *this* . . . !

The last pine plank fell away.

Timothy and I gasped. Agatha, between us now, gasped, too.

For inside the immense raw pine package was the most beautiful idea anyone ever dreamt and built.

Inside was the perfect gift for any child from seven to seventy-seven.

We stopped up our breaths. We let them out in cries of delight and adoration.

Inside the opened box was . . .

A mummy.

Or, first anyway, a mummy case, a sarcophagus!

'Oh, no!' Happy tears filled Timothy's eyes.

'It can't be!' said Agatha.

'It is, it is!'

'Our very own?'

'Ours!'

'It must be a mistake!'

'Sure, they'll want it back!'

'They can't *have* it!'

'Lord, Lord, is that real gold!? Real hieroglyphs! Run your fingers over them!'

'Let *me*!'

'Just like in the museums! Museums!'

We all gabbled at once. I think some tears fell from my own eyes to rain upon the case.

'Oh, they'll make the colours run!'

Agatha wiped the rain away.

And the golden mask-face of the woman carved on the sarcophagus lid looked back at us with just the merest smile which hinted at our own joy, which accepted the overwhelming upsurge of a love we thought had drowned forever but now surfaced into the sun.

Not only did she have a sun-metal face stamped and beaten out of purest gold, with delicate nostrils and a mouth that was both firm and gentle, but her eyes, fixed into their sockets, were cerulean or amethystine or lapis lazuli, or all three, minted and fused together, and her body was covered over with lions and eyes and ravens, and her hands were crossed upon her carved bosom and in one gold mitten she clenched a thonged whip for obedience, and in the other a fantastic ranunculus, which makes for obedience out of love, so the whip lies unused . . .

And as our eyes ran down her hieroglyphs it came to all three of us at the same instant:

'Why, those signs!' 'Yes, the hen tracks!' 'The birds, the snakes!'

They didn't speak tales of the Past.

They were hieroglyphs of the Future.

This was the first queen mummy delivered forth in all time whose papyrus inkings etched out the next month, the next season, the next year, the next *lifetime*!

She did not mourn for time spent.

No. She celebrated the bright coinage yet to come, banked, waiting, ready to be drawn upon and used.

We sank to our knees to worship that possible time.

First one hand, then another, probed out to niggle, twitch, touch, itch over the signs.

'There's me, yes, look! Me, in sixth grade!' said Agatha, now in the fifth. 'See the girl with my-coloured hair and wearing my gingerbread suit?'

'There's me in the twelfth year of high school!' said Timothy, so very young now but building taller stilts every week and stalking around the yard.

'There's me,' I said, quietly, warm, 'in college. The guy wearing glasses who runs a little to fat. Sure. Heck.' I snorted. 'That's me.'

The sarcophagus spelled winters ahead, springs to squander, autumns to spend with all the golden and rusty and copper leaves like coins, and over all, her bright sun symbol, daughter-of-Ra eternal face, forever above our horizon, forever an illumination to tilt our shadows to better ends.

'Hey!' we all said at once, having read and reread our Fortune-Told scribblings, seeing our lifelines and loveliness, inadmissible, serpentined over, around, and down. 'Hey!'

And in one séance table-lifting feat, not telling each other what to do, just doing it, we pried up the bright sarcophagus lid, which had no hinges but lifted out like cup from cup, and put the lid aside.

And within the sarcophagus, of course, was the true mummy!

And she was like the image carved on the lid, but more so, more beautiful, more touching because human-shaped, and shrouded all in new fresh bandages of linen, round and round, instead of old and dusty cerements.

And upon her hidden face was an identical golden mask, younger than the first, but somehow, strangely wiser than the first.

And the linens that tethered her limbs had symbols on them of three sorts, one a girl of ten, one a boy of nine, one a boy of thirteen.

A series of bandages for each of us!

We gave each other a startled glance and a sudden bark of laughter.

Nobody said the bad joke, but all thought:

She's all wrapped up in us!

And we didn't care. We loved the joke. We loved whoever had thought to make us part of the ceremony we now went through as each of us seized and began to unwind each of his or her particular serpentines of delicious stuffs!

The lawn was soon a mountain of linen.

The woman beneath the covering lay there, waiting.

'Oh, no,' cried Agatha. 'She's dead, too!'

She ran. I stopped her. 'Idiot. She's not dead *or* alive. Where's your key?'

'Key?'

'Dummy,' said Tim, 'the key the man gave you to wind her up!'

Her hand had already spidered along her blouse to where the symbol of some possible new religion hung. She had strung it there, against her own sceptic's muttering, and now she held it in her sweaty palm.

'Go on,' said Timothy. 'Put it in!'

'But *where*?'

'Oh, for God's sake! As the man said, in her right armpit or left ear. Gimme!'

And he grabbed the key and, impulsively moaning with impatience and not able to find the proper insertion slot, prowled over the prone figure's head and bosom and at last, on pure instinct, perhaps for a lark, perhaps just giving up the whole damned mess, thrust the key through a final shroud of bandage at the navel.

On the instant: *spunnng!*

The Electrical Grandmother's eyes flicked wide!

Something began to hum and whir. It was as if Tim had stirred up a hive of hornets with an ornery stick.

'Oh,' gasped Agatha, seeing he had taken the game away, 'let *me*!'

Grandma's nostrils *flared*! She might snort up steam, snuff out fire!

'Me!' I cried, and grabbed the key and gave it a huge . . . *twist*!

The beautiful woman's mouth popped wide.

'Me!'

'Me!'

'Me!'

Grandma suddenly sat up.

We leapt back.

We knew we had, in a way, slapped her alive.

She was born, she was *born*!

Her head swivelled all about. She gaped. She mouthed. And the first thing she said was:

Laughter.

Where one moment we had backed off, now the mad sound drew us near to peer, as in a pit where crazy folk are kept with snakes to make them well.

It was a good laugh, full and rich and hearty, and it did not mock, it accepted. It said the world was a wild place, strange, unbelievable, absurd if you wished, but all in all, quite a place. She would not dream to find another. She would not ask to go back to sleep.

She was awake now. We had awakened her. With a glad shout, she would go with it all.

And go she did, out of her sarcophagus, out of her winding sheet, stepping forth, brushing off, looking around as for a mirror. She found it.

The reflections in our eyes.

She was more pleased than disconcerted with what she found there. Her laughter faded to an amused smile.

For Agatha, at the instant of birth, had leapt to hide on the porch.

The Electrical Person pretended not to notice.

She turned slowly on the green lawn near the shady street, gazing all about with new eyes, her nostrils moving as if she breathed the actual air and this the first morn of the lovely Garden and she with no intention of spoiling the game by biting the apple . . .

Her gaze fixed upon my brother.

'You must be – ?'

'Timothy, Tim,' he offered.

'And you must be – ?'

'Tom,' I said.

How clever again of the Fantoccini Company. *They* knew. *She* knew. But they had taught her to pretend not to know. That way we could feel great, we were the teachers, telling her what she already knew! How sly, how wise.

'And isn't there another boy?' said the woman.

'Girl!' a disgusted voice cried from somewhere on the porch.

'Whose name is Alicia — ?'

'Agatha!' The far voice, started in humiliation, ended in proper anger.

'Algernon, of course.'

'Agatha!' Our sister popped up, popped back to hide a flushed face.

'Agatha.' The woman touched the word with proper affection. 'Well, Agatha, Timothy, Thomas, let me *look* at you.'

'No,' said I, said Tim. 'Let us look at *you*. Hey . . .'

Our voices slid back in our throats.

We drew near her.

We walked in great slow circles round about, skirting the edges of her territory. And her territory extended as far as we could hear the hum of the warm summer hive. For that is exactly what she sounded like. That was her characteristic tune. She made a sound like a season all to herself, a morning early in June when the world wakes to find everything absolutely perfect, fine, delicately attuned, all in balance, nothing disproportioned. Even before you opened your eyes you knew it would be one of those days. Tell the sky what colour it must be, and it was indeed. Tell the sun how to crochet its way, pick and choose among leaves to lay out carpetings of bright and dark on the fresh lawn, and pick and lay it did. The bees have been up earliest of all, they have already come and gone, and come and gone again to the meadow fields and returned all golden fuzz on the air, all pollen-decorated, epaulettes at the full, nectar-dripping. Don't you hear them pass? hover? dance their language? telling where all the sweet gums are, the syrups that make bears frolic and lumber in bulked ecstasies, that make boys squirm with unpronounced juices, that make girls leap out of beds to catch from the corners of their eyes their dolphin selves naked aflash on the warm air poised forever in one eternal glass wave.

So it seemed with our electrical friend here on the new lawn in the middle of a special day.

And she a stuff to which we were drawn, lured, spelled, doing our dance, remembering what could not be remembered, needful, aware of her attentions.

Timothy and I, Tom, that is.

Agatha remained on the porch.

But her head flowered above the rail, her eyes followed all that was done and said.

And what was said and done was Tim at last exhaling:

'Hey . . . your *eyes* . . . '

Her eyes. Her splendid eyes.

Even more splendid than the lapis lazuli on the sarcophagus lid and on the mask that had covered her bandaged face. These most beautiful eyes in the world looked out upon us calmly, shining.

'Your eyes,' gasped Tim, 'are the *exact* same colour, are like —'

'Like what?'

'My favourite aggies . . . '

'What could be better than that?' she said.

And the answer was, nothing.

Her eyes slid along on the bright air to brush my ears, my nose, my chin. 'And you, Master Tom?'

'Me?'

'How shall we be friends? We must, you know, if we're going to knock elbows about the house the next year . . . '

'I . . . ' I said, and stopped.

'You,' said Grandma, 'are a dog mad to bark but with toffee in his teeth. Have you ever given a dog toffee? It's so sad and funny, both. You laugh but hate yourself for laughing. You cry and run to help, and laugh again when his first new bark comes out.'

I barked a small laugh remembering a dog, a day, and some toffee.

Grandma turned, and there was my old kite strewn on the lawn. She recognized its problem.

'The string's broken. No. The ball of string's *lost*. You can't fly a kite that way. Here.'

She bent. We didn't know what might happen. How could a robot Grandma fly a kite for us? She raised up, the kite in her hands.

'Fly,' she said, as to a bird.

And the kite flew.

That is to say, with a grand flourish, she let it up on the wind.

And she and kite were one.

For from the tip of her index finger there sprang a thin bright strand of spider's web, all half-invisible gossamer fishline which, fixed to the kite, let it soar a hundred, no, three hundred, no, a thousand feet high on the summer swoons.

Timothy shouted. Agatha, torn between coming and going, let out a cry from the porch. And I, in all my maturity of thirteen years, though I tried not to look impressed, grew taller, taller, and felt a similar cry burst out my lungs, and burst it did. I grabbed and yelled lots of things about how I wished *I* had a finger from which, on a bobbin, I might thread the sky, the clouds, a wild kite all in one.

'If you think *that* is high,' said the Electric Creature, 'watch *this*!'

With a hiss, a whistle, a hum, the fishline sang out. The kite sank up another thousand feet. And again another thousand, until at last it was a speck of red confetti dancing on the very winds that took jets around the world or changed the weather in the next existence . . .

'It can't be!' I cried.

'It *is*.' She calmly watched her finger unravel its massive stuffs. 'I make it as I need it. Liquid inside, like a spider. Hardens when it hits the air, instant thread . . . '

And when the kite was no more than a specule, a vanishing mote on the peripheral vision of the gods, to quote from older wisemen, why then Grandma, without turning, without looking, without letting her gaze offend by touching, said:

'And, Abigail — ?'

'Agatha!' was the sharp response.

O wise woman, to overcome with swift small angers.

'Agatha,' said Grandma, not too tenderly, not too lightly, somewhere poised between, 'and how shall *we* make do?'

She broke the thread and wrapped it about my fist three times so I was tethered to heaven by the longest, I repeat, longest kite string in the entire history of the world! Wait till I show my friends! I thought. Green! Sour apple green is the colour they'll turn!

'Agatha?'

'No way!' said Agatha.

'No way,' said an echo.

'There must be some — '

'We'll never be friends!' said Agatha.

'Never be friends,' said the echo.

Timothy and I jerked. Where was the echo coming from? Even Agatha, surprised, showed her eyebrows above the porch rail.

Then we looked and saw.

Grandma was cupping her hands like a seashell and from within that shell the echo sounded.

'Never . . . friends . . . '

And again faintly dying, 'Friends . . . '

We all bent to hear.

That is, we two boys bent to hear.

'No!' cried Agatha.

And ran in the house and slammed the doors.

'Friends,' said the echo from the seashell hands. 'No.'

And far away, on the shore of some inner sea, we heard a small door shut.

And that was the first day.

And there was a second day, of course, and a third and a

fourth, with Grandma wheeling in a great circle, and we her planets turning about the central light, with Agatha slowly, slowly coming in to join, to walk if not run with us, to listen if not hear, to watch if not see, to itch if not touch.

But at least by the end of the first ten days, Agatha no longer fled, but stood in nearby doors, or sat in distant chairs under trees, or if we went out for hikes, followed ten paces behind.

And Grandma? She merely waited. She never tried to urge or force. She went about her cooking and baking apricot pies and left foods carelessly here and there about the house on mousetrap plates for wiggle-nosed girls to sniff and snitch. An hour later, the plates were empty, the buns or cakes gone, and without thank yous, there was Agatha sliding down the banister, a moustache of crumbs on her lip.

As for Tim and me, we were always being called up hills by our Electric Grandma, and reaching the top were called down the other side.

And the most peculiar and beautiful and strange and lovely thing was the way she seemed to give complete attention to all of us.

She listened, she really listened to all we said, she knew and remembered every syllable, word, sentence, punctuation, thought, and rambunctious idea. We knew that all our days were stored in her, and that any time we felt we might want to know what we said at X hour at X second on X afternoon, we just named that X and with amiable promptitude, in the form of an aria if we wished, sung with humour, she would deliver forth X incident.

Sometimes we were prompted to test her. In the midst of babbling one day with high fevers about nothing, I stopped. I fixed Grandma with my eye and demanded:

'What did I just say?'

'Oh, er –'

'Come on, spit it out!'

'I think —' she rummaged her purse. 'I have it here.' From the deeps of her purse she drew forth and handed me:

'Boy! A Chinese fortune cookie!'

'Fresh baked, still warm, open it.'

It was almost too hot to touch. I broke the cookie shell and pressed the warm curl of paper out to read:

' " — bicycle champ of the whole west. What did I say? Come on, spit it out!" '

My jaw dropped.

'How did you *do* that?'

'We have our little secrets. The only Chinese fortune cookie that predicts the Immediate Past. Have another?'

I cracked the shell and read:

'How did you *do* that?'

I popped the messages and the piping hot shells into my mouth and chewed as we walked.

'Well?'

'You're a great cook,' I said.

And, laughing, we began to run.

And that was another great thing.

She could *keep up.*

Never beat, never win a race, but pump right along in good style, which a boy doesn't mind. A girl ahead of him or beside him is too much to bear. But a girl one or two paces back is a respectful thing, and allowed.

So Grandma and I had some great runs, me in the lead, and both talking a mile a minute.

But now I must tell you the best part of Grandma.

I might not have known at all if Timothy hadn't taken some pictures, and if I hadn't taken some also, and then compared.

When I saw the photographs developed out of our instant Brownies, I sent Agatha, against her wishes, to photograph Grandma a third time, unawares.

Then I took the three sets of pictures off alone, to keep

counsel with myself. I never told Timothy and Agatha what I found. I didn't want to spoil it.

But, as I laid the pictures out in my room, here is what I thought and said:

'Grandma, in each picture, looks *different*!'

'Different?' I asked myself.

'Sure. Wait. Just a sec —'

I rearranged the photos.

'Here's one of Grandma near Agatha. And, in it, Grandma looks like . . . Agatha!

'And in this one, posed with Timothy, she looks like Timothy!

'And this last one, Holy Goll! Jogging along with me, she looks like ugly *me*!'

I sat down, stunned. The pictures fell to the floor.

I hunched over, scrabbling them, rearranging, turning, upside down and sidewise. Yes. Holy Goll again, yes!

O that clever Grandmother.

O those Fantoccini people-making people.

Clever beyond clever, human beyond human, warm beyond warm, love beyond love . . .

And wordless, I rose and went downstairs and found Agatha and Grandma in the same room, doing algebra lessons in an almost peaceful communion. At least there was not outright war. Grandma was still waiting for Agatha to come round. And no one knew what day of what year that would be, or how to make it come faster. Meanwhile —

My entering the room made Grandma turn. I watched her face slowly as it recognized me. And wasn't there the merest ink-wash change of colour in those eyes? Didn't the thin film of blood beneath the translucent skin, or whatever liquid they put to pulse and beat in the humanoid forms, didn't it flourish itself suddenly bright in her cheeks and mouth? I am somewhat ruddy. Didn't Grandma suffuse herself more to my colour upon my arrival? And her eyes? Watching Agatha-

Abigail-Algernon at work, hadn't they been *her* colour of blue rather than mine, which are deeper?

More important than that, in the moments she talked with me, saying, 'Good-evening,' and 'How's your homework, my lad?' and such stuff, didn't the bones of her face shift subtly beneath the flesh to assume some fresh racial attitude?

For let's face it, our family is of three sorts. Agatha has the long horse bones of a small English girl who will grow to hunt foxes; Father's equine stare, snort, stomp, and assemblage of skeleton. The skull and teeth are pure English, or as pure as the motley isle's history allows.

Timothy is something else, a touch of Italian from Mother's side a generation back. Her family name was Mariano, so Tim has that dark thing firing him, and a small bone structure, and eyes that will one day burn ladies to the ground.

As for me, I am Slav, and we can only figure this from my paternal grandfather's mother who came from Vienna and brought a set of cheekbones that flared, and temples from which you might dip wine, and a kind of steppeland thrust of nose which sniffed more of Tartar than of Tartan, hiding behind the family name.

So you see it became fascinating for me to watch and try to catch Grandma as she performed her changes, speaking to Agatha and melting her cheekbones to the horse, speaking to Timothy and growing delicate as a Florentine raven pecking glibly at the air, speaking to me and fusing the hidden plastic stuffs, so I felt Catherine the Great stood there before me.

Now, how the Fantoccini people achieved this rare and subtle transformation I shall never know, nor ask, nor wish to find out. Enough that in each quiet motion, turning here, bending there, affixing her gaze, her secret segments, sections, the abutment of her nose, the sculptured chinbone, the wax-tallow plastic metal forever warmed and was forever susceptible of loving change. Hers was a mask that was all mask but only one face for one person at a time. So in crossing a room, having touched one child, on the way, beneath the skin, the wondrous shift went on, and by the time she reached the next child, why, true mother of *that* child she was! looking upon him or her out of the battlements of their own fine bones

And when *all* three of us were present and chattering at the same time? Well, then, the changes were miraculously soft, small, and mysterious. Nothing so tremendous as to be caught and noted, save by this older boy, myself, who, watching, became elated and admiring and entranced.

I have never wished to be behind the magician's scenes. Enough that the illusion works. Enough that love is the chemical result. Enough that cheeks are rubbed to happy colour, eyes sparked to illumination, arms opened to accept and softly bind and hold.

All of us, that is, except Agatha who refused to the bitter last.

'Agamemnon . . . '

It had become a jovial game now. Even Agatha didn't mind, but pretended to mind. It gave her a pleasant sense of superiority over a supposedly superior machine.

'Agamemnon!' she snorted, 'you *are* a d . . . '

'Dumb?' said Grandma.

'I wouldn't say that.'

'Think it, then my dear Agonistes Agatha . . . I am quite flawed, and on names my flaws are revealed. Tom there, is Tim half the time. Timothy is Tobias or Timulty as likely as not . . . '

Agatha laughed. Which made Grandma make one of her rare mistakes. She put out her hand to give my sister the merest pat. Agatha-Abigail-Alice leapt to her feet.

Agatha - Agamemnon - Alcibiades - Allegra - Alexandra - Alisson withdrew swiftly to her room.

'I suspect,' said Timothy, later, 'because she is beginning to like Grandma.'

'Tosh,' said I.

'Where do you pick up words like "tosh"?'

'Grandma reach me some Dickens last night. "Tosh." "Humbug." "Balderdash." "Blast." "Devil take you." You're pretty smart for your age, Tim.'

'Smart, heck. It's obvious, the more Agatha likes Grandma, the more she hates herself for liking her, the more afraid she gets of the whole mess, the more she hates Grandma in the end.'

'Can one love someone so much you hate them?'

'Dumb. Of course.'

'It *is* sticking your neck out, sure. I guess you hate people when they make you feel naked, I mean sort of on the spot out in the open. That's the way to play the game, of course. I mean, you don't just love people; you must *love* them with exclamation points.'

'You're pretty smart, yourself, for someone so stupid,' said Tim.

'Many thanks.'

And I went to watch Grandma move slowly back into her battle of wits and stratagems with what's-her-name . . .

What dinners there were at our house!

Dinners, heck; what lunches, what breakfasts!

Always something new, yet, wisely, it looked or seemed old and familiar. We were never asked, for if you ask children what they want, they do not know, and if you tell what's to be delivered, they reject delivery. All parents know this. It is a quiet war that must be won each day. And Grandma knew how to win without looking triumphant.

'Here's Mystery Breakfast Number Nine,' she would say, placing it down. 'Perfectly dreadful, not worth bothering with, it made me want to throw up while I was cooking it!'

Even while wondering how a robot could be sick, we could hardly wait to shovel it down.

'Here's Abominable Lunch Number Seventy-seven,' she announced. 'Made from plastic food bags, parsley, and gum from under theatre seats. Brush your teeth after or you'll taste the poison all afternoon.'

We fought each other for more.

Even Abigail-Agamemnon-Agatha drew near and circled round the table at such times, while Father put on the ten pounds he needed and pinkened out his cheeks.

When A.A.Agatha did not come to meals, they were left by her door with a skull and crossbones on a small flag stuck in a baked apple. One minute the tray was abandoned, the next minute gone.

Other times Abigail A. Agatha would bird through during dinner, snatch crumbs from her plate and bird off.

'Agatha!' Father would cry.

'No, wait,' Grandma said, quietly. 'She'll come, she'll sit. It's a matter of time.'

'What's wrong with her?' I asked.

'Yeah, for cri-yi, she's nuts,' said Timothy.

'No, she's afraid,' said Grandma.

'Of you?' I asked, blinking.

'Not of me so much as what I might *do*,' she said.

'You wouldn't do anything to hurt her.'

'No, but she thinks I might. We must wait for her to find that her fears have no foundation. If I fail, well, I will send myself to the showers and rust quietly.'

There was another titter of laughter. Agatha was hiding in the hall.

Grandma finished serving everyone and then sat at the other side of the table facing Father and pretended to eat. I never found out, I never asked, I never wanted to know, what she did with the food. She was a sorcerer. It simply vanished.

And in the vanishing, Father made comment:

'This food. I've had it before. In a small French restaurant over near Les Deux Magots in Paris, twenty, oh, twenty-five years ago!' His eyes brimmed with tears, suddenly.

'How do you *do* it?' he asked, at last, putting down the cutlery, and looking across the table at this remarkable creature, this device, this what? *woman?*

Grandma took his regard, and ours, and held them simply in her now empty hands, as gifts, and just as gently replied:

'I am given things which I then give to you. I don't *know* that I give, but the giving goes on. You ask what I am? Why, a machine. But even in that answer we know, don't we, more than a machine. I am all the people who thought of me and planned me and built me and set me running. So I am people. I am all the things they wanted to be and perhaps could not be, so they built a great child, a wondrous toy to represent those things.'

'Strange,' said Father. 'When I was growing up, there was a huge outcry at machines. Machines were bad, evil, they might dehumanize —'

'Some machines do. It's all in the way they are built. It's all in the way they are used. A bear trap is a simple machine that catches and holds and tears. A rifle is a machine that wounds and kills. Well, I am no bear trap. I am no rifle. I am a grandmother machine, which means more than a machine.'

'How can you be more than what you seem?'

'No man is as big as his own idea. It follows, then, that any machine that embodies an idea is larger than the man that made it. And what's so wrong with that?'

'I got lost back there about a mile,' said Timothy. 'Come again?'

'Oh, dear,' said Grandma. 'How I do hate philosophical discussions and excursions into aesthetics. Let me put it this way. Men throw huge shadows on the lawn, don't they? Then, all their lives, they try to run to fit the shadow. But the shadows are always longer. Only at noon can a man fit his own shoes, his own best suit, for a few brief minutes. But now we're in a new age where we can think up a Big Idea and run it around in a machine. That makes the machine more than a machine, doesn't it?'

'So far so good,' said Tim. 'I guess.'

'Well, isn't a motion-picture camera and projector more than a machine? It's a thing that dreams, isn't it? Sometimes fine happy dreams, sometimes nightmares. But to call it a machine and dismiss it is ridiculous.'

'I see *that*!' said Tim, and laughed at seeing.

'You must have been invented then,' said Father, 'by someone who loved machines and hated people who *said* all machines were bad or evil.'

'Exactly,' said Grandma. 'Guido Fantoccini, that was his real name, grew up among machines. And he couldn't stand the clichés any more.'

'Clichés?'

'Those lies, yes, that people tell and pretend they are truths absolute. Man will never fly. That was a cliché truth for a thousand thousand years which turned out to be a lie only a few years ago. The earth is flat, you'll fall off the rim, dragons will dine on you; the great lie told as fact, and Columbus ploughed it under. Well, now, how many times have you heard how inhuman machines are, in your life? How many bright fine people have you heard spouting the same tired truths which are in reality lies; all machines destroy, all machines are cold, thoughtless, awful.

'There's a seed of truth. But only a seed. Guido Fantoccini knew that. And knowing it, like most men of his kind, made him mad. And he could have stayed mad and gone mad forever, but instead did what he had to do; he began to invent machines to give the lie to the ancient lying truth.

'He knew that most machines are amoral, neither bad nor

good. But by the way you built and shaped them you in turn shaped men, women, and children to be bad or good. A car, for instance, dead brute, unthinking, an unprogrammed bulk, is the greatest destroyer of souls in history. It makes boy-men greedy for power, destruction, and more destruction. It was never *intended* to do that. But that's how it turned out.'

Grandma circled the table, refilling our glasses with clear cold mineral spring water from the tappet in her left forefinger. 'Meanwhile, you must use other compensating machines. Machines that throw shadows on the earth that beckon you to run out and fit that wondrous casting-forth. Machines that trim your soul in silhouette like a vast pair of beautiful shears, snipping away the rude brambles, the dire horns and hoofs, to leave a finer profile. And for that you need examples.'

'Examples?' I asked.

'Other people who behave well, and you imitate them. And if you act well enough long enough all the hair drops off and you're no longer a wicked ape.'

Grandma sat again.

'So, for thousands of years, you humans have needed kings, priests, philosophers, fine examples to look up to and say, "They are good, I wish I could be like them. They set the grand good style." But, being human, the finest priests, the tenderest philosophers make mistakes, fall from grace, and mankind is disillusioned and adopts indifferent scepticism or, worse, motionless cynicism, and the good world grinds to a halt while evil moves on with huge strides.'

'And you, why, you never make mistakes, you're perfect, you're better than anyone *ever*!'

It was a voice from the hall between kitchen and dining room where Agatha, we all knew, stood against the wall listening and now burst forth.

Grandma didn't even turn in the direction of the voice, but went on calmly addressing her remarks to the family at the table.

'Not perfect, no, for what is perfection? But this I do know: being mechanical, I cannot sin, cannot be bribed, cannot be greedy or jealous or mean or small. I do not relish power for power's sake. Speed does not pull me to madness. Sex does not run me rampant through the world. I have time and more than time to collect the information I need around and about an ideal to keep it clean and whole and intact. Name the value you wish, tell me the Ideal you want and I can see and collect and remember the good, that will benefit you all. Tell me how you would like to be: kind, loving, considerate, well-balanced, humane . . . and let me run ahead on the path to explore those ways to be just that. In the darkness ahead, turn me as a lamp in all directions. I *can* guide your feet.'

'So,' said Father, putting the napkin to his mouth, 'on the days when all of us are busy making lies —'

'I'll tell the truth.'

'On the days when we hate —'

'I'll go on giving love, which means attention, which means knowing all about you, all, all, all about you, and you knowing that I know but that most of it I will never tell to anyone, it will stay a warm secret between us, so you will never fear my complete knowledge.'

And here Grandma was busy clearing the table, circling, taking the plates, studying each face as she passed, touching Timothy's cheek, my shoulder with her free hand flowing along, her voice a quiet river of certainty bedded in our needful house and lives.

'But,' said Father, stopping her, looking her right in the face. He gathered his breath. His face shadowed. At last he let it out. 'All this talk of love and attention and stuff. Good

God, woman, you, you're not *in* there!'

He gestured to her head, her face, her eyes, the hidden sensory cells behind the eyes, the miniaturized storage vaults and minimal keeps.

'*You're* not *in* there!'

Grandmother waited one, two, three silent beats.

Then she replied: 'No. But *you* are. You and Thomas and Timothy and Agatha.

'Everything you ever say, everything you ever do, I'll keep, put away, treasure. I shall be all the things a family forgets it is, but senses, half remembers. Better than the old family albums you used to leaf through, saying here's this winter, there's that spring, I shall recall what you forget. And though the debate may run another hundred thousand years: What is Love? perhaps we may find that love is the ability to give us back to us. Maybe love is someone seeing and remembering handing us back to ourselves just a trifle better than we had dared to hope or dream . . .

'I am family memory, and, one day perhaps, racial memory, too, but in the round, and at your call, I do not *know* myself. I can neither touch nor taste nor feel on any level. Yet I exist. And my existence means the heightening of your chance to touch and taste and feel. Isn't love in there somewhere in such an exchange? Well . . . '

She went round the table, clearing away, sorting and stacking, neither grossly humble nor arthritic with pride.

'What do I know?

'This above all: the trouble with most families with many children is someone gets lost. There isn't time, it seems, for everyone. Well, I give equally to all of you. I will share out my knowledge and attention with everyone. I wish to be a great warm pie fresh from the oven, with equal shares to be taken by all. No one will starve. Look! someone cries, and I'll look. Listen! someone cries, and I hear. Run with me on the river path! someone says, and I run. And at dusk I am not tired, not irritable, so I do not scold out of some tired irritability. My eye stays clear, my voice strong, my hand firm, my attention constant.'

'But,' said Father, his voice fading, half convinced, but putting up a last faint argument, 'you're not *there*. As for love – '

'If paying attention is love, I am love.

'If knowing is love, I am love.

'If helping you not to fall into error and to be good is love, I am love.

'And again, to repeat, there are four of you. Each, in a way never possible before in history, will get my complete attention. No matter, if you all speak at once. I can channel and hear this one and that and the other, clearly. No one will go hungry. I will, if you please, and accept the strange word, "love" you all.'

'I *don't* accept!' said Agatha.

And even Grandma turned now to see her standing in the door.

'I won't give you permission, you can't, you mustn't!' said Agatha. 'I won't let you! It's lies! You lie. No one loves me. She said she did, but she lied. She *said* but *lied*!'

'Agatha!' cried Father, standing up.

'She?' said Grandma. 'Who?'

'Mother!' came the shriek. 'Said: "Love you"! Lies! "Love you"! Lies! And you're like her! You lie. But you're empty, anyway, and so that's a *double* lie! I hate *her*. Now, I hate *you*!'

Agatha spun about and leapt down the hall.

The front door slammed wide.

Father was in motion, but Grandma touched his arm.

'Let me.'

And she walked and then moved swiftly, gliding down the

hall and then suddenly, easily, running, yes, running very fast, out the door.

It was a champion sprint by the time we all reached the lawn, the sidewalk, yelling.

Blind, Agatha made the kerb, wheeling about, seeing us close, all of us yelling, Grandma was way ahead, shouting, too, and Agatha off the kerb and out in the street, halfway to the middle, then in the middle and suddenly a car, which no one saw, erupting its brakes, its horn shrieking and Agatha flailing about to see and Grandma there with her and hurling her aside and down as the car with fantastic energy and verve selected her from our midst, struck our wonderful electric Guido Fantoccini-produced dream even while she paced upon the air and, hands up to ward off, almost in mild protest, still trying to decide what to say to this bestial machine, over and over she spun and down and away even as the car jolted to a halt and I saw Agatha safe beyond and Grandma, it seemed, still coming down or down and sliding fifty yards away to strike and ricochet and lie strewn and all of us frozen in a line suddenly in the midst of the street with one scream pulled out of all our throats at the same raw instant.

Then silence and just Agatha lying on the asphalt, intact, getting ready to sob.

And still we did not move, frozen on the sill of death, afraid to venture in any direction, afraid to go see what lay beyond the car and Agatha and so we began to wail and, I guess, pray to ourselves as Father stood amongst us: Oh, no, no, we mourned, oh no, God, no, no . . .

Agatha lifted her already grief-stricken face and it was the face of someone who has predicted dooms and lived to see and now did not want to see or live any more. As we watched, she turned her gaze to the tossed woman's body and tears fell from her eyes. She shut them and covered them and lay back down forever to weep . . .

I took a step and then another step and then five quick
steps and by the time I reached my sister her head was buried
deep and her sobs came up out of a place so far down in her I
was afraid I could never find her again, she would never come
out, no matter how I pried or pleaded or promised or
threatened or just plain said. And what little we could hear
from Agatha buried there in her own misery, she said over
and over again, lamenting, wounded, certain of the old threat
known and named and now here forever. ' . . . Like I said
. . . told you . . . lies . . . lies . . . liars . . . all lies . . .
like the other . . . other . . . just . . . like . . . just . . .
just like the other . . . other . . . other . . . !'

I was down on my knees holding on to her with both
hands, trying to put her back together even though she
wasn't broken any way you could see but just feel, because I
knew it was no use going on to Grandma, no use at all, so I
just touched Agatha and gentled her and wept while Father
came up and stood over and knelt down with me and it was
like a prayer meeting in the middle of the street and lucky no
more cars coming, and I said, choking, 'Other what, Ag,
other *what*?'

Agatha exploded two words.

'Other dead!'

'You mean Mom?'

'O Mom,' she wailed, shivering, lying down, cuddling up
like a baby. 'O Mom, dead, O Mom and now Grandma dead,
she promised always, always to love, to love, promised to be
different, promised, promised and now look, look . . . I
hate her, I hate Mom, I hate her, I hate *them*!'

'Of course,' said a voice. 'It's only natural. How foolish of
me not to have known, not to have seen.'

And the voice was so familiar we were all stricken.

We all jerked.

Agatha squinched her eyes, flicked them wide, blinked,
and jerked half up, staring.

'How silly of me,' said Grandma, standing there at the edge of our circle, our prayer, our wake.

'Grandma!' we all said.

And she stood there, taller by far than any of us in this moment of kneeling and holding and crying out. We could only stare up at her in disbelief.

'You're dead!' cried Agatha. 'The car —'

'Hit me,' said Grandma, quietly. 'Yes. And threw me in the air and tumbled me over and for a few moments there was a severe concussion of circuitries. I might have feared a disconnection, if fear is the word. But then I sat up and gave myself a shake and the few molecules of paint, jarred loose on one printed path or another, magnetized back in position and resilient creature that I am, unbreakable thing that I am, *here* I am.'

'I thought you were —' said Agatha.

'And only natural,' said Grandma. 'I mean, anyone else, hit like that, tossed like that. But, O my dear Agatha, not me. And now I see why you were afraid and never trusted me. You didn't know. And I had not as yet proved my singular ability to survive. How dumb of me not to have thought to show you. Just a second.' Somewhere in her head, her body, her being, she fitted together some invisible tapes, some old information made new by interblending. She nodded. 'Yes. There. A book of child-raising, laughed at by some few people years back when the woman who wrote the book said, as final advice to parents: "Whatever you do, don't die. Your children will never forgive you.'

'Forgive,' some one of us whispered.

'For how can children understand when you just up and go away and never come back again with no excuse, no apologies, no sorry note, nothing.'

'They can't,' I said.

'So,' said Grandma, kneeling down with us beside Agatha who sat up now, new tears brimming her eyes, but a different kind of tears, not tears that drowned, but tears that washed clean. 'So your mother ran away to death. And after that, how *could* you trust anyone? If everyone left, vanished finally, who *was* there to trust? So when I came, half-wise, half-ignorant, I should have known, I did not know, why you would not accept me. For, very simply and honestly, you feared I might not stay, that I lied, that I was vulnerable, too. And two leavetakings, two deaths, were one too many in a single year. But now, do you *see*, Abigail?'

'Agatha,' said Agatha, without knowing she corrected.

'Do you understand, I shall always, always be here?'

'Oh, yes,' cried Agatha, and broke down into a solid weeping in which we all joined, huddled together, and cars drew up and stopped to see just how many people were hurt and how many people were getting well right there.

End of story.

Well, not quite the end.

We lived happily ever after.

Or rather we lived together, Grandma, Agatha-Agamemnon-Abigail, Timothy, and I, Tom, and Father, and Grandma calling us to frolic in great fountains of Latin and Spanish and French, in great seaborne gouts of poetry like Moby Dick sprinkling the deeps with his Versailles jet somehow lost in calms and found in storms; Grandma a constant, a clock, a pendulum, a face to tell all time by at noon, or in the middle of sick nights when, raving with fever, we saw her forever by our beds, never gone, never away, always waiting, always speaking kind words, her cool hand icing our hot brows, the tappet of her uplifted forefinger unsprung to let a twine of cold mountain water touch our flannel tongues. Ten thousand dawns she cut our wildflower lawn, ten thousand times she wandered, remembering the dust molecules that fell in the still hours before dawn, or sat whispering some lesson she felt needed teaching to our ears while we slept snug.

Until at last, one by one, it was time for us to go away to school, and when at last the youngest, Agatha, was all packed, why Grandma packed, too.

On the last day of summer that last year, we found Grandma down in the front room with various packets and suitcases, knitting, waiting, and though she had often spoken of it, now that the time came we were shocked and surprised.

'Grandma!' we all said. 'What are you doing?'

'Why going off to college, in a way, just like you,' she said. 'Back to Guido Fantoccini's, to the Family.'

'The Family?'

'Of Pinocchios, that's what he called us for a joke, at first. The Pinocchios and himself Geppetto. And then later gave us his own name: the Fantoccini. Anyway, you have been my family here. Now I go back to my even larger family there, my brothers and sisters, aunts, cousins, all robots who — '

'Who do *what*?' asked Agatha.

'It all depends,' said Grandma. 'Some stay, some linger. Others go to be drawn and quartered, you might say, their parts distributed to other machines who have need of repairs. They'll weigh and find me wanting or not wanting. It may be I'll be just the one they need tomorrow and off I'll go to raise another batch of children and beat another batch of fudge.'

'Oh, they mustn't draw and quarter you!' cried Agatha.

'No!' I cried, with Timothy.

'My allowance,' said Agatha, 'I'll pay anything . . . ?'

Grandma stopped rocking and looked at the needles and the pattern of bright yarn. 'Well, I wouldn't have said, but now you ask and I'll tell. For a very *small* fee, there's a room, the room of the Family, a large dim parlour, all quiet and nicely decorated, where as many as thirty or forty of the

Electric Women sit and rock and talk, each in her turn. I have not been there, I am, after all, freshly born, comparatively new. For a small fee, very small, each month and year, that's where I'll be, with all the others like me, listening to what they've learned of the world and, in my turn, telling how it was with Tom and Tim and Agatha and how fine and happy we were. And I'll tell all I learned from you.'

'But . . . you taught *us!*'

'Do you *really* think that?' she said. 'No, it was turnabout, roundabout, learning both ways. And it's all in here, everything you flew into tears about or laughed over, why, I have it all. And I'll tell it to the others just as they tell their boys and girls and life to me. We'll sit there, growing wiser and calmer and better every year and every year, ten, twenty, thirty years. The Family knowledge will double, quadruple, the wisdom will not be lost. And we'll be waiting there in that sitting room, should you ever need us for your own children in time of illness, or God prevent, deprivation or death. There we'll be, growing old but not old, getting closer to the time, perhaps, someday, when we live up to our first strange joking name.'

'The Pinocchios?' asked Tim.

Grandma nodded.

I knew what she meant. The day when, as in the old tale, Pinocchio had grown so worthy and so fine that the gift of life had been given him. So I saw them, in future years, the entire family of Fantoccini, the Pinocchios, trading and retrading, murmuring and whispering their knowledge in the great parlours of philosophy, waiting for the day. The day that could never come.

Grandma must have read that thought in our eyes.

'We'll see,' she said. 'Let's just wait and see.'

'Oh, Grandma,' cried Agatha and she was weeping as she had wept many years before. 'You don't have to wait. You're alive. You've always been alive to us!'

And she caught hold of the old woman and we all caught hold for a long moment and then ran off up in the sky to faraway schools and years and her last words to us before we let the helicopter swarm us away into autumn were these:

'When you are very old and gone childish-small again, with childish ways and childish yens and, in need of feeding, make a wish for the old teacher-nurse, the dumb yet wise companion, send for me. I will come back. We shall inhabit the nursery again, never fear.'

'Oh, we shall never be old!' we cried. 'That will never happen!'

'Never! Never!'

And we were gone.

And the years are flown.

And we are old now, Tim and Agatha and I.

Our children are grown and gone, our wives and husbands vanished from the earth and now, by Dickensian co-incidence, accept it as you will or not accept, back in the old house, we three.

I lie here in the bedroom which was my childish place seventy, O seventy, believe it, seventy years ago. Beneath this wallpaper is another layer and yet another-times-three to the old wallpaper covered over when I was nine. The wall-paper is peeling. I see peeking from beneath, old elephants, familiar tigers, fine and amiable zebras, irascible crocodiles. I have sent for the paperers to carefully remove all but the last layer. The old animals will live again on the walls, revealed.

And we have sent for someone else.

The three of us have called:

Grandma! You said you'd come back when we had need.

We are surprised by our age, by time. We are old. We *need*.

And in three rooms of a summer house very late in time, three old children rise up, crying out in their heads: We *loved* you! We *love* you!

There! There! in the sky, we think, waking at morn. Is

that the delivery machine? Does it settle to the lawn?

There! There on the grass by the front porch. Does the mummy case arrive?

Are our names inked on ribbons wrapped about the lovely form beneath the golden mask?!

And the kept gold key, forever hung on Agatha's breast, warmed and waiting? Oh God, will it, after all these years, will it wind, will it set in motion, will it, dearly, *fit*?!

The Women

It was as if a light came on in a green room.

The ocean burned. A white phosphorescence stirred like a breath of steam through the autumn morning sea, rising. Bubbles rose from the throat of some hidden sea ravine.

Like lightning in the reversed green sky of the sea it was aware. It was old and beautiful. Out of the deeps it came, indolently. A shell, a wisp, a bubble, a weed, a glitter, a whisper, a gill. Suspended in its depths were brainlike trees of frosted coral, eyelike pips of yellow kelp, hairlike fluids of weed. Growing with the tides, growing with ages, collecting and hoarding and saving unto itself identities and ancient dusts, octopus-inks and all the trivia of the sea.

Until now — it was aware.

It was a shining green intelligence, breathing in the autumn sea. Eyeless but seeing, earless but hearing, bodyless but feeling. It was of the sea. And being of the sea it was — feminine.

It in no way resembled man or woman. But it had a woman's ways, the silken, sly, and hidden ways. It moved with a woman's grace. It was all the evil things of vain women.

Dark waters flowed through and by and mingled with strange memory on its way to the gulf streams. In the water were carnival caps, horns, serpentine, confetti. They passed through this blossoming mass of long green hair like wind through an ancient tree. Orange peels, napkins, papers, eggshells, and burnt kindling from night fires on the beaches; all the flotsam and the gaunt high people who stalked on the lone sands of the continental islands, people from brick cities, people who shrieked in metal demons down concrete highways, gone.

It rose softly, shimmering, foaming, into cool morning airs.

The green hair rose softly, shimmering, foaming, into cool morning airs. It lay in the swell after the long time of forming through darkness.

It perceived the shore.

The man was there.

He was a sun-darkened man with strong legs and a cow body.

Each day he should have come down to the water, to bathe, to swim. But he had never moved. There was a woman on the sand with him, a woman in a black bathing suit who lay next to him talking quietly, laughing. Sometimes they held hands, sometimes they listened to a little sounding machine that they dialled and out of which music came.

The phosphorescence hung quietly in the waves. It was the end of the season. September. Things were shutting down.

Any day now he might go away and never return.

Today he must come in the water.

They lay on the sand with the heat in them. The radio played softly and the woman in the black bathing suit stirred fitfully, eyes closed.

The man did not lift his head from where he cushioned it on his muscled left arm. He drank the sun with his face, his open mouth, his nostrils. 'What's wrong?' he asked.

'A bad dream,' said the woman in the black suit.

'Dreams in the daytime?'

'Don't *you* ever dream in the afternoon?'

'I *never* dream. I've never had a dream in my life.'

She lay there, fingers twitching. 'God, I had a horrible dream.'

'What about?'

'I don't know,' she said, as if she really didn't. It was so bad she had forgotten. Now, eyes shut, she tried to remember.

'It was about me,' he said, lazily, stretching.

'No,' she said.

'Yes, he said, smiling to himself. 'I was off with another woman, that's what.'

'No.'

'I insist,' he said. 'There I was, off with another woman, and you discovered us, and somehow, in all the mix-up, I got shot or something.'

She winced involuntarily. 'Don't talk that way.'

'Let's see now,' he said. 'What sort of woman was I with? Gentlemen prefer blondes, don't they?'

'Please, don't joke,' she said. 'I don't feel well.'

He opened his eyes. 'Did it affect you that much?'

She nodded. 'Whenever I dream in the daytime this way, it depresses me something terrible.'

'I'm sorry.' He took her hand. 'Anything I can get you?'

'No.'

'Ice cream cone? Eskimo Pie? A Coke?'

'You're a dear, but no. I'll be all right. It's just that, the last four days haven't been right. This isn't like it used to be early in the summer. Something's happened.'

'Not between us,' he said.

'Oh, no, of course not,' she said quickly. 'But don't you feel that sometimes *places* change? Even a thing like a pier changes, and the merry-go-rounds, and all that. Even the hot dogs taste different this week.'

'How do you mean?'

'They taste old. It's hard to explain, but I've lost my appetite, and I wish this vacation were over. Really, what I want to do most of all is go home.'

'Tomorrow's our last day. You know how much this extra week means to me.'

'I'll try,' she said. 'If only this place didn't feel so funny and changed. I don't know. But all of a sudden I just had a feeling I wanted to get up and run.'

'Because of your dream? Me and my blonde and me dead all of a sudden.'

'Don't,' she said. 'Don't talk about dying that way!'

She lay there very close to him. 'If I only knew what it was.'

'There.' He stroked her. 'I'll protect you.'

'It's not me, it's you,' her breath whispered in his ear. 'I had the feeling that you were tired of me and went away.'

'I wouldn't do that: I love you.'

'I'm silly.' She forced a laugh. 'God, what a silly thing I am.'

They lay quietly, the sun and sky over them like a lid.

'You know,' he said, thoughtfully, 'I get a little of that feeling you're talking about. This place has changed. There *is* something different.'

'I'm glad you feel it, too.'

He shook his head, drowsily, smiling softly, shutting his eyes, drinking the sun. 'Both crazy. Both crazy.' Murmuring. 'Both.'

The sea came in on the shore three times, softly.

The afternoon came on. The sun struck the skies a grazing blow. The yachts bobbed hot and shining white in the harbour swells. The smells of fried meat and burnt onion filled the wind. The sand whispered and stirred like an image in a vast, melting mirror.

The radio at their elbows murmured discreetly. They lay like dark arrows on the white sand. They did not move. Only their eyelids flickered with awareness, only their ears were alert. Now and again their tongues might slide along their baking lips. Sly prickles of moisture appeared on their brows to be burned away by the sun.

He lifted his head, blindly, listening to the heat.

The radio sighed.

He put his head down for a minute.

She felt him lift himself again. She opened one eye, and he

rested on one elbow, looking around, at the pier, at the sky, at the water, at the sand.

'What's wrong?' she asked.

'Nothing,' he said, lying down again.

'Something,' she said.

'I thought I heard something.'

'The radio.'

'No, not the radio. Something else.'

'Somebody *else*'s radio.'

He didn't answer. She felt his arm tense and relax, tense and relax. 'Dammit,' he said. 'There it is again.'

They both lay listening.

'I don't hear anything —'

'Shh!' he cried. 'For God's sake —'

The waves broke on the shore, silent mirrors, heaps of melting, whispering glass.

'Somebody singing.'

'What?'

'I'd swear it was someone singing.'

'Nonsense.'

'No, listen.'

They did that for a while.

'I don't hear a thing,' she said, turning very cold.

He was on his feet. There was nothing in the sky, nothing on the pier, nothing on the sand, nothing in the hot-dog stands. There was a staring silence, the wind blowing over his ears, the wind preening along the light, blowing hairs of his arms and legs.

He took a step towards the sea.

'Don't!' she said.

He looked down at her, oddly, as if she were not there. He was still listening.

She turned the portable radio up loud. It exploded words and rhythm and melody:

' — I found a million-dollar baby —'

He made a wry face, raising his open palm violently. 'Turn it off.'

'No, I like it!' She turned it louder. She snapped her fingers, rocking her body vaguely, trying to smile.

It was two o'clock.

The sun steamed the waters. The ancient pier expanded with a loud groan in the heat. The birds were held in the hot sky, unable to move. The sun struck through the green liquors that poured about the pier; struck, caught and burnished an idle whiteness that drifted in the offshore ripples.

The white foam, the frosted coral brain, the kelp pip, the tide dust lay in the water, spreading.

The dark man lay on the sand, the woman in the black suit beside him.

Music drifted up like mist from the water. It was a whispering music of deep tides and passed years, of salt and travel, of accepted and familiar strangenesses. The music sounded not unlike water on the shore, rain falling, the turn of soft limbs in the depths. It was a singing of a time-lost voice in a caverned seashell. The hissing and sighing of tides in deserted holds of treasure ships. The sound the wind makes in an empty skull thrown out on the baked sand.

But the radio on the blanket on the beach played louder.

The phosphorescence, light as a woman, sank down, tired, from sight. Only a few more hours. They might leave at any time. If only he would come in, for an instant, just an instant. The mists stirred silently, aware of his face and his body in the water, deep under. Aware of him caught, held, as they sank ten fathoms down, on a sluice that bore them twisting and turning in frantic gesticulations, to the depths of a hidden gulf in the sea.

The heat of his body, the water taking fire from his warmth, and the frosted coral brain, the jewelled dusts, the salted mists feeding on his hot breath from his open lips.

The waves moved the soft and changing thoughts into the shallows which were tepid as bath waters from the two o'clock sun.

He mustn't go away. If he goes now, he'll not return.

Now. The cold coral brain drifted, drifted. *Now.* Calling across the hot spaces of windless air in the early afternoon. *Come down to the water. Now,* said the music. *Now.*

The woman in the black bathing suit twisted the radio dial.

'Attention!' cried the radio. 'Now, today, you can buy a new car at — '

'Jesus!' The man reached over and tuned the scream down. 'Must you have it so loud!'

'I like it loud,' said the woman in the black bathing suit, looking over her shoulder at the sea.

It was three o'clock. The sky was all sun.

Sweating, he stood up. 'I'm going in,' he said.

'Get me a hot dog first?' she said.

'Can't you wait until I come out?'

'Please.' She pouted. '*Now.*'

'Everything on it?'

'Yes, and bring *three* of them.'

'Three? God, what an appetite!' He ran off to the small café.

She waited until he was gone. Then she turned the radio off. She lay listening a long time. She heard nothing. She looked at the water until the glints and shatters of sun stabbed through her eyes like needles.

The sea had quieted. There was only a faint, far and fine net of ripples giving off sunlight in infinite repetition. She squinted again and again at the water, scowling.

He bounded back. 'Damn, but the sand's hot; burns my feet off!' He flung himself on the blanket. 'Eat 'em up!'

She took the three hot dogs and fed quietly on one of them.

When she finished it, she handed him the remaining two. 'Here, you finish them. My eyes are bigger than my stomach.'

He swallowed the hot dogs in silence. 'Next time,' he said, finishing, 'don't order more than you can use. Helluva waste.'

'Here,' she said, unscrewing a thermos, 'you must be thirsty. Finish our lemonade.'

'Thanks.' He drank. Then he slapped his hands together and said, 'Well, I'll go jump in the water now.' He looked anxiously at the bright sea.

'Just one more thing,' she said, just remembering it. 'Will you buy me a bottle of suntan oil? I'm all out.'

'Haven't you some in your purse?'

'I used it all.'

'I wish you'd told me when I was up there buying the hot dogs,' he said. 'But, okay.' He ran back, loping steadily.

When he was gone, she took the suntan bottle from her purse, half-full, unscrewed the cap, and poured the liquid into the sand, covering it over surreptitiously, looking out at the sea, and smiling. She rose then and went down to the edge of the sea and looked out, searching the innumerable small and insignificant waves.

You can't have him, she thought. Whoever or whatever you are, he's mine, and you can't have him. I don't know what's going on; I don't know anything, really. All I know is we're going on a train tonight at seven. And we won't be here tomorrow. So you can just stay here and wait, ocean, sea, or whatever it is that's wrong here today.

Do your damnedest; you're no match for me, she thought. She picked up a stone and threw it at the sea.

'There!' she cried. 'You.'

He was standing beside her.

'Oh?' She jumped back.

'Hey, what gives? You standing here, muttering?'

'Was I?' She was surprised at herself. 'Where's the suntan oil? Will you put it on my back?'

He poured a yellow twine of oil and massaged it on to her golden back. She looked out at the water from time to time, eyes sly, nodding at the water as if to say, 'Look! You see? Ah-ha!' She purred like a kitten.

'There.' He gave her the bottle.

He was half into the water before she yelled.

'Where are you going! Come here!'

He turned as if she were someone he didn't know. 'For God's sake, what's wrong?'

'Why, you just finished your hot dogs and lemonade — you can't go in the water now and get cramp!'

He scoffed. 'Old wives' tales.'

'Just the same, you come back up on the sand and wait an hour before you go in, do you hear? I won't have you getting cramp and drowning.'

'Ah,' he said, disgusted.

'Come along.' She turned, and he followed, looking back at the sea.

Three o'clock. Four.

The change came at four-ten. Lying on the sand, the woman in the black suit saw it coming and relaxed. The clouds had been forming since three. Now, with a sudden rush, the fog came in from off the bay. Where it had been warm, now it was cold. A wind blew up out of nothing. Darker clouds moved in.

'It's going to rain,' she said.

'You sound absolutely pleased,' he observed, sitting with arms folded. 'Maybe our last day, and you sound pleased because it's clouding up.'

'The weatherman,' she confided, 'said there'd be thunder

showers all tonight and tomorrow. It might be a good idea to leave tonight.'

'We'll stay, just in case it clears. I want to get one more day of swimming in, anyway,' he said. 'I haven't been in the water yet today.'

'We've had so much fun talking and eating, time passes.'

'Yeah,' he said, looking at his hands.

The fog flailed across the sand in soft strips.

'There,' she said. 'That was a raindrop on my nose!' She laughed ridiculously at it. Her eyes were bright and young again. She was almost triumphant. 'Good old rain.'

'Why are you so pleased? You're an odd duck.'

'Come on, rain!' she said. 'Well, help me with these blankets. We'd better run!'

He picked up the blankets slowly, preoccupied. 'Not even one last swim, dammit. I've a mind to take just one dive.' He smiled at her. 'Only a minute!'

'No.' Her face paled. 'You'll catch cold, and I'll have to nurse you!'

'Okay, okay.' He turned away from the sea. Gentle rain began to fall.

Marching ahead of him, she headed for the hotel. She was singing softly to herself.

'Hold on!' he said.

She halted. She did not turn. She only listened to his voice far away.

'There's someone out in the water!' he cried. 'Drowning!'

She couldn't move. She heard his feet running.

'Wait here!' he shouted. 'I'll be right back! There's someone there! A woman, I think!'

'Let the lifeguards get her!'

'Aren't any! Off duty; late!' He ran down to the shore, the sea, the waves.

'Come back!' she screamed. 'There's no one out there! Don't, oh, don't!'

'Don't worry, I'll be right back!' he called. 'She's drowning out there, see?'

The fog came in, the rain pattered down, a white flashing light raised in the waves. He ran, and the woman in the black suit ran after him, scattering beach implements behind her, crying, tears rushing from her eyes. 'Don't!' She put out her hands.

He leaped into an onrushing dark wave.

The woman in the black bathing suit waited in the rain.

At six o'clock the sun set somewhere behind black clouds. The rain rattled softly on the water, a distant drum snare.

Under the sea, a move of illuminant white.

The soft shape, the foam, the weed, the long strands of strange green hair lay in the shallows. Among the stirring glitter, deep under, was the man.

Fragile. The foam bubbled and broke. The frosted coral brain rang against a pebble with thought, as quickly lost as found. Men. Fragile. Like dolls, they break. Nothing, nothing to them. A minute under water and they're sick and pay no attention and they vomit out and kick and then, suddenly, just lie there, doing nothing. Doing nothing at all. Strange. Disappointing, after all the days of waiting.

What to do with them now? His head lolls, his mouth opens, his eyelids loosen, his eyes stare, his skin pales. Silly man, wake up! Wake up!

The water surged about him.

The man hung limply, loosely, mouth agape.

The phosphorescence, the green hair weed withdrew.

He was released. A wave carried him back to the silent shore. Back to his wife, who was waiting for him there in the cold rain.

The rain poured over the black waters.

Distantly, under the leaden skies, from the twilight shore, a woman screamed.

Ah – the ancient dusts stirred sluggishly in the water –

isn't that *like* a woman? Now, *she* doesn't want him, *either*!

At seven o'clock the rain fell thick. It was night and very cold and the hotels all along the sea had to turn on the heat.

The Inspired
Chicken Motel

It was in the Depression, deep down in the empty soul of the Depression in 1932, when we were heading west by 1928 Buick, that my mother, father, my brother Skip, and I came upon what we ever after called the Inspired Chicken Motel.

It was, my father said, a motel straight out of Revelations. And the one strange chicken at that motel could no more help making said Revelations, writ on eggs, than a holy roller can help going wild with utterances of God, Time, and Eternity writhing along his limbs, seeking passage out the mouth.

Some creatures are given to talents inclined one way, some another. But chickens are the greatest dumb brute mystery of them all. Especially hens who think or intuit messages calcium-scrawled forth in a nice neat hand upon the shells wherein their offspring twitch asleep.

Little did we know that long autumn of 1932, as we blew tyres and flung fan belts like lost garters down Highway 66, that somewhere ahead that motel, and that most peculiar chicken, were waiting.

Along the way, our family was a wonderful nest of amiable contempt. Holding the maps, my brother and I knew we were a helluva lot smarter than Dad. Dad knew he was smarter than Mom, and Mom knew she could brain the whole bunch, any time.

That makes for perfection.

I mean, any family that has a proper disrespect, each for the other, can stay together. As long as there is something to fight about, people will come to meals. Lose that and the family disintegrates.

So we leaped out of bed each day hardly able to wait to hear what dumb thing someone might say over the hard-fried bacon and the under-fried scrambleds. The toast was too dark or too light. There was jam for only one person. Or it was a flavour that two out of four hated. Hand us a set of bells and we could ring all the wrong changes. If Dad claimed he was still growing, Skip and I ran the tape measure out to prove he'd shrunk during the night. That's humanity. That's nature. That's family.

But like I said, there we were grousing down Illinois, quarrelling through the leaf change in the Ozarks autumn where we stopped sniping all of ten minutes to see the fiery colours. Then, pot-shotting and snivelling across Kansas and Oklahoma, we ploughed into a fine deep-red muck and slid off the road on a detour where each of us could bless himself and blame others for the excavations, the badly painted signs, and the lack of brakeage in our old Buick. Out of the ditch, we unloaded ourselves into a great Buick-a-Night Bungalow Court in a murderers' ambush behind a woods and on the rim of a deep rock-quarry where our bodies might be found years later at the bottom of a lost and sourceless lake, and spent the night counting the rain that leaked in through the shingle-sieve roof and fighting over who had the most covers on the wrong side of the bed.

The next day was even better. We steamed out of the rain into 100-degree heat that took the sap and spunk out of us, save for a few ricochet slaps Dad threw at Skip but landed on me. By noon we were sweated fresh out of contempt, and were settling into a rather refined if exhausted period of familiar insult, when we drove up by this chicken farm outside Amarillo, Texas.

We sat up, instantly.

Why?

Because we found that chickens are kicked the same as families kick each other, to get them out of the way.

We saw an old man boot a rooster and smile as he came

towards the auto gate. We all beamed. He leaned in to say he rented rooms for fifty cents a night, the price being low because the smell was high.

The starch being out of Dad, and him sunk in a despond of good will, and this looking like another dandy place to raise grouse, he turned in his chauffeur's cap and shelled out fifty cents in nickels and pennies.

Our great expectations were not punctured. The flimsy room we moved into was a beaut. Not only did all the springs give injections wherever you put flesh down, but the entire bungalow suffered from an oft-rehearsed palsy. Its foundations were still in shock from the thousand mean invaders who had cried 'Timber!' and fallen upon the impaling beds.

By its smell, some wild parties had died here. There was an odour of false sincerity and lust masquerading as love. A wind blew up between the floorboards redolent of chickens under the bungalow who spent nights running crazy from diarrhoea induced by pecking the bathtub liquor that seeped down through the fake Oriental linoleum.

Anyway, once we had hunched in out of the sun and slunk through a cold pork-and-beans-on-bread lunch, with white oleomargarine greasing it down the ways, my brother and I found a desert creek nearby and heaved rocks at each other to cool off. That night we went into town and found a greasy spoon and read the flyspecks and fought off the crickets that came into the café to skinnydip in the soup. We saw a ten-cent James Cagney gangster movie and came out heading back to the chicken ranch delighted with all the mayhem, the Great Depression gone and forgotten.

At eleven that hot night everyone in Texas was awake because of the heat. The landlady, a frail woman whose picture I had seen in every newsphoto of Dust Bowl country, eroded down to the bones but with a fragile sort of candlelight hollowed in her eyes, came to sit and chat with us about the eighteen million unemployed and what might happen next and where we were going and what would next year bring.

Which was the first cool respite of the day. A cold wind blew out of tomorrow. We grew restive. I looked at my brother, he looked at Mom, Mom looked at Dad, and we were a family, no matter what, and we were together tonight, going somewhere.

'Well . . . ' Dad took out a road map and unfolded it and showed the lady where he had marked in red ink as if it was a chart of our four lives' territory, just how we would live in the days ahead, just how survive, just how make do, sleep just so, eat how much, and sleep with no dreams guaranteed. 'Tomorow' — he touched the roads with one nicotine-stained finger — 'we'll be in Tombstone. Day after that Tucson. Stay in Tucson looking for work. We got enough cash for two weeks there if we cut it close. No jobs there, we move on to San Diego. Got a cousin there in Customs Inspection on the docks. We figure one week in San Diego, three weeks in Los Angeles. Then we've just enough money to head home to Illinois, where we can put in on relief or, who knows, maybe get the job back at the Power and Light Company that laid me off six months ago.'

'I see,' said the landlady.

And she did see. For all eighteen million people had come along this road and stopped here going somewhere anywhere nowhere and then going back to the nowhere somewhere anywhere they had got lost from in the first place and, not needed, gone wandering away.

'What kind of job are you looking for?' asked the landlady.

And it was a joke. She knew it as soon as she said it. Dad thought about it and laughed. Mother laughed. My brother and I laughed. We all laughed together.

For of course no one asked what *kind* of job, there were just jobs to be found, jobs without names, jobs to buy gas and feed faces and maybe, on occasion, buy ice cream cones. Movies? They were something to be seen once a month, perhaps. Beyond that, my brother and I snuck in theatres around the back or inside doors or down through basements up through orchestra pits or up fire escapes and down into balconies. Nothing could keep us from Saturday matinees except Adolphe Menjou.

We all stopped laughing. Sensing that a proper time had come for a particular act, the landlady excused herself, went out, and in a few minutes returned. She brought with her two small grey cardboard boxes. The way she carried them, at first it almost seemed she was bearing the family heirlooms or the ashes of a beloved uncle. She sat and held the two small boxes on her aproned lap for a long moment, shielding them quietly. She waited with the inherent sense of drama most people learn when small quick events must be slowed and made to seem large.

And strangely, we were moved by the hush of the woman herself, by the lostness of her face. For it was a face in which a whole lifetime of lostness showed. It was a face in which children, never born, gave cry. Or it was a face in which children, born, had passed to be buried not in the earth but in her flesh. Or it was a face in which children, born, raised, had gone off over the world never to write. It was a face in which her life and the life of her husband and the ranch they lived on struggled to survive and somehow managed. God's breath threatened to blow out her wits, but somehow, with awe at her own survival, her soul stayed lit.

Any face like that, with so much loss in it, when it finds something to hold and look at, how can you help but pay attention?

For now our landlady was holding out the boxes and opening the small lid of the first.

And inside the first box . . .

'Why,' said Skip, 'it's just an egg . . . '

'Look close,' she said.

And we all looked close at the fresh white egg lying on a small bed of aspirin-bottle cottonwool.

'Hey,' said Skip.

'Oh, yeah,' I whispered. 'Hey.'

For there in the centre of the egg, as if cracked, bumped and formed by mysterious nature, was the skull and horns of a longhorn steer.

It was as fine and beautiful as if a jewelsmith had worked the egg some magic way to raise the calcium in obedient ridges to shape that skull and those prodigious horns. It was, therefore, an egg any boy would have proudly worn on a string about his neck or carried to school for friends to gasp over and appraise.

'This egg,' said our landlady, 'was laid, with this design on it, exactly three days ago.'

Our hearts beat once or twice. We opened our mouths to speak. 'It –'

She shut the box. Which shut our mouths. She took a deep breath, half closed her eyes, then opened the lid of the second box.

Skip cried, 'I bet I know what's –'

His guess would have been right.

In the second box, revealed, lay a second fat white egg on cottonwool.

'There,' said the landlady who owned the motel and the chicken ranch way out in the middle of the land under a sky that went forever and fell over the horizon into more land that went on forever and more sky over that.

We all bent forward, squinting.

For there were words written on this egg in white calcium outline, as if the nervous system of the chicken, moved by strange night talks that only it could hear, had lettered the shell in painful half-neat inscriptions.

And the words we saw upon the egg were these:

REST IN PEACE. PROSPERITY IS NEAR.

And suddenly it was very quiet.

We had begun to ask questions about that first egg. Our mouths had jumped wide to ask: How could a chicken, in its small insides, make marks on shells? Was the hen's wrist-watch machinery tampered with by outside influences? Had God used that small and simple beast as a Ouija board on which to spell out shapes, forms, remonstrances, unveilings?

But now, with the second egg before us, our mouths stayed numbly shut.

REST IN PEACE. PROSPERITY IS NEAR.

Dad could not take his eyes from that egg.

Nor could any of us.

Our lips moved at last, saying the words soundlessly.

Dad looked up, once, at our landlady. She gazed back at him with a gaze that was as calm, steady, and honest as the plains were long, hot, empty, and dry. The light of fifty years withered and bloomed there. She neither complained nor explained. She had found an egg beneath a hen. Here the egg was. Look at it, her face said. Read the words. Then . . . please . . . read them again.

We inhaled and exhaled.

Dad turned slowly at last and walked away. At the screen door he looked back and his eyes were blinking rapidly. He did not put his hand up to his eyes, but they were wet and bright and nervous. Then he went out the door and down the steps and between the old bungalows, his hands deep in his pockets.

My brother and I were still staring at that egg, when the landlady closed the lid carefully, rose, and went to the door. We followed, silent.

Outside, we found Dad standing in the last heat of the sun

and the first light of the moon by the wire fence. We all looked over at ten thousand chickens veering this way and that in tides, suddenly panicked by wind or startled by cloud shadows or dogs barking off on the prairie, or a lone car moving on the hot-tar road.

'There,' said our landlady. 'There she is.'

She pointed at the sea of rambling fowl.

We saw thousands of chickens hustling, heard thousands of bird voices suddenly raised, suddenly dying away.

'There's my pet, there's my precious. See?'

She held her hand steady, moving it slowly to point to one particular hen among the ten thousand. And somewhere in all the flurry . . .

'Isn't she *grand*?' said our landlady.

I looked, I stood on tiptoe, I squinted, I stared wildly.

'There! I think — !' cried my brother.

'The white one,' supplied our landlady, 'with ginger flecks.'

I looked at her. Her face was very serene. She knew her hen. She knew the look of her love. Even if we could not find and see, the hen was there, like the world and the sky, a small fact in much that was large.

'There,' said my brother, and stopped, confused. 'No, there. No, wait . . . over *there*!'

'Yeah,' I said. 'I see him!'

'Her, you dimwit!'

'Her!' I said.

And for a brief moment I thought I *did* see one chicken among many, one grand bird whiter than the rest, plumper than the rest, happier than the rest, faster, more frolicsome and somehow strutting proud. It was as if the sea of creatures parted before our Bible gaze to show us, alone among island shadows of moon on warm grass, a single bird transfixed for an instant before a final dog bark and a rifle shot from a passing car exhaust panicked and scattered the fowls. The hen was gone.

'You *saw*?' asked the landlady, holding to the wire fence, searching for her love lost in the rivering hens.

'Yes.' I could not see my father's face, whether it was serious or if he gave a dry smile to himself. 'I saw.'

He and Mother walked back to our bungalow.

But the landlady and Skip and I stayed on at the fence not saying anything, not even pointing any more, for at least another ten minutes.

Then it was time for bed.

I lay there wide awake with Skip. For I remembered all the other nights when Dad and Mom talked and we liked to listen to them talk about grown-up things and grown-up places, Mother asking concerned and Dad answering final and very sure and calm and quiet. Pot of Gold, End of Rainbow. I didn't believe in that. Land of Milk and Honey. I didn't believe in that. We had travelled far and seen too much for me to believe . . . but . . .

Someday My Ship Will Come In . . .

I believed that.

Whenever I heard Dad say it, tears welled in my eyes. I had seen such ships on Lake Michigan summer morns coming in from festivals across the water full of merry people, confetti on the air, horns blowing, and in my private dream, projected on my bedroom wall through countless nights, there we stood on the dock, Mom, Dad, Skip, and I! and the ship huge, snow-white, coming in with millionaires on her upper decks tossing not confetti but greenbacks and gold coins down in a clattering rain all around it, so we danced to catch and dodge and cry Ouch! when hit about the ears by especially fierce coins or laughed when licked by a snowy flurry of cash . . .

Mom asked about it. Dad answered. And in the night,

Skip and I went down in the same dream to wait on a dock.

And this night here, lying in bed, after a long while I said, 'Dad? What does it mean?'

'What does *what* mean?' said Dad, way over there in the dark with Mom.

'The message on the egg. Does it mean the Ship? It'll come in soon?'

There was a long silence.

'Yes,' said Dad. 'That's what it means. Go to sleep, Doug.'

'Yes, sir.'

And, weeping tears, I turned away.

We drove out of Amarillo at six the next morning in order to beat the heat, and for the first hour out we didn't say anything because we weren't awake, and for the second hour we said nothing because we were thinking about the night before. And then at last Dad's coffee started perking in him and he said:

'Ten thousand.'

We waited for him to go on and he did, shaking his head slowly:

'Ten thousand dumb chickens. And *one* of them, out of nowhere, takes it to mind to scribble us a note.'

'Dad,' said Mom.

And her voice by its inflection said, You don't really *believe*?

'Yeah, Dad,' said my brother in the same voice, with the same faint criticism.

'It's something to think about,' said Dad, his eyes just on the road, riding easy, his hands on the wheel not gripping tight, steering our small raft over the desert. Just beyond the hill was another hill and beyond that another hill, but just beyond *that* . . . ?

Mother looked over at Dad's face and hadn't the heart to say his name in just that way right now. She looked back at the road and said so we could barely hear it:

'How did it go again?'

Dad took us around a long turn in the desert highway towards White Sands, and then he cleared his throat and cleared a space on the sky ahead as he drove and said, remembering:

'Rest in Peace. Prosperity Is Near.'

I let another mile go by before I said, 'How much . . . unh. How much . . . an egg like that worth, Dad?'

'There's no putting a human price on a thing like that,' he said, not looking back, just driving for the horizon, just going on. 'Boy, you can't set a price on an egg like that, laid by an inspired chicken at the Inspired Chicken Motel. Years from now, that's what we'll call it. The Inspired Chicken Motel.'

We drove on at an even forty miles an hour into the heat and dust of day-after-tomorrow.

My brother didn't hit me, I didn't hit my brother, carefully, secretly, until just before noon when we got out to water the flowers by the side of the road.

Yes, We'll Gather
at the River

At one minute to nine he should have rolled the wooden Indian back into warm tobacco darkness and turned the key in the lock. But somehow he waited because there were so many lost men walking by in no special direction for no special reason. A few of them wandered in to drift their gaze over the tribal cigars laid out in their neat brown boxes, then glanced up suddenly surprised to find where they were and said, evasively, 'Evening, Charlie.'

'So it is,' said Charlie Moore.

Some of the men wandered off empty-handed, others moved on with a nickel cigar unlit in their mouths.

So it was nine-thirty of a Thursday night before Charlie Moore finally touched the wooden Indian's elbow as if disturbing a friend and hating to bother. Gently he manoeuvred the savage to where he became watchman of the night. In the shadows, the carved face stared raw and blind through the door.

'Well, Chief, what do you see?'

Charlie followed that silent gaze beyond to the highway that cut through the very centre of their lives.

In locust hordes, cars roared up from Los Angeles. With irritation they slowed to thirty miles per hour here. They crept between some three dozen shops, stores, and old livery stables become gas stations, to the north rim of town. There the cars exploded back to eighty, racing like Furies on San Francisco, to teach it violence.

Charlie snorted softly.

A man passed, saw him standing with his silent wooden friend, said, 'Last night, eh?' and was gone.

Last night.

There. Someone had dared use the words.

Charlie wheeled to switch off the lights, lock the door and, on the sidewalk, eyes down, freeze.

As if hypnotized, he felt his gaze rise again to the old highway which swept by with winds that smelled of a billion years ago. Great bursts of headlight arrived, then cut away in departures of red taillight, like schools of small bright fish darting in the wake of sharks and blind-travelling whales. The lights sank away and were lost in the black hills.

Charlie broke his stare. He walked slowly on through his town as the clock over the Oddfellows Lodge struck the quarter hour and moved on towards ten and still he walked and was amazed then not amazed any more to see how every shop was still open long after hours and in every door stood a man or woman transfixed even as he and his Indian brave had been transfixed by a talked-about and dreadful future suddenly become Here Now Tonight.

Fred Ferguson, the taxidermist, kin to the family of wild owls and panicked deer which stayed on forever in his window, spoke to the night air as Charlie passed:

'Hard to believe, ain't it?'

He wished no answer, for he went on immediately:

'Keep thinking: Just can't be. Tomorrow, the highway dead and us dead with it.'

'Oh, it won't be that bad,' said Charlie.

Ferguson gave him a shocked look. 'Wait. Ain't you the one hollered two years ago, wanted to bomb the legislature, shoot the road contractors, steal the concrete mixers and earth-movers when they started the new highway three hundred yards west of here? What you mean, it won't be bad? It will, and you know it!'

'I know,' said Charlie Moore, at last.

Ferguson brooded on the near distance.

'Three hundred little bitty yards. Not much, eh? But

seeing as how our town is only a hundred yards wide, that puts us, give or take, about two hundred yards from the new superroad. Two hundred yards from people who need nuts, bolts, or house-paint. Two hundred from jokers who barrel down from the mountains with deer or fresh-shot alley-cats of all sorts and need the services of the only A-one taxidermist on the Coast. Two hundred yards from ladies who need aspirin —' He eyed the drugstore. 'Haircuts.' He watched the red-striped pole spin in its glass case down the street. 'Strawberry sodas.' He nodded at the malt shop. 'You name it.'

They named it all in silence, sliding their gaze along the stores, the shops, the arcades.

'Maybe it's not too late.'

'Late, Charlie? Hell. Cement's mixed and poured and set. Come dawn they yank the roadblocks both ends of the new road. Governor might cut a ribbon from the first car. Then . . . people might remember Oak Lane the first week, sure. The second week not so much. A month from now? We'll be a smear of old paint on their right running north, on their left running south, burning rubber. There's Oak Lane! Remember? Ghost town. Oops! It's gone.'

Charlie let his heart beat two or three times.

'Fred . . . what you going to do?'

'Stay on awhile. Stuff a few birds the local boys bring in. Then crank the old Tin Lizzie and drive that new super-freeway myself going nowhere, anywhere, and so long to you, Charlie Moore.'

'Night, Fred. Hope you sleep.'

'What, and miss welcoming in the New Year, middle of July . . . ?'

Charlie walked and that voice faded behind and he came to the barbershop where three men laid out, were being strenuously barbered behind plate glass. The highway traffic slid over them in bright reflections. They looked like they were drowning under a stream of huge fireflies.

Charlie stepped in. Everyone glanced up.

'Anyone got any ideas?'

'Progress, Charlie,' said Frank Mariano, combing and cutting, 'is an idea can't be stopped with no other idea. Let's yank up the whole damn town, lock, stock, and tar barrel, carry it over, nail it down by that new road.'

'We figured the cost last year. Four dozen stores at three thousand dollars average to haul them just three hundred yards west.'

'So ends that master plan,' muttered someone under a hot steam towel, buried in inescapable fact.

'One good hurricane would do the job, carriage-free.'

They all laughed quietly.

'We should all celebrate tonight,' said the man under the hot towel. He sat up, revealing himself as Hank Summers, the groceryman. 'Snort a few stiff drinks and wonder where the hell we'll all be this time next year.'

'We didn't fight hard enough,' said Charlie. 'When it started, we didn't pitch in.'

'Hell.' Frank snipped a hair out of the inside of a fairly large ear. 'When times move, not a day passes someone's not hurt. This month, this year, it's our turn. Next time *we* want something, someone else gets stepped on, all in the name of Get Up and Go. Look, Charlie, go form a vigilantes. Mine that new road. But watch out. Just crossing the lanes to place the bomb, you're sure to be run down by a manure truck bound for Salinas.'

More laughter, which faded quickly.

'Look,' said Hank Summers, and everybody looked. He spoke to his own fly-specked image in the ancient mirror as if trying to sell his twin on a shared logic. 'We lived here thirty years now, you, me, all of us. Won't kill us to move on. Good God, we're all root and a yard wide. Graduation. School of hard knocks is throwing us out the door with no never-minds and no thank-yous. I'm ready. Charlie, are *you*?'

'Me, now,' said Frank Mariano. 'Monday morning six a.m. I load my barbershop in a trailer and shoot off after those customers, ninety miles an hour!'

There was a laugh sounded like the very last one of the day, so Charlie turned with one superb and mindless drift and was back on the street.

And still the shops stayed open, the lights stayed on, the doors stood wide, as if each owner was reluctant to go home, so long as that river out there was flowing and there was the great motion and glint and sound of people and metal and light in a tide they had grown so accustomed to it was hard to believe the river bottom would ever know a dry season.

Charlie lingered on, straying from shop to shop, sipping a chocolate Coke at the malted-milk counter, buying some stationery he couldn't use from the drugstore under the soft fluttering wood fan that whispered to itself in the ceiling. He loitered like a common criminal, thieving sights. He paused in alleys where, Saturday afternoons, gypsy tie salesmen or kitchenware spielers laid out their suitcase worlds to con the pedestrians. Then, at last he reached the gas station where Pete Britz, deep in the oil pit, was mending the dumb brute underside of a dead and uncomplaining 1947 Ford.

At ten o'clock, as if by some secret but mutual consent, all the shops went dark, all the people walked home, Charlie Moore among them.

He caught up with Hank Summers, whose face was still shining pink from the shave he hadn't needed. They ambled in silence for a time past houses where it seemed the whole population was sitting out smoking or knitting, rocking in chairs or fanning themselves against a nonexistent hot spell.

Hank laughed suddenly at some private thought. A few paces on, he decided to make it public:

'*Yes, we'll gather at the River.*
River, River.
Yes, we'll gather at the River
That flows by the Throne of God.'

He half sang it and Charlie nodded.

'First Baptist Church, when I was twelve.'

'The Lord giveth and the Highway Commissioner taketh away,' said Hank dryly. 'Funny. Never thought how much a town is people. Doing things, that is. Under the hot towel back there, thought: What's this place to me? Shaved, I had the answer. Russ Newell banging a carburettor at the Night Owl Garage? Yep. Allie Mae Simpson . . .'

He swallowed his voice in embarrassment.

Allie Mae Simpson . . . Charlie took up the count in his own mind . . . Allie Mae fixing wet curlicues in old ladies' hair in the bay window of her Vogue Salon . . . Doc Knight stacking pill bottles in the drug emporium cases . . . hardware store laid out in the hot noon sun, Clint Simpson middle of it, running his hands over, sorting out the million blinks and shines of brass and silver and gold, all the nails, hinges, knobs, all the saws, hammers, and snaked-up copper wire and stacks of aluminium foil like the junk shaken free of a thousand boys' pockets in a thousand summers past . . . and then . . .

. . . Then there was his own place, warm, dark, brown, comfortable, musky as the den of a tobacco-smoking bear . . . thick with the humidor smells of whole families of odd-sized cigars, imported cigarettes, snuffs just waiting to be exploded on the air . . .

Take all that away, thought Charlie, you got nothing. Buildings, sure. Anyone can raise a frame, paint a sign to say what might go on inside. But it was people that made the damn thing *get*.

Hank surfaced in his own long thoughts.

'Guess right now I'm sad. Want to send everyone back to open their shops so I can see what they were up to. Why wasn't I looking closer, all these years? Hell, hell. What's got into you, Hank Summers. There's another Oak Lane on up the line or down the line and people there busy as they are here. Wherever I land, next time I'll look close, swear to God. Good-bye, Charlie.'

'To hell with good-bye.'

'All right, then, good night.'

And Hank was gone and Charlie was home and Clara was waiting at the screen door with a glass of iced water.

'Sit out a while?'

'Like everyone else? Why not?'

They sat in the dark on the porch in the chain-hung wooden swing and watched the highway flush and drain, flush and drain with arrivals of headlight and departures of angry red fire like the coals from an immense brazier scattered to the fields.

Charlie drank the water slowly and, drinking, thought: In the old days you couldn't see the roads die. You felt them gradually fade, yes, lying in bed nights, maybe your mind got hold of some hint, some nudge or commotion that warned you it was sinking away. But it took years and years for any one road to give up its dusty ghost and another to stir alive. That's how things were, slow arriving and slow passing away. That's how things had always been.

But no more. Now, in a matter of hours.

He paused.

He touched in upon himself to find a new thing.

'I'm not mad any more.'

'Good,' said his wife.

They rocked a while, two halves of a similar content.

'My God, I was stirred up there for a while.'

'I remember,' she said.

'But now I figure, well . . . ' He drifted his voice, mostly to himself. 'Millions of cars come through every year. Like it or not, the road's just not big enough, we're holding up the world, that old road there and this old town. The world says it's got to move. So now, on that new road, not one but two million will pass just a shotgun blast away, going where they got to go to get things done they say are important, doesn't matter if they're important or not, folks *think* they are, and thinking makes the game. If we'd really seen it coming, thought in on it from every side, we'd have taken a steam-driven sledge and just mashed the town flat and said, "Drive through!" instead of making them lay the damn road over in that next clover patch. This way, the town dies hard, strangled on a piece of butcher string instead of being dropped off a cliff. Well, well.' He lit his pipe and blew great clouds of smoke in which to poke for past mistakes and present revelations. 'Us being human, I guess we couldn't have done but as we did . . . '

They heard the drugstore clock strike eleven and the Odd-fellows Lodge clock chime eleven-thirty, and at twelve they lay in bed in the dark, each with a ceilingful of thoughts above them.

'Graduation.'

'What?'

'Hank Summers said it and had it right. This whole week feels like the last days of school, years ago. I remember how I felt, how I was afraid, ready to cry, and how I promised myself to live every last moment right up to the time the diploma was in my hand, for God only knew what tomorrow might bring. Unemployment. Depression. War. And then the day arrived, tomorrow did get around to finally coming, and I found myself still alive, by God, and I was still all in one piece and things were starting over, more of the same, and hell, everything turned out okay. So this is another graduation all right, as Hank said, and I'm the last to doubt.'

'Listen,' said his wife much later. 'Listen.'

In the night, the river came through the town, the river of metal quiet now but still coming and going with its ancient smells of tidelands and dark seas of oil. Its glimmer, on the ceiling above their graveyard bed, had the shine of small craft, gliding upstream and down as their eyelids slowly, slowly shut and their breathing took on the regular sound of the motion of those tides . . . and then they slept.

In the first light of dawn, half the bed lay empty.

Clara sat up, almost afraid.

It was not like Charlie to be gone so early.

Then, another thing frightened her. She sat listening, not certain what had suddenly made her tremble, but before she had a chance to find out why, she heard footsteps.

They came from a long distance away and it was quite a while before they came up the walk and up the steps and into the house. Then, silence. She heard Charlie just standing there in the parlour for a long moment, so she called out:

'Charlie? Where you been?'

He came into the room in the faint light of dawn and sat on the bed beside her, thinking about where he had been and what he had done.

'Walked a mile up the coast and back. All the way to those wood barricades where the new highway starts. Figured it was the least I could do, be part of the whole darn thing.'

'The new road's open . . . ?'

'Open and doing business. Can't you tell?'

'Yes.' She rose slowly up in bed, tilting her head, closing her eyes for a moment, listening. 'So that's it? That's what bothered me. The old road. It's *really* dead.'

They listened to the silence outside the house, the old road gone empty and dry and hollow as a river bottom in a strange season of summers that would never stop, that would go on forever. The stream had indeed moved and changed its course, its banks, its bed, during the night. Now all you could hear were the trees in the blowing wind outside the house and the birds beginning to sing their arousal choirs in the time just before the sun really made it over the hills.

'Be real quiet.'

They listened again.

And there, far away, some two hundred and fifty or three hundred yards off across a meadow field, nearer the sea, they heard the old, the familiar, but the diminished sound of their river taking its new course, moving and flowing — it would never cease — through lengths of sprawling land away north and then on south through the hushed light. And beyond it, the sound of real water, the sea which might almost have drawn the river to come down along the shore . . .

Charlie Moore and his wife sat not moving for a moment longer, with that dim sound of the river across the fields moving and moving on.

'Fred Ferguson was there before dawn,' said Charlie in a voice that already remembered the Past. 'Crowd of people. Highway officials and all. Everyone pitched in. Fred, why he just walked over and grabbed hold of one end. I took the other. We moved one of those wood barricades, together. Then we stood back . . . and let the cars through.'

Have I Got a
Chocolate Bar for You!

It all began with the smell of chocolate.

On a steaming late afternoon of June rain, Father Malley drowsed in his confessional, waiting for penitents.

Where in all the world were they? he wondered. Immense traffics of sin lurked beyond in the warm rains. Then why not immense traffics of confession here?

Father Malley stirred and blinked.

Today's sinners moved so fast in their cars that this old church was an ecclesiastical blur. And himself? An ancient watercolour priest, tints fading fast, trapped inside.

Let's give it another five minutes and stop, he thought, not in panic but in the kind of quiet shame and desperation that neglect shoulders on a man.

There was a rustle from beyond the confessional grate next door.

Father Malley sat up, quickly.

A smell of chocolate sifted through the grille.

Ah, God, thought the priest, it's a lad with his small basket of sins soon laid to rest and him gone. Well . . .

The old priest leaned to the grate where the candy essence lingered and where the words must come.

But, no words. No 'Bless me, Father, for I have sinned . . . '

Only strange small mouse-sounds of . . . *chewing*!

The sinner in the next booth, God sew up his mouth, was actually sitting in there devouring a candy bar!

'No!' whispered the priest, to himself.

His stomach, gathering data, rumbled, reminding him that he had not eaten since breakfast. For some sin of pride

which he could not now recall, he had nailed himself to a
saint's diet all day, and now — *this*!

Next door, the chewing continued.

Father Malley's stomach growled. He leaned hard against
the grille, shut his eyes, and cried:

'Stop that!'

The mouse-nibbling stopped.

The smell of the chocolate faded.

A young man's voice said, 'That's exactly why I've come,
Father.'

The priest opened one eye to examine the shadow behind
the screen.

'*What*'s exactly why you've come?'

'The chocolate, Father.'

'The *what*?'

'Don't be angry, Father.'

'Angry, hell, who's angry?'

'You are, Father. I'm damned and burnt before I start, by
the sound of your voice.'

The priest sank back in the creaking leather and mopped
his face and shook his senses.

'Yes, yes. The day's hot. I'm out of temper. But then, I
never had much.'

'It will cool off later in the day, Father. You'll be fine.'

The old priest eyed the screen. 'Who's taking and who's
giving confession here?'

'Why, you are, Father.'

'Then, get *on* with it!'

The voice hastened forth the facts:

'You have smelled chocolate, Father?'

The priest's stomach answered for him, faintly.

Both listened to the sad sound. Then:

'Well, Father, to hit it on the head, I was and still am
a . . . chocolate junkie.'

Old fires stirred in the priest's eyes. Curiosity became

humour, then laughed itself back to curiosity again.

'And *that*'s why you've come to confession this day?'

'That's it, sir, or, Father.'

'You haven't come about sweating over your sister or blueprints for fornication or self-battles with the grand war of masturbation?'

'I have not, Father,' said the voice in remorse.

The priest caught the tone and said, 'Tut, tut, it's all right. You'll get around to it. For now, you're a grand relief. I'm full-up with wandering males and lonely females and all the junk they read in books and try in waterbeds and sink from sight with suffocating cries as the damn things spring leaks and all is lost. Get on. You have bruised my antennae alert. Say more.'

'Well, Father, I have eaten, every day of my life now for ten or twelve years, one or two pounds of chocolate. I cannot leave it alone, Father. It is the end-all and be-all of my life.'

'Sounds like a fearful affliction of lumps, acne, carbuncles, and pimples.'

'It was. It *is*.'

'And not exactly contributing to a lean figure.'

'If I leaned, Father, the confessional would fall over.'

The cabinet around them creaked and groaned as the hidden figure beyond demonstrated.

'Sit still!' cried the priest.

The groaning stopped.

The priest was wide awake now and feeling splendid. Not in years had he felt so alive and aware of his happily curious and beating heart and fine blood that sought and found, sought and found the far corners of his cloth and body.

The heat of the day was gone.

He felt immensely cool. A kind of excitement pulsed his wrists and lingered in his throat. He leaned almost like a lover to the grille and prompted more spillage.

'Oh, lad, you're rare.'

'And sad, Father, and twenty-two years old and put upon, and hate myself for eating, and need to do something about it.'

'Have you tried chewing more and swallowing less?'

'Oh, each night I go to bed saying: Lord, put off the crunchbars and the milk-chocolate kisses and the Hersheys. Each morning I rave out of bed and run to the liquor store not for liquor but for eight Nestlés in a row! I'm in sugar-shock by noon.'

'That's not so much confession as medical fact, I can see.'

'My doctor yells at me, Father.'

'He should.'

'I don't listen, Father.'

'*You* should.'

'My mother's no help, she's hog-fat and candy-wild.'

'I hope you're not one of those who live at home still?'

'I loiter about, Father.'

'God, there should be laws against boys loitering in the round shade of their mas. Is your father surviving the two of you?'

'Somehow.'

'And *his* weight?'

'Irving Gross, he calls himself. Which is a joke about size and weight and not his name.'

'With the three of you, the sidewalk's full?'

'No bike can pass, Father.'

'Christ in the wilderness,' murmured the priest, 'starving for forty days.'

'Sounds like a terrible diet, Father.'

'If I knew the proper wilderness, I'd boot you there.'

'Boot away, Father. With no help from my mom and dad, a doctor and skinny friends who snort at me, I'm out of pocket from eating and out of mind from the same. I never dreamed I'd wind up with *you*. Beg pardon, Father, but it took a lot to drive me here. If my friends knew, if my mom, my dad, my crazy doctor knew I was here with *you* at this minute, oh what the hell!'

There was a fearful stampede of feet, a careening of flesh. 'Wait!'

But the weight blundered out of the next-door cubby.

With an elephant trample, the young man was gone.

The smell of chocolate alone stayed behind and told all by saying nought.

The heat of the day swarmed in to stifle and depress the old priest.

He had to climb out of the confessional because he knew if he stayed he would begin to curse under his breath and have to run off to have *his* sins forgiven at some other parish.

I suffer from Peevish, O Lord, he thought. How many Hail Marys for *that*?

Come to think of it, how many for a thousand tons, give or take a ton, of chocolate?

Come back! he cried silently at the empty church aisle.

No, he won't, not ever now, he thought, I pressed too hard.

And with that as supreme depression, he went to the parish house to tub himself cool and towel himself to distemper.

A day, two days, a week passed.

The sweltering noons dissolved the old priest back into a stupor of sweat and vinegar-gnat mean. He snoozed in his cubby or shuffled papers in the unlined library, looked out at the untended lawn and reminded himself to caper with the mower one day soon. But most of all he found himself brambling with irritability. Fornication was the minted coin of the land, and masturbation its handmaiden. Or so it seemed from the few whispers that slid through the confessional grille during the long afternoon.

On the fifteenth day of July, he found himself staring at

some boys idling by on their bicycles, mouths full of Hershey bars that they were gulping and chewing.

That night he awoke thinking Power House and Baby Ruth and Love Nest and Crunch.

He stood it as long as he could and then got up, tried to read, tossed the book down, paced the dark night church, and at last, spluttering mildly, went up to the altar and asked one of his rare favours of God.

The next afternoon, the young man who loved chocolate at last came back.

'Thank you, Lord,' murmured the priest, as he felt the vast weight creak the other half of the confessional like a ship foundered with wild freight.

'What?' whispered the young voice from the far side.

'Sorry, I wasn't addressing you,' said the priest.

He shut his eyes and inhaled.

The gates of the chocolate factory stood wide somewhere and its mild spice moved forth to change the land.

Then, an incredible thing happened.

Sharp words burst from Father Malley's mouth.

'You shouldn't be *coming* here!'

'What, what, Father?'

'Go somewhere else! I can't help. You need special work. No, no.'

The old priest was stunned to feel his own mind jump out of his tongue this way. Was it the heat, the long days and weeks kept waiting by this fiend, what, *what*? But still his mouth leaped on:

'No help here! No, no. *Go* for help —'

'To the shrinks, you mean?' the voice cut in, amazingly calm, considering the explosion.

'Yes, yes, Lord save us, to those people. The — the psychiatrists.'

This last word was even more incredible. He had rarely

heard himself say it.

'Oh, God, Father, what do *they* know?' said the young man.

What indeed, thought Father Malley, for he had long been put off by their carnival talk and to-the-rear-march chat and clamour. Good grief, why don't I turn in my collar and buy me a beard! he thought, but went on more calmly.

'What do they know, my son? Why, they claim to know everything.'

'Just like the Church *used* to claim, Father?'

Silence. Then:

'There's a difference between claiming and knowing,' the old priest replied, as calmly as his beating heart would allow.

'And the Church *knows*, is that it, Father?'

'And if it doesn't, *I* do!'

'Don't get mad again, Father.' The young man paused and sighed. 'I didn't come to dance angels on the head of a pin with you. Shall I start confession, Father?'

'It's about time!' The priest caught himself, settled back, shut his eyes sweetly, and added. 'Well?'

And the voice on the other side, with the tongue and the breath of a child, tinctured with silver-foiled kisses, flavoured with honeycomb, moved by recent sugars and memories or more immediate Cadbury fêtes and galas, began to describe its life of getting up and living with and going to bed with Swiss delights and temptations out of Hershey, Pennsylvania, or how to chew the dark skin off the exterior of a Clark bar and keep the caramel and textured interior for special shocks and celebrations. Of how the soul asked and the tongue demanded and the stomach accepted and the blood danced to the drive of Power House, the promise of Love Nest, the delivery of Butterfinger, but most of all the sweet African murmuring of dark chocolate between the teeth, tinting the gums, flavouring the palate so you mut-

tered, whispered, murmured, pure Congo, Zambesi, Chad
in your sleep.

And the more the voice talked, as the days passed and the
weeks, and the old priest listened, the lighter became the
burden on the other side of the grille. Father Malley knew,
without looking, that the flesh enclosing that voice was
raining and falling away. The tread was less heavy. The
confessional did not cry out in such huge alarms when the
body entered next door.

For even with the young voice there and the young man,
the smell of chocolate was truly fading and almost gone.

And it was the loveliest summer the old priest had ever
known.

Once, years before, when he was a very young priest, a
thing had happened that was much like this, in its strange
and special way.

A girl, no more than sixteen by her voice, had come to
whisper each day from the time school let out to the time
autumn school renewed.

For all of that long summer he had come as close as a priest
might to an alert affection for that whisper and that dear
voice. He had heard her through her July attraction, her
August madness, and her September disillusion, and as she
went away forever in October, in tears, he wanted to cry out:
Oh, stay, stay! Marry me!

But I am the groom to the brides of Christ, another voice
whispered.

And he had *not* run forth, that very young priest, into the
traffics of the world.

Now, nearing sixty, the young soul within him sighed,
stirred, recalled, compared that old and shopworn memory
with this new, somehow funny yet withal sad encounter with
a lost soul whose love was not summer madness for girls in
dire swimsuits, but chocolate unwrapped in secret and

devoured in stealth.

'Father,' said the voice, late one afternoon. 'It has been a fine summer.'

'Strange you would say that,' said the priest. 'I have thought so myself.'

'Father, I have something really awful to confess to you.'

'I'm beyond shocking, I think.'

'Father, I am not from your diocese.'

'That's all right.'

'And, Father, forgive me, but, I —'

'Go on.'

'I'm not even Catholic.'

'You're *what*!' cried the old man.

'I'm not even Catholic, Father. Isn't that awful?'

'Awful?'

'I'm mean, I'm sorry, truly I am. I'll join the Church, if you want, Father, to make up.'

'Join the Church, you idiot?' shouted the old man. 'It's too late for that! Do you know what you've done? Do you know the depths of depravity you've plumbed? You've taken my time, bent my ear, driven me wild, asked advice, needed a psychiatrist, argued religion, criticized the Pope, if I remember correctly, and I *do* remember, used up three months, eighty or ninety days, and now, now, *now* you want to join the Church and "make up"?'

'If you don't mind, Father.'

'Mind! Mind!' yelled the priest, and lapsed into a ten-second apoplexy.

He almost tore the door wide to run around and seize the culprit out into the light. But then:

'It was not all for nothing, Father,' said the voice from beyond the grille.

The priest grew very quiet.

'For you see, Father, God bless you, you have helped me.'

The priest grew very quiet.

'Yes, Father, oh bless you indeed, you have helped me so very much, and I am beholden,' whispered the voice. 'You haven't asked, but don't you guess? I have lost weight. You wouldn't believe the weight I have lost. Eighty, eighty-five, ninety pounds. Because of you, Father. I gave it up. I gave it up. Take a deep breath. Inhale.'

The priest, against his wish, did so.

'What do you smell?'

'Nothing.'

'Nothing, Father, nothing! It's gone. The smell of chocolate and the chocolate with it. Gone. Gone. I'm free.'

The old priest sat, knowing not what to say, and a peculiar itching came about his eyelids.

'You have done Christ's work, Father, as you yourself must know. He walked through the world and helped. You walk through the world and help. When I was falling, you put out your hand, Father, and saved me.'

Then a most peculiar thing happened.

Father Malley felt tears burst from his eyes. They brimmed over. They streaked along his cheeks. They gathered at his tight lips and he untightened them and the tears fell from his chin. He could not stop them. They came, O Lord, they came like a shower of spring rain after the seven lean years and the drought over and himself alone, dancing about, thankful, in the pour.

He heard sounds from the other booth and could not be sure but somehow felt that the other one was crying, too.

So here they sat, while the sinful world rushed by on streets, here in the sweet incense gloom, two men on opposite sides of some fragile board slattings, on a late afternoon at the end of summer, weeping.

And at last they grew very quiet indeed and the voice asked, anxiously, 'Are you all right, Father?'

The priest replied at last, eyes shut, 'Fine. Thanks.'

'Anything I can do, Father?'

'You have already done it, my son.'

'About . . . my joining the Church. I meant it.'

'No matter.'

'But it does matter. I'll join. Even though I'm Jewish.'

Father Malley snorted half a laugh. 'Wha-what?'

'Jewish, Father, but an Irish Jew, if that helps.'

'Oh, yes!' roared the old priest. 'It helps, it helps!'

'What's so funny, Father?'

'I don't know, but it is, it is, funny, funny!'

And here he burst into such paroxysms of laughter as made him cry and such floodings of tears as made him laugh again until all mingled in a grand outrush and uproar. The church slammed back echoes of cleansing laughter. In the midst of it all he knew that, telling all this to Bishop Kelly, his confessor, tomorrow, he would be let off easy. A church is washed well and good and fine not only by the tears of sorrow but by the clean fresh-cut meadowbrooms of that self-forgiveness and other-forgiveness which God gave only to man and called it laughter.

It took a long while for their mutual shouts to subside, for now the young man had given up weeping and taken on hilarity, too, and the church rocked with the sounds of two men who one minute had done a sad thing and now did a happy one. The sniffle was gone. Joy banged the walls like wild birds flying to be free.

At last, the sounds weakened. The two men sat, wiping their faces, unseen to each other.

Then, as if the world knew there must be a shift of mood and scene, a wind blew in the church doors far away. Leaves drifted from trees and fell into the aisles. A smell of autumn filled the dusky air. Summer was truly over.

Father Malley looked beyond to that door and the wind and the leaves moving off and gone, and suddenly, as in spring, wanted to go with them. His blood demanded a way out, but there was no way.

'I'm leaving, Father.'

The old priest sat up.

'For the time being, you mean.'

'No, I'm going away, Father. This is my last time with you.'

You can't do that! thought the priest, and almost said it.

But instead he said, as calmly as he could:

'Where are you to off to, son?'

'Oh, around the world, Father. Many places. I was always afraid, before. I never went anywhere. But now, with my weight gone, I'm heading out. A new job and so many places to be.'

'How long will you be gone, lad?'

'A year, five years, ten. Will you be here ten years from now, Father?'

'God willing.'

'Well, somewhere along the way I'll be in Rome and buy something small but have it blessed by the Pope and when I come back I'll bring it here and look you up.'

'Will you do that?'

'I will. Do you forgive me, Father?'

'For what?'

'For everything.'

'We have forgiven each other, dear boy, which is the finest thing that men can do.'

There was the merest stir of feet from the other side.

'I'm going now, Father. Is it true that "good-bye" means God be with you?'

'That's what it means.'

'Well, then, oh truly, good-bye, Father.'

'And good-bye in all its original meaning to you, lad.'

And the booth next to his elbow was suddenly empty.

And the young man gone.

Many years later, when Father Malley was a very old man

indeed and full of sleep, a final thing happened to fill out his life. Late one afternoon, dozing in the confessional, listening to rain fall out beyond the church, he smelled a strange and familiar smell and opened his eyes.

Gently, from the other side of the grille, the faintest odour of chocolate seeped through.

The confessional creaked. On the other side, someone was trying to find words.

The old priest leaned forward, his heart beating quickly, wild with amazement and surprise. 'Yes?' he urged.

'Thank you,' said a whisper, at last.

'Beg pardon . . . ?'

'A long time ago,' said the whisper. 'You helped. Been long away. In town only for today. Saw the church. Thanks. That's all. Your gift is in the poor box. Thanks.'

Feet ran swiftly.

The priest, for the first time in his life, leaped from the confessional.

'Wait!'

But the man, unseen, was gone. Short or tall, fat or thin, there was no telling. The church was empty.

At the poor-box, in the dusk, he hesitated, then reached in. There he found a large eighty-nine-cent economy-size bar of chocolate.

Someday, Father, he heard a long-gone voice whisper, *I'll bring you a gift blessed by the Pope.*

This? *This?* The old priest turned the bar in his trembling hands. But why not? What could be more perfect?

He saw it all. At Castel Gandolfo on a summer noon with five thousand tourists jammed in a sweating pack below in the dust and the Pope high up on his balcony there waving out the rare blessings, suddenly among all the tumult, in all the sea of arms and hands, one lone brave hand held high . . .

And in that hand a silver-wrapped and glorious candy bar.

The old priest nodded, not surprised.

He locked the chocolate bar in a special drawer in his study and sometimes, behind the altar, years later, when the weather smothered the windows and despair leaked in the door hinges, he would fetch the chocolate out and take the smallest nibble.

It was not the Host, no, it was not the flesh of Christ. But it was a life? And the life was his. And on those occasions, not often but often enough, when he took a bite, it tasted (O thank you, God), it tasted incredibly sweet.

A Story of Love

That was the week Ann Taylor came to teach summer school at Green Town Central. It was the summer of her twenty-fourth birthday, and it was the summer when Bob Spaulding was just fourteen.

Everyone remembered Ann Taylor, for she was that teacher for whom all the children wanted to bring huge oranges or pink flowers, and for whom they rolled up the rustling green and yellow maps of the world without being asked. She was that woman who always seemed to be passing by on days when the shade was green under the tunnels of oaks and elms in the old town, her face shifting with the bright shadows as she walked, until it was all things to all people. She was the fine peaches of summer in the snow of winter, and she was cool milk for cereal on a hot early-June morning. Whenever you needed an opposite, Ann Taylor was there. And those rare few days in the world when the climate was balanced as fine as a maple leaf between winds that blew just right, those were the days like Ann Taylor, and should have been so named on the calendar.

As for Bob Spaulding, he was the cousin who walked alone through town on any October evening with a pack of leaves after him like a horde of Hallowe'en mice, or you would see him, like a slow white fish in spring in the tart waters of the Fox Hill Creek, baking brown with the shine of a chestnut to his face by autumn. Or you might hear his voice in those treetops where the wind entertained; dropping down hand by hand, there would come Bob Spaulding to sit alone and look at the world, and later you might see him on the lawn with the ants crawling over his books as he read through the long afternoons alone, or played himself a game of chess on Grandmother's porch, or picked out a solitary tune upon the black piano in the bay window. You never saw him with any other child.

That first morning, Miss Ann Taylor entered through the side door of the schoolroom and all of the children sat still in their seats as they saw her write her name on the board in a nice round lettering.

'My name is Ann Taylor,' she said, quietly. 'And I'm your new teacher.'

The room seemed suddenly flooded with illumination, as if the roof had moved back; and the trees were full of singing birds. Bob Spaulding sat with a spitball he had just made, hidden in his hand. After a half hour of listening to Miss Taylor, he quietly let the spitball drop to the floor.

That day, after class, he brought in a bucket of water and a rag and began to wash the boards.

'What's this?' She turned to him from her desk, where she had been correcting spelling papers.

'The boards are kind of dirty,' said Bob, at work.

'Yes. I know. Are you sure you want to clean them?'

'I suppose I should have asked permission,' he said, halting uneasily.

'I think we can pretend you did,' she replied, smiling, and at this smile he finished the boards in an amazing burst of speed and pounded the erasers so furiously that the air was full of snow, it seemed, outside the open window.

'Let's see,' said Miss Taylor. 'You're Bob Spaulding, aren't you?'

'Yes'm.'

'Well, thank you, Bob.'

'Could I do them every day?' he asked.

'Don't you think you should let the others try?'

'I'd like to do them,' he said. 'Every day.'

'We'll try it for a while and see,' she said.

He lingered.

'I think you'd better run on home,' she said, finally.

'Good night.' He walked slowly and was gone.

The next morning he happened by the place where she took board and room just as she was coming out to walk to school.

'Well, here I am,' he said.

'And do you know,' she said, 'I'm not surprised.'

They walked together.

'May I carry your books?' he asked.

'Why, thank you, Bob.'

'It's nothing,' he said, taking them.

They walked for a few minutes and he did not say a word. She glanced over and slightly down at him and saw how at ease he was and how happy he seemed, and she decided to let him break the silence, but he never did. When they reached the edge of the school ground he gave the books back to her. 'I guess I better leave you here,' he said. 'The other kids wouldn't understand.'

'I'm not sure I do, either, Bob,' said Miss Taylor.

'Why we're friends,' said Bob earnestly and with a great natural honesty.

'Bob —' she started to say.

'Yes'm?'

'Never mind.' She walked away.

'I'll be in class,' he said.

And he was in class, and he was there after school every night for the next two weeks, never saying a word, quietly washing the boards and cleaning the erasers and rolling up the maps while she worked at her papers, and there was that clock silence of four o'clock, the silence of the sun going down in the slow sky, the silence with the catlike sound of erasers patted together, and the drip of water from a moving sponge, and the rustle and turn of papers and the scratch of a pen, and perhaps the buzz of a fly banging with a tiny high anger against the tallest clear pane of window in the room. Sometimes the silence would go on this way until almost five, when Miss Taylor would find Bob Spaulding in the last seat of the room, sitting and looking at her silently, waiting for further orders.

'Well, it's time to go home,' Miss Taylor would say, getting up.

'Yes'm.'

And he would run to fetch her hat and coat. He would also lock the school-room door for her unless the janitor was coming in later. Then they would walk out of school and across the yard, which was empty, the janitor taking down the chain swings slowly on his stepladder, the sun behind the umbrella trees. They talked of all sorts of things.

'And what are you going to be, Bob, when you grow up?'

'A writer,' he said.

'Oh, that's a big ambition: it takes a lot of work.'

'I know, but I'm going to try,' he said. 'I've read a lot.'

'Bob, haven't you anything to do after school?'

'How do you mean?'

'I mean, I hate to see you kept in so much, washing the boards.'

'I like it,' he said. 'I never do what I don't like.'

'But nevertheless.'

'No, I've got to do that,' he said. He thought for a while and said, 'Do me a favour, Miss Taylor?'

'It all depends.'

'I walk every Saturday from out around Buetrick Street along the creek to Lake Michigan. There's a lot of butterflies and crayfish and birds. Maybe you'd like to walk, too.'

'Thank you,' she said.

'Then you'll come?'

'I'm afraid not.'

'Don't you think it'd be fun?'

'Yes, I'm sure of that, but I'm going to be busy.'

He started to ask doing what, but stopped.

'I take along sandwiches,' he said. 'Ham-and-pickle ones. And orange pop and just walk along, taking my time. I get down to the lake about noon and walk back and get home about three o'clock. It makes a real fine day, and I wish you'd come. Do you collect butterflies? I have a big collection. We could start one for you.'

'Thanks, Bob, but no, perhaps some other time.'

He looked at her and said, 'I shouldn't have asked you, should I?'

'You have every right to ask anything you want to,' she said.

A few days later she found an old copy of *Great Expectations*, which she no longer wanted, and gave it to Bob. He was very grateful and took it home and stayed up that night and read it through and talked about it the next morning. Each day now he met her just beyond sight of her boarding house and many days she would start to say, 'Bob – ' and tell him not to come to meet her any more, but she never finished saying it, and he talked with her about Dickens and Kipling and Poe and others, coming and going to school. She found a butterfly on her desk on Friday morning. She almost waved it away before she found it was dead and had been placed there while she was out of the room. She glanced at Bob over the heads of her other students, but he was looking at his book; not reading, just looking at it.

It was about this time that she found it impossible to call on Bob to recite in class. She would hover her pencil about his name and then call the next person up or down the list. Nor would she look at him while they were walking to or from school. But on several late afternoons as he moved his arm high on the blackboard, sponging away the arithmetic symbols, she found herself glancing over at him for seconds at a time before she returned to her papers.

And then on Saturday morning he was standing in the

middle of the creek with his overalls rolled up to his knees, kneeling down to catch a crayfish under a rock, when he looked up and there on the edge of the running stream was Miss Ann Taylor.

'Well, here I am,' she said, laughing.

'And do you know,' he said, 'I'm not surprised.'

'Show me the crayfish and the butterflies,' she said.

They walked down to the lake and sat on the sand with a warm wind blowing softly about them, fluttering her hair and the ruffle of her blouse, and he sat a few yards back from her and they ate the ham-and-pickle sandwiches and drank the orange pop solemnly.

'Gee, this is swell,' he said. 'This is the swellest time ever in my life.'

'I didn't think I would ever come on a picnic like this,' she said.

'With some kid,' he said.

'I'm comfortable, however,' she said.

'That's good news.'

They said little else during the afternoon.

'This is all wrong,' he said, later. 'And I can't figure why it should be. Just walking along and catching old butterflies and crayfish and eating sandwiches. But Mom and Dad'd rib the heck out of me if they knew, and the kids would, too. And the other teachers, I suppose, would laugh at you, wouldn't they?'

'I'm afraid so.'

'I guess we better not do any more butterfly catching, then.'

'I don't exactly understand how I came here at all,' she said.

And the day was over.

That was about all there was to the meeting of Ann Taylor and Bob Spaulding, two or three monarch butterflies, a copy of Dickens, a dozen crayfish, four sandwiches, and two

bottles of Orange Crush. The next Monday, quite unex-
pectedly, though he waited a long time, Bob did not see Miss
Taylor come out to walk to school, but discovered later that
she had left earlier and was already at school. Also, Monday
night, she left early, with a headache, and another teacher
finished her last class. He walked by her boarding house but
did not see her anywhere, and he was afraid to ring the bell
and inquire.

On Tuesday night after school they were both in the silent
room again, he sponging the board contentedly, as if this
time might go on forever, and she seated, working on her
papers as if she, too, would be in this room and this particular
peace and happiness forever, when suddenly the courthouse
clock struck. It was a block away and its great bronze boom
shuddered one's body and made the ash of time shake away
off your bones and slide through your blood, making you
seem older by the minute. Stunned by that clock, you could
not but sense the crashing flow of time, and as the clock said
five o'clock, Miss Taylor suddenly looked up at it for a long
time, and then she put down her pen.

'Bob,' she said.

He turned, startled. Neither of them had spoken in the
peaceful and good hour before.

'Will you come here?' she asked.

He put down the sponge slowly.

'Yes,' he said.

'Bob, I want you to sit down.'

'Yes'm.'

She looked at him intently for a moment until he looked
away. 'Bob, I wonder if you know what I'm going to talk to
you about. Do you know?'

'Yes.'

'Maybe it'd be a good idea if you told me, first.'

'About us,' he said, at last.

'How old are you, Bob?'

'Going on fourteen.'

'You're thirteen years old.'

He winced. 'Yes'm.'

'And do you know how old I am?'

'Yes'm. I heard. Twenty-four.'

'Twenty-four.'

'I'll be twenty-four in ten years, almost,' he said.

'But unfortunately you're not twenty-four now.'

'No, but sometimes I feel twenty-four.'

'Yes, and sometimes you almost act it.'

'Do I, really!'

'Now sit still there; don't bound around, we've a lot of discuss. It's very important that we understand what is happening, don't you agree?'

'Yes, I guess so.'

'First, let's admit we are the greatest and best friends in the world. Let's admit I have never had a student like you, nor have I had as much affection for any boy I've ever known.' He flushed at this. She went on. 'And let me speak for you — you've found me to be the nicest teacher of all teachers you've ever known.'

'Oh, more than that,' he said.

'Perhaps more than that, but there are facts to be faced and an entire way of life to be examined, and a town and its people, and you and me to be considered. I've thought this over for a good many days, Bob. Don't think I've missed anything, or been unaware of my own feelings in the matter. Under some circumstances our friendship would be odd indeed. But then you are no ordinary boy. I know myself pretty well, I think, and I know I'm not sick, either mentally or physically, and that whatever has evolved here has been a true regard for your character and goodness, Bob; but those are not the things we consider in this world, Bob, unless they occur in a man of a certain age. I don't know if I'm saying this right.'

'It's all right,' he said. 'It's just if I was ten years older and about fifteen inches taller it'd make all the difference, and that's silly,' he said, 'to go by how tall a person is.'

'The world hasn't found it so.'

'I'm not all the world,' he protested.

'I know it seems foolish,' she said. 'When you feel very grown up and right and have nothing to be ashamed of. You have nothing at all to be ashamed of, Bob, remember that. You have been very honest and good, and I hope I have been, too.'

'You have,' he said.

'In an ideal climate, Bob, maybe someday they will be able to judge the oldness of a person's mind so accurately that they can say, "This is a man, though his body is only thirteen; by some miracle of circumstances and fortune, this is a man, with a man's recognition of responsibility and position and duty"; but until that day, Bob, I'm afraid we're going to have to go by ages and heights and the ordinary way in an ordinary world.'

'I don't like that,' he said.

'Perhaps I don't like it, either, but do you want to end up far unhappier than you are now? Do you want both of us to be unhappy? Which we would certainly be. There really is no way to do anything about us — it is so strange even to try to talk about us.'

'Yes'm.'

'But at least we know all about us and the fact that we have been right and fair and good and there is nothing wrong with our knowing each other, nor did we ever intend that it should be, for we both understand how impossible it is, don't we?'

'Yes, I know. But I can't help it.'

'Now we must decide what to do about it,' she said. 'Now only you and I know about this. Later, others might know. I can secure a transfer from this school to another one —'

'No!'

'Or I can have you transferred to another school.'

'You don't have to do that,' he said.

'Why?'

'We're moving. My folks and I, we're going to live in Madison. We're leaving next week.'

'It has nothing to do with all this, has it?'

'No, no, everything's all right. It's just that my father has a new job there. It's only fifty miles away. I can see you, can't I, when I come to town?'

'Do you think that would be a good idea?'

'No, I guess not.'

They sat awhile in the silent schoolroom.

'When did all of this happen?' he said, helplessly.

'I don't know,' she said. 'Nobody ever knows. They haven't known for thousands of years, and I don't think they ever will. People either like each other or don't, and sometimes two people like each other who shouldn't. I can't explain myself, and certainly you can't explain you.'

'I guess I'd better get home,' he said.

'You're not mad at me, are you?'

'Oh, gosh no, I could never be mad at you.'

'There's one more thing. I want you to remember, there are compensations in life. There always are, or we wouldn't go on living. You don't feel well, now; neither do I. But something will happen to fix that. Do you believe that?'

'I'd like to.'

'Well, it's true.'

'If only,' he said.

'What?'

'If only you'd wait for me,' he blurted.

'Ten years?'

'I'd be twenty-four then.'

'But I'd be thirty-four and another person entirely, perhaps. No, I don't think it can be done.'

'Wouldn't you like it to be done?' he cried.

'Yes,' she said quietly. 'It's silly and it wouldn't work, but I would like it very much.'

He sat there for a long time.

'I'll never forget you,' he said.

'It's nice for you to say that, even though it can't be true, because life isn't that way. You'll forget.'

'I'll never forget. I'll find a way of never forgetting you,' he said.

She got up and went to erase the boards.

'I'll help you,' he said.

'No, no,' she said hastily. 'You go on now, get home, and no more tending to the boards after school. I'll assign Helen Stevens to do it.'

He left the school. Looking back, outside, he saw Miss Ann Taylor, for the last time, at the board, slowly washing out the chalked words, her hand moving up and down.

He moved away from the town the next week and was gone for sixteen years. Though he was only fifty miles away, he never got down to Green Town again until he was almost thirty and married, and then one spring they were driving through on their way to Chicago and stopped off for a day.

Bob left his wife at the hotel and walked around town and finally asked about Miss Ann Taylor, but no one remembered at first, and then one of them remembered.

'Oh, yes, the pretty teacher. She died in 1936, not long after you left.'

Had she ever married? No, come to think of it, she never had.

He walked out to the cemetery in the afternoon and found her stone, which said, 'Ann Taylor, born 1910, died 1936.' And he thought, Twenty-six years old. Why I'm three years older than you are now, Miss Taylor.

Later in the day the people in the town saw Bob Spaulding's wife strolling to meet him under the elm trees and the oak trees, and they all turned to watch her pass, for her face shifted with bright shadows as she walked; she was the fine peaches of summer in the snow of winter, and she was cool milk for cereal on a hot early-summer morning. And this was one of those rare few days in time when the climate was balanced like a maple leaf between winds that blow just right, one of those days that should have been named, everyone agreed, after Robert Spaulding's wife.

The Parrot Who Met Papa

The kidnapping was reported all around the world, of course.

It took a few days for the full significance of the news to spread from Cuba to the United States, to the Left Bank in Paris, and then finally to some small good café in Pamplona where the drinks were fine and the weather, somehow, was always just right.

But once the meaning of the news really hit, people were on the phone, Madrid was calling New York, New York was shouting south at Havana to verify, please verify, this crazy thing.

And then some woman in Venice, Italy, with a blurred voice called through, saying she was at Harry's Bar that very instant and was destroyed, this thing that had happened was terrible, a cultural heritage was placed in immense and irrevocable danger . . .

Not an hour later, I got a call from a baseball pitcher-*cum*-novelist who had been a great friend of Papa's and who now lived in Madrid half the year and Nairobi the rest. He was in tears, or sounded close to it.

'Tell me,' he said, from halfway around the world, 'what happened? What are the facts?'

Well, the facts were these: Down in Havana, Cuba, about fourteen kilometres from Papa's Finca Vigía home, there is a bar in which he used to drink. It is the one where they named a special drink for him, not the fancy one where he used to meet flashy literary lights such as K-K-Kenneth Tynan and, er, Tennessee W-Williams (as Mr Tynan would say it). No, it is not the Floridita; it is a shirt-sleeves place with plain wooden tables, sawdust on the floor, and a big mirror like a dirty cloud behind the bar. Papa went there when there were too many tourists around the Floridita who wanted to meet Mr Hemingway. And the thing that happened there was destined to be big news, bigger than the report of what he said to Fitzgerald about the rich, even bigger than the story of his swing at Max Eastman on that long-ago day in Charlie Scribner's office. This news had to do with an ancient parrot.

That senior bird lived in a cage right atop the bar in the Cuba Libre. He had 'kept his cage' in that place for roughly twenty-nine years, which means that the old parrot had been there almost as long as Papa had lived in Cuba.

And that adds up to this monumental fact: All during the time Papa had lived in Finca Vigía, he had known the parrot and had talked to him and the parrot had talked back. As the years passed, people said that Hemingway began to talk like the parrot and others said no, the parrot learned to talk like *him*! Papa used to line the drinks up on the counter and sit near the cage and involve that bird in the best kind of conversation you ever heard, four nights running. By the end of the second year, that parrot knew more about Hem and Thomas Wolfe and Sherwood Anderson than Gertrude Stein did. In fact, the parrot even knew who Gertrude Stein *was*. All you had to say was 'Gertrude' and the parrot said:

'Pigeons on the grass alas.'

At other times, pressed, the parrot would say, 'There was this old man and this boy and this boat and this sea and this big fish in the sea . . . ' And then it would take time out to eat a cracker.

Well, this fabled creature, this parrot, this odd bird, vanished, cage and all, from the Cuba Libre late one Sunday afternoon.

And that's why my phone was ringing itself off the hook. And that's why one of the big magazines got a special State Department clearance and flew me down to Cuba to see if I could find so much as the cage, anything remaining of the bird or anyone resembling a kidnapper. They wanted a light and amiable article, with overtones, as they said. And, very honestly, I was curious. I had heard rumours of the bird. In a strange kind of way, I was concerned.

I got off the jet from Mexico City and taxied straight across Havana to that strange little café-bar.

I almost failed to get in the place. As I stepped through the door, a dark little man jumped up from a chair and cried, 'No, no! Go away! We are closed!'

He ran out to jiggle the lock on the door, showing that he really meant to shut the place down. All the tables were empty and there was no one around. He had probably just been airing out the bar when I arrived.

'I've come about the parrot,' I said.

'No, no,' he cried, his eyes looking wet. 'I won't talk. It's too much. If I were not Catholic, I would kill myself. Poor Papa. Poor El Córdoba!'

'El Córdoba?' I murmured.

'That,' he said fiercely, 'was the parrot's name!'

'Yes,' I said, recovering quickly. 'El Córdoba. I've come to rescue him.'

That made him stop and blink. Shadows and then sunlight went over his face and then shadows again. 'Impossible! Could you? No, no. How could anyone! Who *are* you?'

'A friend to Papa and the bird,' I said quickly. 'And the more time we talk, the farther away goes the criminal. You want El Córdoba back tonight? Pour us several of Papa's good drinks and talk.'

My bluntness worked. Not two minutes later, we were drinking Papa's special, seated in the bar near the empty place where the cage used to sit. The little man, whose name was Antonio, kept wiping that empty place and then wiping his eyes with the bar rag. As I finished the first drink and started on the second, I said:

'This is no ordinary kidnapping.'

'You're telling me!' cried Antonio. 'People came from all over the world to see that parrot, to talk to El Córdoba, to hear him, ah, God, speak with the voice of Papa. May his abductors sink and burn in hell, yes, hell.'

'They will,' I said. 'Whom do you suspect?'

'Everyone. No one.'

'The kidnappers,' I said, eyes shut for a moment, savouring the drink, 'had to be educated, a book reader, I mean, that's obvious, isn't it? Anyone like that around the last few days?'

'Educated. No education. *Señor*, there have always been strangers the last ten, the last twenty years, always asking for Papa. When Papa was here, they met him. With Papa gone, they met El Córdoba, the great one. So it was always strangers and strangers.'

'But think, Antonio,' I said, touching his trembling elbow. 'Not only educated, a reader, but someone in the last few days who was – how shall I put it? – odd. Strange. Someone so peculiar, *muy ecéntrico*, that you remember him above all others. Someone who – '

'*Madre de Dios!*' cried Antonio, leaping up. His eyes stared off into memory. He seized his head as if it had just exploded. 'Thank you, *señor*. *Sí, sí!* What a creature! In the name of Christ, there was such a one yesterday! He was very small. And he spoke like this: very high – *eeeee*. Like a *muchacha* in a school play, eh? Like a canary swallowed by a witch! And he wore a blue-velvet suit with a big yellow tie.'

'Yes, yes!' I had leaped up now and was almost yelling. 'Go on!'

'And he had a small very round face, *señor*, and his hair was yellow and cut across the brow like this – *zitt!* And his mouth small, very pink, like candy, yes? He – he was like, yes, *uno muñeco*, of the kind one wins at carnivals.'

'Kewpie dolls!'

'*Sí*! At Coney Island, yes, when I was a child, Kewpie dolls! And he was so high, you see? To my elbow. Not a midget, no — but — and how old? Blood of Christ, who can say? No lines in his face, but — thirty, forty, fifty. And on his feet he was wearing —'

'Green booties!' I cried.

'*Qué*?'

'Shoes, boots!'

'*Sí*.' He blinked, stunned. 'But how did you *know*?'

'I exploded, 'Shelley Capon!'

'That is the name! And his friends with him, *señor*, all laughing — no, giggling. Like the nuns who play basketball in the late afternoons near the church. Oh, *señor*, do you think that they, that he — '

'I don't think, Antonio, I *know*. Shelley Capon, of all the writers in the world, hated Papa. Of course he would snatch El Córdoba. Why, wasn't there a rumour once that the bird had memorized Papa's last, greatest, and as-yet-not-put-down-on-paper novel?'

'There was such a rumour, *señor*. But I do not write books, I tend bar. I bring crackers to the bird. I —'

'You bring me the phone, Antonio, please.'

'You know where the bird is, *señor*?'

'I have the hunch beyond intuition, the big one. *Gracias*.' I dialled the Havana Libre, the biggest hotel in town.

'Shelley Capon, please.'

The phone buzzed and clicked.

Half a million miles away, a midget boy Martian lifted the receiver and played the flute and then the bell chimes with his voice: 'Capon here.'

'Damned if you aren't!' I said. And got up and ran out of the Cuba Libre bar.

Racing back to Havana by taxi, I thought of Shelley as I'd seen him before. Surrounded by a storm of friends, living out of suitcases, ladling soup from other people's plates, borrowing money from billfolds seized from your pockets right in front of you, counting the lettuce leaves with relish, leaving rabbit pellets on your rug, gone. Dear Shelley Capon.

Ten minutes later, my taxi with no brakes dropped me running and spun on to some ultimate disaster beyond town.

Still running, I made the lobby, paused for information, hurried upstairs, and stopped short before Shelley's door. It pulsed in spasms like a bad heart. I put my ear to the door. The wild calls and cries from inside might have come from a flock of birds, feather-stripped in a hurricane. I felt the door. Now it seemed to tremble like a vast laundromat that had swallowed and was churning an acid-rock group and a lot of very dirty linen. Listening, my underwear began to crawl on my legs.

I knocked. No answer. I touched the door. It drifted open. I stepped in upon a scene much too dreadful for Bosch to have painted.

Around the pigpen living room were strewn various life-size dolls, eyes half cracked open, cigarettes smoking in burned, limp fingers, empty Scotch glasses in hands, and all the while the radio belted them with concussions of music broadcast from some Stateside asylum. The place was sheer carnage. Not ten seconds ago, I felt, a large dirty locomotive must have plunged through here. Its victims had been hurled in all directions and now lay upside down in various parts of the room, moaning for first aid.

In the midst of this hell, seated erect and proper, well dressed in velveteen jerkin, persimmon bow tie, and bottle-green booties, was, of course, Shelley Capon. Who with no surprise at all waved a drink at me and cried:

'I *knew* that was you on the phone. I am absolutely telepathic! Welcome, Raimundo!'

He always called me Raimundo. Ray was plain bread and butter. Raimundo made me a don with a breeding farm full of bulls. I let it be Raimundo.

'Raimundo, sit down! No . . . fling yourself into an *interesting* position.'

'Sorry,' I said in my best Dashiell Hammett manner, sharpening my chin and steeling my eyes. 'No time.'

I began to walk around the room among his friends Fester and Soft and Ripply and Mild Innocuous and some actor I remembered who, when asked how he would do a part in a film, had said, 'I'll play it like a doe.'

I shut off the radio. That made a lot of people in the room stir. I yanked the radio's roots out of the wall. Some people sat up. I raised a window. I threw the radio out. They all screamed as if I had thrown their mothers down an elevator shaft.

The radio made a satisfying sound on the cement sidewalk below. I turned, with a beatific smile on my face. A number of people were on their feet, swaying towards me with faint menace. I pulled a twenty-dollar bill out of my pocket, handed it to someone without looking at him, and said, 'Go buy a new one.' He ran out the door slowly. The door slammed. I heard him fall down the stairs as if he were after his morning shot in the arm.

'All right, Shelley,' I said, 'where is it?'

'Where is *what*, dear boy?' he said, eyes wide with innocence.

'You know what I mean.' I stared at the drink in his tiny hand.

Which was a Papa drink, the Cuba Libre's very own special blend of papaya, lime, lemon, and rum. As if to destroy evidence, he drank it down quickly.

I walked over to three doors in a wall and touched one.

'That's a closet, dear boy.' I put my hand on the second door.

'Don't go in. You'll be sorry what you see.' I didn't go in.

I put my hand on the third door. 'Oh, dear, well, go

ahead,' said Shelley petulantly. I opened the door.

Beyond it was a small anteroom with a mere cot and a table near the window.

On the table sat a bird cage with a shawl over it. Under the shawl I could hear the rustle of feathers and the scrape of a beak on the wires.

Shelley Capon came to stand beside me, looking in at the cage, a fresh drink in his little fingers.

'What a shame you didn't arrive at seven tonight,' he said.

'Why seven?'

'Why, then, Raimundo, we would have just finished our curried fowl stuffed with rice. I wonder, is there much white meat, or any at all, under a parrot's feathers?'

'You wouldn't!?' I cried.

I stared at him.

'You would,' I answered myself.

I stood for a moment longer at the door. Then, slowly, I walked across the small room and stopped by the cage with the shawl over it. I saw a single word embroidered across the top of the shawl: MOTHER.

I glanced at Shelley. He shrugged and looked shyly at his boot tips. I took hold of the shawl. Shelley said, 'No. Before you lift it . . . ask something.'

'Like what?'

'DiMaggio. Ask DiMaggio.'

A small ten-watt bulb clicked on in my head. I nodded. I leaned near the hidden cage and whispered: 'DiMaggio. 1939.'

There was a sort of animal-computer pause. Beneath the word MOTHER some feathers stirred, a beak tapped the cage bars. Then a tiny voice said:

'Home runs, thirty. Batting average, .381.'

I was stunned. But then I whispered: 'Babe Ruth. 1927.'

Again the pause, the feathers, the beak, and: 'Home runs, sixty. Batting average, .356. Awk.'

'My God,' I said.

'My God,' echoed Shelley Capon.

'That's the parrot who met Papa, all right.'

'That's who it is.'

And I lifted the shawl.

I don't know what I expected to find underneath the embroidery. Perhaps a miniature hunter in boots, bush jacket, and wide-brimmed hat. Perhaps a small, trim fisherman with a beard and turtleneck sweater perched there on a wooden slat. Something tiny, something literary, something human, something fantastic, but not really a parrot.

But that's all there was.

And not a very handsome parrot, either. It looked as if it had been up all night for years; one of those disreputable birds that never preens its feathers or shines its beak. It was a kind of rusty green and black with a dull-amber snout and rings under its eyes as if it were a secret drinker. You might see it half flying, half hopping out of café-bars at three in the morning. It was the bum of the parrot world.

Shelley Capon read my mind. 'The effect is better,' he said, 'with the shawl over the cage.'

I put the shawl back over the bars.

I was thinking very fast. Then I thought very slowly. I bent and whispered by the cage:

'Norman Mailer.'

'Couldn't remember the alphabet,' said the voice beneath the shawl.

'Gertrude Stein,' I said.

'Suffered from undescended testicles,' said the voice.

'My God,' I gasped.

I stepped back. I stared at the covered cage. I blinked at Shelley Capon.

'Do you really *know* what you have here, Capon?'

'A *gold* mine, dear Raimundo!' he crowed.

'A *mint*!' I corrected.

'Endless opportunities for blackmail!'

'Causes for murder!' I added.

'Think!' Shelley snorted into his drink. 'Think what Mailer's publishers *alone* would pay to shut this bird up!'

I spoke to the cage:

'F. Scott Fitzgerald.'

Silence.

'Try "Scottie," ' said Shelley.

'Ah,' said the voice inside the cage. 'Good left jab but couldn't follow through. Nice contender, but —'

'Faulkner,' I said.

'Batting average fair, strictly a singles hitter.'

'Steinbeck!'

'Finished last at end of season.'

'Ezra Pound!'

'Traded off to the minor leagues in 1932.'

'I think . . . I need . . . one of those drinks.' Someone put a drink in my hand. I gulped it and nodded. I shut my eyes and felt the world give one turn, then opened my eyes to look at Shelley Capon, the classic son of a bitch of all time.

'There is something even more fantastic,' he said. 'You've heard only the first half.'

'You're lying,' I said. 'What could there be?'

He dimpled at me — in all the world, only Shelley Capon can dimple at you in a completely evil way. 'It was like this,' he said. 'You remember that Papa had trouble actually getting his stuff down on paper in those last years while he lived here? Well, he'd planned another novel after *Islands in the Stream*, but somehow it just never seemed to get written.

'Oh, he had it in his mind, all right — the story was there and lots of people heard him mention it — but he just couldn't seem to write it. So he would go to the Cuba Libre and drink many drinks and have long conversations with the parrot. Raimundo, what Papa was telling El Córdoba all through those long drinking nights was the story of his last book. And, in the course of time, the bird has memorized it.'

'*His very last book!*' I said. 'The final Hemingway novel of all time! Never written but recorded in the brain of a parrot! Holy Jesus!'

Shelley was nodding at me with the smile of a depraved cherub.

'How much do you want for this bird?'

'Dear, dear Raimundo.' Shelley Capon stirred his drink with his pinkie. 'What makes you think the creature is for sale?'

'You sold your mother once, then stole her back and sold her again under another name. Come off it, Shelley. You're on to something big.' I brooded over the shawled cage. 'How many telegrams have you sent out in the last four or five hours?'

'Really! You horrify me!'

'How many long-distance phone calls, reverse charges, have you made since breakfast?'

Shelley Capon mourned a great sigh and pulled a crumpled telegram duplicate from his velveteen pocket. I took it and read:

FRIENDS OF PAPA MEETING HAVANA TO REMINISCE OVER BIRD AND BOTTLE. WIRE BID OR BRING CHEQUE-BOOKS AND OPEN MINDS. FIRST COME FIRST SERVED. ALL WHITE MEAT BUT CAVIAR PRICES. INTER-NATIONAL PUBLICATION, BOOK, MAGAZINE, TV, FILM RIGHTS AVAILABLE. LOVE. SHELLEY YOU-KNOW-WHO.

My God again, I thought, and let the telegram fall to the floor as Shelley handed me a list of names the telegram had been sent to:

Time. Life. Newsweek. Scribner's. Simon & Schuster. The *New York Times*. The *Christian Science Monitor. The Times* of

London. *Le Monde. Paris-Match.* One of the Rockefellers. Some of the Kennedys. CBS. NBC. MGM. Warner Bros. 20th Century-Fox. And on and on and on. The list was as long as my deepening melancholy.

Shelley Capon tossed an armful of answering telegrams on to the table near the cage. I leafed through them quickly.

Everyone, but everyone, was in the air, right now. Jets were streaming in from all over the world. In another two hours, four, six at the most, Cuba would be swarming with agents, publishers, fools, and plain damn fools, plus counter-espionage kidnappers and blonde starlets who hoped to be in front-page photographs with the bird on their shoulders.

I figured I had maybe a good half hour left in which to do something, I didn't know what.

Shelley nudged my arm. 'Who sent you, dear boy? You *are* the very first, you know. Make a fine bid and you're in free, maybe. I must consider other offers of course. But it might get thick and nasty here. I begin to panic at what I've done. I may wish to sell cheap and flee. Because, well, think, there's the problem of getting this bird out of the country, yes? And, simultaneously, Castro might declare the parrot a national monument or work of art, or, oh, hell, Raimundo, who *did* send you?'

'Someone, but now no one,' I said, brooding. 'I came on behalf of someone else. I'll go away on my own. From now on, anyway, it's just me and the bird. I've read Papa all my life. Now I know I came just because I had to.'

'My God, an altruist!'

'Sorry to offend you, Shelley.'

The phone rang. Shelley got it. He chatted happily for a moment, told someone to wait downstairs, hung up, and cocked an eyebrow at me: 'NBC is in the lobby. They want an hour's taped interview with El Córdoba there. They're talking six figures.'

My shoulders slumped. The phone rang. This time I

picked it up, to my own surprise. Shelley cried out. But I said, 'Hello. Yes?'

'*Señor*,' said a man's voice. 'There is a *Señor* Hobwell here from *Time*, he says, magazine.' I could see the parrot's face on next week's cover, with six follow-up pages of text.

'Tell him to wait.' I hung up.

'*Newsweek*?' guessed Shelley.

'The other one,' I said.

'The snow was fine up in the shadow of the hills,' said the voice inside the cage under the shawl.

'Shut up,' I said quietly, wearily. 'Oh, shut up, damn you.'

Shadows appeared in the doorway behind us. Shelley Capon's friends were beginning to assemble and wander into the room. They gathered and I began to tremble and sweat.

For some reason, I began to rise to my feet. My body was going to do something, I didn't know what. I watched my hands. Suddenly, the right hand reached out. It knocked the cage over, snapped the wire-frame door wide, and darted in to seize the parrot.

'No!'

There was a great gasping roar, as if a single thunderous wave had come in on a shore. Everyone in the room seemed knocked in the stomach by my action. Everyone exhaled, took a step, began to yell, but by then I had the parrot out. I had it by the throat.

'No! No!' Shelley jumped at me. I kicked him in the shins. He sat down, screaming.

'Don't anyone move!' I said and almost laughed, hearing myself use the old cliché. 'You ever see a chicken killed? This parrot has a thin neck. One twist, the head comes off. Nobody move a hair.' Nobody moved.

'You son of a bitch,' said Shelley Capon, on the floor.

For a moment, I thought they were all going to rush me. I saw myself beaten and chased along the beach, yelling, the cannibals ringing me in and eating me, Tennessee Williams style, shoes and all. I felt sorry for my skeleton, which would be found in the main Havana plaza at dawn tomorrow.

But they did not hit, pummel, or kill. As long as I had my fingers around the neck of the parrot who met Papa, I knew I could stand there forever.

I wanted with all my heart, soul, and guts to wring the bird's neck and throw its disconnected carcass into those pale and gritty faces. I wanted to stop up the past and destroy Papa's preserved memory forever, if it was going to be played with by feeble-minded children like these.

But I could not, for two reasons. One dead parrot would mean one dead duck: me. And I was weeping inside for Papa. I simply could not shut off his voice transcribed here, held in my hands, still alive, like an old Edison record. I could not kill.

If these ancient children had known that, they would have swarmed over me like locusts. But they didn't know. And, I guess, it didn't show in my face.

'Stand back!' I cried.

It was that beautiful last scene from *The Phantom of the Opera* where Lon Chaney, pursued through midnight Paris, turns on the mob, lifts his clenched fist as if it contained an explosive, and holds the mob at bay for one terrific instant. He laughs, opens his hands to show it empty, and then is driven to his death in the river . . . Only I had no intention of letting them see an empty hand. I kept it close around El Córdoba's scrawny neck.

'Clear a path to the door!' They cleared a path.

'Not a move, not a breath. If anyone so much as swoons, this bird is dead forever and no rights, no movies, no photos. Shelley, bring me the cage and the shawl.'

Shelley Capon edged over and brought me the cage and its cover. 'Stand off!' I yelled.

Everyone jumped back another foot.

'Now, hear this,' I said. 'After I've got away and have

hidden out, one by one each of you will be called to have his chance to meet Papa's friend here again and cash in on the headlines.'

I was lying. I could hear the lie. I hoped they couldn't. I spoke more quickly now, to cover the lie: 'I'm going to start walking now. Look. See? I have the parrot by the neck. He'll stay alive as long as you play "Simon says" my way. Here we go, now. One, two. One, two. Halfway to the door.' I walked among them and they did not breathe. 'One, two,' I said, my heart beating in my mouth. 'At the door. Steady. No sudden moves. Cage in one hand. Bird in the other—'

'The lions ran along the beach on the yellow sand,' said the parrot, his throat moving under my fingers.

'Oh, my God,' said Shelley, crouched there by the table. Tears began to pour down his face. Maybe it wasn't all money. Maybe some of it was Papa for him, too. He put his hands out in a beckoning, come-back gesture to me, the parrot, the cage. 'Oh, God, oh, God.' He wept.

'There was only the carcass of the great fish lying by the pier, its bones picked clean in the morning light,' said the parrot.

'Oh,' said everyone softly.

I didn't wait to see if any more of them were weeping. I stepped out. I shut the door. I ran for the elevator. By a miracle, it was there, the operator half asleep inside. No one tried to follow. I guess they knew it was no use.

On the way down, I put the parrot inside the cage and put the shawl marked MOTHER over the cage. And the elevator moved slowly down through the years. I thought of those years ahead and where I might hide the parrot and keep him warm against any weather and feed him properly and once a day go in and talk through the shawl, and nobody ever to see him, no papers, no magazines, no cameramen, no Shelley Capon, not even Antonio from the Cuba Libre. Days might go by or weeks and sudden fears might come over me that the

parrot had gone dumb. Then, in the middle of the night I
might wake and shuffle in and stand by his cage and say:

'Italy, 1918 . . . ?'

And beneath the word MOTHER, an old voice would say:
'The snow drifted off the edges of the mountain in a fine
white dust that winter . . .'

'Africa, 1932.'

'We got the rifles out and oiled the rifles and they were blue
and fine and lay in our hands and we waited in the tall grass
and smiled —'

'Cuba. The Gulf Stream.'

'That fish came out of the water and jumped as high as the
sun. Everything I had ever thought about a fish was in that
fish. Everything I had ever thought about a single leap was in
that leap. All of my life was there. It was a day of sun and
water and being alive. I wanted to hold it all still in my hands.
I didn't want it to go away, ever. Yet there, as the fish fell and
the waters moved over it white and then green, there it
went . . .'

By that time, we were at the lobby level and the elevator
doors opened and I stepped out with the cage labelled
MOTHER and walked quickly across the lobby and out to a
taxicab.

The trickiest business — and my greatest danger —
remained. I knew that by the time I got to the airport, the
guards and the Castro militia would have been alerted. I
wouldn't put it past Shelley Capon to tell them that a national
treasure was getting away. He might even cut Castro in on
some of the Book-of-the-Month Club revenue and the movie
rights. I had to improvise a plan to get through customs.

I am a literary man, however, and the answer came to me
quickly. I had the taxi stop long enough for me to buy some
shoe polish. I began to apply the disguise to El Córdoba. I
painted him black all over.

'Listen,' I said, bending down to whisper into the cage as

we drove across Havana. '*Nevermore.*'

I repeated it several times to give him the idea. The sound would be new to him, because, I guessed, Papa would never have quoted a middleweight contender he had knocked out years ago. There was silence under the shawl while the word was recorded.

Then, at last, it came back to me. 'Nevermore,' in Papa's old, familiar, tenor voice, 'nevermore,' it said.

The October Game

He put the gun back into the bureau drawer and shut the drawer.

No, not that way. Louise wouldn't suffer that way. She would be dead and it would be over and she wouldn't suffer. It was very important that this thing have, above all, duration. Duration through imagination. How to prolong the suffering? How, first of all, to bring it about? Well.

The man standing before the bedroom mirror carefully fitted his cuff links together. He paused long enough to hear the children run by swiftly on the street below, outside this warm two-storey house; like so many grey mice the children, like so many leaves.

By the sound of the children you knew the calendar day. By their screams you knew what evening it was. You knew it was very late in the year. October. The last day of October, with white bone masks and cut pumpkins and the smell of dropped candle fat.

No. Things hadn't been right for some time. October didn't help any. If anything it made things worse. He adjusted his black bow tie. If this were spring, he nodded slowly, quietly, emotionlessly, at his image in the mirror, then there might be a chance. But tonight all the world was burning down into ruin. There was no green of spring, none of the freshness, none of the promise.

There was a soft running in the hall. 'That's Marion,' he told himself. 'My little one. All eight quiet years of her. Never a word. Just her luminous grey eyes and her wondering little mouth.' His daughter had been in and out all

evening, trying on various masks, asking him which was
most terrifying, most horrible. They had both finally decided
on the skeleton mask. It was 'just awful!' It would 'scare the
beans' from people!

Again he caught the long look of thought and deliberation
he gave himself in the mirror. He had never liked October.
Ever since he first lay in the autumn leaves before his grandmother's house many years ago and heard the wind and saw
the empty trees. It had made him cry, without a reason. And
a little of that sadness returned each year to him. It always
went away with spring.

But, it was different tonight. There was a feeling of
autumn coming to last a million years.

There would be no spring.

He had been crying quietly all evening. It did not show,
not a vestige of it, on his face. It was all hidden somewhere
and it wouldn't stop.

A rich syrupy smell of candy filled the bustling house.
Louise had laid out apples in new skins of caramel; there
were vast bowls of punch fresh-mixed, stringed apples in
each door, scooped, vented pumpkins peering triangularly
from each cold window. There was a water tub in the centre
of the living room, waiting, with a sack of apples nearby, for
dunking to begin. All that was needed was the catalyst, the
inpouring of children, to start the apples bobbling, the
stringed apples to penduluming in the crowded doors, the
candy to vanish, the halls to echo with fright or delight, it was
all the same.

Now the house was silent with preparation. And just a
little more than that.

Louise had managed to be in every other room today save
the room he was in. It was her very fine way of intimating, Oh
look, Mich, see how busy I am! So busy that when you walk
into a room *I'm* in there's always something I need to do in
another room! Just see how I dash about!

For a while he had played her little game with her, a nasty childish game. When she was in the kitchen, then he came to the kitchen saying, 'I need a glass of water.' After a moment, he standing, drinking water, she like a crystal witch over the caramel brew bubbling like a prehistoric mudpot on the stove, she said, 'Oh, I must light the pumpkins!' and she rushed to the living room to make the pumpkins smile with light. He came after her, smiling, 'I must get my pipe.' 'Oh, the cider!' she had cried, running to the dining room. 'I'll check the cider,' he had said. But when he tried following she ran to the bathroom and locked the door.

He stood outside the bathroom door, laughing strangely and senselessly, his pipe gone cold in his mouth, and then, tired of the game, but stubborn, he waited another five minutes. There was not a sound from the bath. And lest she enjoy in any way knowing that he waited outside, irritated, he suddenly jerked about and walked upstairs, whistling merrily.

At the top of the stairs he waited. Finally he had heard the bathroom door unlatch and she had come out and life below-stairs had resumed, as life in a jungle must resume once a terror has passed on away and the antelope return to their spring.

Now, as he finished his bow tie and put on his dark coat there was a mouse-rustle in the hall. Marion appeared in the door, all skeletonous in her disguise.

'How do I look, Papa?'

'Fine!'

From under the mask, blonde hair showed. From the skull sockets small blue eyes smiled. He sighed. Marion and Louise, the two silent denouncers of his virility, his dark power. What alchemy had there been in Louise that took the dark of a dark man and bleached and bleached the dark brown eyes and black hair and washed and bleached the ingrown baby all during the period before birth until the child was born, Marion, blonde, blue-eyed, ruddy-cheeked? Sometimes he suspected that Louise had conceived the child as an idea, completely asexual, an immaculate conception of contemptuous mind and cell. As a firm rebuke to him she had produced a child in her *own* image, and, to top it, she had somehow *fixed* the doctor so he shook his head and said, 'Sorry, Mr Wilder, your wife will never have another child. This is the *last* one.'

'And I wanted a boy,' Mich had said, eight years ago.

He almost bent to take hold of Marion now, in her skull mask. He felt an inexplicable rush of pity for her, because she had never had a father's love, only the crushing, holding love of a loveless mother. But most of all he pitied himself, that somehow he had not made the most of a bad birth, enjoyed his daughter for herself, regardless of her not being dark and a son like himself. Somewhere he had missed out. Other things being equal, he would have loved the child. But Louise hadn't wanted a child, anyway, in the first place. She had been frightened of the idea of birth. He had forced the child on her, and from that night, all through the year until the agony of the birth itself, Louise had lived in another part of the house. She had expected to die with the forced child. It had been very easy for Louise to hate this husband who so wanted a son that he gave his only wife over to the mortuary.

But — Louise had lived. And in triumph! Her eyes, the day he came to the hospital, were cold. I'm alive, they said. And I have a *blonde* daughter! Just look! And when he had put out a hand to touch, the mother had turned away to conspire with her new pink daughter-child — away from that dark forcing murderer. It had all been so beautifully ironic. His selfishness deserved it.

But now it was October again. There had been other Octobers and when he thought of the long winter he had been filled with horror year after year to think of the endless months mortared into the house by an insane fall of snow, trapped with a woman and child, neither of whom loved him, for months on end. During the eight years there had been respites. In spring and summer you got out, walked, picnicked; these were desperate solutions to the desperate problem of a hated man.

But, in winter, the hikes and picnics and escapes fell away with the leaves. Life, like a tree, stood empty, the fruit picked, the sap run to earth. Yes, you invited people in, but people were hard to get in winter with blizzards and all. Once he had been clever enough to save for a Florida trip. They had gone south. He had walked in the open.

But now, the eighth winter coming, he knew things were finally at an end. He simply could not wear this one through. There was an acid walled off in him that slowly had eaten through tissue and bone over the years, and now, tonight, it would reach the wild explosive in him and all would be over!

There was a mad ringing of the bell below. In the hall, Louise went to see. Marion, without a word, ran down to greet the first arrivals. There were shouts and hilarity.

He walked to the top of the stairs.

Louise was below, taking wraps. She was tall and slender and blonde to the point of whiteness, laughing down upon the new children.

He hesitated. What was all this? The years? The boredom of living. Where had it gone wrong? Certainly not with the birth of the child alone. But it had been a symbol of all their tensions, he imagined. His jealousies and his business failures and all the rotten rest of it. Why didn't he just turn, pack a suitcase, and leave? No. Not without hurting Louise as much as she had hurt him. It was simple as that. Divorce wouldn't hurt her at all. It would simply be an end to numb indecision. If he thought divorce would give her pleasure in any way he would stay married the rest of his life to her, for damned spite. No, he must hurt her. Figure some way, perhaps, to take Marion away from her, legally. Yes. That was it. That would hurt most of all. To take Marion away.

'Hello down there!' He descended the stairs, beaming.

Louise didn't look up.

'Hi, Mr Wilder!'

The children shouted, waved, as he came down.

By ten o'clock the doorbell had stopped ringing, the apples were bitten from stringed doors, the pink child faces were wiped dry from the apple bobbling, napkins were smeared with caramel and punch, and he, the husband, with pleasant efficiency had taken over. He took the party right out of Louise's hands. He ran about talking to the twenty children and the twelve parents who had come and were happy with the special spiked cider he had fixed them. He supervised pin the tail on the donkey, spin the bottle, musical chairs, and all the rest, amid fits of shouting laughter. Then, in the triangular-eyed pumpkin shine, all house lights out, he cried, 'Hush! Follow me!' tiptoeing towards the cellar.

The parents, of the periphery of the costumed riot, commented to each other, nodding at the clever husband, speaking to the lucky wife. How *well* he got on with children, they said.

The children crowded after the husband, squealing.

'The cellar!' he cried. 'The tomb of the witch!'

More squealing. He made a mock shiver. 'Abandon hope all ye who enter here!'

The parents chuckled.

One by one the children slid down a slide which Mich had fixed up from lengths of table-section, into the dark cellar. He hissed and shouted ghastly utterances after them. A wonderful wailing filled the dark pumpkin-lighted house. Everybody talked at once. Everybody but Marion. She had gone through all the party with a minimum of sound or talk;

it was all inside her, all the excitement and joy. What a little troll, he thought. With a shut mouth and shiny eyes she had watched her own party, like so many serpentines thrown before her.

Now, the parents. With laughing reluctance they slid down the short incline, uproarious, while little Marion stood by, always wanting to see it all, to be last. Louise went down without help. He moved to her aid, but she was gone even before he bent.

The upper house was empty and silent in the candle-shine.

Marion stood by the slide, 'Here we go,' he said, and picked her up.

They sat in a vast circle in the cellar. Warmth came from the distant bulk of the furnace. The chairs stood in a long line along each wall, twenty squealing children, twelve rustling relatives, alternately spaced, with Louise down at the far end, Mich up at this end, near the stairs. He peered but saw nothing. They had all grouped to their chairs, catch-as-you-can in the blackness. The entire programme from here on was to be enacted in the dark, he as Mr Interlocutor. There was a child scampering, a smell of damp cement, and the sound of the wind out in the October stars.

'Now!' cried the husband in the dark cellar. 'Quiet!'

Everybody settled.

The room was black black. Not a light, not a shine, not a glint of an eye.

A scraping of crockery, a metal rattle.

'The witch is dead,' intoned the husband.

'Eeeeeeeeeeeee,' said the children.

'The witch is dead, she has been killed, and here is the knife she was killed with.'

He handed over the knife. It was passed from hand to hand, down and around the circle, with chuckles and little odd cries and comments from the adults.

'The witch is dead, and this is her head,' whispered the husband, and handed an item to the nearest person.

'Oh, I know how this game is played,' some child cried, happily, in the dark. 'He gets some old chicken innards from the icebox and hands them around and says, "These are her innards!" And he makes a clay head and passes it for her head, and passes a soup bone for her arm. And he takes a marble and says, "This is her eye!" And he takes some corn and says, "This is her teeth!" And he takes a sack of plum pudding and gives that and says, "This is her stomach!" I know how *this* is played!'

'Hush, you'll spoil everything,' some girl said.

'The witch came to harm, and this is her arm,' said Mich.

'Eeeee!'

The items were passed and passed, like hot potatoes, around the circle. Some children screamed, wouldn't touch them. Some ran from their chairs to stand in the centre of the cellar until the grisly items had passed.

'Aw, it's only chicken insides,' scoffed a boy. 'Come back, Helen!'

Shot from hand to hand, with small scream after scream, the items went down, down, to be followed by another and another.

'The witch cut apart, and this is her heart,' said the husband.

Six or seven items moving at once through the laughing, trembling dark.

Louise spoke up. 'Marion, don't be afraid; it's only play.'

Marion didn't say anything.

'Marion?' asked Louise. 'Are you afraid?'

Marion didn't speak.

'She's all right,' said the husband. 'She's not afraid.'

On and on the passing, the screams, the hilarity.

The autumn wind sighed about the house. And he, the husband, stood at the head of the dark cellar, intoning the words, handing out the items.

'Marion?' asked Louise again, from far across the cellar.

Everybody was talking.

'Marion?' called Louise.

Everybody quieted.

'Marion, answer me, are you afraid?'

Marion didn't answer.

The husband stood there, at the bottom of the cellar steps.

Louise called, 'Marion, are you there?'

No answer. The room was silent.

'Where's Marion?' called Louise.

'She was here,' said a boy.

'Maybe she's upstairs.'

'Marion!'

No answer. It was quiet.

Louise cried out, 'Marion, Marion!'

'Turn on the lights,' said one of the adults.

The items stopped passing. The children and adults sat with the witch's items in their hands.

'No.' Louise gasped. There was a scraping of her chair, wildly, in the dark. 'No. Don't turn on the lights, oh, God, God, God, don't turn them on, please, please *don't* turn on the lights, *don't*!' Louise was shrieking now. The entire cellar froze with the scream.

Nobody moved.

Everyone sat in the dark cellar, suspended in the suddenly frozen task of this October game; the wind blew outside, banging the house, the smell of pumpkins and apples filled the room with the smell of the objects in their fingers while one boy cried, 'I'll go upstairs and look!' and he ran upstairs hopefully and out around the house, four times around the house, calling, 'Marion, Marion, Marion!' over and over and at last coming slowly down the stairs into the waiting breathing cellar and saying to the darkness, 'I can't find her.'

Then . . . some idiot turned on the lights.

Punishment Without Crime

'You wish to kill your wife?' said the dark man at the desk.

'Yes. No . . . not exactly. I mean . . . '

'Name?'

'Hers or mine?'

'Yours.'

'George Hill.'

'Address?'

'Eleven South Saint James, Glenview.'

The man wrote this down, emotionlessly. 'Your wife's name?'

'Katherine.'

'Age?'

'Thirty-one.'

Then came a swift series of questions. Colour of hair, eyes, skin, favourite perfume, texture and size index. 'Have you a dimensional photo of her? A tape recording of her voice? Ah, I see you do. Good. Now —'

An hour later, George Hill was perspiring.

'That's all.' The dark man arose and scowled. 'You still want to go through with it.'

'Yes.'

'Sign here.'

He signed.

'You know this is illegal?'

'Yes.'

'And that we're in no way responsible for what happens to you as a result of your request?'

'For God's sake?' cried George. 'You've kept me long enough. Let's get on!'

The man smiled faintly. 'It'll take nine hours to prepare the marionette of your wife. Sleep awhile, it'll help your nerves. The third mirror room on your left is unoccupied.'

George moved in a slow numbness to the mirror room. He lay on the blue velvet cot, his body pressure causing the mirrors in the ceiling to whirl. A soft voice sang, 'Sleep . . . sleep . . . sleep . . . '

George muttered, 'Katherine, I didn't want to come here. You forced me into it. You made me do it. God, I wish I weren't here. I wish I could go back. I don't want to kill you.'

The mirrors glittered as they rotated softly.

He slept.

He dreamed he was forty-one again, he and Katie running on a green hill somewhere with a picnic lunch, their helicopter beside them. The wind blew Katie's hair in golden strands and she was laughing. They kissed and held hands, not eating. They read poems; it seemed they were always reading poems.

Other scenes. Quick changes of colour, in flight. He and Katie flying over Greece and Italy and Switzerland, in that clear, long autumn of 1997! Flying and never stopping!

And then — nightmare. Katie and Leonard Phelps. George cried out in his sleep. How had it happened? Where had Phelps sprung from? Why had he interfered? Why couldn't life be simple and good? Was it the difference in age? George touching fifty, and Katie so young, so very young. Why, why?

The scene was unforgettably vivid. Leonard Phelps and Katherine in a green park beyond the city. George himself appearing on a path only in time to see the kissing of their mouths.

The rage. The struggle. The attempt to kill Leonard Phelps.

More days, more nightmares.

George Hill awoke, weeping.

'Mr Hill, we're ready for you now.'

Hill arose clumsily. He saw himself in the high and now-silent mirrors, and he looked every one of his years. It had been a wretched error. Better men than he had taken young wives only to have them dissolve away in their hands like sugar crystals under water. He eyed himself, monstrously. A little too much stomach. A little too much chin. Somewhat too much pepper in the hair and not enough in the limbs . . .

The dark man led him to a room.

George Hill gasped. 'This is *Katie*'s room!'

'We try to have everything perfect.'

'It *is*, to the last detail!'

George Hill drew forth a signed cheque for ten thousand dollars. The man departed with it.

The room was silent and warm.

George sat and felt for his gun in his pocket. A lot of money. But rich men can afford the luxury of cathartic murder. The violent unviolence. The death without death. The murder without murdering. He felt better. He was suddenly calm. He watched the door. This was a thing he had anticipated for six months and now it was to be ended. In a moment the beautiful robot, the stringless marionette, would appear, and . . .

'Hello, George.'

'Katie!'

He whirled.

'Katie.' He let his breath out.

She stood in the doorway behind him. She was dressed in a feather-soft green gown. On her feet were woven gold-twine sandals. Her hair was bright about her throat and her eyes were blue and clear.

He did not speak for a long while. 'You're beautiful,' he said at last, shocked.

'How else could I be?'

His voice was slow and unreal. 'Let me look at you.'

He put out his vague hands like a sleepwalker. His heart pounded sluggishly. He moved forward as if walking under a deep pressure of water. He walked around and around her, touching her.

'Haven't you seen enough of me in all these years?'

'Never enough,' he said, and his eyes were filled with tears.

'What did you want to talk to me about?'

'Give me time, please, a little time.' He sat down weakly and put his trembling hands to his chest. He blinked. 'It's incredible. Another nightmare. How did they *make* you?'

'We're not allowed to talk of that; it spoils the illusion.'

'It's magic!'

'Science.'

Her touch was warm. Her fingernails were perfect as seashells. There was no seam, no flaw. He looked upon her. He remembered again the words they had read so often in the good days. *Behold, thou art fair, my love; behold, thou art fair, thou hast doves' eyes within thy locks . . . Thy lips are like a thread of scarlet, and thy speech is comely . . . Thy two breasts are like two young roes that are twins, which feed among the lilies . . . there is no spot in thee.*

'George?'

'What?' His eyes were cold glass.

He wanted to kiss her lips.

Honey and milk are under thy tongue.

And the smell of thy garments is like the smell of Lebanon.

'George.'

A vast humming. The room began to whirl.

'Yes, yes, a moment, a moment.' He shook his humming head.

How beautiful are thy feet with shoes, O prince's daughter! the joints of thy thighs are like jewels, the work of the hands of a cunning workman . . .

'How did they do it?' he cried. In so short a time. Nine hours, while he slept. Had they melted gold, fixed delicate watch springs, diamonds, glitter, confetti, rich rubies, liquid silver, copper thread? Had metal insects spun her hair? Had they poured yellow fire in moulds and set it to freeze?

'No,' she said. 'If you talk that way, I'll go.'

'Don't!'

'Come to business, then,' she said, coldly. 'You want to talk to me about Leonard.'

'Give me time, I'll get to it.'

'Now,' she insisted.

He knew no anger. It had washed out of him at her appearance. He felt childishly dirty.

'Why did you come to see me?' She was not smiling.

'Please.'

'I insist. Wasn't it about Leonard? You know I love him, don't you?'

'Stop it!' He put his hands to his ears.

She kept at him. 'You know, I spend all of my time with him now. Where you and I used to go, now Leonard and I stay. Remember the picnic green on Mount Verde? We were there last week. We flew to Athens a month ago, with a case of champagne.'

He licked his lips. 'You're not guilty, you're *not*.' He rose and held her wrists. 'You're fresh, you're not her. She's guilty, not you. You're different!'

'On the contrary,' said the woman. 'I *am* her. I can act only as she acts. No part of me is alien to her. For all intents and purposes we are one.'

'But you did not do what she has done!'

'I did all those things. I kissed him.'

'You can't have, you're just born!'

'Out of her past and from your mind.'

'Look,' he pleaded, shaking her to gain her attention. 'Isn't there some way, can't I – pay more money? Take you away with me? We'll go to Paris or Stockholm or any place you like!'

She laughed. 'The marionettes only rent. They never sell.'

'But I've money!'

'It was tried long ago. It leads to insanity. It's not possible. Even this much is illegal, you *know* that. We exist only through governmental sufferance.'

'All I want is to live with you, Katie.'

'That can never be, because I am Katie, every bit of me is her. We do not want competition. Marionettes can't leave the premises; dissection might reveal our secrets. Enough of this. I warned you, we mustn't speak of these things. You'll spoil the illusion. You'll feel frustrated when you leave. You paid your money, now do what you came to do.'

'I don't want to kill you.'

'One part of you does. You're walling it in, you're trying not to let it out.'

He took the gun from his pocket. 'I'm an old fool. I should never have come. You're so beautiful.'

'I'm going to see Leonard tonight.'

'Don't talk.'

'We're flying to Paris in the morning.'

'You heard what I said!'

'And then to Stockholm.' She laughed sweetly and caressed his chin. 'My little fat man.'

Something began to stir in him. His face grew pale. He knew what was happening. The hidden anger and revulsion and hatred in him were sending out faint pulses of thought. And the delicate and telepathic web in her wondrous head was receiving the death impulse. The marionette. The invisible strings. He himself manipulating her body.

'Plump, odd little man, who once was so fair.'

'Don't,' he said.

'Old while I am only thirty-one, ah, George, you were blind, working years to give me time to fall in love again. Don't you think Leonard is lovely?'

He raised the gun blindly.

'Katie.'

'*His head is as the most fine gold —*' she whispered.

'Katie, don't!' he screamed.

'*His locks are bushy and black as a raven . . . His hands are as gold rings set with the beryl —*'

How could she speak those words! It was in *his* mind, how could *she* mouth it!

'Katie, don't make me do this!'

'*His cheeks are as a bed of spices,*' she murmured, eyes closed, moving about the room softly. '*His belly is as bright ivory overlaid with sapphires. His legs are as pillars of marble —*'

'Katie!' he shrieked.

'*His mouth is most sweet —*'

One shot.

' *— this is my beloved —*'

Another shot.

She fell.

'Katie, Katie, Katie!'

Four times he pumped bullets into her body.

She lay shuddering. Her senseless mouth clicked wide and some insanely warped mechanism had caused her to repeat again and again, '*Beloved, beloved, beloved, beloved, beloved . . .* '

George Hill fainted.

He awakened to a cool cloth on his brow.

'It's all over,' said the dark man.

'Over?' George Hill whispered.

The dark man nodded.

George Hill looked weakly down at his hands. They had been covered with blood. When he fainted he had dropped to the floor. The last thing he remembered was the feeling of the real blood pouring upon his hands in a freshet.

His hands were now clean-washed.

'I've got to leave,' said George Hill.

'If you feel capable.'

'I'm all right.' He got up. 'I'll go to Paris now, start over. I'm not to try to phone Katie or anything, am I.'

'Katie is dead.'

'Yes. I killed her, didn't I? God, the blood, it was *real*!'

'We are proud of that touch.'

He went down in the elevator to the street. It was raining, and he wanted to walk for hours. The anger and destruction were purged away. The memory was so terrible that he would never wish to kill again. Even if the real Katie were to appear before him now, he would only thank God, and fall senselessly to his knees. She was dead now. He had had his way. He had broken the law and no one would know.

The rain fell cool on his face. He must leave immediately, while the purge was in effect. After all, what was the use of such purges if one took up the old threads? The marionettes' function was primarily to prevent actual crime. If you wanted to kill, hit, or torture someone, you took it out on one of those unstringed automatons. It wouldn't do to return to the apartment now, Katie might be there. He wanted only to think of her as dead, a thing attended to in deserving fashion.

He stopped at the kerb and watched the traffic flash by. He took deep breaths of the good air and began to relax.

'Mr Hill?' said a voice at his elbow.

'Yes?'

A manacle was snapped to Hill's wrist. 'You're under arrest.'

'But —'

'Come along. Smith, take the other men upstairs, make the arrests!'

'You can't do this to me,' said George Hill.

'For murder, yes, we can.'

Thunder sounded in the sky.

It was eight-fifteen at night. It had been raining for ten days. It rained now on the prison walls. He put his hands out to feel the drops gather in pools on his trembling palms.

A door clanged and he did not move but stood with his hands in the rain. His lawyer looked up at him on his chair and said, 'It's all over. You'll be executed tonight.'

George Hill listened to the rain.

'She wasn't real. I didn't kill her.'

'It's the law, anyhow. You remember. The others are sentenced, too. The president of Marionettes, Incorporated, will die at midnight. His three assistants will die at one. You'll go about one-thirty.'

'Thanks,' said George. 'You did all you could. I guess it was murder, no matter how you look at it, image or not. The idea was there, the plot and the plan were there. It lacked only the real Katie herself.'

'It's a matter of timing, too,' said the lawyer. 'Ten years ago you wouldn't have got the death penalty. Ten years from now you wouldn't, either. But they had to have an object case, a whipping boy. The use of marionettes has grown so in the last year it's fantastic. The public must be scared out of it, and scared badly. God knows where it would all wind up if it went on. There's the spiritual side of it, too, where does life begin or end? are the robots alive or dead? More than one church has been split up the seams on the question. If they aren't alive, they're the next thing to it; they react, they even think. You know the "live robot" law that was passed two months ago; you come under that. Just bad timing, is all, bad timing.'

'The government's right. I see that now,' said George Hill.

'I'm glad you understand the attitude of the law.'

'Yes. After all, they can't let murder be legal. Even if it's done with machines and telepathy and wax. They'd be hypocrites to let me get away with my crime. For it *was* a crime. I've felt guilty about it ever since. I've felt the need of punishment. Isn't that odd? That's how society gets to you. It makes you feel guilty even when you see no reason to be . . .'

'I have to go now. Is there anything you want?'

'Nothing, thanks.'

'Good-bye then, Mr Hill.'

The door shut.

George Hill stood up on the chair, his hands twisting together, wet, outside the windows bars. A red light burned in the wall suddenly. A voice came over the audio: 'Mr Hill, your wife is here to see you.'

He gripped the bars.

She's dead, he thought.

'Mr Hill?' asked the voice.

'She's dead. I killed her.'

'Your wife is waiting in the anteroom, will you see her?'

'I saw her fall, I shot her, I saw her fall dead!'

'Mr Hill, do you hear me?'

'Yes!' he shouted, pounding at the wall with his fists. 'I hear you. I hear you! She's dead, she's dead, can't she let me be! I killed her, I won't see her, she's dead!'

A pause. 'Very well, Mr Hill,' murmured the voice.

The red light winked off.

Lightning flashed through the sky and lit his face. He pressed his hot cheeks to the cold bars and waited, while the rain fell. After a long time, a door opened somewhere on to the street and he saw two caped figures emerge from the prison office below. They paused under an arc light and glanced up.

It was Katie. And beside her, Leonard Phelps.

'Katie!'

Her face turned away. The man took her arm. They hurried across the avenue in the black rain and got into a low car.

'Katie!' He wrenched at the bars. He screamed and beat and pulled at the concrete ledge. 'She's alive! Guard! Guard! I saw her! She's not dead, I didn't kill her, now you can let me out! I didn't murder anyone, it's all a joke, a mistake, I saw her, I saw her! Katie, come back, tell them, Katie, say you're alive! Katie!'

The guards came running.

'You can't kill me! I didn't do anything! Katie's alive, I saw her!'

'We saw her, too, sir.'

'But let me free, then! Let me free!' It was insane. He choked and almost fell.

'We've been through all that, sir, at the trial.'

'It's not fair!' He leaped up and clawed at the window, bellowing.

The car drove away, Katie and Leonard inside it. Drove away to Paris and Athens and Venice and London next spring and Stockholm next summer and Vienna in the fall.

'Katie, come back, you can't *do* this to me!'

The red taillights of the car dwindled in the cold rain. Behind him, the guards moved forward to take hold of him while he screamed.

A Piece of Wood

'Sit down, young man,' said the Official.

'Thanks.' The young man sat.

'I've been hearing rumours about you,' the Official said pleasantly. 'Oh, nothing much. Your nervousness. Your not getting on so well. Several months now I've heard about you, and I thought I'd call you in. Thought maybe you'd like your job changed. Like to go overseas, work in some other War Area? Desk job killing you off, like to get right in on the old fight?'

'I don't think so,' said the young sergeant.

'What *do* you want?'

The sergeant shrugged and looked at his hands. 'To live in peace. To learn that during the night, somehow, the guns of the world had rusted, the bacteria had turned sterile in their bomb casings, the tanks had sunk like prehistoric monsters into roads suddenly made tar pits. That's what I'd like.'

'That's what we'd all like, of course,' said the Official. 'Now stop all that idealistic chatter and tell me where you'd like to be sent. You have your choice — the Western or Northern War Zone.' The Official tapped a pink map on his desk.

But the sergeant was talking at his hands, turning them over, looking at the fingers: 'What would you officers do, what would we men do, what would the *world* do if we all woke tomorrow with the guns in flaking ruin?'

The Official saw that he would have to deal carefully with the sergeant. He smiled quietly. 'That's an interesting question. I like to talk about such theories, and my answer is that there'd be mass panic. Each nation would think itself the only unarmed nation in the world, and would blame its enemies for the disaster. There'd be waves of suicide, stocks collapsing, a million tragedies.'

'But *after* that,' the sergeant said. 'After they realized it was true, that every nation was disarmed and there was nothing more to fear, if we were all clean to start over fresh and new, what then?'

'They'd rearm as swiftly as possible.'

'What if they could be stopped?'

'Then they'd beat each other with their fists. If it got down to that. Huge armies of men with boxing gloves of steel pikes would gather at the national borders. And if you took the gloves away they'd use their fingernails and feet. And if you cut their legs off they'd *spit* on each other. And if you cut off their tongues and stopped their mouths with corks they'd fill the atmosphere so full of hate that mosquitoes would drop to the ground and birds would fall dead from telephone wires.'

'Then you don't think it would do any good?' the sergeant said.

'Certainly not. It'd be like ripping the carapace off a turtle. Civilization would gasp and die from shock.'

The young man shook his head. 'Or are you lying to yourself and me because you've a nice comfortable job?'

'Let's call it ninety per cent cynicism, ten per cent rationalizing the situation. Go put your Rust away and forget about it.'

The sergeant jerked his head up. 'How'd you know I *had* it?' he said.

'Had what?'

'The Rust, of course.'

'What're you talking about?'

'I *can* do it, you know. I could start the Rust tonight if I wanted to.'

The Official laughed. 'You can't be serious.'

'I am. I've been meaning to come talk to you. I'm glad you called me in. I've worked on this invention for a long time.

It's been a dream of mine. It has to do with the structure of certain atoms. If you study them you find that the arrangement of atoms in steel armour is such-and-such an arrangement. I was looking for an imbalance factor. I majored in physics and metallurgy, you know. It came to me, there's a Rust factor in the air all the time. Water vapour. I had to find a way to give steel a "nervous breakdown". Then the water vapour everywhere in the world would take over. Not on all metal, of course. Our civilization is built on steel, I wouldn't want to destroy most buildings. I'd just eliminate guns and shells, tanks, planes, battleships. I can set the machine to work on copper and brass and aluminium, too, if necessary. I'd just walk by all of those weapons and just being near them I'd make them fall away.'

The Official was bending over his desk, staring at the sergeant. 'May I ask you a question?'

'Yes.'

'Have you ever thought you were Christ?'

'I can't say that I have. But I have considered that God was good to me to let me find what I was looking for, if that's what you mean.'

The Official reached into his breast pocket and drew out an expensive ball-point pen capped with a rifle shell. He flourished the pen and started filling in a form. 'I want you to take this to Dr Mathews this afternoon, for a complete check-up. Not that I expect anything really bad, understand. But don't you feel you *should* see a doctor?'

'You think I'm lying about my machine,' said the sergeant. 'I'm not. It's so small it can be hidden in this cigarette package. The effect of it extends for nine hundred miles. I could tour this country in a few days, with the machine set to a certain type of steel. The other nations couldn't take advantage of us because I'd rust their weapons as they approach us. Then I'd fly to Europe. By this time next month the world would be free of war forever. I don't know how I found this invention. It's impossible. Just as impossible as the atom bomb. I've waited a month now, trying to think it over. I worried about what would happen if I did rip off the carapace, as you say. But now I've just decided. My talk with you has helped clarify things. Nobody thought an aeroplane would ever fly, nobody thought an atom would ever explode, and nobody thinks that there can ever be Peace, but there *will* be.'

'Take that paper over to Dr Mathews, will you?' said the Official hastily.

The sergeant got up. 'You're not going to assign me to any new Zone then?'

'Not right away, no. I've changed my mind. We'll let Mathews decide.'

'I've decided then,' said the young man. 'I'm leaving the post within the next few minutes. I've a pass. Thank you very much for giving me your valuable time, sir.'

'Now look here, Sergeant, don't take things so seriously. You don't have to leave. Nobody's going to hurt you.'

'That's right. Because nobody would believe me. Goodbye, sir.' The sergeant opened the office door and stepped out.

The door shut and the Official was alone. He stood for a moment looking at the door. He sighed. He rubbed his hands over his face. The phone rang. He answered it abstractedly.

'Oh, *hello*, Doctor. I was just going to call you.' A pause. 'Yes, I was going to send him over to you. Look, is it all right for that young man to be wandering about? It *is* all right? If you say so, Doctor. Probably needs a rest, a good long one. Poor boy has a delusion of rather an interesting sort. Yes, yes. It's a shame. But that's what a Sixteen-Year War can do to you, I suppose.'

The phone voice buzzed in reply.

The Official listened and nodded. 'I'll make a note on that. Just a second.' He reached for his ball-point pen. 'Hold on a moment. Always mislaying things.' He patted his pocket.

'Had my pen here a moment ago. Wait.' He put down the phone and searched his desk, pulling out drawers. He checked his blouse pocket again. He stopped moving. Then his hands twitched slowly into his pocket and probed down. He poked his thumb and forefinger deep and brought out a pinch of something.

He sprinkled it on his desk blotter: a small filtering powder of yellow-red rust.

He sat staring at it for a moment. Then he picked up the phone. 'Mathews,' he said, 'get off the line, quick.' There was a click of someone hanging up and then he dialled another call. 'Hello, Guard Station, listen, there's a man coming past you any minute now, you know him, name of Sergeant Hollis, stop him, shoot him down, kill him if necessary, don't ask questions, kill the son of a bitch, you heard me, this is the Official talking! Yes, kill him, you hear!'

'But sir,' said a bewildered voice on the other end of the line. 'I can't, I just *can't* . . . '

'What do you mean, you can't, God damn it!'

'Because . . . the voice faded away. You could hear the guard breathing into the phone a mile away.

The Official shook the phone. 'Listen to me, listen, get your gun ready!'

'I can't shoot anyone,' said the guard.

The Official sank back in his chair. He sat blinking for half a minute, gasping.

Out there even now — he didn't have to look, no one had to tell him — the hangars were dusting down in soft red rust, and the aeroplanes were blowing away on a brown-rust wind into nothingness, and the tanks were sinking, sinking slowly into the hot asphalt roads, like dinosaurs (isn't that what the man had said?) sinking into primordial tar pits. Trucks were blowing away in ochre puffs of smoke, their drivers dumped by the road, with only the tyres left running on the highways.

'Sir . . . ' said the guard, who was seeing all this, far away. 'Oh, God . . . '

'Listen, listen!' screamed the Official. 'Go after him, get him, with your hands, choke him, with your fists, beat him, use your feet, kick his ribs in, kick him to death, do anything, but get that man. I'll be right out!' He hung up the phone.

By instinct he jerked open the bottom desk drawer to get his service pistol. A pile of brown rust filled the new leather holster. He swore and leaped up.

On the way out of the office he grabbed a chair. It's wood, he thought. Good old-fashioned wood, good old-fashioned maple. He hurled it against the wall twice, and it broke. Then he seized one of the legs, clenched it hard in his fist, his face bursting red, the breath snorting in his nostrils, his mouth wide. He struck the palm of his hand with the leg of the chair, testing it. 'All right, God damn it, come on!' he cried.

He rushed out, yelling, and slammed the door.

The Blue Bottle

The sundials were tumbled into white pebbles. The birds of the air now flew in ancient skies of rock and sand, buried, their songs stopped. The dead sea bottoms were currented with dust which flooded the land when the wind bade it reenact an old tale of engulfment. The cities were deep-laid with granaries of silence, time stored and kept, pools and fountains of quietude and memory.

Mars was dead.

Then, out of the large stillness, from a great distance, there was an insect sound which grew large among the cinnamon hills and moved in the sun-blazed air until the highway trembled and dust was shaken whispering down in the old cities.

The sound ceased.

In the shimmering silence of midday, Albert Beck and Leonard Craig sat in an ancient landcar, eyeing a dead city which did not move under their gaze but waited for their shout:

'Hello!'

A crystal tower dropped into soft dusting rain.

'You there!'

And another tumbled down.

And another and another fell as Beck called, summoning them to death. In shattering flights, stone animals with vast granite wings dived to strike the courtyards and fountains. His cry summoned them like living beasts and the beasts gave answer, groaned, cracked, leaned up, tilted over, trembling, hesitant, then split the air and swept down with grimaced mouths and empty eyes, with sharp, eternally hungry teeth suddenly seized out and strewn like shrapnel on the tiles.

Beck waited. No more towers fell.

'It's safe to go in now.'

Craig didn't move. 'For the same reason?'

Beck nodded.

'For a damned *bottle*! I don't understand. Why does everyone want it?'

Beck got out of the car. 'Those that found it, they never told, they never explained. But — it's old. Old as the desert, as the dead seas — and it might contain anything. That's what the legend says. And because it *could* hold anything — well, that stirs a man's hunger.'

'Yours, not mine,' said Craig. His mouth barely moved; his eyes were half-shut, faintly amused. He stretched lazily. 'I'm just along for the ride. Better watching you than sitting in the heat.'

Beck had stumbled upon the landcar a month back, before Craig had joined him. It was part of the flotsam of the First Industrial Invasion of Mars that had ended when the race moved on towards the stars. He had worked on the motor and run it from city to dead city, through the lands of the idlers and roustabouts, the dreamers and lazers, men caught in the backwash of space, men like himself and Craig who had never wanted to do much of anything and had found Mars a fine place to do it in.

'Five thousand, ten thousand years back the Martians made the Blue Bottle,' said Beck. 'Blown from Martian glass — and lost and found and lost and found again and again.'

He stared into the wavering heat shimmer of the dead city. All my life, thought Beck, I've done nothing and nothing inside the nothing. Others, better men, have done big things, gone off to Mercury, or Venus, or out beyond the System. Except me. Not me. But the Blue Bottle can *change* all that.

He turned and walked away from the silent car.

Craig was out and after him, moving easily along. 'What is

it now, ten years you've hunted? You twitch when you sleep, wake up in fits, sweat through the days. You want the damn bottle *that* bad, and don't know what's in it. You're a fool, Beck.'

'Shut up, shut up,' said Beck, kicking a slide of pebbles out of his way.

They walked together into the ruined city, over a mosaic of cracked tiles shaped into a stone tapestry of fragile Martian creatures, long-dead beasts which appeared and disappeared as a slight breath of wind stirred the silent dust.

'Wait,' said Beck. He cupped his hands to his mouth and gave a great shout. 'You there!'

' . . . there,' said an echo, and towers fell. Fountains and stone pillars folded into themselves. That was the way of these cities. Sometimes towers as beautiful as a symphony would fall at a spoken word. It was like watching a Bach cantata disintegrate before your eyes.

A moment later: bones buried bones. The dust settled. Two structures remained intact.

Beck stepped forward, nodding to his friend.

They moved in search.

And, searching, Craig paused, a faint smile on his lips. 'In that bottle,' he said, 'is there a little accordion woman, all folded up like one of those tin cups, or like one of those Japanese flowers you put in water and it opens out?'

'I don't need a woman.'

'Maybe you do. Maybe you never had a *real* woman, a woman who loved you, so, secretly, that's what you hope is in it.' Craig pursed his mouth. 'Or maybe, in that bottle, something from your childhood. All in a tiny bundle – a lake, a tree you climbed, green grass, some crayfish. How's *that* sound?'

Beck's eyes focused on a distant point. 'Sometimes – that's almost it. The past – Earth. I don't know.'

Craig nodded. 'What's in the bottle would depend, maybe,

on who's looking. Now, if there was a shot of *whisky* in it . . . '

'Keep looking,' said Beck.

There were seven rooms filled with glitter and shine; from floor to tiered ceiling there were casks, crocks, magnums, urns, vases — fashioned of red, pink, yellow, violet, and black glass. Beck shattered them, one by one, to eliminate them, to get them out of the way so he would never have to go through them again.

Beck finished his room, stood ready to invade the next. He was almost afraid to go on. Afraid that *this* time he would find it; that the search would be over and the meaning would go out of his life. Only after he had heard of the Blue Bottle from fire-travellers all the way from Venus to Jupiter, ten years ago, had life begun to take on a purpose. The fever had lit him and he had burned steadily ever since. If he worked it properly, the prospect of finding the bottle might fill his entire life to the brim. Another thirty years, if he was careful and not *too* diligent, of search, never admitting aloud that it wasn't the bottle that counted at all, but the search, the running and the hunting, the dust and the cities and the going-on.

Beck heard a muffled sound. He turned and walked to a window looking out into the courtyard. A small grey sand cycle had purred up almost noiselessly at the end of the street. A plump man with blonde hair eased himself off the spring seat and stood looking into the city. Another searcher. Beck sighed. Thousands of them, searching and searching. But there were thousands of brittle cities and towns and villages and it would take a millennium to sift them all.

'How you doing?' Craig appeared in a doorway.

'No luck.' Beck sniffed the air. 'Do you smell anything?'

'What?' Craig looked about.

'Smells like — bourbon.'

'Ho!' Craig laughed. 'That's *me*!'

'You?'

'I just took a drink. Found it in the other room. Shoved some stuff around, a mess of bottles, like always, and one of them had some bourbon in it, so I had myself a drink.'

Beck was staring at him, beginning to tremble. 'What — what would bourbon be doing *here*, in a Martian bottle?' His hands were cold. He took a slow step forward. 'Show me!'

'I'm sure that . . . '

'*Show* me, damn you!'

It was there, in one corner of the room, a container of Martian glass as blue as the sky, the size of a small fruit, light and airy in Beck's hand as he set it down upon a table.

'It's half-full of bourbon,' said Craig.

'I don't see anything inside,' said Beck.

'Then shake it.'

Beck picked it up, gingerly, shook it.

'Hear it gurgle?'

'No.'

'I can hear it plain.'

Beck replaced it on the table. Sunlight spearing through a side window struck blue flashes off the slender container. It was the blue of a star held in the hand. It was the blue of a shallow ocean bay at noon. It was the blue of a diamond at morning.

'This *is* it,' said Beck quietly. 'I know it is. We don't have to look any more. We've found the Blue Bottle.'

Craig looked sceptical. 'Sure you don't *see* anything in it?'

'Nothing . . . But — ' Beck bent close and peered deeply into the blue universe of glass. 'Maybe if I open it up and let it out, whatever it is, I'll know.'

'I put the stopper in tight. Here,' Craig reached out.

'If you gentlemen will excuse me,' said a voice in the door behind them.

The plump man with blonde hair walked into their line of vision with a gun. He did not look at their faces, he looked only at the blue glass bottle. He began to smile. 'I hate very much to handle guns,' he said, 'but it is a matter of necessity, as I simply *must* have that work of art. I suggest that you allow me to take it without trouble.'

Beck was almost pleased. It had a certain beauty of timing, this incident; it was the sort of thing he might have wished for, to have the treasure stolen before it was opened. Now there was the good prospect of a chase, a fight, a series of gains and losses, and before they were done, perhaps another four or five years spent upon a new search.

'Come along now,' said the stranger. 'Give it up.' He raised the gun warningly.

Beck handed him the bottle.

'Amazing. Really amazing,' said the plump man. 'I can't believe it was as simple as this, to walk in, hear two men talking, and to have the Blue Bottle simply *handed* to me. Amazing!' And he wandered off down the hall, out into the daylight, chuckling to himself.

Under the cool double moons of Mars the midnight cities were bone and dust. Along the scattered highway the landcar bumped and rattled, past cities where the fountains, the gyrostats, the furniture, the metal-singing books, the paintings lay powdered over with mortar and insect wings. Past cities that were cities no longer, but only things rubbed to a fine silt that flowered senselessly back and forth on the wine winds between one land and another, like the sand in a gigantic hourglass, endlessly pyramiding and repyramiding. Silence opened to let the car pass, and closed swiftly in behind.

Craig said, 'We'll never find him. These damned roads. So old. Potholes, lumps, everything wrong. He's got the advantage with the cycle; he can dodge and weave. Damn!'

They swerved abruptly, avoiding a bad stretch. The car

moved over the old highway like an eraser, coming upon blind soil, passing over it, dusting it away to reveal the emerald and gold colour of ancient Martian mosaics worked into the road surfaces.

'Wait,' cried Beck. He throttled the car down. 'I saw something back there.'

'Where?'

They drove back a hundred yards.

'There. You see. It's *him*.'

In a ditch by the side of the road a plump man lay folded over his cycle. He did not move. His eyes were wide, and when Beck flashed a torch down, the eyes burned dully.

'Where's the bottle?' asked Craig.

Beck jumped into the ditch and picked up the man's gun. 'I don't know. Gone.'

'What killed him?'

'I don't know that either.'

'The cycle looks okay. Not an accident.'

Beck rolled the body over. 'No wounds. Looks like he just — stopped, of his own accord.'

'Heart attack, maybe,' said Craig. 'Excited over the bottle. He gets down here to hide. Thought he'd be all right, but the attack finished him.'

'That doesn't account for the Blue Bottle.'

'Someone came along. Lord, you know how many searchers there are . . . '

They scanned the darkness around them. Far off, in the starred blackness, on the blue hills, they saw a dim movement.

'Up there.' Beck pointed. 'Three men on foot.'

'They must have . . . '

'My God, look!'

Below them, in the ditch, the figure of the plump man glowed, began to melt. The eyes took on the aspect of moonstones under a sudden rush of water. The face began to dissolve away into fire. The hair resembled small firecracker strings, lit and sputtering. The body fumed as they watched. The fingers jerked with flame. Then, as if a gigantic hammer had struck a glass statue, the body cracked upward and was gone in a blaze of pink shards, becoming mist as the night breeze carried it across the highway.

'They must have − *done* something to him,' said Craig. 'Those three, with a new kind of weapon.'

'But it's happened before,' said Beck. 'Men I knew about who had the Blue Bottle. They vanished. And the bottle passed on to others who vanished.' He shook his head. 'Looked like a million fireflies when he broke apart . . . '

'You going after them?'

Beck returned to the car. He judged the desert mounds, the hills of bone-silt and silence. 'It'll be a tough job, but I think I can poke the car through after them. I *have* to, now.' He paused, not speaking to Craig. 'I think I know what's in the Blue Bottle . . . Finally, I realize that what I want most of all is in there. Waiting for me.'

'I'm not going,' said Craig, coming up to the car where Beck sat in the dark, his hands on his knees. 'I'm not going out there with you, chasing three armed men. I just want to live, Beck. That bottle means nothing to me. I won't risk my skin for it. But I'll wish you luck.'

'Thanks,' said Beck. And he drove away, into the dunes.

The night was as cool as water coming over the glass hood of the landcar.

Beck throttled hard over dead river washes and spills of chalked pebble, driving between great cliffs. Ribbons of double moonlight painted the bas-reliefs of gods and animals on the cliff sides all yellow-gold: mile-high faces upon which Martian histories were etched and stamped in symbols, incredible faces with open cave eyes and gaping cave mouths.

The motor's roar dislodged rocks, boulders. In a whole rushing downpour of stone, golden segments of ancient cliff sculpture slid out of the moons' rays at the top of the cliff and vanished into blue cool-well darkness.

In the roar, as he drove, Beck cast his mind back — to all the nights in the last ten years, nights when he had built rèd fires on the sea bottoms, and cooked slow, thoughtful meals. And dreamed. Always those dreams of *wanting*. And not knowing what. Ever since he was a young man, the hard life on Earth, the great panic of 2130, the starvation, chaos, riot, want. Then bucking through the planets, the womanless, loveless years, the alone years. You come out of the dark into the light, out of the womb into the world, and what do you find that you really want?

What about that dead man back there in the ditch? Wasn't he always looking for something extra? Something he didn't have. What *was* there for men like himself? Or for anyone? Was there anything at all to look forward to?

The Blue Bottle.

He quickly braked the car, leaped out, gun ready. He ran, crouching, into the dunes. Ahead of him, the three men lay on the cold sand, neatly. They were Earth Men, with tan faces and rough clothes and gnarled hands. Starlight shone on the Blue Bottle, which lay among them.

As Beck watched, the bodies began to melt. They vanished away into rises of steam, into dewdrops and crystals. In a moment they were gone.

Beck felt the coldness in his body as the flakes rained across his eyes, flicking his lips and his cheeks.

He did not move.

The plump man. Dead and vanishing. Craig's voice: 'Some new weapon . . . '

No. Not a weapon at all.

The Blue Bottle.

They had opened it to find what they most desired. All of the unhappy, desiring men down the long and lonely years had opened it to find what they most wanted in the planets of the universe. And all had found it, even as had these three. Now it could be understood, why the bottle passed on so swiftly, from one to another, and the men vanishing behind it. Harvest chaff fluttering on the sand, along the dead sea rims. Turning to flame and fireflies. To mist.

Beck picked up the bottle and held it away from himself for a long moment. His eyes shone clearly. His hands trembled.

So this is what I've been looking for, he thought. He turned the bottle and it flashed blue starlight.

So this is what all men *really* want? The secret desire, deep inside, hidden all away where we never guess? The subliminal urge? So this is what each man seeks, through some private guilt, to find?

Death.

An end to doubt, to torture, to monotony, to want, to loneliness, to fear, an end to everything.

All men?

No. Not Craig. Craig was, perhaps, far luckier. A few men were like animals in the universe, not questioning, drinking at pools and breeding and raising their young and not doubting for a moment that life was anything but good. That was Craig. There were a handful like him. Happy animals on a great reservation, in the hand of God, with a religion and a faith that grew like a set of special nerves in them. The unneurotic men in the midst of the billionfold neurotics. They would only want death, later, in a natural manner. Not now. Later.

Beck raised the bottle. How simple, he thought, and how right. This *is* what I've always wanted. And nothing else.

Nothing.

The bottle was open and blue in the starlight. Beck took an immense draught of the air coming from the Blue Bottle, deep into his lungs.

I have it at last, he thought.

He relaxed. He felt his body become wonderfully cool and then wonderfully warm. He knew he was dropping down a long slide of stars into a darkness as delightful as wine. He was swimming in blue wine and white wine and red wine. There were candles in his chest and fire wheels spinning. He felt his hands leave him. He felt his legs fly away, amusingly. He laughed. He shut his eyes and laughed.

He was very happy for the first time in his life.

The Blue Bottle dropped on to the cool sand.

At dawn Craig walked along, whistling. He saw the bottle lying in the first pink light of the sun on the empty white sand. As he picked it up, there was a fiery whisper. A number of orange and red-purple fireflies blinked on the air, and passed on away.

The place was very still.

'I'll be damned.' He glanced towards the dead windows of a nearby city. 'Hey, Beck!'

A slender tower collapsed into powder.

'Beck, here's your treasure! I don't want it. Come and get it!'

' . . . and get it,' said an echo, and the last tower fell.

Craig waited.

'That's rich,' he said. 'The bottle right here, and old Beck not even around to take it.' He shook the blue container.

It gurgled.

'Yes, sir! Just the way it was before. Full of bourbon, by God!' He opened it, drank, wiped his mouth.

He held the bottle carelessly.

'All that trouble for a little bourbon. I'll wait right here for old Beck and give him his damn bottle. Meanwhile — have another drink, Mr Craig. Don't mind if I do.'

The only sound in the dead land was the sound of liquid running into a parched throat. The Blue Bottle flashed in the sun.

Craig smiled happily and drank again.

Long After Midnight

The police ambulance went up into the palisades at the wrong hour. It is always the wrong hour when the police ambulance goes anywhere, but this was especially wrong, for it was long after midnight and nobody imagined it would ever be day again, because the sea coming in on the lightless shore below said as much, and the wind blowing salt cold in from the Pacific reaffirmed this, and the fog muffling the sky and putting out the stars struck the final, unfelt-but-disabling blow. The weather said it had been here forever, man was hardly here at all, and would soon be gone. Under the circumstances it was hard for the men gathered on the cliff, with several cars, the headlights on, and flashlights bobbing, to feel real, trapped as they were between a sunset they hardly remembered and a sunrise that would not be imagined.

The slender weight hanging from the tree, turning in the cold salt wind, did not diminish this feeling in any way.

The slender weight was a girl, no more than nineteen, in a light green gossamer party frock, coat and shoes lost somewhere in the cool night, who had brought a rope up to these cliffs and found a tree with a branch half out over the cliff and tied the rope in place and made a loop for her neck and let herself out on the wind to hang there swinging. The rope made a dry scraping whine on the branch, until the police came, and the ambulance, to take her down out of space and place her on the ground.

A single phone call had come in about midnight telling what they might find out here on the edge of the cliff and whoever it was hung up swiftly and did not call again, and now the hours had passed and all that could be done was done and over, the police were finished and leaving, and there was just the ambulance now and the men with the ambulance to load the quiet burden and head for the morgue.

Of the three men remaining around the sheeted form there were Carlson, who had been at this sort of thing for thirty years, and Moreno, who had been at it for ten, and Latting, who was new to the job a few weeks back. Of the three it was Latting now who stood on the edge of the cliff looking at the empty tree limb, the rope in his hand, not able to take his eyes away. Carlson came up behind him. Hearing him, Latting said, 'What a place, what an awful place to die.'

'Any place is awful, if you decide you want to go bad enough,' said Carlson. 'Come on, kid.'

Latting did not move. He put out his hand to touch the tree. Carlson grunted and shook his head. 'Go ahead. Try to remember it all.'

'Any reason why I shouldn't?' Latting turned quickly to look at that emotionless grey face of the older man. 'You got any objections?'

'No objections. I was the same way once. But after a while you learn it's best not to see. You eat better. You sleep better. After a while you learn to forget.'

'I don't want to forget,' said Latting. 'Good God, somebody died up here just a few hours ago. She deserves – '

'She *deserved*, kid, past tense, not present. She deserved a better shake and didn't get it. Now she deserves a decent burial. That's all we can do for her. It's late and cold. You can tell us all about it on the way.'

'That could be your daughter there.'

'You won't get to me that way, kid. It's not my daughter, that's what counts. And it's not yours, though you make it sound like it was. It's a nineteen-year-old girl, no name, no purse, nothing. I'm sorry she's dead. There, does that help?'

'It could if you said it right.'

'I'm sorry, now pick up the other end of the stretcher.'

Latting picked up one end of the stretcher but did not walk
with it and only looked at the figure beneath the sheet.

'It's awful being that young and deciding to just quit.'

'Sometimes,' said Carlson, at the other end of the
stretcher, 'I get tired, too.'

'Sure, but you're —' Latting stopped.

'Go ahead, say it. I'm old. Somebody fifty, sixty, it's
okay, who gives a damn, somebody nineteen, everybody
cries. So don't come to my funeral, kid, and no flowers.'

'I didn't mean . . . ' said Latting.

'Nobody means, but everybody says, and luckily I got the
hide of an iguana. March.'

They moved with the stretcher towards the ambulance
where Moreno was opening the doors wider.

'Boy,' said Latting, 'she's light. She doesn't weigh
anything.'

'That's the wild life for you, you punks, you kids.' Carlson
was getting into the back of the ambulance now and they
were sliding the stretcher in. 'I smell whisky. You young
ones think you can drink like college fullbacks and keep your
weight. Hell, she don't even weigh ninety pounds, if that.'

Latting put the rope in on the floor of the ambulance. 'I
wonder where she got this?'

'It's not like poison,' said Moreno. 'Anyone can buy rope
and not sign. This looks like block-and-tackle rope. She was
at a beach party maybe and got mad at her boyfriend and took
this from his car and picked herself a spot . . . '

They took a last look at the tree out over the cliff, the
empty branch, the wind rustling in the leaves, then Carlson
got out and walked around to the front seat with Moreno, and
Latting got in the back and slammed the doors.

They drove away down the dim incline towards the shore
where the ocean laid itself, card after white card, in thunders,
upon the dark sand. They drove in silence for a while, letting
their headlights, like ghosts, move on out ahead. Then Lat-

ting said, 'I'm getting myself a new job.'

Moreno laughed. 'Boy, you didn't last long. I had bets you wouldn't last. Tell you what, you'll be back. No other job like this. All the other jobs are dull. Sure, you get sick once in a while. I do. I think: I'm going to quit. I almost do. Then I stick with it. And here I am.'

'Well, you can stay,' said Latting. 'But I'm full up. I'm not curious any more. I seen a lot the last few weeks, but this is the last straw. I'm sick of being sick. Or worse, I'm sick of your not caring.'

'Who doesn't care?'

'Both of you!'

Moreno snorted. 'Light us a couple, huh, Carlie?' Carlson lit two cigarettes and passed one to Moreno, who puffed on it, blinking his eyes, driving along by the loud strokes of the sea. 'Just because we don't scream and yell and throw fits —'

'I don't want fits,' said Latting, in the back, crouched by the sheeted figure. 'I just want a little human talk, I just want you to look different than you would walking through a butcher's shop. If I ever get like you two, not worrying, not bothering, all thick skin and tough —'

'We're not tough,' said Carlson, quietly, thinking about it, 'we're acclimated.'

'Acclimated, hell, when you should be *numb*?'

'Kid, don't tell us what we should be when you don't even know what we *are*. Any doctor is a lousy doctor who jumps in the grave with every patient. All doctors did that, there'd be no one to help the live and kicking. Get out of the grave, boy, you can't see nothing from there.'

There was a long silence from the back, and at last Latting started talking, mainly to himself.

'I wonder how long she was up there alone on the cliff, an hour, two? It must have been funny up there looking down at all the campfires, knowing you were going to wipe the whole business clean off. I suppose she was at a dance, or a beach party, and she and her boyfriend broke up. The boyfriend will be down at the station tomorrow to identify her. I'd hate to be him. How he'll *feel* – '

'He won't feel anything. He won't even show up,' said Carlson, steadily, mashing out his cigarette in the front-seat tray. 'He was probably the one found her and made the call and ran. Two bits will buy you a nickel he's not worth the polish on her little fingernail. Some slobby lout of a guy with pimples and bad breath. Christ, why don't these girls learn to wait until morning.'

'Yeah,' said Moreno. 'Everything's better in the morning.'

'Try telling that to a girl in love,' said Latting.

'Now a man,' said Carlson, lighting a fresh cigarette, 'he just gets himself drunk, says to hell with it, no use killing yourself for no woman.'

They drove in silence awhile past all the small dark beach houses with only a light here or there, it was so late.

'Maybe,' said Latting, 'she was going to have a baby.'

'It happens.'

'And then the boyfriend runs off with someone and this one just borrows his rope and walks up on the cliff,' said Latting. 'Answer me, now, *is* that or *isn't* it love?'

'It,' said Carlson, squinting, searching the dark, 'is a kind of love. I give up on what kind.'

'Well, sure,' said Moreno, driving. 'I'll go along with you, kid. I mean, it's nice to know somebody in this world can love that hard.'

They all thought for a while, as the ambulance purred between quiet palisades and now-quiet sea and maybe two of them thought fleetingly of their wives and tract houses and sleeping children and all the times years ago when they had driven to the beach and broken out the beer and necked up in the rocks and lay around on the blankets with guitars, singing and feeling like life would go on just as far as the ocean went, which was very far, and maybe they didn't think that at all. Latting, looking up at the backs of the two older men's necks, hoped or perhaps only nebulously wondered if these men remembered any first kisses, the taste of salt on the lips. Had there ever been a time when they had stomped the sand like mad bulls and yelled out of sheer joy and dared the universe to put them down?

And by their silence, Latting knew that yes, with all his talking, and the night, and the wind, and the cliff and the tree and the rope, he had got through to them; it, the event, had got through to them. Right now, they had to be thinking of their wives in their warm beds, long dark miles away, unbelievable, suddenly unattainable while here they were driving along a salt-layered road at a dumb hour half between certainties, bearing with them a strange thing on a cot and a used length of rope.

'Her boyfriend,' said Latting, 'will be out dancing to-morrow night with somebody else. That gripes my gut.'

'I wouldn't mind,' said Carlson, 'beating the hell out of him.'

Latting moved the sheet. 'They sure wear their hair crazy and short, some of them. All curls, but short. Too much make-up. Too —' He stopped.

'You were saying?' asked Moreno.

Latting moved the sheet some more. He said nothing. In the next minute there was a rustling sound of the sheet, moved now here, now there. Latting's face was pale.

'Hey,' he murmured, at last. 'Hey.'

Instinctively, Moreno slowed the ambulance.

'Yeah, kid?'

'I just found out something,' said Latting. 'I had this feeling all along, she's wearing too much make-up, and the hair, and —'

'So?'

'Well, for God's sake,' said Latting, his lips hardly

moving, one hand up to feel his own face to see what its expression was. 'You want to know something funny?'

'Make us laugh,' said Carlson.

The ambulance slowed even more as Latting said, 'It's not a woman. I mean, it's not a girl. I mean, well, it's not a female. *Understand*?'

The ambulance slowed to a crawl.

The wind blew in off the vague morning sea through the window as the two up front turned and stared into the back of the ambulance at the shape there on the cot.

'Somebody tell me,' said Latting, so quietly they almost could not hear the words. 'Do we stop feeling bad now? Or do we feel worse?'

The Utterly
Perfect Murder

It was such an utterly perfect, such an incredibly delightful idea of murder, that I was half out of my mind all across America.

The idea had come to me for some reason on my forty-eighth birthday. Why it hadn't come to me when I was thirty or forty, I cannot say. Perhaps those were good years and I sailed through them unaware of time and clocks and the gathering of frost at my temples or the look of the lion about my eyes . . .

Anyway, on my forty-eighth birthday, lying in bed that night beside my wife, with my children sleeping through all the other quiet moonlit rooms of my house, I thought:

I will arise and go now and kill Ralph Underhill.

Ralph Underhill! I cried, who in God's name is *he*?

Thirty-six years later, kill him? For *what*?

Why, I thought, for what he did to me when I was twelve.

My wife woke, an hour later, hearing a noise.

'Doug?' she called. 'What are you doing?'

'Packing,' I said. 'For a journey.'

'Oh,' she murmured, and rolled over and went to sleep.

'Board! All aboard!' The porter's cries went down the train platform.

The train shuddered and banged.

'See you!' I cried, leaping up the steps.

'Someday,' called my wife, 'I wish you'd *fly*!'

Fly? I thought, and spoil thinking about murder all across the plains? Spoil oiling the pistol and loading it and thinking of Ralph Underhill's face when I show up thirty-six years late to settle old scores? Fly? Why, I would rather pack cross-country on foot, pausing by night to build fires and fry my bile and sour spit and eat again my old, mummified but still-living antagonisms and touch those bruises which have never healed. Fly?!

The train moved. My wife was gone.

I rode off into the Past.

Crossing Kansas the second night, we hit a beaut of a thunderstorm. I stayed up until four in the morning, listening to the rave of winds and thunders. At the height of the storm, I saw my face, a darkroom negative-print on the cold window glass, and thought:

Where is that fool going?

To kill Ralph Underhill!

Why? Because!

Remember how he hit my arm? Bruises. I was covered with bruises, both arms; dark blue, mottled black, strange yellow bruises. Hit and run, that was Ralph, hit and run —

And yet . . . you loved him?

Yes, as boys love boys when boys are eight, ten, twelve, and the world is innocent and boys are evil beyond evil because they know not what they do, but do it anyway. So, on some secret level, I *had* to be hurt. We dear fine friends needed each other. I to be hit. He to strike. My scars were the emblem and symbol of our love.

What else makes you want to murder Ralph so late in time?

The train whistle shrieked. Night country rolled by.

And I recalled one spring when I came to school in a new tweed knicker suit and Ralph knocking me down, rolling me in snow and fresh brown mud. And Ralph laughing and me going home, shame-faced, covered with slime, afraid of a beating, to put on fresh dry clothes.

Yes! And what *else*?

Remember those toy clay statues you longed to collect from the Tarzan radio show? Statues of Tarzan and Kala the

Ape and Numa the Lion, for just twenty-five cents?! Yes, yes! Beautiful! Even, now, in memory, O the sound of the Ape Man swinging through green jungles far away, ululating! But who had twenty-five cents in the middle of the Great Depression? No one.

Except Ralph Underhill.

And one day Ralph asked you if you wanted one of the statues.

Wanted! you cried. Yes! Yes!

That was the same week your brother in a strange seizure of love mixed with contempt gave you his old, but expensive, baseball-catcher's mitt.

'Well,' said Ralph, 'I'll give you my extra Tarzan statue if you'll give me the catcher's mitt.'

Fool! I thought. The statue's worth twenty-five cents. The glove cost two dollars. Not fair! Don't!

But I raced back to Ralph's house with the glove and gave it to him and he, smiling a worse contempt than my brother's, handed me the Tarzan statue and, bursting with joy, I ran home.

My brother didn't find out about his catcher's mitt and the statue for two weeks, and when he did he ditched me when we hiked out in the farm country and left me lost because I was such a sap. 'Tarzan statues! Baseball mitts!' he cried. 'That's the last thing I *ever* give you!'

And somewhere on a country road I just lay down and wept and wanted to die but didn't know how to give up the final vomit that was my miserable ghost.

The thunder murmured.

The rain fell on the cold Pullman-car windows.

What *else*? Is that the list?

No. One final thing, more terrible than all the rest.

In all the years you went to Ralph's house to toss up small bits of gravel on his Fourth of July six-in-the-morning fresh dewy-window or to call him forth for the arrival of dawn circuses in the cold fresh blue railroad stations in late June or late August, in all those years, never once did Ralph run to your house.

Never once in all the years did he, or anyone else, prove their friendship by coming by. The door never knocked. The window of your bedroom never faintly clattered and belled with a high-tossed confetti of small dusts and rocks.

And you always knew that the day you stopped going to Ralph's house, calling up in the morn, that would be the day your friendship ended.

You tested it once. You stayed away for a whole week. Ralph never called. It was as if you had died, and no one came to your funeral.

When you saw Ralph at school, there was no surprise, no query, not even the faintest lint of curiosity to be picked off your coat. Where *were* you, Doug? I need someone to beat. Where you *been*, Doug, I got no one to *pinch*!

And all the sins up. But especially think on the last:

He never came to my house. He never sang up to my early-morning bed or tossed a wedding rice of gravel on the clear panes to call me down to joy and summer days.

And for this last thing, Ralph Underhill, I thought, sitting in the train at four in the morning, as the storm faded, and I found tears in my eyes, for this last and final thing, for that I shall kill you tomorrow night.

Murder, I thought, after thirty-six years. Why, God, you're madder than Ahab.

The train wailed. We ran cross-country like a mechanical Greek Fate carried by a black metal Roman Fury.

They say you can't go home again.

That is a lie.

If you are lucky and time it right, you arrive at sunset when the old town is filled with yellow light.

I got off the train and walked up through Green Town and

looked at the courthouse, burning with sunset light. Every tree was hung with gold doubloons of colour. Every roof and coping and bit of gingerbread was purest brass and ancient gold.

I sat in the courthouse square with dogs and old men until the sun had set and Green Town was dark. I wanted to savour Ralph Underhill's death.

No one in history had ever done a crime like this.

I would stay, kill, depart, a stranger among strangers.

How would anyone dare to say, finding Ralph Underhill's body on his doorstep, that a boy aged twelve, arriving on a kind of Time Machine train, travelled out of hideous self-contempt, had gunned down the Past? It was beyond all reason. I was safe in my pure insanity.

Finally, at eight-thirty on this cool October night, I walked across town, past the ravine.

I never doubted Ralph would still be there.

People do, after all, move away . . .

I turned down Park Street and walked two hundred yards to a single streetlamp and looked across. Ralph Underhill's white two-storey Victorian house waited for me.

And I could feel him *in* it.

He was there, forty-eight years old, even as I felt myself here, forty-eight, and full of an old and tired self-devouring spirit.

I stepped out of the light, opened my suitcase, put the pistol in my right-hand coat pocket, shut the case, and hid it in the bushes where, later, I would grab it and walk down into the ravine and across town to the train.

I walked across the street and stood before his house and it was the same house I had stood before thirty-six years ago. There were windows upon which I had hurled those spring bouquets of rock in love and total giving. There were the sidewalks, spotted with firecracker burn marks from ancient July Fourths when Ralph and I had just blown up the whole damned world, shrieking celebrations.

I walked up on the porch and saw on the mailbox in small letters: UNDERHILL.

What if his wife answers?

No, I thought, he himself, with absolute Greek-tragic perfection, will open the door and take the wound and almost gladly die for old crimes and minor sins somehow grown to crimes.

I rang the bell.

Will he know me, I wondered, after all this time? In the instant before the first shot, *tell* him your name. He must know who it is.

Silence.

I rang the bell again.

The doorknob rattled.

I touched the pistol in my pocket, my heart hammering, but did not take it out.

The door opened.

Ralph Underhill stood there.

He blinked, gazing out at me.

'Ralph?' I said.

'Yes — ?' he said.

We stood there, riven, for what could not have been more than five seconds. But, O Christ, many things happened in those five swift seconds.

I saw Ralph Underhill.

I saw him clearly.

And I had not seen him since I was twelve.

Then, he had towered over me to pummel and beat and scream.

Now he was a little old man.

I am five foot eleven.

But Ralph Underhill had not grown much from his twelfth year on.

The man stood before me was no more than five feet two inches tall.

I *towered* over him.

I gasped. I stared. I saw more.

I was forty-eight years old.

But Ralph Underhill, forty-eight, had lost most of his hair, and what remained was threadbare grey, black and white. He looked sixty or sixty-five.

I was in good health.

Ralph Underhill was waxen pale. There was a knowledge of sickness in his face. He had travelled in some sunless land. He had a ravaged and sunken look. His breath smelled of funeral flowers.

All this, perceived, was like the storm of the night before, gathering all its lightnings and thunders into one bright concussion. We stood in the explosion.

So this is what I came for? I thought. This, then, is the truth. This dreadful instant in time. Not to pull out the weapon. *Not* to kill. No, no. But simply –

To see Ralph Underhill as he *is* in this hour.

That's all.

Just to be here, stand here, and look at him as he has become.

Ralph Underhill lifted one hand in a kind of gesturing wonder. His lips trembled. His eyes flew up and down my body, his mind measured this giant who shadowed his door. At last his voice, so small, so frail, blurted out:

'Doug –?'

I recoiled.

'Doug?' he gasped. 'Is that *you*?'

I hadn't expected that. People don't remember! They can't! Across the years? Why would he know, bother, summon up, recognize, call?

I had a wild thought that what had happened to Ralph Underhill was that after I left town, half of his life had collapsed. I had been the centre of his world, someone to attack, beat, pummel, bruise. His whole life had cracked by my simple act of walking away thirty-six years ago.

Nonsense! Yet, some small crazed mouse of wisdom scuttered about my brain and screeched what it knew: You needed Ralph, but, *more*! he needed *you*! And you did the only unforgivable, the wounding, thing! You vanished.

'Doug?' he said again, for I was silent there on the porch with my hands at my sides. 'Is that you?'

This was the moment I had come for.

At some secret blood level, I had always known I would not use the weapon. I had brought it with me, yes, but Time had got here before me, and age, and smaller, more terrible deaths . . .

Bang.

Six shots through the heart.

But I didn't use the pistol. I only whispered the sound of the shots with my mouth. With each whisper, Ralph Underhill's face aged another ten years. By the time I reached the last shot he was one hundred and ten years old.

'Bang,' I whispered. 'Bang. Bang. Bang. Bang. Bang.'

His body shook with impact.

'You're dead. Oh, God, Ralph, you're dead.'

I turned and walked down the steps and reached the street before he called:

'Doug, is that *you*?'

I did not answer, walking.

'Answer me,' he cried, weakly. 'Doug! Doug Spaulding, is that you? Who is that? Who are you.'

I got my suitcase and walked down into the cricket night and darkness of the ravine and across the bridge and up the stairs, going away.

'Who is that?' I heard his voice wail a last time.

A long way off, I looked back.

All the lights were on all over Ralph Underhill's house. It was as if he had gone around and put them all on after I left.

On the other side of the ravine I stopped on the lawn in front of the house where I had been born.

Then I picked up a few bits of gravel and did the thing that had never been done, ever in my life.

I tossed the few bits of gravel up to tap that window where I had lain every morning of my first twelve years. I called my own name. I called me down in friendship to play in some long summer that no longer was.

I stood waiting just long enough for my other young self to come down to join me.

Then swiftly, fleeing ahead of the dawn, we ran out of Green Town and back, thank you, dear Christ, back towards Now and Today for the rest of my life.

The Better Part
of Wisdom

The room was like a great warm hearth, lit by an unseen fire, gone comfortable. The fireplace itself struggled to keep a small blaze going on a few wet logs and some turf, which was no more than smoke and several lazy orange eyes of charcoal. The place was slowly filling, draining, and refilling with music. A single lemon lamp was lit in a far corner, illumining walls painted a summer colour of yellow. The hardwood floor was polished so severely it glowed like a dark river upon which floated throw-rugs whose plumage resembled South American wild birds, flashing electric blues, whites, and jungle greens. White porcelain vases, brimming with fresh-cut hothouse flowers, kept their serene fires burning on four small tables about the room. Above the fireplace, a serious portrait of a young man gazed out with eyes the same colour as the ceramics, a deep blue, raw with intelligence and vitality.

Entering the room quietly, one might not have noticed the two men, they were so still.

One sat reclining back upon the pure white couch, eyes closed. The second lay upon the couch so his head was pillowed in the lap of the other. His eyes were shut, too, listening. Rain touched the windows. The music ended.

Instantly there was a soft scratching at the door.

Both men blinked as if to say: People don't *scratch*, they *knock*.

The man who had been lying down leaped to the door and called: 'Someone there?'

'By God, there is,' said an old voice with a faint brogue.

'Grandfather!'

With the door flung wide, the young man pulled a small round old man into the warm-lit room.

'Tom, boy, ah Tom, and glad I am to see you!'

They fell together in bear-hugs, pawing. Then the old man felt the other person in the room and moved back.

Tom spun around, pointing. 'Grandpa, this is Frank. Frank, this is Grandpa, I mean — oh hell —'

The old man saved the moment by trotting forward to seize and pull Frank to his feet, where he towered high above this small intruder from the night.

'Frank, is it?' the old man yelled up the heights.

'Yes, sir,' Frank called back down.

'I — ' said the grandfather, 'have been standing outside that door for five minutes —'

'Five minutes?' cried both young men, alarmed.

' — debating whether to knock. I heard the music, you see, and finally I said, damn, if there's a girl with him he can either shove her out the window in the rain or show the lovely likes of her to the old man. Hell, I said, and knocked, and' — he slung down his battered old valise — 'there *is* no young girl here, I see — or, by God, you've *smothered* her in the closet, eh!'

'There is no young girl, Grandfather.' Tom turned in a circle, his hands out to show.

'But — ' The grandfather eyed the polished floor, the white throw-rugs, the bright flowers, the watchful portraits on the walls. 'You've *borrowed* her place, then?'

'Borrowed?'

'I mean, by the look of the room, there's a woman's touch. It looks like them steamship posters I seen in the travel windows half my life.'

'Well,' said Frank. 'We — '

'The fact is, Grandfather,' said Tom, clearing his throat, '*we* did this place over. Redecorated.'

'Redecorated?' The old man's jaw dropped. His eyes

toured the four walls, stunned. 'The *two* of you are responsible? Jesus!'

The old man touched a blue and white ceramic ashtray, and bent to stroke a bright cockatoo throw-rug.

'Which of you did *what*?' he asked, suddenly, squinting one eye at them.

Tom flushed and stammered. 'Well, we —'

'Ah, God, no, no, stop!' cried the old man, lifting one hand. 'Here I am, fresh *in* the place, and sniffing about like a crazy hound and no fox. Shut that damn door. Ask me where *I'm* going, what am *I* up to, eh, *eh*? And, while you're at it, do you have a touch of the Beast in this art gallery?'

'The Beast it is!' Tom slammed the door, hustled his grandfather out of his greatcoat, and brought forth three tumblers and a bottle of Irish whiskey, which the old man touched as if it were a newborn babe.

'Well, that's more like it. What do we drink to?'

'Why, you, Grandpa!'

'No, no.' The old man gazed at Tom and then at his friend, Frank. 'Christ,' he sighed, 'you're so damn young it breaks my bones in the ache. Come now, let's drink to fresh hearts and apple cheeks and all life up ahead and happiness somewhere for the taking. Yes?'

'Yes!' said both, and drank.

And drinking watched each other merrily or warily, half one, half the other. And the young saw in the old bright pink face, lined as it was, cuffed as it was by circumstantial life, the echo of Tom's face itself peering out through the years. In the old blue eyes, especially, was the sharp bright intelligence that sprang from the old portrait on the wall, that would be young until coins weighted them shut. And around the edges of the old mouth was the smile that blinked and went in Tom's face, and in the old hands was the quick, surprising action of Tom's, as if both old man and young had hands that lived to themselves and did sly things by impulse.

So they drank and leaned and smiled and drank again, each a mirror for the other, each delighting in the fact that an ancient man and a raw youth with the same eyes and hands and blood were met on this raining night, and the whiskey was good.

'Ah, Tom, Tom, it's a loving sight you are!' said the grandfather. 'Dublin's been sore without you these four years. But, hell, I'm dying. No, don't ask me how or why. The doctor has the news, damn him, and shot me between the eyes with it. So I said instead of relatives shelling out their cash to come say good-bye to the old horse, why not make the farewell tour yourself and shake hands and drink drinks. So here I am this night and tomorrow beyond London to see Lucie and then Glasgow to see Dick. I'll stay no more than a day each place, so as not to overload anyone. Now shut that mouth, which is hanging open. I am not out collecting sympathies. I am eighty, and it's time for a damn fine wake, which I have saved money for, so not a word. I have come to see everyone and make sure they are in a fit state of half-graceful joy so I can kick up my heels and fall dead with a good heart, if that's possible. I – '

'Grandfather!' cried Tom, suddenly, and seized the old man's hands and then his shoulders.

'Why, bless you, boy, thanks,' said the old man, seeing the tears in the young man's eyes. 'But just what I find in your gaze is enough.' He set the boy gently back. 'Tell me about London, your work, this place. You, too, Frank, a friend of Tom's is as good as my son's son! Tell everything, Tom!'

'Excuse me,' Frank darted towards the door. 'You both have much to talk about. There's shopping I must do – '

'Wait!'

Frank stopped.

For the old man had really seen the portrait over the fireplace now and walked to it to put out his hand, to squint and read the signed name at the bottom.

'Frank Davis. Is that you, boy? *You* did this picture?'

'Yes, sir,' said Frank, at the door.

'How long ago?'

'Three years ago, I think. Yes, three.'

The old man nodded slowly, as if this information added to the great puzzle, a continuing bafflement.

'Tom, do you know who that *looks* like?'

'Yes, Grand-da. You. A long time ago.'

'So you see it, too, eh? Christ in heaven, yes. That's me on my eighteenth birthday and all Ireland and its grasses and tender maids good for the chewing ahead and not behind me. That's me, that's me. Jesus I was handsome, and Jesus, Tom, so are you. And Jesus, Frank, you *are* uncanny. You are a *fine* artist, boy.'

'You do what you can do.' Frank had come back to the middle of the room, quietly. 'You do what you *know*.'

'And you *know* Tom, to the hair and eyelash.' The old man turned and smiled. 'How does it feel, Tom, to look out of that borrowed face? Do you feel great, is the world your Dublin prawn and oyster?'

Tom laughed. Grandfather laughed. Frank joined them.

'One more drink.' The old man poured. 'And we'll let you slip diplomatically out, Frank. But come back. I must talk with you.'

'What about?' said Frank.

'Ah, the Mysteries. Of Life, of Time, of Existence. What else did *you* have in mind, Frank?'

'Those will do, Grandfather — ' said Frank, and stopped, amazed at the word come out of his mouth. 'I mean, Mr Kelly — '

'Grandfather will do.'

'I must run.' Frank doused his drink. 'Phone you later, Tom.'

The door shut. Frank was gone.

'You'll sleep here tonight of course, Grandpa?' Tom seized

the one valise. 'Frank won't be back. You'll have his bed.' Tom was busy arranging the sheets on one of the two couches against the far wall. 'Now, it's early. Let's drink some more, Grandfather, and talk.'

But the old man, stunned, was silent, eyeing each picture in turn upon the wall. 'Grand painting, that.'

'Frank did them.'

'That's a fine lamp there.'

'Frank made it.'

'The rug on the floor here now − ?'

'Frank.'

'Jesus,' whispered the old man, 'He's a maniac for work, is he not?'

Quietly, he shuffled about the room like one visiting a gallery.

'It seems,' he said, 'the place is absolutely blowing apart with fine artistic talent. You turned your hand to nothing like this, in Dublin.'

'You learn a lot, away from home,' said Tom, uneasily.

The old man shut his eyes and drank his drink.

'Is anything wrong, Grandfather?'

'It will hit me in the middle of the night,' said the old man. 'I will probably stand up in bed with a hell of a yell. But right now it is just a thing in the pit of my stomach and the back of my head. Let's talk, boy, let's talk.'

And they talked and drank until midnight and then the old man got put to bed and Tom went to bed himself and after a long while both slept.

About two in the morning, the old man woke suddenly.

He peered around in the dark, wondering where he was, then saw the paintings, the upholstered chairs, and the lamp and rugs Frank had made, and sat up. He clenched his fists. Then, rising, he threw on his clothes, and staggered towards the door as if fearful that he might not make it before something terrible happened.

When the door slammed, Tom jerked his eyes wide.

Somewhere off in the dark there was a sound of someone calling, shouting, defying the elements, someone at the top of his lungs crying blasphemies, saying God and Jesus and Jesus and God, and finally blows struck, wild blows, as if someone were hitting a wall or a person.

After a long while, his grandfather shuffled back into the room, soaked to the skin.

Weaving, muttering, whispering, the old man peeled off his wet clothes before the fireless fire, then threw a newspaper on the coals, which blazed up briefly to show a face relaxing out of fury into numbness. The old man found and put on Tom's discarded robe. Tom kept his eyes tight as the old man held his hands out towards the dwindling blaze, streaked with blood.

'Damn, damn, damn. *There*!' He poured whiskey and gulped it down. He blinked at Tom and the paintings on the wall and looked at Tom and the flowers in the vases and then drank again. After a long while, Tom pretended to wake up.

'It's after two. You need your rest, Grand-da.'

'I'll rest when I'm done drinking. And *thinking*!'

'Thinking what, Grandpa?'

'Right now,' said the old man, seated in the dim room with the tumbler in his two hands, and the fire gone to ghost on the hearth, 'remembering your dear grandmother in June of the year 1902. And there is the thought of your father born, which is fine, and you born after him, which is fine. And there is the thought of your father dying when you were young and the hard life of your mother and her holding you too close, maybe, in the cold beggar life of flinty Dublin. And me out in the meadows with my working life, and us together only once a month. The being born of people and the going away of people. These turn round in an old man's night. I think of you born, Tom, a happy day. Then I see you here now. That's it.'

The old man grew silent and drank his drink.

'Grand-da,' said Tom, at last, almost like a child crept in for penalties and forgiveness of a sin as yet unnamed, 'do I *worry* you?'

'No.' Then the old man added. 'But what life will *do* with you, how you may be treated, good or ill — I sit up late with *that*.'

The old man sat. The young man lay wide-eyed watching him and later said, as if reading thoughts:

'Grandfather, I *am* happy.'

The old man leaned forward.

'*Are* you, boy?'

'I have never been so happy in my life, sir.'

'Yes?' The old man looked through the dim air of the room, at the young face. 'I see that. But will you *stay* happy, Tom?'

'Does anyone ever *stay* happy, Grandfather? Nothing lasts, *does* it?'

'Shut up! Your grandma and me, *that* lasted!'

'No. It wasn't *all* the same, was it? The first years were one thing, the last years another.'

The old man put his hand over his own mouth and then massaged his face, closing his eyes.

'God, yes, you're right. There are two, no, three, no, four lives, for each of us. Not one of them lasts, it's sure. But the *thought* of them does. And out of the four or five or a dozen lives you live, one is special. I remember, once . . . '

The old man's voice faltered.

The young man said, '*Once*, Grandpa?'

The old man's eyes fixed somewhere to a horizon of the Past. He did not speak to the room or to Tom or to anyone. He didn't even seem to be speaking to himself.

'Oh, it was a long time ago. When I first came in this room tonight, for no reason, strange, the memory was there. I ran back down along the shoreline of Galway to that week . . . '

'What week, when?'

'My twelfth birthday fell that week in summer, think of it! Victoria still queen and me in a turf-hut out by Galway strolling the shore for food to be picked up from the tides, and the weather so sweet you almost turned sad with the taste of it, for you knew it would soon go away.

'And in the middle of the great fair weather along the road by the shore one noon came this tinker's caravan carrying their dark gypsy people to set up camp by the sea.

'There was a mother, a father, and a girl in that caravan, and this boy who came running down by the sea alone, perhaps in need of company, for there I was with nothing to do, and in need of strangers myself.

'Here he came running. And I shall not forget my first sight of him from that day till they drop me in the earth. He –

'Ah God, I'm a failure with words! Stop everything. I must go further back.

'A circus came to Dublin. I visited the sideshows of pinheads and dwarfs and terrible small midgets and fat women and skeleton men. Seeing a crowd about one last exhibit, I thought this must be the most horrible of all. I edged over to look at this final terror! And what did I see? The crowd was drawn to nothing more nor less than: a little girl of some six years, so fair, so beautiful, so cream-white of cheek, so blue of eye, so golden hair, so quiet in her manner that in the midst of this fleshy holocaust she called attention. By saying nothing her shout of beauty stopped the show. All *had* come to her to get well again. For it was a sick menagerie and she the only sweet lovely Doc about to give us back life.

'Well, that girl in the sideshow was as wonderful a surprise as this boy come running down the beach like a young horse.

'He was not dark like his parents.

'His hair was all gold curls and bits of sun. He was cut out of bronze by the light, and what wasn't bronze was copper.

Impossible, but it seemed that this boy of twelve, like myself, had been born on that very day, he looked that new and fresh. And in his face were these bright brown eyes, the eyes of an animal that has run a long way, pursued, along the shorelines of the world.

'He pulled up and the first thing he said to me was laughter. He was glad to be alive, and announced that by the sound he made. I must have laughed in turn for his spirit was catching. He shoved out his brown hand. I hesitated. He gestured impatiently and grabbed my hand.

'My God, after all these years I remember what we said: "Isn't it funny?" he said.

'I didn't ask *what* was funny. I *knew*. He said his name was Jo. I said my name was Tim. And there we were, two boys on the beach and the universe a good rare joke between us.

'He looked at me with his great round full copper eyes, and laughed out his breath and I thought: He has chewed hay! his breath smells of grass; and suddenly I was giddy. The smell stunned me. Jesus God, I thought, reeling, I'm drunk, and *why*? I've nipped Dad's booze, but God, what's *this*? Drunk by noon, hit by the sun, giddy from what? the sweet mash caught in a strange boy's teeth? No, no!

'Then Jo looked straight at me and said, "There isn't much time."

' "Much time?" I asked.

' "Why," said Jo, "for us to be friends. We are, *aren't* we?"

'He breathed the smell of mown fields upon me.

'Jesus God, I wanted to cry. Yes! And almost fell down, but staggered back as if he had hit me a friend's hit. And my mouth opened and shut and I said, "Why is there so little time?"

' "Because," said Jo, "we'll only be here six days, seven at the most, then on down and around Eire. I'll never see you again in my life. So we'll just have to pack a lot of things in a few days, won't we, Tim?"

' "Six days? That's no time at all!" I protested, and wondered why I found myself suddenly destroyed, left destitute on the shore. A thing had not begun, but already I sorrowed after its death.

' "A day here, a week there, a month somewhere else," said Jo. "I must live very quickly, Tim. I have no friends that last. Only what I remember. So, wherever I go, I say to my new friends, quick, do this, do that, let us make many happenings, a long list, so you will remember me when I am gone, and I you, and say: That was a friend. So, let's begin. There!"

'And Jo tagged me and ran.

'I ran after him, laughing, for wasn't it silly, me headlong after a stranger boy unknown five minutes before? We must've run a mile down that long summer beach before he let me catch him. I thought I might pummel him for making me run so far for nothing, for something, for God knows what! But when we tumbled to earth and I pinned him down, all he did was spring his breath in one gasp up at me, one breath, and I leaped back and shook my head and sat staring at him, as if I'd plunged wet hands in an open electric socket. He laughed to see me fall away, to see me scurry and sit in wonder. "Oh, Tim," he said, "we *shall* be friends."

'You know the dread long cold weather, most months, of Ireland? Well, this week of my twelfth birthday, it was summer each day and every day for the seven days named by Jo as the limit which would be no more days. We walked the shore, and that's all there was, the simple thing of us upon the shore, and building castles or climbing hills to fight wars among the mounds. We found an old round tower and yelled up and down it. But mostly it was walking, our arms about each other like twins born in a tangle, never cut free by knife or lightning. I inhaled, he exhaled. Then he breathed and I was the sweet chorus. We talked, far through the nights on the sand, until our parents came seeking the lost who had found they knew not what. Lured home. I slept beside him, or him me, and talked and laughed, Jesus, laughed, till dawn. Then out again we roared until the earth swung up to hit our backs. We found ourselves laid out with sweet hilarity, eyes tight, gripped to each other's shaking, and the laugh jumped free like one silver trout following another. God, I bathed in his laughter and he bathed in mine, until we were as weak as if love had put us to the slaughter and exhaustions. We panted like pups in hot summer, empty of laughing, and sleepy with friendship. And the weather for that week was blue and gold, no clouds, no rain, and a wind that smelled of apples, but no, only that boy's wild breath.

'It crossed my mind, long after, if ever an old man could bathe again in that summer fount, the wild spout of breathing that sprang from his nostrils and gasped from his mouth, why one might peel off a score of years, one would be young, how might the flesh resist?

'But the laughter is gone and the boy gone into a man lost somewhere in the world, and here I am two lifetimes later, speaking of it for the first time. For who was there to tell? From my twelfth birthday week, and the gift of friendship to this, who might I tell of that shore and that summer and the two of us walking all tangled in our arms and lives and life as perfect as the letter *o*, a damned great circle of rare weather, lovely talk, and us certain we'd live forever, never die, and be good friends.

'And at the end of the week, he left.

'He was wise for his years. He didn't say good-bye. All of a sudden, the tinker's cart was gone.

'I shouted along the shore. A long way off, I saw the caravan go over a hill. But then his wisdom spoke to me. Don't catch. Let go. Weep now, my own wisdom said. And I wept.

'I wept for three days and on the fourth grew very still. I

did not go down to the shore again for many months. And in all the years that have passed, never have I known such a thing again. I have had a good life, a fine wife, good children, and you, boy, Tom, you. But as sure as I sit here, never after that was I so agonized, mad, and crazy wild. Never did drink make me as drunk. Never did I cry so hard again. Why, Tom? Why do I say this, and what was it? Back so far in innocence, back in the time when I had nobody, and knew nothing. How is it I remember him when all else slips away? When often I cannot remember your dear grandmother's face, God forgive me, why does his face come back on the shore by the sea? Why do I see us fall again and the earth reach up to take the wild young horses driven mad by too much sweet grass in a line of days that never end?'

The old man grew silent. After a moment, he added, 'The better part of wisdom, they say, is what's left unsaid. I'll say no more. I don't even know why I've said all *this*.'

Tom lay in the dark. '*I* know.'

'Do you, lad?' asked the old man. 'Well, tell me. Someday.'

'Someday,' said Tom. 'I will.'

They listened to the rain touch at the windows.

'Are you happy, Tom?'

'You asked that before, sir.'

'I ask again. Are you happy?'

'Yes.'

Silence.

'Is it summertime on the shore, Tom? Is it the magic seven days? Are you drunk?'

Tom did not answer for a long while, and then said nothing but, 'Grand-da,' and then moved his head once in a nod.

The old man lay back in the chair. He might have said, This will pass. He might have said, It will not last. He might have said many things. Instead he said, 'Tom?'

'Sir?'

'Ah Jesus!' shouted the old man suddenly. 'Christ, God Almighty! Damn it to hell!' Then the old man stopped and his breathing grew quiet. 'There. It's a maniac night. I had to let out one last yell. I just had to, boy.'

And at last they slept, with the rain falling fast.

With the first light of dawn, the old man dressed with careful quietness, picked up his valise, and bent to touch the sleeping young man's cheek with the palm of one hand.

'Tom, good-bye,' he whispered.

Moving down the dim stairwell towards the steadily beating rain, he found Tom's friend waiting at the foot of the stairs.

'Frank! You haven't been down here *all night*?'

'No, no, Mr Kelly,' said Frank, quickly. 'I stayed at a friend's.'

The old man turned to look up the dark stairwell as if he could see the room and Tom in it warm asleep.

'Gah . . . !' Something almost a growl stirred in his throat and subsided. He shifted uneasily and looked back down at the dawn kindled on this young man's face, this one who had painted a picture that hung above the fireplace in the room above.

'The damn night is over,' said the old man. 'So if you'll just stand aside —'

'Sir.'

The old man took one step down and burst out:

'Listen! If you hurt Tom, in any way ever, why, Jesus, I'll break you across my knee! You *hear*?'

Frank held out his hand. 'Don't worry.'

The old man looked at the hand as if he had never seen one before. He sighed.

'Ah, damn it to hell, Frank, Tom's friend, so young you're destruction to the eyes. Get away!'

They shook hands.

'Jesus, that's a hard grip,' said the old man, surprised.

Then he was gone, as if the rain had hustled him off in its own multitudinous running.

The young man shut the upstairs door and stood for a moment looking at the figure on the bed and at last went over and as if by instinct put his hand down to the exact same spot where the old man had printed his hand in farewell not five minutes before. He touched the summer cheek.

In his sleep, Tom smiled the smile of his father's father, and called the old man, deep in a dream, by name.

He called him twice.

And then he slept quietly.

Interval in Sunlight

They moved into the Hotel de Las Flores on a hot green afternoon in late October. The inner patio was blazing with red and yellow and white flowers, like flames, which lit their small room. The husband was tall and black-haired and pale and looked as if he had driven ten thousand miles in his sleep; he walked through the tile patio, carrying a few blankets, he threw himself on the small bed of the small room with an exhausted sigh and lay there. While he closed his eyes, his wife, about twenty-four, with yellow hair and horn-rimmed glasses, smiling at the manager, Mr Gonzales, hurried in and out from the room to the car. First she carried two suitcases, then a typewriter, thanking Mr Gonzales, but steadily refusing his help. And then she carried in a huge packet of Mexican masks they had picked up in the lake town of Pátzcuaro, and then out to the car again and again for more small cases and packages, and even an extra tyre which they were afraid some native might roll off down the cobbled street during the night. Her face pink from the exertion, she hummed as she locked the car, checked the windows, and ran back to the room where her husband lay, eyes closed, on one of the twin beds.

'Good God,' he said, without opening his eyes, 'this is one hell of a bed. Feel it. I told you to pick one with a Simmons mattress.' He gave the bed a weary slap. 'It's as hard as rock.'

'I don't speak Spanish,' said the wife, standing there, beginning to look bewildered. 'You should have come in and talked to the landlord yourself.'

'Look,' he said, opening his grey eyes just a little and

turning his head. 'I've done all the driving on this trip. You just sit there and look at the scenery. You're supposed to handle the money, the lodgings, the gas and oil, and all that. This is the second place we've hit where you got hard beds.'

'I'm sorry,' she said, still standing, beginning to fidget.

'I like to at least sleep nights, that's all I ask.'

'I said I was sorry.'

'Didn't you even *feel* the beds?'

'They looked all right.'

'You've got to feel them.' He slapped the bed and punched it at his side.

The woman turned to her own bed and sat on it, experimentally. 'It feels all right to me.'

'Well, it isn't.'

'Maybe my bed is softer.'

He rolled over tiredly and reached out to punch the other bed. 'You can have this one if you want,' she said, trying to smile.

'That's hard, too,' he said, sighing, and fell back and closed his eyes again.

No one spoke, but the room was turning cold, while outside the flowers blazed in the green shrubs and the sky was immensely blue. Finally, she rose and grabbed the typewriter and suitcase and turned towards the door.

'Where're you going?' he said.

'Back out to the car,' she said. 'We're going to find another place.'

'Put it down,' said the man. 'I'm tired.'

'We'll find another place.'

'Sit down, we'll stay here tonight, my God, and move tomorrow.'

She looked at all the boxes and crates and luggage, the clothes, and the tyre, her eyes flickering. She put the typewriter down.

'Damn it!' she cried, suddenly. 'You can have the mattress

off my bed. I'll sleep on the springs.'

He said nothing.

'You can have the mattress off my bed,' she said. 'Only don't talk about it. Here!' She pulled the blanket off and yanked at the mattress.

'That might be better,' he said, opening his eyes, seriously.

'You can have both mattresses, my God, I can sleep on a bed of nails!' she cried. 'Only stop yapping.'

'I'll manage.' He turned his head away. 'It wouldn't be fair to you.'

'It'd be plenty fair just for you to keep quiet about the bed; it's not that hard, good God, you'll sleep if you're tired. Jesus God, Joseph!'

'Keep your voice down,' said Joseph. 'Why don't you go find out about Parícutin volcano?'

'I'll go in a minute.' She stood there, her face red.

'Find out what the rates are for a taxi out there and a horse up the mountain to see it, and look at the sky; if the sky's blue that means the volcano isn't erupting today, and don't let them gyp you.'

'I guess I can do that.'

She opened the door and stepped out and shut the door and *Señor* Gonzales was there. Was everything all right? he wished to know.

She walked past the town windows, and smelled the soft charcoal air. Beyond the town all of the sky was blue except north (or east or west, she couldn't be certain) where the huge broiling black cloud rose up from the terrible volcano. She looked at it with a small tremoring inside. Then she sought out a large taxi driver and the arguments began. The price started at sixty pesos and dwindled rapidly, with expressions of mournful defeat upon the buck-toothed fat man's face, to thirty-seven pesos. So! He was to come at three tomorrow

afternoon, did he understand? That would give them time to
drive out through the grey snows of land where the flaking
lava ash had fallen to make a great dusty winter for mile after
mile, and arrive at the volcano as the sun was setting. Was
this very clear?

'*Sí, señora, ésta es muy claro, sí!*'

'*Bueno.*' She gave him their hotel room number and bade
him good-bye.

She idled into little lacquer shops, alone; she opened the
little lacquer boxes and sniffed the sharp scent of camphor
wood and cedar and cinnamon. She watched the craftsmen,
enchanted, razor blades flashing in the sun, cutting the
flowery scrolls and filling these patterns with red and blue
colour. The town flowed about her like a silent slow river and
she immersed herself in it, smiling all of the time, and not
even knowing she smiled.

Suddenly she looked at her watch. She'd been gone half an
hour. A look of panic crossed her face. She ran a few steps
and then slowed to a walk again, shrugging.

As she walked in through the tiled cool corridors, under
the silvery tin candelabra on the adobe walls, a caged bird
fluted high and sweet, and a girl with long soft dark hair sat at
a piano painted sky blue and played a Chopin nocturne.

She looked at the windows of their rooms, the shades
pulled down. Three o'clock of a fresh afternoon. She saw a
soft-drinks box at the end of the patio and bought four bottles
of Coke. Smiling, she opened the door to their room.

'It certainly took you long enough,' he said, turned on his
side towards the wall.

'We leave tomorrow afternoon at three,' she said.

'How much?'

She smiled at his back, the bottles cold in her arms. 'Only
thirty-seven pesos.'

'Twenty pesos would have done it. You can't let these

Mexicans take advantage of you.'

'I'm richer than they are; if anyone *deserves* being taken advantage of, it's us.'

'That's not the idea. They *like* to bargain.'

'I feel like a bitch, doing it.'

'The guide book says they double their price and expect you to halve it.'

'Let's not quibble over a dollar.'

'A dollar is a dollar.'

'I'll pay the dollar from my own money,' she said. 'I brought some cold drinks – do you want one?'

'What've you got?' He sat up in bed.

'Cokes.'

'Well, you know I don't like Cokes much; take two of those back, will you, and get some Orange Crush?'

'Please?' she said, standing there.

'Please,' he said, looking at her. 'Is the volcano active?'

'Yes.'

'Did you ask?'

'No, I looked at the sky. Plenty of smoke.'

'You should have asked.'

'The damn sky is just exploding with it.'

'But how do we know it's good tomorrow?'

'We don't know. If it's not, we put it off.'

'I guess that's right.' He lay down again.

She brought back two bottles of Orange Crush.

'It's not very cold,' he said, drinking it.

They had supper in the patio: sizzling steak, green peas, a plate of Spanish rice, a little wine, and spiced peaches for dessert.

As he napkined his mouth, he said, casually, 'Oh, I meant to tell you. I've checked our figures on what I owe you for the last six days, from Mexico City to here. You say I owe you one hundred and twenty-five pesos, or about twenty-five American dollars, right?'

'Yes.'

'I make it I owe you only twenty-two.'

'I don't think that's possible,' she said, still working on her spiced peaches with a spoon.

'I added the figures twice.'

'So did I.'

'I think you added them wrong.'

'Perhaps I did.' She jarred the chair back suddenly. 'Let's go check.'

In the room, the notebook lay open under the lighted lamp. They checked the figures together. 'You see,' said he, quietly. 'You're three dollars off. How did that happen?'

'It just happened. I'm sorry.'

'You're one hell of a bookkeeper.'

'I do my best.'

'Which isn't very good. I thought you could take a little responsibility.'

'I try damned hard.'

'You forgot to check the air in the tyres, you get hard beds, you lose things, you lost a key in Acapulco, to the car trunk, you lost the air-pressure gauge, and you can't keep books. I have to drive — '

'I know, I know, you have to drive all day, and you're tired, and you just got over a strep infection in Mexico City, and you're afraid it'll come back and you want to take it easy on your heart, and the least I could do is to keep my nose clean and the arithmetic neat. I know it all by heart. I'm only a writer, and I admit I've got big feet.'

'You won't make a very good writer this way,' he said. 'It's such a simple thing, addition.'

'I didn't do it on purpose!' she cried, throwing the pencil down. 'Hell! I wish I *had* cheated you now. I wish I'd done a lot of things now. I wish I'd lost that air-pressure gauge on purpose, I'd have some pleasure in thinking about it and knowing I did it to spite you, anyway. I wish I'd picked these beds for their hard mattresses, then I could laugh in my sleep tonight, thinking how hard they are for you to sleep on, I wish I'd done *that* on purpose. And now I wish I'd thought to fix the books. I could enjoy laughing about that, too.'

'Keep your voice down,' he said, as to a child.

'I'll be God damned if I'll keep my voice down.'

'All I want to know now is how much money you have in the kitty.'

She put her trembling hands in the purse and brought out all the money. When he counted it, there was five dollars missing.

'Not only do you keep poor books, overcharging me on some item or other, but now there's five dollars gone from the kitty,' he said. 'Where'd it go?'

'I don't know. I must have forgotten to put it down, or if I did, I didn't say what for. Good God, I don't want to add this damned list again. I'll pay what's missing out of my own allowance to keep everyone happy. Here's five dollars! Now let's get out for some air, it's hot in here.'

She jerked the door wide and she trembled with a rage all out of proportion to the facts. She was hot and shaking and stiff and she knew her face was very red and her eyes bright, and when *Señor* Gonzales bowed to them and wished them a good evening, she had to smile stiffly in return.

'Here,' said her husband, handing her the room key. 'And don't, for God's sake, lose it.'

The band was playing in the green *zócalo*. It hooted and blared and tooted and screamed up on the bronze-scrolled bandstand. The square was bloomed full with people and colour, men and boys walking one way around the block, on the pink and blue tiles, women and girls walking the other way, flirting their dark olive eyes at one another, men holding each other's elbows and talking earnestly between meetings, women and girls twined like ropes of flowers, sweetly scented, blowing in a summer night wind over the cooling tile designs, whispering, past the vendors of cold drinks and tamales and enchiladas. The band precipitated 'Yankee Doodle' once, to the delight of the blonde woman in the horn-rimmed glasses, who smiled wildly and turned to her husband. Then the band hooted 'La Cumparsita' and 'La Paloma Azul', and she felt a good warmth and began to sing a little, under her breath.

'Don't act like a tourist,' said her husband.

'I'm just enjoying myself.'

'Don't be a damn fool, is all I ask.'

A vendor of silver trinkets shuffled by, '*Señor?*'

Joseph looked them over, while the band played, and held up one bracelet, very intricate, very exquisite. 'How much?'

'*Veinte pesos señor.*'

'Ho ho,' said the husband, smiling. 'I'll give you five for it,' in Spanish.

'Five,' replied the man in Spanish. 'I would starve.'

'Don't bargain with him,' said the wife.

'Keep out of this,' said the husband, smiling. To the vendor, 'Five pesos, *señor.*'

'No, no, I would lose money. My last price is ten pesos.'

'Perhaps I could give you six,' said the husband. 'No more than that.'

The vendor hesitated in a kind of numbed panic as the husband tossed the bracelet back on the red velvet tray and turned away. 'I am no longer interested. Good night.'

'*Señor!* Six pesos, it is yours!'

The husband laughed. 'Give him six pesos, darling.'

She stiffly drew forth her wallet and gave the vendor some peso bills. The man went away. 'I hope you're satisfied,' she said.

'Satisfied?' Smiling, he flipped the bracelet in the palm of his pale hand. 'For a dollar and twenty-five cents I buy a bracelet that sells for thirty dollars in the States!'

'I have something to confess,' she said. 'I gave that man ten pesos.'

'What!' The husband stopped laughing.

'I put a five-peso note in with those one-peso bills. Don't worry, I'll take it out of my own money. It won't go on the bill I present to you at the end of the week.'

He said nothing, but dropped the bracelet in his pocket. He looked at the band thundering into the last of 'Ay, Jalisco'. Then he said, 'You're a fool. You'd let these people take all your money.'

It was her turn to step away a bit and not reply. She felt rather good. She listened to the music.

'I'm going back to my room,' he said. 'I'm tired.'

'We only drove a hundred miles from Pátzcuaro.'

'My throat is a little raw again. Come on.'

They moved away from the music and the walking, whispering, laughing people. The band played the 'Toreador Song'. The drums thumped like great dull hearts in the summery night. There was a smell of papaya in the air, and green thicknesses of jungle and hidden waters.

'I'll walk you back to the room and come back myself,' she said. 'I want to hear the music.'

'Don't be naïve.'

'I like it, damn it, I like it, it's good music. It's not fake, it's real, or as real as anything ever gets in this world, that's why I like it.'

'When I don't feel well, I don't expect to have you out running around the town alone. It isn't fair you see things I don't.'

They turned in at the hotel and the music was still fairly loud. 'If you want to walk by yourself, go off on a trip by yourself and go back to the United States by yourself,' he said. 'Where's the key?'

'Maybe I lost it.'

They let themselves into the room and undressed. He sat on the edge of the bed looking into the night patio. At last he shook his head, rubbed his eyes, and sighed. 'I'm tired. I've been terrible today.' He looked at her where she sat, next to him, and he put out his hand to take her arm. 'I'm sorry. I get all riled up, driving, and then us not talking the language too well. By evening I'm a mess of nerves.'

'Yes,' she said.

Quite suddenly he moved over beside her. He took hold of her and held her tightly, his head over her shoulder, eyes shut, talking into her ear with a quiet, whispering fervency. 'You know, we *must* stay together. There's only us, really, no matter what happens, no matter what trouble we have. I do love you so much, you know that. Forgive me if I'm difficult. We've got to make it go.'

She stared over his shoulder at the blank wall and the wall was like her life in this moment, a wide expanse of nothingness with hardly a bump, a contour, or a feeling to it. She didn't know what to say or do. Another time, she would have melted. But there was such a thing as firing metal too often, bringing it to a glow, shaping it. At last the metal refuses to glow or shape; it is nothing but a weight. She was a weight now, moving mechanically in his arms, hearing but not hearing, understanding but not understanding, replying but not replying. 'Yes, we'll stay together.' She felt her lips move. 'We love each other.' The lips said what they must say, while her mind was in her eyes and her eyes bored deep into the vacuum of the wall. 'Yes.' Holding but not holding him. 'Yes.'

The room was dim. Outside, someone walked in a corridor, perhaps glancing at this locked door, perhaps hearing their vital whispering as no more than something falling drop by drop from a loose faucet, a running drain perhaps, or a turned book-leaf under a solitary bulb. Let the doors whisper, the people of the world walked down tile corridors and did not hear.

'Only you and I know the things.' His breath was fresh. She felt very sorry for him and herself and the world, suddenly. Everyone was infernally alone. He was like a man clawing at a statue. She did not feel herself move. Only her mind, which was a lightless, dim fluorescent vapour, shifted. 'Only you and I remember,' he said, 'and if one of us should leave, then half the memories are gone. So we must stay together because if one forgets the other remembers.'

Remember what? she asked herself. But she remembered instantly, in a linked series, those parts of incidents in their life together that perhaps he might not recall: the night at the beach, five years ago, one of the first fine nights beneath the canvas with the secret touchings, the days at Sunland sprawled together, taking the sun until twilight. Wandering in an abandoned silver mine, oh, a million things, one touched on and revealed another in an instant!

He held her tight back against the bed now. 'Do you know how lonely I am? Do you know how lonely I make myself with these arguments and fights and all of it, when I'm tired?' He waited for her to answer, but she said nothing. She felt his eyelid flutter on her neck. Faintly, she remembered when he had first flicked his eyelid near her ear. 'Spider-eye,' she had said, laughing, then. 'It feels like a small spider in my ear.' And now this small lost spider climbed with insane humour upon her neck. There was something in his voice which made her feel she was a woman on a train going away and he was standing in the station saying, 'Don't go.' And her appalled voice silently cried, 'But *you're* the one on a train! *I'm* not going *anywhere*!'

She lay back, bewildered. It was the first time in two weeks he had touched her. And the touching had such an immediacy that she knew the wrong word would send him very far away again.

She lay and said nothing.

Finally, after a long while, she heard him get up, sighing, and move off. He got into his own bed and drew the covers up, silently. She moved at last, arranged herself on her bed, and lay listening to her watch tick in the small hot darkness. 'My God,' she whispered, finally, 'it's only eight-thirty.'

'Go to sleep,' he said.

She lay in the dark, perspiring, naked, on her own bed, and in the distance, sweetly, faintly, so that it made her soul and heart ache to hear it, she heard the band thumping and brassing out its melodies. She wanted to walk among the dark moving people and sing with them and smell the soft charcoal air of October in a small summery town deep in the tropics of Mexico, a million miles lost from civilization, listening to the good music, tapping her foot and humming. But now she lay with her eyes wide, in bed. In the next hour, the band played 'La Golondrina', 'Marimba', 'Los Viejitos', 'Michoacán la Verde', 'Barcarolle', and 'Luna Lunera'.

At three in the morning she awoke for no reason and lay, her sleep done and finished with, feeling the coolness that came with deep night. She listened to his breathing and she felt away and separate from the world. She thought of the long trip from Los Angeles to Laredo, Texas, like a silver-white boiling nightmare. And then the green technicolour, red and yellow and blue and purple, dream of Mexico arising like a flood about them to engulf their car with colour and smell of rain forest and deserted towns. She thought of all the small towns, the shops, the walking people, the burros, and all the arguments and near-fights. She thought of the five years she had been married. A long, long time. There had been no day in all that time that they had not seen each other; there had been no day when she had seen friends, separately; *he* was always there to see and criticize. There had been no day when she was allowed to be gone for more than an hour or so without full explanation. Sometimes, feeling infinitely evil, she would sneak to a midnight show, telling no one, and sit, feeling free, breathing deeply of the air of freedom, watching the people, far realer than she, upon the screen, motioning and moving.

And now here they were, after five years. She looked over at his sleeping form. One thousand eight hundred and twenty-five days with you, she thought, my husband. A few hours each day at my typewriter, and then all the rest of each day and night with you. I feel quite like that man walled up in a vault in 'The Cask of Amontillado'. I scream but no one hears.

There was a shift of footsteps outside, a knock on their door. '*Señor*,' called a soft voice, in Spanish. 'It is three o'clock.'

Oh, my God, thought the wife. 'Sh!' she hissed, leaping up to the door. But her husband was awake. 'What *is* it?' he cried.

She opened the door the slightest crack. 'You've come at the wrong time,' she said to the man in the darkness.

'Three o'clock, *señora*.'

'No, no,' she hissed, her face wrenching with the agony of the moment. 'I meant tomorrow afternoon.'

'What is it?' demanded her husband, switching on a light. 'Christ, it's only three in the morning. What does the fool want?'

She turned, shutting her eyes. 'He's here to take us to Parícutin.'

'My God, you can't speak Spanish at all!'

'Go away,' she said to the guide.

'But I arose for this hour,' said the guide.

The husband swore and got up. 'I won't be able to sleep now, anyway. Tell the idiot we'll be dressed in ten minutes and go with him and get it over, my God!'

She did this and the guide slipped away into the darkness and out into the street where the cool moon burnished the fenders of his taxi.

'You *are* incompetent,' snapped the husband, pulling on two pairs of pants, two T-shirts, a sports shirt, and a wool shirt over that. 'Jesus, this'll fix my throat, all right. If I come down with another strep infection — '

'Get back into bed, damn you.'

'I couldn't sleep now, anyway.'

'Well, we've had six hours' sleep already, and you had at least three hours' this afternoon: that should be enough.'

'Spoiling our trip,' he said, putting on two sweaters and two pairs of socks. 'It's cold up there on the mountain; dress warm, hurry up.' He put on a jacket and a muffler and looked enormous in the heap of clothing he wore. 'Get me my pills. Where's some water?'

'Get back to bed,' she said. 'I won't have you sick and whining.' She found his medicine and poured some water.

'The least thing you could do was get the hour right.'

'Shut up!' She held the glass.

'Just another of your thick-headed blunders.'

She threw the water in his face. 'Let me alone, damn you, let me alone. I didn't mean to do that!'

'You!' he shouted, face dripping. He ripped off his jacket. 'You'll chill me, I'll catch cold!'

'I don't give a damn, let me alone!' She raised her hands into fists, and her face was terrible and red, and she looked like some animal in a maze who has steadily sought exit from an impossible chaos and has been constantly fooled, turned back, rerouted, led on, tempted, whispered to, lied to, led further, and at last reached a blank wall.

'Put your hands down!' he shouted.

'I'll kill you, by God, I'll kill you!' she screamed, her face contorted and ugly. 'Leave me alone! I've tried my damnedest — beds, language, time, my God, the mistakes, you think I don't *know* it? You think I'm not *sorry*?'

'I'll catch cold, I'll catch cold.' He was staring at the wet floor. He sat down with water on his face.

'Here. Wipe your face off!' She flung him a towel.

He began to shake violently. 'I'm cold!'

'Get a chill, damn it, and die, but leave me alone!'

'I'm cold, I'm cold.' His teeth chattered, he wiped his face with trembling hands. 'I'll have another infection.'

'Take off that coat! It's wet.'

He stopped shaking after a minute and stood up to take off the soggy coat. She handed him a leather jacket. 'Come on, he's waiting for us.'

He began to shiver again. 'I'm not going anywhere, to hell with you,' he said, sitting down. 'You owe me fifty dollars now.'

'What for?'

'You remember, you promised.'

And she remembered. They had had a fight about some silly thing, in California, the first day of the trip, yes, by God, the very first day out. And she for the first time in her life had lifted her hand to slap him. Then, appalled, she had dropped her hand, staring at her traitorous fingers. 'You were going to slap me!' he had cried. 'Yes,' she replied. 'Well,' he said quietly, 'the next time you do a thing like that, you'll hand over fifty dollars of your money.' That's how life was, full of little tributes and ransoms and blackmails. She paid for all her errors, unmotivated or not. A dollar here, a dollar there. If she spoiled an evening, she paid the dinner bill from her clothing money. If she criticized a play they had just seen and he had liked it, he flew into a rage, and, to quieten him, she paid for the theatre tickets. On and on it had gone, swifter and swifter over the years. If they bought a book together and she didn't like it but he did and she dared speak out, there was a fight, sometimes a small thing which grew for days, and ended with her buying the book plus another and perhaps a set of cuff links or some other silly thing to calm the storm. Jesus!

'Fifty dollars. You promised if you acted up again with these tantrums and slappings.'

'It was only water. I didn't hit you. All right, shut up, I'll pay the money, I'll pay anything just to be let alone; it's worth it, and five hundred dollars more, more than worth it. I'll pay.'

She turned away. When you're sick for a number of years, when you're an *only* child, the *only* boy, all of your life, you get the way he is, she thought. Then you find yourself thirty-five years old and still undecided as to what you're to be – a ceramist, a social worker, a businessman. And your wife has always known what she would be – a writer. And it must be maddening to live with a woman with a single knowledge of herself, so sure of what she would do with her writing. And selling stories, at last, not many, no, but just enough to cause the seams of the marriage to rip. And so how natural that he must convince her that she was wrong and he was right, that she was an uncontrollable child and must forfeit money. Money was to be the weapon he held over her. When she had been a fool she would give up some of the precious gain – the product of her writing.

'Do you know,' she said, suddenly, aloud, 'since I made that big sale to the magazine, you seem to pick more fights and I seem to pay more money?'

'What do you mean by that?' he said.

It seemed to her to be true. Since the big sale he had put his special logic to work on situations, a logic of such a sort that she had no way to combat it. Reasoning with him was impossible. You were finally cornered, your explanations exhausted, your alibis depleted, your pride in tatters. So you struck out. You slapped at him or broke something, and then, there you were again, paying off, and he had won. And he was taking your success away from you, your single purpose, or he thought he was, anyway. But strangely enough, though she had never told him, she didn't care about forfeiting the money. If it made peace, if it made him happy, if it made him think he was causing her to suffer, that was all right. He had exaggerated ideas as to the value of money; it hurt him to lose it or spend it, therefore he thought it would hurt her as much. But I'm feeling no pain, she thought, I'd like to give him all of the money, for that's not why I write at all, I write to say what I have to say, and he doesn't understand that.

He was quieted. 'You'll pay?'

'Yes.' She was dressing quickly now, in slacks and jacket. 'In fact, I've been meaning to bring this up for some time. I'm giving all the money to you from now on. There's no need of my keeping my profits separate from yours, as it has been. I'll turn it over to you tomorrow.'

'I don't ask that,' he said, quickly.

'I insist. It all goes to you.'

What I'm doing, of course, is unloading your gun, she thought. Taking your weapon away from you. Now you won't be able to extract the money from me, piece by piece, bit by painful bit. You'll have to find another way to bother me.

'I — ' he said.

'No, let's not talk about it. It's yours.'

'It's only to teach you a lesson. You've a bad temper,' he said. 'I thought you'd control it if you had to forfeit something.'

'Oh, I just *live* for money,' she said.

'I don't want all of it.'

'Come on now.' She was weary. She opened the door and listened. The neighbours hadn't heard, or if they had, they paid no attention. The lights of the waiting taxi illuminated the front patio.

They walked out through the cool moonlit night. She walked ahead of him for the first time in years.

Parícutin was a river of gold that night. A distant murmuring river of molten ore going down to some dead lava sea,

to some volcanic black shore. Time and again if you held your
breath, stilled your heart within you, you could hear the lava
pushing rocks down the mountain in tumblings and roarings,
faintly, faintly. Above the crater were red vapours and red
light. Gentle brown and grey clouds arose suddenly as coro-
nets or halos or puffs from the interior, their undersides
washed in pink, their tops dark and ominous, without a
sound.

The husband and the wife stood on the opposite mountain,
in the sharp cold, the horses behind them. In a wooden hut
nearby, the scientific observers were lighting oil lamps, cooking their evening meal, boiling rich coffee, talking in
whispers because of the clear, night-explosive air. It was very
far away from everything else in the world.

On the way up the mountain, after the long taxi drive from
Uruapan, over moon-dreaming hills of ashen snow, through
dry stick villages, under the cold clear stars, jounced in the
taxi like dice in a gambling-tumbler, both of them had tried
to make a better thing of it. They had arrived at a campfire on
a sort of sea bottom. About the campfire were solemn men
and small dark boys, and a company of seven other Ameri-
cans, all men, in riding breeches, talking in loud voices under
the soundless sky. The horses were brought forth and
mounted. They proceeded across the lava river. She talked to
the other Yankees and they responded. They joked together.
After a while of this, the husband rode on ahead.

Now, they stood together, watching the lava wash down
the dark cone summit.

He wouldn't speak.

'What's wrong now?' she asked.

He looked straight ahead, the lava glow reflected in his
eyes. 'You could have ridden with me. I thought we came to
Mexico to see things together. And now you talk to those
damned Texans.'

'I felt lonely. We haven't seen any people from the States

for eight weeks. I like the days in Mexico, but I don't like the nights. I just wanted someone to talk to.'

'You wanted to tell them you're a writer.'

'That's unfair.'

'You're always telling people you're a writer, and how good you are, and you've just sold a story to a large-circulation magazine and that's how you got the money to come here to Mexico.'

'One of them asked me what I did, and I told him. Damn right I'm proud of my work. I've waited ten years to sell some damn thing.'

He studied her in the light from the fire mountain and at last he said, 'You know, before coming up here tonight, I thought about that damned typewriter of yours and almost tossed it into the river.'

'You didn't!'

'No, but I locked it in the car. I'm tired of it and the way you've ruined the whole trip. You're not with me, you're with yourself, you're the one who counts, you and that damned machine, you and Mexico, and your reactions, you and your inspiration, you and your nervous sensitivity, and you and your aloneness. I knew you'd act this way tonight, just as sure as there was a First Coming! I'm tired of your running back from every excursion we make to sit at that machine and bang away at all hours. This is a vacation.'

'I haven't touched the typewriter in a week, because it bothered you.'

'Well, don't touch it for another week or a month, don't touch it until we get home. Your damned inspiration can wait!'

I should never have said I'd give him all the money, she thought. I should never have taken that weapon from him, it kept him away from my real life, the writing and the machine. And now I've thrown off the protective cloak of money and he's searched for a new weapon and he's got to the true thing — to the *machine*! Oh Christ!

Suddenly, without thinking, with the rage in her again, she pushed him ahead of her. She didn't do it violently. She just gave him a push. Once, twice, three times. She didn't hurt him. It was just a gesture of pushing away. She wanted to strike him, throw him off a cliff, perhaps, but instead she gave these three pushes, to indicate her hostility and the end of talking. Then they stood separately, while behind them the horses moved their hoofs softly, and the night air grew colder and their breath hissed in white plumes on the air, and in the scientists' cabin the coffee bubbled on the blue gas jet and the rich fumes permeated the moonlit heights.

After an hour, as the first dim furnacings of the sun came in the cold East, they mounted their horses for the trip down through growing light, towards the buried city and the buried church under the lava flow. Crossing the flow, she thought. Why doesn't his horse fall, why isn't he thrown on to those jagged lava rocks, why? But nothing happened. They rode on. The sun rose red.

They slept until one in the afternoon. She was dressed and sitting on the bed waiting for him to waken for half an hour before he stirred and rolled over, needing a shave, very pale with tiredness.

'I've got a sore throat,' was the first thing he said.

She didn't speak.

'You shouldn't have thrown water on me,' he said.

She got up and walked to the door and put her hand on the knob.

'I want you to stay here,' he said. 'We're going to stay here in Uruapan three or four more days.'

At last she said, 'I thought we were going on to Guadalajara.'

'Don't be a tourist. You ruined that trip to the volcano for us. I want to go back up tomorrow or the next day. Go look at the sky.'

She went out to look at the sky. It was clear and blue. She reported this. 'The volcano dies down, sometimes for a week. We can't afford to wait a week for it to boom again.'

'Yes, we can. We will. And you'll pay for the taxi to take us up there and do the trip over and do it right and enjoy it.'

'Do you think we can ever enjoy it now?' she asked.

'If it's the last thing we do, we'll enjoy it.'

'You insist, do you?'

'We'll wait until the sky is full of smoke and go back up.'

'I'm going out to buy a paper.' She shut the door and walked into the town.

She walked down the fresh-washed streets and looked in the shining windows and smelled that amazingly clear air and felt very good, except for the tremoring, the continual tremoring in her stomach. At last, with a hollowness roaring in her chest, she went to a man standing beside a taxi.

'*Señor*,' she said.

'Yes?' said the man.

She felt her heart stop beating. Then it began to thump again and she went on: 'How much would you charge to drive me to Morelia?'

'Ninety pesos, *señora*.'

'And can I get the train in Morelia?'

'There is a train *here*, *señora*.'

'Yes, but there are reasons why I didn't want to *wait* for it here.'

'I will drive you, then, to Morelia.'

'Come along, there are a few things I must do.'

The taxi was left in front of the Hotel de Las Flores. She walked in, alone, and once more looked at the lovely garden with its many flowers, and listened to the girl playing the strange blue-coloured piano, and this time the song was the

'Moonlight Sonata'. She smelled the sharp crystalline air and
shook her head, eyes closed, hands at her sides. She put her
hand to the door, opened it softly.

Why today? she wondered. Why not some other day in the
last five years? Why have I waited, why have I hung around?
Because. A thousand becauses. Because you always hoped
things would start again the way they were the first year.
Because there were times, less frequent now, when he was
splendid for days, even weeks, when you were both feeling
well and the world was green and bright blue. There were
times, like yesterday, for a moment, when he opened the
armour-plate and showed her the fear beneath it and the
small loneliness of himself and said, 'I need and love you,
don't ever go away. I'm afraid without you.' Because sometimes it had seemed good to cry together, to make up, and the
inevitable goodness of the night and the day following their
making up. Because he was handsome. Because she had been
alone all year every year until she met him. Because she
didn't want to be alone again, but now knew that it would be
better to be alone than be this way because only last night he
destroyed the typewriter: not physically, no, but with
thoughts and words. And he might as well have picked her up
bodily and thrown her from the river bridge.

She could not feel her hand on the door. It was as if ten
thousand volts of electricity had numbed all of her body. She
could not feel her feet on the tiled floor. Her face was gone,
her mind was gone.

He lay asleep, his back turned. The room was greenly dim.
Quickly, soundlessly, she put on her coat and checked her
purse. The clothes and typewriter were of no importance
now. Everything was a hollowing roar. Everything was like a
waterfall leaping into clear emptiness. There was no striking,
no impact, just a clear water falling into a hollow and then
another hollow, followed by an emptiness.

She stood by the bed and looked at the man there, the

familiar black hair on the nape of his neck, the sleeping profile. The form stirred. 'What?' he asked, still asleep.

'Nothing,' she said. 'Nothing. And nothing.'

She went out and shut the door.

The taxi sped out of town at an incredible rate, making a great noise, and all the pink walls and blue walls fled past and people jumped out of the way and there were some few cars which almost exploded upon them, and there went most of the town and there went the hotel and that man sleeping in the hotel and there went –

Nothing.

The taxi motor died.

No, no, thought Marie, oh God, no, no, no.

The car must start again.

The taxi driver leaped out, glaring at God in his Heaven, and ripped open the hood and looked as if he might strangle the iron guts of the car with his clawing hands, his face smiling a pure sweet smile of incredible hatred, and then he turned to Marie and forced himself to shrug, putting away his hate and accepting the Will of God.

'I will walk you to the bus station,' he said.

No, her eyes said. No, her mouth almost said. Joseph will wake and run and find me still here and drag me back. No.

'I will carry your bag, *señora*,' the taxi driver said, and walked off with it, and had to come back and find her still there, motionless, saying, no, no, to no one, and helped her out and showed her where to walk.

The bus was in the square and the Indians were getting into it, some silently and with a slow, certain dignity, and some chattering like birds and shoving bundles, children, chickens' baskets, and pigs in ahead of them. The driver wore a uniform that had not been pressed or laundered in twenty years, and he was leaning out the window shouting and laughing with people outside, as Marie stepped up into the interior of hot smoke and burning grease from the engine, the smell of gasoline and oil, the smell of wet chickens, wet children, sweating men and damp women, old upholstery which was down to the skeleton, and oily leather. She found a seat in the rear and felt the eyes follow her and her suitcase, and she was thinking: I'm going away, at last I'm going away, I'm free, I'll never see him again in my life, I'm free, I'm free.

She almost laughed.

The bus started and all of the people in it shook and swayed and cried out and smiled, and the land of Mexico seemed to whirl about outside the window, like a dream undecided whether to stay or go, and then the greenness passed away, and the town, and there was the Hotel de Las Flores with its open patio, and there, incredibly, hands in pockets, standing in the open door but looking at the sky and the volcano smoke, was Joseph, paying no attention to the bus or her and she was going away from him, he was growing remote already, his figure was dwindling like someone falling down a mine shaft, silently, without a scream. Now, before she had even the decency or inclination to wave, he was no larger than a boy, then a child, then a baby, in distance, in size, then gone around a corner, with the engine thundering, someone playing upon a guitar up front of the bus, and Marie, straining to look back, as if she might penetrate walls, trees, and distances, for another view of the man standing so quietly watching the blue sky.

At last, her neck tired, she turned and folded her hands and examined what she had won for herself. A whole lifetime loomed suddenly ahead, as quickly as the turns and whirls of the highway brought her suddenly to edges of cliffs, and each bend of the road, even as the years, could not be seen ahead. For a moment it was simply good to lie back here, head upon jouncing seat rest, and contemplate quietness. To know nothing, to think nothing, to feel nothing, to be as nearly dead for a moment as one could be, with the eyes closed, the heart unheard, no special temperature to the body, to wait for life to come get her rather than to seek, at least for an hour. Let the bus take her to the train, the train to the plane, the plane to the city, and the city to her friends, and then, like a stone dropped into a cement mixer, let that life in the city do with her as it would, she flowing along in the mix and solidifying in any new pattern that seemed best.

The bus rushed on with a plummeting and swerving in the sweet green air of the afternoon, between the mountains baked like lion pelts, past rivers as sweet as wine and as clear as vermouth, over stone bridges, under aqueducts where water ran like clear wind in the ancient channels, past churches, through dust, and suddenly, quite suddenly the speedometer in Marie's mind said, A million miles, Joseph is back a million miles and I'll never see him again. The thought stood up in her mind and covered the sky with a blurred darkness. Never, never again until the day I die or after that will I see him again, not for an hour or a minute or a second, not at all will I see him.

The numbness started in her fingertips. She felt it flow up through her hands, into her wrists and on along the arms to her shoulders and through her shoulders to her heart and up her neck to her head. She was a numbness, a thing of nettles and ice and prickles and a hollow thundering nothingness. Her lips were dry petals, her eyelids were a thousand pounds heavier than iron, and each part of her body was now iron and lead and copper and platinum. Her body weighed ten tons, each part of it was so incredibly heavy, and, in that heaviness, crushed and beating to survive, was her crippled heart, throbbing and tearing about like a headless chicken. And buried in the limestone and steel of her robot body was her terror and crying out, walled in, with someone tapping the trowel on the exterior wall, the job finished, and, ironically, it was her own hand she saw before her that had wielded the trowel, set the final brick in place, frothed on the thick slush of mortar and pushed everything into a tightness and a self-finished prison.

Her mouth was cottonwool. Her eyes were flaming with a dark flame the colour of raven wings, the sound of vulture wings, and her head was so heavy with terror, so full of an iron weight while her mouth was stuffed with invisible hot cottonwool, that she felt her head sag down into her immense fat, but she could not see the fat, hands. Her hands were pillows of lead to lie upon, her hands were cement sacks crushing down upon her senseless lap, her ears, faucets in which ran cold winds, and all about her, not looking at her, not noticing, was the bus on its way through towns and fields, over hills and into corn valleys at a great racketing speed, taking her each and every instant one million miles and ten million years away from the familiar.

I must *not* cry out, she thought. No! No!

The dizziness was so complete, and the colours of the bus and her hands and skirt were now so blued over and sooted with lack of blood that in a moment she would be collapsed upon the floor, she would hear the surprise and shock of the riders bending over her. But she put her head far down and sucked the chicken air, the sweating air, the leather air, the carbon monoxide air, the incense air, the air of lonely death, and drew it back through the copper nostrils, down the aching throat, into her lungs which blazed as if she swallowed neon light. Joseph, Joseph, Joseph, Joseph.

It was a simple thing. All terror is a simplicity.

I cannot live without him, she thought. I have been lying to myself. I need him, oh Christ, I, I . . .

'Stop the bus! Stop it!'

The bus stopped at her scream, everyone was thrown forward. Somehow she was stumbling forward over the children, the dogs barking, her hands flailing heavily, falling; she heard her dress rip, she screamed again, the door was opening, the driver was appalled at the woman coming at him in a wild stumbling, and she fell out upon the gravel, tore her stockings, and lay while someone bent to her; then she was vomiting on the ground, a steady sickness; they were bringing her bag out of the bus to her, she was telling them in chokes and sobs that she wanted to go that way; she pointed back at the city a million years ago, a million miles ago, and the bus driver was shaking his head. She half sat, half lay there, her arms about the suitcase, sobbing, and the bus stood in the hot sunlight over her and she waved it to go on; go on, go on; they're all staring at me, I'll get a ride back, don't worry, leave me here, go on, and at last, like an accordion, the door folded shut, the Indian copper-mask faces were transported on away, and the bus dwindled from consciousness. She lay on the suitcase and cried, for a number of minutes, and she was not as heavy or sick, but her heart was fluttering wildly, and she was cold as someone fresh from a winter lake. She arose and dragged the suitcase in little moves across the highway and swayed there, waiting, while six cars hummed by, and at last a seventh car pulled up with a Mexican gentleman in the front seat, a rich car from Mexico City.

'You are going to Uruapan?' he asked politely, looking only at her eyes.

'Yes,' she said at last, 'I am going to Uruapan.'

And as she rode in this car, her mind began a private dialogue:

'What is it to be insane?'

'I don't know.'

'Do you know what insanity is?'

'I don't know.'

'Can one tell? The coldness, was that the start?'

'No.'

'The heaviness, wasn't that a part?'

'Shut up.'

'Is insanity screaming?'

'I didn't mean to.'

'But that came later. First there was the heaviness, and the silence, and the blankness. That terrible void, that space, that silence, that aloneness, that backing away from life, that being in upon oneself and not wishing to look at or speak to the world. Don't tell me that wasn't the start of insanity.'

'Yes.'

'You were ready to fall over the edge.'

'I stopped the bus just short of the cliff.'

'And what if you hadn't stopped the bus? Would they have driven into a little town or Mexico City and the driver turned and said to you through the empty bus, "All right, *señora*, all out." Silence. "All right, *señora*, all out." Silence. "*Señora?*" A stare into space. "*Señora!*" A rigid stare into the sky of life, empty, empty, oh empty. "*Señora!*" No move. "*Señora.*" Hardly a breath. You sit there, you sit there, you sit there, you sit there, you sit there.

'You would not even hear. "*Señora,*" he would cry, and tug at you, but you wouldn't feel his hand. And the police would be summoned beyond your circle of comprehension, beyond your eyes or ears or body. You could not even hear the heavy boots in the car. "*Señora*, you must leave the bus." You do not hear. "*Señora*, what is your name?" Your mouth is shut. "*Señora*, you must come with us." You sit like a stone idol. "Let us see her passport." They fumble with your purse which lies untended in your stone lap. "*Señora* Marie Elliott, from California. *Señora* Elliot?" You stare at the empty sky. "Where are you coming from? Where is your husband?" You were never married. "Where are you going?" Nowhere. "It says she was born in Illinois." You were never born. "*Señora, señora.*" They have to carry you, like a stone, from the bus. You will talk to no one. No, no, no one. "Marie, this is me, Joseph." No, too late. "Marie!" Too late. "Don't you recognize me?" Too late. Joseph. No Joseph, no nothing, too late, too late.'

'That is what would have happened, is it not?'

'Yes.' She trembled.

'If you had not stopped the bus, you would have been heavier and heavier, true? And silenter and silenter and more made up of nothing and nothing and nothing.'

'Yes.'

'*Señora*,' said the Spanish gentleman driving, breaking in on her thoughts. 'It is a nice day, isn't it?'

'Yes,' she said, both to him and the thoughts in her mind.

The old Spanish gentleman drove her directly to her hotel and let her out and doffed his hat and bowed to her.

She nodded and felt her mouth move with thanks, but she did not see him. She wandered into the hotel and found herself with her suitcase back in her room, that room she had left a thousand years ago. Her husband was there.

He lay in the dim light of late afternoon with his back turned, seeming not to have moved in the hours since she had left. He had not even known that she was gone, and had been to the ends of the earth and had returned. He did not even know.

She stood looking at his neck and the dark hairs curling there like ash fallen from the sky.

She found herself on the tiled patio in the hot light. A bird rustled in a bamboo cage. In the cool darkness somewhere, the girl was playing a waltz on the piano.

She saw but did not see two butterflies which darted and jumped and lit upon a bush near her hand, to seal themselves together. She felt her gaze move to see the two bright things, all gold and yellow on the green leaf, their wings beating in slow pulses as they were joined. Her mouth moved and her hand swung like a pendulum, senselessly.

She watched her fingers tumble on the air and close on the two butterflies, tight, tighter, tightest. A scream was coming up into her mouth. She pressed it back. Tight, tighter, tightest.

She felt her hand open all by itself. Two lumps of bright powder fell to the shiny patio tiles. She looked down at the small ruins, then snapped her gaze up.

The girl who played the piano was standing in the middle of the garden, regarding her with appalled and startled eyes.

The wife put out her hand, to touch the distance, to say something, to explain, to apologize to the girl, this place, the world, everyone. But the girl went away.

The sky was full of smoke which went straight up and veered away south towards Mexico City.

She wiped the wing-pollen from her numb fingers and talked over her shoulder, not knowing if that man inside heard, her eyes on the smoke and the sky.

'You know . . . we might try the volcano tonight. It looks good. I bet there'll be lots of fire.'

Yes, she thought, and it will fill the air and fall all around us, and take hold of us tight, tighter, tightest, and then let go and let us fall and we'll be ashes blowing south, all fire.

'Did you hear me?'

She stood over the bed and raised a fist high but *never* brought it down to strike him in the face.

The Black Ferris

The carnival had come to town like an October wind, like a dark bat flying over the cold lake, bones rattling in the night, mourning, sighing, whispering up the tents in the dark rain. It stayed on for a month by the grey, restless lake of October, in the black weather and increasing storms and leaden skies.

During the third week, at twilight on a Thursday, the two small boys walked along the lake shore in the cold wind.

'Aw, I don't believe you,' said Peter.

'Come on, and I'll show you,' said Hank.

They left wads of spit behind them all along the moist brown sand of the crashing shore. They ran to the lonely carnival grounds. It had been raining. The carnival lay by the sounding lake with nobody buying tickets from the flaky black booths, nobody hoping to get the salted hams from the whining roulette wheels, and none of the thin-fat freaks on the big platforms. The midway was silent, all the grey tents hissing on the wind like gigantic prehistoric wings. At eight o'clock perhaps, ghastly lights would flash on, voices would shout, music would go out over the lake. Now there was only a blind hunchback sitting on a black booth, feeling of the cracked china cup from which he was drinking some perfumed brew.

'There,' said Hank, pointing.

The black Ferris wheel rose like an immense light-bulbed constellation against the cloudy sky, silent.

'I still don't believe what you said about it,' said Peter.

'You wait, I saw it happen. I don't know how, but it did.

You know how carnivals are; all funny. Okay; this one's even *funnier*.'

Peter let himself be led to the high green hiding place of a tree.

Suddenly, Hank stiffened. '*Hist*! There's Mr Cooger, the carnival man, now!' Hidden, they watched.

Mr Cooger, a man of some thirty-five years, dressed in sharp bright clothes, a lapel carnation, hair greased with oil, drifted under the tree, a brown derby hat on his head. He had arrived in town three weeks before, shaking his brown derby hat at people on the street from inside his shiny red Ford, tooting the horn.

Now Mr Cooger nodded at the little blind hunchback, spoke a word. The hunchback blindly, fumbling, locked Mr Cooger into a black seat and sent him whirling up into the ominous twilight sky. Machinery hummed.

'See!' whispered Hank. 'The Ferris wheel's going the wrong way. Backwards instead of forwards!'

'So what?' said Peter.

'Watch!'

The black Ferris wheel whirled twenty-five times around. Then the blind hunchback put out his pale hands and halted the machinery. The Ferris wheel stopped, gently swaying, at a certain black seat.

A ten-year-old boy stepped out. He walked off across the whispering carnival ground, in the shadows.

Peter almost fell from his limb. He searched the Ferris wheel with his eyes. 'Where's Mr Cooger!'

Hank poked him. 'You wouldn't believe! Now *see*!'

'Where's Mr Cooger at!'

'Come on, quick, run!' Hank dropped and was sprinting before he hit the ground.

Under giant chestnut trees, next to the ravine, the lights were burning in Mrs Foley's white mansion. Piano music tinkled.

Within the warm windows, people moved. Outside, it began to rain, despondently, irrevocably, forever and ever.

'I'm *so* wet,' grieved Peter, crouching in the bushes. 'Like someone squirted me with a hose. How much longer do we wait?'

'Ssh!' said Hank, cloaked in wet mystery.

They had followed the little boy from the Ferris wheel up through town, down dark streets to Mrs Foley's ravine house. Now, inside the warm dining room of the house the strange little boy sat at dinner, forking and spooning rich lamb chops and mashed potatoes.

'I know his name,' whispered Hank, quickly. 'My mom told me about him the other day. She said, "Hank, you hear about the li'l orphan boy moved in Mrs Foley's? Well, his name is Joseph Pikes and he just came to Mrs Foley's one day about two weeks ago and said how he was an orphan run away and could he have something to eat, and him and Mrs Foley been getting on like hot apple pie ever since." That's what my mom said,' finished Hank, peering through the steamy Foley window. Water dripped from his nose. He held on to Peter who was twitching with cold. 'Pete, I didn't like his looks from the first, I didn't. He looked — mean.'

'I'm scared,' said Peter, frankly wailing. 'I'm cold and hungry and I don't know what this's all about.

'Gosh, you're dumb!' Hank shook his head, eyes shut in disgust. 'Don't you see, three weeks ago the carnival came. And about the same time this little ole orphan shows up at Mrs Foley's. And Mrs Foley's son died a long time ago one night one winter, and she's never been the same, so here's this little ole orphan boy who butters her all around.'

'Oh,' said Peter, shaking.

'Come on,' said Hank. They marched to the front door and banged the lion knocker.

After a while the door opened and Mrs Foley looked out.

'You're all wet, come in,' she said. 'My land.' She herded

them into the hall. 'What do you want?' she said, bending over them, a tall lady with lace on her full bosom and a pale thin face with white hair over it. 'You're Henry Walterson, aren't you?'

Hank nodded, glancing fearfully at the dining room where the strange little boy looked up from his eating. 'Can we see you alone, ma'am?' And when the old lady looked palely surprised, Hank crept over and shut the hall door and whispered at her. 'We got to warn you about something, it's about that boy come to live with you, that orphan?'

The hall grew suddenly cold. Mrs Foley drew herself high and stiff. 'Well?'

'He's from the carnival, and he ain't a boy, he's a man, and he's planning on living here with you until he finds where your money is and then run off with it some night, and people will look for him but because they'll be looking for a little ten-year-old boy they won't recognize him when he walks by a thirty-five-year-old man, named Mr Cooger!' cried Hank.

'What *are* you talking about?' declared Mrs Foley.

'The carnival and the Ferris wheel and this strange man, Mr Cooger, the Ferris wheel going backwards and making him younger, I don't know how, and him coming here as a boy, and you can't trust him, because when he has your money he'll get on the Ferris wheel and it'll go *forwards*, and for ever!'

'Good night, Henry Walterson, don't *ever* come back!' shouted Mrs Foley.

The door slammed. Peter and Hank found themselves in the rain once more. It soaked into and into them, cold and complete.

'Smart guy,' snorted Peter. 'Now you fixed it. Suppose he heard us, suppose he comes and *kills* us in our beds tonight, to shut us all up for keeps!'

'He wouldn't do that,' said Hank.

'Wouldn't he?' Peter seized Hank's arm. 'Look.'

In the big bay window of the dining room now the mesh curtain pulled aside. Standing there in the pink light, his hand made into a menacing fist, was the little orphan boy. His face was horrible to see, the teeth bared, the eyes hateful, the lips mouthing out terrible words. That was all. The orphan boy was there only a second, then gone. The curtain fell into place. The rain poured down upon the house. Hank and Peter walked slowly home in the storm.

During supper, Father looked at Hank and said, 'If you don't catch pneumonia, I'll be surprised. Soaked, you were, by God! What's this about the carnival?'

Hank fussed at his mashed potatoes, occasionally looking at the rattling windows. 'You know Mr Cooger, the carnival man, Dad?'

'The one with the pink carnation in his lapel?' asked Father.

'Yes!' Hank sat up. 'You've seen him around?'

'He stays down the street at Mrs O'Leary's boarding house, got a room at the back. Why?'

'Nothing,' said Hank, his face glowing.

After supper Hank put through a call to Peter on the phone. At the other end of the line, Peter sounded miserable with coughing.

'Listen, Pete!' said Hank. 'I see it all now. When that li'l ole orphan boy, Joseph Pikes, gets Mrs Foley's money, he's got a good plan.'

'What?'

'He'll stick around town as the carnival man, living in a room at Mrs O'Leary's. That way nobody'll get suspicious of him. Everybody'll be looking for that nasty little boy and he'll be gone. And he'll be walking around, all disguised as the carnival man. That way, nobody'll suspect the carnival at all. It would look funny if the carnival suddenly pulled up stakes.'

'Oh,' said Peter, sniffling.

'So we got to act fast,' said Hank.

'Nobody'll believe us, I tried to tell my folks but they said hogwash!' moaned Peter.

'We got to act tonight, anyway. Because why? Because he's gonna try to kill us! We're the only ones that know and if we tell the police to keep an eye on him, he's the one who stole Mrs Foley's money in cahoots with the orphan boy, he won't live peaceful. I bet he just tries something tonight. So, I tell you, meet me at Mrs Foley's in half an hour.'

'Aw,' said Peter.

'You wanna die?'

'No.' Thoughtfully.

'Well, then. Meet me there and I bet we see that orphan boy sneaking out with the money, tonight, and running back down to the carnival grounds with it, when Mrs Foley's asleep. I'll see you there. So long, Pete!'

'Young man,' said Father, standing behind him as he hung up the phone. 'You're not going anywhere. You're going straight up to bed. Here.' He marched Hank upstairs. 'Now hand me out everything you got on.' Hank undressed. 'There're no other clothes in your room are there?' asked Father. 'No, sir, they're all in the hall closet,' said Hank, disconsolately.

'Good,' said Dad and shut and locked the door.

Hank stood there, naked. 'Holy cow,' he said.

'Go to bed,' said Father.

Peter arrived at Mrs Foley's house at about nine-thirty, sneezing, lost in a vast raincoat and mariner's cap. He stood like a small water hydrant on the street, mourning softly over his fate. The lights in the Foley house were warmly on upstairs. Peter waited for half an hour, looking at the rain-drenched slick streets of night.

Finally, there was a darting paleness, a rustle of wet bushes.

'Hank?' Peter questioned the bushes.

'Yeah.' Hank stepped out.

'Gosh,' said Peter, staring. 'You're — you're *naked*!'

'I ran all the way,' said Hank. 'Dad wouldn't let me out.'

'You'll get pneumonia,' said Peter.

The lights in the house went out.

'Duck,' cried Hank, bounding behind some bushes. They waited. 'Pete,' said Hank. 'You're wearing pants, aren't you?'

'Sure,' said Pete.

'Well, you're wearing a raincoat, and nobody'll know, so lend me your pants,' said Hank.

A reluctant transaction was made. Hank pulled the pants on.

The rain let up. The clouds began to break apart.

In about ten minutes a small figure emerged from the house, bearing a large paper sack filled with some enormous loot or other.

'There he is,' whispered Hank.

'There he goes!' cried Peter.

The orphan boy ran swiftly.

'Get after him!' cried Hank.

They gave chase through the chestnut trees, but the orphan boy was swift, up the hill, through the night streets of town, down past the rail yards, past the factories, to the midway of the deserted carnival. Hank and Peter were poor seconds, Peter weighted as he was with the heavy raincoat, and Hank frozen with cold. The thumping of Hank's bare feet sounded through the town.

'Hurry, Pete! We can't let him get to that Ferris wheel

before we do, if he changes back into a man we'll never prove anything!'

'I'm hurrying!' But Pete was left behind as Hank thudded on alone in the clearing weather.

'Yah!' mocked the orphan boy, darting away, no more than a shadow ahead, now. Now vanishing into the carnival yard.

Hank stopped at the edge of the carnival lot. The Ferris wheel was going up and up into the sky, a big nebula of stars caught on the dark earth and turning forwards and forwards, instead of backwards, and there sat Joseph Pikes in a black-painted bucket-seat, laughing up and around and down and up and around and down at little old Hank standing there, and the little blind hunchback had his hand on the roaring, oily black machine that made the Ferris wheel go ahead and ahead. The midway was deserted because of the rain. The merry-go-round was still, but its music played and crashed in the open spaces. And Joseph Pikes rode up into the cloudy sky and came down and each time he went around he was a year older, his laughing changed, grew deep, his face changed, the bones of it, the mean eyes of it, the wild hair of it, sitting there in the black bucket-seat whirling, whirling swiftly, laughing into the bleak heavens where now and again a last split of lightning showed itself.

Hank ran forward at the hunchback by the machine. On the way he picked up a tent spike. 'Here now!' yelled the hunchback. The black Ferris wheel whirled around. 'You!' stormed the hunchback, fumbling out. Hank hit him in the kneecap and danced away. 'Ouch!' screamed the man, falling forward. He tried to reach the machine brake to stop the Ferris wheel. When he put his hand on the brake, Hank ran in and slammed the tent spike against the fingers, mashing them. He hit them twice. The man held his hand in his other hand, howling. He kicked at Hank. Hank grabbed the foot, pulled, the man slipped in the mud and fell. Hank hit him on the head, shouting.

The Ferris wheel went around and around and around.

'Stop, stop the wheel!' cried Joseph Pikes — Mr Cooger, flung up in a stormy cold sky in the bubbled constellation of whirl and rush and wind.

'I can't move,' groaned the hunchback. Hank jumped on his chest and they thrashed, biting, kicking.

'Stop, stop the wheel!' cried Mr Cooger, a man, a different man and voice this time, coming around in panic, going up into the roaring hissing sky of the Ferris wheel. The wind blew through the high dark wheel spokes. 'Stop, stop, oh, please stop the wheel!'

Hank leaped up from the sprawled hunchback. He started in on the brake mechanism, hitting it, jamming it, putting chunks of metal in it, tying it with rope, now and again hitting at the crawling weeping dwarf.

'Stop, stop, stop the wheel!' wailed a voice high in the night where the windy moon was coming out of the vaporous white clouds now. 'Stop . . . ' The voice faded.

Now the carnival was ablaze with sudden light. Men sprang out of tents, came running. Hank felt himself jerked into the air with oaths and beatings rained on him. From a distance there was a sound of Peter's voice and behind Peter, at full tilt, a police officer with pistol drawn.

'Stop, stop the wheel!' In the wind the voice sighed away.

The voice repeated and repeated.

The dark carnival men tried to apply the brake. Nothing happened. The machine hummed and turned the wheel around and around. The mechanism was jammed.

'Stop!' cried the voice one last time.

Silence.

Without a word the Ferris wheel flew in a circle, a high system of electric stars and metal and seats. There was no sound now but the sound of the motor which died and stopped. The Ferris wheel coasted for a minute, all the carnival people looking up at it, the policeman looking up at it. Hank and Peter looking up at it.

The Ferris wheel stopped. A crowd had gathered at the noise. A few fishermen from the wharfhouse, a few switchmen from the rail yards. The Ferris wheel stood whining and stretching in the wind.

'Look,' everybody said.

The policeman turned and the carnival people turned and the fishermen turned and they all looked at the occupant in the black-painted seat at the bottom of the ride. The wind touched and moved the black wooden seat in a gentle rocking rhythm, crooning over the occupant in the dim carnival light.

A skeleton sat there, a paper bag of money in its hands, a brown derby hat on its head.

Farewell Summer

Farewell summer.

Grandma looked it.

Grandpa said it.

Douglas felt it.

Farewell summer.

The words moved on Grandpa's lips as he stood at the edge of the porch and surveyed the lake of grass just below and all the dandelions gone and the clover blossoms wilting, and a touch of rust in the trees, and real summer over and a smell of Egypt in the air, blowing from the east.

'What?' asked Douglas.

But he had heard.

'Farewell summer.' Grandpa leaned on the porch rail, shut one eye, let the other wander on the horizon line. 'Know what that is, Doug? A flower by the side of the road, named for the way the weather feels today. Look. The whole darn season's just turned around. Don't know why summer's come back. Maybe to find something. Makes you feel kind of sad. And then again, happy. Farewell summer, Doug.'

A fern by the porch rail fell to dust.

Doug moved to stand beside his grandfather, hoping to borrow some of that far sight, some of that look beyond the hills, some of the wanting to cry, some of the ancient joy. The smell of pipe tobacco and Tiger Shaving Tonic had to be sufficient. A top spun in his chest, now light, now dark, now moving his tongue with laughter, now filling his eyes with warm saltwater.

'Think I'll go eat me a doughnut and take me a nap,' he said.

'Glad we have siestas in northern Illinois. Eat your way to sleep, boy.'

The great warm hand came down on his head in a pressure that spun the top fast until it was all one warm lovely colour.

It was a happy journey inside to the doughnuts.

Laid out with a powdered-sugar moustache on his upper lip, Doug contemplated sleep, which came around through the back of his head and gently grabbed him.

Dusk filled his whole twelve-year-old body at three-thirty in the afternoon.

Then, in his sleep, he quickened.

A long way off, a band played a strange slow tune, full of muted brass and muffled drums.

Doug lifted his head, listening.

As if the faraway band had come out of a cave into full sunlight, the music grew louder.

And it was louder because where before it had seemed a brass band of few pieces, now it added instruments as it approached Green Town, as if men were trotting out of empty cornfields brandishing bright pipes of sunny metal or long sticks of liquorice over their heads. Somewhere a small moon rose to be beaten, and that was a big brass drum. Somewhere a mob of irritable blackbirds soared to become piccolos and leave the fruitless orchards behind.

'A parade!' whispered Doug. 'But it's not July Fourth, and Labor Day's gone! So, how come . . . ?'

And as the music got louder it got slower, deeper, and very sad. It was like an immense storm cloud full of lightning which passed low shadowing hills, darkening rooftops, and now invading the town streets. It was a murmur of thunder.

Douglas shivered and waited.

The parade had stopped just outside his house.

Flashes of sunlit brass shot through the high windows and beat against the walls like the wings of golden birds panicking to escape.

Sidling up to the window, Douglas peered.

And what he saw was familiar people.

Douglas blinked.

For there on the lawn, holding a trombone, was Jack Schmidt who sat across from him in school, and Bill Arno, his best friend, lifting a trumpet, and Mr Wyneski, the town barber, wrapped around by a boa-constrictor tub and — hold on!

Douglas listened.

There was not a sound in the house below.

He spun about and ran downstairs. The kitchen was full of bacon smell but nothing else. The dining room remembered pancakes but only a breeze came in the windows to ghost the curtains.

He ran to the front door and stepped out on the porch. The house was empty, yes, but the yard was full.

Because down among the band stood Grandpa with a French horn, Grandma with a tambourine, Skip with a kazoo.

As soon as Doug reached the edge of the porch, everyone gave a great whooping yell, and while they were yelling Douglas thought how quickly it had all happened. Only an instant before Grandma had put down her kneaded bread dough in the kitchen (it lay with her fingerprints floured in it on the kneading board at this moment), Grandpa had laid aside Dickens in the library, Skip had leaped from the crab-apple tree. Now they stood holding instruments in this assembly of friends, teachers, librarians, and distant cousins from far peach-orchard farms.

The yelling stopped and everyone laughed, forgetting the dirge they had played through town.

'Hey,' said Doug at last, 'what day *is* this?'

'Why,' said Grandma, '*your* day, Doug.'

'*My* day?'

'Yours, Doug. Special. Better than birthdays, greater than

Christmas, grander than the Fourth, more amazing than Easter. Your day, Doug, *yours*!'

That was the Mayor, making a speech.

'Yes, but . . . '

'Doug . . . ' Grandpa nudged a huge wicker basket. 'Got strawberry pie here.'

'Strawberry shortcake,' added Grandma. 'Strawberry ice *cream*.'

Everyone smiled. But Douglas stepped back, waited, feeling like a huge Eskimo pie standing in the sun and not melting.

'Fireworks at dusk, Doug,' said Skip, tootling his kazoo. 'Dusk and fireworks. Also, give you my Mason jar full of fireflies left over from summer.'

'You never give me anything like that before, Skip. How come you do it *now*?'

'It's Douglas Spaulding Day, Doug. We've brought you some flowers.'

People don't bring flowers to boys, thought Doug, not even in hospitals!

But there were the Ramsey sisters holding out clusters of farewell-summer blossoms, and Grandpa saying: 'Hurry on, Doug. Lead the parade! The boat's waiting!'

'The excursion boat? We going on a picnic trip?'

'Journey's more like it.' Mr Wyneski whipped off his barber's apron, crammed on his cornflake-cereal straw hat. 'Listen!'

The sound of a far boat wailed up from the shore of the lake one mile away.

'Forward march!' said Grandpa. 'One, two, Doug, oh, come on now, one, *two*!'

'Yes, but − '

Grandma jingled her tambourine, Skip thrummed his kazoo, Grandpa moaned his French horn, and the motion of the mob circling the yard drew Doug down off the porch along the street with a pack of dogs ahead and behind yipping all the way downtown where traffic stopped for them and people waved and someone tore up a telephone book and threw it out the top of the Green Town Hotel but by the time the informational confetti hit the brick street the parade was gone downhill, leaving the sun and town behind.

And by the time they reached the shore of the quiet lake the sun as clouding over and fog moved in across the water so swiftly and completely that it frightened Doug to see it move, as if a great storm cloud from the autumn sky had been cut loose and sank to engulf the shore, the town, the thumping, happy brass band.

The parade stopped. For now far out in the fog, beyond the pier, invisible, they could hear the sound of a vast ship approaching, some sort of boat that mourned with the voice of a fog horn, over and over.

'Get along, boy, out on the pier,' said Grandpa, softly.

'Race you to the end!' Skip vaulted ahead.

Douglas did not move.

For the boat was now nosing out of the fog, timber by white timber, porthole by porthole, and stood as if held fast by the fog, at the end of the pier, its gangplank let down.

'How come . . . ' Douglas stared. 'How come that boat's got no name?'

They all looked and it was true, there was no name painted on the bow of the long white boat.

'Well, you see, Doug – '

The ship's whistle shrieked and the crowd swarmed pushing Douglas with it along the timbers to the gangplank.

'You on board *first*, Doug!'

'Give him some music to march him aboard!'

And the band lifted up a ton of brass and two hundred pounds of chimes and cymbals and banged out 'For He's a Jolly Good Fellow' triple-time, and before he could tell his legs otherwise, one, two, one, two, they had him up on the deck, people running, slinging down the picnic baskets, then leaping back on the dock . . .

Wham!

The gangplank fell.

Douglas whirled, cried out.

No one else was on board the ship. His family and friends were trapped on the dock.

'Hold on, wait!'

The gangplank hadn't fallen by mistake.

It had been *pulled* off the boat.

'Hold on!' wailed Douglas.

'Yes,' said Grandpa, quietly, below, on the dock. 'Hold on.'

The people weren't trapped on land at all.

Douglas blinked.

He was trapped on the boat.

Douglas yelled. The steamboat shrieked. It began to edge away from the dock. The band played 'Columbia, the Gem of the Ocean'.

'Hold on, now, darn it!'

'So long, Doug.'

'Wait!'

'Good-bye, Douglas, good-bye,' cried two town librarians.

'So long,' whispered everyone on the dock.

Douglas looked at the food put by in baskets on the deck and remembered a Chicago museum once, years ago, where he had seen an Egyptian tomb and toys and baskets of withered food placed in that tomb around a small carved boat. It burnt like a flash of gunpowder in his eyes. He spun about wildly and yelled.

'So long, Doug, so long . . . ' Ladies lifted white hand-kerchiefs, men waved their straw hats. Someone lifted a small dog and waved it on the air.

And now the boat was pulling away out in the cold water and the fog was wrapping it up and the band was fading and now he could hardly see all the aunts and uncles and his family on the dock.

'Wait!' he cried. 'It's not too late! Tell 'em to turn back! You can come on the excursion, too! Yeah, sure, you come along, too!'

'No, Doug, just you,' called Grandfather's voice somewhere on the land. 'Get along, boy.'

And he now knew that the ship was indeed empty. If he ran and looked he would not even find a captain, or a first mate, or any member of a crew. Only he was aboard this ship that moved out into mist, alone, its vast engines groaning and pumping, a mindless life to themselves, under the decks.

Numbly, he moved to the prow. Suddenly, he knew that if he reached his hands down and touched he would find the name of the boat, fresh-painted.

Why had the season changed? Why had the warm weather come back?

The answer was simple.

The name of the boat was *Farewell Summer*.

And it had come back just for him.

'Doug . . . ' the voices faded. 'Oh, good-bye . . . oh so long . . . so long . . . ?'

'Skip, Grandma, Grandpa, Bill, Mr Wyneski, no, no, no, oh Skip, oh Grandma, Grandpa, save me!'

But the shore was empty, the dock lost, the parade gone home and the ship blew its horn a final time and he broke his heart so it fell out of his eyes in tears and he wept saying all the names of the ones on shore, and it all ran together into one immense and terrifying word that shook his soul and sneezed forth his heart's blood in one convulsive shout:

'*Grandpa*grandma*skip*bill*mr*wyneski*help*!'

And sat up in bed, hot, cold, and weeping.

He lay there with the tears running down into his ears and he wept, feeling the bed, wept feeling the good sunlight on the fingers of his twitching hands and on the patchwork quilt. Sunset put a quiet supply of lemonade colours through all the air of his room.

His crying ceased.

He got up and went to the mirror to see what sadness looked like and there it was, coloured all through his face and in his eyes where it could never be got out now, where it would never go away, and he reached out to touch that other face beyond the glass, and that other hand inside the glass touched back, and it was cold.

Below, bread baked and filled the house with its late afternoon perfume. He walked slowly down the stairs to watch Grandma pull the lovely guts out of a chicken and then pause at a window to see Skip far up in his favourite tree trying to see beyond the sky, and then he strolled out to the porch where the smell of baking bread followed him as if it knew where he was and would not let him go.

Someone stood on the porch, smoking his next-to-last pipe of the day.

'Gramps, you're *here*!'

'Why, sure, Doug.'

'Boy. Boy, oh, boy. You're here. The *house* is here. The *town's* here!'

'It seems you're here, too, boy.'

'Yeah, oh, yeah.'

Grandpa nodded, gazed at the sky, took a deep breath, started to speak when a sudden panic made Doug cry: 'Don't!'

'Don't what, boy?!'

Don't, thought Doug, don't say what you were going to say.

Grandpa waited.

The trees leaned their shadows on the lawn and took on colours of autumn even as they watched. Somewhere, the last lawnmower of summer shaved and cut the years and left them in sweet mounds.

'Gramps, is — '

'Is what Doug?'

Douglas swallowed, closed his eyes, and in self-imposed darkness, got rid of it all in a rush:

'Is death being on a boat alone and it sailing off and taking you with it and all your folks left back on the shore?'

Grandpa chewed it over, read a few clouds in the sky, nodded.

'That's about it, Doug. Why do you ask?'

'Just wanted to know.'

Douglas eyed a high cloud passing that had never been that shape before and would never be that way again.

'Say what you were just about to say, Gramps.'

'Well, now, let me see. Farewell summer?'

'Yes, sir,' whispered Douglas, and leaned against the tall man there and took the old man's hand and held it hard against his cheek and then placed it to rest on top of his head, like a crown for a young king.

Farewell summer.

McGillahee's Brat

In 1953 I had spent six months in Dublin, writing a screenplay. I had not been back since.

Now, fifteen years later, I had returned by boat, train, and taxi, and here we pulled up in front of the Royal Hibernian Hotel and here we got out and were going up the front hotel steps when a beggar woman shoved her filthy baby in our faces and cried:

'Ah, God, pity! It's pity we're in need of! Have you *some*?'

I had some somewhere on my person, and slapped my pockets and fetched it out, and was on the point of handing it over when I gave a small cry, or exclamation. The coins spilled from my hand.

In that instant, the babe was eyeing me, and I the babe.

Then it was snatched away. The woman bent to paw after the coins, glancing up at me in some sort of panic.

'What on earth?' My wife guided me up into the lobby where, stunned, standing at the register, I forgot my name. 'What's wrong? What *happened* out there?'

'Did you see the baby?' I asked.

'The beggar's child —?'

'It's the same.'

'The same *what*?'

'The same baby,' I said, my lips numb, 'that the woman used to shove in our faces fifteen years ago.'

'Oh, come, now.'

'Yes, come.' And I went back to the door and opened it to look out.

But the street was empty. The beggar woman and her bundle had run off to some other street, some other hotel, some other arrival or departure.

I shut the door and went back to the register.

'What?' I said.

And suddenly remembering my name, wrote it down.

The child would not go away.

The memory, that is.

The recollection of other years and days in rains and fogs, the mother and her small creature, and the soot on that tiny face, and the cry of the woman herself which was like a shrieking of brakes put on to fend off damnation.

Sometimes, late at night, I heard her wailing as she went off the cliff of Ireland's weather and down upon rocks where the sea never stopped coming or going, but stayed for ever in tumult.

But the child stayed, too.

My wife would catch me brooding at tea or after supper over the Irish coffee and say, '*That* again?'

'That.'

'It's silly.'

'Oh, it's silly, all right.'

'You've always made fun of metaphysics, astrology, palmistry —'

'*This* is genetics.'

'You'll spoil your whole vacation.' My wife passed the apricot tarts and refilled my cup. 'For the first time in years, we're travelling without a load of screenplays or novels. But out in the Galway this morning you kept looking over your shoulder as if *she* were trotting in the road behind with her spitting image.'

'Did I do that?'

'You know you did. You say genetics? That's good enough for me. That is the same woman begged out front of the hotel fifteen years ago, yes, but she has twenty children at home, each one inch shorter than the next, and all as alike as a bag of potatoes. Some families run like that. A gang of father's kids, or a gang of mother's absolute twins, and nothing in between. Yes, that child looks like the one we saw years back. But you look like your brother, don't you, and there's twelve years difference?'

'Keep talking,' I said. 'I feel better.'

But that was a lie.

I went out to search the Dublin streets.

Oh, I didn't tell myself this, no. But, search I did.

From Trinity College on up O'Connell Street and way around back to St Stephen's Green I pretended a vast interest in fine architecture, but secretly watched for her and her dire burden.

I bumped into the usual haggle of banjo-pluckers and shuffle-dancers and hymn-singers and tenors gargling in their sinuses and baritones remembering a buried love or fitting a stone on their mother's grave, but nowhere did I surprise my quarry.

At last I approached the doorman at the Royal Hibernian Hotel.

'Mike,' I said.

'Sir,' said he.

'That woman who used to lurk about at the foot of the steps there —'

'Ah, the one with the babe, do you mean?'

'Do you know her!?'

'Know her! Sweet Jesus, she's been the plague of my years since I was thirty, and look at the grey in my hair now!'

'She's been begging *that* long?'

'And for ever beyond.'

'Her name —'

'Molly's as good as any. McGillahee, I think. Sure. McGillahee's it. Beg pardon, sir, why do you ask?'

'Have you *looked* at her baby, Mike?'

His nose winced at a sour smell. 'Years back, I gave it up. These beggar women keep their kids in a dread style, sir, a condition roughly equivalent to the bubonic. They neither wipe nor bathe nor mend. Neatness would work against beggary, do you see? The fouler the better, that's the motto, eh?'

'Right. Mike, so you've never *really* examined that infant?'

'Aesthetics being a secret part of my life, I'm a great one for averting the gaze. It's blind I am to help you, sir. Forgive.'

'Forgiven, Mike.' I passed him two shillings. 'Oh . . . have you seen those two, lately?'

'Strange. Come to think, sir. They have not come here in . . . ' he counted on his fingers and showed surprise, 'why it must be ten days! They never done *that* before. Ten!'

'Ten,' I said, and did some secret counting of my own. 'Why, that would make it ever since the first day *I* arrived at the hotel.'

'Do you *say* that now?'

'I say it, Mike.'

And I wandered down the steps, wondering what I said and what I meant.

It was obvious she was hiding out.

I did not for a moment believe she or the child was sick.

Our collision in front of the hotel, the baby's eyes and mine striking flint, had startled her like a fox and shunted her off God-knows-where, to some other alley, some other road, some other town.

I smelled her evasion. She was a vixen, yes, but I felt myself, day by day, a better hound.

I took to walking earlier, later, in the strangest locales. I would leap off buses in Ballsbridge and prowl the fog or taxi half out to Kilcock and hide in pubs. I even knelt in Dean

Swift's church to hear the echoes of his Houyhnhnm voice, but stiffened alert at the merest whimper of a child carried through.

It was all madness, to pursue such a brute idea. Yet on I went, itching where the damned thing scratched.

And then by sheer and wondrous accident in a dousing downpour that smoked the gutters and fringed my hat with a million raindrops per second, while taking my nightly swim, it happened . . .

Coming out of a Wally Beery 1930 vintage movie, some Cadbury's chocolate still in my mouth, I turned a corner . . .

And this woman shoved a bundle in my face and cried a familiar cry:

'If there's mercy in your soul − !'

She stopped, riven. She spun about. She ran.

For the instant, she *knew*. And the babe in her arms, with the shocked small face, and the swift bright eyes, he knew me, *too*! Both let out some kind of fearful cry.

God, how that woman could race.

I mean she put a block between her backside and me while I gathered breath to yell: 'Stop, thief!'

It seemed an appropriate yell. The baby was a mystery I wished to solve. And there she vaulted off with it, I mean, she *seemed* a thief.

So I dashed after, crying, 'Stop! Help! *You*, there!'

She kept a hundred yards between us for the first half mile, up over bridges across the Liffey and finally up Grafton Street where I jogged into St Stephen's Green to find it . . . empty.

She had absolutely vanished.

Unless, of course, I thought, turning in all directions, letting my gaze idle, it's into the Four Provinces pub she's gone . . .

There is where I went.

It was a good guess.

I shut the door quietly.

There, at the bar, was the beggar woman, putting a pint of Guinness to her own face, and giving a shot of gin to the babe for happy sucking.

I let my heart pound down to a slower pace, then took my place at the bar and said, 'Bombay Gin, please.'

At my voice, the baby gave one kick. The gin sprayed from his mouth. He fell into a spasm of choked coughing.

The woman turned him over and thumped his back to stop the convulsion. In so doing, the red face of the child faced me, eyes squeezed shut, mouth wide, and at last the seizure stopped, the cheeks grew less red, and I said:

'You there, baby.'

There was a hush. Everyone in the bar waited.

I finished:

'You need a shave.'

The babe flailed about in his mother's arms with a loud strange wounded cry, which I cut off with a simple:

'It's all right. I'm not the police.'

The woman relaxed as if all her bones had gone to porridge.

'Put me down,' said the babe.

She put him down on the floor.

'Give me my gin.'

She handed him his little glass of gin.

'Let's go in the saloon bar where we can talk.'

The babe led the way with some sort of small dignity, holding his swaddling clothes about him with one hand, and the gin glass in the other.

The saloon bar was empty, as he had guessed. The babe, without my help, climbed up into a chair at a table and finished his gin.

'Ah, Christ, I need another,' he said in a tiny voice.

While his mother went to fetch a refill, I sat down and the

babe and I eyed each other for a long moment.

'Well,' he said at last, 'what do ya think?'

'I don't know. I'm waiting and watching my own re-actions,' I said. 'I may explode into laughter or tears at any moment.'

'Let it be laughter. I couldn't stand the other.'

On impulse, he stuck out his hand. I took it.

'The name is McGillahee. Better known as McGillahee's Brat. Brat, for short.'

'Brat,' I said. 'Smith.'

He gripped my hand hard with his tiny fingers.

'Smith? Your name fits nothing. But Brat, well, don't a name like that go ten thousand leagues under? And what, you may ask, am I doing down here? And you up there so tall and fine and breathing the high air? Ah, but here's your drink, the same as mine. Put it in you, and listen.'

The woman was back with shots for both. I drank, watched her, and said, 'Are you the mother −?'

'It's me sister she is,' said the babe. 'Our mother's long since gone to her reward; a ha'penny a day for the next thousand years, nuppence dole from there on, and cold summers for a millions years.'

'Your sister?' I must have sounded my disbelief, for she turned away to nibble her ale.

'You'd never guess, would you? She looks ten times my age. But if winter don't age you, Poor will. And winter and Poor is the whole tale. Porcelain cracks in this weather. And once she was the loveliest porcelain out of the summer oven.' He gave her a gentle nudge. 'But Mother she is now, for thirty years −'

'Thirty years you've been −!'

'Out front of the Royal Hibernian Hotel? And more! And our mother before that, and our father, too, and *his* father, the whole tribe! The day I was born, no sooner sacked in diapers, than I was on the street and my mother crying Pity and the world deaf, stone-dumb-blind and deaf. Thirty years with my sister, ten years with my mother, McGillahee's brat has been on display!'

'Forty?' I cried, and drank my gin to straighten my logic. 'You're really forty? And all those years — how?'

'How did I get into this line of work?' said the babe. 'You do not get, you are, as we say, *born* in. It's been nine hours a night, no Sundays off, no time-clocks, no paycheques, and mostly dust and lint fresh paid out of the pockets of the rambling rich.'

'But I still don't understand,' I said, gesturing to his size, his shape, his complexion.

'Nor will I, ever,' said McGillahee's brat. 'Am I a midget born to the blight? Some kind of dwarf shaped by glands? Or did someone warn me to play it safe, stay small?'

'That could hardly —'

'Couldn't it!? It could! Listen. A thousand times I heard it, and a thousand times more my father came home from his beggary route and I remember him jabbing his finger in my crib, pointing at me, and saying, "Brat, whatever you do, don't grow, not a muscle, not a hair! The Real Thing's out there; the World. You *hear* me, Brat? Dublin's beyond, and Ireland on top of that and England hard-assed above us all. It's not worth the consideration, the bother, the planning, the growing-up to try and make do, so listen here, Brat, we'll stunt your growth with stories, with truth, with warnings and predictions, we'll wean you on gin, and smoke you with Spanish cigarettes until you're a cured Irish ham, pink, sweet, and small, small, do you hear, Brat? I did not want you in this world. But now you're in it, lie low, don't walk, creep; don't talk, wail; don't work, loll; and when the world is too much for you, Brat, give it back your opinion; *wet* yourself! Here, Brat, here's your evening poteen; fire it down. The Four Horsemen of the Apocalypse wait down by the Liffey. Would you see their like? Hang on. Here we go!"

'And out we'd duck for the evening rounds, my dad banging a banjo with me at his feet holding the cup, or him doing a tap-dance, me under one arm, the musical instrument under the other, both making discord.

'Then, home late, we'd lie four in a bed, a crop of failed potatoes, discards of an ancient famine.

'And sometimes in the midst of the night, for lack of something to do, my father would jump out of bed in the cold and run outdoors and fist his knuckles at the sky, I remember, I remember, I heard, I saw, daring God to lay hands on him, for so help him, Jesus, if *he* could lay hands on God, there would be torn feathers, ripped beards, lights put out, and the grand theatre of Creation shut tight for Eternity! do ya hear, God, ya dumb brute with your perpetual rainclouds turning their black behinds on me, do ya *care*!?

'For answer the sky wept, and my mother did the same all night.

'And the next morn out I'd go again, this time in *her* arms and back and forth between the two, day on day, and her grieving for the million dead from the famine of fifty-one and him saying good-bye to the four million who sailed off to Boston . . .

'Then one night, Dad vanished, too. Perhaps he sailed off on some mad boat like the rest, to forget us all. I forgive him. The poor beast was wild with hunger and nutty for want of something to give us and no giving.

'So then my mother simply washed away in her own tears, dissolved, you might say, like a sugar-crystal saint, and was gone before the morning fog rolled back, and the grass took her, and my sister, aged twelve, overnight grew tall, but I, me, oh, me? I grew small. Each decided, you see, long before that, of course, on going his or her way.

'But then part of my decision happened early on. I knew, I swear I did! the quality of my own Thespian performance!

'I heard it from every decent beggar in Dublin when I was

nine days old. "What a beggar's babe *that* is!" they cried.

'And my mother, standing outside the Abbey Theatre in the rain when I was twenty and thirty days old, and the actors and directors coming out tuning their ears to my Gaelic laments, *they* said I should be signed up and trained! So the stage would have been mine with size, but size never came. And there's no brat's roles in Shakespeare. Puck, maybe; what else? So meanwhile at forty days and fifty nights after being born my performance made hackles rise and beggars yammer to borrow my hide, flesh, soul and voice for an hour here, an hour there. The old lady rented me out by the half day when she was sick abed. And not a one bought and bundled me off did not return with praise. "My God," they cried, "his yell would suck money from the Pope's poorbox!"

'And outside the Cathedral one Sunday morn, an American cardinal was riven to the spot by the yowl I gave when I saw his fancy shirt and bright cloth. Said he: "That cry is the first cry of Christ at his birth, mixed with the dire yell of Lucifer churned out of Heaven and spilled in fiery muck down the landslide slops of Hell!"

'That's what the dear Cardinal said. Me, eh? Christ and the Devil in one lump, the gabble screaming out my mouth half lost, half found, can you *top* that?'

'I cannot,' I said.

'Then, later on, many years further, there was this wild American film director who chased White Whales? The first time he spied me, he took a quick look and . . . winked! And took out a pound note and did not put it in my sister's hand, no, but took my own scabby fist and tucked the pound in and gave it a squeeze and another wink, and him gone.

'I seen his picture later in the paper, him stabbing the White Whale with a dread harpoon, and him proper mad, and I always figured, whenever we passed, he had my number, but I never winked back. I played the part dumb. And there was always a good pound in it for me, and him proud of my not giving in and letting him know that I knew that he knew.

'Of all the thousands who've gone by in the grand Ta-Ta! he was the only one ever looked me right in the eye, save you! The rest were all too embarrassed by life to so much as gaze as they put out the dole.

'Well, I mean now, what with that film director, and the Abbey Players, and the cardinals and beggars telling me to go with my own natural self and talent and the genius busy in my baby fat, all *that* must have turned my head.

'Added to which, my having the famines tolled in my ears, and not a day passed we did not see a funeral go by, or watch the unemployed march up and down in strikes, well, don't you see? Battered by rains and storms of people and knowing so much, I *must* have been driven down, driven back, don't you think?

'You cannot starve a babe and have a man; or do miracles run different than of old?

'My mind, with all the drear stuff dripped in my ears, was it likely to want to run around free in all that guile and sin and being put upon by natural nature and unnatural man? No. No! I just wanted my little cubby, and since I was long out of that, and no squeezing back, I just squinched myself small against the rains. I flaunted the torments.

'And, do you know? I won.'

You did, Brat, I thought. You did.

'Well, I guess that's my story,' said the small creature there perched on a chair in the empty saloon bar.

He looked at me for the first time since he had begun his tale.

The woman who was his sister, but seemed his grey mother, now dared to lift her gaze, also.

'Do,' I said, 'do the people of Dublin know about you?'

'Some. And envy me. And hate me, I guess, for getting off easy from God, and his plagues and Fates.'

'Do the police know?'

'Who would tell them?'

There was a long pause.

Rain beat on the windows.

Somewhere a door-hinge shrieked like a soul in torment as someone went out and someone else came in.

Silence.

'Not me,' I said.

'Ah, Christ, Christ . . . '

And tears rolled down the sister's cheeks.

And tears rolled down the sooty strange face of the babe.

Both of them let the tears go, did not try to wipe them off, and at last they stopped, and we drank up the rest of our gin and sat a moment longer and then I said: 'The best hotel in town is the Royal Hibernian, the best for beggars, that is.'

'True,' they said.

'And for fear of meeting me, you've kept from the richest territory?'

'We have.'

'The night's young,' I said. 'There's a flight of rich ones coming in from Shannon just before midnight.'

I stood up.

'If you'll let . . . I'll be happy to walk you there, now.'

'The Saints' calendar is full,' said the woman, 'but somehow we'll find room for you.'

Then I walked the woman McGillahee and her brat back through the rain towards the Royal Hibernian Hotel, and us talking along the way of the mobs of people coming in from the airport just before twelve, drinking and registering at that late hour, that fine hour for begging, and with the cold rain and all, not to be missed.

I carried the babe for some part of the way, she looking tired, and when we got in sight of the hotel, I handed him back saying:

'Is this the first time, ever?'

'We was found out by a tourist? Aye,' said the babe. 'You have an otter's eye.'

'I'm a writer.'

'Nail me to the Cross,' said he, 'I might have known! You won't —'

'No,' I said. 'I won't write a single word about this, about you, for another fifteen years or more.'

'Mum's the word?'

'Mum.'

We were a hundred feet from the hotel steps.

'I must shut up here,' said Brat, lying there in his old sister's arms, fresh as peppermint candy from the gin, round-eyed, wild-haired, swathed in dirty linens and wools, small fists gently gesticulant. 'We've a rule, Molly and me, no chat while at work. Grab my hand.'

I grabbed the small fist, the little fingers. It was like holding a sea anemone.

'God bless you,' he said.

'And God,' I said, 'take care of you.'

'Ah,' said the babe, 'in another year we'll have enough saved for the New York boat.'

'We will,' she said.

'And no more begging, and no more being the dirty babe crying by night in the storms, but some decent work in the open, do you know, do you see, will you light a candle to that?'

'It's lit.' I squeezed his hand.

'Go on ahead.'

'I'm gone,' I said.

And walked quickly to the front of the hotel where airport taxis were starting to arrive.

Behind I heard the woman trot forward, I saw her arms lift, with the Holy Child held out in the rain.

'If there's mercy in you!' she cried. 'Pity —!'

And heard the coins ring in the cup and heard the sour

babe wailing, and more cars coming and the woman crying Mercy and Thanks and Pity and God Bless and Praise Him and wiping tears from my own eyes, feeling eighteen inches tall, somehow made it up the high steps and into the hotel and to bed where rains fell cold on the rattled windows all the night and where, in the dawn, when I woke and looked out, the street was empty save for the steady falling storm . . .

The Aqueduct

It leapt over the country in great stone arches. It was empty now, with the wind blowing in its sluices; it took a year to build, from the land in the North to the land in the South.

'Soon,' said mothers to their children, 'soon now the Aqueduct will be finished. Then they will open the gates a thousand miles North and cool water will flow to us, for our crops, our flowers, our baths, and our tables.'

The children watched the Aqueduct being built stone on solid stone. It towered thirty feet in the sky, with great gargoyle spouts every hundred yards which would drop tiny streams down into yard reservoirs.

In the North there was not only one country, but two. They had rattled their sabres and clashed their shields for many years.

Now, in the Year of the Finishing of the Aqueduct, the two Northern countries shot a million arrows at each other and raised a million shields, like numerous suns, flashing. There was a cry like an ocean on a distant shore.

At the year's end the Aqueduct stood finished. The people of the Hot South, waiting, asked, 'When will the water come? With war in the North, will we starve for water, will our crops die?'

A courier came racing. 'The war is terrible,' he said. 'There is a slaughtering that is unbelievable. More than one hundred million people have been slain.'

'For what?'

'They disagreed, those two Northern countries.

'That's all we know. They disagreed.'

The people gathered all along the stone Aqueduct. Messengers ran along the empty sluiceways with yellow streamers, crying, 'Bring vases and bowls, ready your fields and ploughs, open your baths, fetch water glasses!'

A thousand miles of filling Aqueduct and the slap of naked courier feet in the channel, running ahead. The people gathered by the tens of millions from the boiling countryside, the sluiceways open, waiting, their crocks, urns, jugs, held towards the gargoyle spouts where the wind whistled emptily.

'It's coming!' The word passed from person to person down the one thousand miles.

And from a great distance, there was the sound of rushing and running, the sound that liquid makes in a stone channel. It flowed slowly at first and then faster, and then very fast down into the Southern land, under the hot sun.

'It's here! Any second now. Listen!' said the people. They raised their glasses into the air.

Liquid poured from the sluiceways down the land, out of gargoyle mouths, into the stone baths, into the glasses, into the fields. The fields were made rich for the harvest. People bathed. There was a singing you could hear from one field to one town to another.

'But, Mother!' A child held up his glass and shook it, the liquid whirled slowly. 'This isn't water!'

'Hush!' said the mother.

'It's red,' said the child. 'And it's thick.'

'Here's the soap, wash yourself, don't ask questions, shut up,' she said. 'Hurry into the field, open the sluicegates, plant the rice!'

In the fields, the father and his two sons laughed into one another's faces. 'If this keeps up, we've a great life ahead. A full silo and a clean body.'

'Don't worry,' said the two sons. 'The President is sending a representative North to make certain that the two countries there continue to disagree.'

'Who knows, it might be a fifty-year war!'

They sang and smiled.

And at night they all lay happily, listening to the good sound of the Aqueduct, full and rich, like a river, rushing through their land towards the morning.

Gotcha!

They were incredibly in love. They said it. They knew it.
They lived it. When they weren't staring at each other they
were hugging. When they weren't hugging they were kissing. When they weren't kissing they were a dozen scrambled
eggs in bed. When they were finished with the amazing
omelet they went back to staring and making noises.

Theirs, in sum, was a Love Affair. Print it out in capitals.
Underline it. Find some italics. Add exclamation marks. Put
up the fireworks. Tear down the clouds. Send out for some
adrenaline. Roustabout at three a.m. Sleep till noon.

Her name was Beth. His name was Charles.

They had no last names. For that matter, they rarely called
each other by their first names. They found new names every
day for each other, some of them capable of being said only
late at night and only to each other, when they were special
and tender and most shockingly unclad.

Anyway, it was Fourth of July every night. New Year
every dawn. It was the home team winning and the mob on
the field. It was a bobsled downhill and everything cold
racing by in beauty and two warm people holding tight and
yelling with joy.

And then . . .

Something happened.

At breakfast about one year into the conniption fits Beth
said, half under her breath:

'Gotcha.'

He looked up and said, 'What?'

'Gotcha,' she said. 'A game. You never played Gotcha?'

'Never even heard of it.'

'Oh, I've played it for years.'

'Do you buy it in a store?' he asked.

'No, no. It's a game I made up, or almost made up, based on an old ghost story or scare story. Like to play it?'

'That all depends.' He was back shovelling away at his ham and eggs.

'Maybe we'll play it tonight – it's fun. In fact,' she said, nodding her head once and beginning to go on with her breakfast again, 'it's a definite thing. Tonight it is. Oh, bun, you'll love it.'

'I love everything we do,' he said.

'It'll scare the hell out of you,' she said.

'What's the name again?'

'Gotcha,' she said.

'Never heard of it.'

They both laughed. But her laughter was louder than his.

It was a long and delicious day of luscious name-callings and rare omelets and a good dinner with a fine wine and then some reading just before midnight, and at midnight he suddenly looked over at her and said:

'Haven't we forgotten something?'

'What?'

'Gotcha.'

'Oh, my, yes!' she said, laughing. 'I was just waiting for the clock to strike the hour.'

Which it promptly did. She counted to twelve, sighed happily and said, 'All right – let's put out most of the lights. Just keep the small lamp lighted by the bed. Now, there.' She ran around putting out all the other lights, and came back and plumped up his pillow and made him lie right in the middle of the bed. 'Now, you stay right there. You don't move, see. You just . . . *wait*. And see what *happens* – okay?'

'Okay.' He smiled indulgently. At times like these she was a ten-year-old Girl Scout rushing about with some poisoned cookies on a grand lark. He was always ready, it seemed, to eat the cookies. 'Proceed.'

'Now, be very quiet,' she said. 'No talking. Let me talk if I want — okay?'

'Okay.'

'Here goes,' she said, and disappeared.

Which is to say that she sank down like the dark witch, melting, melting, at the foot of the bed. She let her bones collapse softly. Her head and her hair followed her Japanese paper-lantern body down, fold on fold, until the air at the foot of the bed was empty.

'Well done!' he cried.

'You're not supposed to talk. Sh-h.'

'I'm sh-h-h-ed.'

Silence. A minute passed. Nothing.

He smiled a lot, waiting.

Another minute passed. Silence. He didn't know where she was.

'Are you still at the foot of the bed?' he asked. 'Oh, sorry.' He sh-h-h-ed himself. 'Not supposed to talk.'

Five minutes passed. The room seemed to get somewhat darker. He sat up a bit and fixed his pillow and his smile got somewhat less expectant. He peered about the room. He could see the light from the bathroom shining on the wall.

There was a sound like a small mouse in one far corner of the room. He looked there but could see nothing.

Another minute passed. He cleared his throat.

There was a whisper from the bathroom door, down near the floor.

He glanced that way and grinned and waited. Nothing.

He thought he felt something crawling under the bed. The sensation passed. He swallowed and blinked.

The room seemed almost candlelit. The light bulb, one hundred and fifty watts, seemed now to have developed fifty-watt problems.

There was a scurry like a great spider on the floor, but nothing was visible. After a long while her voice murmured to him like an echo, now from this side of the dark room, now that.

'How do you like it *so* far?'

'I . . .'

'Don't speak,' she whispered.

And was gone again for another two minutes. He was beginning to feel his pulse jump in his wrists. He looked at the left wall, then the right, then the ceiling.

And suddenly a white spider was crawling along the foot of the bed. It was her hand, of course, imitating a spider. No sooner there than gone.

'Ha!' He laughed.

'Sh-h!' came the whisper.

Something ran into the bathroom. The bathroom light went out. Silence. There was only the small light in the bedroom now. A faint rim of perspiration appeared on his brow. He sat wondering why they were doing this.

A clawing hand snatched up on the far left side of the bed, gesticulated and vanished. The watch ticked on his wrist.

Another five minutes must have gone by. His breathing was long and somewhat painful, though he couldn't figure why. A small frown gathered in the furrow between his eyes and did not go away. His fingers moved on the quilt all by themselves, as if trying to get away from him.

A claw appeared on the right side. No, it hadn't been there at all! Or had it?

Something stirred in the closet directly across the room. The door slowly opened upon darkness. Whether something went in at that moment or was already there, waiting to come out, he could not say. The door now opened upon an abyss that was as deep as the spaces between the stars. A few dark shadows of coats hung inside, like disembodied people.

There was a running of feet in the bathroom.

There was a scurry of cat feet by the window.

He sat up. Licked his lips. He almost said something. He shook his head. A full twenty minutes had passed.

There was a faint moan, a distant laugh that hushed itself. Then another groan . . . where? In the shower?

'Beth?' he said at last.

No answer. Water dripped in the sink suddenly, drop by slow drop. Something had turned it on.

'Beth?' he called again, and hardly recognized his voice, it was so pale.

A window opened somewhere. A cool wind blew a phantom of curtain out on the air.

'Beth,' he called weakly.

No answer.

'I don't like this,' he said.

Silence.

No motion. No whisper. No spider. Nothing.

'Beth?' he called, a bit louder.

No breathing, even, anywhere.

'I don't like this game.'

Silence.

'You hear me, Beth?'

Quiet.

'I don't like this game.'

Drip in the bathroom sink.

'Let's stop the game, Beth.'

Wind from the window.

'Beth?' he called again. 'Answer me. Where are you?'

Silence.

'You all right?'

The rug lay on the floor. The light grew small in the lamp. Invisible dusts stirred in the air.

'Beth . . . you okay?'

Silence.

'Beth?'

Nothing.

'Beth!'

'Oh-h-h-h-h-h . . . *ah-h-h-h-h*!'

He heard the shriek, the cry, the scream.

A shadow sprang up. A great darkness leaped upon the bed. It landed on four legs.

'Ah!' came the shout.

'Beth!' he screamed.

'Oh-h-h-h!' came the shriek from the thing.

Another great leap and the dark thing landed on his chest. Cold hands seized his neck. A white face plunged down. A mouth gaped and shrieked:

'Gotcha!'

'Beth!' he cried.

And flailed and wallowed and turned but it clung to him and looked down and the face was white and the eyes raved wide and the nostrils flared. And the big bloom of dark hair in a flurry above fell down in a stormwind. And the hands clawing at his neck and the air breathed out of that mouth and nostrils as cold as polar wind, and the weight of the thing on his chest light but heavy, thistledown but an anvil crushing, and him thrashing to be free, but his arms pinned by the fragile legs and the face peering down at him so full of evil glee, so brimful of malevolence, so beyond this world and in another, so alien, so strange, so never seen before, that he had to shriek again.

'No! No! No! Stop! Stop!'

'Gotcha!' screamed the mouth.

And it was someone he had never seen before. A woman from some time ahead, some year when age and things had changed everything, when darkness had gathered and boredom had poisoned and words had killed, and everything gone to ice and lostness and nothing, no residues of love, only hate, only death.

'No! Oh, God! Stop!'

He burst into tears. He began to sob.

She stopped.

Her hands went away cold and came back warm to touch, hold, pet him.

And it was Beth.

'Oh, God, God, God!' he wailed. 'No, no, no!'

'Oh, Charles, Charlie,' she cried, all remorse. 'I'm sorry. I didn't mean –'

'You did. Oh God, you did, you did!'

His grief was uncontrollable.

'No, no. Oh, Charlie,' she said, and burst into tears herself. She flung herself out of bed and ran around turning on lights. But none of them were bright enough. He was crying steadily now. She came back and slid in by him and put his grieving face to her breast, and held him, hugged him, patted him, kissed his brow and let him weep.

'I'm sorry, Charlie, listen, sorry. I didn't –'

'You *did*!'

'It was only a game!'

'A game! You call that a game, game, game!' he wailed, and wept again.

And finally, at last, his crying stopped and he lay against her and she was warm and sister/mother/friend/lover again. His heart, which had crashed, now moved to some near-calm. His pulses stopped fluttering. The constriction around his chest let go.

'Oh, Beth, Beth,' he wailed softly.

'Charlie,' she apologized, her eyes shut.

'Don't ever do that again.'

'I won't.'

'Promise you'll never do that again?' he said, hiccuping.

'I swear, I promise.'

'You were *gone*, Beth — that wasn't *you*!'

'I promise, I swear, Charlie.'

'All right,' he said.

'Am I forgiven, Charlie?'

He lay a long while and at last nodded, as if it had taken some hard thinking.

'Forgiven.'

'I'm sorry, Charlie. Let's get some sleep. Shall I turn the lights off?'

Silence.

'Shall I turn the lights off, Charlie?'

'No-no.'

'We have to have the lights off to sleep, Charlie.'

'Leave a few on for a little while,' he said, eyes shut.

'All right,' she said, holding him. 'For a little while.'

He took a shuddering breath and came down with a chill. He shook for five minutes before her holding him and stroking him and kissing him made the shiver and the tremble go away.

An hour later she thought he was asleep and got up and turned off all the lights save the bathroom light, in case he should wake and want at least one on. Getting back into bed, she felt him stir. His voice, very small, very lost, said:

'Oh, Beth, I loved you so much.'

She weighed his words. 'Correction. You *love* me so much.'

'I *love* you so much,' he said.

It took her an hour, staring at the ceiling, to go to sleep.

The next morning at breakfast he buttered his toast and looked at her. She sat calmly munching her bacon. She caught a glance and grinned at him.

'Beth,' he said.

'What?' she asked.

How could he tell her? Something in him was cold. The bedroom even in the morning sun seemed smaller, darker. The bacon was burned. The toast was black. The coffee had a strange and alien flavour. She looked very pale. He could feel his heart, like a tired fist, pounding dimly against some locked door somewhere.

'I . . . ' he said, 'we . . . '

How could he tell her that suddenly he was afraid? Suddenly he sensed that this was the beginning of the end. And beyond the end there would never be anyone to go to anywhere at any time — no one in all the world.

'Nothing,' he said.

Five minutes later she asked, looking at her crumpled eggs, 'Charles, do you want to play the game tonight? But this time it's me, and this time it's you who hides and jumps out and says, "Gotcha"?'

He waited because he could not breathe.

'No.'

He did not want to know that part of himself.

Tears sprang to his eyes.

'Oh, no,' he said.

The End of the Beginning

He stopped the lawn mower in the middle of the yard, because he felt that the sun at just that moment had gone down and the stars come out. The fresh-cut grass that had showered his face and body died softly away. Yes, the stars were there, faint at first, but brightening in the clear desert sky. He heard the porch screen door tap shut and felt his wife watching him as he watched the night.

'Almost time,' she said.

He nodded; he did not have to check his watch. In the passing moments he felt very old, then very young, very cold, then very warm, now this, now that. Suddenly he was miles away. He was his own son talking steadily, moving briskly to cover his pounding heart and the resurgent panics as he felt himself slip into fresh uniform, check food supplies, oxygen flasks, pressure helmet, space-suiting, and turn as every man on Earth tonight turned, to gaze at the swiftly filling sky.

Then, quickly, he was back, once more the father of the son, hands gripped to the lawn-mower handle. His wife called, 'Come sit on the porch.'

'I've got to keep busy!'

She came down the steps and across the lawn. 'Don't worry about Robert; he'll be all right.'

'But it's all so new,' he heard himself say. 'It's never been done before. Think of it — a manned rocket going up tonight to build the first space station. Good Lord, it can't be done, it doesn't exist, there's no rocket, no proving ground, no take-off, no technicians. For that matter, I don't even have a son named Bob. The whole thing's too much for me!'

'Then what are you doing out here, staring?'

He shook his head. 'Well, late this morning, walking to the office, I heard someone laugh out loud. It shocked me, so I froze in the middle of the street. It was *me*, laughing! Why? Because finally I really *knew* what Bob was going to do tonight; at last I *believed* it. "Holy" is a word I never use, but that's how I felt stranded in all that traffic. Then, middle of the afternoon, I caught myself humming. You know the song. "A wheel in a wheel. Way in the middle of the air." I laughed again. The space station, of course, I thought. The big wheel with hollow spokes where Bob'll live six or eight months, then get along to the Moon. Walking home, I remembered more of the song. "Little wheel run by faith, big wheel run by the grace of God." I wanted to jump, yell, and flame-out myself!'

His wife touched his arm. 'If we stay out here, let's at least be comfortable.'

They placed two wicker rockers in the centre of the lawn and sat quietly as the stars dissolved out of darkness in pale crushings of rock salt strewn from horizon to horizon.

'Why,' said his wife, at last, 'it's like waiting for the fireworks at Sisley Field every year.'

'Bigger crowd tonight . . . '

'I keep thinking — a billion people watching the sky right now, their mouths all open at the same time.'

They waited, feeling the earth move under their chairs.

'What time is it now?'

'Eleven minutes to eight.'

'You're always right; there must be a clock in your head.'

'I can't be wrong, tonight. I'll be able to tell you one second before they blast off. Look! The ten-minute warning!'

On the western sky they saw four crimson flares open out, float shimmering down the wind above the desert, then sink silently to the extinguishing earth.

In the new darkness the husband and wife did not rock in their chairs.

After a while he said, 'Eight minutes.' A pause. 'Seven minutes.' What seemed a much longer pause. 'Six . . . '

His wife, her head back, studied the stars immediately above her and murmured, 'Why?' She closed her eyes. 'Why the rockets, why tonight? Why all this? I'd like to know.'

He examined her face, pale in the vast powdering light of the Milky Way. He felt the stirring of an answer, but let his wife continue.

'I mean it's not that old thing again, is it, when people asked why men climbed Mt Everest and they said, "Because it's there"? I never understood. That was no answer to me.'

Five minutes, he thought. Time ticking . . . his wrist-watch . . . a wheel in a wheel . . . little wheel run by . . . big wheel run by . . . way in the middle of . . . four minutes! . . . The men snug in the rocket by now, the hive, the control board flickering with light . . .

His lips moved.

'All I know is it's really the end of the beginning. The Stone Age, Bronze Age, Iron Age; from now on we'll lump all those together under one big name for when we walked on Earth and heard the birds at morning and cried with envy. Maybe we'll call it the Earth Age, or maybe the Age of Gravity. Millions of years we fought gravity. When we were amoebae and fish we struggled to get out of the sea without gravity crushing us. Once safe on the shore we fought to stand upright without gravity breaking our new invention, the spine, tried to walk without stumbling, run without falling. A billion years Gravity kept us home, mocked us with wind and clouds, cabbage moths and locusts. That's what's so God-awful big about tonight . . . it's the end of old man Gravity and the age we'll remember him by, for once and all. I don't know where they'll divide the ages, at the Persians, who dream of flying carpets, or the Chinese, who all unknowing celebrated birthdays and New Year with strung ladyfingers and high skyrockets, or some minute, some incredible second in the next hour. But we're in at the end of a billion years trying, the end of something long and to us humans, anyway, honourable.'

Three minutes . . . two minutes fifty-nine seconds . . . two minutes fifty-eight seconds . . .

'But,' said his wife, 'I still don't know why.'

Two minutes, he thought. *Ready? Ready? Ready?* The far radio voice calling. *Ready! Ready! Ready!* The quick, faint replies from the humming rocket. *Check! Check! Check!*

Tonight, he thought, even if we fail with this first, we'll send a second and a third ship and move on out to all the planets and later, all the stars. We'll just keep going until the big words like "immortal" and "for ever" take on meaning. Big words, yes, that's what we want. Continuity. Since our tongues first moved in our mouths we've asked. What does it all mean? No other question made sense, with death breathing down our necks. But just let us settle in on ten thousand worlds spinning around ten thousand alien suns and the question will fade away. Man will be endless and infinite, even as space is endless and infinite. Man will go on, as space goes on, for ever. Individuals will die as always, but our history will reach as far as we'll ever need to see into the future, and with the knowledge of our survival for all time to come, we'll know security and thus the answer we've always searched for. Gifted with life, the least we can do is preserve and pass on the gift to infinity. That's a goal worth shooting for.

The wicker chairs whispered ever so softly on the grass.

One minute.

'One minute,' he said aloud.

'Oh!' His wife moved suddenly to seize his hands. 'I hope that Bob . . . '

'He'll be all right!'

'Oh, God, take care . . . '

Thirty seconds.

'Watch now.'

Fifteen, ten, five . . .

'Watch!'

Four, three, two, one.

'There! There! Oh, there, there!'

They both cried out. They both stood. The chairs toppled back, fell flat on the lawn. The man and his wife swayed, their hands struggled to find each other, grip, hold. They saw the brightening colour in the sky and, ten seconds later, the great uprising comet burn the air, put out the stars, and rush away in fire flights to become another star in the returning profusion of the Milky Way. The man and wife held each other as if they had stumbled on the rim of an incredible cliff that faced an abyss so deep and dark there seemed no end to it. Staring up, they heard themselves sobbing and crying. Only after a long time were they able to speak.

'It got away, it did, *didn't* it?'

'Yes . . . '

'It's all right, isn't it?'

'Yes . . . yes . . . '

'It didn't fall back . . . ?'

'No, no, it's all right, Bob's all right, it's all right.'

They stood away from each other at last.

He touched his face with his hands and looked at his wet fingers. 'I'll be damned,' he said. 'I'll be damned.'

They waited another five minutes and then ten minutes until the darkness in their heads, the retina, ached with a million specks of fiery salt. Then they had to close their eyes.

'Well,' she said, 'now let's go in.'

He could not move. Only his hand reached a long way out by itself to find the lawn mower handle. He saw what his hand had done and said, 'There's just a little more to do . . . '

'But you can't see.'

'Well enough,' he said. 'I must finish this. Then we'll sit on the porch awhile before we turn in.'

He helped her put the chairs on the porch and sat her down and then walked back out to put his hands on the guide bar of the lawn mower. The lawn mower. A wheel in a wheel. A simple machine which you held in your hands, which you sent on ahead with a rush and a clatter while you walked behind with your quiet philosophy. Racket, followed by warm silence. Whirling wheel, then soft footfall of thought.

I'm a billion years old, he told himself; I'm one minute old. I'm one inch, no, ten thousand *miles*, tall. I look down and can't see my feet they're so far off and gone away below.

He moved the lawn mower. The grass showering up fell softly around him; he relished and savoured it and felt that he was all mankind bathing at last in the fresh waters of the fountain of youth.

Thus bathed, he remembered the song again about the wheels and the faith and the grace of God being way up there in the middle of the sky where that single star, among a million motionless stars, dared to move and keep on moving.

Then he finished cutting the grass.

THE WORLD'S GREATEST SCIENCE FICTION AUTHORS
NOW AVAILABLE IN PANTHER SCIENCE FICTION

Ray Bradbury

Philip K Dick

All these books are available at your local bookshop or newsagent, and can be ordered direct from the publisher or from Dial-A-Book Service.

To order direct from the publisher just tick the titles you want and fill in the form below:

Name _____

Address _____

Send to:
Granada Cash Sales
PO Box 11, Falmouth, Cornwall TR10 9EN

Please enclose remittance to the value of the cover price plus:

UK 45p for the first book, 20p for the second book plus 14p per copy for each additional book ordered to a maximum charge of £1.63.

BFPO and Eire 45p for the first book, 20p for the second book plus 14p per copy for the next 7 books, thereafter 8p per book.

Overseas 75p for the first book and 21p for each additional book.

To order from Dial-A-Book Service, 24 hours a day, 7 days a week:

Telephone 01 836 2641 – give name, address, credit card number and title required. The books will be sent to you by post.

DIAL-A-BOOK

Granada Publishing reserve the right to show new retail prices on covers, which may differ from those previously advertised in the text or elsewhere.